DUSTIES

MW00613087

Book 1
of the 5-part
Dusties Series

Brett Murrell

WARNING!

This is no normal tale.

It is mouse to your cat, fox to your hound, Moriarty to your Sherlock, and it will dash ahead of you calling, "Catch me if you can!"

And if you can, you are not normal either.

Cast off where you are and what you know and gather together in the dark with the Dusties.

THE DUSTIES SERIES
DUSTIES — DEVOURERS — MALFAER — DALMAR — CAMPAIGN

To Jessica, my fellow sleuth.

Cover art by Kerem Beyit.
Ravenhair illustrations by Caroline Zina.
Interior illustrations by Elwira Pawlikowska.

Many thanks to the early beta-reader cadre: Jessica, Sherry, James, Shirley, Cody, Lynette, Mitchel, Matthew, Joe, Colby, Curtis, Josh, Bern, and the others who enjoyed the chase.

This book is polished like silver because of Lisa Dawn Martinez, The Finicky Editor.

This appears to be a work of fiction. No character, place, or incident described in this work correlates with any character, place, or incident existing on planet Earth within several decades of the year 2016.

Copyright © 2016 by Brett Murrell. All rights reserved. No part of this book may be reproduced, stored in a retrieval system, or transmitted in any form, or by any means, electronic, mechanical, photocopying, recording or otherwise, without prior permission of the author.

ISBN-13: 978-1-938826-10-8

ISBN-10: 1-938826-10-8

Worldspanner® is a trademark of Worldspanner, Inc.

PART I:

DARKNESS

1 : FALL

It began unpleasantly.

A boy of seventeen dreamt of a dark place and a monster so large, so swift, and so terrifying that the sight of it stole his breath away.

He awoke.

Strong calloused hands held his arms and legs like vises, keeping him painfully stretched out, face up over a pressing, roiling mob. Dozens of pole lanterns bobbed around him while streaks of dimly luminous blue tendrils drifted across the dark, starless sky above. At times the boy could glimpse a city out of the corner of his eye, lit by the flames of hundreds of lamps and built against a cliff— a cliff that rose skyward, seemingly forever, lost in the darkness and the not-light of the sky tendrils.

The mob did not carry him in celebration but in anger and fear. They yelled at him, screamed at him.

"Demon!"

"Murderer!"

Hands pulled at his black hair and fists pummeled his lean ribs, interrupting his attempts at shouting a question. He began again, and again.

"What-"

"Why-"

He fought against blind horror, as if he were falling and could not see.

He needed time to recover his fogged senses, a moment to speak.

But he did not have that time.

A roaring sound grew nearer. Flecks of wetness spattered his face. He tried to lever himself up, his stomach muscles quivering with the effort. But a hand took hold of his hair and forced his head back and down, drawing a groan of pain from his stretched throat. He hung there, arched over and backward, his head held upside down, struggling to breathe.

Rodrigo's eyes tried to adjust. He caught sight of six legs, their feet planted in deep sand bordering a narrow river of swift water. A multi-colored glow, bright enough to cause him to blink, covered the nearby ground and spread down into the water, turning the river into a ribbon of light. Rodrigo thought it might be the plants that glowed, but his attention snapped to two of the legs as they strode forward.

A lean, bony hand rapped sharply against his ear. The flash of a middle-aged woman's face swung across his view, her expression tightened in fury and sorrow.

Mutters and cruel laughter filtered into his stinging ear.

"Give him another, Katya!" said a voice. "That one we won't count."

"Yes!" said others.

The hand struck him in the ear again, harder, and the fingernails dug flesh from his cheek. A cheer followed.

The second set of legs shifted in front of him, and instantly a sledgehammer of force struck his cheek, spreading a shower of swirling stars through his vision. The hand that held his head kept his neck from snapping with the impact. Cheers arose.

The third legs approached, though Rodrigo could barely see them through his quivering eyes. The crowd fell silent. He felt a woman's hand at his neck. Then sand poured into his nostrils, bringing the sting of sensitive tissue and a panic of drowning. His reflexes wrenched away from the woman's grip, but other hands held him tightly as the crowd urged on her torture with shouts and vengeful laughter.

"Why-" Rodrigo managed to choke out, but the woman's hand flashed above him and a handful of sand pitched through his open lips. Stretched as he was, he couldn't spit it out and couldn't clear his throat. His arms and legs spasmed in suffocation until a ragged rasp of air squeezed out and in through his sand-swollen nostrils.

The warm wet of spit spattered his face, the woman turned aside, and Rodrigo was lifted higher. Only a few hands held him now—strong hands, expertly gripping to keep him from struggling. The beach passed by, rock appeared, and the roar of the water grew suddenly louder as he found himself on a large spur of rock. Below him, the swift water dropped violently away over a tumbling falls.

A building roar of avenging shouts arose from the riverbank. The hands drew him back, a voice barked a command, and Rodrigo found himself launched in the air. For a moment he hung there, his sand-crusted eyes flicking frantically over the city, the mob, and the swift glowing river beneath him. Then he struck the water and it bore him over the edge, down into a misty, depthless void.

———

"Aren't you overplaying your part?"

The boy awoke in sand on the bank of an underground river. Every strand of him felt bruised and sore—so sore that he hesitated to move for fear of discovering that his bones had been smashed.

Although he lay in a cave, he could see. Luminous multi-colored growth covered every solid surface of the cavern, extending into the riverbed and giving the whole scene a disorienting, otherworldly cast.

In the twisted light, an equally twisted man leaned over him.

The man was big—not merely tall but heavy boned, his half-naked body wrapped in various strips that had long ago ceased to be clothing. No part of his face was without wrinkle or crease, including one shredded ear and a nose that bulged and folded. The battered face suggested age, yet he moved like a younger man and his pale eyes shone with an active intensity.

"What will I call you?" said the man.

"Call me?" said the boy.

"Come now, you're making me nervous. First you lay here for a few days acting unconscious, now you act confused. Either my mind is slipping or it's becoming more creative after all these years. Do you have a name?"

"Yes, it's—it's Rodrigo."

"Rodrigo?" The man rubbed his lopsided, poorly cropped beard. "That's a strange name. I hope it isn't a name that a lunatic would make up. You can call me Talen. I rescued you from certain death as you floated face down in the river, and now you will recover slowly over the weeks as we engage in profound conversations and unlock the secrets of the universe. Or maybe I intend you to be nothing more than an avid Creekle player. Are you intelligent?"

"I am...confused. Are you making sense?"

"I sincerely hope so, for my sake. Let's start over. Who are you and where are you from?"

Rodrigo did not answer immediately, turning inward for a moment. "I do not know."

Talen shook his head. "I must be running out of stories. You have nothing to say?"

"I remember a city full of lanterns, and a cliff, and a mob of people yelling."

"Ah, that's better," said Talen. "So you're from Drift. Go on."

"Drift, is that the cliff city?"

"Yes, of course, the one above us, at least. What else?"

Rodrigo blinked, his eyes losing focus, his mind grasping for memories. "I do not remember anything, even about the city. I just saw it in a glance. I was being carried by a group of people. They were yelling things at me and hitting me. They threw me into a river and I went over a cliff. I remember falling, and that is it."

"Ah, and what did you do to deserve death?"

"I do not know. I do not remember anything before the mob."

"Nothing? You've nothing else to say?"

"I—I have no memory at all. I have lost my memory!"

"So, your story is that you're a Dustie."

"A Dustie?"

Talen shook his head in frustration. "A speck of human dust blown here by the capricious winds—really, this is getting old. I'm the only one with meaningful things to say. You're boring me."

Rodrigo worked himself to his feet, surprised to find nothing broken. He traced a long, angry wound that ran from his right shoulder to his stomach, breathing a sigh of relief when the gash turned out to be nothing more than a scrape. He was about to apologize to Talen for his lack of entertaining qualities, but Talen turned away from him.

"Ah, Indra, did you sleep well?" said Talen. "Yes, I've scraped up another playmate, although he's not top quality. Says he's a Dustie, though why I would dream up someone so dull I cannot imagine. Rodrigo, meet my wife, Indra."

As Talen waited for a response, Rodrigo thought of what to say. He understood now. The place where Indra stood contained nothing but air.

"Greetings, Indra," said Rodrigo, playing along. He glanced about the small growth-choked cavern, seeing no exit, no escape.

Talen continued his one-way conversation. "I fished him out of the river. Yes, a joke, I know. No one drops over a waterfall fifteen hundred feet high and then filters down to the underground without dying most thoroughly. But I dreamed him up for some reason, Indra, so let's at least humor him. For now."

Rodrigo glanced at the river. Upriver the inrushing water roiled in a surging pool. Downriver the tunnel shrank quickly until the water filled it entirely. Drowning would be certain either way.

Talen grew quieter, retreating a short distance away, still in conversation with his nonexistent mate. He spoke in whispers, glancing at Rodrigo now and then. Finally he threw up his hands and returned.

"Indra has taken more than a mild dislike to you. Downright hatred, actually. I'm sorry, but I must move on to someone more entertaining, so you'll need to die."

Rodrigo took several steps back, feeling the water's edge swirl around his feet. "You think I am a delusion?"

"Of course."

"I am no delusion, Talen. Indra is the delusion."

"This is very disconcerting," said Talen, searching about the riverbank. "You're a very bad delusion to begin with, and I won't stand here arguing with myself about it. And now that you've said unfavorable things about Indra, I'm disposed to kill you violently myself rather than dream up some gallant means of death." Talen found what he sought and began prying a large stone out from under the growth.

"You intend to bash my head in?"

"Yes, just…hold on a moment. It's stuck."

Rodrigo's mind wrestled to come to grips with the lunatic's casually planned execution, but his body acted swiftly. He bent, pried out a fist-sized stone at his own feet, and flung it at Talen's back. *Can a delusion make a bruise, Talen?*

The rock sailed high and struck Talen squarely on the back of the head. The big man crashed forward and lay there unmoving.

Rodrigo gasped and rushed to Talen's side. The man moved a feeble hand up to his head.

"Are you all right?" asked Rodrigo. "My apologies, I did not mean to do that, but you *were* planning to kill me."

"I'm not…not a vengeful man," muttered Talen as he fought to clear his vision. "But this will only end happily if I pretend to strangle you slowly with my bare hands."

As Talen tried to regain his feet, Rodrigo lifted the now loosened stone that Talen had intended to use and poised it over the dazed man. But the stone remained poised, and Rodrigo groaned in uncertainty. Heaving it away, he retreated back to the water's edge and cast desperately about.

How had he survived the fall and the passage through to the roiling pool? It didn't seem possible. The narrowed tunnel downstream promised the same fate.

Talen stalked him now, fully on his feet with his hands outstretched. Earlier the man looked imposing, but now, closing in on Rodrigo with deadly intent, he seemed enormous, overpowering.

Rodrigo made his choice. If he could survive the first impossibility, he would trust to the second. He flung himself back into the river.

"Die your own way then!" yelled Talen as Rodrigo bobbed to the surface. Rodrigo caught a momentary glance back, and his heart froze.

There, next to Talen, he thought that he could see something—a shape outlined in the penetrating glow of the cavern's moss-growth.

Water slapped into his eyes and, before he could clear them, his head bumped into the cavern roof and he was swept into the airless flow.

Water is a powerful creature, and the flow of the river gave no regard to Rodrigo. Though he flailed desperately, the current spun him about, slamming and scraping him repeatedly along the water-worn black walls. Here and there the spotty glow of stubborn growth flashed by. He felt the air escape from his lungs and water replace it, and he panicked fully.

The water abruptly changed course, pushing him upward violently. He felt air about him and then a falling sensation. He landed painfully, though thick growth cushioned his fall. The water in his lungs rushed out and he gasped life back into his body as the torrent of the massive artesian fountain beat down on him. Crawling away from the geyser of water, he fell unconscious atop a heap of brightly glowing red moss-growth.

2 : SHADOW

Rodrigo awoke, stretching flexibly, discovering that his youthful body had taken the abuse with resilience. For a time—a day, perhaps two, for with no sun he had no way of knowing—Rodrigo rested, rinsed away the sand in his sinuses, dabbed at his battered face, and tried to eat a small bulb that looked close enough to a mushroom for his comfort. The bright yellowish glow of the bulb faded quickly after he plucked it from the rocks.

He held it before him, sighed out a breath, uttered a hopeful prayer, and took a modest nibble. To his surprise, it tasted sweet, and he gorged himself on others like it.

He began to explore, finding that water flowed out of the fountain cave through a number of cracks and crevices too narrow for Rodrigo to fit into. He started searching drier gaps that sloped upward, discovering in the process that he disliked tight places to the point of panic. Disregarding his fear, he crawled and squeezed his way into each space, disappointed every time when the crack ended or narrowed down too closely.

He ate, and rested, and tried again, his mind numbed by the string of terrors, the isolation, and the groaning weight of the massive mountain under which he found himself entombed. Another narrow tunnel dead-ended, and another. But the next one, higher up on the jagged walls, gave him hope. A breeze blew lightly through it, bringing in drier and warmer air. He pushed on, feeling his way blindly upward in the darkness of the dry, sloping tunnel where the growth did not extend.

The crack opened more, and the floor became less rock-strewn, covered over with a heavy clay and sand that must have been laid down by an old watercourse.

Rodrigo's spirits lifted. He would gather up a bundle of yellow growth for food, use the large bulbs to carry water, and he would press on.

He had not quite finished his thought when he heard a sharp grating sound and rumble behind him. Scrambling back through the crack, he came to what he feared most.

Fallen rock blocked the way back—to water, and food, and light.

———

Time passed, although Rodrigo no longer understood time. His existence extended to the tips of his fingers, the bruises on his forehead, the dry, rough movement of his parched tongue, the pang in his empty stomach, and the thin lines of dried blood tracing down from his rock-savaged knees. Right, left, up, down—

but mostly up—he found nothing but wandering tunnels, jagged ledges, and mind-spinning twists in direction.

He tried piling rocks, and it helped. He could navigate a small area, but as he pushed outward he always found himself, sooner or later, reaching out and discovering one of his rock piles, having somehow looped back. And everywhere he pushed, he found dry stone—nothing to drink and no cheery, glowing moss-growth to eat.

His body did not suffer alone. His mind fought a long, grand campaign against an encroaching fear, and slowly, slice by slice, he was losing. But he did not blame this on the darkness. He blamed it on the Other Darkness.

Something, he was certain, had joined him in the maze.

It followed him. He could feel it at his heels, prowling along the rock at his side, drifting just behind the hairs at the back of his neck. It made no sound, placed no claw upon him, nor even disturbed the dry, warm air. He called it Shadow, although no shadow could be made here. It ate at him, scraped away his life fleck by fleck, using fear like sharpened fangs. Rodrigo fought against every bite by the Shadow, wrestling frantically, in a world not visible to the eye, to keep the devoured flecks small. And, when in the real world, he turned suddenly to reach out and touch the monster, to catch it by surprise, he felt nothing.

But he knew better.

———

There came a moment in his agonized timelessness that he lay stretched out at the wall of rock that had trapped him, feeling the light rumble of the artesian fountain in his fingertips and placing his eye so that he could see a ghost of moss-light through a seam of rock. The main obstacle back to the fountain was nothing but a slab of rock—a massive, immovable barrier. He had tried to chip away at it with another rock, but accomplished little more than a small rough spot in its surface.

The Shadow chose this time to speak to him. Rodrigo did not hear the words with his ears, but he did not let this fact concern him.

"Get up," said the Shadow.

Rodrigo believed that he raised his head. Yes, he did, for he could no longer see the nothing-glow of the moss-light. "My pardons, but…did you speak to me?"

"Get up." The Shadow floated above him, drifting back and forth, or so Rodrigo imagined, for he could see nothing.

Rodrigo laughed. It started as little more than a dry-mouthed chuckle, but it rose until his body seized with the effort. "I think not." He slowly lowered his

8

head, trying to control the shaking of his shrunken, exhausted muscles so that he could align one eye back to the tantalizing glow coming through the rock seam.

"Why?" said the Shadow.

"Consider my options," said Rodrigo with a last grunt of humor.

The Shadow remained silent for a time. But it returned. "You wonder if I am real. If real, and nibbling away on you, then I am an enemy and one does not obey an enemy. If not real, then there is also no reason to obey."

"So you *have* been nibbling away on me."

The Shadow grew darker, if that were possible. "Get up. You must live."

"Why?"

"Because your life means my life," said the Shadow.

Despite Rodrigo's exhaustion, he rose to his feet. The Shadow gave no ground, towering over him.

"I will die soon," said Rodrigo, his throat-choked words emphasizing his shrunken, thirsting state. "Perhaps it will be good for the world that you die as well."

Again the Shadow fell silent. Rodrigo faced the darkness, his body swaying lightly in an attempt to remain standing.

"Then you leave me no choice. I must live." The Shadow boiled down over the boy. Its rending fear, so deftly but lightly applied in feeding upon him before, struck upon Rodrigo now without reserve, without limit.

Where before it had nibbled, it would now swallow whole.

Rodrigo remained standing, his eyes closed, his face lifted, his sunken features tightened by a trembling grimace as soundless words hissed out through his cracked lips.

The Shadow recoiled, gathered, and struck again, bringing with the fear a clawing desperation. Rodrigo stumbled back against the slab of stone. His muttered words turned to cries. Slowly he slid to the ground, his chest heaving in ragged gasps and his eyelids tightened into bulging creases.

There came the hint of passing, like a monstrous thunderstorm flashing slightly farther away on its latest bolt. He took a desperate, ragged swallow, fought for a breath...

The assault wavered, failed, and died.

With a final exhausted shudder, Rodrigo released the clench in his chest. Slowly he opened his pained eyes.

He could feel no Shadow.

He concentrated on breathing, shifting his back weakly on the uneven floor and feeling at his scrapes. Blood stained the rock where his bony ribs had dragged down along the stone.

How long he laid there, he did not know.

But his rest did not continue long. The Shadow's presence brushed against him once again.

"Get up, I beg you," said the Shadow.

3: VISION

Rodrigo's fingers touched against a small pile of rock—a pyramid that he recognized, despite the tatters in his mind. Feeling the nearby stones and their alignment, he knew that he had already passed onward into three different exits, whether tunnel, fissure, cavern, or nothing more than a crack.

Four other stones reminded him that he still had four untried directions remaining from here. A hundred other options awaited him at other stone piles in this endless labyrinth.

His hands touched one of the untried stones. It stood on end. When he'd put the stone here, he'd had a reason for setting it on end. What was it? Ah, the passage must be above him, or at least going up. Here…yes…to the right, this steep upward slope.

He aligned his body slowly and began to crawl over the uneven stone. Many places had clay or sand covering the floor. He had tried those first, being easier on his knees, but they'd led nowhere.

He fooled his mind away from his battered knees by closing his eyes and pulling forth daydreams of horses—fine, graceful racing steeds and mighty, wide-shouldered war mounts. And with each, he thanked his god for the beautiful vision and found—or at least hoped—that he had covered a meaningful distance.

The Shadow followed. Its fear-fangs ripped at Rodrigo on occasion, but the battle fell into a stalemate. Rodrigo did not resist a small nibble, and the Shadow did not try for more.

The slope turned slowly into a level, sand-layered tunnel. Rodrigo dug fingers into the sand and offered up a grateful, ragged prayer.

Through his eyelids, he thought he saw light.

He opened his eyes.

There, floating in the tall, narrow crease of tunnel, was a female. Rodrigo could not only see the vision clearly, but the tunnel as well, for a blue-white light streamed from her with such intensity that his eyes refused to open fully until he had rubbed them repeatedly and blinked away the crust of abuse.

He managed to stand and he shuffled forward.

Although perfectly beautiful, she was not perfectly human. Her hair—if indeed hair—flowed outward to form a brilliant corona that lit her finely curved features. Except that light came from behind and shone through her face, as if she were nothing more than a gossamer curtain through which a bright moon shimmered.

Within her large moonglow eyes, he saw worlds.

His lips tried to form words, but they stumbled over each other. The words caught, not in his throat but in his mind. He tried desperately to weave them back into coherence.

Her hand rose, and a finger of light touched his lips. "A gift," came a musical, softly echoing voice which he imagined to be hers.

The touch flashed through his flesh and into his mind, pulling unseen threads into contact. His head rocked momentarily, and then words snapped from his lips. "Gracia de Dios! Eres una angel!"

The words thrilled him, their grace and cadence lifting his soul, and he croaked out a laugh. But a harder, sharp-edged part of him rose up and brought forcefully to mind the desperate state of his flesh. He had very little time.

"Do you know the way?" he asked.

"You have found it," came the voice, and she gestured a hand forward.

He forced his eyes from staring through hers and shuffled past her, his feet finding solid footing by her light. He came to a natural rock wall, slightly higher than his head and topped by a ledge, but he could see the tunnel continue from there.

"Why am I here?" he asked as he placed one weary foot on a jut of stone. A desperate hope rose in him, awaiting the answer.

"To live. To trust. To set right."

"Do you know who I am...who I was?"

"Be...who...you...*are,*" drifted the voice, and with each word, the light faded.

"Wait!" Rodrigo slipped from the stone, trying to turn to catch sight of the moonlit vision. But he crumpled against the wall with a groan.

Nothing remained except the darkness.

In his building despair he felt for the presence of the Shadow, but found no hint of it.

"Are you there?" he called, for it came to his mind that something terrible in the dark might be better than nothing at all, anywhere.

No answer came.

He turned and gripped the ledge, digging for toeholds with his feet. A reservoir of strength driven by desperation propelled him, allowing him progress in levering himself up. One hand stretched out on the ledge's top, struggling for a grip. For a brief moment his fingers slid along something that felt like slick stone.

An exploding sphere of brilliant white light expanded on the ledge in front of him and slammed him back into the sand below.

4: YUN

Not far away there was a cave of vast size.

A lake had once filled it, polishing smooth the walls of banded black-and-pale stone and depositing terraces of speckled sand on the floor. Ages passed and the lake retreated far enough to expose a full two hundred feet of beach. At several points, thin cascades of water fell from the ceiling like veils and flowed through the sand to the lake's edge.

Mounds of the strange moss-growth spread in and around the water and the mists of the waterfalls—odd assortments of fat bulbous growths and wide plant-like fronds glowing in a riot of luminous colors, bright enough to reveal the high, water-sculpted ceiling. At one place in the cavern wall, there was a dry, dark tunnel entrance.

Out of this darkness appeared Rodrigo.

He crawled, dragging a burden behind him in short bursts that left his breath ragged and his muscles quivering. The lean angles of his battered, filthy face contorted in exhaustion with each pull, his haunted nut-brown eyes squinting and blinking rapidly even in the soft moss-light of the cave. His clothes, especially the knees of his loose trousers, were beyond mending.

"Over and past," he breathed out, and repeated it. He muttered other less meaningful things, bits and pieces of a fevered conversation between the loosened ends of his mind. A trickle of water ran down the cavern wall, and he licked hungrily at it for several minutes until he retched and tried again.

The burden he dragged lay upon an old tapestry put to use as a makeshift sled. It was a girl, oriental in appearance, younger than him. She remained as he had placed her, curled up, her breathing shallow and slow. Her eyes rolled under their lids and her lips formed unspoken words, as if frantic dreams battled for attention inside her.

The boy crawled back to the tapestry, gave a final heave forward, and let his grip slip, lurching into the sand. He lay there, panting, until sudden alarm came over him and he levered up into a sitting position, facing the dark tunnel from where he had come.

His eyes narrowed with intensity, searching the shifting of even deeper shadow within the tunnel's darkness. His breath caught, and though his cracked lips stretched in fear, he bared his teeth in a triumphant snarl. He stabbed a finger at the tunnel, and managed to rasp out between breaths, "I can...see you!"

A low, giggling laugh escaped him, turning quickly into a wracking cough. His head sank low. He slid prone onto the sand and fell asleep between breaths.

Water light played over the two, and the tunnel darkness watched.

When Rodrigo awoke later, the tapestry—and the girl—were gone.

His eyes immediately turned to the dark tunnel exit, and his breath caught in his throat. He rose to his feet unsteadily and took a first step toward it, but not a second. His legs would not readily obey a return to that horror, even if the girl had foolishly gone that way.

But a scan of the ground gave him relief. Something had made wide, shallow drag marks in the sand. The meandering trail led to the nearby fall of water from the ceiling and the small brook that it birthed. He worked his way to the waterfall and, to his relief, found the girl curled up beneath the tapestry near the water's edge, asleep.

He bent to her.

Her fevered state had obviously passed, her heart-shaped face relaxed and her breathing steady and soft. Mist collected in her long, straight, ebony hair and trickled down across the tapestry. Despite the lightness of her small body, his arms could not lift her, and he dragged her on the tapestry, away from the wet sand.

He removed his shirt, placed it beneath her head, and brushed at the collected moisture around her. As he did, an object fell from her hand. He arranged the tapestry over her and picked up the item—a strip of brown paper rolled tightly around a stick of charcoal. He remembered them in her pocket when he'd found her.

On the paper were a few words, in shaky script:

Chakri Blue Silver Dance

With a small, puzzled grunt he placed the paper and stick in her pocket.

Rodrigo bent to the stream and, to his delight, found it teeming with small fish. After drinking carefully, he scooped several out and swallowed them down without even bothering to kill them first.

"Rodrigo."

His name came softly, startling him nonetheless. He turned to her, and her lips made his name again. "Rodrigo."

He bent close to her. "How do you know my name?"

Her large eyes opened farther, but she made no move to rise. A weak smile came to her. "You told me."

"I did? I do not remember."

Her eyes closed again, and she sighed. "I'm glad you hear me. I thought you were a dream, like the others."

"What is your name?"

"Yun…Yun…" She fell silent for a time. Finally, "I can't remember my name."

Rodrigo watched a tear trickle across her nose.

She brought a trembling hand to her cheek. "I can't remember *anything*. I don't know who I am."

He watched her tense and begin to crawl inside of herself as the fear of her memory loss took hold. He remembered how his own panic had built as he'd discovered that he knew nothing of himself. For him, the panic had competed with the more immediate terror of being stoned to death by the insane brute in the cave. *Was his name Talen? Did I merely imagine him?*

"Yun, listen to me."

Her eyes opened slightly, but the tears came harder.

"I am Rodrigo, and that is all I know as well. So you are not alone, and neither am I. We are alive, and in a cave with light, and we are safe. That is as good a place to start as any. So rest. Do you like fish?"

Yun listened to him, though her tears continued. "Yes."

"Raw fish?"

"Yes."

"Good, because there is plenty of fish but no fire. Can you stand?"

Yun tried, feebly and without much enthusiasm. "No." She started crying more openly again.

Rodrigo bit back his frustration. She was just a girl, he reminded himself—scared and tired and without any memory. He sat back a moment, trying not to let her crying grate on his nerves. Then he remembered the paper.

"Yun, you wrote something on your paper."

"W-What?"

"The paper in your pocket. You wrote something while I slept."

Yun's crying died down as she fumbled around her pocket. Eventually she pulled out a scattering of the brown paper and charcoal. She gasped and her tears ended instantly. "What did I write?"

"Not those. The rolled up one."

She found it. "Chakri Blue Silver Dance." Her gentle, halting but finely enunciated voice died after reading the words.

"What did you mean? Why did you write that?"

She didn't answer immediately, rereading the words. "I—I don't know. The chakri is a dress. And I do like to dance." Her eyes grew larger, and she sat up. "Yes, I do!"

Rodrigo patted her shoulder. "There, you are getting better as we speak. Things will come to us in time. For now, I will catch some fish. They are small. I just swallowed them whole, head and all."

Yun nodded absently as Rodrigo turned down to the water's edge. She retrieved all of her paper, counted it, and carefully uncurled the used one. She began to write deftly with small, neat letters.

Day 1

I like to dance.

5: FLOTSAM

Yun's diary, Day 2

My name is Yun. I do not remember my last name. I am not even sure how old I am.

I have three bits of charcoal and twenty-four leaves of brown paper, and the clothes I wear. Good and sturdy, but not very pretty.

Rodrigo found me. He has not told me where. I was asleep to start. My sleep was full of dreams. I can't remember any of them now.

Rodrigo is hurt, with terrible scrapes and cuts. Just looking at them made my knees ache. I helped him take care of them.

The two finished their small pile of fish.

"Rodrigo?"

"Yes?"

"Where did you find me?"

He pointed to the dark tunnel. "Out there. I was trying to climb up on a ledge and there was this strange explosion of light that knocked me off. When I tried the ledge again, you were lying there."

"Sounds scary."

"I was delighted, actually." He smiled. "Someone else besides me."

"Where were you all that time?" asked Yun.

Rodrigo's mirth left him. "Out there."

"What were you doing?"

"Little to tell," said Rodrigo.

"Please tell me," said Yun. "It helps. To hear you talk, I mean."

Rodrigo paused and nodded. He related to her the city, the river, the lunatic Talen, and his entry into the dark tunnels, but he said nothing of the Shadow or the angel.

Yun was silent for a moment. Then she looked at him, her deep brown eyes full of concern. "You had no lamp or fire?"

"No. It was quite dark."

"For how long?"

"Three or four days, I would guess. I crawled around in the dark so long that I was dying of thirst. I stumbled onto you, and soon after found this entrance and this glorious haven."

"I would have gone mad," said Yun.

Rodrigo went silent, his head resting on his knee. Then he took hold of her hand and faced her, his chestnut eyes steady but rimmed with moisture.

"I did go mad," he said. "And it will take a lifetime to erase that shame."

He lowered his eyes, seeking to avoid the pain by studying his hand and the smallness of hers, cupped in his palm.

Then, her eyes met his and she smiled a girl's smile. "You saved me. A madman couldn't do that."

Rodrigo snorted, then smiled, and withdrew his hand. "That was not enough to eat. You can eat the yellow mushroom things, like that over there. I will taste some of these other plants, or mushrooms, or whatever they are. One at a time, so we know if any are poisonous. Just a nibble."

"Me too," said Yun.

"No-" started Rodrigo, but she picked a small round bulb and popped it in her mouth before he could protest further. She managed one chew, then bent forward and retched it out.

"Ugh. That's horridly bitter!" After wiping away the offending juice and swishing a mouthful of water, she broke off the tip of an upright fern-like frond and nibbled at it.

"You let me take the risks." Rodrigo looked around for a likely candidate. In the shallows of the stream a purplish plant grew, like watercress but fully submerged. He gathered several strands and chewed them. They were surprisingly tasty, and he craved to eat more, but he stepped away.

"Good, like eating scallions. How was yours?"

"Chalky," said Yun. "But not bad."

"Can you stand?"

"Probably, but I'm very sleepy again."

"Then rest." Rodrigo pointed to the lake's edge. "I will explore—not far, just around over there, by the lake."

Yun curled herself up, not looking particularly excited about the idea. "Okay, not far."

"I promise." He walked the hundred paces to the lake's edge. The lake view opened up as he approached it, and his breath caught at the strange, spectacular scene. He could see the moss-glow along other shorelines, some close, some far away.

He waded into the clear water and found it pleasantly warm. A riotous landscape of luminescent growth lit the water far into its depths. After splashing a remainder of crusted dirt off his arms, he returned to shore and gazed out over the slight ripples of the lake.

To his left, he spotted what appeared to be a large mound. He strode in that direction and was surprised by what he saw.

A waterfall fell from the ceiling and formed a shallow creek that flowed to the lake. A pile of refuse and flotsam lay strewn along that creek. Rodrigo edged near it and tried to peer up into the fissure from where the water came, but the scattering of glowmoss within the gap revealed little. He imagined that the pile of debris somehow fell from whatever lay above, although the constricted, jagged appearance of the opening made that unlikely.

Judging by this pile, there would be other people nearby—many others, considering the pile's size. Perhaps it came from the city of Drift, not that he wished another toss over the waterfall.

Some of the debris looked fairly new, but Rodrigo remembered his promise and returned to Yun before digging about. When he reached her side, she was asleep again, clutching her papers in both hands.

6: TREASURES

Yun's diary, Day 3

I can stand and walk about.

Rodrigo guesses that I am 13. He's a horrid guesser. I know I am small and look more girl than woman. But I am much older than that, 16 or so. I feel it.

Rodrigo is like a tree next to me, very tall and lean of face. He looks like he is still growing into his body, all arms and legs, but he moves with grace. Rodrigo believes he is 18. I am sure he is a little younger.

Today I used up two of my papers. I hope we can find more. Both of us feel okay, so we ate more of my fronds and his seaweed. There must be a hundred kinds of growing things. Maybe if we like another three or four new kinds, we can stop so we don't try the wrong thing and get poisoned to death.

We are going to explore a pile of debris that Rodrigo found, out there next to the lake. Rodrigo has started calling it Vida Lake. He says vida means life, and this lake gave it back to him.

"This is paraffin, I am sure of it. A hundred pound block of paraffin!" Rodrigo wrestled with the translucent block of wax to remove it from a pile of other debris.

Firelight bathed him and the nearby piles with a cheery orange glow, a result of Rodrigo's skill at starting a fire with nothing more than a string and a dry old stick. Yun fed the bonfire more pieces of driftwood and splintered lumber. At first they worried about the smoke, but a steady draft pushed it out over the lake and beyond.

"We can make candles," said Yun.

"Hundreds of big, fat candles, enough to chase away the dark for a lifetime," said Rodrigo. "Enough to make a proper dedication to San..." He paused and went silent.

"San?" asked Yun after a moment.

"I—I am not sure. San is a name—perhaps." Rodrigo's brows knit together closer and closer as he wrestled to drag something from the edge of his memory. The remembrance refused to cooperate, and presently he smiled. "No matter.

We might be in the warrens of purgatory for all I know, but the Lord of All is favoring us even so."

The debris had already given up a wealth of practical treasures, including an assortment of rusting weapons, a fine knife in a sheath, lanterns and lamps and tools and an entire barrel of what Rodrigo thought was whale oil. Yun found additional papers and a sturdy oilskin case, which she declared to be the greatest discoveries possible.

Rodrigo stepped back and looked around at the piles yet to be searched. "This is the strangest treasure trove. I would say some of it looks like shipwreck but there is not much in the way of ship parts. Old things are mixed in with new— see? Perhaps a flood came down through that fissure and swept all this with it. But the gap is so narrow…Just strange, so many things smashed to bits and others untouched."

Rodrigo returned to his pilfering while Yun made up a torch with a wrap of old canvas and a dip of the whale oil. Rodrigo heard her say something about statues or such, but his interest latched onto the next pile, which immediately rewarded him with a roll of light netting and a large rusty hook.

He dug in with fervor, sorting out many small treasures, though most of them were admittedly dubious in value. Here and there he found electric devices, but cast them aside. Their fragility and the lack of electricity made them valueless. The pile shrank slowly as the once vigorous light from the bonfire waned.

Rodrigo was about to step back and take a break when his hands uncovered an object of fine, dark wood. He grasped and pulled, expecting a difficult tug, but the object slid easily from the pile—a battered but polished oblong box, its center carved elegantly with a silver symbol of a charging bull.

He carried it to the sand, broke the heavy wax seals, and opened it. A whistle of delight escaped his lips as he drew out a long, slim sword from a silver-trimmed scabbard. Not a speck of rust tainted the blade, and the edge proved dangerously keen as Rodrigo nicked his finger. The same charging bull graced the finely crafted hilt.

He held the sword before his eyes, turning it slightly to cause the torchlight to run along its polished edge and over the lines of the stylistic bull symbol. A minute passed, his eyes drinking in every detail, his mouth moving silently with unspoken appreciation.

He was barely aware that he had fallen into a sitting position in the sand. The other treasures were lost to him, swept away in their insignificance.

He blinked. "Yun! Come see!"

He rose and turned to show her, but she was gone.

———

I found stairs carved into the cavern wall next to the lake. From where I am, and you can see around all the far shores because of the glowing plants.

The stairs end on a ledge above the lake. There's water dripping from the walls, and growth covers everything except for a dry patch around some statues. I can imagine there's an entrance to a gnome kingdom here, or a troll cave full of treasure.

Vida Lake is beautiful, and this spot will be My Place.

Despite being in the cave only a few days, Yun's mind already accepted the lake as home, and therefore safe. So when she spied three figures high on a growth-crusted cliff side, and when she realized that they weren't moving, she decided to take a closer look without bothering Rodrigo as he sorted through debris.

Torch in hand, she reached the cave's edge. To her surprise, the beach ended in carved steps leading up to the statues. The stone stairs were wide and shallow, easing her ascent. In no time she reached an end to the steps and a wide landing where the three statues rested.

But the view took Yun's attention first. She dared herself to sit at the edge with her legs dangling free, and she gazed out over the lake. Being forty feet up from its surface, she could see its entire expanse. Below her, spots of luminescence dotted the flanks of bulky fish that swam above the glowing underwater landscape. Those fish were much larger than the ones near the sand shore.

Although the growths of moss gave off a respectable light, that light came mainly from the ground, casting its illumination upward and giving everything an eerie, sinister nature, throwing shadows that crept and crawled along the rock overhead. Even with the cheery addition of firelight, shadows and gloom dominated this world and gave uncertainty to what awaited in the dark.

She propped up her torch, nursed a few lines of writing into her makeshift diary, then spun herself around to look at the statues.

My Place has three statues. I can't guess why someone would drag them up here. They are nicely done. The first is a big angry-looking man carved from a dark green jade. Beside him is an old man, regal like a king. He's carved of white stone, like marble. And behind them is a tall woman without proper clothing at all. I hope Rodrigo doesn't come up here.

Yun stored her papers, stood, and ran her hand over the arm of the king. It felt utterly strange—slippery like oil but not oily. It seemed as though the surface pushed back against her.

She moved in front of the big angry man, careful of the cliff edge, and reached out to touch his fist-clenched hand.

The world exploded in thunder and light—a searing flash that left her blinded. What felt like a giant hand slammed into her. Her shock turned to panic as she realized that she plummeted through dark, empty air.

———

"Yun?" said Rodrigo, walking around the fire. Yun did not answer. He called louder, but he heard no response.

"Stupid girl, no sense in her at all!" He sighed, feeling guilty at his muttered words—and a bit panicked at her sudden disappearance. Perhaps not "sudden," considering how long he had worked at his treasure hunting.

He tried to read tracks, but the sand had already been stirred to uselessness. He scanned about, trying to spot torch fire among the different shades of glowing growth, and his eyes had almost caught sight of it up on the ledge when a blinding burst of white erupted. There came a momentary total silence, then a shattering, echoing roar.

It was familiar—the same as when he'd found Yun.

Although partially night-blinded, Rodrigo could see the torch arcing through the air and splashing out into the lake's less-lit, deep water. A much larger splash rose beyond it.

Yun?

He raced to the water's edge, spotted the steps, and sprinted recklessly up. Halfway along, he thought he saw an object in the deep water where the bigger splash had been. He launched himself over the edge.

The fall took forever and he struck hard, but he battled to the surface and tried to orient himself. "Yun!" he yelled.

A small splashing sound came from his right, and he swam frantically toward it. Nothing. He treaded water and spun. "Yun!"

A sputtering cough, close by. He reached out with his hands, searching blindly, the odd underwater light twisting his vision. His left hand touched cloth and he grabbed hold.

As he did so, a slash of pain ran along his leg and a weight dragged at it.

He cried out and tried to see down into the water. Two large, luminous eyes stared back at him from a fat fish-like body nearly as long as himself. He thrust his hand at the eyes, felt the soft sinking of the eye sockets, and dug in with his fingernails. The finned body shook violently, more pain struck Rodrigo, and then his leg swung free of the monster's grip.

He lost track of the next moments in a haze of pain and panic. Dragging his unknown burden back to shore, he discovered that it was indeed Yun, unconscious—or dead. He leaned her over his knee, slapping hard on her back.

"Gracia de Dios! Do not leave me! I cannot be here alone. Not again."

No response, and no breath.

"What were you *doing!*" he yelled at her and pounded her back none too gently.

Yun coughed a gout of water and sucked in a ragged breath. Rodrigo dropped to the sand and cradled her. She continued to cough but her breathing firmed up. She shook uncontrollably, and he realized he did the same.

A trickle ran down the back of his ankle. He turned his leg, discovering blood dripping from a long, curved series of small gashes along the inside of his calf. He felt a similar curving pattern on the other side. Gritting his teeth and probing the wounds, he discovered, to his relief, that while fearsome looking, they were shallow. He removed his shirt and bound the calf tightly.

They both fell asleep, exhausted, as if transported back in time to their first hour in the cave.

7 : BOAR

...and Rodrigo said I was dead for a little while until he got me to breathe again. My back is terribly sore where he beat me.

The oiled case saved my papers. Only a little bit of water got in.

Rodrigo is mad at me.

Rodrigo gave Yun a clumsy series of lectures through the next day, so much so that she spent several hours just curled up and silent, pouting behind her veil of hair.

Rodrigo eventually took a softer tone, and even coaxed her into agreeing to return to the ledge to see what had happened. She thought briefly about taking a cloth with her to drape over the tall female sculpture, but decided never again to touch any statue.

Before going, Rodrigo removed his shirt from the bitten calf, grunted in satisfaction at seeing the clean knit of the wound, and redressed the bite with light cloth from the treasure piles. The blood refused to fully wash from his shirt.

Refreshed, the two ascended the stairs, but upon reaching the ledge Yun froze and took in a breath.

The statue of the angry man was gone. But lying in its place was a man—a real man.

He appeared to be in his mid-twenties. His thick shoulders topped a body that fully rippled with muscle. Reddish-blond hair spiked up in a short crewcut, shaved near to baldness on the sides of a face that was all angles and blocks.

The man's ghostly gray eyes fluttered open as they approached, sending Yun's nape hairs twitching. Several hours passed before the stranger was able to stand and navigate the stairs. And in those hours, he uttered not a word.

Day 5

The stranger won't talk. I thought he might be mute, but he doesn't even try to make gestures or write or anything. He just stares at you with those scary eyes.

26

He's almost a head taller than Rodrigo, and Rodrigo must be almost six feet. I hope the man behaves himself.

"He sets me on edge," whispered Rodrigo to her when the stranger went off to the cavern edge that was reserved for the latrine. "There's something wrong about him. I do not know what it is, but I cannot sleep knowing he is here. He cuts straight to the soul."

"What do we do?" whispered Yun.

"Be careful what you say around him."

Day 7

Last night I cut my ankle on a pointy edge that sticks out of my bathing rock. Rodrigo used a piece of his pant leg to make a bandage. When I went for my bath tonight, that pointy rock was smashed off. Rodrigo never said anything about it.

What if someone like that stranger had found me instead of Rodrigo? Loa protected me.

Yun put her charcoal stick back into her pouch, smoothed the journal pages, rolled them up carefully, and slid them into her oilskin case. Taking hold of her folded blanket, she stretched over to blow out her lamp.

And her body and breath seized in fear.

Crouched atop the rock that served as the head of her sand-bed, Boar stared down at her. His pale eyes drifted their attention down over her hair and along the tattering clothes of her birth.

"You sh…" started Yun, but her voice trailed away. Her body remained rigid, except that the hand holding the folded blanket slowly dragged it up to her neck.

The stranger's eyes snapped back to hers, gripping them like a mouse in the talons of an owl. His lips stretched in a smug sneer.

Then a commanding voice caused Yun to yelp.

"Get up!"

Rodrigo strode into the lamplight, his eyes hawk-fierce, his hand tensed atop the hilt of his bull-engraved sword.

The stranger did not react. He kept his gaze on Yun's panicked eyes.

Rodrigo scanned the nearby sand, then took another step toward the stranger, whose eyes now swung toward him.

"The broken rock, there." Rodrigo pointed. "You will come no closer to her place than that, night or day."

The stranger shifted his ghost-pale eyes back to Yun, a smile curled his lips, and he stood. Without a glance at Rodrigo, he turned and strode away.

Day 10

I can't sleep. I wish that monster would try something, then Rodrigo can use his sword to defend us, and we would be done with him.

The stranger helped himself to the mixture of glowmoss and fish, nearly emptying the pot. Rodrigo, who had built the fire and prepared the stew, shot him a look of disgust. Yun remained sitting, too afraid of the stranger to get up and pour her share.

"My stew is worth at least your name," said Rodrigo.

"Boar," said the man.

Rodrigo froze at the first word uttered by the stranger, but he quickly recovered himself, dropping a splintered board into the fire. "A fitting name. Yun has not eaten yet."

"Da! I make sure she have plenty." Boar's voice came out low and powerful, with an odd curl to each syllable. He returned to the pot, tilted it with his hand-carved wooden spoon, and dumped the remainder of the contents into his large bowl. Picking up another makeshift spoon, he sat down above Yun so that the bowl hovered near her head. He held out the extra spoon to her.

Yun slowly lowered her hands to the sand and slid away from Boar, her eyes fixed on her knees.

Boar grunted a laugh and began filling his mouth as fast as he could work his spoon.

Fury rose in Rodrigo, but he kept his face passive. He brought a curl of humor to his lips as he set aside his own untouched bowl. "I can stop worrying about the poison. You will certainly eat enough of it."

Boar's spoon paused.

"Yes, bad poison!" blurted Yun.

The hopeless lie in Yun's words caused another grunt from Boar as his lips spread in a smug smile. He resumed his feast, but he wagged his spoon momentarily.

"You are children, good, nice little children. Strut around with fancy swords...this you do. Poison? This you do not do."

Rodrigo felt at his sword and wondered if he would soon need it. "If we cannot come to an agreement on how civilized men act, I will forget that I am a nice little child."

Boar brought the bowl to his lips and downed the remainder in a fit of gulping gluttony. Then his gray eyes locked on Rodrigo.

"This is nice, safe place for children. Nice little cage. I don't like cage, not so much. So I leave."

"Through the tunnel?" asked Rodrigo.

"Da, of course through tunnel. I am not frightened little child."

Rodrigo's eyes narrowed. "I have already been in those tunnels. There is nothing to eat or drink, and I am not recovered—and why do you want to go there?"

Boar smiled a predator's smile. "I make them mine."

"Well, by all means, go forth," said Rodrigo.

"I receive blessing from child! Good! Now I go confident."

Rodrigo tried to shake off the man's blatant contempt, but his fury continued to build. "What about us?"

"You? You are safe in little cage. Grow to man, maybe. Yun grow to woman. Live and die in little cage. Now, I get stuff ready. You give me sword."

Boar rose and reached out his hand to indicate the bull sword hanging at Rodrigo's belt.

"What?" Rodrigo jumped to his feet, took a step back, and put his hand on the weapon's hilt. "Whoever you think you are, you are free to take what you need. There are plenty of other weapons here. But this sword will be the death of you if you try to take it."

"It is finest weapon. Here in little cage, why do you need? I have need. Da?"

In one swift, fluid motion Boar leapt forward and drove a kick into Rodrigo's belly that sent the boy sprawling. As Rodrigo tried to regain his feet, he found one of Boar's arms vise-like around his neck, and his own sword arm pinned painfully behind his back.

"Now," said Boar into Rodrigo's ear, "I do not like kill children. But if I need, I kill children. You see?" He pulled the arm back farther, and Rodrigo cried out.

"You cry, but not say da. Da?"

"Yes," said Rodrigo.

"Good, now I take sword. You happy to give sword, da?"

It took more pain, and his arm dangerously close to dislocation, before Rodrigo finally gasped out a word.

"No."

Boar shook his head and clicked his tongue several times. "You are stubborn child." He unstrapped Rodrigo's belt and shoved him toward the fire. "I go pack things now. You sit by fire, be good children. Nobody be kill today."

Rodrigo nursed his arm and sat down by the fire. Yun curled up beside him and clung to his shirt, as though trying to become invisible.

Boar sorted through the provisions, stuffing the best of it into a sizable canvas bag. He prepared a stack of torches and several large water flasks, slung these on his back, and, despite the mountain of material, he hardly seemed burdened.

As he passed by on his way to the tunnel, he stopped and gave Yun a wide grin. "Grow up, little girl, and I come back for you."

Yun tried to curl up tighter, and her eyes grew larger, if possible, as she peered up through her bangs at the angular brute.

Boar struck a torch, and without further comment strode into the tunnel and disappeared from view.

Day 11

Rodrigo and I have vowed never to touch any statue here again.

8: Excursion

— 8 days later

Yun's diary, Day 19

Rodrigo is furious. Not in a fiery way, but cold. When he is not cleaning out the debris piles, he makes me run and lift objects and other exercise with him. He wants me to be fit, he says. But I am more fit than he is.

I told him he needs rest, because he has never fully recovered from all of his past difficulties. He's normally so stubborn, but he must have listened to me, because he sleeps often now. I leave him alone. He is not much fun to be around right now anyway.

Rodrigo awoke and rolled on his side, his sleep-filled gaze wandering toward the glowing line of the lake. A silhouetted figure moved in this glow, causing Rodrigo to sit up in alarm.

He saw Yun's empty bedroll nearby. *It must be her, but best not to take chances.* He dressed quickly and slipped quietly toward the lake.

As he closed in on the figure, it became outlined more clearly, until he knew without doubt that it was Yun. She moved rhythmically, spinning and leaping lightly in the air while forming graceful patterns with her arms and hands.

Rodrigo watched her from the darkness, mesmerized, wishing to move closer to see her as more than just a silhouette, but not wanting to break the spell. If she had wanted an audience, she would have asked.

The dance continued, until, at last, Rodrigo realized he must have been watching for at least an hour. At times the pace of her dance slowed, but she never stopped. Like living water, she moved without jerking or hesitation, her small body flowing effortlessly from one stance to the next.

A bookish little girl she might be, but she certainly doesn't tire quickly. Best leave her to her solitude. He returned to his bedroll and tried to return to slumber, but his eyes would not close and his gaze would not leave the tiny, graceful figure.

Day 21

Rodrigo told me that he plans to go after Boar and get his sword back. I knew that he wanted to. I would rather never see that monster again, *but I won't stay here alone, so I agreed. Boar will kill him, but Rodrigo won't listen to me. Hopefully we will find a way home, and the sword won't matter.*

"Pumpkin bread and smoked pork," whispered Yun, bending over Rodrigo with a wooden plate piled high with assorted growth.

Rodrigo awoke and roused himself. "Ahh—thank you. Pork and bread, my favorite." The meals had become a game, pretending that the growth was something more familiar.

Yun strapped a wide belt across her waist, tucking in it an old knife so rusty that Rodrigo doubted it could survive a twist in a butterball.

"I will need to protect myself too," said Yun.

"Indeed. May I see the dagger?"

She pulled the decrepit thing from her belt and handed it to him. He inspected it, laid it aside, and turned back to her. "Poke me in the eye."

"What?"

"Poke me in the eye."

She tried, hesitantly pushing her right hand up toward his face. He stopped her hand with practiced ease.

She tried again. Again Rodrigo deftly caught up her hand far short of his face. "If you want to carry a weapon, you must have the confidence to use it. I will teach you sometime." He picked up his plate and set to work on his breakfast. "I remember being taught rigorously. But for the life of me I cannot remember who my teacher was. It is aggravating to remember some events in my past in detail, but nothing about the people or places."

"Your father," said Yun.

"My father?"

"Your father must have given you the eye test. A mother would never approve."

"Ah," said Rodrigo, smiling through a mouthful of pale leafy growth. "Agreed. Fine logic on your part. Unless it was an uncle."

"Rodrigo?"

"Yes?"

Yun's left hand flashed up and her index finger caught Rodrigo on the inside corner of his eye. He dropped the plate and clutched his face, losing his balance and rolling backward off his log. What might have been a string of colorful phrases was choked off by the inhalation of half-chewed growth. He righted himself and fumbled around for his cup in between ragged coughing fits.

Yun smiled brightly. "I'm ambidextrous. That means I'm good with both hands. I can even write with either one. Did I pass the test?"

"You—*echh*—fight dirty," Rodrigo managed. "Good for you. But you still need a better dagger."

Day 23

Rodrigo let me have his long knife—dagger, he calls it. The sheath is very pretty, carved with animals and made of soft leather.

"Talen called me a Dustie," said Rodrigo. "He made it sound like I traveled here by accident. Like I had lost my way somehow."

Yun watched Rodrigo through her bangs, enjoying his sudden talkative streak. She liked hearing his voice—the graceful, careful enunciation and the way he drew out certain words to emphasize them, often with a light shake of a finger or flair of a hand.

She sat curled up, her arms across her knees, as was her habit. Rodrigo had returned to good health and spirits over the past weeks. He remained thin but his muscles grew and took on definition, developed by hours of focused exercise. He talked often of his stolen bull sword.

"If we are these Dusties," said Yun, "how do we get home?"

"I don't know," said Rodrigo. "But Boar was right about one thing. It might be safe by this lake, but there are no answers here. We need to begin searching for answers."

Day 24

The day to explore has come. I had hoped that Rodrigo would change his mind, but he is as stubborn now as before. He sits by himself and prays a lot. I am sure that my prayers are not asking for the same things his are, except to find answers and a way out.

He found another sword that is not too rusty—a heavy sabre, he called it—and I can tell he wants a fight. When Rodrigo is killed, I will be left with Boar. But I can't stay here alone.

Boar left two weeks ago. I hope we never find him.

Rodrigo plans to take little trips first. I am supposed to draw maps as we go. I've never done that before.

He is packed. After I packed my bag, he said it was too much for me to carry and made me dump out half of it. I snuck most of it back in.

It's time to go.

"We will take it slow and not try too much to begin," said Rodrigo. "Ready?"

Yun lied by nodding her head.

"Off we go then."

But as the two approached the black void of the tunnel entrance, Rodrigo slowed and stopped.

Yun waited beside him, her expressive eyes widening as they passed from Rodrigo to the tunnel. Her hand clutched his shirt. "What's wrong," she whispered. "Did you hear something?"

"No," whispered Rodrigo back, swallowing hard. "There is something I need to tell you from before. I had gone mad, remember?"

"Yes."

"I believed there was a…a thing in the tunnels. I thought I had imagined it."

Yun blinked, her eyes trying to search Rodrigo's. "What thing?"

His voice dropped lower. "It is there. That Shadow. I can feel it."

Yun moved in closer to Rodrigo, her eyes fixed on the tunnel. "This isn't helping me."

"Me either," said Rodrigo. "But you needed to know. Besides, it is different this time. We will see how it likes big, bright lanterns. With me?"

"You're still going?"

"Yes."

"And I'm still not staying here alone," said Yun, "so, here we go."

"That is the spirit! Deep breath, then."

Yun took that breath, and the two stepped into the tunnel.

Rodrigo led the way, swinging a finely crafted bronze-and-glass lantern filled with whale oil. Yun held a smaller lamp. Between the two, the shadows of the tunnel retreated. But each step came slowly.

A dread pressed against them, a fear that ripped away at their courage, sliced away tattered ribbons of their confidence and consumed it. At one point Yun stopped. Rodrigo took her hand and pulled her forward each step. Tears came to her eyes, but she kept from whimpering.

And then, after a hundred paces, the terrifying presence suddenly eased. The release of fear sprang so strongly that Rodrigo sighed involuntarily.

34

"What was that?" asked Yun.

"Ah, you felt it too."

"Yes, that's why I asked." Yun wiped away a tear.

Rodrigo turned back to her with a confident, triumphant grin. "I am pleased to hear that, very much."

"Because you didn't go insane? The thing was real?"

"Yes. And now it has run away." Rodrigo started forward again at a faster pace.

The tunnel appeared to be a natural lava tube, its floor covered in sand and clay. The black rock gobbled up the light of the lamps, while frequent layers of nearly white ash glowed in sharp relief. The tunnel curved slightly upward, and soon climbed sharply into a vertical shaft. At the curve, however, the wall had fractured, opening out into a large cavern.

"I remember this cursed place," said Rodrigo. "There are a dozen tunnels leaving it and junk is scattered everywhere. I must have tripped in the dark a hundred times. But at least the floor is smooth."

He was right. Blown sand weaved in thin layers over the smooth, flat stone of the floor, which had been carved expertly from the multi-colored rock. The smooth curved ceiling vaulted high into darkness.

"This is the strangest jumble," whispered Yun.

A clutter of odds and ends greeted their light as they crossed the chamber. They made their way through a randomly scattered collection of finely crafted chairs and other furniture. On the other side rose a respectable stack of firewood, and yet no pit or hearth could be seen for its burning. Passing around the pile, they found a heavy, bloodstained table. Rodrigo inspected the table's surface and its cabinets.

"Ah, definitely of use." He pulled an assortment of cooking tools and a heavy butcher's blade from a drawer and placed them carefully in his pack.

"Why is any of this here?" called Yun from ahead. "Look at these tapestries laying all over the floor. Royal, I think. They show kings and princesses and hunts and battles and such."

"I used one of those to drag you to the lake," said Rodrigo. "There should a big…something…up ahead of you."

He rejoined her, and they pressed forward. Out of the gloom in front of them, a giant shape appeared—an immense marble throne lying sideways but perfectly intact, surrounded by a clutter of braziers and gold-lined candelabras.

"That's a throne fit for a giant," said Yun.

"Or a madman."

They circled around the imposing bulk of the throne.

"Careful." Rodrigo pointed out shapes in the gloom.

Scattered here and there were statues, all of light stone, appearing perfectly carved. Rodrigo and Yun avoided them all.

"You walked through here without light, how did you not touch them?" said Yun.

"I did touch them. A few, at least."

"And no explosion?"

"No explosion."

Then Yun let out a little squeal and Rodrigo turned to find her pulling at something sticking out from under a large toppled armoire. He saw what she pulled at, leaned into the armoire, and tipped it up sideways with a grunt. Clothes tumbled from the armoire's drawers, and Yun delightfully dug in.

Seeing the well-preserved finery contrasted against Yun's weeks-old rags, he knew that their first foray would be cut short. "Let me find a suitable rug and we can drag this treasure home."

9: EMBERS

Yun's diary, Day 25

> I have new clothes! I was scared that my old rags were simply going to
> fall apart, but now I have clothes to spare. They were made for someone
> much taller than me, but I can fix that. I even found a shirt for Rodrigo
> that could pass for boy clothes, but I had to convince him to wear it.

They did go out again, this time for a lengthy foray. Yun brought a makeshift journal. On the front of it she drew the word "MAPS" with beautiful lettering. Her handwriting was impeccable, but her mapping skills turned out to be horrid. Rodrigo fared no better. The end result was a pitiful series of stick drawings, heavily amended with notes on discovered landmarks and instructions to ignore this line or that smudge.

A number of passages exited the large chamber, some filled with fancy carvings and statues and various debris, others entirely natural. They took one at random, which led to a smaller chamber similar to the large one. This one had seven exits of various sizes, a jumble of old boards, several faded murals, and a single statue.

"He was happy," said Yun.

Rodrigo turned back from the far exit. "What?"

Yun held her lamp up near the statue's face. "He was happy. The sculptor carved him that way. That is, if he had a sculptor."

The face of dark green stone grinned slyly back at them, mocking the dread that Rodrigo felt.

"Let us try this way," he said, coaxing Yun to move along. He turned and advanced toward the nearest outgoing passage.

Yun screamed.

Rodrigo's nerves, on edge for so long, overreacted. He spun and lost his balance while his fingers fumbled for the sabre, but he steadied himself and drew the thick-bladed weapon slowly and deliberately.

Yun's lamp had dropped to the stone, erupting into a lively blaze. In the flickering light, Rodrigo could see the arm wrapped around Yun's chest, pinning her arms. Compared to Yun, the arm looked obscenely huge. It belonged to an imposing human shape behind her.

The shape of Boar.

The man held his face close to hers, his deep-set ghost eyes studying Rodrigo warily. Rodrigo realized that the man held Yun up off the ground with little apparent difficulty.

"You have new sword," said Boar. "Not fine as mine, of course. Lay sword down and slide it over here."

Rodrigo lowered the sabre's point and took a step toward Yun and her hulking captor. "I have better idea. You lay girl down and slide her over *here*."

"You mock me?" said the man.

"Da." Rodrigo managed a challenging, confident grin.

Panic filled Yun's eyes, but her hand gamely struggled to get a grip on the dagger. Boar's other arm reached down to quiet her, then drew the knife from her sheath. The bull sword sat in its scabbard at his hip.

In the middle of the room, the jumble of wood caught fire. Rodrigo could clearly see the man's face now. It truly was like a wild boar, strong-boned but all sharp angles and edges. His close-cut hair bristled upward. There were several old scars and three fresh, parallel ones down the shoulder. Certainly nothing Yun had done.

Rodrigo pointed at Boar's shoulder with his sword. "You had a disagreement with someone else? I wonder who?"

The intruder grinned, grating his teeth together. "It died before I get name."

It? That surprised Rodrigo, but made sense. The cuts ran parallel, like a raking strike from a big cat or bear, which meant that Boar had to have come from the surface. There would be no such animal down here.

It also meant that a big predator had come out the loser against this man.

Boar slid the canteen off of Yun's shoulder and downed its contents without pause. Yun struggled briefly, but a sharp shake from the massive arm ended that. Keeping his eyes on Rodrigo, Boar opened her pack and rooted about, pulling out and consuming whatever food he found.

Rodrigo paced, edging closer.

Boar stroked Yun's lace collar. "New blouse, very nice. Pretty on girl." He eyed Rodrigo's new shirt, meant for a female. "Not so pretty on boy."

"I trust we will not stain either of them red," said Rodrigo. "I am surprised to find you so close to home. The girl and the sword, please."

"Why do you put nice girl in danger? Do as *I* say." Boar's voice came smoother and bolder now that he had drunk and eaten.

Rodrigo darted in closer. Boar took a step back and pressed the dagger to Yun's throat.

Firelight flickered in Rodrigo's eyes. "You harm the girl and I will finish the work on your shoulder. Take the food and water. Stop trying my patience."

Boar backed away several steps, then sighed and returned his attention to the pack. "Patience, I have plenty. It is your impatience will kill girl."

Rodrigo circled Boar, uncertain how to proceed, but certain that he could not give Boar his way. "Release her."

Boar backed another step. His shoulder bumped into the statue.

Rodrigo was aware of an eye-searing white glare and a sudden absence of all sound. Then, an expanding sphere of ghost-light from the statue propelled him backward. A wild cascade of half-thunder battered at his ears, like an ice wall exploding under a giant's fist. A burning plank struck painfully on his ankle as the blazing fire scattered across the room. Though forced back a pace, he managed to keep his feet.

When Rodrigo finally reoriented, he saw Yun, ten feet from where she had been, unmoving. Boar lay near her, trying to regain his feet.

Rodrigo leapt over Yun and confronted Boar with the point of his sabre as the big man reached a kneeling position.

"Yun? Can you hear me?" said Rodrigo, keeping his eyes on Boar.

After a moment Yun stirred. Rodrigo kicked aside a bit of the scattered fire close to her moving legs. "Move back away from us, Yun."

"Rodrigo? What happened?"

"Just move back. Careful of the fires."

Yun shook herself, then slid quickly back when she caught sight of Boar.

"The sword, Boar," said Rodrigo.

Boar unhooked the scabbard and tossed it at Rodrigo's feet, using that motion to snatch up a burning log. He rose unsteadily to his feet but took a step toward Rodrigo, brandishing the log in front of him. Rodrigo shuffled back several steps and dropped into a fighting crouch, his sabre tip looping repeatedly in a tiny figure eight. The seconds ticked by as the two read each other's eyes.

Slowly, Boar's face shifted into a broad, predatory grin. "I believe you could kill," he said. "I remember this next time. I treat you as man now. Enemy of Boar now." Boar retreated backward but did not let down his guard.

Rodrigo scooped up the bull sword, drew it, then tossed the heavy sabre at Boar's feet. "Judging by your shoulder, you need this."

For a split second, confusion registered in Boar's eyes. Then he retrieved the sabre. "This changes nothing." He stepped back and faded into the darkness of a side tunnel, carrying the sabre and the burning log with him.

Rodrigo did not move until the bobbing embers of the log disappeared entirely. Then he let out a sharp exhale, blinked hard, and lowered the sword point. His eyes remained on the tunnel.

"Yun? Are you up?"

"I hurt," came the quiet reply.

"Where?"

"My head. And my side. And my knee. And my foot. Both feet."

Rodrigo picked up a burning board and tossed it into the tunnel entrance where Boar had left. He turned to Yun, relieved to see her on her feet, though she wavered, teary-eyed and obviously dazed.

"That explosion? What was that?" she said.

Yun swayed, and Rodrigo put his arm around her. "That was exactly the same devilry that hit me when I was finding you. Sit back down and let me see you."

Yun had a wealth of scrapes, a few burns, and a swelling bump of respectable size on her right temple. But nothing seemed broken or out of place. She began sniffling, then crying quietly. Rodrigo sat down beside her and rested her head on his chest.

He let her cry. The energy in his own system played out, and a numbing fatigue set in. The scattered fire died slowly.

Yun's canteen lay nearby. She picked it up and rubbed the spout repeatedly with her sleeve, trying to remove Boar's taint. "Can we trade canteens?"

"Of course."

"I lost your knife."

Rodrigo patted her. "Boar did not have it, so it must be here somewhere. I saw you try to draw it. That was very brave."

"I was going to poke his eye."

"Good for you. Ready to go home?"

"Yes."

The dagger and Yun's lamp both happened to be nearby. Rodrigo refilled her lamp and gave both back to her. As he glanced again around the chamber, something nagged at him. "Yun, do you know which tunnel we came in from?"

"Ummm..." She looked around, and her eyes turned fearful. "No!" Then they brightened again. "The statue! We came in across from it."

Rodrigo searched for the statue. A vague shape lay on the ground where he thought the statue had been. He stepped closer. Then his brows rose in surprise, and his lips curled upward slightly.

"Well, here we go again," he breathed.

"What do you mean?"

Rodrigo held the lamp aloft and pointed with his sword. The robed statue was gone, replaced by a robed, unconscious young man.

10: SCARLET

Yun's diary, Day 26

...and we brought the man back. Rodrigo keeps calling him a man, but he looks just as young as Rodrigo. He is still bedridden, but his name is Scarlet.

He has a very pleasant face, full of relaxed confidence, like a prince who is dressed as a peasant.

"He's sleeping again?" asked Rodrigo, newly awake from three hours of restless sleep. The trip back had proved grueling, dragging the young stranger on an old, tattered tapestry through the tunnels.

"I think so," said Yun, yawning. She had spent most of the past hours sitting next to the man, though she needed sleep herself. "He wakes up every so often and talks to me, then dozes off again. Maybe he isn't even awake when he talks. It's mostly nonsense anyway. He says his name is Scarlet."

Rodrigo knelt down beside the man's head. "Unusual looking," he said.

Even in his unkempt and unconscious state, Scarlet looked like a young man relaxing contentedly on a palm-lined beach. His unruly mass of wavy hair faded from golden blond near the top to a tawny brown at the ears, framing a good-natured face with thick, naturally smiling lips and a long, lean nose.

In stature he appeared entirely ordinary—neither tall nor short—and medium in build. However, despite the initial impression that the scholarly robe gave him, he was wide-shouldered, wiry-muscled, and fit. This gave him the initial impression of being older, but studying him more closely, Rodrigo realized that he was probably no older than Rodrigo himself.

"I hope he's nice—like you," said Yun.

"I hope he has sense—like you," answered Rodrigo. "You've done very well this past day. Get some rest."

Yun smiled warmly and rose unsteadily to her feet.

"A Spaniard!"

Rodrigo looked down at the voice. Scarlet's green eyes peered back at him.

"Spaniard?" asked Rodrigo.

Scarlet cocked his head, raised one unsteady hand and tapped Rodrigo on the chest. "You're a Spaniard!"

"Am I?" answered Rodrigo. "Are you a Spaniard too?"

Scarlet shot Rodrigo a glance that one ordinarily reserves for lunatics spouting nonsense. "Are you daft? Do I look like a Spaniard? Do I sound like a Spaniard?"

"I am not sure. What is a Spaniard?"

For a moment Scarlet stared at Rodrigo, something to be said on the tip of his lips. Then he dropped his head back down, squinting as if trying to see through heavy mist. "Dash it, I haven't the slightest idea. Isn't that odd?"

Rodrigo glanced up at Yun and shrugged with his eyes. When he looked back down again, Scarlet was asleep.

Day 27

Rodrigo saved my life. He also gave Boar his other sword, even after Boar said that they were mortal enemies now. I feel bad calling Rodrigo a grouchy hothead before, but I won't go back and erase all that. That wouldn't be right.

He's still stubborn though.

Day 32

Scarlet had his bad time, like me, but he got past it. He's a naturally cheerful sort, and I very much like having him around.

He and Rodrigo practice swords with each other, and they joke back and forth so much that my sides hurt from laughing during dinner last night. Scarlet makes up these ridiculous stories and Rodrigo adds to them with clever comments. I think they are better with their wits than they are with their swords.

"Well—we're rich!" declared Scarlet. "I can mark that off of my list of lifetime accomplishments. That is to say, if I could only remember my lifetime. Or my accomplishments."

Scarlet stood atop the overturned throne in the large chamber that they had dubbed Royalty Hall, surveying the expanse of it through the light of the four large braziers that he and Rodrigo had brought to life. The firelight successfully illuminated much of the chamber, but produced a host of flickering shadows that made a clear view difficult. Scarlet suggested placing the braziers atop the throne, but had not yet thought of a way to manhandle the heavy iron pots up there.

A steady draft blew through the chamber, making the fires dance, and stirring the sand and dust. A faint wavering moan rose and fell—they hoped it was just wind through a crack somewhere—giving an ominous ambiance to an already spooky environment. Despite this, the three young Dusties were anything but apprehensive. Yun sat engrossed in a thick old book, surrounded by a stack of old tomes and useful female accoutrements discovered in their initial quick search through the chamber. Rodrigo carefully bundled a newly acquired wardrobe of sturdy linen work clothes, while Scarlet tried on several outfits of outlandish royal foppery before settling on a pair of tawny hunting pants and a forest-green touring shirt hemmed off at the elbows. A set of fine opera glasses hung at his neck. He tried to strap a lightly curved naval captain's sword onto his back, but his makeshift straps failed him.

"Wherever we are, it's off the beaten path," said Scarlet. "These treasures would have been nicked long ago otherwise." He strapped on a thick, supple belt with a simple but elegant symbol of a flying seabird engraved on the buckle. "Soaring free, that's me!" announced Scarlet to the flickering darkness.

"I have seen few tracks," said Rodrigo. "The air scatters the dust. Boar came through here, but his tracks are mostly gone already."

Scarlet sat down on the edge of the throne and drew out the map journal. "Let's hope your big chap is long gone," he said. "Right now, time to make a map."

Rodrigo nodded, hefted two pole lanterns, and worked his way to the edge of the chamber. Moving along the curving wall, he shouted back discoveries. He remembered most of it from the earlier expedition: the tunnel leading back to Vida Lake, several wide corridors with wedge-like ceilings, and a narrow tunnel that ended at a blank wall. Off to his left was a carved and ornamented passage that looked more like a royal catacomb. Not far from that a large, plain tunnel led to the chamber where Scarlet was found.

Although Scarlet's maps weren't perfect, they were a step up from the previous work of Yun and Rodrigo. Returning to the throne, Rodrigo looked over the sketches and nodded his approval. "How do you want to tackle these tunnels?"

"Systematic," said Scarlet, tracing a circle clockwise around his chamber sketch. He leaned in and lowered his voice, tipping a finger toward Yun, who remained enthralled with her book. "Should Yunnie tag along? And by that I mean, can she keep up?"

Rodrigo gave a small half-smile. "I do not think that will be a problem."

"Right, then, let's haul back our plunder and get to work."

———

For dinner that night, Scarlet insisted on preparing "the mix"—a heap of uncooked, tastefully tossed glowmoss topped with a tart moss juice. Yun helped him gather the right mosses.

They built the fire extra-large this night, and, as they each prepared to take their first mouthful of the mix, Scarlet's eyes flicked up, secretively watching Rodrigo. Yun kept her head down, her bangs shielding her face and the crawling smile that she tried desperately to contain.

The makeshift fork came slowly to Rodrigo's mouth. Scarlet held his breath. The pieces of bitter bulb that he and Yun had hidden in Rodrigo's mix were small, but they would most certainly do the trick. He hoped Yun could keep from giggling too soon, before that mouthful…

But the fork paused, and Rodrigo looked to the others. "Everything all right, Yun? Not hungry, Scarlet?"

"Oh, starving!" answered Scarlet.

"Me too!" said Yun.

And they dug in.

It wasn't until the third chew of his first forkful that Scarlet realized his mouth felt like it had been doused with pitch and set afire. He retched out the mouthful onto his plate, half of his mix spilling into the sand. His flailing hand knocked his cup off the rock, but managed to get ahold of Yun's drink. He downed half the water and rinsed vigorously with the other half.

Yun, who had taken her own small bite but managed the heat well, rocked back and forth in laughter.

Rodrigo sat impassively, the forkful near his mouth, and a slight upward curl on his lips. "Is something wrong, Scarlet?" he said smoothly, giving a light emphasis to *wrong*.

"How…how did you know?" managed Scarlet.

"Know *what*, Scarlet?" Rodrigo's smirk rose just a little higher.

"What we did…to your mix."

"My mix?" Rodrigo crammed the forkful into his mouth, bitter bulb and all. He chewed slowly, deliberately. Other than a strained intensity in his eyes, he didn't flinch.

Yun quieted, watching Rodrigo manage the bitter bulb's assault. She glanced down at her own mix, somehow spiked with bitter bulb juice by Rodrigo. Her fork descended, she gathered up a generous supply, and she stuffed the mouthful in.

Scarlet's eyes grew wide as the other two chewed at each other.

Rodrigo downed his mouthful, composed himself, and gave Scarlet a tiger's smile. "Tangy, but it could use a little more kick."

Scarlet wagged a finger. "No, stop the nonsense and tell me how you found out. I took great pains…"

Rodrigo turned his face toward Yun but kept his eyes on Scarlet. "It was a delight to see Scarlet helping with dinner tonight. Such a treat. First time, I think."

Yun snickered. "Yeah. Pretty lazy."

"I'm not lazy!" protested Scarlet. "Just…busy. You're telling me that you actually have a suspicion if I try to lend a hand? Never mind, don't answer that."

Rodrigo prepared for another mouthful, smiling like a professor after a fine lesson. "Do you think Scarlet has learned anything here tonight, Yun?"

Yun spat out part of her mouthful, her laughter ruining her chewing.

Scarlet staggered to his feet. "I've learned you're both nutters. If either of you need me to restart your heart, I'll be at the lake, drinking it."

11: SKYHALL

Yun's diary, Day 36

We are resting in the chamber where we fought Boar. We found no way out yet and there are only two passages left to be checked. But there were several places where we think there might be a way through. One of the tunnels ends in a bronze wall covered in engravings, and there's a cavern with a big beautiful waterfall. The waterfall cavern is full of chains and levers that might open something. A few tunnels go straight up, but none of us could climb them.

Time to go.

The passageway had the feel of Royalty Hall, tall and broad, and lined with ornate corbels topped with all manner of strange beasts. A brass lamp hung from the mouth or tail or paw of each. Murals lined the walls, displaying fantastic scenes and exotic creatures.

As they progressed, they noticed that the floor began tilting side to side. Soon, the corridor had twisted itself to the point where they were forced to walk on the right-hand wall.

"Who would build this?" said Rodrigo.

"I doubt anyone did," said Scarlet. "I would think it got this way later, though I couldn't imagine how."

"Earthquake?" said Yun.

"Look at the murals and the carvings, they aren't even damaged. I doubt earthquake," said Scarlet.

Soon they had to switch to walking on the trefoiled arch of the ceiling, then to the left-hand wall. Again and again the passage twisted over, seeming to do so more and more quickly, and it continued, on and on.

But just as they reached the opinion that the passage might indeed be endless, and as the floor once again become the actual floor, they came to a pair of wide open doors. Crafted of dark brass and reinforced with abundant bands of rust-free metal, they towered twelve feet high on either side of the exit. Through this opening streamed a pale blue light.

The three entered the room—at first with caution, then with astonishment, and, finally, with uncontrolled excitement. They rushed through a large open room full of exotic odds and ends, past tall library shelves packed with books right up to the wooden ceiling, and finally to a series of bay windows that covered one entire wall. Through the exquisitely traced panes of glass, they saw a sky. And though that dark, starless sky drifted eerily with dull blue tendrils, they cheered, for they knew now that they were not buried alive. Several of the glass panes were broken, and Yun put her face to the breeze that blew through them.

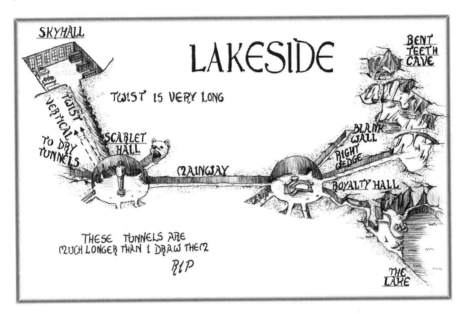

"We made it!" she cried.

"I never believed I would be so excited to see that ugly sky again," said Rodrigo. The ghostly tendrils took him back to his torture in Drift, and the panic he had felt there.

"Aye!" said Scarlet, looking around at the massive beams crossing the raftered ceiling. "A shame there are no pigeons living in here. I should like a plate of squab."

"Fog below," said Rodrigo.

Yun followed his gaze downward. A slightly shimmering haze drifted and stirred not far below. Although it appeared thin, nothing could be seen of the ground.

Looking left and right, they came to the realization that the structure clung to the side of a cliff that rose sheer for as far as they could see. Bands of bright moss-glow streaked it where waterfalls tumbled downward.

"What is that?" Yun pointed up, along the cliff face. High above and close to the far curve of the cliff, a rim of yellow fire-glow lit the night.

"A city!" said Scarlet. "Drift, do you think?"

"Possibly," said Rodrigo. "We are looking from below, so we would not be able to see it well."

Their attention returned to the room. This too was new. Unlike the chaotic and seemingly meaningless jumble of artifacts found everywhere else, this large wood-wrought structure had a clear, organized purpose. It divided into four joining sections—a library to the left and long-dead arboretum to the right, a neatly organized warehouse in the back and a laboratory for some long-lost discipline arrayed near the windows. And nowhere could be seen a statue.

Yun started for the library.

But Rodrigo caught her arm and pointed at the floor nearby. She recognized the pile of equipment that Rodrigo pointed to.

It included a number of items taken by Boar.

She turned to Rodrigo and started to speak, but Rodrigo put up his hand to silence her. He motioned to Scarlet to follow him, drew his sword slowly, and moved off toward the arboretum. Scarlet shadowed Rodrigo, his own sword ready.

Alarmed at being left alone, Yun crouched down behind a table covered in anatomical sketches and jars of dead things, her hand on her dagger.

She pressed her back against the shelves of the laboratory table, trying to tell where Rodrigo had gone but unable to hear past her frantic heartbeat. She wanted to rise up and peek but couldn't move. Staring out at the blue-tinted darkness through the huge windows, she felt terribly exposed.

Slowly she mustered the courage to rise, but at that moment something flashed close by the window. She heard a long, terrifying scream and realized only slowly that it came from herself.

She heard movement, something heavy falling, cursing, and then Scarlet slipped around the table. Yun grabbed him by the collar and he fell over her legs.

"Myriads, Yun. Let go!" he said, trying to undo her death grip on his shirt. "Why'd you scream?"

"Something flew by the window," she whispered.

"Just a bat." Scarlet pushed himself up next to her. "Hmm...your hair smells like-"

"My what?" said Yun, staring at him.

Scarlet ran a finger in her hair. "Your hair, it smells like a spice of some kind. Can't quite place it."

Yun smelled her hair, wondering what spice Scarlet was thinking of. Thoughts of bats and Boars and scary things were momentarily pushed aside, and her heart slowed from frantic to fast.

She had begun to wonder whether he had complimented her on purpose just to distract from her fear, when Rodrigo appeared, standing over them. "If Boar is here, he certainly knows about us now." He cupped a hand to his mouth and shouted, "No need to hide, Boar!"

The only answer came from the soft moan of wind rushing through the broken panes.

Rodrigo recovered his lamp and turned it toward the pile of equipment. Next to the pile, a ladder ascended to the ceiling. He handed his lamp to Yun and inspected the ladder, but found no obvious signs of use. "I want to see where this goes."

"Right behind you," said Scarlet.

"And me," added Yun quickly, not wishing to be left with the tables of dead things.

The ladder led to a trapdoor. Expecting a loft, Yun was surprised to see that the hatch opened out onto the roof. A section of the roofline along the cliff ran flat, surrounded by a sloping outer rim covered in shingles. Two rusting instruments resembling telescopes were propped to one side.

"Not exactly the safest place to play." Scarlet peered down the sloping edge into the mists. No barrier surrounded the flat area.

"Not what I expected," said Rodrigo. "There are tracks up here. Boar must have inspected it as well."

Yun caught sight of something out of place and pointed at the cliff face. "I think he spiked the wall." Sure enough, a sturdy spike with an eyelet had been driven into the dark rock. "And there's another one, I think, up there."

They saw those and more, ascending up and toward the glowing ring of the city. And with a gasp Yun made the connection.

"He climbed! Or at least he tried to."

Scarlet whistled and shook his head. "This cliff has a decent amount of handholds, but they're small. He'd need to be very, very good to go from here all the way up to the city. That's a mile up and over, at least."

"Hard to imagine he would take the risk," said Rodrigo. "He seemed the coldly calculating type."

"You a climber?" asked Scarlet.

"No. You?"

Scarlet shrugged. "Aye, I think, but not a mile's worth."

Then, Yun's eyes caught movement. She let out a little yip. "Is that the bat?" She pointed under a cliff ledge near the trapdoor and backed up behind Scarlet.

Rodrigo and Scarlet turned their lanterns toward the ledge. They could all see the large shadow-black wings of the bat, curled tightly around its body as it dangled under the ledge. Scarlet whistled at its exceptional size, nearly as long as his forearm.

The wings unfurled, revealing the creature, and the three Dusties were suddenly confronted with the terrifying fact that they were not dealing with a bat.

———

For a flash of a second, a large single eye stared at Rodrigo, its depths filled with a pale blue luminescence. And then the creature launched outward. It drove immediately for Scarlet's face, but Scarlet brought his clenched hand up in self-defense. The terror latched onto Scarlet's fist. He winced as the creature drove something into his flesh between two knuckles.

He cried out and tried to slam the terror into the cliff, but it released its grip and shot skyward, its wings beating powerfully. Rodrigo slashed with his sword, but it met with empty air.

Scarlet and Rodrigo pushed Yun between them and tried to keep back to back. The terror swooped by close, its dark shape a faint blur against the midnight blue of the sky. The two boys struck at it hesitantly. Circling tightly, the terror closed again and again in a dizzying dance that left Scarlet and Rodrigo disoriented and swinging at empty air.

The two boys drifted away from Yun, and the bat-thing arrowed directly at the girl, slamming into the back of her neck. Yun shrieked wildly and clawed at her head. The flapping fiend clutched at her hair, attempting to gain sufficient purchase to sting her. Scarlet tried to swipe away the monster with his fist, but it launched itself back into the air.

Scarlet leapt high, swinging desperately.

Rodrigo saw the sword catch the creature's wing, flipping it sideways. The monster dropped to the shingles, flapping crazily as it slid down the roof and disappeared over the edge. Scarlet seemed to balance like an acrobat at the periphery of the roof's flat, trying to recover from the wild sword swing. Then his leg buckled and he tumbled onto the roof slope.

"Scarlet!" Rodrigo raced toward the fallen boy. Scarlet began to go into a roll, and Rodrigo had no time. He launched himself, reaching out his hand. He landed painfully on the flat's edge and his breath left him. He felt his grip sink into fabric but Scarlet rolled and Rodrigo slid with him.

Rodrigo tried to grab the shingled surface with his free hand. Splinters drove into his fingers, but it slowed his slide.

Gradually he brought breath back into his lungs. He could tell now that he had a grip on Scarlet's pant leg, but the fabric began slipping from his hand. With each breath he took, he could feel his body creep, inch by inch, farther down the slope.

"Scarlet!" he called. But the boy did not respond.

Scarlet's arm slipped over the edge and Rodrigo cried out in despair as he felt his grip loosen. His heart twisted as he realized that he would have to let go if he were to save himself.

Something brushed by his arm and he saw Yun's silhouette in front of him, kneeling at the very edge of the shingles. She worked at Scarlet's leg, then gripped Rodrigo's shoulder. "I tied his leg to the ladder," she said in his ear. "You can let go. Can you get up?"

"Gracia de Dios! You saved him, Yun."

"We both did."

12: BITTER

Yun's diary, Day 37

Scarlet is poisoned. Rodrigo says he will pull through, but I can see the doubt in his eyes.

Yun brought a bucket of water from the lake and knelt next to Scarlet. The boy did not move, his shallow breathing barely lifting the blanket. His stung left hand lay on the blanket like a shapeless purple club. Scarlet's bluish lips moved as if he conversed with Death.

"What do we do?" asked Yun for the fifth time.

"The poison must run its course," repeated Rodrigo. "Keep him drinking. That is all you can do."

"What if his hand gets worse?"

Rodrigo's expression and his glance at her dagger told her all she needed to know.

He built the fire higher and cleaned equipment, while Yun remained at Scarlet's side.

Scarlet mumbled and lifted his good hand, which found Yun's shoulder, and he pulled her weakly down toward him. She leaned to his mouth.

"Bitter," whispered Scarlet. "Hope."

"What did you say?"

"Bitter," he repeated, and motioned to his mouth.

"Rodrigo!" cried Yun.

He came and knelt beside her.

"He is saying, 'Bitter'. And 'Hope,' I think. And he's motioning to his mouth."

"Bitter?" mused Rodrigo. "I hope he is not saying Bitter Hope, as in he is…"

"Does he mean eating that bitter bulb?" said Yun.

"That makes little sense, but I have no answers, so try as you wish."

Yun nodded and cast about the stream bank for the bulb. It wasn't common, but she found a pair of them soon enough and brought them back to Scarlet.

He reached for one and tried to get down a piece, but he choked on it. His hand squeezed the soft bulb and he smeared it on his neck before his energy gave out. He made a few feeble circle motions with his hand before lying still.

Yun squeezed the bulbs and smeared it on Scarlet's skin. She smothered his swollen hand in the remainder. Then she sat back, helpless, and a tear streaked down her cheek. An hour later she fell asleep holding Scarlet's good hand. His breathing remained dangerously shallow.

Rodrigo checked on Scarlet, shook his head, and bedded down himself.

When Yun awoke, she found Scarlet's wounded hand considerably less swollen and discolored, and his breathing natural and strong again.

"How did you know about the bitter bulb?" she asked him when he awoke.

"Hope told me," he replied.

"Hope is a person?"

"Yes," said Scarlet. "I saw her in a dream, and she's nice. Like you."

Yun blushed and smiled, but his words confused her. "You saw her in a dream? And she told you the cure?"

He nodded. There appeared every bit of sincerity in his eyes.

"That is very strange, Scarlet."

"I certainly agree. Still, it's true. But I hear you saved me first. Kept me from falling off that roof. How did you get a rope so fast to tie on me?"

"I always keep rope in my pack. Rodrigo says it's best to be prepared, but he doesn't like me to carry much. I have lots of things in my pack he doesn't know about."

"Well, Sneaky, I owe you my life. Thanks."

"You saved me from the flying thing," said Yun.

"That makes us blood brother and sister, so we're stuck with each other." He ran his hand down through her raven hair.

Yun kept silent and her eyes down, but her smile said everything.

Day 42

We have seen the city, but can't reach it. We have to find another way.

"Stop calling it a demon bat," said Scarlet. "I like bats."

"How do you know you like bats?" said Rodrigo.

Scarlet brought his fingers fluttering over his head. "Anyone with a shred of flair would like bats. They're so agile they positively dance in the air."

"Where have you seen bats?"

"I—well, I can't remember, of course, as you both know."

The three Dusties sat in front of the engraved wall of bronze that brought one of the tunnels to a dead-end—a place they aptly named Bronzewall. They had packed plenty of lanterns, but they discovered that the air here did not circulate well, so only one lantern was lit. It cast a shadow-framed glow over the Dusties and the circular wall of etched metal.

"We can call it a Poison Demon Wing," said Rodrigo.

Scarlet shook his head. "Too long. You don't want to be caught trying to say all that in an emergency. 'Look out, it's a Poison Demon Wing!' You'd be stung before you finish. And why do you want to call it a demon? It doesn't look like any demon I know."

"You know demons?" said Yun.

"As well as I know bats."

Rodrigo stood and tapped at several of the knobs on the bronze surface as he spoke. "That is what I find odd. We seem to know our facts, but not our history. You remember seeing bats flying and demons, but cannot remember where, or who you were with, or what your mother and father and brothers and sisters thought of bats and demons. In reality, we remember nearly everything, except those pieces that would put everything together."

"That's profound," said Scarlet. "Here I thought you were little more than a tightlipped soldier of duty, and all the while you've been untying the mystery of our universe."

Rodrigo chuckled as he traced a finger along the tight seam of the circular barrier. "I may be an ox, but I can pull more than one wagon if I put my mind to it."

"You're a bull. Says so on your sword," said Scarlet. "Certainly explains the stubborn bit."

"And the get-out-of-bed-let's-move-it bit," said Yun.

Scarlet pointed a confirming finger at her. "Well said!"

"You both need a little pushing..." Rodrigo's response trailed off, a new thought crowding it out. "Also, none of us recognized the...Thing. We know bats, and demons, but we did not know that evil creature."

"Which means?"

"Which means, Scarlet, we are not from around here. So, Dusties we may be, like Talen called me."

Scarlet joined Rodrigo in front of the wall, sighing at its puzzling surface. "Well, your insane friend's Dustie explanation is certainly possible. It would also explain the scattered odds and ends around here. If people can drift by accident into this place, it's clear that things can do the same."

"That's a sad thought, Scarlet."

"What's that, Yun?"

She cupped her chin in her hands. "Being here, without a purpose, without family. I wish I knew who my mom and dad were. Whoever they are, I miss them."

The two boys nodded to that and there was silence for a time.

"We will just have to find a new purpose," said Rodrigo.

"Says the bull," added Scarlet. "By the way, I thought about us not being from around here. There's another answer. Maybe we are at home, and that creature isn't."

"True," said Rodrigo. "I had not considered that."

Yun straightened, her eyes rising with a dawning thought. "Flying Eye. Is that a good name?"

Scarlet and Rodrigo looked at each other and nodded.

"Perfect!" said Scarlet. "We'll call it a *fleye* for short. Look out! Fleye!" He shielded his face in mock terror. "You can see the advantage."

"I hope we don't see another one forever," said Yun. "I'm glad you barred up that door…though, I wish I could get more books."

Scarlet gave her a martyr's look. "I carried a mountain of them back to the lake! I've a sore back as a result."

"You have seen how she reads," said Rodrigo.

"We need to find a fat history book that tells us all about this place," said Scarlet.

Despite Yun's excitement, the library contained only bizarre fictional stories, odd poetry, and shelf upon shelf of puzzling arcane studies.

"That Skyhall door is fit for a fortress," said Scarlet. "Why it would lead out to an isolated laboratory makes little sense. I know…that's normal here, apparently."

"I wonder if Boar made it," said Yun. "To the city, I mean."

Scarlet wandered back from the bronze wall. "Likely got punctured by a Fleye or two while trying that insane climb."

"Anyone have an idea about these engravings?" Rodrigo pointed to the bronze wall.

"No, not really," said Scarlet. "The outer ring is just like a clock but with only eight hours, and they're all mixed up—the number three is down at the bottom there and nine is right next to it, you see? And…seven is missing. And a center full of constellations, which doesn't help at all considering there are no stars here."

"Constellations?" said Yun. "Oh. I see now."

"What I don't see," continued Scarlet, "is a keyhole, doorknob, latch, or something that gets me through this big metal dead-end. I suggest we go to that cave with the waterfall and monkey with the machinery until something happens."

Rodrigo glanced back at other two. "There is one thing else that we could do."

"I'm all ears," said Scarlet.

"We could inspect statues."

Scarlet whistled and Yun stood up, surprise on her face.

"There could be others here," said Rodrigo. "You and Yun were both statues at one time."

Yun grimaced. "So was Boar."

"Doesn't that involve getting blown up?" asked Scarlet.

"Yes, it does." Yun pointed at her ankle. "I have scars."

"And we have no idea if we are rousing a saint or murderer?"

"True, Scarlet," said Rodrigo.

"And you won't know which one they are until they murder you," added Yun.

Scarlet flipped a hand up. "Well, considering our lot, sounds like entertainment."

13: Triangle

Yun's diary, Day 43

> I cannot say that I like it here, but I can say that it has become home. I never tire of looking out at the lake. The many colors of the glowmoss and the little ripples of the beautiful clear water delight me every time we return. And even though they have a mean temper, the luminescent big fish make graceful patterns in the deep water. We've never found a good way to fish for them yet. I really wish we had a boat.
>
> Scarlet and Rodrigo plan to awaken people tomorrow. It's a bad idea, but they don't listen to me. I'll just pray for a friend and hope. Scarlet thinks the statues are Dusties turned to stone by whatever force pulls them here. He has volunteered to be the one to touch each statue.
>
> Scarlet and Rodrigo are arguing over ways to keep Scarlet from getting hurt when he is blown up. They argue a lot, but I can tell they like each other. They are both so cute. No, Rodrigo isn't cute, but he is very handsome.
>
> I wish Scarlet would touch my hair again.
>
> They are still arguing. I'll just enjoy my time at the lake and not worry about it.

Yun danced, turning about her little arena of carefully swept sand near the lake's edge. There were no kicks or spins in her dance this time, but a slow, graceful pace, using her hands, arms, and legs to tell the story that played in her mind…There was a quiet river, and cattails, and woods rustling with fairy creatures, a soft breeze and a breaking dawn, a boy and a girl…

"I must say, you dance divinely," said a voice nearby.

Yun gasped and recoiled.

Scarlet sat on a rock, his hands under his chin, gazing at her with a bright, clear expression. "I know I am being terribly rude, your dance is your own, but I am delighted by it. It is the most beautiful dancing that I have ever seen. Now that I have told you, and have been privileged to see it up close, I will leave if you want."

"You can stay." Yun looked at Scarlet through her bangs. "I don't know if I can keep dancing though."

"I know of a dance," said Scarlet, rising from the rock. "It's simple, nothing like what you can do, but it takes two people. Would you try it with me?"

Yun didn't answer immediately, digging with a toe in the sand. Finally, she curtsied and held out her hand.

Scarlet smiled a broad joyous smile, then came and took her hand. "Now, I'll be rusty, so bear with me." He positioned her hand on his waist and his on her shoulder. "It's mostly just a series of steps with some twirling in between. Ready?"

She nodded, her head down but her eyes fixed up at him.

"Right foot back, left foot back, you follow, and we spin—just this far—then slide, curl over, I catch you, slide—sorry, I am rusty—then we do the opposite, back and over. There! Now keep going right back into it. See? There's more you can do, but this is the easy part."

The two continued, making mistakes, laughing, the tall Scarlet working to keep himself flowing well with the tiny Yun. They danced until they had worn an hourglass shape in the sand, and they slowed and moved through natural steps as their whim took them.

"If I can be overly bold one last time, Yun, how old are you?" asked Scarlet.

"Old enough," said Yun.

"Enough?"

"Enough not to be called a little girl."

"Ah," said Scarlet. The dance continued in silence for a time.

Finally, he coughed and stepped back. "Well, I would have to say that is the most delightful time I could have ever imagined. But I do need my sleep, considering my task at being blown up tomorrow, and as a gentleman, I bid you goodnight."

Scarlet bowed deeply, kissed Yun's hand, turned, and strode to his sleeping quarters.

Yun watched him leave, then ran and found her journal. For the next hour she wrote furiously.

———

In the far dark, Rodrigo watched Scarlet end the dance and leave. His brows knit down tightly against his dark eyes, and his jaws clenched and unclenched. An hour passed before he was able to turn to his bed and descend into a fitful sleep.

Day 44

I pray Scarlet does not hurt himself.

"What are you doing?" yelled Rodrigo.

Scarlet—rolled up like a scroll in a silk-laced, down-stuffed bedspread—was in the act of reaching for the outstretched foot of a dancing lady, his head turned away, eyes closed and teeth clenched. A grossly oversized turban made of soft cloth clung to his head.

He opened one eye. "What?"

"You are seized up and tight," said Rodrigo. "Do you want to strain something? Loosen up and go with the blast."

"Easy for you to say," said Scarlet. "This is nerve-wracking!"

"Why do we have to start with her?" said Yun.

"Why would we not?" said Rodrigo.

"Never mind," muttered Yun and put her hands to her chin.

"Just stay natural!" called Rodrigo. He and Yun hunched a safe distance, twenty paces away, behind an iron stove. They were in Royalty Hall, now well lit due to the braziers that the boys had painstakingly winched up atop the overturned throne.

"Heya, I had a sad thought." Scarlet held up his hands and wiggled the fingers. "What if I don't have the magic touch?"

Rodrigo snorted. "Had not thought of that. If nothing happens, I will touch after you. But I will get my own armor. Yours is ridiculous."

"Fine. Here we go then." Scarlet took a few breaths and reached out to touch the foot.

Nothing happened. He ran his hand along more of the statue, but it remained stone.

"Feels strange," said Scarlet.

"Like it's vibrating, or pushing back?" called Yun.

"The pushing back part, exactly," said Scarlet.

"My turn," said Rodrigo. Scarlet backed off. Rodrigo threw a blanket behind him, wrapped a thick cloth around his head, and touched the foot.

Nothing.

"Crying shame," said Scarlet. "We could use another feminine soul around. For Yun's sake."

"For everyone's sake," said Rodrigo, glancing at Scarlet.

But Scarlet didn't notice, waving Yun up. "Put a bow on her, Yun."

"What if I have the magic fingers?" said Yun.

"Be careful," suggested Scarlet, turning to select a new target.

Yun hesitantly touched the statue, and when nothing happened she snipped a strip of royal-blue ribbon from a large roll and tied it to the leg.

The three Dusties tried, again and again. They worked through Royalty Hall, down the wide, statue-choked corridor to Coachman's Chamber, and an equally choked passage to the expansive Bent Teeth Cave, where the many stalactites all tilted at the same strange angle. After finishing the numerous dead-ends from Royalty Hall, they made their way down the Mainway, through Scarlet Hall, into the thin slit known as Creep, and then along Jagged, where the tunnel appeared as if they had been sliced and reconnected poorly. Most of the statues had the strange vibration and felt like they were covered in oil.

After ten hours, Scarlet became positively reckless with his preparation, trudging up to each statue and slapping his hand on it. The overstuffed turban had fallen off his head hours ago.

About the mid-point of Jagged, in a particularly long and statue-scattered section, Scarlet threw up his hands. "Shrikes! I cannot believe there were this many statues. Have more been planted since we got here? This is utterly ridiculous."

"I would say we have covered much more than a third," said Rodrigo. "Disappointing, but good work. Take a break?"

"A long break. I need a dip in the lake. This down blanket has made me powerfully itchy."

"Do you want to go back alone?" asked Rodrigo. "I would like to dig around in this place, there is a lot here."

"How about you, Yun?" asked Scarlet.

"Yun will stay with me," said Rodrigo, stone-faced.

Scarlet cocked an eyebrow. "Mm-kay. See you soon." He grabbed up a lantern, lit it, and strode off.

After Scarlet left, Rodrigo turned back to Yun, who stood staring at him.

"Yes, I saw the dancing with Scarlet," he said.

"He was a perfect gentleman," said Yun, her eyes gathering storms and her hands inching to her waist.

"I would expect nothing less from him," said Rodrigo. "And it would be none of my business, but just the three of us are stuck here. I would rather not have complications."

To Rodrigo's surprise, a tear trickled down Yun's cheek. "Well, it's too late. What makes you think I love you less than him?"

"I...what are you saying?"

Yun sat down on a stone frog, a royal-blue bow tied around its fat neck. She wiped her cheeks and took a ragged breath. "You're dense and you're stubborn. And I care about you. Why didn't *you* ever come dance with me?"

Rodrigo had no idea what to say next. He paced, trying to think. Yun had gone silent and he thought she might be crying quietly behind her hair.

How could he have been so stupid? He did care for Yun, but he always held back, knowing it was only the two of them, and it would be unfair to her when she had no choices. And she was so young, nothing more than a girl. He tried to treat her like a little sister, to keep her at arm's length. Yet when Scarlet had arrived, he'd discovered that his feelings for Yun sank far deeper than he admitted to himself. He had determined to be only the big brother, but now, instead of yelling at him like a little sister would about keeping out of her business, she admitted her love for him.

They were trapped here, the three together, and Rodrigo knew in his heart that this would not end well. That would be a lingering cruelty to all of them.

After so many unresponsive statues, his hope of finding others had dimmed. Slowly he came to the determination that there was only one option. He would make it clear to Yun, sternly and coldly, that he was not someone to love, but only to respect.

He could not imagine a more painful lie.

His mind reeling, Rodrigo reached out to lean against a miniature statue, of the type found in manicured gardens. It was clearly just a statue, a rendition of an adventuresome boy fishing, formed of black-green rock. No bow graced it yet.

The bright white blast lifted Rodrigo off his feet.

Scarlet made good time down the narrow, high-ceilinged tunnel that connected Gargoyle Cave with Royalty Hall, avoiding the many statues dotting this passageway. They would check through them soon, and he didn't want to have something happen while he was alone.

Scarlet liked this passage, nicknamed Meander. The ceiling was lost in darkness but chains descended down from the gloom. Strange contraptions made of metal hung from the chains, and Scarlet studied their designs in fascination. He would need to inspect them closely one day.

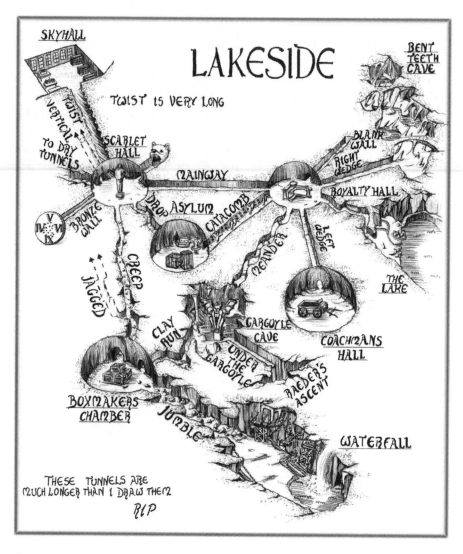

He continued on slowly, the tunnel snaking back and forth like the flow of a dark river. Numerous statues cluttered the passageway, forming creeping shadows along the walls as he passed.

Scarlet stopped.

Something watched him from up ahead.

He couldn't see it. Whatever it was, it stayed just out of range of the light, hidden beyond the outstretched shadows from the scattering of statues. But Scarlet could feel its stare on him, a stare that drilled through him, laid him bare, exposed his vulnerabilities.

He tried to advance but could not. If he moved forward, it would just retreat, keeping its revealing eye on him, stripping him of all secrets. The thought of being so exposed pressed at him, pushed at his confidence, scratched against his nerves. If he moved back, it would be the same, stalking him relentlessly, awaiting the vulnerability of his retreating back.

It could see him but he could not see it. It reached out toward him, its claws fear and its fangs emptiness. It could see him.

But without the light of the lantern, it would be blind as well.

Maybe it could see in the darkness?

A part of Scarlet sneered at that idea. An insistent corner of his brain knew without a doubt that whatever it was, it could not see Scarlet if there were no light.

But, if the lantern remained lit, it couldn't come any closer.

The insistent voice mocked that idea. What would it matter getting close? Its gaze was already scratching his soul. And that vision could be ended only with the snuffing of the lantern's light.

But he needed the light to get home.

There could be no going home, as long as its gaze fell on him.

Snuff the light.

But—

Snuff the light!

Scarlet's hands opened the lantern and extinguished the flame. The passageway fell into cloaking obscurity. He felt a sense of immense relief, of victory brought about by the darkness.

And then it struck, a terrifying fear so violent that Scarlet felt as if he were disemboweled. Every muscle in his body twitched and writhed, trying to escape the monstrous force that consumed him as surely and thoroughly as a pack of lions. His lungs sucked in air spasmodically, and he burst out with a ragged, tearing scream like that of an animal being dragged to its death.

He ran blindly, having little idea that his legs were even moving. Something struck his forehead a smashing blow, a flash of brilliant light seared his quivering eyes, and he fell into a convulsive unconsciousness.

Yun's diary, Day 45

I'm too tired to write. Maybe tomorrow.

I've gotten blood on my journal. Loa, give me strength.

No strength remained in Yun's small body. She had done what she could with the giant welt along Rodrigo's side, and his painful ribs and hip that caused him to stumble when he walked. With Rodrigo's limited help she dragged Scarlet back to the lake, weeping every time she looked at the terrible gash on his forehead and the blood that caked his face and throat and shirt. She had bound the wound as best she could, terrified by the small convulsions that rocked the unconscious boy's body. And somehow, despite legs reduced to uncontrolled quivering, she and Rodrigo dragged two others back with them, inch by inch, hour by hour.

The newcomers were opposites. One appeared where Rodrigo had touched the small statue—a small man with wavy brown locks, gray-violet eyes, a pixieish face and features, and a strong, well-exercised build. And yet he was not human, for his ears curled and trimmed back to a point, almost like a cat's, and were he standing he would barely be taller than Rodrigo's belt, even though he looked mature beyond boyhood. He lay where they had placed him, eyes darting about under his closed lids and suffering through a fit of unconscious dreams.

The other newcomer was discovered close by the stricken Scarlet. He now lay near the cavern exit—a giant, well over a foot taller than Rodrigo, barrel-chested and powerfully built. He had the look of one from the lands of olives and dates— lightly tan skin, looping black hair and a heavy, ugly, lantern-jawed face. Like Boar, he appeared fully adult but youthful. He was the last to be dragged here, and Yun and Rodrigo lost the strength to drag him farther. Unlike the small one, the giant hovered close to death, his pulse and breathing barely detectable. Yun could not be certain that he was still alive on her last check, and she fully expected him to pass away before she awoke.

Yun fell into a deep sleep, her first rest in many hours.

15: DREAM

Yun's diary, Day 46

   Scarlet is missing.

Scarlet began to dream a dream so vivid that he thought he lived it. He didn't want the dream, but he had no choice, as if someone had tied him down and forced him to watch.

The consuming fear remained, though only lightly, as if something that had feasted on him was now just nibbling on crumbs.

And the dream played on.

Scarlet realized that he could see, but unnaturally. He saw clearly, but everything appeared more as replicas, artificial in a way that he could not describe.

He drifted away from the lake, floating through familiar corridors.

He passed through Royalty Hall, Gargoyle Cave, the Boxmaker's Chamber, and the long difficult passage called Jumble, which led to Waterfall. And as he traveled down the passage, something came up it from the other direction. He floated to the wall and remained still, watching.

A small creature appeared, skin a deepest black, much like the Fleye. However, this creature had two eyes, large and golden and owl-like, with oversized ears tufted heavily with hair. It wore a cloth at the hip, a long ebony cloak, a crossbow at its back, a satchel, and a belt with assorted small weapons and tools. What appeared, at first, to be white facial hair was actually a sizable fan of whiskers.

Despite his size, the creature demonstrated considerable strength in dragging a human on a piece of tent canvas, the retractable claws on each of its fingers latched tightly to the end of the canvas as he strained forward, making slow but steady time over the rocky surface of Jumble.

As the creature passed, Scarlet gained a clear view of the human on the canvas. It was a woman in her mid-twenties, dressed in a plain, dark gray work dress, her eyes closed. She seemed fevered, tossing her head slightly and whispering to herself, as if she had just been awakened from stone. Her straight locks of brown hair fell in disarray over her face and shoulders and across the canvas. The face…

Scarlet knew the face. It was Hope.

He remembered Hope from the dream when he was poisoned, her strong, pleasant face and expressive mouth delighting him as she told him about the

65

bitter bulb as cure for the poison. How could she now be in this dream? He remembered when he told Rodrigo—that was his friend's name, wasn't it?—that everything was likely a dream. Now he was no longer sure which of his seemingly endless dreams reflected reality.

Hope and the creature passed by, and Scarlet's sight faded to darkness momentarily. Then he floated again, hovering near the wall of a different passage. This one was Twist, because he could see the barred fortress doors to Skyhall in front of him.

The owl-eyed creature removed the last bar. He slowly swung the doors open enough to drag Hope through into Skyhall. She lay sideways now and her hands were tied behind her back, with many loops of rope pinning her legs together.

Owleye stopped inside. Scarlet floated inside as well, just as the creature pulled the doors closed. Owleye cut the bonds holding Hope, said something to her that Scarlet could not overhear, then leapt to the ladder and ascended to the roof.

Scarlet floated to the windows, where lightning flashed from the mists below. The thunder that should have been deafening came tinny and distant, as if he had pillows over his ears. In the flashes, he saw Owleye making its way along the cliff toward the city. The creature picked its path with apparently little effort, rarely pausing, swinging easily from grip to grip and spike to spike like a monkey.

Save her. You must save her, came a thought that might have been his.

The dream twisted like a wind-tortured fog and faded away, and he found himself waking. But he was not in bed. He was standing in the sands by Vida Lake.

Although he knew this was no longer a dream, his vision kept that same artificial feel. There were others around him, but they all slept.

He had to make haste, if he were save Hope. He knew this, because it whispered again and again in his mind.

He walked quickly to the cavern exit, stepping around the corpse of a giant black-haired man that he had never seen before. He remembered his need for a lantern, then realized that he could see as well without one, and he pressed forward.

He was physically too hurt and exhausted to stand, much less walk all the way along Twist and to Skyhall. But some fountain of energy propelled him, urging on his muscles, clearing his disoriented mind for the task. He passed through Royalty Hall, then Scarlet Hall, and entered Twist. As he did so, his vision, so clear to begin with, had begun to fade to ghostly shapes.

He pressed on, one step at a time, singing drifting patches of songs about stormy seas and treasures laid deep.

And then, at one step more, he was all but blind in the darkness. He gasped, rested his hands on his knees, and laughed in a manner not at all humorously. "No," he said in a wheedling voice as if he were a scolded youth. "No," he said with a growl. He straightened up, drew a long breath, and staggered on, groaning in between snatches of tattered song.

He tripped on debris and on the uneven floor of Twist, until at last he bumped into something. It was metal, and tall, and heavy.

The doors of Skyhall.

He leaned and pulled with all of his remaining strength on the iron loop handles. The doors would not budge. He slid over, pulling with all of his might on just one of the doors. It swung an inch with agonizing slowness.

But his energy passed away.

They found him.

"His forehead is bleeding again!" said Yun.

"Hold the lantern, I'll get a cloth," said Rodrigo. "And help me pull him in here where he can lie flat."

The two dragged Scarlet into Skyhall. Rodrigo cast about for a clean cloth among the extensive laboratory tables and storage areas.

Lightning flashed low in the mist, followed by a rolling rumble of thunder.

"Hello?" came a female voice.

Rodrigo jumped and reached for his sword, until he saw an unmistakable feminine dress, silhouetted in the blue glow from the windows.

"Who are you?" said Rodrigo. And then he added, "Where is Boar?"

"Who is Boar?" said the silhouette.

"That is a good answer. And who am I addressing?"

"My name is Hope. Do you intend me harm?"

Rodrigo limped up to her. She looked at him pensively, her features drawn and colorless with fatigue.

"I have never harmed a lady in my life," he said. "You are safe. I have a wounded friend that I must attend to immediately."

"Something that sounded like an animal was forcing the doors open," said Hope. "Did you see anything?"

"That must have been my friend Scarlet. He's lying here hurt," said Rodrigo, a touch of accusation in his voice. He turned, pulled a cloth from a pigeonhole, and limped back to Scarlet.

Blood oozed slowly from Scarlet's wound, trickling to his ear. When Rodrigo felt for a pulse, he couldn't find one. "No pulse," he said to Yun, barely keeping distress from his voice.

Yun covered her mouth and choked back her agony.

"You haven't your finger in the right place," said the voice behind him. Hope knelt down beside Rodrigo and put her finger farther back under Scarlet's chin. "It's there, and steady, but not strong. Can you help me lift him onto the table over there?"

The three managed this with some effort. Yun held the lantern pole high, and Hope inspected Scarlet's face, opening his eyes and probing at the gash along his forehead.

"Find a blanket, keep him warm." Hope stepped to a set of metal tables lined with various sharp and pointed instruments, her hard shoes clacking on the stone. She came back with a bottle of clear liquid, a thin knife, a small hook, and a spool of what looked like silk thread.

"This will hurt like a fury," said Hope. "If he has fight left in him, he will use it, so hang on to him tightly."

Hope tilted his head and trickled the liquid into the gash, letting it run out from one end to the other. The smell of alcohol drifted into Rodrigo's nostrils.

Scarlet came alive, crying out in agony and seizing up. Yun held a bear hug on Scarlet's legs while Rodrigo pinned his arms.

"Any clean water? I found none in here," said Hope.

"My pack," said Yun.

Hope used the water and alcohol liberally, cleaning the wound with the cloth. "Next step. This won't hurt him as badly, but if you're squeamish, best look away. Hold his head—I'm sorry, you gave no name."

"Rodrigo."

"Steady then, Rodrigo." Hope doused the needle and her hands in alcohol and sewed up the wound, swiftly and steadily. Scarlet moaned and thrashed weakly. When Hope straightened up and clipped the final thread, the gash was little more than a swollen crease, matched expertly.

Yun and Rodrigo slumped, exhausted. They had set out in search of Scarlet hours ago, failing to find him at Bronzewall and trying for Skyhall second. The pain in Rodrigo's hip returned over the effort so that now, each step gave agony.

"Any food?" asked Hope. "I haven't eaten in days."

Yun pointed to her pack, and Hope found the bundle of growth. She dug in hungrily and drank the rest of Yun's water.

"I should bring two canteens," whispered Yun. "Everybody's always drinking mine."

"Your name is Hope?" said Rodrigo. "Scarlet—this man here—had a dream about a young lady named Hope. So I must say, I am surprised to meet a real Hope. Do you recognize Scarlet?"

"No," said Hope. "But I've little to offer there. I awakened from a coma a few days ago and I've lost much of my memory."

"Ah," said Rodrigo. "Well, welcome to the fold, Miss Hope. We are all fellow amnesiacs. How long have you been here?"

"More than a day, I should think. The lack of a sun is unnerving, to say the least. And when the lightning starts up, the thunder can be deafening."

A soft thump came from the roof.

Rodrigo and Yun jumped and stared up at the ceiling. The trapdoor swung open, revealing the silhouette of a rounded, fan-eared head and the glitter of two large, owl-like eyes. The head moved slightly, then the trapdoor slammed back down.

Rodrigo drew his sword and limped to the corner window. In the dull blue glow he saw a dim figure moving along the cliff with the aid of rope, no more than sixty feet from the roof.

The figure was unmistakably Boar.

"We have to leave, now." Rodrigo hastened back to Yun and lifted Scarlet to get a grip under his shoulder.

"Are you sure?" said Hope.

"Now!" Rodrigo pointed to Scarlet's other shoulder.

"Boar?" whispered Yun.

Rodrigo nodded, seeing the fear rise in Yun's eyes.

"One moment." Hope hurried back through the tables.

"We do not have time," called Rodrigo. He motioned for Yun to get Scarlet's shoulder. Yun obeyed, but she had no reserve of strength, and they dragged him slowly. Rodrigo realized that they were also leaving the lantern and Yun's pack.

"Hope!" He turned, found her hauling a large rucksack, in which she scooped the equipment she had used on Scarlet. She threw Yun's pack on top of it, picked up the lantern, and headed to the door.

A second thump came from the roof, heavier this time.

"Move!" growled Rodrigo and he forced himself to quicken his pace, his hip shooting unbearable pain into his leg. He carried Scarlet through the door as sounds of crashing came behind him. Dropping Scarlet none too gently, he shoved his back into the doors while Hope strained above him.

"The bar!" he cried, but Yun had already dragged one near to the door. Rodrigo grabbed it, twisted it over his head, and Hope guided it into place.

It dropped no more than an inch into the slot when a heavy weight struck against the door from the inside.

The bar threatened to slip, but Hope shoved down with all of her weight, and it slid inch by inch into place, despite the pressure on the door.

"Another!" gasped Rodrigo. The second bar dropped into place, and the third. He slid down the door and worked on breathing. The pressure on the door eased.

"Rodrigo, old friend, is that you?" said a familiar rough voice from beyond the door.

"Greetings, Boar, how is the city?" managed Rodrigo.

"A real challenge. I did not come to fight you, old friend. Open door and we talk, da?"

"No," said Rodrigo.

Silence from the other side, until at last, "This girl, you must leave her here. I will take her to city. She become safe there."

"Past history, Boar," said Rodrigo. "It has not changed. You proved yourself untrustworthy, and I would rather die than give over a lady to you."

Boar's voice rose, and even through the inches of metal it caused Rodrigo to flinch. "This is second time you stab me in back, Rodrigo! You are no longer enemy that I regard, dog! When next time we meet, there is sword through your back and I watch you die! You hear me, Rodrigo!"

Rodrigo took a breath. "When next we meet, Boar, I will have the decency to put my sword through your chest, and you will see the thrust that kills you. Take your little demon friend and go."

"Mark the days, dog!" answered Boar, and he said no more.

17: LARGE AND SMALL

— 2 days later

Yun's diary, Day 48

We have Hope. There, I wrote it.

"Try to pull your leg back against me. Pain?"

Rodrigo groaned. "Pain."

"Here?"

"Yes."

"Lie flat. This might hurt in earnest, but just bear through it."

Hope started kneading the muscles at the base of Rodrigo's back, while he closed his eyes and grimaced silently. Several minutes later, she motioned for Yun.

"Get in front of him and hold tight to his arm—up and over, right there. Keep pulling."

"What are you doing?" asked Rodrigo.

"Just let yourself go slack," said Hope.

"Yes—arrrr!" yelled Rodrigo as Hope slammed down on his hip and leg. Rodrigo felt a grinding shift in his hip, and then a numbing relief.

"Any pain now?" asked Hope.

"It is sore," said Rodrigo.

"Yes, but do you have any stinging pain?"

"No," said Rodrigo, rubbing his leg gently.

"Then you are fortunate, merely dislocation and seized muscles. Is your side better?"

"Sore," said Rodrigo. She had manhandled his ribs and middle back earlier, finding strains and bruises but nothing broken.

"You will have your fill of sore the next few days." Hope gave that amiable smile that made her normally passive face brighten delightfully.

Rodrigo was amazed at her strength and confidence, and the ramrod bearing of her athletic, agreeably curved figure. He found himself fascinated by the dance of her ponytail as she went about her work, until the inner Rodrigo shook his head sternly at the childish infatuation of a patient to his healer. He turned over, rubbing his hip tenderly.

"She's a beaut," said the small man propped up in a bedroll next to him. He was bare-chested, his body lean in the legs and hips but rope-muscled in the chest and shoulders. Odd bands of extra muscle ran from rip cage to hip and over the flat stomach, giving his waist a tight streamlining that looked not quite human.

"You are awake," said Rodrigo.

"Been awake for a day. Yer the sleepy-head. Heard yeh been through a grinder the last few days."

"I would relish boredom for a time. We have not met formally. I am Rodrigo."

"Rip, at yer service. Heard yer the top dillie."

"If by 'dillie' you mean leader, I would have to disagree."

"Boggyknot!" said Rip. "Yer the boss, everyone says. A laurel-limbed hero, I hear. Good on yeh. Mess of Dusties like us need to be organized."

"Hope explained the Dustie idea to you?"

"Ahey," said the little man.

"No memory?"

"N'hardly. All us in the same Dustie tub, right?"

"Unfortunately," said Rodrigo.

"That's a blight." Rip's animated pixie-like features scrunched in distaste as he looked around the cavern, his lively gray-violet eyes flashing. "Not much for being stuck in a hole. Green grass and a babbling brook for me. But we do have a lake and fish."

"Little fish," said Rodrigo.

"Hoy, there's bigguns as well!"

"We cannot catch them. No nets or fishing gear."

Rip smiled brightly. "I can catch a whale with a wishbone, I can! You'll see."

"That is good news," said Rodrigo. "If you can catch one and get us real meat, you will be the laurel-rimmed hero."

"Laurel-*limbed*, Boss," corrected Rip. He looked up past Rodrigo.

"Can you lend your arms, gentlemen?" said Hope from behind Rodrigo.

"Comes my muscle, m'lady," piped Rip, and he popped up.

Rodrigo followed more gingerly.

Hope led them to the large man. He lay still as death, without any immediate indication of life. His loosely curled black hair framed a tanned, ugly face as wide as it was tall. Rodrigo guessed that the man was in his late twenties.

"I must have him set properly, over there," said Hope.

The three dragged the man across the sand, his weight easily equaling all three of them combined. They propped him in a rocky crevice padded with blankets.

"Thought he was good as gone," said Rip.

"Close," said Hope. "His trouble is unusual. Frightfully weak blood, as though he were in the last days of starvation, except his body isn't wasted away. Doesn't fit. He is in a coma yet he responds, which also makes little sense. I was able to manage some syrup down him, and he perked up noticeably."

"Strange one," said Rodrigo. "He is having a much tougher struggle coming out of stone than the others."

"Perhaps it is his size," said Hope. "He must be at least twenty inches taller than me."

"Let's hope he's not a Boar," said Rodrigo.

Rip waved a dismissive hand. "Meaning no disrespect to your unfortunate size, Boss, but big is clumsy. Still, I'd hate to knock knuckles with him."

"Regardless," said Rodrigo, "I would say we picked up two sterling additions to our lost little clan. I am glad to find myself side by side with both of you."

Hope gave the smile that Rodrigo craved, and Rip jumped to his feet. "I'll be pulling my oar right now, then, and drop consternation down on the fishies. Meat for dinner!"

"Careful, Rip. They have a big bite." Rodrigo pointed to his leg, but realized that the scars of the old bite had all but disappeared. He rubbed his calf gratefully and checked the long scratch down his chest from being thrown over the cliff. It too had faded completely.

"How is Scarlet?" he asked.

"See for yourself," said Hope. "He's awake now."

Rodrigo walked over to the sandbar on which Scarlet had been isolated to give him quiet. The boy greeted Rodrigo with a sleepy smile. Rodrigo dropped down next to him.

"I heard we won," said Scarlet.

"Victory, thanks to you," said Rodrigo. "How did you know to find her?"

"The oddest thing," said Scarlet. "I floated in a dream state, seeing that little Owleye demon take her and stuff her into Skyhall. Then I woke up, and I couldn't help but try to reach her there. My eyesight was all strange...I can't explain it."

Rodrigo stretched his sore leg. "However it happened, Hope was worth it. She fixed the wound on your head with superb skill. And she likely saved the life of the big man. But what happened to you earlier? How did you get that wound? Hope said you had this unnatural fear just before you were knocked out."

"That's putting it mildly," said Scarlet. "Frightened completely out of my senses. It's a wonder I'm still sane, seriously."

Rodrigo raised an eyebrow and nodded. "It is likely the same Shadow that dogged me in the dark. It was like fear that ate away at you."

Scarlet nodded emphatically. "I honestly don't know how you managed to stay in one piece, four days in the dark with that thing. Might it be a ghost or such? Have you actually seen it? How do we tackle it?"

"I have not seen it," said Rodrigo, "nor heard it, though I imagined it talked to me. I only knew it was there when the fear struck me."

"I haven't the foggiest idea how to defend against that," said Scarlet. "But it's over now."

Scarlet smiled, but something in his eyes gave Rodrigo pause.

"Are you certain you are past it?" said Rodrigo. "It took me some time to recover, and I am not fully there yet. I dread its return."

"Here's to hoping it never will," said Scarlet, his eyes evasive. "Speaking of Hope…"

"Yes?"

"Oh, come now."

Rodrigo raised an eyebrow. "Well, let me see…She is your dream come true. Literally."

"And every other way," said Scarlet.

"Where does that leave Yun?"

Scarlet's smile faded. "That's a low blow. But I see your point."

"No, my real point is this, Scarlet. I watched you dance with Yun. You were every bit a gentleman. Unfortunately, girls like Yun will fall for that harder than if you were an unprincipled rogue. You have everything a girl is looking for, and that is your curse. Yun and Hope need friends right now, not lovers."

"I say, are you seventeen or seventy? You sound like my grandfather."

"As if you remember your grandfather!" said Rodrigo. "He could very well have been the king of rogues. And trust me, I am entirely seventeen. But right now I am trying to give them a fair chance to sort things out."

"It's their fault, you know. Had they been ugly, bickering crows there wouldn't be an issue. I understand what you are digging at. But it won't be easy to turn off my charming self."

"Just be charming at arm's length."

Scarlet grinned impishly. "Yes, Grandfather."

18: Bait

— *6 days later*

Yun's diary, Day 54

Seven days have gone by since our newcomers arrived and things are so busy that I haven't had a chance to just sit and watch them. But today I had nothing to do at all—I am out of good books—and so I spied on everyone. Nobody notices me much anyway.

Scarlet is back to his cheerful self, or mostly. He danced with me again. It was nice, but not the same, maybe because others were watching, but I don't think so. He likes Hope, I can tell.

I like Hope, too. She has taught me all kinds of healing secrets, and I helped her a lot this week. It's just hard having her here. She's the real woman now, and I'm back to being the little girl.

Rodrigo is—well, he's the same old Rodrigo. He treats me very nice when he isn't telling me what to do. Everyone else just naturally accepted him as leader, even though he never said so. He's a good man, and I still love him more than ever. He hasn't shown a lot of interest in Hope, at least in a man way. He's a strange one. I heard Scarlet call him Grandfather yesterday, and I laughed so loud they heard me. Rodrigo just doesn't act his age.

The big man—Trace—has problems. Even after a week he is still clumsy on his feet and has trouble talking. Hope says he might have hurt something in his brain. He is quiet, and a little out of sorts, but he seems nice otherwise. He has the strangest eyes—such a colorful deep blue that they look like pools rather than eyes. You would not believe what he can lift. He's not fat, just muscles all over, and his face is like an ox. I have never seen anyone eat as much as he can.

I haven't quite gotten used to Rip. He looks human, but he isn't. I just wasn't ever expecting there to be anything other than humans. It's like finding out that gnomes really do live in your garden. He has a strange way of talking, and he is always picking on Scarlet, which is funny. Serves Scarlet right. Rip is a sharp dancer, but he dances too fast for me.

Rip begged for paper and charcoal. I saw him drawing on the paper, and he is good! He made a beautiful sketch of me and let me have it. He should be making our maps.

Rip is heading to the lake. He caught some smaller fish a few days ago, but the big ones just don't come anywhere close enough to shore.

Rip led Trace up the cliff stairs to where Rodrigo had jumped in to save Yun. "Perfect!" he called. "I can see a few of the bigguns circling. Sit down here, big man, and get ready."

Trace sat back against the cliff wall. Rip looked like a cat next to a buffalo as he tied a rope tightly around himself and gave the remaining length to Trace.

"You're insane," called Scarlet from the shore.

"If by insane yeh mean devilishly clever, you're dead on, Mr. Pantaloons!" Rip couldn't get enough of teasing Scarlet about the fancy attire that the boy favored.

"Do you intend to stop him?" said Hope to Rodrigo.

"No. I would never even consider doing what I think he is about to do, but this is his decision."

"Those shabby clothes will not protect him well enough," said Hope. "He'll be hurt."

"His decision." Rodrigo kept his eyes on the tiny figure at the edge of the cliff.

Hope readied more complaints, but Yun gave her a little kick to the ankle. "Man stuff. Best let it go."

Rip stepped into a makeshift woolen suit. He hefted an equally makeshift barbed wooden spear, gave Trace a slap on the shoulder, and leapt over the edge. "Comes yer wooooooooorm!"

He hit the water with a fat splash.

Two oiled canvas pouches filled with air prevented him from sinking, but he clearly couldn't swim or even move well in the heavy wool.

"Have you considered," yelled Scarlet, "that you might scare up a fish much bigger than Rodrigo's?"

"Of course!" came back the reply. "Which is to say, no I didn't! But if I get swallowed, Trace will just have to pop me out!"

Trace stood up and pointed. "Eyes!"

"Where?" said Rip, trying to turn himself about.

"Behind!" yelled Trace. "Left!"

"You better go up and steady Trace," said Rodrigo to Scarlet.

"Right." Scarlet raced off to the stairs.

The scene below became clear as Scarlet reached Trace's side. Not one but two sets of luminous eyes closed in on Rip, the dark shapes of the big fish distorted in the ripples from Rip's splashing about.

"You've made yourself two friends," shouted Scarlet. "Can you see them?"

"No!"

"They're moving off," said Scarlet as the two sets of eyes drifted lazily away.

"Come on, you wollybokkins, bite me!" Rip splashed his arms and flailed about.

One set of eyes swung back, circling.

"He's back," shouted Scarlet.

"He better—*ahhhhgh!*"

The fish arrowed in so quickly that Scarlet didn't have time to warn Rip.

"He's got me, *arrhhhh, noooooaaagh!* My leg! I can't feel my leg!"

Yun let out a little scream and clutched Hope, who gave Rodrigo a panicked version of the I-told-you-so glare.

"*Argh*, my hand! Where's my hand! It's floating to shore, snatch it!"

"This is fun...for the girls...you know," said Trace to Scarlet, an amiable smile on his blocky face as he managed the rope.

"Gotchee!" shouted Rip.

"He s-s-said secret word," said Trace. "I pull him up."

Trace drew in the line, pulling Rip to the cliff edge and up out of the water.

"Stop! Stop!" yelled Rip. "Crawkies! This fishie is too heavy! You'll have to pull me to shore instead! She's a fat monster! She's beating me blue!"

Trace and Scarlet descended to the base of the stairs and hauled Rip in. The fish fought furiously, roiling and splashing the water so violently that nothing could be seen of Rip. The little man finally appeared, coughing water, and the three dragged the wildly flopping catch onto the sand.

The fish was indeed big, easily the same mass as Rip himself. It looked back at them with its monster-ugly face and luminous eyes, but the fire in those eyes faded. Rip slapped its wide, stubby body and worked at removing his spear from where it had pierced the gills. "Real meat, laddies! Hooah that was an adventure!"

Hope stormed up. "That was not in the least funny! You should be ashamed of yourself!"

"I've no shame, of that I attest, dear girl," said Rip, bowing. "And of that I'm terrible ashamed. But I am not ashamed of this mountain of *meat!*" The wet little manling gave a whooping cry and tried to stand atop the fish, wobbling unsteadily, his woolen suit sagging woefully. Everyone whooped along with him, even, eventually, Hope.

19: ED

Yun's diary, Day 65

We finished checking all of the statues, and found two more Dusties, both down in the Asylum. Rodrigo was right—the new Dusties were made of greenish-black stone, the same as Scarlet, Boar, and Rip. It looks like we have discovered a common thread. It will make searching for others easier.

The two new Dusties babbled a lot, just like everyone else for the first day. Rodrigo told me to write down as much as I could. He thinks it may be important. I wrote everything down, but it just looks like gibberish to me. One mumbled lots of talk about seeing lights and sounds, and the other seemed to be trying to get away from something.

The first one calls himself Raeder. He's older like Boar, and handsome, and he knows it. He chats with me and Hope whenever he gets the chance. I should have known by the moustache and the goatee that he would be one of *those* kind of men.

Raeder spends most of his time collecting things and finding useful stuff. Rodrigo says he has an eye for it. He found a little pin with a lotus flower on it and gave it to me. He loves to explore and climb, and does not mind tight places at all, which Rodrigo is grateful for.

The other one—his name is Ed—doesn't talk much. In fact, he isn't very sociable at all. He treats everyone as nuisances, except Rodrigo. He will sometimes get into a talking binge and go on and on to Rodrigo and Scarlet about something or other, usually about machines or tools, which he seems to have an obsession about. I can tell Rodrigo doesn't understand half of it, but he's a good faker. I guess that comes with being a good leader.

Ed is taller than Rodrigo, with pale skin, big stooped shoulders, a horse-like face and muddy-colored eyes. His hair is either very dark brown or black. I haven't gotten close enough to him to tell for sure. He must be older than Rodrigo by at least five years.

Ed has spent the last five days far down the tunnels at the big cavern called Waterfall. He won't come home, he says, until he figures out what *the machinery does down there. Once he yelled at me and said I was "meddling." I was just looking at the machinery like everyone else has a hundred times.*

Maybe we can give him to Boar.

"I have it," shouted Ed over the roar of the waterfall, the namesake of this tall, elongated cavern. He stood at what was obviously intended as a control center for the machinery that dominated the cavern—lines of chains that crisscrossed the walls before disappearing into holes in the rock and reappearing elsewhere, arrays of pulleys and lifts, crane-like guides, complicated gear sets, and the control center itself consisting of all manner of cranks and levers along a wall made entirely of metal. Spray from the thundering waterfall soaked everything, allowing growth to cover the cave top to bottom on the natural rock, though it avoided all metal surfaces.

"You know what it does?" asked Rodrigo.

"Yes. Or no. I don't know what it does, but I do know why it was built this way."

"What do you mean, *this way*?" asked Scarlet.

"It's a sly mess. There is machinery in this room that does nothing—complete nonsense—but it's cleverly designed to look as if it did. Or, it's doing a useless job. This, for instance. These chain sets and two levers here do nothing more than raise and lower gates for small water channels over there. You could do the same work easier by hand."

"Seems like a terrific waste," said Scarlet.

"Exactly," said Ed, his intense mud-colored eyes flicking from Scarlet to Rodrigo. "But they were clever little toadies. Do you know why?"

Ed stared at them expectantly. Scarlet and Rodrigo glanced uncomfortably at each other. "We do not have a guess," said Rodrigo at last. "Would you mind?"

Ed sniffed self-importantly. "Favorite story—wish I could remember the author. A man caught a leprechaun and forced it to reveal its gold pot. The gold lay under a tree, and the man tied a red ribbon around the trunk. 'You must promise not to touch this ribbon or move your gold,' demanded the man. The leprechaun promised, and the man returned home to get his cart to carry the gold. When he returned, every tree had a red ribbon, and he could not find the gold."

"That was…quite interesting," said Rodrigo. "And what does it mean? You said that you think you know what the machinery might do."

Ed sighed and gestured as if he were dealing with small children. "Never mind. I can see you'll need a show and tell." He motioned for them to follow. They climbed a ladder onto a narrow metal bridge, and Ed pointed halfway up and to the right of where the thundering waterfall cascaded down into its established pool.

"See the big ledge, how it dips toward the back? Looks like it's carved by machinery, but also worn by water. Right?"

"I see," said Rodrigo. "But I have not caught on to the signifi-"

"It's a diversion," interrupted Ed impatiently. "That waterfall has a heapload of power. When it is diverted, it must cause something big to happen in here. With me?"

"With you," said Scarlet. "Can you puzzle out what that is?"

"Yes and no," shouted Ed over the roar of the falls. "See the row of large levers toward the bottom of the wall? Thirteen in all. I can tell by working them that there's real power behind them, serious hydraulic horsepower."

"Can we try setting them?" asked Rodrigo.

"Yes and no. The levers are interesting. You can position them up, down, left, right, or center."

"So, have you figured out how to operate it?" said Scarlet.

"I'm getting there," snapped Ed. "Those thirteen levers are a giant combination lock. And *we* don't know the combination. Now, we could mine into that wall and try to force the issue, but considering the genius behind this work, I would bet on that being a bad idea."

"And the other machinery?" said Rodrigo.

"As I just explained, useless by design," said Ed. "If you blunder into this cave and you see thirteen mysterious levers alone, you've got your curiosity tickled. But if you see a tangle of machinery doing menial tasks, you don't even notice the important levers. Like red ribbons on all the trees. The builders pulled the leprechaun's trick."

Rodrigo and Scarlet raised their eyes in understanding.

"Considering the hard work to set all this up, it must be a very important secret," said Rodrigo.

"To be kept from powerful enemies," added Scarlet. "Any idea how old it is?"

Ed shook his head. "Hard to tell. Whoever made this had a top-notch foundry to work with. No rust anywhere, which is downright magical. But considering the water wear, I would say fifty to a hundred years."

Rodrigo gestured to the levers. "Any chance you could just-"

"Over a billion combinations," interrupted Ed. "Not a chance to find the correct combination by tugging at Lady Luck."

"A genius setup," said Rodrigo. "Good work in digging out its secret, Ed."

"Easy enough for me."

"Quite," said Scarlet, grinning dubiously and shaking his head.

But Ed had already turned and focused his attention elsewhere.

20: RAEDER

— 2 days later

Yun's diary, Day 67

> Raeder asked me to dance today. He's a very good dancer, like Scarlet, but he likes to get close. I think he's exciting, but Hope despises him. She yelled at him the other day over something. I was too far away to hear.

> Raeder is a good climber. He wanted to climb to Drift like Boar did, but Rodrigo said no. They argued about it for a while. I think Raeder and Rodrigo are wrestling over who is boss.

> We haven't found a way out yet, but Raeder thinks he might have discovered one in Gargoyle Cave.

> Gargoyle Cave—what a terrible name. The most beautiful water-garden cave in our home, and just because there's one big gargoyle monument in there, it gets stuck with an ugly name. That's the problem with boys.

Of all the strange locations in Lakeside, the one Rodrigo now entered impressed him the most. The massive chamber extended in a dome, like many of the others. Water flowed everywhere, pouring down through a hundred seams in the dome and creating its own miniature watersheds through the mounded landscape of the floor. The streams and rivulets eventually made their way to the center of the chamber and formed a lazy whirlpool. Growth covered every inch, producing a respectable light that almost made Rodrigo blink.

Across the chamber from Rodrigo, a gargantuan monument rose sixty feet or more out of the mounded glowmoss of the floor, its greenish metal surface free of growth. Atop the square structure hunched a massive gargoyle, its wings arched outward. Water cascaded over its surface and off the great wings, but the dark metal had not rusted or burnished.

Rodrigo chose a path and threaded his way through the streams and falls of water, selecting the patches of hard, flathead glowmoss for sure footing. He heard a "Hahlay!" and saw Rip wave to him from the monument.

Raeder squeezed out from a slit in the ground near monument's base as Rodrigo approached.

"What did you find?" said Rodrigo.

"A way out!" Raeder's powder-blue eyes were intense with excitement under his tilted brows. He pushed back his lengthy brown hair and patted at globs of dirt and glowmoss on his wet shirt. "Or, a possible way out. I'll show you."

Rodrigo looked at the terribly narrow slit. "Looks like a tight squeeze."

"A bit," said Raeder. "Not a problem for anyone except Trace—not a big problem, anyway. The channel under the monument is tight, but the other way opens out after just ten feet or so. Want to take a look?"

Rodrigo smiled and shook his head. "No. Just tell me about it."

Raeder glanced at Rodrigo, shrugged to himself, and knelt by the slit, working his arms in explanation. "There's a channel that goes both ways from the slit. One runs under the monument, and the other curves out to a big fissure. The first section of the fissure is dry, dark as pitch, but then farther on the water comes down heavy, so the path is iffy. About two hundred feet along, there's a series of metal rungs and convenient ledges carved out of the cliff, going straight up as far as I can see. Plenty of glowmoss for light too."

"Where are Scarlet and Ed?" said Rodrigo.

"Under the monument."

Rodrigo nodded. "This is an important find, Raeder. Well done."

"Thanks." Raeder stepped back, wiping the moisture off his hands. Raeder had good days and bad days with Rodrigo. On the bad days he clearly chafed under Rodrigo's cautious leadership, and on good days he praised the energy that the boy put through in accomplishing things. Raeder liked to make things happen, and getting out of this underground nest had become his top priority.

Scarlet pushed his way out of the slit, followed by Ed.

"There's machinery under the monument," said Ed. "Mighty strange stuff, likely more tomfoolery like the fake odds and ends in Waterfall. I need tools." Without waiting for a response from Rodrigo, he walked away.

"And I'll get rope," said Scarlet.

"Rope? What for?" said Raeder.

"To tie off with, on the rungs."

"That's no good," said Raeder. "The rope will get wet by the time we make the rungs, and that extra weight will be a problem. The rungs and ledges are safe enough without rope."

Scarlet shrugged cautiously. "Right then, shall we give it a go?"

"Ready," said Raeder, smiling excitedly. "We'll be back in three or four hours, Rodrigo."

Rodrigo nodded. "I'll stay here and wait for Ed."

Scarlet and Raeder squirmed their way through the channel until the floor sloped away and deposited them on a rocky ledge littered with small glowmoss surviving on the spray of the chamber. Darkness enveloped all other directions, and the two lit their lanterns.

"Footing can be a little treacherous, so watch your step," said Raeder.

Scarlet soon found the warning valid as the path turned into a narrow, gravel-strewn crease in the nearly vertical chasm wall. His lantern lit the far side of the fissure, a mere fifteen or twenty feet away, giving the impression of being in a great throat in the act of swallowing them. From above, an eerie sound floated down—a lazy, on-and-off clicking, like tiles or stones struck lightly together. The strange noise came and went, sometimes from directly above, sometimes from farther ahead, and at random intervals. Scarlet's nerves started fraying, waiting for the sound to happen, and his imagination conjured up the nature of the terrible beasts that might be lurking above them.

He disturbed a sizable stone that fell away into the void. The echo of the rock's tumbling fall lasted seemingly forever, causing him to wonder just how deep it was.

Raeder forged on, clearly much more confident than Scarlet. As Scarlet's mind berated Raeder for being reckless and hasty, another part of his mind turned on himself.

Why have you become so hesitant and fearful, Scarlet? What has happened? It was the Fear, wasn't it? That terrible moment in the tunnel, alone in the dark, when the Fear struck you... What part of you did it devour?

The sound came again, from ahead and above. It faded, drifted away.

"Scarlet, what are you doing?" called Raeder.

Scarlet started moving again, slowly, picking his way cautiously, his neck quick to crane upward at the enveloping darkness...and whatever might be there.

The chasm curved sharply and a glimmer of moss-glow showed. The fall of water came loudly now...but there it was...audible, just above the noise of the falls...the clicking, faster now—much faster—high above.

Scarlet moved along by placing his hands against the wall, his face turned upward. Now and then his feet missed their mark and he nearly stumbled fatally. He slowed himself, keeping watch for the nightmare-thing that must be above him.

What has happened to your mind, Scarlet?

He made it around the curve, with the ribbon of glow and the rush of water ahead. Raeder stood on a wider ledge with one arm at his waist, clearly impatient but intending to wait for Scarlet.

The clicking rose, louder, more insistent.

And then Scarlet's eyes saw it—the dark bulk of the Thing, a monstrous being, spread above him against the rock of the chasm. The glowmoss from ahead gave just enough light so that Scarlet could see the shape move, but not enough to get an idea of what it might be.

He opened his mouth to shout, but stopped himself. He waved frantically to Raeder and pointed up.

Why did you do that? This is your own little nightmare, Scarlet.

But his mind was wrong. It was Raeder's nightmare too.

Raeder looked up and his eyes grew wide. "Go! Go!" he shouted to Scarlet, and leapt back along the tiny path at a rapid clip.

Scarlet did the same, taking chances, his nimble feet and fine balance carrying him along even as his terrified mind threatened to pitch him into the abyss. His lantern bumped heavily against the rock wall and the glass shattered.

Above and behind him, the clicking gave chase. He could hear the rockfall as the massive nightmare pursued him along the wall. He could feel its presence, the deadly flow of its agile form against the vertical stone.

A shout came from behind, then an agonized groan, then a scream—a long, fading scream. Scarlet's mind listened to it numbly, as though it were a memory. His body scrambled on, step after perilous step, until he saw the ledge and the dark hole of the channel. He dove headfirst into the narrow passage and clawed forward.

Something heavy slammed against his leg, shoving him sideways. He cried out in fear and pushed himself forward desperately.

He felt his shirt being grabbed and he was pulled upward. He fought against it, screaming, until he recognized it as a hand—Rodrigo's hand. Scarlet had reached the slit and did not realize it. He twisted around and clawed up through the hole, sliding frantically away and into a rivulet of water.

"What is it?" shouted Rodrigo.

"I don't know!" cried Scarlet, his hands and voice trembling. "I don't know! It's big—something big!"

Rodrigo drew his sword and peered down into the slit. "Can it get through here? Scarlet, can it get through here?!"

"I felt it! It hit me—no, I don't think—it was huge!"

"Where's Raeder?"

"He was—he was behind me."

"Where did he go?"

"I think it got to him. I think he fell. He fell."

Rodrigo watched the slit, his sword ready, helpless. An hour passed, and Ed returned to find the two huddled next to each other, watching the dark, silent hole.

Day 68

We've fortified the lake. Everyone is terribly frightened. Whatever monster is in the chasm below the gargoyle, it can climb easily, and that means that it could come down any of the holes.

Day 73

Rodrigo and Rip wanted to go down to look for Raeder, but they could still hear the monster when they tried.

I can tell Scarlet feels guilty, and he's scared. I think we all are. Raeder's death ripped away our belief, however false, of being trapped but safe.

We have no choice but to continue on, day to day.

22: THE TOUR

— *30 days later*

Yun's diary, Day 102

I realized today that over a month has passed since losing Raeder. Although we are a little more cautious, the fright of what happened has passed, like a nightmare dreamt years ago.

Life goes on, with all of its dangers. May Loa lead Raeder to a brighter place than our home.

Day 107

Scarlet went off with Hope. She said she wanted a tour, and that fool fell all over himself offering to take her. I couldn't help but giggle out loud when Rip and Trace invited themselves along.

I should have gone too. It's boring in this prison, and I've no books left to read. The books from Skyhall were horrid—stuffy, dull, and depressing.

Actually, I should have gone with Rodrigo. He and Ed are exploring again. They left before I woke up. I don't know how Rodrigo can spend all day with that man.

It may be bigger now, but this place is still just a prison. I've nothing to do. Rip is usually here, but right now I'm alone. I'm not scared, not really. Just tired.

I'm a Dustie. We all are. Eventually we'll join the dust in this place.

The monster loomed over them.

Hope jumped and let out a quickly stifled yelp. The massive head glared down at her—a giant wolf's-head, but more monster than wolf.

"Catches you the first time, doesn't it?" Scarlet smiled, holding out his lantern closer to the huge bronze work of art facing them.

The wolf's head filled the dead-end of one of the passages extending from Scarlet Hall, over thrice Hope's height. The glinting eye sockets and the closed, snarling jaws extending wall to wall gave Hope the uneasy impression that this too could be awakened, and that she would be devoured soonest should she make that mistake.

88

But that was silly, wasn't it?

"It's horrifying!" said Hope, putting one hand on Scarlet's shoulder. She glimpsed a flicker of a smile on his lips, but he kept his eyes on the metal monster.

"Magnificent workmanship though," he said. "The sculptor knew his art, and his perspective. I can't stare at it too long before I get a touch nervous."

"Who placed it here, do you suppose?" whispered Hope. "Imagine the machinery necessary."

Scarlet shrugged. "The builders had time on their hands, apparently."

"And why hidden away in this dead-end?" Hope continued. "Is it a gate of some kind?" She stepped forward and reached out a hand to touch one of the formidable canine fangs.

Scarlet straightened, took a step toward her as his hand came up. "Please don't do that."

Hope looked back at him, swallowing, happy that he had stopped her. But she couldn't help teasing him with her brave act. "It's merely a sculpture, truly."

"Yes, and I was simply a stone statue in the chamber back there. We've learned not to take things at face value here. That would include this huge beast that could swallow you like a frog with a fly. So, no one touches it."

Hope put her hand down and stepped back, suddenly aware of the nervousness that had built in her under the gaze of the beast.

"A gate, you say?" Scarlet rubbed his chin, then remembered himself and gave her a winning smile. "Time to move on."

Hope nodded and they set off.

The two walked the short distance back to Scarlet Hall, Scarlet carefully keeping with the slower pace of Hope. Hope tried, when possible, to observe the young man walking alongside her. She considered herself a good judge of men, and that judgment generally ruled unfavorably. Scarlet intrigued her, however—not in a romantic way, of course, for she was easily five or more years his senior and he not even out of childhood.

But perhaps that is what intrigued her. Despite his youth, he carried himself confidently. Not in the stiff manner of a young man who wishes desperately to communicate "I am a grown man now," but casually, as if it were as natural as breathing. He had a genius for dressing stylishly from the assorted scavenged pieces, though he rarely went without his thick soaring gull belt. "It defines me," he would say, and would pull Yun or Hope into a few steps of dance to prove it.

What was the word that defined Scarlet? She felt it trying to break the surface of her thoughts…

Men frustrated her—not all men, but those who attempted some form of romantic relationship. They turned from having sound sense into clumsy, ingratiating fools. The more they tried to please her, the more they puffed themselves up to become a mockery of what they should be. She wished she could remember the actual men in her past, but she did remember the distaste that she had for the male sex in general.

Not Scarlet. This man—this boy—didn't make a big show of helping her over a pile of rocks or through a tight spot, as if to say, "Look what I do for you, how you must be impressed!" He simply helped, as casually as possible, never dropping his end of the conversation. He hadn't made any form of romantic displays or even hinted at such in his speech, but she found herself carried along blissfully by his gentle, witty conversation and his soft, charming accent.

Natural talent it must be, because any typical boy of his age would be stumbling over himself in her presence. But what an astounding talent he displayed! She found herself smiling openly. Scarlet would provide her many hours of interesting study—

Irrepressible! That was the word for Scarlet.

"Hahlay!" yelled a voice as they entered Scarlet Hall. Lantern glow issued from one of the natural openings, and the comical contrast of tiny light-footed Rip and lumbering Trace appeared. The two had earlier broken off to explore the dry maze of tunnels beyond Scarlet Hall.

"Hullo, you two," said Scarlet. "Back so soon?"

"Ah-hey!" said Rip. "We stumbled upon a real landmark in the Maze, or Trace did. Yeh know the loud spot in there? Trace pushed a big slab of rock out of the way, and there was Rodrigo's big artesian fountain, just like he described it."

"Well!" said Scarlet. "The old boy wasn't hallucinating then."

"N'hardly," said Rip. "The geyser is a beauty, and another nourishing source of weeds. Here's to hoping that Trace can break us through to a pig farm next."

"Bacon!" said Scarlet dreamily.

"Bacon, is right," answered Rip.

A vision of a true morning breakfast rose in Hope's imagination, and her mouth watered. "Bacon, I can agree."

"Bacon?" Trace scratched at his curly black hair "What is bacon?"

The three looked at him. "There are no words," said Rip sadly, "to describe your impoverity. We must find bacon, if only for you."

Trace grinned broadly. "Good, then?"

"Ahhh-hey," confirmed Rip.

23: RETURN TO SKYHALL

Yun's diary, Day 108

> Rodrigo was all business when we went to visit the artesian fountain where he was first spit up here, but I could tell that old memories were visiting him. I tried to help him cheer up, and he gave me a smile and a hug. It was nice. We know what it was like, alone in those early days.
>
> He gave a speech of sorts, telling everyone to hold up their spirits and keep hard at finding a way out of here. He said that he intends to reopen Skyhall, even if it means fighting. Everyone agreed heartily. We are all getting desperate for something. Freedom, I guess. Or maybe just meaning.

When they unbarred the great metal doors at Skyhall, they found it deserted. Everyone breathed a sigh, put away their weapons, and busied themselves with their formerly agreed upon tasks. Rodrigo and Trace secured chains to the roof trapdoor, then started boarding up the broken panes in the window. Hope searched through the laboratory for useful medical supplies. Rip carefully packed the treasures into a pair of large-wheeled carts salvaged from Coachman's Chamber, and kept up a lively tune with his surprisingly rich gift for song. Ed wandered the room, refusing any assignment, inspecting odds and ends silently.

Yun drew in an excited breath, for her task involved books—a whole wall of books extending to the ceiling, with a sliding ladder for access.

Behind her, Scarlet clapped his hands together and rubbed them vigorously. "Where to start?"

"Bottom up." She took a first book from the lowest shelf and began leafing the pages.

In several hours, the two made a first pass over those books on the lower shelves, resulting in extreme disappointment and some concern. Many were scientific logs of a most cryptic and disturbing nature, with exhaustive details of what seemed to be medical experiments or dissections. Others were attempted explanations of the data, written in the most dry, uninspiring script that Yun could ever imagine reading. They came to identify four specific writers—Tophelas, Marrock, Jan-Jen, and Koyesh—each writing extensive and caustic rebuttals to the theories of the others.

"It's a wonder that they didn't kill each other," said Scarlet.

"I'm ready to kill myself," said Yun. "There's a section over here of fiction—I guess it's fiction—written by Marrock that is the worst storytelling I could imagine. Pure despair."

"These chaps must have been dedicated beyond measure," said Scarlet. "It looks like they wrote most of this. That's quite a feat."

"Years and years," said Yun. "I wish the dates in their notes meant something to me."

"Let's try out our ladder and get higher." Scarlet slid the ladder into position and helped Yun up.

She worked through the upper shelves, eventually coming down with several books under her arm. She laid them on a table and surveyed the top shelf more closely. Something caught her eye—a powder-blue book close to the upper corner. "Can we go up there?"

"Certainly," said Scarlet. "Just need to push away these odds and ends." He started moving a jumble of objects piled on the floor below the book—musical instruments like trumpets and flutes and harps, strange manikins made of stuffed cloth, a large brass flower head, and a lean wolf-looking creature derived from capable taxidermy that Scarlet was at first loath to touch, considering their experience with statues.

Yun's eyes widened and she bent to the pile of junk. "A flute!"

Scarlet stopped rummaging. "You play?"

"Mm-hmm, I think." Yun lifted the heavy flute to her lips and blew into it.

Out came a horrendous screech. She lowered it and dropped it back in the pile, pouting. "The thing isn't even built right. The keys don't work."

"Almost there." Scarlet finished clearing the way and prepared the ladder, offering the big brass flower to Yun in fanciful devotion. She giggled and pretended to smell it before ascending the ladder.

She reached out immediately for the blue book. "This is wonderful! A book of fairytales! 'Ninety-Nine Tales of Ravenhair.' Ravenhair, that's me!" She hopped down off the ladder and held the book out. A finely traced scroll symbol graced the binding and cover, with the title engraved and filigreed with gold.

"A good find?" said Scarlet.

Yun bounced with excitement. "Perfect," she said, and put her own black locks up against the cover. "Stories about me!"

Scarlet chuckled.

Yun smiled, enjoying Scarlet's laugh and willing to act silly just to hear it. But the book drew her attention deeper, and she gave it one last brush of her hand before opening it.

———

Rodrigo glanced over to see what Scarlet and Yun laughed about before returning his attention to the oaken plank that he held for Trace, who worked the wood with a bone-saw. Trace's meaty hands drew the saw back and forth effortlessly.

"You're doing better," said Rodrigo. "Your balance and your walk are steadier. No trembling in your fingers."

"I feel better day by day," said Trace in his earthquake voice. "No shaking now." He held out his hand to demonstrate.

"That is very good news," said Rodrigo. "How is your memory?"

"Empty."

"I hoped that with your different symptoms at awakening that you might eventually remember something."

"Hope says I am lucky to live," said Trace. "I am happy with living, even with empty head."

"A good attitude," said Rodrigo.

"It's his attitude that kept him among the living," said Hope, who had overheard the conversation as she worked nearby.

"Agreed," said Rodrigo. "Attitude is a lifesaver."

———

Hope smiled to herself. She enjoyed studying people, and she took note of Rodrigo's ability to inspire, rally, and keep the peace among this misfit group of Dusties. She found this skill surprising for his age, noting the graceful but firm way that she treated the others and the manner in which he made decisions and handled mistakes. He acted decisively, showed a strong will, and she approved of that.

Admit it, Hope, you like the way he looks too.

She shook her head, trying to return her attention to the objects on the tables in front of her.

Moot point. He's a boy, and a bit skinny, and I have five or six years on him.

But someday he will be more than a boy.

She smiled again. Until someday, she would simply enjoy watching him and his strange confidence.

And yet, at her own young age, was she any less confident in her healing arts? Were her companions truly prodigies, or did her own memory loss skew the facts?

She noted the size and shape of the restraints and basins on the nearby tables. She hadn't told the others, but the sturdy tables gave her shivers. She strongly suspected their use, and the fate of those who had been placed on these cold, metal-plated surfaces.

She kept those thoughts at bay, taking the tools and materials that could be used for healing and not for what she feared. Her path eventually brought her near Ed, who studiously inspected two long, wooden poles taken from a tall wall cabinet. The cabinet's lock mechanism lay on the ground, smashed away by Ed's insistent use of a miniature round anvil.

"What are the poles?" asked Hope.

"Not a clue," said Ed, "which is why I am interested in them. Not much to get the heart racing in this room otherwise. Do you find the operating tables fascinating?"

There was an edge to Ed's voice and a smirk on his lips that unsettled Hope. Apparently he guessed their use as well and found amusement in it.

"No," she said quietly, "and it's best that you keep the matter to yourself."

He said nothing, his attention on his new find. Hope watched him, wondering what could be so interesting about the plain-looking rods.

Ed ran his fingers over the smooth wood. Most of the pole was fashioned of regular hardwood, but a rough, black material covered the rest, interrupted by thin bands of metal. Toward the other end, two carved circles had been set into the wood, one on each side.

He pushed one of the circles and it depressed, causing the other circle to rise and form a knob. He turned the rod and pressed in the raised knob on the opposite side, which caused the other side to rise.

Ed inspected the ends. A small enclosing pouch of leather covered one end, filled with a soft material like goose down and emblazoned with a triple lightning bolt symbol. When he ran his hands over the black end, he nicked himself and found blood dripping from a small cut on his fingertip.

Hope caught a glimpse of the blood. "Need help?"

"No." Ed inspected the end closely. "Flint or obsidian buried in the wood."

He returned to the knobs, pushing them back into place flush with the surface. He squeezed both at once.

"Ah, spring pressure," he muttered.

He pressed both knobs in deeply at the same time.

Hope jumped as a flash, like a ball of lightning, seared the pole, gathering and dissipating on the metal bands. A sharp snap jarred her ears, as though a hundred whips cracked at the same time. Then the bands fell to the floor along with a drift of white ash. The pole jerked powerfully, but Ed managed to retain his hold on it. Nothing remained of the rod's black section.

In the instant after the flash, glass shattered and Trace let out an agonized yell.

"Hope!" yelled Rodrigo.

She turned and saw him straining to pull the staggering giant away from the window and toward one of the tables.

She raced to Rodrigo's side. Trace spun, his face ashen, his hands clutching his thigh. Blood seeped between his fingers.

Hope and Rodrigo guided Trace onto the table. She turned him on his side, called for blankets, and pulled Trace's hand away from the wound. He cried out in pain.

No blankets came. Yun and Scarlet stared at Ed, and Ed stared at the pole, continuing his inspection.

"What in the Hallows was that?" Rip jumped atop a cabinet, his head snapping back and forth between Ed and Trace.

Ed didn't answer. He picked up the second pole and ran his fingers over the black surface.

Trace cried out again.

"You're fine, Trace," said Hope. "You have a pretty wound, but it didn't hit anything that can't heal up fully." She looked up with concern at Rodrigo, who had found thick wool pads and laid them over Trace. "These are deep. Just muscle, but I must stop the bleeding."

He nodded. "Tell me what you need."

She traced a finger along the wounds. Three gashes opened his flesh, almost like sword cuts. Something long and black protruded from a fourth wound running near the surface. Hope inspected it, then pulled the object out to more of Trace's cries. The blood ran freely.

She laid the small bladed projectile aside. "Like an arrow with an obsidian rib. I'll need to look for stray pieces. Alcohol, there."

Rodrigo snatched up the bottle and placed it in her hands.

———

Yun fought the daze of surprise. Beside her, Scarlet recovered and moved toward Ed. "Ed! What happened?"

Ed gestured to the ruins of the first pole. "It's a weapon. Like a rifle, except one and done, press and toss."

A sudden anger burned in Yun, watching Ed casually go about his business. "You just shot Trace with something, don't you care!"

Ed glanced over at Trace, then at Yun. "I'm no doctor." He turned his attention back to the second weapon.

Scarlet's eyes grew wide with disbelief. He reached Ed. "You heartless git! Put that down before you kill someone!"

Ed gave him a disgusted look. "Keep your shirt on, boy. I know how it works now."

Scarlet uttered a kind of growl and punched Ed in the jaw. He stepped back, holding his knuckles and Ed spun around, rubbing his jaw.

And then the two launched into each other, kicking and punching.

"Stop it!" yelled Yun. "Rip, stop them!"

"Stop it?" said Rip, who hopped along several tabletops for a closer view. "The cally-pads need a good pounding. The insane one more so, of a certainty."

Yun turned to Rodrigo, but he was trying valiantly to ignore the brawl and help Hope.

At first Yun feared that Scarlet would go so far as to kill Ed—though she was conflicted about that outcome. But as the fight continued, Ed appeared not only to be holding his own, but wearing Scarlet down. Neither picked up a weapon, but they held nothing back otherwise. And then a kick by Ed hit squarely in Scarlet's midriff. The boy went sprawling, clutching his chest and trying to draw breath.

Ed looked around at the others, breathing raggedly, his eyes spearing fury. "Didn't any of you care to stop this maniac? He attacked me!"

"You shot Trace!" screamed Yun.

"I didn't mean to! Do you have no concept of an accident?"

Yun balled her fists, wanting to leap at Ed herself. "Do you have no concept of compassion? You could at least apologize!"

"It was an accident!" Ed scooped up the second pole and a burnt metal band and found a corner to huddle in.

24: RAVENHAIR

Yun's diary, Day 109

> We reached home, but everyone is exhausted, and Hope is concerned about Trace. He lost a lot of blood.
>
> I slept soundly. Ed is gone again, probably back to his waterfall. Good riddance, we all say. He has that pole with him and I wouldn't doubt he would kill someone without much thought.
>
> Hope says Trace should be okay, if infection doesn't set in.
>
> Once again we have more stuff, but no answers and no escape from our prison. No one says it, but we've all reached the end of our rope. Even Rodrigo is listless.

"Which one are you reading?" mumbled Scarlet through a severely swollen lip. He, Yun, and Rodrigo sat around a small fire near the lakeshore. Rip worked at the water's edge nearby, scrubbing his cooking pots and whistling. Hope attended to Trace.

Scarlet had to repeat his question before Yun drifted back from the book's pages.

"Ninety-Nine Tales of Ravenhair," she said.

"Is it good?"

"It's just a fairytale book, but I like it."

Scarlet dug his feet in the sand and settled back. "You should read us a story."

"It's just for kids," said Yun.

"I'm a kid. Rodrigo's a kid. We could use a story."

Yun sat up and laid the book on her lap, leafing backward several pages. "I just read one that sounded familiar somehow. Yes—it's called Ravenhair and the Five Gluttins. They spelled it with an I instead of an O, because they're monsters."

Yun flicked her eyes between the boys uncertainly, then began reading.

"In all the lands that Ravenhair traveled…"

Tale 3: Ravenhair and the Five Gluttins

In all the lands that Ravenhair traveled, the clever girl had no better friends than the Five Sister Goats living on the slopes of the Sky Mountain, where Lord Sun enters his rest each evening and Lady Moon enters her rest each morn. The Five Sisters—Bah, Beh, Bria, Brohild, and Brunna—were no ordinary goats. Their teeth shone clear as diamonds, which they were, in fact. With their size and their teeth and their strong goat stomachs, they had little problem eating the black vines that grew up each night on Sky Mountain.

Now, there is no such thing as a black vine where Ravenhair grew up, and there is likely no black vine where you are growing up, but these were no ordinary vines. Each night, while Lord Sun slept, the Shadow Stealer who lived under the mountain planted his cursed seeds, giving them power to grow a hand's breadth with every moment's stroke. Each morning the vines threatened to snare Lord Sun, for the Shadow Stealer wanted nothing better than to turn all the lands to shadow. But the Five Sisters sprang to the slopes, chomped their teeth and, quick as a wink, they gobbled down every last vine and even nibbled out their roots.

The Shadow Stealer grew frustrated. The more he planted, the more the sisters ate, and the bigger they grew. And so the Shadow Stealer knew that he must rid himself of the Five Sisters. But how to get rid of goats who could eat anything, especially with their diamond teeth and their strong goat stomachs?

The Shadow Stealer was clever, as clever even as Ravenhair, and he realized that there was something that no goat could ever master—its hunger. The Shadow Stealer knew dark and powerful magic, and while the Five Sisters slept he stole the hunger from each of the sisters. In his undermountain domain, he labored all night on the stolen hungers, until he fashioned from each a frightening and ravenous beast and named them Gluttins.

When Sister Bah sprang to the slopes that morning she found a Gluttin awaiting her. Although it was a huge, terrifying monster, Bah tossed her horns and bleated confidently, "I can eat anything, and I can eat you." But the more she tried, the larger the Gluttin grew. It grew, and grew, and then, with one gulp, it swallowed Bah whole.

Beh looked for her sister, but instead found her own Gluttin. "I can eat anything, and I can eat you," she said, but the Gluttin grew and grew until it swallowed Beh whole.

Soon Bria was swallowed, and Brohild, and finally Brunna. The black vines stretched toward the top of the mountain, and the Shadow Stealer gloated deep under the mountain, awaiting his time.

Ravenhair arrived that day to greet her best friends. "Bah!" she called. "Beh! Bria! Brohild! Brunna!" The sisters did not answer, but she did see the fat and bloated Gluttins, who sat on the slope and cheered on the black vines.

Ravenhair approached Bah's Gluttin. "Have you seen Bah?" she asked.

"Yes," said the Gluttin with gritted teeth. "Bah said she could eat anything, but she couldn't eat me! I am Hunger, and I know nothing else!" He dared not open his jaws, for Bah refused to stop trying to eat him. A goat can eat anything, they say, and the Gluttin had become genuinely concerned that a goat could even eat a Gluttin.

"You know nothing other than Hunger?" asked Ravenhair.

"Nothing," said the Gluttin.

"Not even laughter?" asked Ravenhair.

"Laughter?" wondered the Gluttin.

"I will show you," said Ravenhair. She found her flute and played a lively tune, skipping and dancing so comically that the Gluttin couldn't help but laugh. But the second he opened his jaws to laugh, Bah leapt from his mouth and sprang away.

"Come back and gobble me!" roared the Gluttin.

"No!" cried Bah. "The more I eat of you, the more you eat of me!"

The Gluttin gave a wailing scream and shriveled and shriveled, until it looked the piglet and scuttled into the brush.

"My sisters have been swallowed too," she warned Ravenhair.

Ravenhair saw another Gluttin nearby. "Have you seen Beh?" she asked.

"Yes," said the Gluttin with gritted teeth. "Beh said she could eat anything, but she couldn't eat me! I am Hunger, and I know nothing else! Except I do know laughter, and I shall not do it."

"You know nothing other than hunger?" asked Ravenhair.

"And laughter," said the Gluttin.

"But not sadness?" asked Ravenhair.

"Sadness?" wondered the Gluttin.

"I will show you," said Ravenhair. She found her violin and played such a heart-rending dirge that the Gluttin burst out crying. But the second he opened his jaws to cry, Beh leapt from his mouth and sprang away, and it shriveled and shriveled until it looked the piglet and scuttled away into the brush.

Another Gluttin watched this happen. "Bria will not escape me," he said. "I am Hunger, and I know nothing else. Except I do know laughter and crying, which I will not do."

"You know nothing other than hunger?" asked Ravenhair.

"And laughter, and crying," said the Gluttin.

"But not pride?" asked Ravenhair.

"Pride?" wondered the Gluttin.

"I will show you," said Ravenhair. She found her horn and played such a stirring, noble fanfare that the Gluttin burst into a shout. But the second he opened his jaws, Bria leapt from his mouth and sprang away, and it shriveled and shriveled until it looked the piglet and scuttled away.

The fourth Gluttin said, "I have Brohild in my jaws. I am Hunger, and I know nothing else. Except I do know laughter, and crying, and pride, which I will not do."

"You know nothing other than hunger?" asked Ravenhair.

"And laughter, and crying, and pride," said the Gluttin.

"But not contentment?" asked Ravenhair.

"Contentment?" wondered the Gluttin.

"I will show you," said Ravenhair. She found her harp and played such a quiet, peaceful lullaby that the Gluttin sighed happily. But the second he opened his jaws to sigh, Brohild leapt from his mouth.

The final Gluttin, the biggest and fiercest of the five, stared down at Ravenhair. "I would eat you if I could, for I am Hunger. And I have learned of laughter, and sadness, and pride, and contentment. I will not open my mouth for anything you play."

"Then I shall not play," said Ravenhair. "I will simply smell the beautiful flowers."

"Flowers?" asked the Gluttin, and he bent to sniff the flowers growing on the slope. But this made his nose itch, so much so that he let loose a sneeze. The second he opened his jaws to sneeze, Brunna leapt from his mouth and sprang away. And quick as a wink, the Five Sisters gobbled up the black vines, and even nibbled out their roots.

"Seems best to graze wide and free," said Ravenhair to the goats, "rather than be consumed by one passion."

"True," said the Five Sisters, but they never gave up their hunger, and remained far and away the most knowledgeable creatures in the land when it came to eating.

And the Shadow Stealer shook and shivered in mad frustration deep under the mountain, vowing revenge on Ravenhair.

100

"I told you, a little child's story," finished Yun.

"Wonderful," said Rodrigo. "I almost fell asleep."

"Yes," said Scarlet quietly, staring up at the cavern ceiling.

"You okay, Scarlet?" asked Yun. "You hurting?"

"No, I'm fine, just a little loose in the head, I think," said Scarlet, his voice drifting off. Then he shook himself. "Sorry, thank you very much for the story, Yun. You read delightfully and you must do it again sometime. It's just...odd."

Yun nodded, smiling. She gave Scarlet a final, quizzical look and returned to her own silent reading.

25: AN INSANE THOUGHT

Rodrigo felt someone shaking his arm and he started awake. He turned over to see Scarlet's bruised face close to his own. "It must be the middle of sleep, Scarlet."

"I'm all apologies, truly, but I'm quite sure I've completely lost my mind. Can you help me?"

"Of course," said Rodrigo, trying to shake himself awake. "Though, if you have lost your mind, I doubt it will find a way out of this place."

Scarlet grinned sheepishly. "All you need do is take a little trip with me. And a cart. And Yun. And no one else."

"And it cannot wait until we have our sleep?"

"Then everyone would want to come along to see me prove conclusively that I'm a complete nutter."

"You get Yun then. I will have to tell Hope, just to let her know not to worry."

Yun proved hard to wake, but she dressed dutifully and followed Rodrigo and Scarlet to the exit.

They took one of the tall-wheeled, rickshaw-like carts from Royalty Hall, passed through Scarlet Hall and into the now familiar Twist. Arriving at the fortress door, they listened carefully for movement inside Skyhall, discovered only silence, and entered.

"Over here." Scarlet crossed to the corner where Yun had found the Raven-hair book. He began rooting through the pile of odds and ends that he had moved for Yun. "Hold the lanterns higher."

Rodrigo let Yun hold Scarlet's lantern and turned to check the trapdoor and the boarded up window. Both appeared secure. He looked out at the city, then noted that the mists crept higher today. Lightning lit the cliffs, but it came from far away, and made little sound. He hoped to see daylight, but the sky had not seemed to change at all. *What I would not give for one minute of sun on my face!*

He heard Yun gasp and he returned quickly to her and Scarlet, who stood looking down at something on the floor. He lifted his lantern and moved up between them.

On the floor sat five objects in a row. A flute, a violin, a trumpet, a harp, and a large brass flower head.

"I moved this stuff to get to the books Yun found," whispered Scarlet. "It struck me as very strange that the pile had all of those items in the story."

"Brilliant!" Rodrigo grinned. "You have a sound mind. This is no coincidence. Someone set this up carefully, though why they would bury the clue in a book for small children eludes me. No offense to you, Yun."

Yun punched him playfully on the arm. "I remember you liking the story just as much. What do we do with these things though?"

"Well," said Scarlet, "that actually came to me before I even thought of the items themselves. Bear with me. Let's just get them back to Scarlet Hall."

They loaded the five heavy brass objects onto the cart and made their way back to Scarlet Hall. When they entered the hall, Scarlet led them down the large circular passageway, where a familiar figure soon loomed out of the darkness.

Scarlet stepped forward, held his light high on the massive jaws and wicked face of the bronze wolf-monstrosity.

"Gluttin," he said.

Yun gasped, and Rodrigo snorted in amazement.

"Hope mentioned that it might be a gate when she first saw it, and that set me thinking," said Scarlet. "Now, here's the rub. Assuming that we haven't just stirred each other up into the wildest and weirdest of goose chases, what do we do with these things? Anyone know how to play a harp?"

"Not at all," said Rodrigo.

"I couldn't play that flute, remember?" said Yun. "It didn't work right."

"Regardless," said Rodrigo, holding out the brass flower. "You cannot play this."

Scarlet looked up at the statue. "Maybe these things are like keys. We just need to find a keyhole."

"We may have to climb up on the snout," said Rodrigo.

Scarlet gave him a sober look. "That means touching the statue."

Rodrigo rubbed his chin and Yun looked at the boys with alarm. Scarlet turned to face the statue. "It's my crazy theory. I'll do it."

Rodrigo and Yun stepped back, offering no argument to Scarlet. Scarlet gave one last uncomfortable glance back at his friends, pulled in a breath, reached out, and touched a sword-like canine tooth.

Nothing happened.

The three released their breaths and Scarlet raised a finger. "Okay then, not eaten, there's an important hurdle cleared."

They searched its considerable surface, poring over the exceptional work of art. Finding nothing at ground level, Rodrigo helped Scarlet up onto the snout of the beast.

"Wait," said Scarlet excitedly. "Here's a depression, just behind the nose. It's squarish, with leaner curves on the side. Something in the middle, too, like a starburst shape."

Rodrigo and Yun looked through the items, and they both shouted, "Got it!" when they turned over the harp and looked at its base. Lifting the harp to the snout, Scarlet found it fit perfectly into place. But nothing happened.

Scarlet gave a shrug and Rodrigo returned to stroking his chin.

"That starburst is shaped like a gear," suggested Rodrigo. "Can you turn the harp?"

Scarlet tried to swivel the harp. It resisted, until suddenly it spun smoothly clockwise.

Deep in the walls, the rumble of machinery came to their ears. Scarlet scampered down and the three backed up to the limit of their lantern light.

The dark stone rumbled beneath their feet, and slowly the monster's mouth opened. Rodrigo knew that this was merely a piece of machinery, and yet his neck hairs stood on end as the jaws gaped wide and seemed to move toward them. With a thunderous clang the lower jaw settled into the floor and the upper locked into the high round ceiling. Where before the air had sat stale and unmoving, a strong draft now grew from behind them and rushed into the dark passageway beyond.

"Looks like you read the right story at the right time, Yun," said Rodrigo. "Well done, Scarlet."

Scarlet shrugged. "Yun would have figured it out soon enough. I just happened to be the lucky one that moved that pile." He stepped to the new passageway and gestured onward. "Shall we?"

"We shall not," said Rodrigo. "We need to tell the others, but first we need to know how to close this back up. There could be a cloud of fleyes just ahead."

The three peered into the darkness of the great circular tunnel. For one moment, Scarlet thought that he heard a moan or cry from far off, but when he cocked his head and tried to listen more carefully, he could pick up nothing.

The breeze pushed past them strongly now, ruffling Yun's dress as the air whirled into the gloom ahead.

Scarlet sighed, hating the very concept of walking away from a newly revealed mystery. "Right, then, as long as we come right back. My curiosity will eat at me otherwise. How do we close this?"

Yun pointed. "Is that a wheel in there?"

Scarlet followed her point and caught sight of a large metal wheel set into the wall beyond the jaws. "Let's at least give it a go, then we can run home."

Rodrigo nodded, and they passed through the jaws. The three gripped the wheel and cranked slowly, straining at the resistance it gave, hearing the clank of gear locks preventing the apparatus from slipping back. After a length of familiar machinery rumble, the jaws levered slowly back together, closing the passage.

"Probably should have left Yun on the other side," said Rodrigo. "Try the wheel in reverse." The wheel did turn, the jaws rumbled open, and they breathed a sigh of relief.

But when the jaws stopped opening, the rumbling didn't. They spun around.

Within the mist and water-crash of Waterfall Cavern, Ed kept his mind busy by puzzling over the thirteen mysterious levers in the wall. This also kept him from having to deal with the others—those who unfairly treated him like a craven criminal for his innocent mistake with the obsidian pole and Trace. He rubbed at a sore patch on his chin where Scarlet had punched him, wondering why the boy was not in chains for his savage assault.

He glanced over to see Rip approaching.

"Hey-o," said Rip.

Ed nodded, his eyes on the levers.

"You're a balmer, big man," declared Rip over the pounding of the waterfall, "but yeh did take Pantaloons down a notch, and I have to give yeh credit for that. Didn't think yeh had the starch, but yeh proved otherwise."

Ed kept at his work, trying to ignore the impudent little manling. "I will not go back until Scarlet apologizes."

"Hope needs yeh," said Rip.

"And?"

"And she's Hope, and unless yeh plan on never getting sick or hurt, I'd do what she asks."

Ed closed his eyes in frustration and pulled himself to his feet. "Fine, I'll go."

"Now yer thinking straight."

———

Rip led Ed back to Vida Lake, where Hope waited for them, standing by Trace's healing bed.

"Thank you for coming," said Hope, her voice all business.

"What's the emergency?" asked Ed.

"Rodrigo, Scarlet, and Yun have gone missing. They've been away over a day now. Could you-"

"Rip and I will hunt up for them," interrupted Ed, looking around for supplies.

"Thank you," said Hope. "It's good that you brought your firepole. Hopefully you'll have no cause to need it."

"Firepole...Good name, better than mine," said Ed. "Mine had five syllables."

"Ed." Trace turned over carefully, wincing. "Good you are here. I know you had accident."

"It *was* an accident," said Ed. "Sorry it hit you, but I didn't mean for it."

"I know," said Trace. "Not problem. Hope cure me."

Ed nodded uncomfortably and busied himself with packing. Before long, Rip and Ed set out, passing through the exit tunnel and on through Royalty Hall.

"Can I carry the boomstick?" said Rip.

"Firepole," said Ed. "And keep your Lilliputian mitts off it. Too big for you."

"How does it work?"

Ed laughed sarcastically without answering.

"It shoots arrows, right?"

"More like crossbow bolts with obsidian for a cutting edge."

"Nasty."

"Effective."

"Can you make more?"

"Eventually."

"What if yeh can't? What if yer not smart enough?"

"Then I'll shoot you with it and enjoy the peace and quiet."

"A joke! There's hope for yeh, cally-pad," said Rip.

"What in all misery is a cally-pad?"

Rip threw up his hands at Ed's ignorance. "Cally-pad, someone so goofy-tall that he can't lace his own boots. Everyone knows that."

"*No one* knows that! What are you, a leprechaun or some such?"

"*I'm* a human! You're the weirdy. I think yer what they call an ettin."

"You have the ears of a feline! Humans don't have cat ears."

"I do *not* have cat ears. They're just more streamlined than yer bulging ettin ears."

Ed wagged a finger at Rip as he walked. "Ettins are creatures of folklore, just a myth-"

"A myth, yeh say? Yeh look real enough to me."

"You're saying that Yun is an ettin?" said Ed.

"A very sweet ettin," smiled Rip.

"Bah!"

But something else had caught Rip's attention.

"Hey-o, a cart is missing."

———

They had reached Scarlet Hall. Rip shone his lantern on the pair of tall-wheeled carts and the empty spot for the third. But Ed, as usual, wasn't paying attention. He stared at his lantern and circled the room.

"There's a draft in here," he said.

"There's always been a draft," said Rip.

Ed ignored him. When he reached the large circular tunnel, he slowed, took a few steps into the passage, and motioned for Rip to follow.

"By the Hallows…" started Rip when they reached the open jaws, but Ed shushed him. After inspecting the mechanics of the jaws, the two pressed on quietly. Slowly a sound came to their ears—a quavering howl that rose and died, like a pack of wolves prowling in distant woods.

The passageway curved gradually, the howling increased, and the walls opened out and disappeared into the darkness. Or, not quite darkness. Far away they could see a spot of firelight, while closer by to the right, there shone a cluster of greenish-yellow will-o-wisps. The howling continued from high above.

Ed pointed upward.

"Wind," he said. "Just wind. Must be an airshaft."

"I thought we were sneaking-" said Rip.

"Rodrigo!" yelled Ed. "Rodrigohhhh!"

"Seems not," muttered Rip.

Then, a voice called over the distance from the firelight.

"Run!"

"Did he just say run?" said Ed, his hearing less than perfect. He turned, but Rip and his lantern had already sprinted down the passage, gathering speed.

Ed heard a rumble behind him and saw a rising wash of light. Turning back, he gaped in shock.

Where the will-o-wisps had been, a monstrous machine now came to life, its long, low-slung metal form coursing with a glaring greenish gaslight that shone through its many seams. It lifted itself on two long-footed bent legs and loped toward Rip's fleeing form like a great metal dinosaur on the hunt, passing right over the stunned Ed.

———

Rip had a lengthy head start and a knack for speed, but his stride could be measured in feet and the metal monster's in yards. It loped after him, crouching smoothly down as it entered the tunnel, folding its legs and steadying itself with two thick arms protruding from its flanks while reaching out toward Rip with a pair of long, many-clawed front arms.

Rip had almost reached the great jaws when he realized he wouldn't make it, the two long mechanical claws extending out over him. He saw the claws descend and he dodged left, running up along the curved wall of the circular passageway. The claws missed. Rip chanced one look back.

Six gleaming green eyes of the monstrosity stared down at him, its claws extended and readying another strike.

Rip shouted in alarm, forcing his legs to churn faster.

But as he raced into Scarlet Hall and turned to dash toward Royalty Hall, he realized that the monster no longer pursued him. He slowed his sprint, but did not stop running, all the way to the lake.

27: GOLEM

Ed had not moved from his spot when the terrifying machine loped back into the great chamber, pulsing with its exertions and throwing off jets of flaming gas. It slammed its two front sets of claws around Ed, scooped him up, and bore him none too gently to the firelight. The scooped claws lowered and spread, and Ed tumbled to the ground at the feet of Scarlet. Yun and Rodrigo stood nearby.

"I see running isn't your cup of tea," said Scarlet.

"Who was with you?" asked Rodrigo.

"Rip," gasped Ed, trying to gather his breath. Yun's hand appeared at his shoulder and she helped him to his feet. She had a long welt across her forehead and around her left eye.

"Did he get away?" asked Rodrigo.

"Ask that *thing*." Ed turned to look at the infernal machine. It crouched nearby, settling itself, its fires slowly dying down. Now that the chase was over, Ed's fear ebbed away and his excitement rose as he looked over the monstrous construct. He kicked away an urge to walk over and inspect it. It easily outsized an elephant, though its streamlined, open-frame body was made mainly of arms and legs, or whatever the machine-like appendages would be called. It did not appear to be painted or marked, until it half-turned and the lantern-light revealed a large 'III' on what could be considered its head. Below the roman numeral three was an infinity symbol. The green fires of the six eyes faded, returning to a will-o-wisp glow.

"A very good thing that you held on to your lantern," said Rodrigo. "We are almost out of oil." He picked up Ed's lantern, quenched it, checked the oil basin, and gave a frustrated snort. "Except that you did not fill it before you left."

Ed ignored Rodrigo, his interest drawn by the machinery lining the wall. There were controls—not the deceptive jumble found in Waterfall, but meaningful, real. The complex array spread over the wall. Like those at Waterfall, they had no instructive labels, but he immediately recognized groups of controls.

"You have any water in your pack?" asked Yun. "We ran out a while ago."

Ed shook his head, distracted. "Why didn't you just hop on home when the golem settled down?"

"The what?" asked Yun.

"Golem, living machine," said Ed, waving a hand at the metal monster.

"When we try to leave this spot," said Scarlet, "the machine—the golem—gets his hackles up and drags us back here. And he's rather rough about it."

"Hmm," mumbled Ed, looking at the bank of controls. "That's interesting."

"Any clue how it-" started Scarlet.

"Be quiet, will you?" interrupted Ed. "Let me think."

Rodrigo stepped in front of Scarlet and guided his friend back to the lantern. The battering to Scarlet's face had been added to by the golem.

"Let it go," said Rodrigo. "You already look like a battle casualty. Hope will need to give you extra attention. Sometimes I think you get yourself hurt on purpose."

Ed relit his lantern and paced along the wall. No other control stations could be seen to either side. He looked at the golem, back at the controls, and then strolled past them.

Fires roiled up in the golem and it regained its feet. Ed hurried back to the group. The golem paced for a moment, its steps sending vibrations through the stone floor. Then it settled back and its gaslight died.

When Ed walked past the controls on the other side, the same event occurred.

"We already knew that," said Scarlet.

Rodrigo moved to Ed's side. "It wants something."

"Mm-hmm." Ed stepped close to the wall, muttering to himself, his fingers tracing over the controls as he paced along slowly. Rodrigo followed, silently. When Ed reached the end, he turned and repeated his walk, slower this time, tapping at the empty glass indicators set into the metal, testing the levers, trying the wheels, but careful not to engage anything.

"Feel free to talk through it," offered Rodrigo.

"Mmm? Right, not a bad idea. The controls are grouped logically, nine functional sets in all. No idea what they do, but most of them look like they bring something to a certain state—like water, or heat, or pressure or such."

"Do they control the golem?"

"Doubt it. The golem isn't hooked into anything. He's clearly self-powered."

Rodrigo stroked his chin. "Should we try one?"

Ed nodded. "Let's have a go at this one."

He pointed to the easiest control group—merely an oval glass indicator and a wheel. Ed began turning the wheel. He spun it twenty times before giving up. The indicator remained unchanged and nothing visible occurred out in the darkness.

"We're losing a lamp!" called Yun. She lit Ed's lamp as the flame in Rodrigo's dwindled and finally died, leaving a tiny drift of smoke.

Ed wandered down the wall and chose a more-complicated control. He pressed the grip-lock of a lever and drew it downward slowly. He then tried the wheel next to it. A small bubble of silvery liquid sputtered up at the bottom of the indicator.

In the distant darkness, an angry hissing and clank rose up from multiple locations. Fires relit in the golem. Ed stepped back to see the controls better, when Rodrigo pointed.

The indicator from the original control was filling rapidly.

"Spin it!" yelled Ed, cranking back the wheel and disengaging the lever. He hurried to Rodrigo's side just as he finished spinning his wheel. The indicator had stopped rising, but it hovered near the top. In the darkness, the clanking ended but the hissing sounded, loudly and insistently. A slight odor reached them, like rotten cabbage. Ed took over the wheel, cranking it in the same manner as before, and the indicator slowly drained away, along with the hissing. He then closed it back up.

Ed paced. The minutes ticked by.

Rodrigo gave terse updates on the dwindling state of the oil in the lamp. "Minutes left, if that," he warned Ed.

"I think I may have it," said Ed. "It's not nine separate controls, but nine separate steps to accomplish one task. Yun?"

"Yes?"

"Your books read left to right, correct?" said Ed.

"Yes."

"All right, then, Rodrigo, you watch me, in case we have to undo what we do. Shot in the dark. Ready?"

Ed stepped to the first control set on the left, manipulated it, and gained an immediate reaction on the indicators. Satisfied of the result, he moved to the second, and the third. On the fourth, the distant clanking began. He stepped back to check the earlier controls, tweaking several.

The lamplight began to fade.

"Time to be both inspired and fast," urged Rodrigo.

The fifth control set changed the howling wind overhead to a softer moan, and the air around them shifted its movement.

The sixth set seemed to do nothing, but the seventh caused a flurry of pipping sounds, like champagne bottles being opened. Ed tweaked the earlier controls until the pipping sounds slowly died away.

The lantern flame drew swiftly downward, and died entirely.

"Not good!" shouted Scarlet.

Ed felt for the eighth set—the first he had tried. He spun the wheel, unable to see the indicator. In the distance, and all around the apparently circular chamber, a series of faint, greenish glows appeared, like giant versions of the golem's eyes.

Ed peered at the ninth control, the new gaslight not quite providing the light to see it sufficiently. But he remembered the series of small levers, ten in all, and all identical. He disengaged the grip-lock of the first one and pulled it outward.

A momentary rushing sound rose up and a great circle of yellow-green light flared to life high on the curved chamber wall, where one of the new will-o-wisps had been. Ed gave an excited shout and checked the bank of controls in the new light. He pulled the other levers at an even pace until the entire chamber came to life with ten greenish suns of light.

Three larger levers remained. He pulled the first. A bluer light glowed from a depression near the center of the room. The second initiated a flow of water through a canal running across the chamber, and the third caused a row of manufacturing machinery nearby to adjust themselves with a metallic clatter.

In the center of the chamber's ceiling, Ed could now see the opening of a vertical shaft extending up into darkness, drawing a strong pull of air through its extensive maw.

The four Dusties said nothing, but their eyes widened as they took in the fantastic spectacle. The far side of the chamber appeared at least two hundred yards away, and the ceiling vaulted upward more than a hundred feet. Six wide, square corridors fed into the chamber and five circular passageways interspaced them. The stone floor spread out flat and smooth to the point of polish. No ornamentation could be seen, nothing impractical, except for a large gray-tiled mosaic expertly laid into the wall above the controls, displaying the symbol of a lever and fulcrum.

In front of them, the golem fired to life. It gave them a sweep of its gaze, turned and plodded through one of the large square corridors.

"Time to run?" said Scarlet.

Even Ed agreed, although, when he arrived back at Vida Lake he couldn't pack fast enough to return to the new discovery.

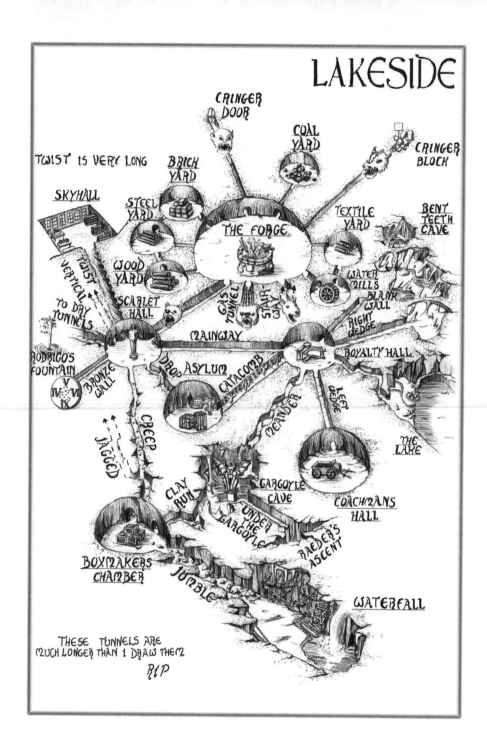

LAKESIDE

CRINGER DOOR

COAL YARD

CRINGER BLOCK

TWIST IS VERY LONG

BRICK YARD

SKYHALL

STEEL YARD

TEXTILE YARD

BENT TEETH CAVE

THE FORGE

TWIST VERTICAL

TO DRY TUNNELS

WOOD YARD

WATER MILLS

SCARLET HALL

GAS TUNNEL

STAIR JAY 3

BLANK WALL

RIGHT WEDGE

RODRIGO'S FOUNTAIN

BRONZE WALL

MAINWAY

ROYALTY HALL

V IV·VI IX

DROP

ASYLUM

CATACOMB

LEFT WEDGE

BOYALTY HALL

CREEP

MEANDER

THE LAKE

JAGGED

CLAY RUN

GARGOYLE CAVE

COACHMANS HALL

UNDER THE GARGOYLE

BOYMAKERS CHAMBER

JUMBLE

RAEDER'S ASCENT

WATERFALL

THESE TUNNELS ARE MUCH LONGER THAN I DRAW THEM

RLP

114

28: Through the Door

Yun's diary, Day 112

We nicknamed it the Forge. I have never seen such a place. There are machines for all manners of tasks, and a very hot forgeworks, hot enough and built the right way to make good steel and other things, according to Ed.

The Forge is surrounded by other large chambers that are full of building materials like wood and pipes and metal blocks, and heaps upon heaps of coal. The golem-machine, which we nicknamed Three, just ignores us now and wanders the Forge. Sometimes it uses the forgeworks to build something or repair one of the other machines. There are so many machines, and even a printing press, and stacks and stacks of paper too. I'm sure we've lost Ed permanently to the Forge. He spends all of his time there. For all his issues, he does have an amazing mind. He saved our lives.

We found four other Big Jaws in the Forge. Each brass "key" fits one (you can pop them out after you turn them), but we came in from the inside of each so we didn't need to use them. Each jaw is beautifully crafted, with a different head. They aren't exactly heads as I know them, but they are close enough for us to nickname:

Wolf: Into Scarlet Hall

Bear: A shaft goes down at a steep angle, and is filled with pipes. Ed says it brings the gas and maybe other things that power the Forge.

Dragon: Ends at a rockfall with strange warning signs on it.

Ogre: An opening to a tunnel that ends in a heavy closed door that we didn't open.

Rat: A large natural passage that goes up. Everyone is excited about that passage, but we are waiting for Trace to heal up.

The boys and I—not Ed—are off to explore those other tunnels. Hope is babysitting Trace.

"I was right," said Scarlet, lifting the twisted metal sign that they had dug out from beneath a pile of castoff rock. "Same sign." He spun it around for Rodrigo, Yun, and Rip to see.

CRINGERS
FOR THE SAKE OF ALL
DO NOT UNSEAL THESE TUNNELS

One of the other Great Jaws led to the same sign, but at a closed-off rockfall. This tunnel lay open, but someone had spent a great deal of effort to create an extensive deadfall that would bring down twenty yards of carefully shattered ceiling if one wooden beam were removed. The beam sat propped at an angle to the floor, and a large sledgehammer lay next to it, covered in the dust of years.

Within the tunnel, looking out of place in the natural rock, a reinforced wooden door hung by heavy hinges in a solid frame.

"I say Pantaloons picks up that pounder and gives the beam a good whack," said Rip, gesturing with his left hand at the sledgehammer and at Scarlet with his right. "Drop it all and be good and done. Don't know what cringers are like and don't want to discover."

"There are no signs of tracks, and this door has clearly not been opened for a while," said Rodrigo. "I hate to close off any area."

"Cringers—doesn't sound good to me either, Rip," said Scarlet. "But we should at least give it a quick go. We can always bury it."

"Not if we're dead," said Rip. "But, hey-o, I'm in as well." He brought out his sketchbook and started up a new map page, his hand deftly stroking the charcoal across the linen paper. Unlike the others, Rip had a genius for mapmaking.

The oak door had several steel crossbars, much like the door into Skyhall. Once the bars were removed, it swung smoothly, revealing not a rock tunnel but a room—a room straight out of a country mansion. The walls contained windows and curtains, but the mottled rock of the tunnel could be seen inches outside them through the broken glass. A fireplace and black woodstove graced the far wall, and a kitchen table with sturdy oaken chairs occupied the middle. Crates sat here and there, containing supplies that were out of place in this thoroughly out-of-place kitchen. A short hallway extended beyond the room, but the natural tunnels began again beyond that.

"Cozy." Scarlet inspected several of the crates, finding mining tools and many torches with heavy cork-like tips. He touched one to his lantern and it ignited in a lively flame. "Should we leave our lanterns on the outside by the beam?"

"Leave one here for a landmark as well," said Rodrigo. They each took a torch and a spare, and passed through the room.

The cavern continued for fifty paces but then divided.

"Stay left," said Scarlet. "Every time. Then we know to stay right to get back."

Rodrigo took the left passage, which soon split into three tunnels.

Then left again, and after that a small rocky cavern with multiple exits.

"I could have used that always-left idea months ago," said Rodrigo, who made the mistake of turning to talk to Scarlet and missed his footing, stumbling headlong into the sharp boulders. Pain raced along his ribs, and his shirt caught and tore.

He rolled to a sitting position. A deep breath caused him some discomfort but not stinging pain.

Scarlet's hand reached down to him. "You okay? That was a nasty tumble."

"Fine." Rodrigo touched at his ribs, peeling away a bloody ribbon of shirt stuck to the oozing blood and tearing it off.

"You need a bandage?" said Yun.

"No, just a scrape." Rodrigo took Scarlet's hand, careful in his embarrassment to avoid the eyes of the others. Recovering his torch, he turned back to the exits. "Let's not waste these torches."

Left again, and the Dusties reached an arch of splintered wood. Passing through the arch, they discovered the wreck of a grand ballroom. Only a corner of the ballroom remained, the rock forming its roof and the sweeping stairs to the left ending in stone. The tunnels continued in four separate directions.

"Quite a maze...Is that a body?" Scarlet pointed to a lump on the floor and approached it. "No. Sends the shivers, though."

The others moved up next to him. Lying tumbled on the floor was a humanoid form, created very shoddily from twisted wooden planks, tiles, and odds and ends. Instead of two eyes it had three grotesque bulges affixed to the wood, and a gaping caricature of a mouth. Frayed pieces of it were scattered across the floor.

"We leave it alone, right?" said Yun.

Everyone nodded and backed away from it, heading for the left. The tunnels continued in the same manner, branching here and there. They passed through a cottage, then a fine brick home, a section of marketplace, and a farmhouse—like fragments of someone's surreal dream. Statues appeared here and there. The eeriness set them on edge; they talked little and only in whispers, and tried to move as silently as possible. Rip's map strokes lost their care and became just lines and notes as they hurried along.

Their first torches were showing signs of weakening when they found the skeleton.

It was the first skeleton that they had seen anywhere in their underground prison. The bones lay scattered, with the skull fractured and propped on a rock.

"Time to go drop that beam," whispered Rip.

"We are not dropping the beam unless we must," said Rodrigo. "We can close the jaws. For all we know, this might be a way out."

"This old boy didn't find a way out," said Scarlet.

"How is the map looking?"

"Iffy," said Rip, holding up his work. "Too many different paths too quickly. Apologies."

"Let's try a little farther left, then take this right passage a short ways to see if there's any change. Then we can go back."

"Right," said Scarlet.

"Doesn't feel right to me," said Rip.

They took the left passage first, but finding nothing of note, they tracked back and took to the right. It twisted side to side and ended at rough-cut stairs that descended into a monstrous circular cavern. As they approached the cavern's center, they discovered a fat spire of natural rock, with steps carved upward in a spiral around its circumference. Rodrigo, Yun, and Scarlet paused at the base of the steps while Rip crept ahead to cross the cavern.

"Someone should duck up there," whispered Scarlet. "Nice to know if anyone's staring down at us."

"We will check it," said Rodrigo, tapping Yun's shoulder. "Keep our path clear."

"Do be quick," said Scarlet as they advanced up the steps. He passed the torch in a semi-circle, squinting into the darkness. "I'm not exactly an army."

———

Rodrigo expected a small fortification at the top of the spire, a place they could retreat to if needed. Instead he found only flat stone and a scattering of dark boulders. He approached the closest, his nostrils stung by a sickly sweet stench in the air.

The boulder stood waist high—a tangled blob of black obsidian-like rock, as though it had been dripped into a ropy pile and left to cool. He reached out to touch it and flinched back, finding it unnaturally cold. Yun did the same.

"These aren't normal," she whispered. "I don't like this, can we go?"

Rodrigo lifted his torch high, the hairs rising on the back of his neck. He had gotten used to the dark, and the underground, and the utterly strange nature of this place. But these mounds—how many were there? forty, fifty?—pricked at him in a way nothing else had done, not even the Shadow following him in his days of darkness.

He backed to the stairs. "Yes...we should absolutely go."

"Right now," she whispered.

He pulled Yun close in front of him protectively, guided her back onto the stairs, and they hurried down. Only once at the bottom did Rodrigo begin breathing normally again.

Scarlet and Rip met them there.

"Want to see something that'll curl yer hair?" said Rip. "Look at this." He moved toward the far cavern wall, lit his second torch, and held both up.

A raised ledge lined the wall about three feet high, cut very roughly and forming many pockets and alcoves. Filling these alcoves were the strange manikins, like the one found in the ballroom. While made of twisted wood or bone and covered here and there with the strange eye-bulges, iron nails and spikes stuck out from their bodies at all angles.

In the darkness to their left, a low groan started and died, like strained wood protesting under pressure.

"We should go," whispered Yun. "Rodrigo...we should-"

Rodrigo brought a finger to his lips, nodding his agreement to her. He motioned to Scarlet and Rip. "Count thirty paces and come back."

Scarlet angled left, Rip right, sweeping their torches back and forth as they took a last, parting scan of the ledges. Rodrigo edged Yun back toward their exit, hoping he had kept its position correctly in his mind.

"Rodrigo!" came Scarlet's voice. "Rodrigo!"

Rodrigo and Yun turned and hurried to Scarlet's torchlight as he lit his second torch and lifted it high. In front of them, a set of stairs ascended out of the cavern. Halfway up these stairs, standing with one of the twisted manikins leaning against it, the light revealed a statue of a girl, slightly younger than Rodrigo, in country dress. The torchlight did not shine brightly off of the statue due to its dark green surface.

"Ah-hey, this is rich," said Rip, hurrying up to them.

Rodrigo stepped up to the statue, stroking his chin. "This is the same stone, no doubt about it."

"Our torches aren't going to last," said Scarlet. "We weren't supposed to be gone this long. Should we leave and come back for her later?"

"Are we gabbing about setting off an explosion in the middle of Boggart Cave?" said Rip. "I'm good and ready to bolt this cursed place, I am. Can't we find blankets or rugs or such and just cart her out of here without touching her? Blow her up on the beach back home."

Rodrigo backed away from the statue. "I agree. Let's come back prepared."

"You can't just leave her!" said Yun, loudly enough that it caused the others to glance nervously about the cavern.

"We can come right back," said Rodrigo.

"How do you know? What if the trap falls and we can never save her? She'd be imprisoned forever—in here! How would you like that?"

The two boys and the manling looked at each other.

"It'll make quite a racket," said Scarlet.

Rip snorted. "We're already making a racket standing here gabbing—no offense, dear girl."

"Rip has a point," said Rodrigo.

"Ah-hey, we blow her up right here," said Rip. "And it's my turn. I hear it's quite a ride. Unlike you ettins, I know how to land on meh feet. Should I move that stickman that's molesting her, or see how far he flies?"

"Launch him," said Scarlet. "Then let's roll a brace of oil barrels in here and torch this whole place."

Rip rubbed his hands and stepped up to the statue. Everyone else gave him room.

"Ready to catch me, Pantaloons?" said Rip, and he touched the stone dress.

There came a silent white flash, and a sharp crack. Rodrigo closed his eyes to protect his sight, and when he opened them, he discovered to his surprise that Rip remained next to the statue—a statue transformed into a real girl.

The girl started to topple. Rip turned to look, discovered the girl falling onto him, and tried to catch her. Despite her diminutive size and slender build, she outmassed the surprised Rip and he fell back under her. Rodrigo and Scarlet raced to the stairs and caught them before they could roll down.

"That's the big scary explosion?" said Rip. "Is this some kind of ettin humor?"

"That wasn't normal," said Scarlet.

The girl stirred weakly.

"And that's not normal either. Usually you're unconscious for a day."

Rodrigo picked up the girl in his arms, and then they heard it—a quavering keen, like a banshee shriek from far away. It came from the spire.

The four turned.

A flickering green glow lined the spire's top edge. Around the Dusties a rustle arose. At their feet the manikin that had leaned against the girl twisted and flexed its spike-covered hand.

"Move!" yelled Rodrigo, and they raced around the spire and toward the steps as the cavern came to life with dark crawling shapes.

29 : CRINGERS

Phoebe dreamt of a dying sun.

The sun struggled to live. It flared weakly, its red heat touching Phoebe's face. Again it died, only to return a moment later.

The dream faded, but the heat did not. With it came a familiar rustling sound. Fire.

Her eyes were closed and would not open. Was she asleep? She was swinging. No, she was being carried. She could feel the grip of a hand on one shoulder, another on her knee.

With great effort she opened one eye, then the other.

The flame of a torch. The torch bobbed like a phantom in the darkness, very close. It followed her. Or the person carrying her.

"Her eyes are open," whispered the torch. No, not the torch. There was a face behind it, visible only in momentary flickers and flashes. A girl's face, delicate, with raven-black hair and almond-shaped eyes. The girl's eyes darted about alertly, wide and fearful.

Phoebe could feel her fingers dig into the shirt collar of her carrier. Her jaws worked sluggishly.

"Stop," she managed.

"I cannot," came the whispered response from above her. The smoothly accented words were spoken between labored breaths.

"I can walk," said Phoebe after further effort.

"I do not think so," said the voice.

"Why?" she asked.

"Because you were just awakened. I am shocked to hear you talking, much less walking."

"What?"

There came a sigh and her carrier stopped. The whisper became softer. "When I am under more restful circumstances, I will tell you everything I know—which is very little. Until then, please do not talk."

Phoebe did not protest the sharp words. Something in his voice alarmed her. He was afraid.

The carrier continued on, the torch and girl bobbing faithfully behind him. Black cavern walls flickered dully in the torchlight, interrupted at times with brick masonry or wood planking.

"Curse me for taking the wrong tunnel!" said the carrier, who stopped once more and spun slowly in a complete circle. "I do not recognize this," he breathed harshly. "Yun, do you see Rip's torch ahead anywhere? Circle around me."

121

"Yes, Rodrigo." The torch obeyed, bobbing around them among the jagged gray rocks.

Rodrigo? Phoebe tried to collect the frayed ends of her thoughts. There was a boy in her town with the same name, wasn't there? And he had a similar accent. But Phoebe's mind refused to conjure up either the boy's face or the town.

Rodrigo snorted in frustration. "Five tunnels. There should be three! Yun, do you see any marks? Which tunnel did we just come out of? We should stay right!"

The light shifted as the girl moved from entrance to entrance.

A sound rose above the sighing of the torch. Phoebe could barely hear it, yet it cut into her brain, sharp as a blade. Giggling?

The man who carried her crouched, his breathing turning ragged. "Yun, hurry!"

"I don't know...Oh, Loa save us, they're coming!"

"Keep looking!" In the darkness, Rodrigo's face bent close to Phoebe's. "I must put you down. Do not be afraid. I will not leave you."

Phoebe was lowered onto rocky ground, which dug cruelly into her side. The pain gave her the strength, however feeble, to rise on one arm.

The giggling again, clearer, closer—and fear lashed Phoebe like tongues of fire. Her body dropped involuntarily back to the hard ground, trying impossibly to squeeze into the cracks.

"Ripped cloth, Rodrigo!" said the girl. "This is where you fell against the rock-"

"Are you sure?"

"Yes!"

"Gracia de Dios! God marks our path even when I fail to. Stay ahead of me."

Phoebe was scooped up again, none too gently, and Rodrigo's steps quickened. The jarring pace and frequent near-falls battered at her body, but Phoebe welcomed the aches—causing the numbness and fatigue to retreat.

Despite their pace, the giggling grew steadily louder. Phoebe pressed her free hand to her ear. Her teeth bit into her upper lip, drawing blood, but she made no sound.

A different light arose behind them—glowing green streaks crawling like living things along the rocks.

"Run, Yun!" Rodrigo gave up all pretense of stealth or safety, hurtling himself and his burden down the rock-strewn black tunnel.

"Do not look back, lady," he said.

Phoebe looked back. A green luminescence filled the tunnel behind them. Shadows of movement flashed along the walls. And then something wooden and twisted dashed into the torchlight, not two paces behind her, from an adjoining tunnel. Phoebe tried to scream but her lungs wouldn't obey. The horror leapt from rock to rock and swung an arm at Phoebe's face. She felt the rush of air as the spiked hand swept by. It leapt again, but lost its footing and fell awkwardly with a clatter. Silhouettes of the twisted shapes filled the tunnel behind them, backlit by the growing green glow. Phoebe reflexively tried to reach the ground and run herself, pushing against Rodrigo's grip.

"Do not look!" Rodrigo grasped the back of her head and pressed her face forcefully into his shoulder. She could feel his grip loosen, but she marshaled the strength to grasp his collar and hang on.

"Rip! Rip!" Rodrigo yelled the name again, ragged and desperate.

Phoebe heard the creak of wood. Rodrigo restored his grip and she looked up. Heavy beams of a room flashed overhead and they passed through a threshold. A very small man stepped from one side and swung a thick oaken door shut behind them. He dropped two crossbars into place, sealing the passage.

The small man turned and followed. Under brown curls of hair his pixyish face set in hard determination, and seeing it gave Phoebe a measure of strength.

After a short distance the tunnel gave way to a larger passageway. Rodrigo dropped to one knee, spilling Phoebe gracelessly onto the floor.

"Drop it, Scarlet," gasped Rodrigo.

"Should we see if the door holds first?" said another boy standing next to a large beam leaning against the ceiling. He looked at Phoebe with concern, his pleasant face flush with exertion and trial. He too had an accent, but different than Rodrigo's.

Phoebe had her first clear look at Rodrigo, on hands and knees beside her. His arms quivered uncontrollably as his chest heaved in ragged gasps. His dusty white shirt sagged open, torn from the arm down, revealing a bloody scrape along his side.

Rodrigo had a face of angles, thinner than the man named Scarlet. Almost gaunt he looked, with deep-set chestnut eyes and a long jaw that clenched and unclenched.

He was hardly more than a boy, perhaps no older than Phoebe herself.

How old am I?

"Drop it!"

Scarlet's expressive face showed disagreement, but he picked up a long hammer from against the wall and hefted it across his shoulders.

A muffled sound ran across the tunnel door—a slow, deliberate scrape, as if its dimensions were being carefully measured and marked.

Something pale crawled out between the seams of the door. Smoke. It curled here and there along the wood, snake-like, as if a light breeze blew it first one way, then another. The door shook.

Scarlet raised the hammer high to one side and brought it crashing against the wooden beam.

The beam shifted slightly.

For a brief moment Scarlet stared at it, as if his eyes were not to be trusted. Then he heaved the hammer up and brought it smashing against the beam again. And again. It moved no farther.

Dark splotches bloomed and spread across the violently shaking door. Loudly protesting layers of wood twisted away in long curls. The smoke thrashed wildly about, as if seeking prey.

Rodrigo tried to rise, but his energy was spent. Scarlet smashed furiously at the unyielding beam, and the small man pushed at its base, bellowing unintelligibly with each push as if his words could force the issue.

Phoebe's mind reeled from the ache that now roared throughout her body as the numbness disappeared entirely. Over the desperate smashing of Scarlet, Rodrigo's ragged shouting, and the screech of tortured wood, the muted giggling from beyond the door crept up to her and crawled about inside her head in anticipation.

Then, two horrifying realizations arose in her like demons of the deep.

First, despite all her efforts, she could not remember her last name.

Second, the door...

The twisted curls of wood on the door sprouted thick, uneven talons. They scrabbled clumsily at the top crossbar. Three dark splotches on the door's face turned milky yellowish and protruded outward, forming a black void in their centers.

Eyes. One turned its baleful, unblinking gaze on Scarlet while the others twisted to focus on the crossbars. The talons found their mark and the top crossbar fell away.

Phoebe lay back, quiet. Out of the protective fog of her mind, the hawkish young face of Rodrigo came. "Close your eyes, lady."

She closed her eyes and felt the press of his heavy linen shirt against her chin. She thought it smelled like sawdust and horses.

But a strange excitement filled her, and her eyes refused to remain closed.

Scarlet stepped back, then raced away a short distance. He turned, held the hammer crosswise in front of him, and charged the beam.

The wooden claws tore the bottom crossbar from its brackets and flung it clattering across the rocks. Nearly free, the door—or the horror it had become—tore savagely at the hinges that bound it to the frame.

Scarlet struck the beam in full sprint. The hammer's handle splintered in two and the beam smashed against his right shoulder.

Scarlet won. The beam tore away from its footing and fell sideways. With a series of protesting snaps the carefully trapped ceiling of the tunnel fell in a domino effect. Loose rock followed in a black waterfall twenty paces deep.

Rodrigo covered Phoebe's small frame as the cavern filled with earth-thunder and choking dust.

30: PHOEBE

Yun's diary, Day 113

We—the four of us who entered that place—are shaken to our soul, and Scarlet is hurt again. But we saved her. Her name is Phoebe. She came awake right when we found her, but tonight she suffered a strange shivering and fell unconscious.

There was a barn filled with beautiful horses. Light filtered through the open door, warming Phoebe in a soft caress. She smiled sleepily and breathed in the smell of fresh sawdust.

The arched roof melted away and dimmed, replaced with a soft glow on gray stone as she awoke. She lay on a rough cot set on sand, in a small, enclosed area lined with hanging blankets. An oil lamp sputtered on a three-legged stool next to her.

The small man—Rip, that was his name—sat curled in a makeshift chair in one corner, breathing lightly in sleep. When she turned over, one of his eyes slipped open.

"Morn, Miss Phoebe," he said.

"Hello," said Phoebe. "How long have I slept?"

"A few hours only," said Rip. "How do yeh feel?"

"Rested."

"Yeh be breaking the mold, miss. I'll be back in a flash."

Rodrigo followed Rip through the blankets that served as the door to Phoebe's room. He stopped short, seeing her sitting up in bed, alert. "You are awake. Did Rip tell you how unusual that is?"

Phoebe shook her head and Rodrigo explained everything to her. She listened quietly, sitting cross-legged on the cot, her dress draped over both sides and her long brown curls doing the same over her shoulders and down her chest.

She had a narrow fox-ish nose like Scarlet, but smaller and more pointed. The fine, strong angles of her chin and jaw clashed with the rounded cheeks of fading childhood, but her startling teal eyes and full, sleek brows stole the attention, and Rodrigo found himself losing his train of thought now and then as her gaze rested on him.

As they spoke, he watched her eyes moisten, and yet she kept her focus on him and her chin straight, quietly composed.

"Will my memory return?" she asked. "When I sleep, I dream of places—a barn, and country, and horses."

"All of us have lost our memories as well, but we have hope," said Rodrigo.

"My deepest appreciation for saving me," she said. "This—being here, and having no memory—is difficult to bear. Would you…allow me time alone, please?" Moisture in her eyes pooled and turned to tears.

"Certainly," said Rodrigo, and left with Rip.

———

They wandered away together, hearing soft, controlled crying coming from Phoebe's blanket-lined room.

"She's a fine lass," said Rip, "and another little slip of a girl like Yun. What are yeh thinking of her?"

"Yes," said Rodrigo absently.

"I see," smiled Rip. "Well, as ettins go, I am still an admirer of this one here." They had reached the cooking fire, where Yun curled next to the small blaze with a book in hand.

"Ravenhair again?" said Rip, spying the cover.

Yun looked up. "Hello, Rip! Hi, Rodrigo. I've read through most all of the stories now, but I can't find anything else that might be a clue."

"Unlikely that they would bury anything else in the same book," said Rodrigo. "But try a few more on us before lunch is ready."

She read them four stories. After each the three bandied about a few theories, shook their heads, and threw up their hands.

"Looks like that well is dry," said Rip.

"Still, keep your eyes open if you read it again," said Rodrigo. "And, Yun, you made the right decision to speak up back in the tunnels."

Yun's face battled between emotions. "But we woke up something, didn't we? I can't even remember much about running away."

"Yeh kept yer head, yeh did," said Rip.

"I remember those twisted things coming into the light right behind us…What were they?"

Rodrigo stirred the fire. "Slaves to whatever masters arose from that spire, I should guess. I am grateful that we caught them asleep. We did not even see the masters, except for their glow, but they whipped my mind like a lash with their cries."

Yun returned to her book, clearly uncomfortable with the conversation. Rodrigo stood, stretched, and changed the subject. "Where is Hope?"

"She's still with Scarlet," said Yun, disgust evident in her voice.

Amused concern registered on Rodrigo's face. He turned to Rip. "Should we see what Trace is up to?"

"Ahey," said Rip. "He's a-wandering Royalty Hall, working his leg. Coming right along, he is."

The two left Yun and passed by the rows of newly erected blanket-lined tents in the sand, built from the abundant supplies found in the Forge. As Rodrigo and Rip passed to the exit, they heard a small yip of pain coming from Hope's makeshift hospice.

"Pantaloons—er, Scarlet—has a habit for taking a hurt, doesn't he?" said Rip.

Rodrigo quirked one raven-black eyebrow. "Gives him a reason to visit the good doctor."

"How did you brewed...browed...emmm, make that up?" asked Scarlet, his speech slow and disjointed. "And why...I say, why did *you* stuff my body off...off over there in the corner like that? I regomnize my boots!"

"Your body is right here." Hope inspected Scarlet's splintered chest.

She unrolled her favorite discovery from Skyhall—a set of fine surgical tools encased in a canvas roll, its cover embroidered in gold thread with the symbol of a climbing vine. She selected a general-use forceps and pulled a wooden splinter from Scarlet's flesh, one of several embedded when the sledge handle had broken and smashed against him. "I didn't brew it up," she said. "I found a bottle of it in Skyhall. To be honest, I don't know exactly what it is. I just know it kills pain."

"I think you gaven—have gaven—me too much. I'm having trouble standing."

"You're lying down, now be still."

"I'm having trouble lying down, then. And I'm suppo...supposed to keep you at arm's length at all times, because you are too wonderful and new and confused. And I'm too wonderful too. Ouch! I felt that."

Hope pulled the last splinter. "I'm sorry, that one required a bit of digging. Now, why must you keep me at arm's length?"

Scarlet gave a wobbly flourish, flopping one hand about. "Grandfather! That's why. He says—said—you would fall to my charms too easy, and I would be a rogue, like my papa. You like me, don't you?"

"You're a nice, amiable fellow. Just relax now, we're nearly there. So, you remember your grandfather, do you?"

Scarlet snorted out a giggle. "Nooooo. No, no. That's the joke, right? He's the same age as me, but he's Grandfather!" The thought amused him considerably, and he laughed without making any noise or breathing.

Hope furrowed her brows and shook her head as she laid a dressing over the clean wounds. "Your grandfather is of the same age as you?"

Scarlet sucked in a big breath. "He's not my *real* grandpapa, he just acts like it." At this Scarlet produced a surprisingly good impression of Rodrigo, considering his current state. This got him laughing again.

Hope wasn't sure whether to be amused or deeply concerned, but it dawned on her that Scarlet was in a highly unguarded state. She played with her ear for a moment, and a rather sly smile developed on her lips.

"Who are you speaking of?" she said.

"Rodrigo!" said Scarlet, and performed the impression again. "You see, now, watch my chin." He stroked his chin dramatically before rolling his head forward and laughing silently.

"And he told you what?"

"He told me," said Scarlet, sighing deeply and concentrating like he had to dredge up a long-lost memory, "that you are a dream come true. And you—as a beautiful example of the feline—feminline species—would be so eager to fall for my manly charms that I would have to—I quite liberably would have to beat you away with a stick. And I would beat Yun too, of course, because I danced with her. It's how dangerous my charming manly apparently has gotten to."

"And would you *want* to beat me with a stick?" she asked, leaning in closely to him and gazing into his eyes.

He quieted down, his eyes trying to concentrate on her face. He brought one hand up and clumsily touched her cheek. "I would love you. But Grandfather won't let me." And he closed his eyes, drifting off to sleep.

Hope kissed him lightly on the cheek. "You are a dear boy, Scarlet. But just a boy. And I must have a discussion with your grandfather."

———

Rodrigo held both fastidious habits and a strong routine, so when Hope rose and went to look for him at the lakeshore an hour before the others normally woke, she found him sitting atop a low crate, preparing to bathe.

"Apologies for disturbing you, Rodrigo, but I haven't seen to your wound."

"I took care of it," he said. "Nothing more than a scrape."

"If you don't mind, allow me."

Rodrigo paused and nodded. "As you wish." He undid the laces and pulled the shirt over his head, laying it aside.

Hope sat down behind him and he twisted to view the wound along his side. The scrape covered a respectable territory but did little more than rough up the surface and leave a bruise. The sly smile returned her face. She probed around the scrape gently.

"You are rough on your ribs, Rodrigo." She ran her hand over his back and to the other side, to the ribs that had previously been bruised by his triggering of Rip. "Let me loosen them." She massaged his back lightly.

Rodrigo closed his eyes and sighed, but it seemed to Hope that the sigh came more from nervousness than relaxation.

"The lake is quite beautiful," said Hope. "Peaceful."

He nodded.

The massage continued for some time. Hope moved along his ribs, around his shoulders and to his neck, keeping a playful conversation going even though Rodrigo remained mostly silent. "Is that feeling better?"

Rodrigo nodded.

"You have excellent skin, quite healthy looking. It's a lovely tan, like a lion."

Rodrigo didn't move. "Lions are gold."

Hope slipped an arm over in front of Rodrigo and leaned so that she faced him. Her other hand continued to massage his back. Her trademark ponytail was missing, replaced by a loose waterfall of straight brown hair cascading over her shoulders and sleeveless nightshirt. "Now, my skin is healthy too, but it's quite pale compared to yours. Alabaster, I believe they call it. Would you say my skin is alabaster?"

Rodrigo didn't immediately answer, his gaze cast down. But slowly his chestnut eyes came up to meet her own hazel ones. He remained silent.

"My alabaster, your tan, would you not say they complement each other?" Hope brought her hand up to rest on his shoulder and she leaned in closer.

"Miss Hope-" whispered Rodrigo, but she moved her hand to his lips and stopped him.

"I must ask a question first, before we progress as we should," crooned Hope.

It was as if Rodrigo had been turned to stone, but his eyes betrayed a flickering array of conflicting emotions. Their faces drifted so closely together that her nose threatened to brush his cheek.

Hope cocked her head slightly and smiled winsomely. "I wish to ask...should you not be heeding the advice you gave Scarlet and beat me away with a stick?"

Rodrigo didn't immediately react, but after a time, a small, knowing smile appeared. "If I recall correctly," he whispered, "my advice to Scarlet did not include a stick, but merely an arm's length."

"I wish you to understand," whispered Hope, "that I am not a mare in your stable. I am no love-struck, empty-headed ninny to be hopelessly led away by shallow charms. Rather, it should be my charms that you are worried about."

To Hope's surprise, Rodrigo did not begin falling about himself in apology as she had expected. Instead, his face turned serious, almost plaintive. "Miss Hope, I am not certain that you gained the whole measure of what I explained to Scarlet. I expressed my concern that there were entirely too many charms possessed by everyone here, and that it would be right to do our part as men to keep matters cordial and uncomplicated until our futures were more certain. So, Miss Hope, at this moment I am reminded that it is precisely your exceedingly abundant charms that I am worried about."

Doubt crept in to Hope's mind. "I thought that you and Scarlet were 'dividing the spoils.'"

"I assure you that that is not the case. You and Yun and now Phoebe are treasures, but never spoils, and I pledge that to you. You have both my protection and respect."

"That is kind," whispered Hope, at a loss to come back with anything witty. This conversation, and her little trap, was spiraling in a direction she did not expect or prepare for. Rodrigo smelled faintly of straw, or saddles, and she breathed in more deeply.

"I told Scarlet one other thing," said Rodrigo.

"What is that?"

"I told him that I was also very much a man. I have discovered that there is a slight dimple on your left cheek and that your smell reminds me of a spring cornfield. I have seen that your coy smile is nearly as enchanting as your natural one. I have noticed that neither one of us has retreated a thread since we began our coming-to-minds, and that I could kiss you with the slightest movement. So, if either your alabaster or my tan does not *flee* soon, things will progress and my pretty promises will not survive the moment."

Hope smiled, and she realized that the spell tangling them had been broken— a spell that had struck her quite by surprise. She pulled away and stood up. "Scarlet is right. You're no boy. But you're no grandfather either. I am intrigued. But, as you say, until our future is certain…"

"And now, if you do not mind, I need time in the lake. Good morning, Miss Hope."

Hope nodded and turned toward the tent community.

———

Once she was lost in the darkness, Rodrigo rubbed his eyes, took an extensive deep breath, uttered a quiet word to his god, and waded out into the lake waters.

32: THE FOUR WINDS

— *8 days later*

Yun's diary, Day 121

We pass the days waiting for everyone to heal. I help Rodrigo and Ed search and catalog everything. The most exciting find has been the clock—a big wooden thing with silver hands and pendulums that works by winding it. Ed dotes on the thing ever since he fixed something in it and got it working. We tried it yesterday, and our typical day is quite close to what it says. It's nice knowing a time and being able to talk in hours again.

Everyone has been getting on well enough. Two nights now we have sat around the fire and taken turns reading from my Ravenhair book, trying to guess its hidden meaning. No one really expects to find something else in it, or maybe deep down we hope but don't want to look silly saying so.

Hope turned out to be a cold fish. Not to me; she's nice to me and I still help her out. I like her. She knows her own mind and she treats Scarlet and Rodrigo as just kids. She's so much older than them, at least five years. It does bother me that everyone says "Miss Hope" and "Miss Phoebe" and I'm just "Yun," especially when Phoebe is my age.

Phoebe likes to cook and sew and organize things. She is quiet, pays no attention to the boys—in that kind of way—and works really hard. I like her, but she doesn't have that close, kindred-spirit manner that Hope has. She also doesn't have any trouble wandering the tunnels by herself, which makes Rodrigo nervous.

She has the prettiest eyes and nicest hair I've ever seen. I see Scarlet and Rodrigo glancing at her a lot. And at Hope. And sometimes at me.

Rodrigo is a true leader now. Everyone just lets him set the pace and make the big decisions, except Ed, who doesn't really pay attention to anything except himself and what he is doing. I think Rodrigo is a good leader because he talks to everyone and gets their ideas and settles disputes with that way he talks. Sometimes I start up conversations with Rodrigo just to hear him say things. Scarlet has a nice voice too. Those two are inseparable now, and Rip also spends a lot of time with them. I noticed that ever since the cringer tunnels, Rip has stopped calling Scarlet names like Pantaloons.

Rip continues to be the showoff. He sings beautifully and I dance with him regularly, and he loves to read and act out the Ravenhair stories. He and Scarlet and Rodrigo are really funny when they get to joking and making up things about the stories, and Rip gets into funny arguments with Ed, too, which, strangely enough, Ed doesn't seem to mind. I think that's one reason why everyone enjoys the night's readings even though they're just kids' stories.

Trace is fully better now, but he's still a little slow in the head. He has this content smile on his big thick face that makes you want to smile as well. He just enjoys being in company and listening to others, and having someone ask him to help out with that monster strength of his. He eats and eats and eats! Everyone is amazed by how much.

I am content. Maybe I would even say I'm happy. I have friends, and books, and my dancing, and my journal. Rodrigo told me yesterday how glad he is that I write this journal, even though I won't let him read it. He thinks it will be something to remember us by.

Tomorrow we open up the jaws to the stairs and see where they lead. Everyone is getting excited.

Time for dinner. I'm tired of fish.

———————

"One more!" said Trace, his happy smile as large as ever.

"Agreed!" said Rip. "But only one. I need more sleep than you ettins."

Rip began the next story in his typical dramatic voice. He used a high, squeaky voice whenever Ravenhair spoke, to tease Yun, and a suitably creepy hissing voice for the Shadow Stealer. Everyone else leaned back and relaxed in the sand, except Ed, who sat on a rock with a little notepad, taking the whole secret-code bit so seriously that the others regularly joked about it.

———————

134

Tale 13: Ravenhair and the Four Winds

Ravenhair loved to dance, and her favorite dance partners were the Four Winds. She always began with a pleasant polka at the hands of the refined East Wind, and then the wild North Wind swirled Ravenhair's blood up with a furious rigadoon. When she tired, she fell into the arms of calm West Wind, who led her gently through the minuet, and, refreshed, she finished finely in a tango with the dashing South Wind.

"Yun needs more dancers," said Rodrigo. "Scarlet brings her East and Rip the North."

"And I'm waiting for my West," added Yun, grinning impishly at Hope.

Although they were all brothers, or because they were brothers, the Four Winds argued constantly. They could not agree on dance, or clouds, or rain, or sun. "You're too hot!" said North to South.
"And you're too cold," South said in return.
"You're too brisk!" said West to East.
"And you're too slow," cried East to West.
The Lord Sun and the Lady Moon did not interfere with the wild bickering of the four brothers. Although they disliked the bickering, they knew that the lands needed each of the four winds. And so, when the West Wind had his way, the lands knew quiet and clouds like cotton, and when the East pushed back he brought lightning and nourishing rain. When the South Wind won out, the lands knew heat and sun that made the corn

grow tall, until the North whirled in to bring the snow for a blanket of sleep.

But the Four Winds brought their changes too strongly. The heat was too hot and the cool too cold. The rain came in buckets and the snow came in piles and the clouds came in stacks that covered Lord Sun. The lands were less than happy, but they were less than sad, and the days passed on.

It was ever the Shadow Stealer's desire to destroy the lands of Lord Sun, for without the lands and those who lived there, Lord Sun and Lady Moon would find despair and pass beyond the horizon forever, never to return. So it was, one day, as he scratched and crawled his way up from under the mountain, the Shadow Stealer spied the Four Winds arguing.

"If I caged the Four Winds," he thought, "no rain, no wind, no warmth, and no snow. The land would die, and the peoples would die, and the hearts of the Lord and Lady would die. And even that accursed Ravenhair would be no more!"

The Shadow Stealer drew down into his darkest hole, and there he laid plans. No one could lay plans like he could, except perhaps Ravenhair. He thought and thought, and the Lord and Lady passed many times over the land above before his plans formed complete. He knew the nature of the Four Winds, and because he knew their nature, he knew their weak-nesses. He could never hope to overcome their boundless strength, but he could use that strength to overcome them. He danced his own devilish dance of glee, and then called forth his dark laborers for the great task.

They hollowed out an old volcano and set four colossal swinging gates into it—one in each direction. The gates were easier to push in than out, and the machines that drove the gates worked in such a way that pushing upon one gate pulled upon the others.

"Ingenious," said Ed. "I could tell you the rest."

"Hush!" said Hope.

At the time, the Four Winds loved the Breezes, four beautiful sisters who spent their days dancing through the leaves of the woods. While beau-tiful and soft, they did not have the strength of the winds, and when one night the many-clawed Despair crept into their woods and snatched them up, they were helpless to escape. Despair dragged them to the volcano and threw them in, and the great gates were far too strong for them to open.

When the East Wind discovered this hateful act, he rushed to the vol-cano and called out, "Dear Breezes, are you there?"

"Here!" they cried. "Save us!"

East Wind moved to blow open a gate. But because he was so deter-mined never to blow any way but his, he chose the gate that let him blow east. With all his might and all his strength he blew, and the gate swung inward. He rushed in, and the gate swung closed behind.

"You are saved!" he said to the Breezes. And while he comforted them, his brothers blew in their gates as well, one by one, forcing their way into the volcano to comfort the Breezes. Each time, the gate closed behind them with great force.

The Breezes were grateful to the brothers, but not yet pleased, for they were still trapped in the volcano. "We must escape before Despair comes back and finds us all trapped!" they cried.

"Follow me!" the brothers said in unison, and they approached the gates. But each determined never to blow any way but their own, so each blew with great gusto upon their own gate, the rush of air whistling so strongly through the volcano that the little Breezes swirled about as if in a tornado. The Winds blew and blew and blew, and by doing so made the gates doubly strong.

"Told you," said Ed.

The others clicked their tongues.

The days passed, the Winds blew, and the Breezes cried in hopelessness.

Seeing the land begin to wither and die, Ravenhair went in search of the Four Winds. She heard the stubborn huffing of the Winds and the wailing of the Breezes inside the old black volcano.

"We are trapped!" cried the Breezes. "The Winds blow each upon their own gate with great gusto, but they do not open."

"Yes!" hissed the Shadow Stealer from a deep dark hole at the volcano's foot. "And the Winds have trapped themselves as well. The lands will wither, and the peoples with wither, and you will wither, Ravenhair!"

And then Despair arose and tried to clutch Ravenhair and drag her down the dark hole, but she leapt to the top of the old volcano and called out to the Winds.

"East Wind, West Wind, hear me! North Wind, South Wind, cease your blowing!"

Upon hearing their good friend, the Winds died down. "We are trapped," they said, "but *I* will soon have my gate open."

"No, friends, you will not," shouted Ravenhair. "For the Shadow Stealer knows your determination, and has turned your strength into weakness. Do you love your Breezes?"

"Yes!" said the Winds heartily.

"And do you love your brothers?"

"Of course," said the Winds less heartily.

"Then center upon me in combination. Only by love and not by determination will you unlock this prison."

"If we must," said wild North Wind.

"You must," said Ravenhair. "Blow upon your gate, North Wind!"

"If need be," said West Wind.

"The need is great," said Ravenhair. "Stand and blow with brother North!"

"If there is no other way," said East Wind.

"You must make a way," said Ravenhair. "Make a way with brother North!"

"I'm not one to follow," said South.

"Then lead with your brothers," said Ravenhair. "Lead along with brother North!"

Slowly, the four brothers turned and blew upon the same gate, side to side. Ravenhair urged them on and the Breezes added what help they could. The gate strained but could not hold, and the Breezes and the Winds rushed out, free.

"Thank you!" cried the Breezes.

"It worked!" shouted the Winds.

"Seems better to push as one," said Ravenhair to the Winds, "than to pull against each other in blind determination."

"True," said the Four Winds. The brothers pledged marriage to the four gentle Breezes, and to this day they bicker less. Now the land is fully pleased, for the winds blow quieter, the rain and snow fall softer, and the clouds do not hide Lord Sun for days on end.

The Shadow Stealer smashed the old volcano and his dark laborers with it, and crawled deep down to curl up for a time with Despair.

"That wasn't bad," said Scarlet. "Masterful performance, Rip."

Rip bowed deeply and handed the book back to Yun, who clutched it to her breast happily.

"Stealer needs a good head-lopping," said Trace. Everyone laughed, as much because Trace actually said something.

"Has possibilities," said Rodrigo. "All those directions make it sound like a treasure map."

"True!" said Yun. "Except there aren't any distances. You know, six paces one way, three paces the other, that sort."

"Could it be a set distance each time?" asked Phoebe.

"I didn't hear any distances," said Scarlet.

"But there were numbers," said Phoebe. "Four Winds, and twenty days that the Shadow Stealer thought up his plan."

"So, four or twenty paces?" said Hope.

"Could be," said Rodrigo. "Of course, we would also need a starting point."

Everyone thought on that, but no theories came forth.

"Great little story, though, with Rip's help," said Scarlet.

"Combination!"

The word exploded so loudly from Ed's mouth that the others jumped. He made a diamond in the air with a jabbed finger. "North, South, East, West! And Ravenhair right in the middle!"

He stepped quickly to Yun and ripped the book from her embrace, which brought instant and lively outrage from the others. They all leapt to their feet.

"That's no-" started Hope.

Ed rifled furiously through the book. "What page?"

"First yeh give the book back, Ed," said Rip darkly. "And by Boxley yeh better find finer manners to mind."

"Yes, *ahem*." Ed coughed and passed the book back to Yun. She carefully looked up the page and turned to it, smoothing several others ruffled by Ed. "Fifty-one," she said, handing the book back.

"Keep it," said Ed. "We need to hoof off to Waterfall." He suddenly laughed. "Tale number thirteen...clever, clever."

"That's a long trip for an evening jaunt," said Scarlet.

"I go," said Trace, always helpful.

"Sleep is off the to-do list until I sort out this little mystery," said Ed.

"I know that feeling," said Scarlet.

Rodrigo looked around at the others.

I'm game," said Phoebe.

"I'm along too," said Rip. "And Hope here loves me too dearly to be parted."

Hope blew him a kiss.

"Pack up, then," said Rodrigo. "Ed, you wish to tell us what you know?"

Ed set off. "Show is better than tell on this."

———

Hours later, Ed stood in front of the steel wall containing the many controls of Waterfall. Everyone else huddled around while Yun tried to shelter her book from the drifting mist of the falls.

"Toward the end of the story, when the Winds agree to cooperate," shouted Ed over the falls.

Yun searched through the story and started reading, but Ed cocked his head sideways. "Speak up, Yun. My hearing's no good."

Yun repeated the sentence, shouting it the best she could.

"No, before that," said Ed.

"Before that it says, 'Then center upon me in combination. Only by love and not by determination will you unlock this prison.'"

"Combination! Yes, that part exactly," yelled Ed. "Trace, help me." The two moved to the thirteen levers, which Ed had pointed out weeks before, each with a center and four directional settings. "Go ahead, Yun."

Yun shouted the words, trying to be heard over the waterfall and the preparations of the men. "'If we must,' said wild North Wind. 'You must,' said Ravenhair. 'Blow upon your gate, North Wind!'"

Ed pointed to the levers and shouted over the waterfall's noise. "The Winds are directions of the lever, and Ravenhair is the center point of the lever. The Winds and Ravenhair are mentioned by name thirteen times in this section. In this part, you have North, Ravenhair, and North again, so…"

Trace and Ed shoved the first lever up, left the second in the center, and moved the third up. He gestured to Yun.

She nodded. "'If need be,' said West Wind. 'The need is great,' said Ravenhair. 'Stand and blow with brother North!'"

The two pushed the fourth left, kept five at the center, and levered six up.

Yun flipped the page. "'If there is no other way,' said East Wind. 'You must make a way,' said Ravenhair. 'Make a way with brother North!'"

Right, center, up.

"'I'm not one to follow,' said South. 'Then lead with your brothers,' said Ravenhair. 'Lead along with brother North!' Slowly the four brothers turned and blew upon the same gate, side to side. Ravenhair urged them on and the Breezes added what help they could."

Yun paused and held her breath.

Down, center, up. One lever remained, but it was centered.

The ground shook. Ed shouted in triumph and everyone turned.

The intimidating flow of the falls diminished to a trickle, but deep in the rock the rushing and tumbling of water could be heard and felt. To the waterfall's left, a section of wall twelve feet high and thirty feet wide slid inward by slow, pulsing degrees, provoking groans and ground-shaking thuds from the rock. Ed raced over to the moving rock, inspecting it closely from all angles as it settled slowly inward. The others followed him more cautiously.

Minutes passed. The retreating rock gradually revealed a smooth floor and the beginning of an opening directed downward. Ten minutes passed, then twenty, and finally the rock stopped retreating, leaving the wide, steep descending passage fully exposed. The pool below the lost waterfall slowly drained away down its channel in the floor and into the far wall.

Rip held his lantern over the passage. Regular, precisely cut stairs descended into darkness in a slight curl, wide enough for four of them to comfortably walk abreast.

The eight Dusties looked at each other, and turned to Rodrigo.

Rodrigo gestured a hand to Scarlet. "Scarlet, Trace, Rip, and…Yun and I will give it a look. We will measure off twelve hours of oil in our timing lamps and be back by then. Hope, Ed, and Phoebe stay here, in case this closes on us."

"Doubtful," said Ed, his attention fully entrapped by the secret portal's heavy machinery, now visible in the exposed walls. "This is an ingenious implementation of hydraulics. Unless it fails completely, you haven't got a worry."

Rodrigo quirked his lip. "Well, you have given me something to worry about."

Scarlet and Yun filled their miniature lamps, which served as timepieces. Everyone nodded ready, and Rodrigo stepped onto the smooth, dusty stairs.

33: BIG HOLE

Yun's diary, Day 122

We are resting in a wide-open void of space, I think the biggest cavern I can imagine. We can't see the ceiling anywhere. I'm sitting at the edge of a series of stone terraces, like steps. They curve and disappear both ways. Flashes of light are coming from ahead and below us, and the flashes make the surroundings visible. It looks like the terraces curve all the way around in a giant ring. It's very strange in here, makes me feel weird. Rodrigo thinks there's a big hole in front of us.

Early on we found a huge, twisting circular side-tunnel with rock as smooth as glass. Along it, here and there, were embedded the bottoms of ships—big steel ones, wooden ones, and others made of more modern materials. Some were on the floor, and some were sideways on the walls, and some hung from the ceiling. They weren't stone; they were the real thing. Rope and nets and seafarer stuff lay tangled everywhere. We didn't go far in there because of the debris and the smell, but Rip is excited. We saw the full wreckage of a smaller wooden boat, like a lifeboat. He thinks that he might find a boat to float the lake with.

The explorers backed out of the strange twisting tunnel that Scarlet nicknamed Seagrave and reached a series of terraces cut into the stone like giant stairs, each several paces wide and a few feet down from the next. The terraces curved inward slightly and extended left and right, as though they eventually circled around in a giant ring. Scarlet and Rip split off left to test this theory, walking the curve of the terraces while Rodrigo, Trace, and Yun settled in to wait for them, watching the ever-shrinking lights of their bobbing lanterns.

Rodrigo and Yun sat with their feet dangling, looking down the ring of terraces, watching the reflected glow of white light appear and fade, ahead and below, as though searchlights swung randomly in a pit. The wandering light, the steep terrace slope, and the seemingly infinite darkness disoriented their perceptions and brought on a measure of vertigo, so that finally Yun groaned and scooted around to face the other direction, staring at her feet.

In the quiet, Rodrigo began to hear distant sounds—an irregular and indistinct thumping drifting up from below.

Thirty minutes passed by before Rodrigo nudged Yun and pointed. Scarlet and Rip appeared, coming along the terrace from the other direction.

"So, a ring it is," said Scarlet.

"Are there exits?" asked Rodrigo.

"None," said Rip. "Except the ship-filled tunnel and that giant hungry hole down there, where the bangity sounds and lightning are a-coming."

"We should take a look at what is below," said Rodrigo. "Trace, stay here and hold a rope for us in case we need to leave hastily. Scarlet, carry the other rope."

"Good, my head dizzy," said Trace, sitting down with a thick spear braced across his legs and letting Scarlet pull two lengths of rope from Trace's over-stuffed pack.

Rodrigo climbed down to the next terrace, and the others followed slowly, careful to keep their footing on the polished stone. They soon noticed that the terraces grew both narrower and taller as they progressed, giving the eyes and mind the impression that they were being drawn downward into a black vortex from which they could not back out. The height of the terraces became a problem for Yun and Rip, and they all paused.

Below them the hole clearly opened out—a vast void drilling straight down into the rock, at least three or four hundred paces wide. They could see the source of the light directly now. Great bands of pure-white luminescence appeared, wandered along the curved wall of the big hole, and faded quickly. Something clung to the walls, creating thousands of tiny black specks as the bands of light wandered through them.

Rodrigo fought his vertigo and a rising sense of vulnerability. He looked around at the others. Yun kept her face to the inner wall, clinging there until everyone else jumped down to the next terrace. Rip's height would soon prevent him from climbing back up on his own without the rope.

"Rip, you and Yun hold the rope steady here."

Rip agreed readily. Yun sat down and put a hand on the rope.

Four more terraces, and Scarlet whispered to Rodrigo, "I feel like a worm in a whale's mouth. This is approaching insane."

"Agreed," said Rodrigo. "I am not much for heights. But someone spent immense effort to build that Waterfall entrance. This cannot just be a dead-end."

"Dead-end—how apt," muttered Scarlet.

Rodrigo gave him an appraising glance as they dropped to the next terrace. He remembered the cheerful, undaunted Scarlet strutting atop the Overthrown Throne in their early days, and he wondered how—and why—Scarlet had descended into hesitation and negativity.

Since the day that the fear in the dark had attacked Scarlet, something had changed in his friend. Not immediately, but slowly over time—a withdrawal, as if Scarlet were shrinking in both mind and soul. He kept up the pretenses well, went about with his usual dash and flair, but Rodrigo sensed the increasing hollowness in it.

Rodrigo had no answer, no solution, and he sighed quietly in frustration. But once again he set the matter aside and refocused on the task at hand.

They descended four more terraces, and then dropped down onto a wider ring. Approaching its edge, they discovered that they had reached the hole proper. Far below, at least two hundred paces down, they could see a stone floor, illuminated by spotty sources of soft yellow-green light—much like the gaslight of the Forge.

Rodrigo stretched out prone and inched to the hole's edge. Scarlet followed and held his lantern out.

A few feet below them, a stone carving of a small bird thrust out from the wall. It was not a full carving, merely the head and front of the wings, tilted to one side as if in flight. To the left and right, they saw other such carvings, large and small.

But the bird carvings did not hold their attention. Next to and dwarfing the birds, the front end of a magnificent old flying machine jutted out from the wall. A pair of more advanced aircraft could be dimly seen below that, their streamlined angles represented perfectly in stone. Lying at the edge and watching the bands of light for a time, it became apparent to the two Dusties that the scattered specks on the walls were more of the same—many thousands of birds and hundreds of flying machines.

"Remember my theory that this is all a dream?" said Scarlet. "I offer this as proof."

"Listen," said Rodrigo.

Scarlet went silent. The thumping sounded much more loudly here. They could hear noises before, and after, each thump, but not clearly enough to make out anything distinctly. Sometimes the thumps came in quick succession, and sometimes slowly, and sometimes there would be no thump for several minutes.

Scarlet's eyes widened. "That's no machinery, or anything natural."

"No," said Rodrigo. "Someone is down there."

"Could it be a golem, like Three? That light down there looks familiar."

"Perhaps—ah! Did you see the last light band to the right of us?" said Rodrigo.

"No."

"Something more than birds and air machines is down along the wall over there. A dark strip. Watch."

The two kept their eyes on the area Rodrigo had pointed out, waiting for the next light band.

"This might sound like an odd time to bring it up," said Scarlet, "but I can't make heads nor tails out of Hope."

"Oh?" said Rodrigo, keeping his eyes on the wall below.

"I mean, after my dream of her—such a vivid dream!—and then to have her appear in the flesh, I feel this powerful attachment to her that I cannot shake. But it's maddening trying to figure her out. I can't tell whether she hates me or loves me, but she's always so—I don't know—tricky."

A smile grew on Rodrigo's face, but he kept it hidden by turning his head away. "She does have a number of surprising dimensions," he said.

"Arm's length and all that, of course—There it is! I see the line you're talking about. Should we circle the hole?"

They rose and walked along the edge. No more than twenty paces away, they found a huge, stone flying machine very close to the top—the front half-projecting from the wall like the others they had seen. As they passed it, Rodrigo happened to glance back. Against the side of the flying machine, he spotted something made of iron and wood. He motioned to Scarlet and they both stepped down onto the back of the craft, its round body so wide that they could easily walk side by side.

Not far out, they found cables stretched around the aircraft, anchoring the top of a makeshift but well-built bridge constructed of steel pipe and wooden slats that descended off one side of the machine. This hanging bridge hopped from craft to craft as it followed the curve of the wall downward.

Scarlet shook his head in awe. "The dark line we saw must be this bridge. I would suppose it leads all of the way to the bottom."

As they inspected the top of the swinging staircase, a loud "Hi!" came from behind them, startling both of the boys. Scarlet nearly fell off, grabbing the staircase's handrail to steady himself. He turned and saw Trace's blocky, smiling face.

"Shrikes, Trace, you gave us a fright! I nearly fell off."

"Sorry," said Trace, "but I had to find you. Rip took Yun back to Waterfall. I come see you. Make sure you okay. Less dizzy down here anyway. Find out what the thumping is?"

"No," said Rodrigo. "But I don't want to return until we do. Can you go back and tell the others that we will be another hour or two? It's getting late."

"Rip say you be back in some hours, so I stay with you, okay?"

Rodrigo looked at the narrow, sloping bridge and back at Trace. "We will be going down that. Think you can do it?"

"Yah, no problem," said Trace. "I close my eyes if things get too scaredy."

"Well, don't do that. Just be careful," said Scarlet.

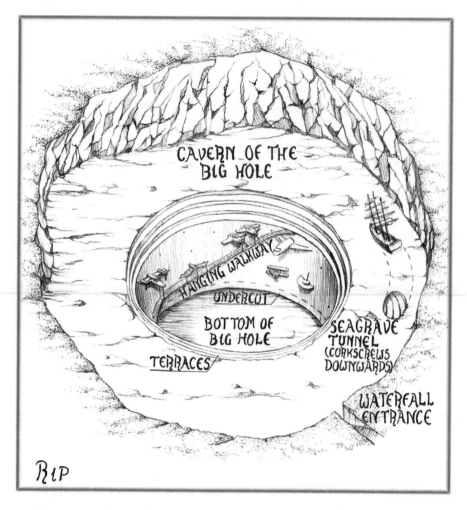

CAVERN OF THE BIG HOLE

HANGING WALKWAY

UNDERCUT

BOTTOM OF BIG HOLE

SEAGRAVE TUNNEL (CORKSCREWS DOWNWARDS)

TERRACES

WATERFALL ENTRANCE

RiP

"You want to be tied to my rope? I catch you if you fall," said Trace.

"No need," said Rodrigo, imagining being tied to Trace when the big man fell off. "But keep your rope handy."

———

The three descended the staircase, fighting off their vertigo as the hanging structure swung slightly with each step. Scarlet took the lead, his heart racing.

146

He could see only to the distance of his lantern—except when the light bands flashed to life—so that he appeared to be walking toward empty air and a long fall into darkness. The staircase swung under another flying machine and became steeper until it fastened onto a series of smaller craft, each with two large propellers. Scarlet reached out to touch one of the propellers. "I say, it has a strange feel. Like ice!"

"Hands off, then," said Rodrigo. "If we awaken anything here, the explosion will likely destroy the staircase."

"Then we die, probly," said Trace.

"Right, probably," said Scarlet, and kept his hands on the rail.

They continued, minute after harrowing minute. Once, a band of light passed along the wall next to them, a huge luminous river sliding by with a faint rushing sound.

"If I wasn't fearful for my life, this would be quite a treat," said Scarlet. His mind wandered back to the dark crevasse beneath the gargoyle monument and Raeder's fall to his death, and though he tried to fight it off, the fear slowly rose in him.

This will end like Raeder. Your other friends will die.

I know, but I can't go back. Rodrigo would never let me.

That is a shame. You will die, too, of course. You were lucky last time. Not this time.

Scarlet pulled in a breath and shook himself. Thankfully he heard no sounds but the thumping from below.

They passed a narrow section where the staircase became little more than a glorified rope bridge that hung from dozens of cables strung over birds. They spread out, hoping the displaced weight would keep the structure from shearing away. The bridge held, and they continued, until it opened out onto a packed line of broad-winged craft that cradled the hanging walkway safely and gently. At last, they saw the gaslights, no more than a dozen paces below. The staircase ended at one of the gaslights, and they stepped off with sighs of relief.

34: IMPACT

A larger, circular area spread out beneath the hole, vaguely defined by soft-burning gaslights that left more darkness than illumination. Like the Forge above, supplies and derelict machinery of all types lay scattered about. A web of dry water channels and long horizontal gear shafts traced through the machinery.

"This place needs a golem like Three to clean up," said Rodrigo. "Where is the thumping coming from? It's echoing."

"Sounds more like giants throwing boulders," said Scarlet. "To our right, I think."

They headed that direction and reached the circular perimeter wall. Following it, they found a large corridor, round except for the flat floor. Rodrigo shone his lantern down the tunnel, and then looked meaningfully at Scarlet.

The passageway ended immediately in a brass-looking barrier, like the one they called the Bronzewall in their home above.

"The markings on this barrier are different," said Scarlet, inspecting the surface. While the Bronzewall up above contained a centerpiece of constellations, the raised design on this barrier formed a complex labyrinth.

"Mystery for another day," said Rodrigo. "The thumping is farther along."

The Dusties left the barred corridor and followed the gradual curve of the wall. The thumping grew louder and louder, until Rodrigo could feel the vibration in his feet. They reached another even larger corridor, and Rodrigo peered around the corner.

This was it—the source of the now distinct smashing, like a giant fist being slammed against a metal object. They could hear the squealing of protesting metal and the clattering fall of stone. A haze of dust filled the air of the passage.

"We're going down there, aren't we?" said Scarlet.

"We have come this far," said Rodrigo.

"Yes, of course. It's just that this feels very much like a bad idea. Whatever is making that racket sounds like it would dwarf even Three. I prefer not to get stepped on."

Rodrigo turned to Trace, who held his spear, inspecting the tip. "Trace, are you willing?" asked Rodrigo.

"We come this far." Trace gave his big smile, but Rodrigo saw another flicker of sentiment in his deep-blue eyes—a sharp and dangerous edge. Rodrigo had never seen that in Trace, and it gave him a new perspective on the big man.

Scarlet's face, downcast and sour since they had first reached the Big Hole, managed an even more bitter state. "Well then, let's remember what we are thinking…for when we come back terribly maimed and they ask us what we were thinking," said Scarlet.

"You have not been terribly maimed for weeks," said Rodrigo.

"Then I'm due." Scarlet shuddered at the memory of the cringer escape.

"Stay together," said Rodrigo.

They each took a final breath and stepped into the passage.

———

The three advanced, hesitantly, down the round corridor. Dust obscured the view, but a gaslight glow slowly took form ahead. The crashes fell with such power that the Dusties had to resist the urge to cringe at each impact. Between the crashes they could now hear other sounds—an intermittent rattling hiss, like sandpaper over a washboard, the shifting of a great weight on loose rock, and, during moments of quiet, an eerie, hollow clattering, like a pit full of writhing skeletons.

Waiting for the next ground-shaking crash, and trying to block the unnatural clattering from overriding their courage, the Dusties inched forward into the darkness. Rodrigo glanced back to see Scarlet readying his curved sword, his face fatefully grim, as if he knew death sat on his shoulder. Rodrigo drew his own sword, despite not knowing the threat ahead, finding comfort in its weight and strength. Turning back, he nearly fell as he tripped on a notch in the floor. The notch ran like a ring around the round passage.

"Watch your-" he said, but noticed Scarlet pointing above, his mouth agape. Rodrigo turned and saw the gaslight on the ceiling move swiftly toward them, and a massive brass-metal shape swung low out of the haze from above. Three yellow-green eyes burned at Rodrigo.

"Golem," whispered Rodrigo, and prepared to run. The head swiveled in turn to view Trace and Scarlet. It occurred to Rodrigo that he could see nothing of the golem's body. He had assumed that it stood over him, but he stepped forward several paces and held his lantern up. He saw no golem body, which meant that this monster either floated or hung from the ceiling.

The golem head swung up and back toward the passageway ahead, muffled clanks from above indicating that it either moved along the ceiling or inside it. Rodrigo followed it, and Scarlet and Trace followed him.

Rising fear nearly overcame the Dusties when they reached the end. They stared speechless at the sight that materialized out of the haze, their eyes blinking each time the ground-shaking sound of the crash rolled over them.

Illuminated dimly by their own lanterns and the gaslight of the golem, a vast brass-metal barrier towered over them. But the barrier had little life left in it.

Twisted and buckled, it hung loosely in a shattered stone notch encircling the round corridor's wall. As they gaped at it, something on the other side smashed violently against the barrier, rocking it and sending stone showering. The Dusties ducked, one sharp-edged stone slicing Rodrigo's cheek.

The golem head swiveled back to Rodrigo, and below its eyes two distinct letters formed in gaslight:

[GO]

The three looked at each other, stepping back.

"Go?" said Scarlet. "As in forward or backward? I'm for backward."

[RUN], blazed the golem, and then it raced away along the ceiling back through the passageway in the direction from which they had just come.

The barrier suffered a powerful blow and gave way, toppling over with an ear-tearing squeal. It wedged sideways in the circular passageway. Something massive moved behind it, its dark body throwing off a dizzying aura of violet luminescence. Three smaller shapes sprang headlong over and under the fallen barrier, sprinting toward the Dusties.

35: NOT IN THE WAY OF FLESH

"Move!" yelled Rodrigo, turning around to run, but the other two were already sprinting in full retreat. Rodrigo raced away from the shattered barrier, clutching the lantern even though it hindered his speed. A deep rumble started up from ahead. Two great discs of brass were rolling in from either side of the wall at the point where he had tripped over the notch, and Rodrigo decided it must be a fallback barrier, in case the other one failed.

Two dark shapes caught up with and moved in on either side of Rodrigo. He could feel their foul presence and hear the skeleton-rustle of their bodies as they loped to easily overtake him. If—when—they brought him down, it would not matter if he fought them off. The new fallback barrier would close, and he would be trapped here with these demons.

But the shapes ignored him, their slightly purplish black forms passing by and reaching Trace and Scarlet. All four shot through the closing fallback barrier with little space to spare.

The two discs nearly touched now, sliding by each other to lock into the notch. Only a gap at the bottom remained. From somewhere deep there came to Rodrigo a surge of final strength. He lowered his head and slid through the gap headfirst, catching and spraining a finger on the notch as he did so and losing the grip on his lantern.

Rolling, he tried to regain the lantern, but a third shape slid through the crack behind him—a split-second too late. The discs pinned it and crushed it in half. What Rodrigo saw then burned in his memory.

The creature did not die in the way of flesh. A rattling hiss escaped its several mouths, and then the misshapen head and body melted and broke apart. Rodrigo most clearly remembered an ear (or perhaps a horn) twisting itself into a small fiendish thing that leapt to the floor to scuttle away on spidery legs. Much of the monster fell away into tiny mite-like creatures—like a pile of black ants boiling and spreading—but larger creatures also formed from the dying monstrosity, all with hideous or unrecognizable shapes.

Then, this one moment of clarity ended as he heard Scarlet shout. He leapt to his feet, sword in hand. The gaslight of the golem overhead lit the scene and Rodrigo oriented himself, searching for his friends.

Scarlet and Trace fought a desperate struggle with the other two creatures.

Rodrigo didn't waste the opportunity. He sprang to the thing battling Trace and slashed at one of its three hind legs.

It felt like hitting gravel. The sword bounced harmlessly off.

Momentarily taken aback, Rodrigo was caught flat-footed as the creature spun and delivered a smashing blow to his leg, throwing him prone. It landed another blow to Rodrigo's chest, knocking the wind out of him, but as it reared back for a killing strike, Rodrigo saw something slide out of its right side.

It was the broad-bladed point of Trace's spear, thrust in from the left side.

The thing hissed and retreated as Trace pulled his spear free. Black insect-globs and shapes dribbled from both holes. Its shape contorted, two of its legs drawing into the body and the remaining legs growing fatter and shorter. With a final rasping snap, an entire chunk of its left side broke free, twisting into a vaguely humanoid monstrosity that scrambled away into the darkness.

The creature recovered, closing off the wounds and reforming itself into a squat blocky thing with two fat tentacle-arms, with which it flailed at Rodrigo as he tried to close. The creature swung wildly, while Rodrigo kept carefully out of reach, timing the swings. Then, he thrust his sword to meet one of the club-fists. The sword point bit home, sliding through the fist.

The black bleeding issued from the fist, and the creature tried to draw the wound into itself. But the arm disintegrated rapidly, fist-inward. Another chunk fell away from its head. But just as it appeared to be falling away toward complete dissolution, the bleeding ended and the remaining creature—no bigger than a spaniel now—pulled away, cowering against the wall, wildly swinging one blunt arm.

Rodrigo glanced back toward Scarlet and Trace. The two circled the last creature, which bled black through multiple wounds from Trace's spear and Scarlet's sword point. Its end came suddenly, the entire beast nearly exploding apart, forming an expanding pile of dark essence. Scarlet stabbed at one of the smaller horrors as it ran by. The sword struck home, and the little creature melted away.

Trace and Scarlet moved to Rodrigo's side. They stared at the cowering survivor of the creatures as it swung its one tentacle.

"This is no dream," spat Scarlet. "It's a nightmare, and I've had my fill of it." He thrust his sword savagely into the thing, receiving a bruising blow to the thigh in return. The creature fell away.

The stone around them streamed with black shapes, flowing to and fro but finding no cracks or hiding spaces. Unlike the larger creatures, they produced no violet luminescence, and they blended in well with the darkness. As Rodrigo recovered his lantern, the golem's head swung low, flashing a clear message.

[RUN]

Without hesitation they retreated down the passage toward the Big Hole, looking back when a bright light and hiss erupted behind them. Jets of flame shot from the golem's head, engulfing the corridor. The small black things hissed and their bone-writhing clatter died away. The golem moved down the passage toward them, burning as it went, and the Dusties continued to retreat until the jets of flame ended. The golem, apparently satisfied, ascended to the ceiling again. A chalky stink filled the corridor.

Scarlet rubbed at his bruises, his face bent into a sour, nauseated grimace. "It's time to leave."

"Not yet," said Rodrigo.

"Yet," said Scarlet, and turned to leave the corridor.

Rodrigo watched him go, sighing wearily. "Trace, can you-"

"I follow him," said Trace, his face lit with a fierce and triumphant elation, and Rodrigo realized then that Trace had found a warrior inside himself.

"Well done, Trace," said Rodrigo. "Your choice of weapon came in handy."

"Spear always handy, fight or no fight," said Trace. "Sword look good, make ladies admire, and also good in a fight. But not as good as spear."

Rodrigo laughed, and the fatigue and despair lifted from him slightly. "I always thought that there might be a surprise or two in you, Trace. I saw one today."

"A surprise or two," grinned Trace, and turned to follow Scarlet.

The Big Hole

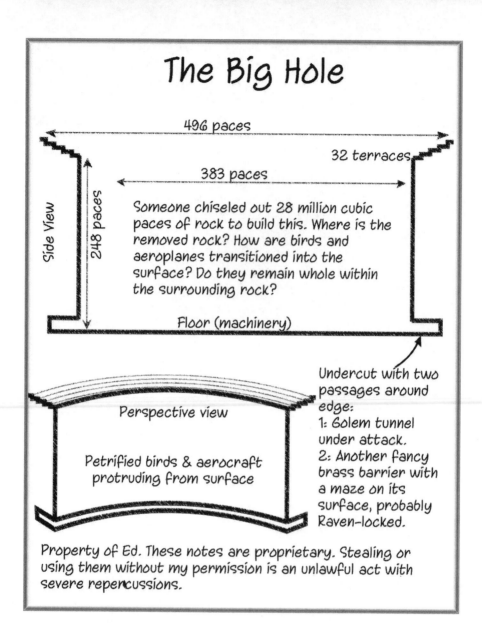

496 paces

32 terraces

383 paces

Side View

248 paces

Someone chiseled out 28 million cubic paces of rock to build this. Where is the removed rock? How are birds and aeroplanes transitioned into the surface? Do they remain whole within the surrounding rock?

Floor (machinery)

Undercut with two passages around edge:
1: Golem tunnel under attack.
2: Another fancy brass barrier with a maze on its surface, probably Raven-locked.

Perspective view

Petrified birds & aerocraft protruding from surface

Property of Ed. These notes are proprietary. Stealing or using them without my permission is an unlawful act with severe repercussions.

36: DESPAIR

Rodrigo walked back along the corridor toward the newly closed barrier, noting that all the creatures had indeed been immolated—or nearly all. One larger, lone-surviving fiend tried to retreat from him. After several attempts, he pinned it with his foot and delivered the killing thrust. The black mites flowed. Rodrigo tried to crush them with his boot, but they were like ticks, scuttling away even after receiving the full force of his heel. He hastily scraped most of the black things together, poured oil on the tiny crab-like creatures and lit it. The monsters shriveled away in a hiss.

The golem hovered just ahead. Rodrigo approached it. In the light of its fires, he saw three golem arms working away at the stone high on the wall—digging a notch for a new barrier, twenty paces away from the recently closed one.

Beyond, a powerful force slammed into the new bronze barrier. Rodrigo's jaws clenched, his eyebrows knit tightly, and his face strained. Then he strode to the wall, holding the lantern up. Another blow fell against the barrier, but it appeared to be holding well.

"Hear me!" yelled Rodrigo.

No answer came, only hissing and death-clatter, but the attempts against the barrier ceased as Rodrigo repeated his words and waited.

"Mark these words," shouted Rodrigo, his head down. "This is my home, my place. Your scouts are dead and burned away. If you continue, if you bring down this barrier, you will meet the same fate. This gate does not protect *me* from you…"

Rodrigo's head came up and a fierce determination burned in him.

"It protects *you* from *us*."

A long, thunderous hiss erupted from the other side of the barrier.

Rodrigo turned and strode away. The hammering assault against the wall resumed.

At the entrance to the corridor, he found Trace standing discreetly nearby, and Scarlet sitting against the wall, with the look of a man who no longer cared.

"Nice speech," said Scarlet. "For a minute there, I actually believed we had the slightest ability to back that up. But, of course, we don't."

Rodrigo approached Scarlet and stood over him. "We will."

Scarlet laughed, but his face went slack again. "I'm sick of this nightmare, Rodrigo. I once thought we needed to break out of a cage. But every time we try, something is there, something bad. And the bad things get worse and worse. We're not in a cage. We're in a dream-trap and we're slowly being squeezed to death in it. But why should I care? Every nightmare ends sooner or later."

"Get up," said Rodrigo.

"Humph, my dreams are bossy," said Scarlet, laughing humorlessly.

Rodrigo grabbed up a fistful of Scarlet's shirt and dragged the boy to his feet. "Remember when I told you about Talen, the one I met after going over those falls?"

Scarlet wagged his head carelessly. "Big ugly insane chap, right?"

"He thought this was his own personal dream," said Rodrigo. "And yet I was able to brain him in the head with a rock. Explain that."

Scarlet grew silent, puzzled. "Sorry, old boy, I'm really just tired."

"I said explain it!"

A lost look crept into Scarlet's eyes. "I know it's not a nightmare, Rodrigo," said Scarlet quietly. "I just wish it were."

Rodrigo pulled Scarlet close. "There are others that need strength from us, Scarlet. Think of Hope and the girls. We cannot falter, even for a second. This place is a razor, and it waits to cut us at the slightest mistake. We cannot make that mistake. And I cannot do this without you."

Scarlet smiled, his eyes showing a glimmer of his old self. "I hear you, friend. Just wish I knew what 'this' was that we are trying to do."

"Survive," said Rodrigo. "Grow. Make every place we set our feet better than when we arrived. Change everything that's wrong and defend everything that's right. Put fear into everything that seeks to harm us or the good people we protect."

"I say, that's ambitious." Scarlet smiled hopelessly. "I'm with you all the way, at least through the 'survive' part."

Rodrigo dusted Scarlet off and stepped back. "That's good enough for now, friend. You've lifted my spirits many times in the past. The old Scarlet needs to fight back and win out."

Scarlet turned grim. "I haven't been honest with you, Rodrigo. Remember when I was struck with fear? I laughed it off, to you. But there's a scar there. Something burned out of me. I'm afraid now, all of the time. Even over little things."

Rodrigo stood there, staring at his friend, unable to respond.

"I'm sorry," said Scarlet. "I couldn't let you know. Like you said, we needed to be strong. I thought I could overcome it. I can't."

"But you already did," rumbled Trace. "You walked in with us."

"I know, but..." Scarlet turned to the man-giant that strode up to face him.

"You do *not* know," said Trace, craning his face to within inches of Scarlet's. "Wounds heal slowly, but your wound *is* healing. Sometimes the pain of recovery is confused with the pain of the hurt."

156

Seconds ticked by. Scarlet said nothing. Trace said nothing. And Rodrigo stood by, uncertain how to react as his two friends stared at each other in immobile silence.

After a minute, Scarlet blinked. "That's good advice, Trace. I'll take it to heart."

"Good." Trace turned and walked to the staircase. Despite a stubborn pride showing on his face, the big man's feet shuffled with fatigue and his great shoulders slumped woefully. Clearly the fight had taken more out of him than he would admit.

"That was...strange," said Scarlet to Rodrigo.

He nodded. "Trace has a surprise or two."

37: DREAM

Yun's diary, Day 124

The night—the clock night—had gone by the time we got back to home. We slept and rested the day away, and Rodrigo told us all about what happened and what they saw. I would like to see that staircase, but I would never want to see those creatures. We decided to call them slivers, because that's what they shatter into when Trace is done with them. Rodrigo told us about Trace's courage and wisdom and his great fighting skill, and Rip said that he would write a song about it, because we all need to remember our heroes for the next fifty generations.

Trace is horribly embarrassed about the whole thing but he just smiles his big smile and doesn't say much.

Scarlet hasn't said much either since he came back, but he did do something strange. When we were alone, he hugged me so hard that he lifted me off the ground. He just whispered, "I've missed you, Yun."

Then he told me about his battle with the strange, unnatural fear, and how Rodrigo and Trace helped him so well that the fear went away. He couldn't explain it. He just makes jokes about Trace hypnotizing him and Rodrigo beating it out of him with the flat of his sword.

We closed up the secret entrance in Waterfall Cave. That leaves only the stairs in the Forge as a way out. I don't know what I will do if we reach another dead-end.

Rip leaned back from the embers of the cooking fire as Phoebe covered it over with sand to trap the heat. Watching her, he thanked the Luckies once again that they had rescued her from the cringer tunnels and the terrible stickmen within.

"Yer a bonnie, dear girl," said Rip. "I haven't an idea what I would have done without yeh, with all these lazy ettins about."

Phoebe glanced up at him and smirked. "Speaking of Scarlet..."

Rip laughed. "Ah-hey!"

"Will he be helping you fish tomorrow morning?"

"If I can wake the sluggy-headed nobbin in time."

Phoebe smiled again—a reserved, girlish stretch of her lips that caused her striking teal eyes to flash. Rip, who knew gemstones, could not imagine any precious stone that could compare with those eyes.

He complimented her often, first because she deserved it. No one worked as hard as she.

Second, to see those eyes...

Phoebe loosed the cloth band around her wavy brown curls, causing her bounteous mane of hair to fall nearly to her waist. She gathered it back together and made the band tighter. "Well, if 'Lord Scarlet' can't be dragged out of bed, I should be up and about if you need me."

Rip laughed again. He never tired of talking to Phoebe. His jokes always fell flat on Hope, who was too proud to be fun. Yun's tender soul sometimes took his teasing hard, so he had to be careful there. But the more he teased Phoebe, the more she teased back.

Phoebe shifted away from the fire, wiping sand from her legs, careful to maintain her modesty in the long dress. "I'm not recovered from yesterday. I think after I take care of the dishes-"

"*I'll* wrestle the dishes tonight, girl."

Phoebe gave a happy sigh and stood, straightening her dress. "Then I will wrestle with dreams."

Rip's eyes narrowed. "Yeh dream, do yeh?"

"Often."

———

The sheets of rain marched eastward, a veil of gray in the far valley. Phoebe kept to the deer trails when possible, but the sodden grass had thoroughly soaked her boots and woolen skirt, which slapped heavily against her shins with each step.

Phoebe barely noticed. The thundercloud could not drown out the late spring warmth, or the renewed birdsong. Fresh smells hung thickly in the damp of the woodlands and fields.

Home awaited over the next ridge. On most days Phoebe would take the much longer creek trail, never eager for her woodland forays to end. But today she needed to be home. An important purpose awaited her there.

So she turned and pushed up the gentle slope, becoming freshly drenched by the thick brush of the ridge. And as the ground grew more level under her, then began to slope away, and when her home could just be seen in the valley below, the evening sun found a way to pierce beneath the heavy clouds.

The valley blazed with color, made more brilliant by the overhanging thundercloud and its wall of rain beyond. Despite her urgency, Phoebe paused. She pushed back her long brown locks, turning now left, then right, then left again. Never had she seen the valley like this. Her eyes flashed from one delight to the next...

The river, risen high and eager to reach the sea. "My River," she called it, when she walked alone on its overgrown banks.

The great crescent of woodlands, brilliant green with new leaves.

The rich, rain-soaked fields, dark brown laced with the thin green lines of young corn.

The homestead, where her mother and her sisters and her brother awaited her.

Phoebe's sharp eyes caught sight of her baby brother and younger sister exiting the back of their log home on their way to the barn. As usual, her sister ran ahead, taunting her young brother to catch her. Her older sister scolded them from the foaling pen. Phoebe waved, knowing it was unlikely they would see her from this distance and with the sun at her back.

One last sweep with her eyes, then a laugh escaped her and she began breathing again.

She must return home.

A furious burst of wings erupted from the brush behind her. Phoebe spun.

But it was not the partridge that caught her attention. It was the sun.

The sun filled the horizon, immense, boiling, crimson red. Life drained from it. Phoebe stumbled back on one knee as the dying star sputtered to a deep flaming ember in a rapidly darkening sky. And before she could turn to face home, it gave a final flaming burst of agony and vanished.

Abject darkness fell upon her, and the way home became lost...

———

With a gasp Phoebe started awake, sitting up in her cot, straining at breath. Her eyes darted wildly, searching for something among her few belongings and the blanket-walls. Slowly she calmed, sighed, and recognized reality.

In her dream, she'd had sisters and a brother, and a mother. But in reality, she was lost and without her family.

But she didn't believe it was a dream. Not entirely. She felt again the sorrow of loss that had plagued her since waking, as if she had just returned from the family cemetery and the fresh graves there.

Or as if the others were walking away from hers.

She needed to find them, find a way to return, prove that she was safe, that they were safe, and life would go on quietly, peacefully.

She shook herself. Until that day, she would manage.

Their long trip to the Big Hole had upset their sleep schedule. Although by Ed's grandfather clock it was late at night, Phoebe had enough of sleeping. She prepared a bundle of clean clothes, slipped quietly out of her tent, and made her way to the lakeshore. The dream had drenched her in sweat, and she brought her damp clothes into the water with her to wash them. The warm water restored her senses, causing the vividness of the dream to fade and her senses to return to their normal sharpness.

She picked up two male voices talking nearby.

Her breath caught and she scanned the shore, stepping back into deeper water and clutching her clothes in front of her. The voices came from the left, near the stream bank. When only her head remained above water, she closed her eyes and listened intently.

At first she could not make out the words being said, but the persons speaking were obvious—the silly drawl of Rip and the smooth, inflected voice of Rodrigo. Slowly the words became clearer too.

"Not one to complain, mind, and Hallows knows that I have my own stash of precious loot, but these are weapons. Yeh could put a nice hole in a sliver, yeh could."

"How many firepoles did you see?"

"Ten to the least, mayhap more," said Rip.

"Was the chest locked?"

"More like a wall-hole. There was machinery and such—pipes and the like. The lid pops out; there's no place for a lock. The firepoles are just sitting with the pipes like that, hiding in plain sight, yeh might say."

"Ed is sleeping here tonight. And you are right, Rip, we need weapons."

Phoebe focused so intently on the words of the conversation that she missed the increasing clarity of it, and she realized suddenly that the two must be very close along the shore. Panicking, she took the only action that came to mind and submerged.

Utterly embarrassed, she remained under water until her lungs screamed, and, finally, she surfaced in a coughing sputter, preparing for the worst moment of her short memory.

But Rodrigo and Rip were gone.

Having escaped this fate, she washed and dressed hurriedly and went in search of Rodrigo. If he and Rip went to the Forge tonight, she would follow.

The golem Three fascinated her, and it would give her a chance to shadow someone without being discovered, which she delighted in and had succeeded at several times before.

She slipped back to her tent, grabbed up a pouch and her special lamp, and peered outside. Rodrigo and Rip were gathering things in their tents. She watched them slip quietly out, light their bullseye lanterns, and exit the cavern. She lit her own little lamp and hurried after them, entering the tunnel only after ensuring that Rodrigo was far enough ahead.

Her lamp was entirely enclosed except for a funnel shape, casting a spot of light at the floor but not shining revealing light elsewhere. Rodrigo and Rip talked as they strolled along, and so far she found little challenge in the pursuit.

Phoebe knew that in many ways she was the odd one out within the little Dustie society. Being quiet and not comfortable with long, aimless conversation, she spent most days being the listener. Phoebe rather enjoyed it. She worked hard, helping Rip with the cleaning and cooking and fishing and gathering of glowmoss, and the little man could carry a conversation all by himself through the entire day. When not working, she liked to explore alone or follow others and listen in on their conversations.

Unlike Yun and Hope, who seemed to talk incessantly about boys—about how Yun liked them and how Hope didn't—Phoebe was still a girl at heart, and more of a tomboy, happily willing to gut a fish while Yun crinkled her nose at the sight. When her time came to marry, she would marry, but until then she had things to do.

Her current quarry moved through Royalty Hall ahead of her, their light causing shadows to drift through the clutter of objects in the chamber. Their conversation had ceased, so Phoebe tried to move as quietly as possible as she rounded the huge marble obstacle that Scarlet had named the Overthrown Throne.

"Hahlay, missy," said a voice from above. It was said softly and didn't startle her too badly. She looked up to see Rip's grinning face peering down from atop the throne.

Phoebe smiled and gave a little shrug of resignation. "What was my mistake?"

"N'hardly much," said Rip, jumping down from the throne. "But I have human bobs," he said, pulling at one cat-like ear. "Not those wrinkly ettin ears like Rodrigo. I can hear your heartbeat at a hundred paces."

"Don't be silly. What could you hear?"

Rip grinned and pointed. "Yer feet. They slap on this smooth stone. Put down first the edge of yer foot, and that will keep the quiet. And now, did yeh intend just to chase us, or are yeh planning to be involved with Rodrigo and mehself in a bit of larceny?"

"What do you mean?" said Phoebe, playing the innocent.

"Oh, come now, yeh had to hear our whole plan, lying wait in the water like that."

Phoebe gasped and clutched at herself reflexively. "You saw me?"

Rip rolled his eyes. "Missy, the water is clear as a spring day, and there's moss aglow beneath yeh. We couldn't miss yeh!"

Phoebe didn't respond. She felt the blood drain from her face.

"Ah, missy, don't trouble yer mind with it. Yeh could have been a jellyfish, for all could be seen of yeh. Must have had yer clothes with yeh, washing them, I suppose? So stop yer fret, yeh should feel sorry for Rodrigo instead!"

"Why?" said Phoebe, feeling like she could pass out with embarrassment, but inwardly grateful that it was Rip who stood before her now, and not Rodrigo.

Rip laughed in that conspiratorial way that meant he was about to share a secret. "When he caught sight of yeh, I thought he'd been shot through the chest with a ballista. A ballista, mind yeh! 'I am terribly sorry!' he says, and he runs away, like he's just burned down the family barn!" Rip's face turned serious, which meant he wasn't done with the joke. "Now I'm all for honor, mind yeh, but if you was a human lass—not that you aren't a fine pretty ettin—I would've been tempted to steal yer clothes if yeh didn't have had them clutched with yeh in the water."

Without waiting for a response, Rip turned and strode away, saying over his shoulder, "Now let's catch up with that awkward young Rodrigo, shall we?"

38: A Meeting of Minds

They caught up with Rodrigo, who greeted Phoebe politely and welcomed her along. The three continued a running conversation through Scarlet Hall and along into the Forge. Although Phoebe prepared to be the listener, Rodrigo regularly drew her into the conversation—a conversation that eventually came around to sleep and dreams.

"I had a strange dream," offered Phoebe.

"Do tell it," said Rip. "My dreams are but glowmoss and tunnels."

Phoebe related her dream, providing only a short summary until Rodrigo began asking questions, and even more questions. His pace slowed as Phoebe fleshed in the full details of the dream.

"It sounds as though you remember the dream well," said Rodrigo.

"Yes, quite."

"In all the time that I have been here," said Rodrigo, "I do not remember a single dream having to do with anything other than this place—glowmoss and tunnels, like Rip said. And when I waken, I have difficulty remembering even those. I think everyone else has mentioned the same. So having a dream like yours is unusual."

"Well, I hope for more," said Phoebe. "At least, the part with the woods, and the farm, and my family."

"You think that is your real family?"

"I like to believe so," said Phoebe, "unless I discover otherwise."

"You are an articulate young lady, when you choose to speak," said Rodrigo.

"Thank you."

Rip rolled his eyes.

"You also work hard," said Rodrigo, "which is causing certain others to take advantage."

"I enjoy hard work."

"Yes, as should everyone, instead of shirking their responsibilities. I am referring to Ed making you wash his clothes."

"I wash Edward's clothes as a favor to everyone," said Phoebe. "I would rather the tunnels not reek of tar and sweat."

They approached the gaslight of the Forge. Phoebe doused her lantern.

"He's taking advantage of you," insisted Rodrigo.

"Ed wouldn't know where to find his pants unless someone pointed them out." Phoebe turned to face Rodrigo. "And if I didn't make him eat, he would starve to death."

"That's no excuse."

"Suit yourself. I, however, will continue to suit Ed, for all our sakes." She turned and walked on into the opening of the Forge.

As they watched her stride away, Rodrigo whispered to Rip, "Does she intend to give me trouble?"

"All yeh can handle, I should hope," said Rip, and he followed her.

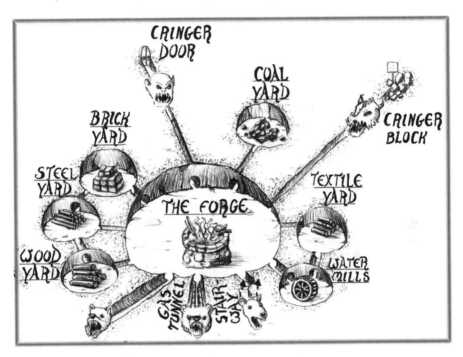

The conversation having been properly spoiled, Phoebe searched about for the golem Three, finding it in the Wood Yard. From what Phoebe could tell, Three labored to keep the Forge clean and operational but constructed nothing himself.

Careful to stay out of Three's way, she watched it work for a time before shouting, "Hello, Three! Do you talk, like the other golem below?"

Three ignored her, continuing its task diligently. Phoebe sat on a barrel and watched it, enjoying the manner in which it spun about and loped along, like a two-legged predator. The last beam dropped into place. Three straightened it, paused a moment, then spun on Phoebe and advanced directly to her.

Phoebe caught her breath, fearing that Three would become aggressive again. But it stopped in front of her and slowly settled into a position of rest, facing sideways, its head swiveled.

Flame came to life on Three's flank, forming:

[YES]

Phoebe gasped. "You can talk!"

[NAME THE GOLEM]

"I...I don't know its name."

[DESCRIBE THE GOLEM]

"Hmm...it hangs from the ceiling, and its head is quite large."

[SIX]

"Is that its name?"

[YES]

"Are there others?"

[?DOES SIX FUNCTION?]

"Well, yes. It's busy fighting slivers down below the waterfall."

Three levered itself up and loped off into the Forge. Phoebe watched it go, a bit nonplussed. It came to a sudden pause at the exit, and Phoebe saw Ed cross the opening, heading to the Steel Yard.

Phoebe cupped a hand to her mouth, hoping she had not been seen, and raced off to the connecting corridor between the yards.

She beat Ed by a few seconds, but his stride was both deliberate and hasty, and he reached Rodrigo and Rip just as she did. Rodrigo had a firepole in his hand, inspecting it. Ed had his own firepole.

"Put them back," said Ed, his ears red and his teeth clenched.

"Why are you keeping these secret, Ed?" said Rodrigo, his manner dangerously calm. "We could have used a few of these down below."

"They are mine, Rodrigo. I found them, I know how to use them. They're mine."

"You can't just keep something as important as this to yourself. There are ten firepoles here. We need to distribute them."

"Is that so?" said Ed. "I'd say you have a nice sword there. How about we distribute that?"

Rodrigo looked up to stare at Ed. "That is different."

"How so?"

Rodrigo did not have an immediate answer.

Ed pointed fingers. "First, you two are no better than thieves coming here to steal these. Second, we each have our things. You haven't taken Hope's medical supplies or Yun's books. Why come here to take my things?"

Rodrigo inspected one of the firepoles closely. "We need the weapons, Ed. It's different."

Ed was getting hotter, Rodrigo was getting colder, and Phoebe truly believed that the two would come to blows. Or worse.

"Edward, I-" said Phoebe.

"Ed," he corrected without looking at her. "Not Edward, just Ed. I've told you that before."

"I spoke to Three, Ed."

"What?" Ed turned on Phoebe.

"Yes, he said that the golem down below was named Six."

"Did he say where One and Two and the others are?"

"I didn't ask," said Phoebe.

"How did you get him to talk?"

"I simply asked, and waited for him to finish his chore."

"Phoebe, you're wonderful!" Ed turned back to Rodrigo. "And these are still mine."

Ed's former hostile mood had snapped, as if he had been robbed of twenty coins only to be handed a hundred by another. He was actually smiling.

Not Rodrigo, who said quietly but grimly, "We need them, Ed. At least some of them." It became Rodrigo's turn to show a flash of anger. "And more, you will do your own laundry from now on. Phoebe is not your wash-maid, and you will stop treating her as such."

Ed strode to Rodrigo and took the firepole out of the boy's hand. "I said you can't have them. But I will sell three of them. Phoebe?"

"Yes?"

"I will trade you this firepole for ninety days of laundry. And, I owe you one other for getting Three to chat. Are we square?"

Phoebe glanced at Rodrigo. Rodrigo still burned, but his mouth quirked up and he gave her a small shrug.

"Square!" said Phoebe, eagerly accepting the two firepoles.

Ed took hold of two other firepoles. "And I will give Hope a down payment on my next life-saving ministration from her. Also, Yun can give me a few months of helping me organize my notes. That's four of the ten. I don't want to sell more, and I wouldn't sell to thieves in any event." He stared at Rodrigo.

Rodrigo had his eyes down, and his voice sounded dangerously calm. "That is acceptable, Ed. I will note, however, that I have been in five life-and-death confrontations since I awoke here. I survived each because Scarlet fought at my side, and Rip, and Trace, and even Yun. But not you." His eyes came up, hardened and uncompromising. "But now that you have weapons, and want them for yourself, you will be at my side the next time we risk death."

Ed blinked. "Agreed. Now, if this preposterous melodrama is concluded, I have a host of critical accomplishments to accomplish."

Rodrigo and Rip walked away, followed by Phoebe, who triumphantly carried the bundle of four firepoles over her shoulder.

Yun's diary, Day 125

Rodrigo announced a need to set times of bathing privacy for parts of the lakeshore. I happened to look over at Phoebe and she was beet red. Something must have happened. I wonder if Rip also stole her clothes.

Rodrigo asked me if I would start writing a copy of Ravenhair. He is afraid we might lose it. He doesn't know how I treat books.

Scarlet danced with me tonight, just like he did the first time. It was very, very nice.

39 : PREPARATION

Yun's diary, Day 127

> Hope told Rodrigo that we are working too hard. We're getting tired and
> crabby. He agreed.

Scarlet sat with Hope and Rodrigo on the lakeside sandbar, watching Yun and Phoebe fly through the obstacle course set up along the dry, softer sand. The two leapt from boulder to crate, cat-walked along narrow bridges and experimented with leaps and vaults in the sand over various obstacles, throwing off all pretense of approaching adulthood, laughing and sharing giggles like schoolchildren.

Rodrigo continued to insist on exercise, not that anyone failed to get their fill in the course of a day. Phoebe and Yun discovered a shared agility and tried to outdo each other, although not in any serious competitive sense.

Yun demonstrated an impressive precision and balance, able to hop on one toe across a plank bridge only a few inches wide. Phoebe had the flexibility and presence of an acrobat, modestly securing her skirt before pulling off fancy handstands and effortless flips. When not acting the part of a flying squirrel, the deft girl would toss a spoon out to her foot and catch it in the cup of her arch, then flip it back to balance on two fingers. Rip became so impressed by this that he demanded that she keep going, toss after toss, until she dropped it on the nineteenth straight attempt. After hours trying, he himself managed to catch it only twice.

"That is the oddest quirk of a trick," he said, watching Phoebe succeed again. "Can yeh do it with the other foot?"

Phoebe, who stood perched on her right leg with her left foot cupping the spoon, tilted her head a bit, pursed her lips, and considered. Then she flipped the spoon up, switched legs in a flash, and caught the spoon with her right foot. It hung there edgewise, barely held, but it didn't drop. An excited smile came to her face.

"Bawley for yeh!" yelled Rip, shaking his head. "However did yeh learn it?"

"I don't know," said Phoebe. "It just seems...natural."

The antics of Rip and the two girls helped Scarlet, who was trying to pull both Rodrigo and Hope out of a moody funk that had settled over them the past few days. Scarlet saw it at times in the others—a frustrated despair at their trapped state, the loss of memory, the litany of surrounding enemies, and the lack of sky and sun. Scarlet learned that it helped Rodrigo to talk, and it helped Hope to hear others talk.

"The stairs are bound to lead somewhere important," said Scarlet. "And I don't agree that they are our final option. The Bronze Wall is an obvious doorway. We just haven't been clever enough to coax it open yet. And there's that other bronze barrier down in the Big Hole—the one with the maze on its surface, not the one with the bashing monster behind it, mind you..."

"I felt certain that Waterfall's secret passage would lead out," said Rodrigo. "It had so many protections on it. There must be *something* down there valuable enough for all that security."

"Like Scarlet said, we do have at least two possible exits out of the Big Hole," said Hope without particular passion. "Not that we would likely get past the slivers."

"So why are the slivers so diligently working to get in?" said Rodrigo, rubbing at his temple.

Scarlet laughed. "You presented your philosophy of life passionately to me down in the Big Hole, friend, and it helped. I'm freed in full from that fear. Now let me give you a different take. Do what needs doing, when you can do it, and don't fret about it until then. The Big Hole can wait. That golem Six has matters in hand for now."

Rodrigo smiled grimly. "I hear you, Scarlet. It is hard not to fret. We have not made much progress."

"Progress?" Scarlet laughed. "On what do we base progress? I consider us still afoot and breathing as a feat of stellar accomplishment! The rescue of Phoebe alone would fill a bard's repertoire. You're harsh on yourself. Learn to lie back and bask in your own greatness now and again."

"Life's an adventure, is that it?" said Hope. "You sound like Rip."

"Rip sounds like me," corrected Scarlet.

"*You* sound like you have little care in even getting home," said Hope.

Scarlet shrugged and threw up his hands. "What's home? It's one thing to lose your memory around people who have not forgotten. But here? Far as I can tell, we've all suffered a complete cut to the quick. This place became home five minutes after I arrived, by necessity." He shook his head and stabbed a finger at the mottled stone of the cavern roof. "For all I know, I was born in a cottage somewhere up there, but for now, this is my home and you're my family."

Hope considered that a moment before nodding and lifting her brows. "I confess I hadn't thought of it that way."

Rodrigo smiled—causing Scarlet to breathe an inward sigh of relief—and playfully flicked sand at Hope's feet. "So what is *your* philosophy of life?"

"I'm a healer," said Hope. "I'm much too busy for a philosophy of life."

"So busy that you invade dreams," said Scarlet. "I never properly thanked you for that, by the way."

"For the dream?" said Hope.

"Yes. If you hadn't pointed out the bitter bulb as the poison cure, I would have been done in."

Hope's gaze sank down to her feet. "Yes, about that. Quite honestly, I haven't the slightest idea what bitter bulb is as a medicine, or what a fleye is. My apologies, but I was embarrassed to tell you before this."

Rodrigo sat up. "Are you sure? You've never heard of them?"

"Positive," said Hope.

Scarlet chewed at his lip, surprised. "Do you remember being in my dream?"

Hope shook her head slowly. "I'm sorry, no, not at all."

Scarlet reclined back in the sand, his mind replaying Hope in his dream. "Dash it, then how could I have dreamed you so clearly?"

———

———

Yun's diary, Day 130

Rodrigo and Scarlet have gotten over their bruises from the sliver fight and it's time to explore again. We are packing for a journey up the stairs. Everyone is going.

Rodrigo wondered where his Shadow—the fear-eating thing in the dark—was hiding. No one has seen it (felt it, actually) for a long time now. Then he said he hoped that it didn't follow us.

Why did he have to say that?

———

It looked like the progression of a thousand-mile pilgrimage—eight Dusties burdened with packs and pouches, their hopes elevated by the belief that the stairs would indeed lead to a way out.

As they approached the stairway that led to the jaws, Three loped to the entrance and settled himself down directly in front of it. The Dusties tilted their heads and scratched their noses, perplexed. Letters of flame appeared on Three's flank:

[TAKE NOTHING]

Ed, who had not been able to evoke a single letter out of Three since his deal with Phoebe, uttered a snort of outrage. "Confounded machine talks only when it demands something, apparently."

Phoebe wandered up to it. "Do you mean our packs, Three?"

[PACKS BELONGINGS WEAPONS]

The Dusties looked around helplessly at each other.

"Next he'll be wanting our boots and trousers," said Rip.

[KEEP CLOTHING]

"Why, I wonder?" said Scarlet. "Phoebe, ask him why?"

Before Phoebe could ask:

[FORGE SECRET SAY NOTHING]

"Say nothing to whom?" asked Scarlet.

[THOSE ABOVE]

Ed's teeth clenched. "He's known all along that there are people at the end of this stairway, and he's kept it a secret."

"Three, who built this place?" asked Yun.

[——]

"Why did they build it?"

[——]

"When did they build you?"

[——]

"Three, have you seen those above?" asked Scarlet.

[NO]

"Who told you about them?"

[——]

"How long ago were you told about those above?"

[21195102Kc]

"What is a Kc?"

[KILOCYCLE]

"How long is a kilocycle?"

[1000C]

Scarlet looked around at the others. "Any suggestions?"

Ed stepped up. "Three, you need to explain kilocycle to us, so that we communicate properly." He held up his hand. "When I drop my hand, wait one kilocycle, then signal with the word kilocycle."

"Wait," said Scarlet. "How do you know one of these kilocycles is not, say, a thousand years? You'll be counting a long time."

Ed slowly turned to face Scarlet, as if confronting a loose-mouthed, drunken lout. "How's your math, boy? Twenty-one *million* kilocycles old. Looking at the minimal wear and tear on the machinery here, the age of this place is less than a century. One hundred years times three hundred sixty-five days times sixty minutes-"

Scarlet conceded with a surrendering wave. "By all means, continue."

Ed turned back to Three. "Ready?" He dropped his hand, and began humming to himself, wagging one finger back and forth.

The time passed in silence, until:

[KILOCYCLE]

"Almost exactly ninety seconds," said Ed.

"Yes!" said Scarlet. "What was it, 21159102Kc?"

"Ninety-five," corrected Yun.

"That's what?" said Scarlet, trying to work the math in his head.

"Almost sixty years," said Ed.

"A lot could change in sixty years," said Hope.

"Exactly," said Scarlet. "Three, are the people above us our enemies?"

[———]

"Cheeky way of keeping time, Ed," said Rip. "Engineer's trick?"

"Piano lessons," said Ed.

"Yeh play, do yeh?"

"Not particularly. Haven't the ears to hear it well enough. But I remembered how to count off seconds."

[LEAVE BELONGINGS]

Rodrigo stepped forward. "Three, I give my word to leave our belongings and not to mention anything about this place or our time here. Is that satisfactory?"

Three levered himself up, spun, and loped off.

"Satisfactory, apparently," said Hope.

"This changes the plan," announced Rodrigo. "I know everyone here is eager to find a larger society, but we will need to take this more cautiously. We will explore the stairway together, but once we find indications of people, only a few should meet them."

"Suits me," said Ed. "I never wanted to leave our cozy domicile in the first place. I'll be with Three if you need me."

Rodrigo ignored Ed as he marched off. "Scarlet, you are a natural fit. If there is trouble, try to talk your way out, not fight."

"I will go," said Hope.

"I am sorry, Hope, but you should not," said Rodrigo.

Hope stiffened and her face reddened. "And why not?"

"Healers are always coveted. If this place finds out you are a doctor, they may never let you leave. That would be a disaster."

"Fair enough," said Hope.

"I go," said Trace.

"That would be good," said Rodrigo. "Ears open, mouth shut, show the muscle."

Trace smiled. "Easy for me."

"That's three," said Scarlet. "That enough?"

Rodrigo shook his head. "Three people would be good, Scarlet, but I am not going. I doubt that this passage leads to Drift, but it would hurt the cause if I am thrown over a waterfall again. Phoebe?"

"Yes?"

"Would you go?"

"Is this simply a way to keep me from Ed's laundry?"

Rodrigo laughed. "No, but that wit of yours is exactly why you should go."

Phoebe smiled demurely. Rodrigo glanced at Scarlet. Scarlet exchanged a dubious shrug with Trace.

"I'm game," said Phoebe, offering a challenging smile over her shoulder at Scarlet, "and Trace can decide which of us proves to be the better scout."

Scarlet raised his brows in delighted shock. "I say, are you making this a competition? Did you hear that, Rodrigo?"

Rodrigo looked to each of them. "Win or lose, stay alive."

40: The Way Out

"Not the gate to Paradise that I expected," said Scarlet.

Everyone except Ed made the journey up the stairway, escorting Scarlet, Trace, and Phoebe. The stairway turned to pathway, twisting along as a meandering, crude trail cut through natural fissures and tunnels, dark except where glowmoss accompanied an occasional cascade of water.

They took belongings, intending to bring them back to the Forge after seeing off the three volunteers. But the trail continued, and they ended up fatigued after more than three miles of gradual climb.

The tunnel ended at a small, thick metal door with iron crossbars. After Scarlet soaked the hinges with oil, they opened it up.

It opened into empty air.

Outside the door, from left to right, ran a strange wedge-shaped passage of pumice-like stone, the floor flat and the walls rising up to meet at a peak thirty feet above. But their hatch did not open at the passageway's floor. Instead, it was set near the top of the wedge, making for a thirty-foot drop to the floor below.

They heard no sound and saw no light, no people, no city. But below them, their lamplight revealed a burned-out torch and a broken weapon.

The drop posed no difficulty, for an old metal-rung rope ladder lay rolled up next to the door.

"Actually, it does make sense," said Scarlet. "This was meant to be a very secret entrance, and had to be undisturbed for at least sixty years. Obviously they couldn't build a frilly gate that opened out onto the city. Even the door is camouflaged to look like stone."

"Strange how the rock goes from the normal stone to this strange pumice lining the walls out here," said Rodrigo, brushing his hand along the walls outside the hatch. "I would-"

Rodrigo stopped mid-sentence as a band of reddish light burst into life along the passageway's walls and shot past from right to left, causing the pumice-stone to smoke and spark. A terrible shriek, like the wail of a stricken cat, clawed at their ears. Rodrigo and Scarlet fell back away from the hatch at the shock of the event.

"Shrikes!" gasped Scarlet. "That's like the Big Hole, except angrier."

"And louder," said Trace.

Rodrigo leaned back out the hatch, contemplating something silently as he tapped his fingers on the hatch frame. "Your call, Scarlet. This is not what we expected, but judging by that torch and weapon, there might be people nearby."

Scarlet looked at Trace. "Let's give it a go. At least scout around a bit. That sounded alarming, but it didn't harm us."

"We do need to change the plan," said Rodrigo. "You cannot return without the ladder down, and we cannot leave it down. One of us will need to stay here and observe. This is a good vantage point for remaining secret."

Rip and Phoebe readied the ladder. Scarlet prepared to go, but caught himself. "I say, we won't have light..."

Rodrigo rubbed his chin and sighed in frustration. "Not our best day for planning. Take a torch, look around, come back before it dies, and we will all head back and rethink this."

Scarlet took a torch and descended. Trace and Phoebe followed. They immediately found more signs of habitation—a filthy old rag, some splinters of wood, and a scattering of bones that looked suspiciously human. Farther on, two human forms appeared—statues of an old woman and a young man.

Phoebe gingerly touched both. Nothing happened. "Just like all those others in our home that we can't wake up. The ones that feel like they're vibrating."

She stepped back and her foot kicked a pile of stones on the ground. Several small black things scuttled out from under it.

Scarlet bent low with his torch. "Sliver essence!" he cried. The three backed away from the stones and peered into the cracks and corners. There were others.

"The place is infested," said Phoebe.

"These aren't a danger," said Scarlet. "But it likely means bigger ones are about."

They turned to retreat and saw the glow of torchlight far down the tunnel behind them. Voices drifted in, muted by the pumice walls.

"This cuts it!" whispered Scarlet.

"This is perfect," said Trace. "Kill your torch and throw it away."

Scarlet gave Phoebe a reassuring nod and killed the torch. "Ready or not, the stage is set. Play dumb."

Lanterns appeared, heralding the arrival of four men in cloth armor, and one in boiled leather armor. The group stopped when the light revealed Trace.

The man in leather stepped forward—a tall, lean, dark-eyed soldier with a severely broken nose. Tattoos littered his pale skin, including a black rook chess piece on his right cheek.

"Who are you?" he demanded.

"I don't know," said Scarlet. "Except—my name is Scarlet."

"Who woke you? Have you been marked?"

"Marked?"

"No one woke you? Are you from Drift?" asked the man.

"Drift, what's that? Where are we?"

The dark-eyed man gave Scarlet a dubious grimace. "I'm Captain Grager, of the Rook Clan. If you haven't been marked yet, then you gain our mark. Who are these others?"

"Trace, and—what was your name, miss?"

"Phoebe."

"Did you wake them?" said Grager to Scarlet.

"I'm—what is this place? I can't…" rambled Scarlet, trying his best to act the fresh Dustie.

Grager appeared to lose interest, seeing the two statues. He glanced over them both, and waved two of his men forward. "Keep him from flailing, we don't want him accidentally waking the old woman."

Two of the soldiers prepared to catch the young male statue. Grager reached out and touched the stone. There came a snap like static electricity, an inward rush of wind, and an instant flash of heavy condensation in the air. A blanket of frozen fog rolled over Scarlet's feet.

The three Dusties glanced secretively at each other, surprised at the result.

The young man, now fully flesh, fell struggling into the arms of the soldiers, babbling incoherently.

Phoebe found one of the soldiers next to her. "Hold still," he said, clasping her shoulder. She tried to remain calm. He brought his finger to her cheek and drew something on it with a thick, black paint. Another soldier worked on Trace, who turned to reveal a rough outline of a rook piece on his own cheek.

"That's a foursome, Cap'n," said one of the soldiers. The soldier broke into an elated grin, and his fellows shared his high mood.

Captain Grager didn't. His narrowed eyes kept flicking to Scarlet. "Let's hightail it. Keep the noise down, we don't want to attract anything that wants to kill us, got it?"

"Mum. Got it," said Scarlet.

"Stuff that kid," said Grager to his fellows. They shoved a cloth in the babbling young man's mouth and anchored it with a strip of tarred canvas.

"All right, let's move." Grager set out at a steady pace, but with caution.

The soldiers all carried spears or crossbows and they kept the weapons at the ready. The pumice tunnel occasionally opened out into natural caverns often split by side tunnels and deep fissures lit by glowmoss-lined cascades of water. Once, they heard the familiar cat-wail in the distance and saw reflected light, but they continued on. Several other patrols of soldiers either passed by or joined their group on the way home, congratulating the Rooks on their daily catch.

To Scarlet's surprise, and relief, they always took the straight path of the pumice tunnel. As far as he could tell, it ran perfectly straight and level, and the soldiers did not deviate until they left the pumice for a wide, well-traveled path that descended sharply and widened out. That path opened into a taller and taller crack until...

The three Dusties stood under the open sky. The familiar ghostly blue tendrils that they had seen from the windows of Skyhall once again drifted in the starless blackness above, and before them a city stretched out over a terrace that sloped up along the great cliff. On the left, the "up" cliff rose to the sky, a thousand feet or more. On the right, the "down" cliff dropped into the dark mists below.

The size of the city surprised Scarlet—at least three miles long and a mile wide. Beyond the high stone walls and fortifications, the buildings rose on the steady slope so that much of the city could be seen from the ledge on which they stood. Bands of smoke and haze drifted with the sluggish breeze. Glowmoss grew everywhere, lighting the sizable expanse with the aid of many lanterns. The city could easily hold tens of thousands, plus large stretches of what seemed like farmland, with neat rows of glowmoss lined out like vineyards.

Captain Grager turned to them, his smile enigmatic. "Welcome to Haven."

PART II:

HAVEN

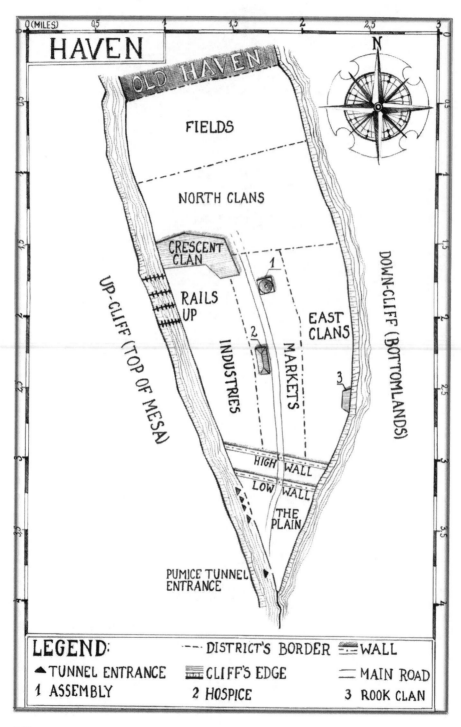

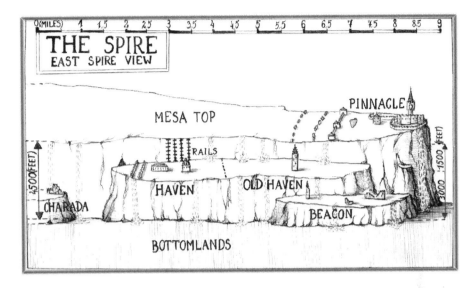

For a time, Phoebe would not move, even with the gentle push of one of the Havenite soldiers. She stared at the sky, and the dark expanse all around them, and her heart leapt.

She loved their tunnel home below—the comforting loneliness, the quiet, and the many interesting places to explore.

But here was sky, and the promise of horizons…once the sun rose.

Grager kept his eye on her as the others strode toward the gate. "Let's move it."

As she leveled her gaze, their eyes met. Alarm spiked in her, for she saw something there—a desire, or familiarity, that put her on edge.

Was he looking at her in *that* way?

He turned away, falling in step behind Scarlet and Trace. Suspicious of him, Phoebe caught up to Scarlet and matched his pace.

The three Dusties passed through the gates of Haven, beneath the low, thick bulk of the outer wall and the tall skirt of the inner wall. The entry turned into a narrow street, bounded by stone structures of impressive quality.

Despite the dark sky, the city contained sufficient light, both from fire and from widespread and carefully cultivated glowmoss. The cliffs above the city ran with ribbons of luminous growth fed by the many small waterfalls that cascaded into the city.

"Trader's town." Scarlet spoke quietly, bending toward Phoebe's ear. He looked nervous behind his smile.

"How so?" she asked.

"The people here, they're all different skins and heights and shapes."

Phoebe looked about and saw the thorough mixture of races. However, nearly all shared similarities, including clothing made of supple woven fabric that rustled lightly when the wearer moved, and a mark or tattoo on the right cheek. Phoebe saw no other Rooks, but there were at least two dozen others—Lion, Ram, Moon, Frog, Lightning Bolt, and so on.

"Chickens!" Phoebe gasped and pointed. In an open side street, the Dusties saw a market, and the nearest stall contained a line of woven cages filled with an assortment of fowl—chickens, bantams and game hens, ducks, geese, pheasants and doves.

"Welcome to civilization," whispered Scarlet.

The soldiers stopped at the wide door of a hospice. It opened, and a stout woman greeted the soldiers. She took the disoriented young man from them and disappeared inside. Grager spoke discreetly to his men and they moved on, leaving the tall captain alone with the three Dusties.

"Come with me." He led them through the curving streets. They turned toward the down-cliff along the outer edge of the city, traveled along a small stream, and twisted through city avenues until they passed beneath a stone arch with the sign of the Rook. In the courtyard beyond, a row of barracks, smithies, warehouses, and an assembly hall lined the edge of the cliff on which Haven nested. Rooks moved about the courtyard and labored in the buildings, but no one yet took notice of them.

"This way," said Grager. Instead of leading them to the buildings, he worked along the edge of the wall on a small path. The path wound through jumbles of large boulders before finally opening out onto a rocky flat bounded by a waist-high stone wall.

Scarlet approached the wall and leaned over it. Below him, the glowmoss-ribboned cliff continued down into darkness and mist. Nothing else could be seen, so that Scarlet felt like he floated over a boundless void.

"This is a long-familiar view, one that reminds us of the cage that we live in. That's why so few come here to look over," said Grager. "We call it Desolation Point, or just Desolation."

"Cheery," said Scarlet.

"Reality." Grager gave each of the newcomers an appraising gaze. "You did not awaken in the tunnels, not recently at least. Are you from Drift?"

Trace turned to look over the cliff wall. Scarlet cleared his throat, but Phoebe ended up answering.

184

"We cannot tell you. Not because we are enemies, but because of a promise we made. We did awaken here, but not where you found us."

Grager smiled, though no mirth could be found in it. "I have little worry that you are enemies. Humans have quite enough enemies, everywhere." He pointed down into the mist-filled darkness over the cliff. "They swarm down in the Bottomlands." His finger turned to the cliff rising to the sky. "And none of the tunnels are safe from the blackspawn. But that is only a few of our enemies, seen—or unseen."

Grager paused, peering along the cliff and outward. "It is unwise to be alone in isolated places, like this."

For a moment, Grager lapsed into silence. Then he shook himself, as if he remembered something terribly important. "Are you familiar with Haven?"

"Not at all," said Phoebe.

"I assume that you know of Pinnacle?"

"No, sir."

"The tantyrs?"

Phoebe shook her head.

Grager scratched his tattooed cheek in what appeared to be satisfaction, but Phoebe caught a glimpse of triumph in his dark eyes. "Well then, it seems you are little better than Sleepers after all."

And a slow, deliberate smile replaced the permanent scowl on Captain Grager's lips.

Just as suddenly, the scowl returned. "Let me tell you about your new home...big man, are you listening?"

Trace turned back from the wall where he had been standing and gazing down. "Oh...yes, Mister Captain."

"Listen carefully. You are on a large mesa called the Spire. Our city sits on a ledge on the side of the cliffs. Pinnacle is the city up on top of the mesa, ruled by four monarchs. Officially, they rule the Spire. Unofficially, they've gone insane. In fact, we rarely hear from them, except through creatures called *tantyrs*. The tantyrs are angels—some would say—and are the only allies of the humans here. They share authority with the monarchs of Pinnacle. There is one specific tantyr representative here in Haven named Berylata. Are you getting this?"

Scarlet closed his eyes and put a hand up, thrusting a new finger in the air at every point. "Spire, Pinnacle, crazy kings, angels called tantyrs led by...by a tantyr with a rather odd name..."

"Berylata," corrected Grager. "You aren't mocking me with your tone, are you, boy? We can converse just as easily with you in chains."

Scarlet hesitated, then bowed, and went silent.

Grager continued to speak quickly and his voice seemed to hush lower with each sentence. "You know of the blackspawn?"

Phoebe raised a brow. "The creatures made of tiny crawling things rather than flesh and blood? We called them slivers."

"Yes," said Grager. "We have been at war with the blackspawn for decades. They attack us from the tunnels, making it more difficult for us to awaken the Sleepers from stone. And in recent times, the blackspawn have assaulted Pinnacle itself."

Grager glanced toward the rising up-cliff. "Pinnacle now gathers recruits from us, promising both treasure and comforts to those who fight the blackspawn at Pinnacle. With our battle losses, the heavy drain of manpower to Pinnacle, and our lack of Sleepers, our city dwindles each year."

"Are the tunnels enemy territory?" said Phoebe. "You seem to have passed back and forth through them safely enough."

"The attacks have died down considerably in the past few months," said Grager, "but we are under no illusion that it will last. We are scrambling to find as many new Sleepers as possible in this lull."

Phoebe nodded. "Captain, you must have many duties to attend to. We appreciate your attention, but why are you spending this time with us?"

Grager looked Phoebe in the eyes for a moment, chewing on his lower lip. Phoebe's nagging sense of alarm returned at the far-too-familiar manner in which he stared at her.

He suddenly straightened, closing himself off. "I have my own secrets. You're no Sleepers, which makes you strangers. Now that I have explained Haven's predicament to you, is there anything that you wish to tell me?"

Scarlet and Phoebe glanced at each other.

"You have us at a loss, sir," said Phoebe. "We have nothing and know of nothing that would bring relief to Haven's situation. We are sorry."

Grager nodded, but he returned to staring at Phoebe, as if he were looking for answers beyond her words. Phoebe found it difficult to maintain her poise, looking into those intense, dark, firelit eyes. She blinked and lowered her gaze.

He led them back on the path. They turned into the courtyard and met up with a young man who had shocking blond hair and a seemingly permanent blush on his nose and cheeks. Grager introduced him as his aide, Kane.

"Get them properly quartered and marked, Mr. Kane, and see to their orientation. I want them at the assembly tonight."

"The assembly, sir? All three?"

"Yes," said Grager.

Kane scratched at his pale tufts of hair. "Will Scarlet and Trace be voting?"

"Yes, Mr. Kane, see to your orders."

Grager turned and strode to the manor house.

Kane faced the Dusties and grinned. "Well, you rate. A voting Rook on your first day—I'll wager that's never been done before. Word's gotten 'round about you already. You were awake when found. From another city?"

The young man met Phoebe's gaze and his voice trailed off momentarily. His eyes flicked over her and he offered his hand, smiling nervously. "Grager's war-boys weren't lying about you."

She smiled pleasantly, shaking his hand. "It is a pleasure to meet you, Mr. Kane. As for our history, your Captain Grager has our answer to that. In reality, we are no different than Sleepers. Assume we know nothing."

"Suit yourself," said Kane. "Expect people to pry harder than I do. Let me give you the speech...By Haven law, having been found and awakened by us, you are legally a member of the Rook Clan. Phoebe, as a woman you are only temporarily Rook. When you take a husband—and you are expected to do so— you will join his clan."

"I am hardly of marriageable age, Mr. Kane."

"In Haven you are," he said. "Also, there are more women than men. Some men—more than some, actually—take two wives, though, it's frowned upon. Are you promised to either of these two?"

"I've promised her nothing as yet," said Scarlet, "though she has been persistent."

Phoebe smiled demurely, but she flashed ice at Scarlet. He gave her a wink.

"Well, no matter, with eyes like those, you'll have little trouble attracting suitors." Kane smiled admiringly.

Scarlet coughed and ducked his head between the two. "If I am to understand, your clan is readily offering us citizenship? No strings attached?"

Kane shrugged. "This is Haven. No kings here. But let me finish. Wear your clan mark on your right cheek. Some men eventually get a tattoo. Otherwise, learn to make the mark.

"Clan members pay taxes to their clan, and the clans pay taxes to the governing clan. The clan that most successfully gathers Sleepers each year becomes the governing clan for the next year. Builds motivation to do sweeps for Sleepers, you see.

"There's more than enough work to be done, and you are expected to take up an occupation. The whole city is striving just to stay alive, so shirkers and deadweights have a rough time of it."

They approached the barracks, but before they entered, Kane turned to the Dusties. "If you want to impress others here, skill with spear or crossbow is key. They are the most effective weapons against the blackspawn."

Scarlet raised his brows. "Excellent! Trace is skilled with the spear, and I believe the crossbow might suit me. Phoebe will bear fifteen sons, so her fame is assured."

Kane grinned hesitantly. "He's joking?"

"It's best not to take Scarlet too seriously," said Phoebe. "Could you excuse us one moment?"

Kane grinned again, nodded, and disappeared into the barracks.

Phoebe edged to the side of the building. Scarlet and Trace followed.

"What do we do?" said Trace.

Scarlet laughed. "Do? We landed in silk, my friend. These are decent folk. I can poke my nose into dark corners over the next week to make sure there are no nasty surprises, then we find a way to go get the others."

Phoebe considered their choices, realizing that there were few. She had to admit that they were being treated more like neighbors than strangers. The worst fears were all past—being sold into slavery, or abused cruelly, or even killed on sight.

"Then that's our plan," agreed Phoebe.

"Sure," added Trace.

Scarlet raised a hand. "Oh, but one more thing, Phoebe. To keep you off the wedding block, be sweet on me. I suggest a kiss or two when we meet the clan."

"Perhaps I should be sweet on Trace instead," suggested Phoebe.

"I don't know how to kiss," mumbled Trace.

"Ah, that's settled then." Scarlet gestured to the door. "Shall we?"

42: PETRA

The Dusties settled into their quarters, Trace and Scarlet in the barracks proper and Phoebe in the maiden's quarters. The Rook Clan slept, and, despite the excitement of the day and Phoebe's many thoughts, she fell asleep as well.

She dreamt of a barn filled with beautiful horses. Light filtered through the arched roof, warming her in a soft caress. She smiled and breathed in the smell of fresh sawdust.

She heard a creak and turned her head to the barn door, but she could not see it. Blocking her view was a man, sitting close by in a chair, his back mostly to her.

He spun, revealing a pale, angular face and midnight-dark eyes that pierced her—eyes and a face much like Captain Grager's.

The pale man opened his mouth to speak but then he flickered away as if a ghost, revealing the half-open barn door in which the silhouettes of three children stood...

The dream faded, the barn melting away, replaced with gray-black stone as she awoke. Phoebe lay on a rough cot in a small room illuminated with glowpots, her heart racing from the images of the dream.

Rough-woven blankets hung over the entryway. They parted slowly and a lamp appeared.

"Oh! My pardons," said a wide-eyed girl who stepped close to the bed, the lamp in one hand and a bundle of cloth in the other. Black, slightly wavy hair framed the girl's wide, high-cheeked face and large coal-black eyes, then fell over an equally dark blouse. Her gray skirt and long socks met at the knees. Phoebe felt an aura of quiet, accepting despair burdening the girl's thin shoulders.

"Did I wake you, m'lady?" asked the girl.

Phoebe rose to an elbow and pulled back an unruly lock of hair. "Not at all. My name is Phoebe. Who are you?"

"Petra," said the girl, glancing shyly at Phoebe from the corner of her eyes. The lamplight created a golden sheen on the girl's tan skin, amplifying the angles of her straight nose and brows. Like Phoebe, there remained a child's roundness to her cheeks, but it was clear that she would be complete with bold angles when she reached adulthood.

"It is good to meet you, Petra. And how old are you?"

"My years are eleven, m'lady. At least, that's what they say."

"And they say I am fifteen, which means I'm just a girl too. So no more m'lady, only Phoebe. It seems someone has taken my garments and my shoes, and the floor looks icy cold. Can you help me?"

Petra broke into a sheepish smile. "Yes, m'—Phoebe." The girl laid a rough-woven dress and two woven slippers on the bed, apparently intended for Phoebe. "I washed your clothes. They are drying now. The slippers are very comfortable. I hope they fit."

Phoebe tried on the slippers and the dress. Although it rustled when she moved, and fit only loosely, the fabric felt smooth against her skin, almost like silk. The slippers fit well and warmed her feet nicely.

"What fabric is this?" asked Phoebe.

"It's wist. Everything is made from it. Most clothing, at least. Wool and leather are too rare and expensive."

"You have a pretty outfit, Petra."

"It's the clothes I woke with. I'm new, like you. You can tell the new ones because they still have their old clothes to wear, for a time."

Phoebe opened the shutters of the small window. The sky had not changed. The blue tendrils floated above in a midnight expanse.

"It's not morning yet," said Phoebe. "What time is it?"

"Beyond seven," said the girl. "You are waiting for a sunrise, aren't you?"

"Yes, of course."

"There is no sunrise."

Phoebe looked at the girl, puzzled. "What do you mean?"

"There is no sun."

Phoebe looked at the sky again. "But how can that be? There *must* be a sun."

"Not here," said Petra, shaking her head morosely. "There was a sun where I came from. But not here."

Phoebe's heart chilled, and she felt a sudden sensation of being terribly lost. She realized that Petra looked the same way, and her heart went out to the girl. "How long have you been here?"

"Twenty days. I was the first of my friends."

"Who are the others?"

"Ana and Ardi. Ardi's a boy. Grager found them about six days ago."

"I would very much like to meet them. Do you live here too?"

"Yes, in the orphan's quarters."

"Bring them by later, and perhaps you can show me the city."

Petra broke into a delighted smile and took Phoebe's hand. "Thank you, m'lady!"

"For what do you thank me?"

"For talking to me," mumbled Petra, turning sheepish again. "I must make my rounds."

As the girl withdrew, Phoebe's mind replayed the dreams of her two sisters and brother racing to the barn under a warm sun and then standing at the threshold of the barn. Her sense of loss and pain at her separation from everything and everyone she knew rose fresh in her, and she wondered how much greater it would be for a little eleven-year-old.

43: ROOK

A cheery fire and rows of glowmoss pots greeted the Dusties when they entered the assembly that evening. A large mead hall took up most of the lower level, sturdily built with large wooden beams crossing the ceiling. The hall could hold five hundred, but half of the stone seats sat empty.

"Are we early?" asked Phoebe.

"No," said Kane. "There's not as many of us as there used to be."

The Dusties sat together, next to Kane. They were greeted by lines of men and women interested in the new and unusual Sleepers, and the Dusties heard so many names that they could remember none.

"I might mention," whispered Kane to Phoebe, "that there are a growing number of men here that have no wife, and are not interested in finding one. They are interested in being recruited to Pinnacle. Pays very well. Having a wife is becoming more of a hindrance to that goal."

"I will try very hard not to be a hindrance then," said Phoebe.

"*I* don't plan on going to Pinnacle," said Kane, smirking boyishly at her.

"Oh, but you're young," said Phoebe, a humoring smile on her lips. "You might change your mind, and then what a burden I would be."

The first course came to the table. Egg soup. The three Dusties gave each other ecstatic glances and dug in. They had not tasted anything so delightful in their entire remembered lives.

"Rip will be mad with envy," whispered Phoebe.

"Careful," whispered Scarlet back.

A serving girl set before Phoebe a cup of milk and a cup of ale. The milk matched her hopes, but the ale proved to be weak and bitter.

"Leather and milk, so cattle," said Scarlet.

"Clearly no barley," said Phoebe, wrinkling her nose at the ale.

"If I might interrupt your private discussion," said Kane. "This is a highly important evening in which Scarlet and Trace will have votes. We currently have no clan lord. Our recent lord disappeared—mysteriously and suspiciously. Grager has been nominated, and will likely win by a slim margin. That's two problems for him. First, some people suspect him of murdering the old clan lord, and second, he's innocent and therefore concerned about being the next victim. By the way, murder and other crimes are severely punished here. The tantyrs— the angels—are a virtuous lot, and they expect us to be the same."

"So, support Grager," said Scarlet.

"Exactly, and two votes might matter."

A hand took Phoebe's milk cup to refill it. She turned and saw Petra, smiling cautiously, her head down.

"Hello, Petra!"

"You shouldn't speak to her, Phoebe," said Kane.

"And why not?" Phoebe turned on Kane.

"She is a child serving in the assembly, and not to speak while here."

Phoebe faced Petra again. "If Ana and Ardi are here, can you point them out?"

Petra nodded, gave a little smile, and pointed to a boy and a girl close by, serving flanking tables. The girl, Ana, bounced along beside her table, filling cups, her long, straight golden hair straying into her flashing blue eyes so that she pulled at it continuously. Phoebe shook her head, wondering why no one had the sense to help her tie it back. She could not have been more than twelve, but her pretty, freckle-sprinkled face already showed fine features. Unlike Petra, she did not seem particularly concerned about her lot in life, carrying herself with a confident, straight-shouldered swagger fit for a boy, and, indeed, her build appeared straight, tall and shoulder-heavy.

The boy, Ardi, moved along quietly, diligent in his table duties. His restless slate-blue eyes darted here and there under a mat of tawny hair that desperately needed a shearing. Phoebe guessed that he was ten or a recent eleven.

Phoebe kept her eyes on the children through the meal. The courses came composed mostly of glowmoss, though a few treasures, like a small slice of cheese, kept the Dusties' interest.

The meal being completed, the women in the assembly began drifting out. Kane leaned to Phoebe. "The assembly and vote are for the men, Phoebe. If you will excuse us."

She nodded and rose. Scarlet gave her an envious look, for it appeared that the young man would be trapped in a long night of political dialogue.

On her way out, she caught sight of Ana carrying a stack of dishes into the draped kitchen archway. Phoebe worked her way through the tables and to the kitchen. Heat and moisture struck her as she entered the long, lantern-lit room, where a cook and a small crowd of maids hurried about.

"May I help you?" asked a sweating, heavy-boned maid, straggles of curly black hair escaping her bonnet and sticking to her copper skin.

Phoebe could see the three children working at dishes by the scrubbing tubs. "I should like to help you, I think, with the dishes."

"Oh, thank you," smiled the maid. "You are the girl who was not awakened, aren't you? Phoebe?"

"Yes, and you are...?"

"Emma," said the maid, blushing and lowering her gaze as if she were addressing royalty.

Phoebe rolled up the sleeves of her wist dress. "I am delighted to meet you, Emma. Let's put our elbows to these dishes, shall we?"

"Yes, ma'am."

The women of the kitchen cleaned for a time, the discussion just shallow enough for the maids to learn the basics about Phoebe without overtly prying. The three children cleaned dishes in tubs on the floor nearby, whispering to each other and glancing often at Phoebe. Eventually the conversation worked around to the children.

"Are these the only orphans?" asked Phoebe.

"Yes, at the moment," answered the maids.

"I would suppose that orphans find a home quickly here," said Phoebe.

The maids shook their heads. "'Tis true for the boys. Not so the girls."

"But Ardi is a boy," said Phoebe.

"Ardi cannot speak," said Emma.

Phoebe dwelt on this, drifting from the conversation as the maids directed the topic elsewhere. But eventually she interrupted. "If the girls are rarely adopted, why are there no other girls here?"

The maids tended carefully to their work, none eager to answer. Emma finally spoke. "They find a home at Pinnacle."

One of the other maids snorted derisively. "A home indeed. Sold as slaves, is the truth."

A second maid nodded. "Rumor is the girls that are sent to Pinnacle find no parents, but serve as slaves to the Greatmother—the ruling queen of the city. The city pays for the girls—with real wood, livestock, exotic clothing, and more."

"We don't know that their lot is difficult," said Emma. "Any more than Ana and Petra here right now. But we do have fears and suspicions."

"Can't you visit the children and see for yourself?" asked Phoebe.

Emma lowered her gaze. "Those who go to Pinnacle remain at Pinnacle."

44: SUSPICIONS

Within the assembly hall, Scarlet and Trace sat with Captain Grager's aide, Kane. On the platform at the hall's front, Grager and a scowling bald warrior named Capul faced off in an extended debate over the fate and direction of the clan. By their words, Scarlet could tell the two had a long, bitter history.

And when Capul's direct accusation of murder came against Grager, the hall grew icy with tension.

"Where is Lord Ulth's body, murderer!" Capul rose to his feet, his fists clenching. He took a step toward Grager.

Warriors under Grager's command rose to their feet in fury, but an angry bark of command from Grager put them back in their seats.

Grager rose slowly, his scowl directed at his opponent, Capul. "You accuse me *now*, seconds before the clan chooses, leaving me with no means to defend myself? So be it. Let the choice begin."

Grager turned and stepped off the platform, leaving Capul and his rage—real or forced—alone for all to witness.

Scarlet glanced at Kane, who turned and gave him an alarmed raise of his blond-white brows. "Ouch," Kane whispered.

"Bad for Grager?" asked Scarlet.

Kane brought his eyes to rest on Capul, and then on Grager, who reached the doors and exited the assembly. "No…Grager handled it perfectly."

Capul appeared ready to make a final appeal to those assembled, but he clamped his mouth shut and followed Grager out of the hall.

Scarlet, whose heart raced at the accusation of murder, bent to Kane's ear. "This Lord Ulth, you say he disappeared?"

Kane nodded. "Forty days ago. Went to bed, left his wives in the middle of the night, and never came back. No idea where he went, and no alibis for anyone else except being in bed themselves."

"I take it Grager and Ulth weren't friends," said Scarlet.

"Hated each other," said Kane. "Grager is the son of our clan's founder, Lord Drake. Ulth was treasure-rich. Basically bought his way into the title and purchased a lot of friends. Capul was Ulth's captain. He'll do anything to keep Grager from lordship."

The time came for the vote. Starting from the front of the hall, men rose and proclaimed their vote one by one. Many offered a reason, while some offered advice, warnings, and even threats to those waiting. An hour crawled by, and Scarlet wondered why the clan didn't simply have a show of hands and be done with it.

The threatening grew worse. The voting reached the back of the hall, the tally nearly tied, when Kane prompted Scarlet to stand.

"He can't vote, he's been here a day!" yelled someone from the crowd. Shouts and counter-shouts cascaded, and many rose, ready to come to blows. The assembly warden worked to bring order. He gestured impatiently to Scarlet. Scarlet signaled his vote and quickly sat back down.

"They've rough politics here," whispered Scarlet to Trace.

Trace said nothing. He stood. Slowly the crowd noticed the silent, powerfully built, seven-and-a-half-foot-tall giant. The hall quieted.

"I only been here a day, but I got this Rook on my cheek. I vote Grager. You people are too angry, and I don't like it."

Scarlet stifled a laugh, which could still be heard in the silence.

And by vote's end, Captain Grager became Lord Grager.

———

A day passed, and another. Scarlet volunteered to help with assembling crossbow bolts. He worked quickly, shearing the shafts off long rods, applying the fletching and anchoring the point. But for every four he finished, he set one aside secretly.

The Mastersmith shook his head at Scarlet's mediocre productivity, accepting the small bundle of completed bolts each day for three days. On the fourth day, Scarlet complained of a stiff neck and excused himself to work on the assembly in his quarters.

And there, he donned soft shoes and made his way to the window, and was not seen again until he placed another small bundle of bolts in the Mastersmith's hands.

———

Scarlet sat across from Phoebe at dinner. The kitchen maid, Emma, perched close to Phoebe's right, her knack for conversation keeping Phoebe busy. Lord Grager's aide, Kane, sat at Scarlet's left, laughingly engaged in the swirl of conversation, his eyes straying often to Phoebe. Trace ate slowly, sitting silently at the end of the table.

Scarlet, not the most delicate of eaters unless he chose to be, finished first, but he sat patiently, quietly, his eyes on Phoebe's plate. And when it appeared that she might excuse herself, he rose, circled the table, and held out his hand to her.

"Shall we take a quiet walk under the moon?" he said in a voice that caused Emma to smirk and blush.

"We will need quite a walk to find a moon," said Phoebe, wiping her lips gently and glancing quickly at Kane. He attempted to hide his flash of jealousy beneath his heavy brows.

"It matters little," said Scarlet. "My eyes will be too busy to even notice a moon."

Emma giggled.

"In that case," said Phoebe, rising, "I had better come along, and tell you when you are about to trip on a stone."

Scarlet bowed slightly, accepting her hand. "You needn't wait for us," he said to their two friends, and with a flashing smile he escorted Phoebe to the doors.

———

It took a few blocks outside the Rook holdings to find a lonely street, where Phoebe gently but firmly removed her hand from his.

"I rather like your hand," said Scarlet.

"I rather like my hand too," answered Phoebe. "Trace said you were up to something today."

Scarlet clasped his hands behind his back and strutted along beside her. "I was. I took a tour of the clan. I found many windows with locks of poor quality."

"You went thieving?"

Scarlet shook his head emphatically. "I stole nothing. Nothing of value at least, except secrets. These Rooks are clumsy with their secrets."

"What did you find?"

Scarlet sobered. "Not entirely good news, I'm afraid. First, our friends Emma and Kane are spying on us. It seems Lord Grager remains very much interested in who we are."

"I forgive them that," said Phoebe airily. "Emma is nice and Kane is charming. Does...does Lord Grager seem familiar to you?"

"Of course not." Scarlet at first gave her a smirk, but noted her seriousness. "What, you think you know him?"

Phoebe shrugged.

"Familiar or not," said Scarlet, "he might well be a murderer."

Phoebe began to laugh, until she saw that Scarlet didn't. "You're not serious."

"Quite. This Capul fellow that Grager competed against for lordship, he has a document and some notes stuffed under his armoire—a written eyewitness account of a maid who saw Grager with Lord Ulth the night Ulth was killed. Apparently Capul's looking for more evidence before he reveals the witness."

"What do you intend to do?"

"I intend to do nothing, yet. Grager treats us oddly. He knows something—something I want to know. I can't very well find out what if they hang him."

"Live and let murder, that's your motto then?"

Scarlet smiled. "Say, I rather like that! For now, there is a mystery to attend to, and I need a sneaky lookout to solve it. Are you willing?"

It didn't take long for Phoebe to nod yes.

"Excellent! You need your trousers and soft shoes-"

"I don't wear *boy* clothes, haven't you noticed by now?"

Scarlet picked at Phoebe's skirt. "Aye, I noticed. But this is hardly practical for a burglar."

Phoebe gave a quick, effortless twirl. "We shall see."

45: GRAGER

The third hour of morning came and, with it, a hush over the holdings of Rook Clan. A shadow passed across the window of an unused gathering room on the third story of the main estate. The window opened silently, having been oiled the night previous.

Above the steady *drip-drip* of the lone glowpot across from the grimy fireplace, there came a light creak of moss-wood, and patches of shadow advanced toward an old, overstuffed couch.

On the couch, a petite form lay in sleep.

A hand hovered along the brown skirt draped over the couch's edge, then reached out silently for the thin blanket pulled up over the head. It gripped a shoulder...

"Don't sit on me!" said a whispered voice.

Scarlet jerked back, his hand jumbling the expertly formed pile of blankets and pillows arranged on the couch to look like Phoebe. At the couch's back, the real Phoebe rested her chin on her fingers, her mouth turned up in the slightest of smiles, but her eyes brimming with victory.

Scarlet slowly let out his shocked intake of breath, bringing his racing heart back under control. "Shrikes, Phoebe! You scared years off me!"

"Imagine Scarlet...scared of girls," crowed Phoebe.

Scarlet recovered quickly, but he remained as he was, his eyes fixed on her. She had the look of a hawk having caught a mouse, and her triumphant intensity gave her a wild, untamed look, turning her pleasant beauty into a goddess of the hunt.

He very much wanted to be hunted more, but he knew her reservation toward his advances. So, he captured her in his memory and rose nonchalantly. "You had no problems staying in here, I see."

She slid from behind the couch and stepped lightly around the study. "I'm just a girl. No one pays me attention. What are we looking for?"

Scarlet loosened the straps holding the sword at his back and resettled the weapon at his belt. "Well, this is the most likely place that...mind if I sit on you?"

"Pardon?"

Scarlet plopped down atop the couch's pillow-person. "This is the most likely place that Grager and Ulth ducked into after being seen by that maid that witnessed them together. And this is a special room."

"How so?"

Scarlet spun to face the fireplace wall across from him. "Because that wall there was built right into the big rock spire outside. Below us is the cistern and above us is the top of the spire."

He rose suddenly, stepped to the fireplace, and ran a hand around its mantle. "So, this is the perfect place for a secret."

Phoebe came to his side. "You mean, a tunnel in the rock? Wouldn't it be hard to build something like that without everyone knowing?"

Scarlet tapped the wall lightly. "Ah, but these buildings are old. The Rook Clan bought them from a previous clan, who bought them from someone else, and so on. This whole collective is far larger than what the Rooks need, so there's a wealth of empty places for secrets."

"You said you needed me as a lookout?" said Phoebe.

"Yes…" said Scarlet, flashing her an appreciative smile. "There's a guard that makes the rounds at this time. He's erratic in his patrol, no sense of routine, very rude. I need you to peek at the door and tell me if you see his shadow on the stairs. I may need to make a little noise in my search."

"Very well," said Phoebe, lighting her small personal lamp and shuttering it. "I'll open the shutter briefly if I see him."

"Perfect!" And Scarlet set to work.

———

An hour passed. Twice the guard came strolling up the stairs and along the hall toward them, and Scarlet went quiet. But Phoebe kept watch at the keyhole, and Scarlet continued at her all-clear signal.

"Unfortunate," said Scarlet finally, plopping back down on the couch. "I've made a mistake, it appears. And here I was trying to impress you."

Phoebe left the door and sat on a low end table. "Could they have gone into one of the nearby rooms?"

"Well, they must have gone *somewhere*…" Scarlet closed his eyes and gave a low chuckle. "Ah, shrikes! The window! I found it so very easy to climb in here, but of course that makes it so easy to climb *out*. Come!"

Scarlet hurried to the window and stepped out onto the unusually wide sill. Phoebe followed. To their right, they could hop onto a jutting roof ledge, and from there another ledge, until they stood upon the small, narrow strip of roofing over the window. Stone surrounded them on three sides, making a small isolated grotto. Scarlet moved to the back of it, felt about, and gave a victorious, whispered cheer as a section of stone swiveled inward with a low grating rumble.

He stood and beckoned a hand. "Coming or staying?"

"Most certainly coming," she answered, and stepped inside.

The tunnel had been cut narrow. Scarlet pushed past Phoebe and moved slowly, searching the floor and walls. After a hundred descending paces along the tunnel, they reached a deep crevasse.

On their left, a wall made of smooth stone rose to the ceiling, high above. Beneath this, a small cave mouth opened out, spewing forth a thunder of water into the rocky, brightly lit ravine below.

Above them, water streamed down the walls and dripped from a vaulted roof, giving extensive illumination.

Thirty feet on the other side of the crevasse, the tunnel continued.

"Bridge," said Scarlet, pointing up. Fifteen feet above, a lightweight metal-mesh bridge hung on cables next to the wall, directly over the crevasse.

"It must drop down to there." Phoebe gestured to where three small, flat metal brackets jutted a foot out from the smooth rock face, spaced floor-level between their side and the opposite tunnel. "The bridge must come down and rest on those."

Scarlet searched about for a bridge mechanism, quickly found it near the edge, and uttered a curse. "Needs a special crank. Wasn't expecting this."

"There's rope over there." Phoebe pointed. In the far tunnel across the chasm, a coil of light rope hung from an ore cart. Other mining equipment lay scattered about the cart.

Scarlet peered across the way. "Does us no good. Can't reach it. I'll need to go back and get rope, and a grapple."

"Others will be waking up by now," said Phoebe. "We don't have time."

"We'll try again tomorrow, perhaps." Scarlet turned to leave.

He took several steps, caught movement behind him, and spun back around. Phoebe raced to the edge, and she leapt.

"No!" yelled Scarlet, chasing her.

Phoebe's jump angled toward the wall along the left. Her effort had no chance to cover even half the distance to the other side, but her foot landed on the first bracket and she pushed off. The wall prevented her from landing vertically and she hit the next bracket on a lean. Her inertia drove her on. Despite her angle, she struck the final bracket true and landed lightly on the far floor.

The two stared at each other across the chasm. Slowly Scarlet shook his head and attempted a diplomatic smile. "That was impressive, missy, but I'd prefer you didn't kill yourself trying to impress me."

"No more risk than stepping across a stream," answered Phoebe. "I'd prefer that you stop underestimating me."

Scarlet nursed a heavy sigh. "Can you toss the rope up around the bridge? Try to get it to fall through the railing."

Phoebe dug through the boxes for a suitable weight. At first she tried a small rock pick tied to the rope, but when she managed to toss it up onto the dangling bridge, it lodged in the metal mesh of the floor. Cutting the stuck rope, she tried a stone. On the second throw, it clattered along the bridge and through the railing. By pulling on it, she set the dangling stone into a swing that Scarlet was able to catch.

She looped the rope onto the ore cart.

Scarlet tested it. "Rather thin," he muttered.

He was about to have Phoebe play out a second length of rope when, with a clatter of gears and chains, the bridge began descending.

Scarlet stopped thinking and acted, swinging out onto the rope and beginning a frantic climb, his hands slipping, the thin cord burning into his flesh. He grunted in pain but kept his hands moving, until he felt metal and grasped the bridge's railing. Pulling himself up, he raced to the far end and jumped down to Phoebe's side as the bridge neared the brackets.

They rushed into the covering darkness of the far tunnel and came immediately to a dead-end, littered with digging implements and piles of loose rock. A faint stench of death stung their nostrils.

Scarlet cast desperately about the scarred, natural walls, searching in vain for signs of a secret access. He stepped atop a rock pile, disturbing it, and then he paused, inspecting something at his feet.

"The bridge is down," whispered Phoebe.

Scarlet stepped off the pile, took several stones, covered over what he had found, and joined her behind the ore cart.

They went quiet, trying to slow their breathing.

In the stone wall, near the middle of the bridge, a hatch opened, and out walked Lord Grager.

He took one step and froze, his eyes on the rope trailing through the railing. His hand suddenly stretched back inside the hatch, and he pushed.

From the hatch came a whisper, so quiet that Scarlet only thought he heard, "What is it?"

"Visitors," muttered Grager. He pulled the hatch closed, and from within came the light squeal of gears.

Grager peered into the darkness of both tunnel directions. He drew up the rope, inspected it, and smiled at one point. Gathering the rope in a pile, he straightened and brought his hands together. Slowly he began clapping.

"Quite resourceful," he called. "Impressive. But you've scraped your hands, and you won't be able to hide that in the morning."

"Stay here," whispered Scarlet to Phoebe.

Scarlet stood and advanced into the light of the chasm's moss-glow, stepping onto the bridge. "You've caught me. What do we do now?"

"Do?" said Grager, approaching him. "I see no reason to *do* anything. You've had a little fun. Nothing wrong in that, but now it's time to behave."

Despite the lord's calm pretense, Scarlet detected the turmoil in Grager's eyes, the strain in his words, and the quivering of his sweating skin. He seemed a man on the edge of balance.

"And the punishment for coming here?" said Scarlet.

Grager waved him off, leaning on the rail, peering down into the chasm. "Will you give me your word that you will not return?"

Scarlet paused, uncertain, confused. Why was Grager not demanding his head? "And the punishment?" he repeated.

Grager turned to him, his teeth clenched. "Swear to me that you will not return, nor tell anyone about this place."

Scarlet couldn't help a puzzled smile. "And that's it, then?"

"Swear it!" shouted Grager, his fists clenching.

The two men faced each other in silence.

"I swear it," said Scarlet, his breath releasing.

"As do I," came Phoebe's voice behind Scarlet.

"Then it is time for you to leave," said Grager, pointing up the tunnel.

———

Back in the study, Phoebe paused to tidy up the couch. "What do we do now?"

Scarlet searched about the room. "Grager is about four inches taller than me, wouldn't you say?"

"Why?"

Scarlet ignored her, positioning a hearth plate on the floor and stepping onto it. It gave him another four inches. "Come over here…yes, about…there."

Phoebe humored him, standing a few feet away.

"Right, then." Scarlet turned to face away from her. In slow motion, he spun at the torso and extended his hand out toward Phoebe, his neck craned down as he watched the angle between his arm and side. He raised his head to see his fingers perilously close to Phoebe's chest.

"That's odd," he muttered.

———

For the hundredth time Scarlet shook his head. "Want to know what nips at me most?"

"Sure," said Trace.

"When Phoebe showed herself, Grager didn't flinch. No surprise at all. It's like he expected her to be there."

"He's crafty," said Trace, more as a question.

"And crazy," said Scarlet.

"What did you tell Phoebe?"

Scarlet scratched nervously at his ear. "About what I saw? About the body in the rock pile?"

"Yeah."

"Nothing at all. I've no doubt Grager and Ulth went down that hole together, and only Grager returned. But let's pretend we don't know that, and try to ride this out in peace."

46: The Thing in the Tunnel

Yun's diary, Day 151

> It has been twelve days since Scarlet went through the door. We have
> watched every day since. We fear for his safety.

> Each day, around clock six or seven, we see—we hear—slivers prowling
> the tunnel. They quiet down around midnight, though every now and then
> they pass by at wrong hours. Rodrigo has started leaving the door open
> only a crack, and braced, in case something manages to reach or fly up
> here. And, we kill the lanterns.

Yun lay curled up under Rodrigo's cloak, wedged between his arm and chest,
her hands clasping patches of his linen shirt. The metal door sat slightly ajar next
to them, but she could not see it. She couldn't see anything.

Ordinarily, she would never think of curling up next to Rodrigo like this, and
she guessed that Rodrigo would not allow her to do so. But other thoughts
crowded her mind—the damp chill of the tunnel, the utter lack of light, her ears
straining to hear the hiss and bone-clatter of slivers passing below…and the unknown fate of Scarlet.

She napped, and when she awoke, the lightless quiet and the comforting smell
of Rodrigo's shirt did bring her back to thoughts of the boy next to her. She
knew that a slow transition had occurred between Rodrigo and herself.

Her mind drifted through the days before Scarlet left. She always watched the
boys carefully around the other girls—especially Scarlet, but also Rodrigo. Rodrigo treated Hope and Phoebe with impeccable honor and a cautious regard—
ever gracious and never close. But not Yun. His arms were more open to her—
welcoming embraces, a hand on the shoulder, sometimes a playful tousle of hair.

She loved it, and she loved him. But she loved Scarlet also, and Scarlet might
well be dead.

Don't think like that.

"Rodrigo, what do we do?" whispered Yun. "About Scarlet, I mean. And the
others."

"I do not know," said Rodrigo. "I fear we are cut by the razor."

"What?"

"Something I said to Scarlet. We made a mistake allowing them to go into
the tunnel without a much better plan. I hope the Lord of All has been gracious

to our friends and protected them from the razor's edge we dance upon. It gnaws at me that I failed them."

"Will we just keep watching?"

"We cannot, Yun. The journey here each day…Hope and Rip doing the same the other half of the day…we are exhausting ourselves. And sitting here doing nothing, listening to the slivers, we would go mad. We may have no choice but to go looking for them."

"I'm willing," said Yun.

"To enter the tunnels?"

"Yes."

"For Scarlet?"

"Yes."

"If we go, we might never come back. Ed might stay, but he would never bother to come up here to let us in again."

"We could leave the door open. Just a crack."

Rodrigo did not answer immediately. "To be honest, Yun, I had never even thought of that. There is a risk, but perhaps not a great one."

"And we can go when the slivers are sleeping, or whatever they do."

"Yes, but not all sleep, or at least at the same time," said Rodrigo. "And we do not know where to go. We could wander right into the middle of a sliver lair."

"I'm willing," said Yun.

———

Rodrigo sighed inwardly. Yun had a fine mind, but her romantic spirit directed her actions. Facing death to see Scarlet again came as a natural decision to her.

And he found himself agreeing with it. He had to know, had to discover, whether his decisions had killed them all. He would give Scarlet another week or so, but after that, he would need to act, despite the danger of the slivers. "We will talk it over with Rip and Hope. And Ed."

"Ed will never leave, he loves that Forge-"

Rodrigo's hand clapped over her mouth. She went silent.

Something moved in the tunnel. Something big. They could hear the creature's bulk slide against the walls, the scraping of rock, and a low clicking. The sounds grew louder. To Rodrigo's sudden shock, he realized that the creature—or some part of the creature—was right outside the door. Something slapped against the metal, but the brace, and Rodrigo's hand, held it in place. He could kick the brace and slam the door shut, if he could leap to his feet fast enough to push the door closed before the creature knew that it was being resisted…

Rodrigo had just worked up his courage to make a move when he noticed that the sounds were now past the door. He paused. The clicking continued to fade, until he could hear the creature no more.

Neither Rodrigo nor Yun could speak for the next two minutes.

"That sliver must have been huge!" whispered Yun.

"That was no sliver," said Rodrigo. "The sounds were all wrong. That could be the monster that Scarlet and Raeder met under the gargoyle."

"Does that change our decision?" said Yun.

"It probably should, but I doubt it will."

47: TWO SISTERS AND A BROTHER

In Haven, two weeks had passed. Scarlet tried twice to sneak back into the pumice tunnel and find Rodrigo and the others, but he discovered the reality of the blackspawn presence. The hissing nightmares nearly trapped him on the first attempt, and on the second he was caught in one of the frequent spawn attacks and forced to retreat hastily to the city walls.

Although Scarlet was desperate for another attempt, the soldiers of Rook Clan began planning a large tunnel sweep in twenty days. It seemed like the perfect opportunity, so Scarlet insisted on being included and began preparing his plans.

While waiting, the three Dusties concentrated on their new duties. Scarlet demonstrated a reliable skill at the crossbow. Trace proved clumsy with the spear but compensated with his exceptional strength. Phoebe took the three orphans under her wing as sisters and brother, and the four minded the washing and cleaning and serving of Rook.

On this night, Phoebe and the children warmed themselves around a fire built on the rocky flat of Desolation Point. As Grager had said, no one came there, leaving them time to themselves.

"Is Ardi your brother?" Phoebe asked Ana.

"No, silly," said Ana, stirring the fire. "He's my husband."

Phoebe laughed. "Married already, are you?"

Ana rolled her eyes and giggled. "Of course not *yet*," she said. "But he promised."

"Did you promise, Ardi?"

Ardi, who now had nicely cropped hair, after Phoebe took the shears to it, shook his head emphatically and closed his eyes.

"Ardi doesn't seem to think so," laughed Phoebe.

"He doesn't tell the truth a lot," whispered Ana.

"Has Ardi always been unable to speak?" asked Phoebe.

Ana gave a little smile and said nothing. Petra pulled on Phoebe's shirt collar and whispered to her. "We didn't tell people he *couldn't* talk. We said he *wouldn't.*"

"What? Why?"

"If he talks, he'll be taken away. And we don't want to be separated."

"I'm...well...shocked," said Phoebe. "You are clever little conspirators."

"Nobody cares for us," said Petra.

"Grager cares for Petra," said Ana in pouty voice.

"Not really," said Petra.

"Oh pooh!" exclaimed Ana. "He found you first. He *always* comes around and talks to you. He never even looks my way."

"Perhaps he will adopt you," said Phoebe.

Petra shook her head, her normally sad eyes sadder. "He'll not adopt me, I can tell. Everyone else just ignores us…except for you. You won't leave us, will you?"

Phoebe hugged Petra close, kissing the top of her head and running a hand through the girl's midnight hair. "Never."

———

In the morning, when Phoebe went to wake the children, she found empty beds. Concerned, she sought out the maids. None of them knew anything. She found Kane, who simply told her to "talk to Grager" and left quickly with his head down.

She found Grager training with his personal guards and inquired about the children, a terrible sinking feeling dragging at her heart.

"They have been sent to Pinnacle," said Grager.

Phoebe felt like passing out, but she instead managed a step forward. "You sold the children into slavery?"

"Slavery? You know little about Pinnacle. The children will be servants, but how is that different from here?"

"Why would you send the children away without even warning me or letting me say goodbye?"

"Who are you to them? And who are you to tell me what to do with children that *we* found, at risk to our own lives?"

Grager's guards backed away a few steps, smirks on their faces.

But Phoebe didn't back away. "Even you…you cared for Petra, didn't you? The children say so. Why could you not adopt them—at least her?"

"Why would I burden myself with orphan brats?"

"I should say-" started Phoebe, anger replacing her grief.

"You have said enough!" exploded Grager, and he stepped up threateningly, looming over her. "You have no standing here, you little sneak. What are you worth, other than as a scullery maid and a mouth to feed? Considering your puny size and your lack of good sense, I have half a mind to sell you to Pinnacle as well! Keep your tongue to yourself or I'll have you flogged!"

Phoebe stumbled away, numb from the shock of Grager's anger. Unable to hold her emotions, she ran through streets and paths until she found herself at Desolation Point, her tears flowing with ever greater intensity until she sank against the rock wall along the cliff's edge and sobbed uncontrollably.

Hours passed. The searing pain of her loss sank to a crushing sorrow, then cooled to a hollow, empty pit in her spirit. She rose, composed herself, and saw to her duties with a dull, soulless efficiency. Around her, the young maids whispered.

Scarlet and Trace came to see her, but she remembered little of the conversation. That night, she slept on the rock flat of Desolation. Toward the fifth hour, she awoke abruptly, whispered, "We shall see, then," to herself, and hurried to her quarters to prepare for the day.

48: Target

Scarlet's aim was off that morning. His irritation saw to that. Irritation at Phoebe for involving herself so quickly and intensely in the affairs of Haven orphans. Irritation at Grager's selling of the children and his harsh response to Phoebe. Contempt at the strong majority of other Rooks who applauded Grager's actions. And, mostly, recrimination at himself for neglecting to stay close enough to Phoebe to help her before all this blew up. Rodrigo would be less than pleased with his handling of matters to date.

Scarlet saw Trace regularly, but the man-giant seemed to have withdrawn into himself, rarely willing to carry on a conversation or do anything beyond practice with his spear and sit sullenly in the courtyard, watching the comings and goings of Rook. He never ventured into the city proper.

Scarlet cocked his crossbow, took aim, and fired. The metal bolt sank into the second ring of the three-ring target. He'd managed only two center rings on his last ten attempts.

He puffed out an exasperated breath and laid the crossbow aside when the call for cleared weapons came on the target range. As he glanced back, he discovered Phoebe inspecting the trainer weapons. She selected a crossbow, strapped on a waist belt, slung a satchel of bolts between shoulder and belt, and sat down to wait for an opening on the shooting range. She gave Scarlet a composed, disinterested glance and straightened the skirt of her dress.

The muscular, dark-skinned man next to Scarlet returned from retrieving his bolts out of the target and caught sight of Phoebe. "Hoy, young lassie…come on up, have my place," he said with a voice that expected to command the center of attention. He gave her a great lopsided grin and urged her forward.

"I was next, Toby," said a heavy-bearded soldier covered in tattoos.

"You can be next, next," shouted Toby, giving the soldier a disgusted grimace and a shove. "Mind your manners, there's a lady present."

Others near the range paused, their eyes turning toward Phoebe.

She glanced about, picked up her crossbow, and moved to Toby's position.

"Thank you. I'm Phoebe, by the-"

"I'd be old and blind not to know who you are, miss. Mastersmith Toby, is who I am. Is this to be your first time?"

"First time," said Phoebe.

The onlookers shuffled in closer, interested in how the diminutive young Phoebe would manage. The crowd included a number of women, all larger and taller than Phoebe.

"Not a tough weapon, lassie," said Toby. "Cock it here, slide a bolt on, aim along this mark, and fire. Easy."

Phoebe nodded, placed her foot on the brace bar, and pulled at the lever. It gave way grudgingly as she strained to bring it around and back. Throwing both hands and her whole body into it, she wrestled it back until it clicked into place. She fished out a bolt and inserted it into the guide and astride the steel wire string.

Phoebe brought the bulky weapon to her shoulder, staggering slightly with its weight. A murmur of humor ran through the onlookers.

Toby gave the crowd a confrontational sweep of his eyes and put a hand on the crossbow. "This isn't a good weapon for you, lassie. You need something a little more elegant, like yourself." Toby spun around and yelled, "Krow! Where are—there you are, boy. Go get Lightning."

A young man, built much like Toby, raced off to the barracks, returning a minute later with a lean, compact crossbow of unusual design. Toby handed it to Phoebe. "I built this for my son when he was ten. Should be just about your size. I put my smithing skills to the test making her; she's a real lady herself. My son named her Lightning. Here, use these bolts. Also my own crafting."

Phoebe cocked the unusual weapon, which gave her much less of a fight. She settled the bolt, brought the weapon to her shoulder, took a breath, and fired. The bolt struck just outside the outer ring.

"Fine!" shouted Toby, nodding encouragement and looking around at the crowd. There came a scattering of applause and the audience began drifting away, back to their own affairs. Toby stood cross-armed next to Phoebe, awaiting the next shot.

The next bolt stuck in the second ring. The third touched the inner ring. The sixth hit nearly dead center.

"Bullseye! Shining!" Toby's features turned from amusement to interest. "You've never shot before, you say?"

"No," said Phoebe. "Testament to your fine craftsmanship, Toby, and a large helping of beginner's luck."

"My eye! Let's try again." Toby went to retrieve the bolts at the range-clear call.

Phoebe turned her attention to Scarlet, who watched her from the next lane, his head slightly tilted.

"You hope to reach Pinnacle on the steadiness of your aim?" said Scarlet. "You think you can be a soldier?"

"Yes, Scarlet. It's a small hope, but I must try to find the children."

"I'd say you have a chance. You have the knack."

"Thank you."

"This means that our association may be ending soon."

"Yes, Scarlet. I am sorry."

"I feel badly teasing you so much."

"I feel badly not teasing you enough."

They shared smiles before Toby interrupted with six bolts and another round of practice.

———

At the end of the day, Phoebe could reliably hit two bullseyes out of six. She could hit four after three days, and five, if not six, by the end of the week. Her practices drew a small crowd, and brought visitors from other clans. She had proposals for marriage, including from Mastersmith Toby's son, Krow, but she politely refused them, explaining that she felt too young to marry. Krow took the refusal graciously and gave her Lighting as a gift of admiration.

Nine days after her first shot, Lord Grager came and stiffly informed Phoebe that Queen Temma of Pinnacle had purchased the intriguing little sharpshooter, and that she must leave for Pinnacle in two days.

49: FEAR AND CHAOS

Haven's soft two-o'clock night chimes filtered through Scarlet's open window. He lay on his long, narrow bed, his eyes gently shut, his breathing slow and soft, and his face set in a relaxed smile, as though he had fallen asleep in the midst of maidens.

But Scarlet was neither relaxed nor asleep. He had picked up the telltale sounds of someone entering through his window.

"Get up, Scarlet. I don't have time for games."

The whispered voice caused Scarlet to open his eyes. "Lord Grager. I'm honored, sir. Does my door offend you?"

Scarlet's smile faded slowly as Grager paced sharply back and forth like a predator trapped too long in a circus cage. He wore all black and had smeared soot on both cheeks. His eyes kept a continuous stare on Scarlet throughout his movements. The edge of madness shone there.

"Stand up," Grager whispered harshly. "I want you alert."

Scarlet slid his hand away from the dagger under his pillow and rose slowly into a standing position, keeping an eye on Grager's sword hand.

"Look at me," said Grager.

Scarlet looked up into the tall man's dark eyes, noticing the sweat beading on his pale skin.

Grager's finger rose up to tap Scarlet's chest. "Listen to me. Every word."

From beyond the door came the muted scrape of another door being opened down the hallway. Grager's head jerked toward the sound, then snapped back to Scarlet. His jaw quivered. He closed his eyes, took a breath, and began speaking quickly, the words coming in a monotone as if he were reciting a memory lesson.

"Time is short. Do not be distracted by the enemy on the far hill and fail to see the foe at your throat. Fear and Chaos crouch in plain sight, readied to spring, their plans, laid long and patiently, come to fruition."

Grager opened his eyes. "Repeat it."

Scarlet tried and failed.

Grager's eyes turned fiery and he gripped Scarlet's shoulder. He began reciting his words again. He stumbled over the first sentence, corrected himself, and finished.

Scarlet repeated it back successfully.

"Again."

Scarlet succeeded again at the third try.

And with that, Grager turned back to the window. But at the sill, he paused, his hands clenched tightly, and he stepped back to Scarlet. His quivering eyes darted back and forth between the door and the young man.

"Listen, boy, you can die a thousand ways here and your thoughts stripped a thousand ways more...you've a thousand enemies...but you must survive, all of you...stay alive at all costs...the Final Assault is coming, and after that, there will be nothing left to-"

Fists pounded at the door. Soldier's voices pierced the silence.

———

A trio of soldiers, their weapons at the ready, awaited an answer at Scarlet's door. The first knock brought no response, but the second pounded on air as Scarlet swept the door open, wiping sleep from his eyes.

"Gentlemen. Is this a very late emergency or a terribly early one?"

The lead soldier pushed into Scarlet's room, scanning it quickly but keeping an eye on Scarlet, alert for any flicker of guilt. "Have you seen Lord Grager since the ten o'clock hour?"

"Is he missing?"

"He is accused of murdering Lord Ulth."

"Ah. And who is accusing him?"

The soldier turned to Scarlet, bringing his face close to the young man. "Maybe you don't remember me, Scarlet, but I'm Wallak, one of Grager's personal guards. As much as I hate this, Grager is guilty."

"Based on?"

Noting the partially open window, Wallak scanned the area outside. "Lord Ulth's body was found in a secret tunnel—a tunnel Lord Grager clearly knew about. When confronted, Grager fled."

Scarlet gave an emphatic grimace. "Ugh. Well, I do hope he doesn't come see me. Make me guilty by association, wouldn't it?"

Wallak took a last pass over the room and returned to the door. "I suggest you get dressed and help. There won't be much sleep for anyone tonight."

"A grand idea," said Scarlet, reaching for his shirt.

———

The six-o'clock morning bell tolled. No sign could be found of Grager, and the search extended into the city and neighboring clans.

Phoebe left breakfast early, tired of the fearful chatter of the clan maids. She crossed to the armory, gave a good morning to the guard, and readied herself for practice, cinching on a belly strap and anchoring the bolt case between shoulder and strap. Taking down her crossbow and turning it over for a quick inspection, she found a paper rolled tightly around the trigger.

Her head snapped around, her eyes flicking to every dark corner of the armory. The long, dusty room lay silent and empty with the soldiers involved in the manhunt.

She unrolled the note:

Must Talk Avoid Notice Meet At Scraphouse
Scarlet

Setting down her crossbow, she exited the armory, her pace tentative, her eyes on the paper. Then she sighed nervously, gripped the paper in her hand, and set off at a more determined pace.

———

Of all the structures in the Rook holdings, the water silo stood the tallest. From his perch atop the silo, Scarlet had a view of most of the Rook rooftops and rock spurs.

Grager clearly had a knack for skulking and climbing about, and Scarlet had more questions for the murderous lord.

He glanced down at the brightly lit central grounds and saw Phoebe crossing by the fish ponds. She paused, studied something in her hand, and moved off again toward the machinist sheds.

Scarlet returned to scanning the rooftops, nibbling at a crispy dried mosscake which he particularly fancied.

But the vision of Phoebe nagged at him. There was something not quite right about her as she stepped lightly along in the gleaming glow of the fish ponds.

He had almost finished the mosscake when it came to him.

Phoebe carried no crossbow, but had her bolt case strapped on. She had left the training grounds without taking it off.

Scarlet gave a final review of the empty rooftops and slid over to the climbing rungs.

———

Phoebe passed through the machine shops and smithies, stepping aside for a squad of searching soldiers. The smithies lay quiet this early in the morning, their forges cold. Silence settled around Phoebe as she turned from the center street into a curving alleyway.

216

The scraphouse lay ahead, its windows dark but for a lone mosspot hanging from a lamppost near the large barn-like doors. Stopping and listening, she heard only distant sounds, and she moved forward, wondering if the door of the scraphouse would be locked.

Her heart raced, but not frantically. Despite the warnings of terrors in the dark waiting for loners, Phoebe regularly walked by herself and enjoyed the exploration of quiet places. She held a strong faith in her prudent sense of danger.

So, when the tall, cloaked man detached from a shadowy corner and glided up behind her, he was not able to fully pull the sack over Phoebe's head before she reacted.

Phoebe kicked back, catching something solid that caused her attacker to grunt in pain. He fell, but clutched at her tightly and bore her to the ground, falling atop her. She flailed out, striking him with her elbows and fists. Her fingers dug furrows into his neck so that they came slick with blood. She thought to scream, but his knee struck her shoulder and pressed her painfully into the stone so that she could not draw a breath. The bag came over her fully, cinched tightly, and the attacker's grip forced her hands behind her and tied them. She kicked with her legs but a crushing weight fell on them and they were bound together. The man's hands came up under the bag and a cloth was shoved roughly in her mouth and tied back.

In the end, she could neither scream nor move.

———

Phoebe came free of the confining bag and felt stone scrape against her hands as she lay on her back. She tried to struggle with her legs but the cords wrapped around her knees prevented it. Above her, the blue wisps drifted slowly in swirling maelstroms, but then a pale, flame-lit face intervened, looking down on her with intense midnight-black eyes.

The face of Rook Lord Grager.

He smiled at her, but his eyes bulged with intensity, their whites showing all around, as though some fit of fear-induced insanity bedeviled him.

Phoebe tried to spit out the choking cloth tied into her mouth, but his hand pressed it farther in and his other shoved up on her jaw.

"Let me make you more comfortable, my dear," he said, and dragged her up into a sitting position, her back against rock. She immediately recognized the gray stone and the low wall of Desolation Point—the quiet, lonely spot overlooking the cliff edge that Phoebe had once cherished as a place of contemplation. It felt cold and isolated now.

His trembling hand stroked her chin. "Such a dear, brave young lady. I am truly sorry for my deceit with the note, and my forceful means of meeting with you. I did not have time for a better plan."

Phoebe tried to reply, but the cloth prevented it.

"They are coming for me now, only a matter of time. They believe I have fled the clan, but they will look here again, sooner or later." His mouth suddenly broke broadly in a grand smile. "But they won't find me. I will be long gone, and swiftly."

His arm came around her neck and he pulled her tightly in an embrace. Her nose was pressed into his cloak and she could not breathe. He kissed her ear and his other hand caressed her back and took hold of her waist. Phoebe reeled and twisted in revulsion.

"So pretty and so brave," he whispered. "And full of spirit too. I'm afraid your kick brought low my knee, so I could not flee even if I wished. If I took out the gag, would you remain silent? No, I suppose not."

Suddenly he let her go and turned, searching the darkness beyond the guttering flames of his lamp. When he spun back to her, his eyes held desperation and fear. The insanity now appeared to hold full sway over the man. He clutched her again, her nose once again buried and her neck strained painfully by his hysterically tight grip. He spoke in a whisper that she could barely hear.

"It's coming for me! Do you feel it?" He clenched a fist and pressed it against one eye. "I needed more time…Phoebe, don't think badly of me. Guard your body and mind. Guard your friends and the children. Learn to trust with your very life. Do you understand? Your very life!"

He set her quickly against the stone, then limped up onto the wall. She tilted her head back and saw him standing above, staring down at her, his fear replaced by a wild triumph. And vengeance.

"If you fall, worlds fall," he rasped.

And then he was gone, tumbling backward over the cliff's edge, plunging into the void with a strangled cry—or was it laughter?

Phoebe's terror reached a breaking point, and she screamed despite the cloth. She tried working it free but made little progress. Her hands twisted and strained frantically at the ropes, the slickness of blood dripping onto her palms from her raw wrists.

And then she stopped and tried desperately not to breathe, and her heart raced painfully as a new terror built in her.

She sensed it—like far-off footsteps in a dream.

It was coming.

Phoebe slowly pressed back against the stone wall, taking great care not to make noise. An acrid stench filled her nostrils. She searched about, trying not to move her head, scanning the bare stretch of rock.

And then a shadow drifted over Desolation Point.

Phoebe tried to scream out again, but something sharp and precise pierced her mind, and her throat refused to function.

———

Searching the smithies and shops and finding no sign of Phoebe, Scarlet remembered his first days in Haven, when Grager led them to Desolation Point. That Grager had kidnapped Phoebe seemed even more likely now, given her disappearance. And so Scarlet sped along the twisted paths through the maze of jumbled stone, his eyes searching the ground for clues, his mind trying to remember the way.

He passed a trail leading left, paused in uncertainty, then leapt onto the rocks next to him, jumping from boulder to boulder until he stood on the highest.

Desolation Point lay close by on his right, and the scene there stopped his breath.

A lone lamp sat on the stone wall, and beneath it a dimly lit, struggling figure. Phoebe.

But Scarlet's eyes left her and lifted higher.

Above her, a shimmering shadow floated in the dead air, silhouetted by the blue glow of the sky. The shadow swirled and boiled, its dark shape indefinable. Beneath it, a cluster of dark tendrils descended, taking their hold on Phoebe.

Its presence touched at Scarlet's mind, spearing him with terror, warning him to run—to escape or face death in hopelessness.

He leapt down the rocks and raced on the path toward Desolation.

———

Phoebe closed her eyes, yet she could see. And she did not want to see.

The nightmare-being stood out clearly now, hovering in a swirling infinity. She felt as though she were falling. Flashes of another reality materialized around her. She saw herself as she truly existed outside the domain of material existence—the electric labyrinth of her brain and the pulsing star of her mind, anchored by the shining cables of her spirit that stretched out to the soul-fog far beyond.

In the material reality, she worked her hands, feeling the blood-wet ropes slip away. But the ghost-cords of the beast drifted into and through her, coiling forcefully but delicately around the nerves just so. Her arms went slack.

219

And her legs, and ears, and eyes. Within her paralyzed body, her panic-stricken heart raced, fluttered, and stopped.

The strands dug, and sliced, and coiled, and her heart resumed—slow, strong and steady.

———

Scarlet raced at the shadow, raised his sword high, and brought it slashing down through the tendrils above Phoebe's head.

The sword struck through empty air.

Scarlet lost his balance on the swing, and he staggered into the path of the tendrils.

Shifting, star-swirled infinity surrounded him.

The immense creature shimmered above him, like a predator of the deep sea, its stinging strands piercing through the essence of Phoebe below, her body and spirit open, exposed, struggling in vain.

Beware, rash little man. Show no spine. She is mine. Leave while you can.

Scarlet felt the ancient intelligence behind the words—words not spoken but formed in his mind.

He raised his sword and struck at a tendril.

But the ordinary reality that Scarlet knew fell fully away from him. He no longer held a sword, nor even had hands or arms. Instead, his talons stretched out and pierced the shimmering strand. It gave momentary resistance before snapping, and its severed length broke into drifting, wilting wisps.

You should have withdrawn. Foolish mistake. She, I will take. You, I will feast upon.

Tendrils rose from Phoebe and struck out toward Scarlet.

He stretched farther and felt the strength of his wings, then wheeled upward and over, shearing another strand with the snap of his beak.

Phoebe could move her arms and hands once again. The bonds fell to the stone, and, despite the paralysis in her legs, she dragged herself away from the hovering horror.

Scarlet dropped into a dive, flicking sideways in a barrel roll as tendrils speared at him and threw coils in his way. One caught him, but he twisted and brought claw and beak together to shred it.

Phoebe's throat released. She yanked out the gag and screamed with all the strength she could muster, but the beast took hold again, and the scream died.

Ghost-cords wrapped one of Scarlet's wings. He fluttered, arched about, and savaged the soul-flesh that held him. More coils caught at him, bound him, and advanced into his brain. He pulled his talons close and raked powerfully outward, ripping away strand after strand, but still they held on.

Lightning flashed below him, and the creature shivered. The essence of Phoebe crackled with energy, sending crooked bolts of searing-white electricity outward from her mind and will as she struck back in desperation. The tendrils that held Phoebe quivered.

She regained her throat and screamed again, and again lost control.

And then the great beast suddenly released her, flung wide its tendrils, brought them swinging together, and jetted away into the swirling dark.

The hard stone pressed into Phoebe's cheek. She rolled over onto her back. The glow of several lamps appeared at the entrance to Desolation, held by a squad of soldiers.

———

"It still feels like a dream, Scarlet," said Phoebe.

They sat together at a basin of bubbling water, a Rook healer having bandaged the raw skin at Phoebe's wrists and looked to her other small wounds.

"In a way, I think it was," said Scarlet. "That...thing struck directly at our minds. We fought back in the manner we imagined."

"Did anyone know what it was?" she said.

Scarlet shook his head. "I received four confident answers, all different."

"No one seems that concerned," said Phoebe.

"Well, Grager was clearly spot on about there being a thousand enemies, seen and unseen, and these people seem to have met up with them all. They're a tough lot."

"So are we." She smiled. "We fought it off."

He grinned. "That we did. I think. The soldiers' arrival might have had something to do with it."

Inwardly, Scarlet shook his head again. He considered what Phoebe had been through not three hours earlier, and here she sat—not quivering in her bed, not sobbing in fear, not lying curled up in a closet being comforted by others. He saw not a single tear fall from her eyes after untying her, merely an "Oh, Scarlet, thank god you came," as she'd brought her breathing quietly under control on the stone of Desolation.

"How did you know I was at Desolation Point?" she said.

He leaned in closer to her. "Saw a pretty girl who, for some reason, had on her bolt case, and I couldn't help but follow."

"Well, you most certainly saved my life," she said, her eyes down, her hand smoothing a rip in her dress.

Scarlet knew then that the kiss was forthcoming, and he leaned gently in toward her.

Phoebe stood. "The captains are expecting us. Hours of questions, I'm sure. We should go."

And she walked hesitantly away.

Scarlet slowly let his head droop with a sigh. "Not the gratitude imagined."

———

The next morning, Phoebe stood in line at the base of the cliff, awaiting transport up the rails to the top of the mesa, and, there, to join the weekly convoy into Pinnacle.

Trace knelt down and gave her a gentle hug. "I don't like you going."

"I'll miss you too, Trace." She squeezed his thick shoulders a last time.

"You go find those kids and say hi for me." He backed away.

"I will."

Scarlet took Phoebe's hand and kissed it. She did not resist.

"Do you suppose Grager's words meant anything?" she said.

"About as much as any words coming from a suicidal murderer. The important thing is, no one dropped any blame on us. The best result we could hope for, I should think."

"I will miss you."

"We'll see each other again," he said.

"How do you know?"

His green eyes flashed with cheer. "I'm sure Rodrigo will come soon, and we'll march on to Pinnacle in a few weeks—after he conquers Haven, of course."

The giant, fat rail cage descended behind Phoebe, its metal screech drowning out any further conversation. Soldiers guided her inside, she turned for a last wave, and the doors closed. With a clatter of reversing gears, the cage rose to the sky.

———

At the Rook Clan, at the tenth hour, Kane came rushing in looking for Scarlet. "Hey, our guys are bringing in people that you may know. They were already awake when we found them, like you."

Kane led Scarlet and Trace to the compound. Near the assembly building, a small knot of soldiers were gathered. The three approached the group. Kane whispered to the captain in charge, who looked over Scarlet and Trace appraisingly and ordered the soldiers to disperse.

As the crowd opened, Scarlet caught sight of Yun slumped on the ground, bruised, battered, and exhausted. Hope, Rip, and Ed sat next to her, looking worse than Yun. Rip's hands bound as if he were a prisoner, and a bloody wrap encircled his leg.

Scarlet shouted and pushed through the crowd.

Yun's eyes drifted upward. "Scarlet!" She stumbled to her feet and fell into his arms.

Scarlet's face sank into her tangled hair as he held her. Neither said anything, Finally, he could hear Trace's voice ask, "Where is Rodrigo?"

He looked up.

Hope, choking back tears, approached Trace and put a hand on his shoulder. "Rodrigo is dead, Trace."

50: A LAST GOODBYE

—Hours before

Yun's diary, Day 153

It's now over three weeks since Scarlet went away. Rodrigo has given up hope that Scarlet will come back, and so he is determined to go find him, despite the slivers in the tunnels. We are going to the Forge to convince Ed.

"Three!" shouted Rodrigo. His voice echoed in the great chamber of the Forge. Surprisingly, Three slowed and turned.

"Three, I must revise my promise to you."

[KEEP SECRET]

"We will keep this place a secret. But there are items we can safely take that will not hint at this place. We must find those of us who are missing—Scarlet, Trace, and Phoebe—and we need the items. Torches, weapons, food, basic items that do not betray the secret."

[YOU ARE THE COMMANDER]

[FORGE MUST NOT BE LOST]

Prepared for an extended debate, Rodrigo looked at Yun, Hope, and Rip. "Three speaks as though we are in a war."

"Could be we are, *'Commander,'*" said Rip. "Everything we meet means to kill us, so we might as well be."

"There may have been a war sixty years ago," said Yun, "and it's long over."

"Regardless, Three handed the keys to you, Rodrigo," said Hope.

"Good," said Rip. "Then we won't need to repack."

"Let us find Ed," said Rodrigo.

They found him in the mill yard, working at a gear-laden machine. Straps from the spinning main shaft of the water wheel drove the bulky device through its process. As they approached, Ed pulled a long round pole from the machine, released the drive belts, and turned to Rodrigo. "Are we ready to go?"

Rodrigo paused in puzzlement. "How did you know?"

"I pay attention more than you think."

Rodrigo shrugged. "I thought you might like the idea of being alone-"

"Not *that* alone!" scoffed Ed. "Who'd cook my meals and take care of the menial tasks? I do know my limitations, sir."

The others glanced at each other, as though wanting to say many things in response, but in the end leaving it to Rodrigo. "Despite our past differences, Ed, it is good to hear that you are coming."

Ed shrugged and turned away. "I have something for us. I'd rather not die by slivers, which means they have to die instead. So…"

He stepped to a table nearby, lifting a pointed stake of metal embedded in a shaft of wood about as long as his forearm. Strips of cloth lined the back end of the shaft, making an effective, sizable dart.

"I managed to get done with six of these. I put barbs on two. The barbs might make the wound worse, or might prevent the dart from penetrating, so I didn't want to risk more until we experiment."

Rip laughed. "Experiment, he says."

"Nicely done, Ed," said Rodrigo.

"And I finished these." Ed lifted three spears of different lengths and tapped at one of the narrow metal points. Behind the point were four blade-edged fins, each backed by metal spokes. "Based on your description, it sounded like once a spear penetrates, it goes through fairly easily, which is not actually the best result. You want to stop and rip that hole wider. So, the fins will open the hole, and the spokes will stop the target from sliding right along the haft and onto you. I made each a different length so we can work a proper phalanx against them."

Ed handed one to Rodrigo and one to Rip. "You can fold the spokes over the fins so you don't accidentally cut yourself."

"Masterly," said Rip, feeling the balance of his short spear.

"Careful with the tip," said Ed. "The machinery here might only be water- and gas-driven, but it is exceptionally engineered."

"You have outdone yourself," said Rodrigo.

"Anything for us?" said Hope.

"You stay behind us," said Ed.

"We will each take a dart," said Hope. "I, for one, won't throw mine."

Ed handed Hope and Yun a dart. "Last but not least…" He lifted a small barrel up to his back and secured it with a strap over his shoulder. He pumped hard at a lever for over a minute, picked up a metal rod attached by canvas hose to the barrel, and pressed a grip release on the rod.

With a harsh hiss, a violent ejection of gas shot from the nozzle and a steel wheel threw up sparks into it, causing an extensive jet of flame to erupt, its radiant heat flashing the startled faces of the other Dusties.

"Hahlay!" shouted Rip.

Rodrigo laughed in amazement. "This is fantastic, Ed. But much as I would love to see it in operation, we cannot take it."

"Why not?" said Ed, ready to be fully indignant.

"We cannot take things that hint at the Forge. These fine spears are already a bit of a problem. The flame-barrel does more than just hint. I am sorry. That goes for anything else you might have packed."

Ed harrumphed. "Fine," he said in the manner of a naughty boy who had just lost his slingshot to his disapproving mother.

Ed repacked, and the Dusties headed to the stairway. Before entering, Yun turned with a sigh to their old home. She waved at Three, who ignored her. Then she turned and left.

51: A LONG, STRAIGHT WAY

Rodrigo and company used a rope to descend to the pumice tunnel. Ed used a string to draw the rope back up into the metal door, and then cut the string high with the blades on his spear.

"We go the way that the strangers took Scarlet, and we move fast," whispered Rodrigo. "Ed and Rip, take lead. I will take rear. Hope and Yun stay in the center. No talking. Keep straight if you can; I will mark the path if we cannot. If you see obvious signs of heavy use on a side path, we will give it consideration. If you see torchlight, signal."

They moved quickly down the tunnel, meeting nothing except for an occasional statue. The pumice itself gave way to natural stone tunnels or open caverns at times, but it reliably reappeared on the other side. The pumice held no marks of any kind, but the natural stone areas contained abundant markings and chiseled directions.

Ed stopped in a small cavern, pointing to the markings. "Drift! See?" he whispered.

The word DRIFT cut across the path, accompanied by an arrow back the way they had come. A second arrow next to the word HAVEN pointed forward.

"You want Drift?" asked Rip.

"Hardly," said Rodrigo, "they threw me over a cliff. Now, stay straight, and hope to heaven that Haven is a city as well."

After thirty minutes, they crossed a solidly built stone bridge over a great earth-splitting chasm. Old, shattered fortifications flanked the bridge, relics of a battle long lost to history and darkness. Rodrigo brought his companions to rest within a rubble-strewn tower on the far side.

Rip and Yun looked fresh, but Rodrigo saw the strain of exertion and fear on Hope. "Rip, can you keep your fine ears at the entrance?"

"Ahey, Boss," whispered Rip, padding back to the rubble near the gaping breach in the tower.

Rodrigo smiled. "Haven, it is a good name. Very kind of them to mark our way."

"Do you believe Scarlet and the others made it?" said Hope.

"Much more certain now," said Rodrigo. "These appear to be well-traveled, or at least well-known, paths. We should see them soon."

He watched some of the fear and uncertainty fade from Hope's face.

"Rodrigo!" whispered Yun, who had wandered a short way toward the back of the tower. "Look!"

Her lantern shone on the statue of a lean, very tall man in loose-fitting clothes suitable for a desert climate, his gaze cast outward and one hand extended in emphasis, as though he were bringing an oration to a stirring conclusion.

Rodrigo caught his breath as the light revealed the green-black stone. "Do not touch it." He rose and inspected the statue. "We need neither a burst nor a helpless extra right now, especially one as big as this. It will be easy to come back here."

Yun nodded. "How many of us are there, I wonder?"

"Perhaps a few more every month—like birds flying into a wall," said Rodrigo.

"You think we are like the birds and air machines sticking out of the wall in the Big Hole?" said Ed.

Rodrigo nodded. "Somehow, yes. I am grateful, though, that we appear here with everything intact, not merely the front half."

Yun smiled and started to respond, but Rip appeared, his face grim.

"Slivers!"

Rodrigo motioned for quiet. They shuttered their lanterns down to focused beams and crept to the opening.

Enough water filtered into the chasm to create strips and patches of glowmoss. Watching the patches, they could pick out five or six shapes moving stealthily over the bridge. They made no hiss, but the Dusties could pick up the slight bone-whisper of their movement. Rodrigo thought he could make out the violet glow of their bodies, so dim that he had to concentrate to see it.

A slight glow appeared in the tunnel on their side of bridge. It grew steadily brighter, until torches appeared.

"People!" whispered Rip.

"To the tunnel, move!" hissed Rodrigo. He ended up pushing Hope, who had frozen in fear. "Go!"

A chorus of hisses came to Rodrigo's ears from the bridge as he closed on the tunnel. Ahead, he saw the torches rush backward into the entrance and heard the shouting of commands. Urging Hope on, he made the entrance, shouting to Rip and Ed to close in on him and prepare.

As Rodrigo turned for a glance back, a blur of black leapt at him. He had no time to swing his spear around. He fell back, and a thin shape slid over him— Ed's spear. The monster charged directly onto its point, burying itself up to the prongs and slamming Ed backward. The stricken monster landed on Rodrigo and flew apart, gobs and dribbles and tiny monstrosities spilling over the boy.

The rain of black disintegration could have tested any man's sanity, but Rodrigo had no time to think about it as his senses focused on the pack of misshapen slivers advancing into the tunnel. The killers moved in more cautiously as Rip, Ed, and Rodrigo presented their wall of spears.

The beasts all bore different shapes—grotesque assemblies of pieces and parts twisted together in a freakish jumble. One bore massively oversized jaws with teeth the length of Rip's forearm. Another appeared designed merely to swing one ponderously long arm with enough force to crush a body.

An unfamiliar voice shouted in Rodrigo's ear. "We have to move, they'll be flanking us!" Rodrigo risked one glance to see a heavily scarred captain as the speaker, backed by two dozen men armed with spears and crossbows. Each bore the mark of a crescent on their cheek. "Jolden, take rear-guard!" shouted the leader. A crew of spearmen and several crossbowmen took up station facing the slivers. "Double-time!" cried the captain, and the rest of the group retreated quickly back down the passage, the rear guard following at a slower pace.

Rodrigo stayed with the rear-guard, keeping behind the crossbowmen, who fired wildly as they retreated. He turned and discovered that his friends had moved onward with the main group. He could see only a confusing jumble amid the bobbing lanterns and torches. He caught a momentary glimpse of Rip, his spear straight up as he trotted among the big men. "Rip, stay with Hope!" he yelled, but he could not be certain if Rip had heard.

Rodrigo thought to chase them, but the pursuing blackspawn pressed the rear-guard, and he brought his spear up to help them as they continued their backpedaling retreat.

Then screams and cries of agony issued from down the tunnel where his friends had gone, accompanied by a chorus of hissing. The slivers following them chose that moment to close and attack. Jolden, Rodrigo, and the rear-guard tried to form up to meet them, not fully prepared for the sudden assault. The spears and bolts took their toll, but several slivers managed to slip through, including the monster with one arm. Its swing smashed down two of the spearmen. The remaining soldiers turned to face Onearm, but this opened their flank and more slivers crashed into them.

Rodrigo found himself in a confused, deadly melee. He stabbed at a sliver, feeling the point drive in, but the body of Jolden struck him in the side and he staggered against the wall, losing hold of his spear. He backed up, dazed, and he felt his thoughts drift. It seemed as though time slowed. In his mind, he saw the others, their bodies broken, the slivers smashing at their corpses, following some deep, malevolent rage known only to them.

Then something within Rodrigo—something hard and uncompromising—smashed the terrifying vision in his mind. His eyes narrowed, and he acted.

Onearm loomed directly in front of him, swinging its monstrous appendage sideways to crush him against the wall. He dove against the monster's leg, the tree-trunk arm brushing his hair as it slammed jarringly against the pumice. He drew his sword and jabbed upward as Onearm tried to step back for another swing. The blade sank deeply into the back of its leg, staggering the creature. Rodrigo spun under the flailing monster, pulled the dart from his belt, and plunged both sword and dart into the monster's hip. A black stream cascaded from the twin wounds.

Rodrigo leapt away, snatched up a stray lantern, and raced in pursuit of Rip and the others.

Shapes moved ahead of him. Slivers appeared, but ones clearly wounded, diminished, and not interested in a further fight. At a side passage he found the main point of battle, a few soldiers dead or terribly wounded, but no sign of his friends. A sliver advanced out of the passage into his path, but Rodrigo flung the dart and the creature backed away, the dart lodged in its neck. Lanterns bobbed like will-o-wisps fifty paces down the tunnel, and with a surge of hope he raced after them.

52: A Last Duty

Seventeen men remained with the other Dusties as they passed into a natural fissure that crossed the path of the pumice tunnel. A wide bridge spanned the narrow gap. The glowmoss grew heavy here, and Yun could see her fellows clearly. But she couldn't see...

"Where's Rodrigo?" she yelled at Rip.

Rip held one hand to his leg, blood oozing between his fingers. He cast about frantically, trying to see through the larger men, then he pointed excitedly. "He's coming!"

Yun turned and saw a lantern closing on them. Soon she recognized Rodrigo's face and the panic tearing at her heart twisted into a spasm of relief.

A strange noise nagged at her. She looked up into the jagged fissure, and her soul froze. She wanted to scream, but what she witnessed clawed away at her will and left her shaking and helpless.

It was big and swift, and it flowed down out of the fissure like a black water-fall. Yun glimpsed ropy appendages, like tentacles, hooked claws on lean climbing legs, and a vertical mouth topped by gloss-black eyes that glinted momentarily her way. Sword-like mandibles flanked the jaws, thrusting out from the tentacled mass. Of the body she could see little, but it must have been lean and agile and powerful.

A soldier threw aside his spear and ran blindly across the bridge, his face an inhuman mask of terror. Others streamed by her, racing across the bridge and away from the colossal nightmare.

And then, Yun remembered Rodrigo. She willed her eyes to look down the tunnel.

Rodrigo was not far now, close to safety.

But the bulk of the monster flowed into the tunnel, blocking Rodrigo from her view, and Yun screamed his name with all of the pent-up horror that had piled within her.

———

Rodrigo saw Yun. He tried to put on a burst of speed to reach her, but his ankle wasn't working right. It came to his mind that his ankle stung painfully with each step, and he slowed.

Then Yun disappeared, replaced by the most horrifying sight he had ever witnessed.

It filled the lower half of the tunnel, sliding toward him on lightning-swift tentacles and long agile legs. It made a staccato clicking and Rodrigo remembered the thing outside the tunnel hatch, days ago.

He turned and ran, his only thought to escape. Despite his fear, a part of his mind considered the side passage. If he could only reach it…

A line of slivers appeared in his lantern light. They had taken up the chase, sealing him off from the side passage.

Rodrigo raised his sword and rushed at them, bellowing a last, bold rallying cry. But a great black presence overshadowed him, a crushing weight struck him from behind like a falling tree, and Rodrigo came to the end.

———————

Yun's diary, Day 159

We sought so long to escape what we believed to be our trap. We freed ourselves into a world of nightmares.

I remember telling myself yesterday, "This is not how it should be." What a laughable thought! As if anything should *be*, for Dusties. We live a life that has been chopped at the roots, lost to that past that made us who we are, and unable to peer even a day forward through the black fog of our future. Tomorrow, we might easily be like Rodrigo.

We are Dusties, and our lot is to survive this world of nightmares for as many days as we can. Sometimes I think the struggle is too much.

———————

53: HAVEN HALL

Yun's diary, Day 160

> Scarlet and I talked most of the night. He told me what Rodrigo told him, about making every place that you go better, and not giving up.
>
> Scarlet mourns strangely. He tells stories about Rodrigo—I already know the stories, of course—and he laughs and carries on as if Rodrigo would be stepping through the doorway any day now. "Everything about Rodrigo was quality," he says, "and I intend to honor that by soldiering on."
>
> Phoebe is gone. She went up to another city called Pinnacle. The queen there bought Phoebe because she learned how to shoot the crossbow like an expert in just a few days.
>
> I read my notes from yesterday. They were scary. I'm glad Scarlet talked to me. I feel much better today, even though we are in trouble with the people of Haven.
>
> We have been sent to the head clan in Haven—the Crescent Clan. They told us we are under house arrest, for now. Apparently we are on trial, although no one has accused us of anything. They say we will be questioned.
>
> We've all had a chance to talk over what we want to say—that we are a small pocket of Sleepers living by an isolated lake in the tunnels. That's the truth. Scarlet feels like we should carefully honor our agreement not to mention the Forge or anything else in our old home.
>
> Rip is the one that is in trouble. Haven people are very much against anyone that is not human—except the tantyr angels, apparently. There is a tantyr in the city, but we have never seen it.

Day 163

> Haven has an Archive! The high lord here in Haven has a son named Ikone, and he took me to see it today.

The Grand Hall of Haven was grand in both size and appearance—a brightly lit vaulted square, rising into a dome with a hole in its apex, designed and built centuries past by a Sleeper with extraordinary skills in architecture. Fine murals, statues, and engravings covered the walls, floor, and ceiling in a chaotic mixture of themes and styles, reflecting perfectly the Sleeper society. A ring of ascending stone terraces, serving as seats, encircled the room, holding a scattering of audience.

The Crescent Clan Lord perched like a raptor at the seat of honor—a sturdy oriental man in loose-fitting, bright cloth, his hair prematurely white, and his dark eyes intense. Wives, counselors, and allied clan lords surrounded him. Competing clan lords and their counselors took seats elsewhere in the circle. The crowd conversed casually with each other, but their eyes drifted often to the Dusties seated in the chamber's center.

Scarlet took everything in, trying to gauge attitudes and intentions of those in the chamber. Considering the suspicion leveled at Rip, Scarlet assumed that this would be a trial or interrogation.

For days, Scarlet and the others had debated their Lakeside secrets and why they might have been arrested. Other than Rodrigo's promise to Three, there seemed no useful purpose or reason to keeping the secrets of their Lakeside home, but they agreed to keep them, based solely on their respect for Rodrigo.

This meant that Scarlet fully intended to lie. He felt a twinge of regret for pursuing such a course, as it could ruin his standing in Haven later. But he also knew he could pull it off. Hope and Rip could manage it as well. Ed and Trace were unknowns. And then there was Yun.

Yun would crack like a quail's egg.

The other Dusties sat behind him. Scarlet turned and presented a reassuring smile to each.

Yun smiled back. Ordinarily she could hide herself behind her curtain of long bangs, but she had cut her bangs shorter and pulled her hair back in a bun in a vain attempt to look older. Now every wave and wrinkle of nerves and anxiety swam like fish through her large expressive eyes. If she lied, everyone in the chamber would know.

Hope gave Scarlet her own sly smile before returning to her professional façade. Word had gotten out that one of the Dusties was a skilled healer, and Hope already had plans to open a hospice. *At least one of us will land on their feet*, thought Scarlet.

In the back sat Ed and Trace. Ed paid no attention, scribbling in a small journal. Trace sagged, his face turned to his lap. Something was definitely wrong with the man-giant. His clumsiness and stumbling speech had returned, but he also acted sickly and withdrawn. When Scarlet asked Trace about his condition, Trace merely said, "I'll be fine," and refused to talk about it further.

Scarlet turned forward and awaited the interrogation's commencement. For a moment he forgot himself and glanced to his left, but of course Rodrigo wasn't there. The conflict between keeping secrets and telling all battled inside him until he felt dizzy and uncertain.

———

Behind Scarlet, guards began pushing closed the tall metal doors of the chamber. But before they shut, a Crescent page slipped through, strode quickly up to the Crescent leader, and whispered, sparking a sudden burst of conversation among the leader's inner circle. Scarlet focused, trying to read the event. Clearly the Crescents had just received unwelcome information and were scrambling to react. The whispered debates became intense, disorganized, almost panicky. Then the Crescent Lord asserted himself, shutting down the conversations and issuing orders. He stood, causing a rapid cessation of all activity in the room. In the new silence, a tall, battle-ready warrior who acted as the assembly warden took his station on the floor and spoke.

"The Haven Council commands order," said the warden in a manner that suggested the words were ceremonial. "High Lord Odami presides! May his words and thoughts be blessed by Shalem."

High Lord Odami stepped down through the crowd and paced the floor in front of the Dusties, his commanding gaze passing from one to the other. The eyes of the Dusties lowered nervously when their turn at scrutiny came. Scarlet had been informed how Odami had achieved the lordship of Haven for most of the past twenty years. Lordship passed each year to the clan most successful at awakening Sleepers, and clearly the Crescents under Odami had no equals in that task.

Odami gave each Dustie a final challenging stare, then settled himself in the first row of seating. "Yun, come forward."

Scarlet turned. Yun, having no thought that she would be immediately singled out, looked close to panic. She gave Scarlet a plaintive glance and stood slowly. The tall warden motioned her to his side, and she obeyed.

Shrikes! The game is up in minutes.

Yun stood uncomfortably, while Odami scratched his cheek absently. Scarlet noticed the page who had brought news sitting behind Odami. The page glanced about impatiently and fearfully, as though the building was about to explode.

"I am told," said Odami, whose strong, cultured voice did not disappoint his full charismatic presence, "that you enjoy books."

Scarlet could barely hear Yun's small voice. "Yes."

"Speak up," ordered Odami.

"Yes."

"And the pen?"

"I do," said Yun.

Odami leaned forward. "For twenty generations and more we have been at war with enemies seeking our eradication. The blackspawn are only the latest of many. There are few among us who have time beyond survival of the city, and few enough of us with skill of the pen to keep a small sense of our history. Those records, as few as they are, reside in the Archives of this city, carefully protected. I am told that my son, Ikone, showed you the Archives this morning."

"Yes."

"Haven has a purpose and place in this world, little one. From it, the human peoples can regain their former prominence. Sleepers enter this world without their past. The proud history of Haven can give them new ground on which to stand confidently—if there is someone with the energy and skill to bring it to life from the dust-covered shelves of the Archives."

Yun had nothing immediately to say, but there was no doubting the building delight in her face. "Are you speaking of me, sir?"

"Of course. The task requires youth, for it may take many years. Who better than you?"

"Thank you, sir!"

"Ikone, escort Yun to the Archives."

A husky young man with his father's piercing eyes rose and stepped down to Yun.

Does he actually mean now? thought Scarlet.

And he did. Ikone took Yun's arm. Yun gave Scarlet a questioning glance and, without another word, was led away through a narrow side exit.

Peculiar, thought Scarlet. *But it does make my task easier.*

"Yusef!" called Odami.

A burly, bald ogre of a man rose. "Yes, Lord?"

"Is the second cage to Pinnacle working yet?"

"Hopefully soon, Lord. The break in the rail is rather high-"

"Ed!" interrupted Odami, pointing his finger at Ed. It took several embarrassing moments for Ed to realize he was being summoned.

"I'm sorry, I seem to have missed something?" said Ed.

Odami rose, his gaze making plain that he did not appreciate being missed. "There are cage lifts to Pinnacle along the cliff. When I was young, four were in operation. Now there are two, and barely two. I want four again, but Yusef tells me that is unreasonable."

"Well," said Ed, standing, "Yusef might be right. But if he isn't, I can fix a cold in a fog."

"Until you do, you are merely a braggart," said Odami.

Ed bristled.

"I suggest that you work on proving me wrong. Yusef, show the braggart to the cages."

Yusef led a visibly angry Ed to the same side exit.

Scarlet couldn't help the satisfied smile that crept across his lips. *Like a hog to the tying*, he thought. *This Odami is not one to be trifled with.*

Another one of us removed. Is it deliberate, I wonder?

"Hope," called Odami. "Come forward. I have hopes that you are better company than Ed."

Hope flashed the trademark smile that brought her beauty to life. She had done nothing with her hair, other than put it in a plain ponytail, which gave her natural attractiveness even more sway. "Ed has his rough surfaces, My Lord. But he's reliable."

"Is his faith in his skills justified?" said Odami.

"Other than a genius for knots and fulcrums, I could not say," said Hope.

"Did he design the spears and darts that you carried?"

"I am sure that he would say so, though I am told that he made only minor changes to ones we scavenged."

Scarlet could only gape at the smooth, casual way in which the outright lies flowed from Hope. One corner of his soul cheered at the brilliant deflection of what was obviously a trap question. Another corner shrunk back. He knew that he remained fascinated by Hope—who wouldn't be fascinated after having a life-saving dream of Hope before even meeting her, when he lay dying of the Fleye sting? But he felt a gap had grown between them, and more than the arm-length he had promised to Rodrigo.

Odami seemed satisfied by the lies, or at least not concerned about pursuing them. "But you are a healer with proven reputation, I hear?"

"I haven't been awake long," said Hope. "I would not say my skills are established."

"They will be soon enough," said Odami. "We suffered casualties in the attack last night. Also, the latest Fever has claimed a second life. Your presence is far more valuable at the hospice than here. My wife Elairee, who is building her own skill at healing, will escort you there."

"As you wish, My Lord."

"And take your big compatriot with you. He's clearly ailing. It's a wonder he even made it here."

At this, Trace rose and headed directly to the side exit, at a pace that argued against any crippling illness. Hope and Elairee followed him up.

Deliberate, without doubt. Just me and Rip left. Why would—

Scarlet's thoughts were interrupted by the metallic groan of the giant doors opening behind him. He turned and saw a sight he had never dreamed nor imagined.

54: BERYLATA

A woman entered the chamber. At first, she seemed human, despite the golden skin. A flowing gown of black and gray hid her feet and gave her movement the impression of floating instead of walking. Snow-white hair fell like a wedding train behind her shoulders.

But as she approached, Scarlet realized it was not hair. Thin frills ran along the sides of her head and over her neck and shoulders. White fur—or was it feathers?—covered the frills and head. Her finely shaped, exotically beautiful face framed two cat-like eyes of brilliant emerald. Those eyes reflected a deep well of confidence, wisdom, and determination, and Scarlet sensed that the creature had seen many years beyond his own.

The creature passed close by Scarlet, his eyes level with her shoulder. So powerful was her close presence that Scarlet felt both fear and inspiration joining in a new sensation that shook him to the soul. He turned numbly to see two short swords resting in shining scabbards that crossed at the small of her back.

All in the room came to their feet in hushed silence. Clearly they had not expected the tantyr to come here. Several warriors moved to clear one section of the seating—unnecessary, as the Havenites there quickly relocated a safe distance. The creature took her place, and the Havenites sat as well, with only Odami remaining standing.

"Greetings, honorable Berylata."

"Greetings, high lord," spoke Berylata in a voice that made Odami's sound weak and tinny. The tantyr cast her gaze on Scarlet and Rip, who now sat alone. "There are only two."

"The others have promising skills but little else to offer," said Odami. "I have kept the two of importance. Did you wish to question them first?"

"Afterward," said Berylata.

Odami nodded and turned his attention to Rip. "Rip, come forth."

Rip hopped up, laid his newly acquired and ridiculously oversized hat in his chair, and strode cheerfully to the front.

Odami regarded him from his seat for a time. This had little impact on Rip, who stood arrow straight with his hands behind his back. Every so often, he lifted himself slightly onto his toes and flashed a contented smile, as though he had just remembered something delightful.

Odami eventually leaned forward. "What kind of being are you?"

"My Lord," said Rip, bowing slightly, "my exceptional height and my catty bobs aside, I do always consider myself quite human."

"Bobs—are you speaking of your ears? They are hardly human."

"We can debate that as brothers," beamed Rip.

Odami stood. "Over the centuries, Haven has met with many races. Some came with open arms, some with weapons bared. In the end, they all proved to be enemies and betrayers. We have benefitted from a strong distrust of anything that calls itself friend."

Rip maintained his composure, but the lightness in his stance faded.

Odami turned to a group of soldiers clustered together nearby. "Cannel, present yourself."

A lean, wiry young soldier stepped down and moved next to Rip, his deep brown features tense with nervousness.

"Give your witness," said Odami.

"Yes, My Lord. I was in the war party that found the…the Dusties, as they like to call themselves. The blackspawn flanked us, and we did not expect their numbers or their size. Our line shattered."

"Was Rip part of this line?"

"Yes. I was knocked backward and fell. Rip killed the blackspawn that downed me. His spear is murder. I tried to regain my feet. Unfortunately my spear point accidentally caught Rip in the leg."

"Did you see the large crawling monster?" asked Odami.

Cannel's face tightened further and his eyes flicked toward Berylata. "Yes."

"And you, Rip, did you have a good view of the monster that killed your leader?"

"Yes," said Rip. "Though I wish not."

Odami nodded. "The monster appeared only in the last few months. We don't know how many there are, but unlike the blackspawn, it can climb with ease. The city walls will not be any use against them. Do either of you remember anything about the one you saw that would give us an indication of weakness?"

Cannel and Rip looked at each other for a moment, then each shook his head slowly. "I am sorry, My Lord," said Rip. "I saw naught but pure, swift killing power. I hope never to see it again."

Odami leaned toward Cannel. "I am told that you and Rip were two of the few who did not run at its sight. Did either of you manage to shoot at it?"

"I did," said Cannel, "but without apparent luck."

"Do you believe Rip acted with honor in the battle?" asked Odami.

"Yes, sir."

"Scarlet," called Odami, "do you defend Rip?"

"All of us would, My Lord," said Scarlet.

"Do not be hasty," said Odami. "You brought Rip to Haven. He fought well at the battle. But he is not human. Should he prove faithless or devious, he will be killed. You will share his fate. Do you understand?"

"I do. My answer remains."

"And if you prove to be something other than what you say you are, you will all be slain. Haven will never again risk itself to outsiders. Do you understand this?"

"I do," said Scarlet, but he wondered what had happened to bring them to such paranoia.

Odami waved Rip away, but as the little man returned to his place, Odami spoke. "Rip, you will be greeted with suspicion, likely for years. Be prepared for this."

Scarlet resisted shaking his head in disgust. *They treat him poorly while demanding his loyalty. Bad form.*

"Scarlet, come forth."

———

As Scarlet stood, the twists and turns in his mind suddenly sorted themselves out, and he felt a refreshing calm radiate down through his soul. He stepped to the side of the warden.

Odami stood, bringing all of the force of his dominant presence to bear. Scarlet knew then that—for him—this would be an interrogation.

"Who is your leader?" said Odami.

"The lord of Rook Clan, and through him, you," said Scarlet.

He held Odami's gaze, and thought for one moment that he saw amusement in Odami's eyes.

"A wise answer," said Odami. "Tell us about your former leader."

"His name was Rodrigo. He awoke near Drift."

"How many live in your home city?"

"City? All of nine, but one died," said Scarlet. "Now seven, with Rodrigo slain, and six with Phoebe gone up to Pinnacle. We lived next to a small lake, isolated underground. There is no city, My Lord, and no one lives there at all now, once we found a tunnel out."

"How long have you been awake?"

"A hundred sixty days, approximately. We did not have the timekeepers like you have in the city."

"And the others?"

"I was the third woken. Rodrigo was only a few weeks earlier."

"Was Rodrigo lying?"

"About how he came awake? And when?" asked Scarlet.

"Yes."

Scarlet smiled, but his face reflected sorrow. "I wish that you could have met him, My Lord. You would have no need to ask that question."

Odami motioned to an aide, who passed him Rip's short spear. The four fin-like side blades glinted as Odami inspected the weapon.

"This is ingenious," said Odami. "The blades pry open the wound. Catastrophic to a blackspawn, I would presume. In eighty years of war against them, no one has thought of this. How did you think of it? Or, was it Edward?"

"Pardon, My Lord, but it's just Ed," said Scarlet. "And yes, Ed might be a braggart and a few other choice words, but he designed those fins just a few days after our first meeting with the blackspawn."

"And where did you find the materials to build these spears in your isolated lake home? This is very fine wood. Quite a treasure."

The spears were a mistake. Rodrigo should have left them back at the Forge. But likely Yun and everyone else would be dead now had they done so.

"Remnants of old battles and inhabitants littered the place," said Scarlet. "Ed has admirable metalsmith skills, as far as I understand it."

Strangely, Odami did not press the issue. He scratched his chin a moment, then turned to his allied clan leaders. A whispered, sometimes heated, conversation ensued in their huddle.

During this interlude, Scarlet caught sight of a statue of a woman. She stood at the wall above and behind Odami's knot of deliberations, her tall, graceful form outlined in a flowing dress that ended above the ankles. Half of her long, swirling hair was up in classical style, while the other half ran like streams around her shoulders. She looked out over the crowd—an exquisite goddess surveying her subjects.

A goddess of green-black stone.

The Havenites must have brought the statue here, probably from the tunnels and certainly due to her beauty.

But they had not awakened her.

A thought formed in Scarlet's mind, an image of Yun telling him how Grager had woken a stone boy in the tunnels by touching him, but there had been no explosion, just cold and mist.

And another thought—Rip telling him about the tall green stone man inside an old tower in the tunnels. Why had no one awakened him yet? And how had no one awakened this jade goddess standing before him?

Abruptly, the puzzle pieces fell together...

242

Green stone versus ivory stone. Havenites could not awaken the Dusties of green stone, and Scarlet and the other Dusties could not awaken the pale stone Sleepers.

Dusties and Sleepers. He and his Dustie friends were different.

Different enough to throw us over a waterfall, I wonder?

55: EMERALD EYES

Berylata rose and glided toward Scarlet in a cat's stride. The restless crowd quickly hushed, except for Odami and his knot of advisors who were distracted by their whispered huddle of conversation. One of the advisors noticed and the knot broke suddenly apart. Odami turned.

"Berylata!"

Berylata's approach slowed and stopped.

Odami stared her down. "There will be no scourging tonight. Ask your questions."

Berylata's eyes shifted between the high lord and Scarlet, then her mouth curled slyly. "Odami has chosen to trust you." She paced gracefully side to side. "He will keep spies on you, of course, until there is no doubt. He is right to worry. There are many who covet this domain for their own, the latest being the blackspawn. Humanity has no allies."

"Except the tantyrs," said Scarlet.

The perfect, golden-gilded face of Berylata smiled widely, and her emerald cat's eyes narrowed. "The tantyrs are not allies."

"You are scourges, then," said Scarlet. "Punishers."

"Let's change subjects," said Berylata. "How old are you?"

Scarlet stepped closer to the creature, thrilled by the exotic rush of peril and mystery that her presence evoked. He heard a quiet murmur from the crowd. "Seventeen, by best guess."

"A boy."

"Without doubt," answered Scarlet.

"And here you are, facing a scourge of the tantyrs, chatting calmly."

"'Calmly' would be a bit of a reach. More than a bit, actually."

"And how old was your leader?"

"Rodrigo? My age, more or less."

"Two boys leading a tribe. Do you not find that exceptional?"

"I would not call nine rather lost Dusties a tribe," said Scarlet.

"Dusties?"

"Sleepers, accidents of fate. Hardly notable or exceptional."

Berylata laughed lightly, a beautiful sound that Scarlet wished would continue. "There are clan lords that lack the presence to stand before me. You are notable and exceptional."

Berylata turned her head to view the Havenites. "Odami is having second thoughts—are you not, Clan Lord?"

"Not so. Haven is in need of exceptional men and women," said Odami.

Berylata smiled. "Four centuries ago, a tribe of exceptional men and women came to settle in Haven, among their human brothers. But the tribe turned out to be wallcrawlers—changelings bent on the destruction of Haven—and they nearly succeeded. One of every five Havenites either fell in battle or was murdered in their sleep in that terrible year. Then, one century ago, a Devourer infiltrated the society of Haven and consumed half of the city. Tell me, Scarlet, do you represent such a threat?"

"No."

"Are you hiding the truth of where you came from?"

"No."

"Are there truths about your past that you are keeping from us?"

Time to lie.

"Yes."

At the moment of speaking, Scarlet chose a new path, and he felt a sudden, calm resolve.

Berylata smiled again—this time a predator's smile. "That will not ease Odami's concerns."

Scarlet turned and stepped toward Odami. "I've told you the truth; we are only six, and human, and loyal. Like all other Sleepers, we have lost our past and desire only a home. But so long as you insist on treating us as outsiders, then we will hold to our own secrets, to be spoken some day when surrounded by friends of Haven, not the suspicious lot that I see today."

Odami rose, the fierce raptor's intensity returning to his eyes. "Despite your disrespect, the promise stands, Scarlet. If you prove loyal, you will be among friends. If you prove false, you will be killed." The high lord fixed his eyes on Berylata. "Tantyr, the time has come to make this clear—you are tolerated here, but your interference is not welcome. Do not overstep your bounds."

"Of course, Lord Odami," said Berylata smoothly. She turned to Scarlet. "We have more to discuss, in time."

The air shivered above her, and around her shoulders there formed bands of quivering light. They spread, fanned, and flared. A vibrating rush filled the air, and Berylata rose, flying swiftly upward through the open apex of the chamber and into the midnight blue.

56: STONE GODDESS

It rained the next morning, an uncommon occurrence in Haven. Scarlet requested time in the Grand Hall to better review its artistic displays. Odami agreed, assigned Scarlet a "bodyguard," and ordered the boy to become more familiar with Haven.

Scarlet stood in the center of the Grand Hall, enjoying the fall of the light rain on his shoulders. The floor's slight slope channeled the water to one corner of the chamber and into a large sunken pool where glowmoss grew in climbing heaps. A diverted stream cascaded from the ceiling, through the trellises and into the pool.

Knocks echoed at the small side door, and Scarlet's bodyguard ushered in the cloaked form of Hope and that of Rip beneath his oversized chapeau. Scarlet moved toward the sunken pool and motioned them over.

"You stirred the nest last night," said Hope once they had gathered. She nodded approvingly toward the fall of water, its constant rush preventing Scarlet's bodyguard from listening in.

"Funny, that," said Scarlet. "Last night was not precisely according to plan, trust me. Where's Yun?"

"At the Archives," said Hope, smirking. "Odami's boy—Ikone, I think—is keeping her close company. He's shot right through the heart, poor boy. And he already has two wives. Don't fret, her nose is entirely in the books."

"How's Trace?"

"Acting like a sickly hermit," said Hope. "I don't know why."

The image of Trace boldly saving Rodrigo against the blackspawn passed through Scarlet's mind. "We've got to find a way to help him. This has gone on too long."

"I know, but he rebuffs me when I attempt to check him," said Hope.

Scarlet nodded and turned to Rip. "How are you?"

"A freak is what I am to them," grumbled Rip. "May as well be the Hairy Boggart himself the way they throw their suspicious eyes my way. Wouldn't surprise me if they tried to do me off before long."

"I had thought the plan was to make everyone amiable by lying," said Hope.

"Yes, my apologies," said Scarlet. "I just got to thinking, this is our home now. I don't want to start it off with a leg in the mire."

"You let me lie readily enough," said Hope, who seemed more amused by the thought than angry.

"Yes, I regret that. You do forgive me?"

"Not yet. Someday."

246

"Of course," said Scarlet. "But there are two other reasons—main reasons, perhaps—for my answers. I'm beginning to think that keeping our secrets, as easy as they seemed to be to keep, might well be impossible."

"Before you explain why," said Hope, "why do we care anymore? The secrets, I mean."

"We promised Three."

"Three is a machine."

"We promised Rodrigo."

"Rodrigo is dead."

Hope swallowed hard and lowered her eyes. "I'm sorry, Scarlet."

Scarlet nodded but did not answer.

"In my heart, I do wish to keep the secrets too," said Hope, "if for no other reason than for Rodrigo. He was…amazing. We should have been dead a dozen times down below if not for him. He kept us together."

"I know."

"And now we will drift apart, won't we?" said Hope.

Scarlet gave her a dubious eye. "I wouldn't necessarily say that. Shall we have a go at the artistry here? Quite eye opening. Follow me."

————

Scarlet had in mind only one specific piece of art, but he kept them in a slow, deliberate clockwise routine, under the bodyguard's watchful eye. After turning his back to the guard, he brought them close and spoke in a low voice. "Please say nice things about these works, good and loud, and have my bodyguard hear a reassuring earful. You see, he's light on guarding and heavy on spying."

Hope brushed against him. "Tell us more about last night."

"First, if Rip didn't already tell you, the tantyr that showed up last night might be the most dangerous thing I have ever met."

"I heard she had the beauty of a goddess," said Hope.

"Right, and the presence of a hungry leopard," said Scarlet. "The Havenites call her a scourge. I was hoping Yun would show up and explain that to me, but I'm quite sure it's not a happy concept. I believe she could have torn the truth right out of me if she was allowed to."

"Why didn't she?" said Hope.

"Odami wouldn't let her. There's a power play between the two, and I think they both want to find out something from us without the other being witness. Again, I need to talk to Yun. I don't understand how the tantyrs fit into this place. The Havenites are paranoid of everything not human, so why do they trust the tantyrs?"

"Do they think the tantyrs are gods?" asked Hope.

"N-hardly a chance," said Rip. "Yeh don't argue politics with gods. Not a reverent soul in the place. Just a room full of Havenites concerned for their own skin and expecting a show."

"A show of what?" said Hope.

"I think a scourging," said Rip. "High theatrics, mayhaps even a mess of blood. I was glad I was the one sitting down."

"Hiding under your hat," said Scarlet.

"Ah-hey! Best course of action near a tantyr, I think."

They reached a grand mural of a lion in summer sun, making them immediately sick for the feel of a real, warm sun, and reminding them that they had not said anything about the art to keep up the act for the guard.

"Splendid!" shouted Scarlet a little too loudly.

"So agreeably warm!" declared Hope.

"I'm touched!" piped up Rip.

"Yes, you are," whispered Hope.

They moved on.

"One thing is of a-certain," said Rip, "that Berylata is all she-cat and no angel."

Scarlet nodded. "Clearly Odami meant to keep us away from her. I think he believes we have vitally important secrets, and he is not interested in sharing those secrets with Berylata."

"Our secrets seem pretty drab to me," said Hope.

"Exactly. I thought about the Forge, and, while that is a fine manufactory, it is over six miles away through contested tunnels, and hasn't nearly the food and materials of Haven. The glowmoss is truly a remarkable resource—food, fibers for clothes and rope, particularly fine oil, medicines, wood, and on, so Haven isn't hurting for any of that. And Haven's artisans are splendid, as far as I can tell. They have farm stock, some trade with Pinnacle, and the benefits of a city. So, they have little need for our secrets."

"They don't know that," said Hope.

"Precisely," said Scarlet. "They will be sorely disappointed at our shabby secrets."

"So we keep the secrets and test their patience, or we tell and test their sense of humor?"

"Smartly stated, Hope," said Scarlet. "And now, let's hasten just a little to the real fly in the washbasin."

They continued along, up the steps to the top of the audience seating.

"To your right," whispered Scarlet.

Rip and Hope made surreptitious glances.

"Ah-hey...green stone! It's one of us," said Rip.

They strolled along the line of artistic excellence until they stood directly in front of the green stone statue of the tall, flowing beauty.

"My, my," said Hope. "A new mare in your stable, Scarlet."

"Mare?"

"Nothing," said Hope. "She is quite the goddess, isn't she?"

Up close, the woman in stone exceeded every expectation of Scarlet's distant introduction to her. He thought it best that he should stop staring at her. It was not until he heard a snicker from Hope that he realized that he had been staring far too long already.

"What do you think of her, Rip?" said Hope.

"I wish she had half the height and twice the bobs," said Rip. "I am impressed, for an ettin."

"Whatever you do, don't touch her." Scarlet noticed the disc of stone supporting the woman, swirled in a vortex pattern around her feet, like a deity arising from the sea before being petrified by fickle magic.

"Why not?" said Hope.

"Because some clan lord had it carried here," said Scarlet. "You see?"

Hope and Rip looked at each other.

"They carried her here *with their hands,*" said Scarlet, mimicking the task as best he could without letting on to the bodyguard.

Rip's eyes widened. Hope uttered an "Oh!" The two passed through the stages of dawning realization, until Scarlet knew they too had completed the puzzle.

"They can touch her but not wake her," said Hope. "How disappointing for the clan lord."

"How disappointing for us," said Scarlet. "And I mean Us with a capital U. We can't wake Them, and they can't wake Us. And when they find this out, when they discover we are different, we will likely be taking a very short swim over a terribly tall waterfall."

"But what does it matter if we are some different 'batch' of Dustie? We're probably just from a different land."

"It shouldn't. But these people are ready to murder Rip solely for the twist in his ears," said Scarlet. "They see a killer behind every bush, a monster in every shadow. As Lord Grager said, they have a thousand enemies and a long history of being attacked and betrayed. So these are neither the most welcoming nor most understanding people in the world."

"It seems easy to keep this a secret," said Hope. "We simply don't touch any green statues."

Scarlet shook his head. "But Trace and I are Rook Clan soldiers now. What happens when they send us into the tunnels to wake up Sleepers? We can't wake up the white stone statues. That'll be the bitter end, right there."

Hope bit her lip and thought it through. "What do we do?"

Scarlet shrugged in frustration. "I haven't the foggiest guess."

57: History

Yun's diary, Day 181

I haven't had a single chance to write a journal, but today I found some completely blank, fancy leather notebooks in the Archives, so here we go.

I've been busy in the Archives, and lost track of the days. Scarlet came looking for me. Has it really been that long? I promised to meet him today.

"Down there." Yun leaned out and pointed down over the low stone wall at the edge of Desolation Point. "Off to the left a little, about fifteen hundred feet down. It was called Beacon. Not as big as Haven, but rich from trade with the bottomlanders. And around the curve to the right there was Charada, very close to the bottom."

"Nothing but black now," said Scarlet, peering down the cliff into the utter black. And yet, there seemed to be a slight shimmer to the mist below.

"Nothing," echoed Yun. "No one has been to the bottomlands for a long time. Charada died long ago too. I don't know how. Beacon died well over a century ago, swallowed by the Malfaer—something really scary hidden in the mists, at least from the little I've read."

"How far down to the bottomlands?" said Scarlet.

"From here? Over three thousand feet. You would have time to regret falling off. And from here it's fifteen hundred feet to the top. They call it the Spire, but from the maps I've seen, it's a big flat mesa on top, over twenty-one miles from north to south, shaped like a teardrop with Pinnacle sitting at the point of the teardrop. Pinnacle is above us, off to the right there. The maps show sheer cliffs all around the Spire, but there are places, like here, where a big shelf opens out before the cliff continues down. Drift is on another big shelf on the other side. Vida Lake must be buried deep down in the Spire between here and Drift."

"There was a war between the cities recently?" asked Scarlet.

"Not too recently, about a century ago. After that, the blackspawn began to show up, first a little, then more and more. Like tonight."

Scarlet and Yun stood quietly together at the edge, alone. At times, the sounds of battle drifted from the south wall of the city. It was late afternoon Haven time, and the blackspawn attack reached its height for this day. Both of them shuddered—Yun in fear, and Scarlet in guilt for not once being at the defenses. Newly elected Rook Lord Capul would not allow him.

Hope would be there, and Trace. *They could both be dead right now*, thought Scarlet. Each attack caused few casualties, but they came almost every day, in the afternoon and sometimes early morning. The murder of a city, one tiny scratch at a time.

Berylata would be there too.

"Tell me about the tantyrs," said Scarlet.

"Yes, that," said Yun. "Haven and Drift and a city called Mirra fought Pinnacle. It was a century ago, about the time of Beacon being lost. Pinnacle had allies—some creatures called wallcrawlers. Sneaky creatures that could climb as easily as we walk. The war must have been complicated—I haven't figured out much of it yet. Something terrible happened here in the city, and Haven went through a catastrophe—a real horror story with monsters and living dead and ghosts and all that stuff, if you want to believe it. Most of the accounts say the city was tossed into some form of hell for one terrifying night, and mostly destroyed."

"Seems to have recovered well enough."

"No," said Yun. "Ikone says there's a whole part of the city, ruined and walled off, and no one goes there because of the ghosts."

"I haven't seen it," said Scarlet.

"It's up beyond the fields, and you can't see it because it slopes the other way. It used to be the old and more magnificent part of the city."

"And the tantyrs?"

"Oh yes, sorry," said Yun. "The tantyrs appeared then, and exposed the fact that the wallcrawlers were fighting on both sides, playing one side off against the other and trying to destroy them both. The war caused a lot of damage and lost lives, crippling the strength of the cities."

"So where did the tantyrs come from?"

"A different domain. Or, like an earthly realm of heaven. It's confusing."

"The Havenites truly think they're angels?"

Yun shook her head. "No, not really, but the servants of angels, maybe—or of devils, if you ask others. The idea of gods and heaven and the like in this place is very confused—the records here are mostly just a patchwork of journals. But the story is that the tantyrs are representatives from a god or a supreme race, to restore virtue and courage to humanity and prevent them from being deceived again. And they're very stern about it."

"Scourging."

"Yes," said Yun. "Beware the coward and liar. Apparently the tantyrs can melt your soul simply by looking at you, turn you into a repentant worm, or force you back into the heat of battle. Only those with steel will or saintly virtue can resist them. The tantyr leaders are supposed to be awe-inspiring, two big giants—titans, they're called—that reside in Pinnacle, one named Shoca and the other I can't remember. They advise the four rulers of Pinnacle and are said to be immortal."

Battle clash and shouts drifted to them again. Scarlet felt his heart being dragged into the darkness over the edge. He stepped back and took Yun's hand.

They danced, slowly, gently, almost hesitantly, until the city's Timekeepers lit the lanterns of the fifth hour and the battle died away. Over two weeks had passed since the Dusties had stood before the clan lords. Scarlet had not seen Yun again until today.

As they danced, Scarlet realized how much he had missed her—the graceful movements of her small body, the long, easy conversations that came so naturally between them, how the smell of her hair reminded him of almonds. He remembered walking into the Archives this morning and finding this delicate young beauty poring so vigorously through the scattered documents of the Archives like the most absent-minded old professor, and he smiled.

"And what about Ikone?" said Scarlet. "Is he nice?"

"Are you jealous?"

"Very."

"He's the son of a powerful clan lord," said Yun, "and he knows it."

"Does he mind his manners?"

"Barely."

"I'd hate to have to kill him."

"I'd hate to have you try. He's supposed to be as good a warrior as his father," said Yun.

"Well, I guess his other wives could move over and let you in."

Yun slugged Scarlet's arm. "I've not got marriage on my list for some time."

"Nor I," said Scarlet. "But I enjoy the dance, and you're the best partner. I'm content with that. For now."

"Me too."

They forgot the battle, the tantyrs, the lost cities—all of it except each other, under the swirling blue.

58: CAGES

Yun's diary, Day 182

> Scarlet was a dream last night. He's the perfect gentleman, and he always treats me like a lady despite my age. He might even be the one for me.
>
> Hope and Trace made it okay through the battle. Hope said it wasn't too bad, only a few serious wounds and not a single loss. But Trace said the attack was a bit stronger than it normally is.
>
> Trace looks much better today. The tantyr Berylata singled him out for his courage in battle. He's all smiles again.
>
> Today the boys are all out helping Ed.

"Steady!" yelled the yardmaster. Slowly the steel rail levered up. The rope stretched, strained, and held, and the rail rose steadily up the cliff. Somewhere above, clinging to the cliff face by rope and climbing gear, Ed and a crew of workmen prepared to anchor the new rail.

Scarlet and Trace manned one of the seven guide ropes with several dozen other sweating, cursing laborers. The ascending rope stopped, moved backward slightly, then forward a bit more as the laborers on high worked the rail into place. Sometime after the ninth hour, a flare of light flashed above, and the rope handlers relaxed their grip. That had been the final replacement rail, and the city's second giant transport cage would soon be working again.

Trace and Scarlet joined Rip at the edge of the work yard. "Our man Ed has fortitude, to be sure," said Rip. "I don't mind a climb, but hanging like a spider for hours over the abyss…that's one beyond me."

The men cleaned up, rubbing their hands and arms with vinegar and soap, only partly successful at removing the oil, tar, and grime of the day's work in the yard. Scarlet had wisely brought a second change of clothes, and as he strapped on his cherished soaring seabird belt, Trace edged up close to him.

"I been spying," he rumbled quietly.

"On who?" said Scarlet.

"Captains. At the city wall. And some lords too."

"Anything juicy?"

"They don't like Berylata."

Scarlet nodded. "No surprise."

"Odami is going to kick her out. It's a big secret."

Scarlet raised his eyebrows dubiously. "Are you serious, Trace? How did you find out?"

"They think I'm stupid, so they say things around me."

"But that might well start a war with Pinnacle or the tantyrs," said Scarlet.

"Odami thinks Berylata is bad."

Scarlet shook his head. "Because she's not human? She's the city's official shining beacon of virtue, and Odami's going to pick a fight with her? That's insane. His prejudice might end up killing this city. I can't believe the other lords would go along with it, especially considering the fight against the blackspawn."

Trace shrugged. "Odami is clever, and powerful."

"Too much so, I think."

"It's my night on the wall," said Trace. "I need to go. Tell Rip to stay out of trouble."

"Take care of yourself, Trace, and thanks for the gossip. I hope it's wrong." Scarlet watched Trace go, then looked about for Rip. He caught sight of the little man near the rocky outcrops where the laborers dried their clothes. It took a moment for him to realize that Rip was holding his hand close to his chest, beckoning frantically to Scarlet.

Scarlet moved to Rip's side. The manling's gaze darted nervously, his eyes swiveling up to Scarlet but his head not turning. He pressed a mirror into Scarlet's hand—not the poor polished silver kind, but a real glass type with a fine reflective surface.

"Careful now, 'tis one of my most cherished," whispered Rip. "Why don't yeh prop it against the rock there, so that yeh can see behind yeh."

"What am I looking for?" murmured Scarlet.

"In the crowd nearby, about ten paces back. Just find the ugliest man and barmiest woman in the history of ettinkind. They have on deep hoods, so you can just see their chins most of the time."

Scarlet nodded. He tilted himself back and forth, until, "Ugh. I agree."

"They follow yeh about, and not just you but Hope and Ed and me as well," said Rip.

"Half the city watches us," said Scarlet.

"Ahey, but not like this. They follow like bloodhounds, and for days now."

"They must be bored."

But Rip made no witty comeback. He cast his gaze nervously about them, then gave Scarlet a guilty look.

"There's more, and I tell yeh now. They cornered me up yesterday. That male has a mole the size of a goose egg, terrible to behold."

"Did they say anything?"

"Ah-hey! Yeh know I like to stir the spice in my stories, but what I'm about to tell yeh is the straight road, right down the middle. That big one, he leans down to me and says, 'Have yeh gone to Old Haven?' I tried to say something back, but that hag grabbed my shoulder and whispered in my ear, 'Old Haven! Old Haven!' over and over. I don't mind saying, they scared me right out of meh pantaloons. I tried to break away but that hag's grip was like iron. Then the big man lifted me off my feet and said, 'Gone to Old Haven!'

"Somehow I got my sword out, I don't even remember. But I stabbed him in the arm, Scarlet, right here in the arm. And he didn't flinch! 'Old Haven,' he said one more time, and threw me down. And I got up to defend myself, and they were gone."

Scarlet searched Rip's face, trying to discover a sparkle of mirth that would indicate the "spice" in this tale. Rip delighted him as a friend, but one could never take his words at face value. In this case, he saw nothing but a haunted seriousness in the little man. "Why didn't you tell me sooner?"

"Helps to spy them in person when I tell the tale, don't it?"

Scarlet watched the two in the mirror. "Most assuredly. So that's why you've been acting like a cat on pins today. Are you sure you stabbed him?"

Rip scratched his ear and tried to look back at the two strangers without being obvious. "I was solid oak sure at the time. But there wasn't any blood on my blade—wasn't anything. So, no."

Scarlet leaned in toward the mirror for a better view and waited for a passing lantern to momentarily reveal the strangers' features. The man looked like a living shipwreck, a battered hulk listing to starboard. His eyes all but disappeared behind heavy brows and his bulging mouth slid unevenly to one side. The sizable arms ended in meaty, oversized hands. A gigantic mole hung from his right jaw and wiggled when he shifted his stance.

The woman had the appearance of a banshee. Rope-tight muscles strained in her neck, her colorless lips stretched wide and thin, and her eyes showed white all around—as if she were permanently preparing to scream. Her rat's-nest hair drifted out of the hood and back and forth in the swirling breeze.

As he leaned over, staring at them through the mirror, Scarlet got the distinct impression that they were staring back at him.

He shuddered and glanced at Rip. "Let's go have a chat with them, what do you say?"

"I'd say no thank yeh, but I will be behind yeh if yeh make that mistake."

Scarlet returned to the mirror, steeling himself for the confrontation, but the two strangers were gone.

He spun around, searching for the two among the yard workers and on-lookers. Nothing.

Rip did the same. "Told yeh. That's that."

"Not likely," said Scarlet, trying to breathe calm back into his body, "but here's to hoping. I've seen enough of them."

Hope left the east door of the hospice and crossed the street as the third hour lit, her steps drifting and erratic, for she had not slept in fifty hours. The Fever had taken a sudden surge, in combination with a deadly morning assault by the blackspawn. The sick and wounded clogged the hospice, and it was not possible to keep the fevered isolated.

It became clear soon after Hope came to Claire Hospice that she brought both skill and stamina beyond any of the other healers. Her presence meant that some lived who should have died, and others restored whole instead of crippled. But for Hope it meant being the first to be turned to and the last to leave in times of crisis. At this moment, Hope had nothing remaining to give away, and little of her left to pay attention to her surroundings. She entrusted her safety to the Rook bodyguard who escorted her to and from work. He was an older man, past his battle prime, and this suited Hope. She wanted nothing to do with an escort who might become enamored with her, and she did not encourage even this man by talking to him. She walked ahead, and he followed her dutifully.

Hope plodded along her usual route through the narrow back alleys to avoid the marketplace. Crimes of the back-alley kind happened occasionally in Haven, but the marketplace teemed with aggressive sellers, and Hope detested their constant pestering. She could hear behind her the irregular steps of the bodyguard, who walked with one stiff leg due to a battle injury.

Hope's shoulder scraped against rock and she realized that she had blundered into the rough-laid building wall to her right.

This cuts it. Not again. Too many hours will be the death of me.

She shook herself and marched on, head buried in the hood of her cloak. A blanket of cold, wet air settled over the city and she pinched the hood close to her face to try to keep it out.

It will be the death of others if I don't. Get some sleep. Eat. Stop acting the child, Hope.

The alley reached a wider cross street. Hope almost stumbled over the lip of the tiny foot-wide canal of water flowing down the middle of the street. She righted herself, shook her head, and felt a hand on her shoulder.

"M'lady, would you wish my arm?" said her bodyguard, a concerned, fatherly look on his face.

"Thank you, but it's not too far now," said Hope, patting the man's armor-padded shoulder. "I should be quite all right."

She turned and bumped into a couple standing at the alleyway's entrance. The two parted to let her by, the face of the shocked and outraged woman flashing by.

Hope continued on. She caught herself counting steps, wrapped her hood tighter, and trudged on. The alley took a quick turn left and back right again, the walls of the surrounding buildings creating a narrow cut to the midnight blue sky above.

She passed a woman hunched in the alley and felt a pang of guilt in not seeing if the woman needed anything. Poor thing looked quite distressed. But Hope needed home and rest.

Her steps slowed. She couldn't just leave without asking.

It occurred to Hope that she had seen the woman before. And then, it occurred to her that she had seen that same woman this evening...in fact, only a few minutes prior. She was the woman whom Hope had bumped into in the cross-street.

But that was impossible.

Uneven footsteps approached from behind her. She turned and caught her breath. Leaning over her like a portent of doom was the terrifying hulk of a man, with a shattered face that bulged out from underneath his own dust-brown hood. He tilted his head to an unnatural angle, his body rustling and cracking like dried leaves.

"M'lady wish *my* arm?" he croaked in a voice like a bottomless void, and he reached swiftly out for Hope's throat.

Yun's diary, Day 183

Hope has gone missing.

At the seventh hour, the Rook Clan discovered that Hope and her bodyguard were neither at the holdings nor at the hospice, and the hunt began. Rook soldiers split into squads and began searching the city. Scarlet, Rook Mastersmith Toby, and Rip left to search the streets immediately, followed quickly by Yun and Phoebe's friend Emma, and their escort, Trace.

For four hours Scarlet's group circled out from the hospice, searching nearly every street in the city. Yun and Emma talked to everyone at and near the hospice. Beyond her leaving around the midnight hour, no one had seen anything.

Emma knew Hope's preferred way home through the alleyways, and so Scarlet, Yun, and the rest decided to return to the Rook holdings by that route, despite having walked it twice already. They took their time, each carrying a lantern, carefully sweeping for clues. At this busy hour, the alleyway contained a press of people. Mastersmith Toby's frustration began showing through, warning people out of his way and moving people who didn't comply.

At a turn in the alleyway, Scarlet tapped Trace. "See if you can calm Toby down."

Trace nodded and moved ahead.

"I'll help," said Yun, following the big man.

A thick rock-shelf extended from the wall about waist high. Scarlet seated himself on the ledge and leaned back, trying not to allow his fear, frustration, and fatigue to escape.

He couldn't lose another, not after Rodrigo. With Hope and her bodyguard missing and no place to be other than the city, the inability to find any trace of her did not leave room for encouragement.

He had to be missing something.

Rip paced, his head barely reaching the level of the ledge on which Scarlet sat. "What do yeh plan after we get back to Rook?"

Scarlet smiled confidently. "Hopefully we discover something before then. There has to be something here, along her path home, unless someone at the hospice is lying about her leaving."

"I've introduced myself to every speck and tibble on this path. We've done this thrice now."

"Then we'll find something on the fourth try," said Scarlet.

"N'hardly, with all these new feet scrambling up things." Rip moved down the alley and back, scanning the walls, a grimace of futility on his face.

Five paces from Scarlet, as Mastersmith Toby calmed down enough to continue and Scarlet slid off the ledge, Rip froze. "Scarlet!"

He raced to Rip's side. Rip peered at something under the ledge. Scarlet knelt down. There, etched in the wall with deep, fresh scratches, were the words:

O.H. NO HOPE FOR RIP

Scarlet's heart raced. "Clever."

"Fiendish," said Rip. "What does it mean?"

Scarlet quickly scanned the alley. "No, very clever. This message was left for you, Rip. It's under the ledge, right at your eye level. A human—er, ettin—would never see it."

260

"There's an arrow scratched in the rock—wait, there's something here." Rip pulled at a bit of cloth in a cleft above a loose stone in the wall. The stone shifted, and Rip dragged out a canvas wrapping from the hole. He unrolled it, revealing a single thin-bladed scalpel—one of Hope's treasured instruments.

Scarlet's heart threatened to leap from his chest, and the ground spun beneath him. He felt a hand on his shoulder and saw Yun there, staring helplessly at the scalpel.

One by one the others noticed and came. No one said a word, until Trace finally spoke. "Who would take her?"

Scarlet stared at the words. "They didn't identify themselves."

"Would another clan attempt this?" said Trace.

Emma shook her head. "They couldn't keep her secret."

"Revenge, perhaps?" said Toby. "But for what, I've no clue. And why kill a new Sleeper who's done naught but good?"

"Or leave clues afterward," said Emma.

Rip stepped back and grabbed his head, pulling at his hair. "Hallows! Darkness and Death! It can't be!" He pointed at the words.

"O.H.—Old Haven."

60: Barrier

Scarlet's bodyguard—a trusted second cousin of Lord Odami—did not intervene when the five remaining Dusties picked up their traveling gear at the Rook barracks. He hung back silently as they passed through the market district. But when the Dusties approached the less populated farmland and the destination became obvious, he disappeared.

Fifteen minutes later, as the Dusties worked their way through the fields and the curious farm hands, Grager's former aide, Kane, caught up with them, his pale face red with exertion.

"Scarlet, stop. You cannot go into Old Haven," said Kane between heaving breaths.

"What are you talking about?" said Scarlet.

Kane raised his hands in a pleading gesture, seeing Scarlet's rising anger. "Old Haven is a death punishment, Scarlet. Odami will carry out that punishment. He will."

Scarlet snorted in frustration. "That makes no sense. Why would you have a death penalty for visiting the dead part of town, ghosts or no?"

"Because something dwells in Old Haven, and when it is disturbed, it comes here to visit. People disappear, and the Fever gets bad. A lot of people could die."

"That's a pretty theory," said Scarlet, "but your Old Haven friends have already visited. Rip's seen them for the past week. And the Fever is up, if you haven't noticed."

"Are you saying you've seen ghosts?" said Kane.

"Yeh have ugly ghosts," said Rip.

"Scarlet, listen," said Kane, "Odami's lieutenant will be here—he's coming up behind you right now. You have to stop. She's gone. Hope is gone. They never come back. Never."

Scarlet lashed out, the back of his hand smashing into Kane's mouth. Kane spun and dropped to a knee.

Trace reached out and grabbed a handful of Scarlet's shirt at the back of his neck. Scarlet tried to pull himself out of the grip, but Trace hauled him off his feet, swinging the boy over so that Trace now stood between Scarlet and Kane. "Cool off, boy," said the big man.

When Scarlet touched the ground and Trace let go, Scarlet didn't hesitate. He turned and ran up the hill. The other Dusties followed, except Trace, who helped Kane to his feet.

"You might have given too much truth at one time, Kane," said Trace.

"Apparently Scarlet has a temper."

"Apparently."

"He'll get himself killed," said Kane. "If not in Old Haven, then by Odami."

"How do you know Odami will kill him?"

"He has every right. The law against entering Old Haven is a matter of survival. The place is deadly and it does not like to be disturbed."

A squad of soldiers led by a Crescent captain rushed by. A scattering of other soldiers could be seen and heard on the slopes.

"We should catch up," said Kane.

"Will Scarlet reach Old Haven before they overtake him?"

"Not a chance."

―――――

The fields terraced up the high slopes of Haven—row upon row of glowmoss fed by thousands of tiny water channels running through the carefully nurtured soil. The glowmoss grew much larger here, mounding up in fast-growing heaps that dwarfed Scarlet, Yun, Rip, and Ed.

In front of them, close now, they could see the sudden break where the farmland ended, like a band of consuming darkness between the fields and the distant cliffs. The bright mounds rushed by, the band of darkness grew larger and larger, and then they understood.

At the topmost height, running unbroken from up-cliff to down-cliff, a smooth-faced wall over twenty feet high blocked their way, its top rounded and without a hold for a hook or grapple. No gate or archway could be seen in their lamplight. There was no mistaking its intent as a permanent seal between the Haven of today and what lay on the other side.

Scarlet began running along its length, stumbling repeatedly over the rough rock-strewn ground. The soldiers had caught up now, and they quickly corralled Yun and Rip. Ahead, Ed put on a burst of speed, caught up with Scarlet, and tackled him. Scarlet fought back as Ed yelled. Then Ed reared back and punched him. Scarlet went slack, breathing raggedly on the ground beneath Ed's pinning weight.

The soldiers dragged the two to their feet as Scarlet glared at Ed and Ed stared back. The Crescent captain issued orders and the entire procession of soldiers, Kane, and the Dusties made their descent to the Grand Hall.

―――――

At the Grand Hall, Yun watched in fear for Scarlet as Odami and his counselors explained, in forceful terms, the deadly penalty for entering Old Haven and the certainty of the verdict if caught. When it became clear that Hope was lost forever to the dead city, as were so many others before her, Scarlet fell to the chamber's cold floor in despair.

Only after the other Dusties stood to acknowledge this reality, and gave the counselors a complete account of their encounters with the two horrid phantoms, did Scarlet rise, pull his cloak tightly about him, and speak. "It is difficult to accept that Hope is gone, but it is clear that she is. Losing two cherished friends in so short a time is too much to bear."

"She was our friend, too, boy," said Ed. "If you spent more time accomplishing something for this city and less time mooning over the girls, we'd all be better off."

Scarlet glared at the engineer but said nothing, his body tensed.

Rip and Yun looked at each other in alarm.

Odami sat back, his eyes narrowed, one finger absently tracing a circle under his ear. His son Ikone sat next to him, leaning forward with piqued interest.

Ed turned to face the counselors. "Odami-"

"Lord Odami!" corrected the warden of the council.

"Lord Odami, I'm not one for words, so here it is straight. We're Sleepers, and that's it. Nothing grand. There's certainly nothing special about this boy Scarlet. He's a buffoon—been one since he woke."

Scarlet sat once again on the cold polished floor. It appeared to Yun that there was no fight left in the boy.

Ed continued. "As for me, I'm a Rook now, and the best engineer on this rock. You call it bragging if you want. I call it fact. I fixed your second rail cage in half the time expected. There's a third that can be fixed as well, with—and only with—my know-how."

Ed stopped, looking to Odami for a response, but Odami kept silent. His son Ikone's impatience got the better of him, however, and he blurted out, "Go on."

So Ed did. "There's a waste pit for the forges at the yard that needs its drain tunnel cleared. It will be dirty, greasy, lonely, one-man work. Give me Scarlet. Let him find out what honest labor is, away from the comforts and the distraction of the ladies."

Yun saw Ikone's attention caught at that last. With Scarlet out of the picture, Ikone would be seeing a sudden clear path to claim her. She swallowed nervously.

Ikone looked expectantly to his father, who had not yet said a word, until now.

"How soon can you get the third cage in operation?" asked Odami.

"Three months, perhaps even a little less."

Odami nodded. "Then Scarlet is yours for three months, if Rook Lord Capul agrees."

"I do," said the clan lord. "And this will serve as full punishment for the attempt by all of you to enter Old Haven."

"It would seem," said Odami to Ed, "that you harbor ill feelings toward Scarlet."

"Only frustration, Lord Odami," said Ed. "He is a sly charmer and he gathers more respect than he deserves."

Odami rose. "Then we are concluded here. Scarlet is in your hands."

There was something about the way Odami said that last sentence that made Yun's neck hairs twitch.

61: TREACHERY

Yun's diary, Day 186

Scarlet is in Ed's hands now. I pray that Loa protects him and brings him back alive and well.

Ed is a cruel monster and I despise him.

"That's...it's...I'm choking!" sputtered Scarlet's bodyguard, backing away from the hole and the stench drifting up from it.

"Everything in this yard that passes out of a machine, forge, or human drops through this hole," said Ed.

"Scarlet's going to die down there," said the bodyguard.

A lopsided grin escaped Ed. "Possibly. That's why it's a punishment. You coming?"

The bodyguard scratched his chin and peered down into the hole. "Where does this go?"

"All the way to the down-cliff. Spills out below the Wolf holdings. And whoever cut it did a lousy job. Not nearly enough fall, and the walls are too rough. Snags things. It'll be a three-act nightmare to get it cleaned out."

"Well, if this is the only way out, then I'm happy sitting right here," said Scarlet's bodyguard, who now acted as more of a prison guard. He sat on a barrel and made himself comfortable with a satchel full of lunch.

"Suit yourself. I have to give instructions. Be right back."

Ed swung onto the ladder and descended into the fume-ridden pit, his thoughts turning grim when out of sight of the guard. He stepped down into the mire, careful to maintain his footing.

He turned. A hint of firelight flickered on the walls and over the sluggish flow of the water channel. The light came from a small chamber cut into the side of the pit.

Scarlet would be there.

Ed moved slowly around the encircling work path, avoiding the patchy mounds of growth. He paused, reached up, and pulled a heavy hand tool from a ledge. He hefted the tool in one strong, calloused hand and moved toward the chamber.

Ed knew metal, and oil, and the fires of the forge. He knew the human body on similar terms—the muscle and sinew and the pulsing pressure of the heart.

He had, on one hand, a great admiration for the impressive design of the human organism, and, on the other, a contempt for the ease with which it could be destroyed.

The light itself came into view—a pair of lanterns prepared for Scarlet's day of labor. Scarlet knelt in front of them, working on cinching up his boots. A shackle encircled each of his hands, bound by a long, light chain that clattered with each movement.

Scarlet did not seem to hear Ed enter the chamber.

Ed raised the hand tool and brought it down on Scarlet's shoulder with a light tap.

"Give me a wrist."

"Ah! Ed, you gave me a fright…oh, the cutters."

Scarlet put his left hand on the chair next to him. Ed positioned the tool and clamped down with all his weight. The shackle's bolt sheared cleanly in half.

"How's my faithful companion?" whispered Scarlet.

"Not faithful enough to endure this saprogenic stench," said Ed, snipping the second restraint. The shackles and chain fell away.

Scarlet rubbed his wrists. "Where are the rope and hooks?"

"In a long, low box right outside the old hole. I managed to have a stack of bricks placed near the hole, so you should have a better chance of getting to the rail without being seen."

"It's an inspired plan, Ed," said Scarlet. "I'm impressed."

"Don't thank me yet. I have no idea whether the cable and ledge extend as far as the wall of Old Haven."

"I must say you sold your story well at the council," said Scarlet.

"Wasn't that hard. Most of it was true," said Ed with a lopsided smile.

Scarlet shook his head and gathered up the small amount of gear that Ed had smuggled into the tunnels. "For a ragged collection of nobodies, we always seem to be bouncing from one tight spot to another."

Ed snorted. "Noose-tight I'd say, since that demon-in-drapes Odami is likely to put us to death even if we succeed."

Scarlet stood and turned to face Ed. "You've made a name for yourself here in Haven. You could cut strings with us and be better off. So why are you putting yourself in jeopardy?"

The two studied each other for a time before Ed sighed lightly. "I ask myself that more than once every day."

Scarlet extended his hand. "I'll find her, Ed."

"You'd better." Ed reached out and shook Scarlet's hand.

With a last glance over his shoulder, Ed climbed from the sewers and drew up the ladder.

———

Scarlet doused his lamps and packed them away. He stooped into a wide-cut side passage and came quickly to a dead-end. Above him, he saw an old, dry grate, and he remembered Ed's instructions from two nights ago, when he'd whispered them to Scarlet, trying not to let the trio of nearby Crescent guards overhear:

> *There's a second source tunnel. It comes out next to the cliff. The falls that fed it must have shifted many years ago and a new tunnel was dug. There's just a dry grate that everyone ignores. I'll loosen it...*

Firelight from the yard filtered through the grate. Scarlet gripped one of the bars and pushed. It did not budge. He tried the next, and the next. The fourth lifted out with a jarring clank that set Scarlet's nerves on edge. The fifth did the same. He listened, but heard no one approach, then he lifted himself up and through.

> *You've got a long journey ahead, and you aren't in as good a shape as me, so take as little as possible. I'll hide the climbing gear near the grate...*

The grate was nicely sandwiched between the cliff and a waist-high stack of bricks. Scarlet found the low box and pulled out two strongly curved hooks and a sizeable length of rope. Feeling the weight of the rope, Scarlet removed one of his lamps from his pack and left it behind in the box.

> *There'll be a heap of activity in the yard, preparing for the repair of the third cage, but you should be able to just walk over to the fifth cage rail. I'll tie a white strip of cloth to it...*

Scarlet peered out from the bricks. The yard swarmed with more workers than he expected, and he realized that Ed had been far too optimistic. He would be noticed immediately.

His hand rested on a large woven cask. He picked it up, concealed as much of his face as possible, and began walking. He tried to keep the cliff on his left and the cask facing right, but a knot of men working on the cliff face caused him to detour. He shifted the cask left, only to find a pair of scrapmen turning toward him. He dropped to a kneeling position, pretending to tighten his bootstraps.

"Heya, boy, I could use some of that," said one of the scrapmen. They approached close in front of him. "Got my hand in a mess of tar."

Scarlet glanced at the cask, marked with VINEGAR in large letters, and silently cursed his luck. He would have to stand up and walk away, hoping that the two would not recognize him...

"Hey-o!" yelled a voice in the near distance—a familiar voice. Scarlet didn't dare look up.

"Gentlemen!—oh, and you too, fine lady—a month in the making and an eternity in the waiting, the finest drink ever to be drafted by human hands, and a cup's worth FREE to yeh, if yeh have a moment's time and the foreman's blessing!"

The scrapmen didn't hesitate, foreman or not. Neither did Scarlet. As the scrapmen hurried through the machinery toward Rip's gift of free spirits, Scarlet snatched up the cask and wove quickly through the greatly thinned crowd. He hurried past the site of the derelict fourth cage and came to the equally ruined fifth. There on the abandoned lower rail, a long strip of white cloth blew fitfully in the lightly swirling wind.

The fifth cage is off the beaten path, and it still has its rail, at least lower down, so you can climb it. Use the hooks on the rail struts...

The fifth rail might have been off the beaten path, but several workers toiled nearby. Scarlet looked at the hooks and the steel of the rail and clenched his teeth. The structure's struts were roughly six feet apart, and the rail itself was held a foot away from the rock face. It would not be a simple ladder-like climb, but rather a series of lifts. And the clanking of the hook on the steel would be sure to draw attention.

Scarlet retreated into a shadow and cast about. No waterfall and therefore no light-giving growth existed nearby, but the fiery glow of a refinery off to his left bathed the area in dull red. Laborers piled great heaps of a roundish glowmoss into the presses and cookers to separate the heavy oils. Casks of light oil and small metal barrels of tar formed stacked pyramids nearby.

A sudden inspiration came to Scarlet. He untied the long cloth strip, tore it in half, and crept through the clutter of the yard to the refinery. He found a waste barrel of old tar, dipped the two hooks, and wrapped the cloths repeatedly around the now coated hooks. Returning to the rail, he took in a breath, anchored the hooks around it and began climbing, setting himself against the cliff with his feet and using the rail itself as a ladder. The cloth and oozing tar prevented noise and kept the hooks from slipping as he leapfrogged them one foot at a time—left, right, left, right.

The thrill of his cleverness and escape wore out about ninety feet up. Exhausted, he wedged himself between rail and rock and rested several minutes before continuing. From this height the city spread out before him—a riotous mix of glowmoss colors and firelight reflecting off a maze of rock surfaces. Far from alarming him, the precarious perch gave Scarlet an exhilarating sense of freedom. He breathed in deeply and let out a small laugh.

He could find Hope.

Scarlet ascended another ninety feet, then another fifty, then thirty more. His muscles shook with the exertion, and he realized that Ed was exactly right—he wasn't in superb shape. He could see nothing looking up, and he knew he didn't have much climb left in him, but he started upward anyway, challenging himself to thirty hooks. "One, two, three…" he counted off through gritted teeth, trying to counteract the shaking in his shoulders by rocking back and forth with each resetting of the hook. "Ten, eleven, twelve…" He realized that the pack, the sword, and the long rope weighed more than he should have brought, but he wasn't sure what he could have left. "Twenty-two, twenty-three…"

And then his foot pushed into a gap. He had reached a narrow ledge lost in the darkness of the dry cliff face.

He pulled himself up and stepped onto the ledge—nothing more than a roughly chiseled notch a foot deep and four feet high. A cable ran horizontally along it, so that a workman could hold on to it as he stepped along the narrow cut.

About three hundred feet up there's a haul line—a horizontal cable with a step-notch along it. You should be able to walk it all the way to Old Haven, since the original big cages were on the Old Haven side of the city…

Scarlet wedged himself between the notch and rail and rested. He pulled a length of yellow cord from his pack, cut a section, and tied it to the rail. He then set his hooks on the cable, undid his rope, and started out. At first he used two hooks, stepping them along, but after a time his strength returned, his confidence rose, and he dragged just one hook along the cable, walking along while leaning out over the city, pausing only to pass over each anchor point.

Ahead, the wall glowed with the wet of multiple waterfalls. Where the water fell heavily, the notch became a cavern, protecting the cable and giving Scarlet a comfortable spot to rest. Farmland spread out below him now, and though he could be seen as he moved along, he doubted anyone would catch sight of him—or be able to stop him.

Just past the third major falls, the haul line simply ended.

Six hundred feet short of Old Haven.

62: HANGING

When Rip explained Ed's plan to Yun, he also sternly told her that in no way would she be allowed to be part of it. If Scarlet did not come back, Rip and Ed would be in trouble—deadly trouble if the council proved truly serious and entirely inflexible about their laws.

After an initially heated argument, Yun had finally agreed, on the condition that she be allowed to spend the time spying on Ikone at the Archives. Understanding that this would give her a solid alibi, Rip had agreed as well.

It was a mistake.

"Why so nervous?" Ikone stared at her from across the reading table, setting aside a large strap-bound tome.

Spying at him through her bangs, Yun had watched him pretending to read it for the past half hour.

"What? No, I'm quite relaxed," she said in a voice that made an obvious liar of her.

Ikone, who was both well-muscled and well-fed, rose and stretched. This offered Yun an extensive view of the bulky muscles in his arms and neck.

"Tell me, is it Scarlet you worry about?" he asked.

"No!" said Yun hastily, immediately realizing that she should have said yes. Then she would have a good excuse for her nerves and an ongoing reason to play keep-away from Ikone. Surely Ikone knew nothing about Scarlet's plan and meant only his punishment.

"That's good," said Ikone.

She could feel his hawk-eyes boring into the top of her head. She kept her face buried in an old journal.

"Scarlet is swiftly running out of future in Haven."

Did Ikone know? Yun's heart skipped. She looked up at him through her bangs again. "What do you mean?"

He folded his arms, as he often did. "He's hot-headed, immature, irresponsible, lazy. It wouldn't surprise me if he went for Old Haven again to try to steal back that woman he lusts after. I don't know why you want to be claimed by him."

A wild storm of emotions swarmed up in Yun—anger at the harsh words against someone she loved, jealousy toward Hope, a gnawing desire for Scarlet to fail to find Hope, a fear that perhaps Ikone knew something and was toying with her, and a building disgust toward this self-important, spoiled clan lord's brat who already had two wives.

"I'm too young to be married, and I never, ever want to be 'owned.' You have two wives already, Ikone."

He stared grimly at her, and she quickly looked down. He pointed a finger at his chest. "I have a solemn duty to build up not only my clan but this city. You are more than old enough. It is time for you to choose."

The words came sternly, and Yun feared to say no. "I'll have to think," she stammered out. She looked around helplessly but already knew that they were alone in this wing of the Archives. Ikone had made sure of that.

He squeezed her shoulder and kissed the top of her head. "The thinking needs to end. Tomorrow is my birthday. Today you must decide. I have battle trials now. Stay here and clear your mind, and when I return, have an answer."

He turned and strode from the room, leaving her alone among the silence of the old records.

———

Scarlet retreated to the cave at the third waterfall, his mind racing furiously and his heart in a knot. He could see no way past the end of the haul line. Many feet above him, he spotted what appeared to be another cable, but the cliff face offered few handholds. He could use the rope to climb down into the farmland, but that would put him on the wrong side of the wall and in the middle of farm workers.

As he considered his options and scanned about for any shred of hope, he noticed the waterfall acting strangely. The cascade fell past his cave, and in it something wavered back and forth, disturbing the fall of water. He tried to pass his hand through the falls but could not reach it. Cutting a length of rope, he tied it to the haul line and leaned out so that he was almost horizontal. The falls slashed down on his head and shoulders as his arm swept through it—and struck something solid. He grabbed ahold and pulled, dragging a rusted cable with him.

Scarlet tried to make sense of this unexpected find. He doubted that someone would hang it in the waterfall on purpose. He thought of the other cable he had seen higher up. Maybe…

Scarlet used a length of rope to anchor the rusted cable to the haul line, then cut two prussic climbing loops from his rope, plus two spares. Setting his feet in the loops, he attached the other end of the ropes to the cable. He cut the haul line rope, grasped the cable, and threw himself onto it.

Instead of holding him in place, the cable gave way. He swung lower and sideways, completely out of the waterfall, scraping painfully along the cliff face, fighting back the panic of being thrown out into half-darkness on a dangling strand. The prussics kept his feet pinned against the cable so that he spun and

272

bumped uncontrollably, and they strained dangerously as the cable swung him back and forth. Groans of agony escaped Scarlet at each collision with the rock.

The swinging slowed and stopped. He gradually opened his eyes. Trickles of blood ran down his shredded shirt, and his hands stung painfully, embedded with tiny spurs of rusted metal. One knee felt like it had been shattered apart, though it obeyed when he bent it.

But he was alive, and the cable held firm, ascending to heaven.

He began climbing slowly, using the friction loops of the prussics, lifting first one leg then the other, sliding the prussic along the wet, rusted metal. He returned to the level of the haul line, securely tied the cable and the haul line together, flagged it using his yellow cord, and kept going up, foot by foot. After ninety feet the cable angled into an anchor, set inside a larger, deeper notch.

Scarlet dragged himself up and rolled into the notch. For a moment he merely breathed, triumphant that his life remained. Then he undid the prussics, kissed the ropes, stuffed them in the pack, and looked around. Unlike the lower notch, this one appeared long abandoned. A tiny streamlet of water trickled along it, fed by the abundant fall of water. Glowmoss grew everywhere, illuminating the notch far into the distance. The cable and notch continued toward Old Haven in what appeared to be a much older haul line. Behind him, the notch had been smashed away long ago, shearing the haul line and leaving its broken length dangling down into the waterfall.

There was only one way to go, but it was the right way.

———

Scarlet followed the notch hastily. His excitement built as the farmland ended, the wall passed, and he found himself above Old Haven.

At least, he supposed so. Glowmoss lit the cliff face at Scarlet's level, but twenty paces down the glowmoss lessened, at forty it thinned, and at sixty it died altogether. An abundant collection of falls fed into Old Haven and yet not even a tiny patch of glowmoss grew anywhere in it. So, when Scarlet looked down, he saw nothing but a lightless void, and for all he knew, no city existed at all.

He remembered looking down over Desolation Point and seeing the same darkness. He assumed that the mist hid the light of the glowmoss lower down, but perhaps this wasn't so. Perhaps this spire of rock contained the only life left in the world.

Despite the depressing thought, Scarlet's mind simply forgot about the difficulty, shoving it away as something of little concern, as it had with the possibility of falling from the cliff and the likelihood of surviving Old Haven. There was a point, back in Lakeside after the fear had taken him, when he had lost this gift, and doubts and worries had piled upon themselves. Unused to such despair, it had almost destroyed him.

But somehow that wound had healed, and he had returned to his irrepressible self, sitting casually on the notch edge, using the point of a thin hunting knife to dig out the metal spurs from his hands. Beside him, a large, ancient rail ascended into the cliffs above—a lost artifact of a brighter past for the humans who had tried to survive here. The wind blew briskly from the direction of Haven, bringing a taint of smoke and barely discernible sounds of human activity. Nothing moved in Old Haven, and nothing could be heard. If the ruins were full of ghostly phantasms, they clearly didn't care to be about at this hour.

Scarlet tied his rope around the cable, tagged it with a length of yellow cord, wrapped his hands and bleeding knee with cloth, and descended into the void below.

63: TRUTH

The silence and the flicker of the lamps kept Yun company. For the past twenty minutes, despair had acted as her closer companion, and the journals in front of her had gone unread.

Scarlet's secret plan should have made her happy, but it merely brought on more dread. No one entered Old Haven and lived. That's what the Archives said.

Scarlet would die doing the right thing.

Not that it mattered for her future. Ikone, son of High Lord Odami, would see to that.

She could marry Ikone and live as a miserable harem wife of a self-important buffoon, treated as a woman but not a treasured companion. Or, she could reject him and earn the ire of the most important family and clan in Haven. The anger of the Crescent Clan would be sure to fall heavily on her friends as well.

Misery or malice—those two wolves prowled about inside Yun's heart, competing for the kill. She cupped her head in her hands and tears dotted the table.

Lost to her dark thoughts in an empty room, she naturally jumped and gasped when a voice came from her left.

"The choice seems clear to me."

There, atop a balcony, along the book-laden wall, leaned a creature that could only be the tantyr Berylata. She read a large journal, the greenish glowmoss fiber rustling softly as she turned a page.

Yun feared to move. Berylata continued reading, letting a period of silence pass.

"This is a journal written by Rook Lord Grager's father, Lord Drake," said Berylata at last, descending the steep balcony stairs with effortless ease. "I have read it several times. It ends well. He married a loyal and accomplished beauty. So many tragedies here on the Spire, but not this one. Well, at least until his son Grager chose murder and suicide. That wasn't storybook, was it?"

"What do you want?" said Yun, finding her voice.

Berylata flowed into the seat left by Ikone. "The boy was right, you do look nervous."

"Don't I have reason to be nervous?"

"Nervous about Ikone? Yes. He is used to getting his way. But why would you not wish to become one of the most influential women in Haven?"

"I don't love him."

"You mean you are not attracted to him," said Berylata. "And you are attracted to someone else. Scarlet, true?"

Yun shrugged, trying to remain calm. *Should I run? She would catch me in a wink, of course. Does she mean to hurt me?*

"Romantic love can be a misplaced emotion," said Berylata, "and often merely a thoughtless weakness. It is hardly a virtue. High Lord Odami's first wife was pledged to a lesser lord before she instead chose to wed Odami. She is now the most powerful woman in Haven."

Yun tried to hide her contempt. "You think marrying for power is a virtue?"

Berylata shook her head slowly. "No, not power. Power is the craving of tyrants. Marry for influence. The ability to change conditions, to protect friends, and to help those who need it."

"You seem to know humans, for not being one yourself."

Berylata smiled, and her normally intense features seemed almost serene and gentle. "Many creatures exist beyond the human, yet most share very familiar personalities and habits. Man, woman, love, hate, care, worry, evil, goodness."

"I don't think the blackspawn or the monster that killed my friend share any of that—especially the goodness part," said Yun.

"Perhaps. But how many blackspawn do you know?"

Yun kept silent.

Berylata tilted her head slightly, looked at the lamps, and leaned back. "You have other thoughts on your mind, and Ikone will return soon. What will your answer be?"

"No," said Yun. "I won't marry him. I just don't know how to tell him without causing too much..."

It crept into Yun's thoughts at that moment that she sat at a reading table in a lonely room, talking about the affairs of her heart with a strange being who could put fear into the sturdiest Havenite. She looked into Berylata's brilliant green cat's eyes, watched those eyes lid down slightly, and a sudden wave of suspicion and alarm rose in her.

"Why are you here?"

Berylata leaned forward slowly. Her face remained passive, but the wiry muscles in her arms twitched as she placed her hands on the table.

"I need you to answer questions, Yun. These questions are important. It is also important that you answer truthfully. This does not need to become difficult. Will you do this?"

Yun nodded slowly, her mind stuck on the word "difficult."

"Why will you not marry Ikone?"

"I—I don't love him. I'm too young. He's already married. He's not nice. Why are you asking me this?"

"Are you lying about being a Sleeper?"

"No!"

"Are you lying about any of your friends being Sleepers?"

"No. I saw all of them being awakened."

"All of them?"

"Well, not Rodrigo, of course. He woke me."

"Did Rodrigo tell you where he woke?"

"In a town…it was…Drift."

"Did he say anything about his waking?"

"No…I…"

"Did he mention any companions or people that he knew in Drift?"

"No! Why are you asking me about Rodrigo?" demanded Yun.

"Did Rodrigo say anything puzzling or cryptic and then refuse to explain it to you?"

"Why are you asking me about Rodrigo!"

Yun discovered that she was on her feet and leaning across the table toward the beautiful but predatory face of Berylata.

Berylata paused, then spoke in a quiet voice. "You loved Rodrigo."

Yun stared defiantly at Berylata. Tears crowded her eyes and fell in unison down her round cheeks.

"Did he love you back?"

"Stop," whispered Yun plaintively, a second set of tears following the track of the first.

Footsteps approached and an Archive guard entered the room. He flinched upon seeing Berylata, his face frozen in shock.

Berylata turned to him. "Leave us. Make sure no one enters this room or the hallway until Ikone arrives. Close the door."

"Yes—yes, m'lady," stammered the guard, backing out in haste.

Berylata watched him go, leaned back, and her demeanor softened. "I will stop asking questions about you and Rodrigo. Please, sit down."

It took a minute before Yun composed herself and settled slowly back into her seat.

"Tell me about Phoebe."

Yun's defiance remained, but she sighed and spoke. "Phoebe came later. She was quiet. I didn't know her very well."

"Did she become close with anyone?"

"No—maybe Rip."

"Did Hope become close with anyone?"

"Me, mainly," said Yun.

"Not with Scarlet?"

"No."

Berylata leaned forward again. "He seemed quite determined to save her from Old Haven."

"Scarlet would come to the rescue of anyone he knows. He's a good man."

"Do you believe he might try again?"

It took only a second of hesitation and a momentary flash of alarm on Yun's face to bring Berylata to her feet and around the table. She towered over Yun and glared down with her cat-eyes in slits. "What is Scarlet planning?"

Yun did not answer and, before Berylata could ask again, Yun sprang under the table on the way to the closed door. But Berylata's long reach caught a handful of Yun's hair and she dragged the girl out. A long lean foot came down on Yun's chest, pinning her painfully.

"This could have been avoided!" growled Berylata, and with a twist of reality the creature became something else—a hurricane of power bearing down on Yun. Yun felt a wrench and a lifting sensation, though her body remained on the ground.

The tables and books and lamps faded into gray silhouettes, and the walls of the Archives ripped asunder and spun away into a maelstrom of whirling, tearing storm clouds. Berylata loomed over her, a howling tempest personified. Yun felt her arms lifted high as if by ropes and she swung in the lashing gale.

The wind intensified. Berylata grew to staggering proportions, merging with the storm. Emerald lightning lanced outward from her and tore streaks of searing brilliance through the hurricane.

Bit by bit, lash by lash, many secrets that Yun desperately wished to keep were stripped from her soul by the terrifying manifestation of the creature known as Berylata.

———

In the foyer of the Archives, the guard caught the rising and falling of the screams from the room down the hall. He paced angrily, appalled that this agony could be allowed to be visited on such a beautiful young girl, and desperately wishing that he could storm down the hall and stop it. But he had neither the power nor the bravery needed to interfere. Visitors came from other rooms to help, but when the guard told them of Berylata, they quickly retreated.

Eventually the screams died away, replaced with agonized sobbing. Only when the guard caught sight of the bands of Berylata's wing-light as she flew swiftly away toward Old Haven did he turn and hurry down the hallway to help Yun.

278

64: OLD HAVEN

The ocean of darkness that was Old Haven made a mockery of Scarlet's small bubble of lamplight. The single lamp revealed nothing beyond thirty feet. With no means to orient himself, except for the shadowy silhouettes of the taller buildings and frequent looks back at the glow-streaked upper cliffs, he chose a direction and began walking.

Buildings appeared immediately—larger and of more elegant architecture than those in the new city. He had imagined struggling through great piles of rubble from shattered structures, but these buildings appeared as though the occupants had gone out for an afternoon walk and had simply never returned. He paused in front of a slightly open pair of wooden doors engraved with a four-pointed star. The engraving read *Daystar Inn*.

It was while he was considering entering that he heard the sound. It came from behind, from the way he had come—a faint scrape, as though something hard had brushed against the stone walls of the nearby ruins.

A small, satisfied smile played across Scarlet's face.

The first scrape was followed quickly by a sound like a dragging foot, close by, off to Scarlet's right. His smile dropped immediately, replaced by a sudden concern. He held the lamp high and spun, but the pathetic circle of firelight revealed nothing. The darkness beyond the thirty feet of illumination crushed in on him like a wall, and whatever closed in on him moved unseen behind it.

As he swung the lantern about and strained his ears to hear, he picked up, to his left, the muffled but distinct sound of metal scraping slowly against metal.

Scarlet drew his own sword and backed against the inn wall, dropping his pack beside him. Lamp in one hand and weapon in the other, he braced himself.

Silence.

Had he waited for several minutes or only a few seconds? He chose to hold his ground for a moment more.

The silence remained, as did a sense of presence just outside the circle of light.

Scarlet lunged forward, the lamplight reaching into the darkness to catch hold of something. He caught a movement out of the corner of his eye and spun to face it.

Nothing moved. The silence remained.

He felt his heartbeat pound against his ribs, and the ring of bloodrush in his ears hampered his hearing. The struggle to catch a sound or a glimpse strained at his nerves.

And worse, he felt a dread crawl over him, an exposure, as if something monstrous and evil crouched atop the nearby buildings, waiting patiently to descend, to lay him open with rending claws and taste him from the inside out.

He backed up, tripped on his pack, and fell against the doors. They swung open with a grinding squeak from their aged hinges.

Scarlet righted himself quickly, grabbed his pack off the ground, and stumbled into the doorway. When those outside refused to pursue, he sheathed his sword, knelt and rifled through his pack, drawing out a small torch. He lit the torch, wedged it between door and frame, and retreated into the inn.

With the entrance safely lit, Scarlet turned his attention to the room.

The lamplight revealed tables, chairs, and benches, all of wood and covered in a layer of dust. Dishes and mugs could be seen here and there, the plates holding dark crumbles of long-decayed food. Scarlet inspected a nearby table. In the center lay a glass bowl containing a fat candle, dry and cracked. He tried lighting it, and to his delight it remained lit, though it sputtered and smoked.

It was during this moment of small triumph that he noticed the disturbed dust. Several of the plates and mugs had been moved—perhaps not recently, for a light layer of new dust had accumulated. Scarlet scanned the floor. Tracks wandered between the tables, some barely visible, some newer, but all entirely human boot and sandal marks.

He wondered if these might be the tracks of the Uglies that had visited Rip. If so, it would be a shocking stroke of luck to blunder immediately into their home out of all the buildings in this midnight city. He doubted the odds. He also doubted that any normal human would choose to live here.

That meant more Uglies. If so, he sincerely hoped that his torchlight would draw only the ones who had kidnapped Hope.

He followed the freshest set of tracks. They wandered to a wide marble staircase leading up into the gloom of an upper floor. In the lamplight the stairway reminded him of a giant pale tongue, ending in the black throat of the unlit upper hall. Scarlet took a breath and stepped onto the stairs, but before he could take the second step he heard a soft clunk behind him.

He spun.

Nothing moved nearby, and the torch at the doorway burned undisturbed. The sound had come from the far darkness of the common room. He pushed forward slowly, through the tables, skirting along a lounge centered by a great stone fireplace.

And then, at last, the lamplight caught a figure. Scarlet's first glimpse was that of a man sitting almost exactly in profile. As he approached, the firelight revealed details—a heavily bearded face, one arm on a large tin ale cup, and two fingers missing from the man's hand. The clothes looked dusty and gray, as did the man's skin. The stranger did not turn as Scarlet approached. He slowly lifted the cup to his lips, held it there a moment, then returned it to the table.

It occurred to Scarlet that, living in this lightless hell, the man might be blind. Scarlet swallowed, and spoke. "Hullo."

The man did not respond. He brought the cup back up and down again, barely moving his body or head. Scarlet edged closer. With rising alarm he noticed the ghastly skin—pale gray, visibly cracked.

The cup came up, almost. The ghastly man stopped short and turned his head slightly. Scarlet started backing away, but then held his ground.

"Hullo. Can you hear me?"

The man put down his drink and turned, preparing to rise. His right eye stared blankly, his beard-covered mouth slack and dry, and, as he turned, Scarlet discovered that the man had no left eye.

In all of the tight spots and frightening circumstances that Scarlet had endured since awakening, this single moment produced in him a heart-shocking fright. The man's eye was missing, as was much of the left side of his face. Scarlet could see into the dark ashen head of the thing, right through the hole in its face—a hollow man made of funeral ashes. The thing rose up, stretched out its arms and slowly swung them about, as if it sensed something nearby and sought to prove it by striking against it.

Scarlet lost his composure and stumbled back, knocking over a table. The thing came toward him, staggering on gray limbs, swinging more and more wildly about. It opened its mouth as if it wished to speak or yell out, though nothing but a soft hiss escaped. A foul, choking odor, like moldy clothes, grew stronger with every swipe of its arms.

Scarlet regained his feet, ducked under a swinging arm and hastily retreated toward the doorway. The ghast staggered after him, sweeping its arms as if it could sense Scarlet but not see him. Scarlet turned to keep an eye on the thing, but in stepping back he tangled with a chair. He flailed desperately to keep his feet, slammed painfully against the doorjamb, and careened outside.

Strong hands latched onto his arm. Scarlet tried to twist away from the grip, but it held him like a vise. He spun toward his assailant, trying to draw his sword with his other hand, but what clutched at him was not the ghastly creature from inside the inn. The terrifying sight of this new attacker stabbed straight to his soul, made all the worse by its female appearance.

After his harrowing climb, the imprisoning darkness, the ominous sounds, and the shock of the ghast-creature, his mind had had enough. He screamed heartily.

The woman-thing that held him stared back, her eyes wide open in shock and her face in the act of a scream herself. When Scarlet finished, a moment of silence fell. Scarlet could hear the ghast shuffling about in the inn. His face calmed slightly. Hers did not, for it remained permanently fixed in that terror-scream expression.

The Uglies had found Scarlet. Or, at least one of the Uglies—the one he knew as Miss Scareface. She opened her mouth, revealing a row of rotted fangs, and uttered these words:

"Young Scarlet! How nice to see you! Are you tired?"

65: SCAREFACE

Scarlet tried to compose himself, his fear only slowly subsiding, Scareface's first words taking him by surprise. Up close the woman's face looked far worse than his former introduction through the mirror at the work yards in Haven. Her pale skin stretched taut and appeared bloodless, as though she were a corpse. Watching her speak casual words with that terrifying expression gave Scarlet the shivers. Her grip felt like an iron press. The severe scrape on his shoulder had opened when he'd hit the doorjamb, so that a fresh trickle of blood meandered down his arm and over her long, claw-like hands.

"What have...no, I'm not tired, why?" said Scarlet.

"What did you want at the inn if not a soft bed, then?" said Scareface.

"I was looking for you," said Scarlet. "But something else is in there."

"Who?"

"Not so much a who as an it, I should think. Gray, dead, hollow, falling apart in the face."

"Ah, that's likely old Barnham. He's a regular patron of the place." She let go of his arm. "Bit of a sot, he is. He didn't touch you, did he?"

"What I-"

"He didn't *touch* you, did he?"

"No. Why?"

"Best if he doesn't." She looked over Scarlet's scraped and bloodied body. "What happened to you?"

"The usual. How did you find me?" He gathered his belongings while keeping one eye on Scareface.

"Your light, of course. How did you expect?"

"Dark sorcery, sight beyond sight, and what not."

"Oooh, exciting!" crooned Scareface through her fangs, looping her arm around his and leading him off into the darkness, toward the center of the city. "But sorry, no. I'm just like you. Mostly."

Scarlet did not resist, uncertain what this creature's game could be. She guided him through the gloomy streets and alleyways at a leisurely pace, chatting about the sights and history of Old Haven, pointing out small landmarks of no interest to Scarlet. Whenever she grew quiet, Scarlet heard noises just outside the range of his lantern, as he had before entering the inn.

"Who is out there?" whispered Scarlet.

"Ah, you hear little noises, do you, see little sights?" said Scareface.

Scarlet nodded.

Scareface stared around at the darkness, her lips curling into a terror-grin. "Those are the many who are, eh…further along in their troubles than old Barnham. Their bodies have gone, but they remain. They are trying to attract your attention—and you do *not* want to give them your attention. So ignore them and, after a while, you will grow deaf to their little haunts."

Scarlet locked his eyes forward and worked to squeeze out the faint noises. The dead city passed by, block by block. Their stroll almost felt commonplace after a bit, until from the corner of his eye he saw his escort bring her gnarled claw-hand to her mouth and lick his blood with a tongue far, far longer than it should be. It reminded him that this was one of two monsters that had stolen Hope—or worse.

"How is my blood? Tasty?" he asked caustically.

"Waste not, want not," Scareface answered casually. "And yes, you taste divine. Pure and lean."

"You sound like an expert."

"Quite," she said. "And to answer your unspoken question, Hope is safe and there's not a piece missing. Not that we weren't tempted, mind you. Flesh firm but not stringy, if I had to guess."

"Why did you kidnap her? For food?"

Scareface laughed, an act that stirred fear and disgust in Scarlet. He tried to avoid looking at her.

"Show and not tell, young Scarlet," she said. "Hope won't be harmed. Her bodyguard does not receive the same guarantee, I am afraid. Now, be on your best behavior. We have arrived."

Before them the lamplight revealed nothing more than a narrow door and a building wall of mottled white stone. The wall extended upward past the extent of the lamplight.

"What is this place?" he asked.

"You don't recognize it?"

"No. I've never been here."

Scareface shrugged. "This is the Victory Tower, by far the tallest in Old Haven. Built centuries ago after defeating a most dangerous enemy. It was built at the height of the city's power, at least in recent times. Do you know how old this city is?"

Scarlet sighed, failing to understand this discussion. "I remember nothing past a couple hundred days ago…so history isn't my specialty."

Scareface produced a ghastly smile and pressed herself to Scarlet's arm. "You play such a good game, young Scarlet, but we both know the truth."

"Which truth is that?"

She clucked her black tongue against her fangs. "The truth of who you are. But, suit yourself. It's time to-"

Her mouth snapped shut in silence and she turned to peer into the darkness behind them. Seconds ticked by as she strained to pick up something. Scarlet kept still and silent, watching her, trying to read her expression. The terror-face revealed little, but the eyes betrayed a hint...

Fear.

Scareface shook herself and turned back to Scarlet, though her eyes flicked often to the surrounding darkness. "Shouldn't keep you waiting then. Let us look in on dear, sweet Hope."

She turned to the door, swiftly unlocked it, and pushed her weight against it. The unusually thick door gave way stubbornly. Scareface beckoned Scarlet inside. He noticed her eyes fixed to the dark street outside, but as he passed she took his arm again, showed her fangs in a wicked smile, and escorted him down a dusty hallway.

Scarlet glanced back at the door. Scareface had left it open, its entrance a rectangle of complete darkness that quickly faded from sight as they moved down the hallway.

"Ah, such a feast of wealth," sighed Scareface, passing her gaze over the numerous statues and paintings along the wall. Rich adornments graced every archway and doorway. They turned left down a wide hallway dedicated extensively to pools and fountains, many still functioning but all empty of the normally abundant glowmoss. "Here was the seat of power of the last lords of Old Haven. The city was entering a golden age, rivaling and even exceeding Pinnacle. And then it died."

"How?"

"There are wicked things in the world, young Scarlet. Wicked and powerful. But no more wicked than your own kind can be. The last lords betrayed the city. They sought power that wasn't theirs. A Devourer came and helped them, and, in the end, betrayed them. And then it ate the city. Or, I should say, it is eating the city. It isn't finished yet."

Scarlet shuddered. The nagging sense of exposure returned to him, as though the terrifying beast that was crouching above now prowled the streets, seconds away from catching sight or scent of him.

"What is this—thing? Does it know we are here?" asked Scarlet.

"It might."

"Is it a friend of yours?"

Scareface laughed. "You are such a wit! No, we are fleas on its back, and we are very careful not to bite it. Wolves do not befriend fleas."

They passed an open doorway, and Scarlet had a sudden start when he glimpsed movement in the room.

"There's someone in there!" he whispered.

"Oh yes, there are still occupants here," said Scareface. "Live and let live. They won't harm you. Unless they touch you."

"Comforting," said Scarlet, giving the next doorway an extra wide berth.

A stairwell appeared to one side, leading downward. Scareface turned to it, took Scarlet's hand, and descended to another strong door, which she unlocked, and, after that, yet another door. She unlocked it and turned to Scarlet.

"Now don't be alarmed by what you see, young Scarlet. Hope is safe."

She pushed the door wide—straight into a catacomb of nightmares.

66: THE MOLE

It began with prison doors and a holding area, followed by a large sectioned chamber. Devices—terrible devices—dominated every space, and, seeing them, Scarlet turned his gaze to the floor. At that moment, were there a way to murder the monster next to him, he would have gladly chosen to do so.

"Scarlet! How good to see you!"

Scarlet raised his eyes to see the man-monster lumbering toward him, his gargantuan mole wagging under his cheek. His oversized, bulky head swayed with every step, perched on a blocky, powerful body with grossly oversized, low-hanging arms suspended from stooped shoulders. The massive hands looked as though they could completely wrap around Scarlet's neck.

"How nice of you to come. It's a shame Rip couldn't be here as well," he said, his dry, cracked skin rustling with every movement. "Tea?"

Scarlet's hand moved to his blade, but he stopped short. "You have tea?"

"No, but it's polite to ask. How was your trip? Oh, I see you have had a little trouble. You've been bleeding."

"Yes. Your mate has been sampling me."

"Indeed. I wouldn't mind a taste myself. Perhaps later."

Scarlet glanced about the room—a room filled end to end with implements of torture. Several bodies littered the chamber. He could control his anger no longer.

"This is who you are then?" he said, his voice rising with each word. "You steal people away from their homes and *eat* them? But you find the need to *torture* them first?"

Mole shrugged his freakish shoulders and looked around the nightmare chamber. "I don't think you've-"

"No, monster, I don't think *you've* gotten it! I don't know why you took Hope, and I don't know what you want from us, but if there's any way for me to swing it, I swear I will see both of you damned souls erased from this world!"

Mole tilted his head unnaturally, and an uncomfortable silence ensued.

"Really, Scarlet," said Mole finally, "that puts a damper on the festivities. Goodness, man, you're actually trembling! You clearly are not in the mood for a chat right now. So, to Hope, straight away."

Mole turned and walked away. Scareface went with him, turned to Scarlet, then beckoned. Scarlet drew his sword and followed.

They wound through prison cells—little more than tiny caves cut into the stone. Skulls decorated the walls and artwork of old bones hung from the low ceiling. Scarlet could only imagine the state of the prisoners brought here, coming to a place designed in every aspect to convey despair and death.

They reached a narrow tunnel that appeared to have been recently dug, or perhaps reopened, the loose rock filling a nearby storage chamber. The tunnel ended at a pit with a ladder. The two monsters simply jumped down the fifteen-foot drop. Scarlet scrambled down the ladder. Reaching a large iron door, Mole unlocked it and swung it open.

Here there was light—a single lamp burning below a narrow smoke chimney, through which a stream of water trickled, meandering to a small grate in the floor. Mole picked up the lamp and followed the wall, lighting torches. Slowly the room was revealed.

It extended in a rectangle, vaulting to a high ceiling. Human-sized notches layered the walls top to bottom, and in each notch old bones lay, held down by long-rotted straps and rusting shackles. Scarlet clutched his sword hilt tightly as his eyes passed over the dust-draped remains.

There, in a notch cleared of bones, lay Hope.

Scarlet returned his sword to its scabbard and raced to her. Mole began talking, lighting a series of torches along one wall. Scarlet paid little attention, checking Hope for a pulse. There it was, slow and steady. He breathed a great, shaking sigh of relief and clutched one hand to his head. A fear had lain in the back of his mind, for days now, that all of this would be folly—that these monsters would never bother to keep Hope alive. He lifted her head, tried to wake her.

"How much did you tell him?" said Mole to Scarface.

She shrugged. "We hadn't quite gotten that far."

After lighting the torches, Mole plodded back up to the far wall. "I need you to pay attention, Scarlet. This tower was built long ago by an ambitiously noble group of humans. They won a great victory over a deadly foe, and so, they named it the Victory Tower. The Daystar was still in the sky at that time.

"Years passed, the human city-states and their non-human allies grew complacent, and then a new enemy came, a most dangerous one, known as a devourer. It gained a victory so tragic that the Daystar fell from the sky, and its human followers, known as the Fallen, held sway over Haven for a time. This is the legend, anyway. Believe what you want. When they captured the tower, the Fallen took it over as a symbol of their victory, and their revenge. Are you following, Scarlet? Really, she is merely sleeping—in a way.

"The new rulers added these prisons, and their foes—young and old—met their fates here. But this chamber, this deepest prison, was reserved for a particular sect of the hated enemy known as the Dalmar.

"That small group, in this prison, changed the flow of history. They did something that burned fear into their victorious foes. They chiseled an image into this wall. It's not spectacular now, but supposedly, when the water flowed down the wall, the glowmoss grew naturally so as to perfectly highlight the etchings. They say that the emperor came in person to witness the Dalmars' wall, and the last prisoner, before he was slain, pronounced the doom of the new empire. The wall, he said, held the secret of that doom.

"Something happened then—some unexplainable miracle—that convinced the emperor of the wall's power. He became obsessed with it. His empire quickly fell into paranoia and chaos, and the Fallen were swept away.

"Through the centuries, other powers rose and fell, cities died, the human race declined, and only Pinnacle, Haven, and a few other cities survive on the Spire. But there remains, in the deepest nightmares of the elite, a belief that the original powers of the Spire would return for their vengeance. And though the Dalmar Wall and its image have been long lost, it all starts right here."

Scarlet slumped to the floor, exhausted. The strain of the dark city, the insanity of these chatty, murderous monsters, and the ultimate relief at finding Hope alive and unharmed sapped his strength. His mind dutifully attended to Mole's words, but they seemed meaningless—an old history being related by an insane monster who delighted in torture and human flesh.

Scarlet rose wearily and turned to Mole. He was about to demand that Hope be revived and that the monsters explain their intentions in luring them here. Instead, his mouth clapped shut, and he looked again at the Dalmar Wall.

Slowly his mind comprehended what he was seeing. His eyes grew wide, and his breath caught.

The wall, brightly lit by torches, contained a pattern of graceful, stylized engravings—sixteen large symbols surrounding a larger symbol of two connected orbs. Chiseled writing dotted the areas in between them.

One of the symbols caught his attention. A stylized seabird in flight. Scarlet undid his belt and lifted it to the light. The symbol on the buckle and the symbol on the wall matched in every detail.

Mole held out his grotesque hand, revealing Hope's treasured medical instrument kit. Its embroidered climbing vine had an exact twin among the images on the wall.

Scarlet closed his eyes...

Rodrigo raised his precious sword, handing the blade to Scarlet. "My one true possession," he said. Scarlet accepted it gingerly and turned it in the light. It was graceful and unblemished, with a blade of fine steel and a symbol of a charging bull engraved in three places...

Ed had done it. With a gasping sigh of relief, Scarlet watched the Forge come alive with gaslight. The chamber was massive, with little decoration except a large gray mosaic expertly laid into the wall above the controls, displaying the symbol of a lever and fulcrum...

Yun clasped her book of children's tales to her breast, smiling happily. "This is me," she said, pointing at the cover—Ninety-Nine Tales of Ravenhair, emblazoned above and below with a stylized scroll symbol...

Trace grunted in pain, and everyone turned in shock at the loud snap of the fire-pole's triggering. Ed seemed unconcerned that Trace had been hurt, and instead studied the remains of the pole. He turned it slowly, revealing to Scarlet the triple lightning bolt symbol on the pole's leather brace...

Scarlet opened his eyes. They were all there, on the wall, engraved in exact detail—charging bull, fulcrum, scroll, and triple bolt.

Mole stared at Scarlet. He raised a hand and pointed a gnarled finger as words formed on his lips.

But he stopped, and all three of them turned to the door.

Each had heard the faint but unmistakable creak of the ladder.

67: FEROCITY

Scarlet hastily rebuckled his belt and slid his sword quietly from the scabbard at his back. He crept to the doorway and edged his head around the frame. The torchlight from the room filtered out into the tunnel, but not quite far enough to reveal the ladder. The shadow caused by his head stretched out across the floor, making a mockery of any attempt at stealth. His skin crawled and his heart pounded, realizing the trap but not being able to see his captor.

His only thought was to even the odds before his nerves tore further. He would grab one of the torches and throw it out into the tunnel. He turned to snatch up a wall torch and, to his shock, discovered why the room behind him had gone so quiet.

He stood alone in the prison cell. Though Hope's unconscious form remained, the monsters Scareface and Mole were gone.

He raced to the back of the cell, searching desperately for the secret door that the two must have used to escape. Nothing moved and nothing appeared disturbed. He slid frantically along the wall, glancing back at the open door. For a moment he thought to slam it shut. But no. *What folly to close yourself in the deepest cell of this horrifying dungeon! Keep searching!*

He continued, all pretense of stealth out of his mind. He could find no crease, no crack, and no secret knob or plate. He slid by Hope's notch, bumped her arm as he passed by, and to his great surprise and relief he heard her groan. He stooped to her.

"Hope! Hope!" he cried, shaking her.

She lifted a trembling hand to her head and opened her eyes. Slowly they focused on him. "Scarlet? What—where are we?" Then her eyes flung open and she sat up in panic. Her forehead slammed against the roof of her notch and she fell back, clutching her head.

"Just lie still, Hope, you're safe now," he lied. He kissed her hand, squeezed it lightly, and rose again to continue his search.

A tall form crouched in the doorway.

He did not recognize it at first—a creature dark and shadowy, its outline difficult to define. But the two eyes shone brilliant green, and Scarlet recognized them then.

The tantyr Berylata had come.

Slowly the creature's skin lightened, shedding its chameleon-like camouflage, taking on definition and returning to the golden-and-white luster that Scarlet knew. The fine, beautiful lines of her face were hard set, and her eyes mere slits of intensity.

She scanned the room slowly, warily, clearly aware that Scareface and Mole should be here, and deeply suspicious of their absence. Her two thin, slightly curved short swords were drawn and prepared for action. Even after verifying the cell's emptiness and advancing into the room, she remained in a battle crouch, taking in every detail.

Scarlet held his ground but kept his sword point resting on the stone floor. She had seemed elegant, regal, on his last meeting with her. But now, in this dark place, he could think of nothing more deadly looking.

"You were not alone," she hissed.

"I do not know where they went," answered Scarlet quietly. "I can find no secret entrance."

Her eyes continued to scan the room carefully. He watched her gaze at first pass over the etchings, but then return suddenly to them. Slowly she straightened and her sword points lowered. For a time she stared in silence at the great, enigmatic artwork.

"This—this is The Wall!" she exclaimed in a whisper. "*The* Wall of Dalmar! It must be!"

Her eyes roved over it, wide with excitement. Then her gaze settled on something and her breathing stopped. Her head turned to regard Scarlet. She regarded his belt, and then the wall again, and her eyes narrowed.

He took several steps toward her. "I don't know why-"

"I have had *enough* of your lying and games!" Berylata's face grew aflame with anger. She brought up her swords. Scarlet raised his own in defense, but she did not attack. Instead, she rose to her full height, extended her arms upward, and screamed, "You will be stripped!"

The world Scarlet knew faded, and the world of Berylata arose.

He stood upon a vast, empty plain. A clarity came over him, as if he were truly aware of himself for the first time, not merely the shell that crouched in the prison cell, awaiting Berylata's attack.

She came as a great storm, pouring inexorably over the plains toward him. The leading winds buffeted Scarlet, an early promise of the force to come.

In a brief flicker of the mundane reality of the chamber, he caught sight of Hope lifting her bruised head, trying to rise. But his own body was frozen as Berylata stared down at him, her hands lifted high, her swords gripped, point down and threatening, her breathing strained and loud. Scarlet hunched facing her, his own sword point touching the worn stone floor, his eyes locked on hers.

Upon the plains that stretched endlessly through the ethereal soul-world of Berylata's conjuring, she struck, her immense presence in the storm directing all its fury at the tiny form of Scarlet. She was a goddess, a force of nature, smashing against his soul like a hurricane, lashing against his will.

For a moment he faced it, leaning into her presence stubbornly. He knew that he would be shattered, stripped bare. The tempest surrounded him, and there was no lee, no safe place.

He closed his eyes and his composure began to leave him. He would be on his knees, whimpering, and all of his secrets and all of his sins would be bared before this vengeful, demanding deity. If he were Rodrigo, he would stand before the storm and call out to his god and, like a great steel ship, he would turn into the fury of the winds and drive forward.

But there was no steel in Scarlet's soul, and though he called out to Rodrigo's god in desperation, the storm would have him.

In that moment, the wind ceased, as though the eye of the great storm passed over. It lasted only a heartbeat, but in that sliver of peace, Scarlet's vision returned with absolute clarity.

There is no steel in me. But I was molded with wings.

He leaned farther into the renewed wind, shouted with exhilaration, and spread his wings. And he flew. The storm had no choice but to carry him skyward.

Within the quiet of the chamber, minutes passed, and minutes more. Then Scarlet opened his eyes and drew in a long, soft breath. Berylata heaved in a great breath, her eyes flew open wide, and she staggered back.

For several heartbeats they stared at each other, a strange flicker of emotions passing between them.

Berylata's swords lowered, and she spoke almost plaintively.

"Who *are* you?"

Scarlet straightened, his hands and shoulders shaking from the intensity of the events in the otherworld. Berylata watched him numbly. Scarlet stepped forward, reached out...

Behind Berylata a dark ripple appeared, as though something were swimming to the surface of a muddy pond. In a moment's flash, a head, then a shoulder, then an entire body appeared.

Mole had returned. He raised one grotesque arm...

Berylata reacted before Scarlet could shout out. She must have read the shock in his face or sensed the ripple. She flung herself sideways, and the blow from Mole struck her back at a glancing angle, but it was enough to stun her.

The monster charged, intending to lock onto the prone tantyr with his mammoth, crushing hands. Scarlet dove low, catching Mole's knee. Mole stumbled, and Scarlet tumbled sideways, his breath smashed out of him.

But that moment of interference allowed Berylata to rise up on one knee, swords readied.

Mole's fist swiped dangerously close to Berylata's head, but her swords flashed lethally, sliding home into the monster's chest and shoulder. Mole backed up, clutching his chest. A dark wisp filtered out of both wounds.

He bellowed and flung himself at Berylata again, striking her powerfully on the shoulder, but not before one blade penetrated the side of his neck.

The other sword clattered to the stone floor, Berylata's whole arm momentarily paralyzed by Mole's crushing blow.

She backed away, but Mole rushed in again. Berylata gripped her one sword and timed a powerful swing. It caught the monster's arm at the elbow and the entire lower arm spun away, disintegrating into a dark vapor. Mole roared in agony, already wreathed in the smoke of the other three blade wounds. Berylata gave him no respite, driving the sword through his belly and side. Tilting sideways, the monster toppled, spilling out into dark smoke as he sank to the ground.

Berylata started to slide her blade out of the disintegrating body when a second ripple thrust Scareface back into reality in the cell. Berylata could not quite reorient herself when Scareface's right claw tore a ragged wound along Berylata's side and her clenched left claw smashed directly into Berylata's neck.

Berylata flew off her feet, landing heavily on the floor, her head crashing against the stone and the slashing wound freely bleeding out a purplish-red stream of blood.

Scareface, her terror-mask triumphant, drew a curved gray dagger from her waist belt and gripped it high. "Now *she*, young Scarlet—she *deserves* to be eaten!" Scareface leapt to Berylata's body, pulled back her feathered head to reveal the long neck...

There was a flash through the cell door. Scareface arched straight, perplexed. Looking down, she noticed the point of a spear protruding from her chest and black smoke pouring from around it.

Scareface turned around slowly, dazed.

A filthy, ragged, shock-eyed Rip glared up at her, and he growled. "For Hope!"

"Rip," gasped Scareface, "this was...my favorite...dress."

Scareface flowed away.

Rip kicked at the black wisps, then helped the struggling Scarlet to his feet. When the two turned, they discovered Hope already working at the gashes in Berylata's side. Her toolkit lay open over the creature's hip, its elegant climbing vine embroidered in gold thread gleaming in the torchlight.

68: And Four Returned

Scarlet lay in the sand-covered rock near the barrier wall between old and new city, concerned only with breathing, his energy spent. He let his exhales form words. "Say nothing about the Dalmar Wall."

The cliff rose up next to him. Reaching the Old Haven side of the wall near the up-cliff, the three Dusties had found a rope ladder and footholds chiseled into the wall—indications that someone had crossed here. They had carefully winched Berylata over, climbed over themselves, and fell to the ground on the Haven side of the barrier, too tired and numb to continue.

"Berylata knows," said Hope. "She'll not stay silent."

"She might," said Scarlet. "Trace says there's no love lost between many of the lords and the tantyrs. I suspect that Berylata and Odami are not interested in sharing information."

Over a day had passed since the finding of Hope, and the way out of Old Haven proved much more difficult than the way in. The three Dusties were tested to their limits in the escape from the darkness. But as they staggered through the cultivated glowmoss, their faces did not sag in despair. They spoke quietly, and when their eyes met, there passed between them a bond like blood.

Scarlet's eyes traveled to the litter and the ashen face of Berylata. He could not tell if she still breathed. He stooped to her ear to whisper words of life, but the others took notice and he stopped himself.

The news spread through Haven—first through the fields, then through the outskirts of the city—the arrival of three travelers, ragged, exhausted, barely able to hold the makeshift litter bearing the stricken tantyr Berylata. They were coming through the terraces, down from the wall that sealed away the awful terrors of Old Haven.

The reaction of the city took two forms. Some citizens ran to their homes and locked themselves away, deathly afraid of the plague, or vengeful spirits, or being stolen away by whatever terrors had been stirred up by the criminal foolishness of Scarlet. Others ran to the fields to see the miracle of the three who had entered Old Haven and lived, or to look upon the mighty Berylata, fallen and helpless, or to witness those who had broken a capital law of Haven. And so the three trudged weakly on, through rows of curious, excited, and suspicious onlookers.

A squad of soldiers arrayed themselves across the path. Scarlet, his head down, concentrating on the next step, nearly bumped into the captain, who stared at him impassively.

"Move off the path and sit down—there," said the captain, indicating a spot near a glowmoss mound.

Hope straightened, her eyes turning combative. "Berylata needs attention. We-"

"You will stay here until the lords arrive," said the captain, planting his spear meaningfully in front of him.

Hope turned red, preparing to respond, but Scarlet swiveled his end of the litter around and plodded silently to the indicated spot.

"We must bring her to the hospice," said Hope as they carefully lowered the litter to the sandy ground. "She's in desperate shape."

Scarlet took Hope's hand and pulled her close. "Please, Hope, sit with me. We need to talk."

They slid to the ground, exhausted. The driving lash of will to survive and escape drifted out of them, and Hope sank her head onto Scarlet's chest. He stroked a hand through her dusty, tangled hair.

"All of that is behind us now, Hope. We made it," he whispered.

"Yes, but-" She did not finish her words. Hope let out a small choking cry, and broke. Sobbing uncontrollably, she clung tightly to Scarlet. Tears moistened her hair, but they were not all hers. Scarlet held his silence, but his grief cascaded down and mingled with hers.

———

Rip lay nearby, his eyes wandering the sky as his heart tried to chase away demons. He kept telling himself how grateful he should be that the plan had worked. He had followed Scarlet's path of yellow cord, dropped into Old Haven, and managed to trail Scarlet and Scareface to the Victory Tower. There he had suffered a moment of panic watching Scareface unlock the heavy door, but surprisingly she had left it open behind her.

He thought of their flight out—of the ghastly hollow dead men and the invisible pursuers trailing them and surrounding them, keeping just outside of the tiny lamplight.

'Twas worth it, he thought to himself. *'Twas worth it*, he silently repeated again and again.

Scarlet turned his head to look at the little man. "Rip."

"Ahey, mate," said Rip quietly, keeping his eyes to the sky.

"You are amazing, my friend. Through the whole city, I could never tell if you were there. Not a hint."

"Bawley for me," said Rip. "The noisy spooks and ghosties made it easy. But I won't do it again. Not ever."

Minutes passed. A trio of ladies pushed through the crowd.

"Hope!" one of them half-screamed.

———

Hope leapt up, drying her eyes. "Emma!" They clasped each other giddily for only a moment, then Hope guided the girl toward Berylata.

"She's badly in need-" said Hope.

"We heard," said Emma. "We brought alcohol and dressings."

"Emma, you are a lifesaver!" Hope moved toward Berylata, but Scarlet took hold of her arm.

"We need to talk, Hope. Let them see to Berylata," he said.

Hope tried to read the seriousness in his eyes. He pulled her close again and whispered in her ear. "There is a law in Haven that no one is allowed to enter Old Haven. They take it very seriously."

Hope held him. "I am grateful that you broke it," she said.

"The penalty for it is death."

Hope looked at him quizzically. She shook her head slightly. "But surely they wouldn't-"

"They left little room for doubt," said Scarlet. "They believe the plague comes from there, among other troubles."

Hope shook her head again and closed her eyes. "They wouldn't."

Scarlet held her and kept the certainty of his thoughts to himself.

———

The lords arrived and this answered the question of why their friends had not yet appeared. Behind the lords came Ed, Yun, and Trace. Trace leaned on his spear among the guards, Yun stood closely at Ikone's side, and Ed dragged along the pole to which he was shackled.

Odami took his place in front of the assembly of lords, who stood off, keeping a dozen paces between themselves and the weary travelers.

"Scarlet!" shouted Odami.

Scarlet stood and faced the high lord.

"You are a brave man," said Odami. "Rip as well. I cannot deny you that."

"We did what had to be done, high lord. Nothing more," said Scarlet. "Ed! A splendid plan. I owe you a favor."

"Fine execution," shouted Ed back. "And yes, you owe me."

Trace pushed himself to the front. "Why didn't you invite me along?" he boomed. "You look like bloody meat."

"Sorry for that, Trace," said Scarlet. "Maybe next time."

A captain moved in front of Trace and scolded him back in line.

Yun whispered to Ikone and walked to Scarlet. The look of agony on her face tore Scarlet's heart. Tears soaked her cheeks.

"I knew I would never see you again," she whispered.

"I knew otherwise," said Scarlet, and moved to embrace her.

She stepped back. "Perhaps, but it matters not, Scarlet. I am to be married, tomorrow."

Scarlet shook his head, disbelieving. "Married?"

Yun nodded.

He looked over at the collection of lords. "Ikone?"

"Yes."

"Is this what you want?"

Yun glanced over at Hope, who had been drawn into the work on Berylata. Yun stared at the stricken creature, and a shadow passed over her eyes.

"I did what had to be done, Scarlet. Nothing more." Without looking at him, she turned and walked away.

Scarlet watched her go, too stunned to speak. He had many expectations for when he returned to Haven, but her sudden decision struck him to his heart. *Why would she—*

"Rip!" shouted Ed.

Rip hopped on a harvest cart for a better view. "Look at yeh, chained like an old gablin. And all the good yeh've done them with fixing the rails. N'hardly right."

"My firepoles, Rip, remember them?"

"Ah-hey! Beauties they are!"

"You can't have them," said Ed.

"I already nicked them."

"What?"

"Afore we left. Safe and sound, and somewhere else. My condolences, cally-pad."

Ed laughed. "I'm afraid I won't be able to get revenge for this."

Rip's eyes darkened and he simply nodded.

Scarlet set his jaw, driving the thought of Yun's rejection out of his mind as the subject of their survival arose. "Lords! This isn't getting easier in the waiting. You came here for a purpose. Hopefully you are discerning men, and honor the spirit of your law rather than the blind letter-"

Odami shouted Scarlet into silence. "You are woefully ignorant, Scarlet! The only two barriers to our extinction are our fighting prowess and strict adherence to our laws. Honor and integrity. And we follow every letter, to the letter."

The reality of the words being uttered sank into Scarlet. They brought fear to his heart, but not despair. Hope was safe, and the upcoming, final punishment could not tarnish that.

"Every letter, Scarlet!" repeated Odami. "The law against entering Old Haven was written before I was born and never put to use. Of those few that broke that law, none ever returned to face punishment. The punishment is short and clear. It states, 'For this crime, a life is forfeit.'"

The words fell as boulders to hard ground. Scarlet closed his eyes, but he heard murmuring and recognized a thread of agitation in the assembled lords.

Odami gave the lords a challenging sweep. "It is my duty to pass judgment for such serious crimes. Therefore, for the act of entering Old Haven, for endangering all citizens of Haven, a life is forfeit. And I have chosen that life. The executioner will see to his duties!"

The assembly of lords erupted. The Bear Lord Maris turned to face Odami. "The law is clear! All who break it must be killed. If you let them live, you leave the city open to the plagues, and worse."

Odami's hawkish eyes bore in on the Bear Lord. "The law *is* clear, Maris. Is it not you who is fond of saying, 'Every letter to the letter'? *A* life is forfeit. One."

The lords conferred, and a murmur rose in the crowd. "Mercy!" yelled a voice. "Mercy!" repeated a few others. "Mercy!" began the chant, until it became a sustained crescendo.

Odami's opponents fell away, chastened by the crowd. "Mercy it is!" shouted Odami, "but for one." He motioned, and the executioner and his crew moved forward.

Scarlet and Rip looked at each other—their worn faces, their wounds and blood, and the bond that only terrifying trials together can produce.

"What's our plan then?" said Rip.

"I have none," said Scarlet. "Never quite got this far in my head. Didn't think it would happen this way, to be honest."

Rip backed up several steps as the executioner closed in. "Do we fight?"

Scarlet's shoulders sagged. "I'm too tired, Rip. I'm sorry. Hope is safe. I'm content."

Rip didn't have time to respond. The executioner and crew stood before them—towering examples of muscle and deadly intent.

"Stand aside," said the executioner.

Rip put his spear in front of him. "Yeh muddled ballards, we've not done anything deserving of death!"

"I said stand aside!" growled the executioner. His men pushed Rip and Scarlet out of the path and strode forward, until the executioner stood over the litter.

Over Hope.

"Have you gone insane!" screamed Scarlet at Odami. "Hope was kidnapped!" He ran toward Hope, but a soldier struck him in the shoulder, sending him sprawling. The soldier pulled Scarlet to his feet, seizing him in an arm-lock.

The executioner towered over the young healer, readying his axe. "Stand aside, all of you."

Emma, who had moved in front of Hope, stepped in the path of the trained killer. "You'll not lay a hand on Hope-"

"Then get her out of my way!" the executioner bellowed. His crew pushed forward and gathered up the young women, who kicked and screamed, until they noticed that Hope herself had been dragged to the side.

A shocked hush fell over the entire assembly. Not a single onlooker had considered this possibility. Not a soul moved or dared to speak.

The life to be taken was Berylata's. Odami intended to execute the powerful, noble scourge of Haven.

Scarlet turned toward Odami. In the glowing, firelit darkness it was often difficult to pick out fine detail at a distance, but Scarlet knew that the hawkish eyes rested directly on him. Their gazes locked, and Scarlet reconsidered the high lord.

Odami has everything that he desires—Berylata under a death penalty, Yun given over to Ikone, me safely out of Yun's path, the useful skills of Hope and Ed returned to Haven. Could he have possibly planned all of it, controlled or foreseen events to that degree of precision?

Scarlet shook his head.

Not possible. Rip and I should have been dead in Old Haven, and Berylata as well.

But did the outcome matter? Death in Old Haven would serve Odami as well as events here. No, all that mattered would be to set events into motion. One single event, actually—Hope's kidnapping, and the inevitable rescue attempt by a romantic young fool who stood between Yun and Ikone.

One event needed. One kidnapping. All conveniently provided by Scareface and Mole.

Scarlet remembered the climbing evidence on the barrier wall. Someone had entered Old Haven, perhaps regularly.

At that moment, with gazes locked, Scarlet came to a certainty that Odami knew Scareface and Mole, had fashioned some form of unholy alliance with them, and had set events into motion.

It seemed to Scarlet as though a small, satisfied smile crossed Odami's face.

"Guards," said the high lord, pointing to Ed, "release this man." As the soldiers worked to undo the shackles around Ed's arms and legs, Odami continued. "The punishment for your lying and deceit is commuted, so long as you serve the needs of Haven in good faith. Do you agree?"

"Do I have a choice?" said Ed.

"Yes." Odami looked meaningfully to the executioner.

Ed nodded silently, and the chains came off.

The executioner prepared Berylata, turning her face down. He placed a block beneath her chin, exposing and stretching the back of her white-plumed neck.

Despite Scarlet's intense fatigue, his senses clarified, as though a cloudy lens slid away to reveal a vivid world. His focus lanced out into his surroundings—Hope struggling against the executioner's henchmen, Emma sobbing, the light whistle in the breath of the soldier behind him, the peculiar smell of the tangled mounds of reddish glowmoss nearby that for some reason reminded him of boating.

Scarlet's eyes narrowed. Something rose in him—a reserve of energy accompanied by a lean, agile keenness. It was as though he felt the fingers on his hands and the muscles in his legs for the first time. A last, focused gasp, perhaps, and he desperately needed it—for Scarlet could not, under any circumstances, allow Berylata to die.

Scarlet sagged. The soldier who held him let the apparently fainting boy fall to the ground. But Scarlet rolled and kicked out, launching himself up and into a sprint, straight for the executioner. His former captor lunged after him, close on his heels, but with the executioner's crew off to the side trying to maintain control of the women, Scarlet had a free path straight at the hefty killer and his axe.

Prepared for the fatal swing, the executioner lowered his axe and grimaced at Scarlet, like a grand chef staring down the oaf who felled his soufflé. He readied a meaty fist for Scarlet. The chasing soldier reached out, almost able to collar and bring down the boy, but only a handful of paces remained between them and the executioner.

Scarlet slammed to a halt and went to his knees. The pursuing soldier showed skillful reflexes and tried to leap the boy, but Scarlet swung an arm up, tripped his legs, and sent the soldier arrowing headfirst into the stomach of the executioner. Both went down in a pile of sweat, dust, and curses.

Scarlet regained his feet and drew his sword—a useless gesture against the host of soldiers and henchmen that circled in on him, but he had no choice. Something wholly unexpected had occurred during his soul-realm confrontation with Berylata at the Dalmar Wall. Because of it, he would die here with her. Any other choice would be unthinkable.

"Don't kill him! Do *not* kill him!" yelled Odami, rushing toward Scarlet. His personal guard followed, shadowed by Ed, who jogged along beside them.

The soldier tripped by Scarlet ignored the command, his nostrils flared and killing intent in his eyes. Scarlet raised his sword to defend himself. A woman's scream pierced Scarlet's ears, close by in the crowd, then came more shouts. The nearby executioner's crew turned to discover the disturbance. Scarlet felt a presence, then a blur passed by his right. The soldier that faced Scarlet hunched over with a startled expression, clutching his side. A stain of crimson expanded there and the soldier pitched to the side.

Something stood next to Scarlet—dark and shadowy, and armed with two soot-covered short blades in its hands. It turned, considered him with gleaming yellow eyes, and reached out.

302

Odami caught sight of a flash of shadow moving near the executioner—tall and dark and quick. His battle sense instantly took command. He shouted to his personal guard and barked orders to the captains behind him. The array of troops accompanying the captains surged forward, settling into formation with the practiced ease of veterans who'd seen a lifetime of combat.

The executioner's crew didn't fare as well. When Odami turned his attention again to the front, neither the executioner nor his crew remained standing. But there was no time to advance to their rescue in any case. A swarm of shadowy, chameleon tantyrs rushed upon them.

In seconds a dozen humans fell to the storm of dark blades, but the steady troops held formation. Human spears and crossbow bolts found their mark here and there as a frantic melee ensued. The tantyrs darted back and forth with an unnatural agility, seeking openings in the array of spears. Odami and his personal guardsmen held at the center, armed with long, lean, slightly curved blades.

A tantyr slipped in to Odami's right and the high lord spun to meet it, blocking one blade thrust with his pronged dagger and parrying the other with his own blade. The tantyr ducked back before Odami's foot could drive into its knee. Sensing the skill of its opponent, the tantyr backed away. Its eyes darted slightly to one side and Odami caught a flash of movement.

A second tantyr leapt toward Odami's exposed back, its blades expertly aligned for the kill. But the high lord rolled left, bringing up his own blade to catch the tantyr through the leg. The tantyr cried out and lashed one sword sideways, trying to sweep at Odami's head. Odami blocked the sweep with his dagger, and the tantyr staggered sideways, directly onto the blade of one of Odami's personal guards. The creature snarled and sank to the ground.

Odami spun to face the first tantyr, but it had retreated. A vibration arose and he turned to see Ed being lifted swiftly to the sky, the bright wing-bands of light from the capturing tantyr illuminating his startled face. Others rose, and more, and soon several dozen tantyrs ascended in flight. Odami caught sight of Scarlet being lifted skyward, and that large one, Trace.

Crossbows were fired as fast as they could be reloaded, and one tantyr wavered, spun over, and plummeted to the ground. Odami ran to the site of the fallen tantyr, followed closely by his personal guard. In the glow of the nearby mounds of glowmoss, Odami found the tantyr breathing raggedly, a bolt through its lung, another through its hip, and a sword gash across its back.

Odami approached the creature. Despite its clear state of agony it kept its eyes steady on the high lord.

"You would kill Berylata, a tantyr commander, in cold blood? You have sealed your doom," it gasped out.

Odami's face twisted in anger. "You know perfectly well why, fiend," he growled, and brought his sword point swiftly down.

Ten minutes later, the crowds that had begun a mad rush for the city as soon as the fighting began were all far gone, and a dutiful hush fell over the battlefield, punctuated by groans and screams from the wounded. Emma and her fellow nurses moved through the field, helping some and comforting those who would not see the next day. Two of Odami's captains approached the high lord. Both of their faces were set grimly.

"We lost eighteen dead, high lord," said one. "Perhaps as many as eight more. And thirty wounded, at least."

"Tantyrs?" said Odami.

"Four. Plus one wounded and captured."

"Kill it."

The two captains glanced at each other. "Yes, high lord. I'm sure we wounded others, but their flight allowed escape."

"We were unprepared," said Odami. "How did they know that Berylata had been brought back? That was no coincidence."

The captains shook their heads silently.

"Who did they capture? I saw Berylata, Scarlet, and the big Lakesider taken," said Odami.

"Rip and Hope are also missing. Yun is safe."

Odami nodded. "Go. We have much to prepare for."

The captains saluted and hurried away. Odami turned to scan the sky and the outline of the wall that barred the way to Old Haven. After nearly a century, Haven had entered, once again into war with Pinnacle. Many in Haven would accuse him of acting rashly, but he knew otherwise, and he had planned long and carefully. His spies in Pinnacle agreed that the time had come to confront Pinnacle and the tantyrs. And for this confrontation, Odami had gained new allies—allies from across that barrier wall between the city of the living and the city of the dead.

70: LOSS AND DESPAIR

Hours later, Yun sat cross-legged on a corner of the flat stone railing around the balcony outside of her bedroom at the high lord's estate. Few other places in Haven reached as high as this room. Considering the height—over a hundred feet—her position on the railing was most unwise.

A book rested in her hands—a book with a blue cover and graceful scroll symbols traced on its spine and front. She read.

"Where are the stars?" shouted Ravenhair. "Where have you taken them?"

"Where they belong," growled the Shadow Stealer. "Away, deep, where they can no longer mar the sky."

No one knew, not even Rodrigo—especially not Rodrigo—that she had secretly hidden the book within her belongings and brought it with her. It seemed so long ago that she and the other seven Dusties had packed carefully for a journey that they'd known nothing about.

They were all gone now. Scarlet, Rip, Hope—all taken to the sky by the tantyrs. Even Ed and Trace were missing. She was alone.

Loa, gracious One, show my path. I cannot see.

Yun had brought herself here, to this railing, to end it. She would leap and the pain would be gone.

Her friends were more than just missing. Scarlet had let her walk away without so much as a protest, but he'd thrown his life to the wind to try to save that hated Berylata.

The physical pain of her scourging by Berylata had long since passed, but the anger and shock and fear of it still lingered. The anger, especially. Yun remembered again the terrifying confrontation, the feel of her soul being stripped naked and shamed, and, on the other hand, the strange disorienting thrill of experiencing that otherworld.

And now her friend, her love, had forsaken her for that monster.

When Yun had come to the railing, climbed up, and actually stood upon it, looking down to the dark rock below, she knew that she could not make herself do it. She could never jump, even though she must.

Gracious One, let it end.

She did what she could, walking along the rail, careful to keep her balance but hoping beyond reason that she would misstep. Nothing came of it, and she crossed her legs on the railing, bringing forth her secret treasure to read—her one, last thing in the world that did not bring her pain.

Odami—that greedy, self-serving soul—had summoned her the very morning that Scarlet had gone to Old Haven, taking her to his secret chambers. There he'd set forth his expectations, his demands, his threats. Scarlet, Rip, and Hope were all destined for death, whether they returned from Old Haven or not. Death would either find them in the dark or at the hands of an executioner's blade.

But, Odami assured Yun, there was hope, a hope that required great risk by Odami, and therefore required a price. Should they return alive, Odami could save all but one. In exchange, Yun must marry Ikone and reject Scarlet openly.

She held anger at Odami's cold, mercenary tact. She held despair and disgust at forced marriage to a man she did not love—and who already had two wives. But regardless, she knew her answer. She could not let her friends die. She could not let Scarlet die.

And then Scarlet had walked away from her.

The landscape of her life had not merely turned to barren waste in front of her. The barrens spread out behind as well—nothing but Rodrigo, a dead love, and Scarlet, a forsaking, faithless one.

"Ravenhair, Ravenhair, why have you come from the light to the dark?" muttered the Ghastlies from the shadows. "These dreary depths are not for you. They are for us, and we grow hungry seeing you."

"The stars have gone, poor souls," whispered Ravenhair to the dark. "And before you devour me, flesh and bone and soul, might you know where they are?"

A single tear fell upon her precious book. "Buried away deep, like me."

———

When Ikone found Yun's door locked, he brought forth his key and unlocked it, stepping boldly into her bedroom. In nine hours, Yun would be his wife, and nothing stood in the way. Certainly not locks.

He did not see her, but like all the thoughts that darted through his mind at this late hour, he envisioned her—tiny, priceless, beautiful, desirable—a magnificent work of the delicate side of nature.

Nine hours.

There were many women in Haven, many beautiful women, and many hungry for a man to claim. Ikone had already married two of his choice, prime beauties who had given him several sons. He expected to continue until a hundred sons stood proudly at his side. But Yun was different. There may not be another for some time after Yun.

Like his father promised, the lure of Ikone had brought Yun around before too long. Despite her apparent devotion to the boy Scarlet, she had ultimately seen the obvious path and rejected the reckless young fool that nearly threw his life away to recover another woman.

Yun was his now, and it would be many days before the thrill of this victory waned.

Victory.

Again the stirring of great feats rose in him. Years of talk and planning had come to pass this very night. They drew the line against the hated tantyrs—the inhuman monsters that dared to set themselves up as judges over the entire human race of the Spire.

The act had come swiftly. The city now rejoiced in the thrown-off shackles of tantyr tyranny. Gods had died tonight. Died pitifully—shot down and struck down, as an animal would die. Many humans had fallen also, but their fall had brought with it a message: The tantyrs can be defeated. And while they are few, men are many.

Pinnacle. That was the important target now—corrupt, weak Pinnacle—relying on Haven to supply their best fighters, and now brimming with soldiers having the mark of a Haven clan. The tantyrs would come to fight here, and they would find their home taken behind them. There would be no place for them to go afterward—only into the sky and the darkness, perhaps to the other fabled Spires out there in the far-away night.

It was said that the true crowns of Pinnacle could not be wrested from their royal owners, but those crowns came with little power today. Soldiers ran Pinnacle, under the yoke of the tantyrs, and once the tantyrs were defeated, the banner of the Crescent would fly above the once-great city.

Odami had promised Pinnacle to Ikone. The four rulers there, the old ones with useless crowns, would continue to sit idly by, helpless and impotent, as soldiers of Haven came to power.

As Ikone came to power.

Under one rule, father and son, the strength and unity of the humans would grow again, and the blackspawn would be stamped out...

It bothered him that he could not find Yun. But on his second pass near the balcony, he saw her where he did not expect to, sitting on top of the protective railing around the balcony. *Foolish girl, did she not think about what could happen?*

Ikone moved to the balcony threshold. Putting his arms akimbo and sucking in his amply muscled but bulging gut, he commanded, "What do you think you're doing?"

Yun gave a taut yelp and pitched over backward. Ikone gaped in surprise and reached out to catch her. He was far too late. Clasping something dark and rectangular to her breast, eyes closed, Yun plummeted silently toward the rocks below.

The darkness swallowed her up, and Ikone turned to race down through the palace.

———

"What do you think you're doing?"

The words lashed through Yun like a whip crack. Having her head down and dwelling on dark anxious thoughts while reading from her closely guarded secret—believing herself entirely alone—she startled violently.

There was a moment, a slim second where she wondered from where the voice had come. And then she understood. She was looking up at the balcony, at Ikone...and she was falling, plunging to the very end she had come there seeking.

She clasped Ravenhair to her breast, closed her eyes, and plummeted silently down.

Something struck, smashing into her so violently that she almost lost her grip on the book. She had impacted against a rock, and her once pretty body was torn into a bloody, horrifying mess...

But despite an initial crush of pain, she lived.

And the dark rocks, still a ways below her, were sliding sideways now, not rushing up at her.

She felt warmth on her back as she dangled upside down. Something had clamped tightly to her thighs, preventing their movement. Above her, a white light shone, and the air was alive with a pulsing vibration.

She dangled helplessly in the air, rising ever upward along a cliff. Two hands with long fingers carefully turned her until she was right side up and held beneath the arms, soaring over a land filled with brightly glowing streams. She watched the lights of a city grow near, and then they were flying over buildings and streets, approaching a vast castle. The tantyr set her down gently in an upper courtyard, and there she found friends.

"Hahlay! Nabbed you up, like they promised," said Rip, sweeping her up into his substantially muscled arms.

Ed nodded to her, rubbing his shackle-worn wrists. "We've been waiting four hours."

"Just three," said Hope, pointing off to the north, to the tall central tower of the castle, and the soaring flames of the gas clock showing the time.

"Hi, Yun, we missed you," said Trace.

Yun's mind tried to orient. She had not fallen to her death, Ikone could not force marriage on her, a tantyr had rescued her, and she had flown through the sky...

A smile grew and grew on her face, and she turned to hug Trace. "I'm so happy to see you all. How...how did they get you up here, Trace?"

"Took two to get that load off the ground," said Ed.

"Where are we?" asked Yun.

A graceful tantyr dressed in blue stepped forward. "You are in Pinnacle Castle. We will be taking you to the royal court immediately. Ready yourselves."

The Dusties were once again borne up into the sky, around to the west side of the castle, and through large open windows into a lavish throne room.

When the tantyr set her softly down on the stone floor of the royal court, Yun staggered, found her balance, and stared around at the crowd of strangers. One stood crisply at the side of a throne, dressed in a blue military uniform with gold braids. He looked remarkably like a friend whom she had lost recently. And then the soldier grinned from ear to ear and raced toward her.

"Yun!" he yelled.

And she knew the truth.

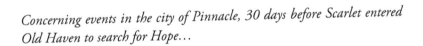

PART III:

PINNACLE

Concerning events in the city of Pinnacle, 30 days before Scarlet entered Old Haven to search for Hope...

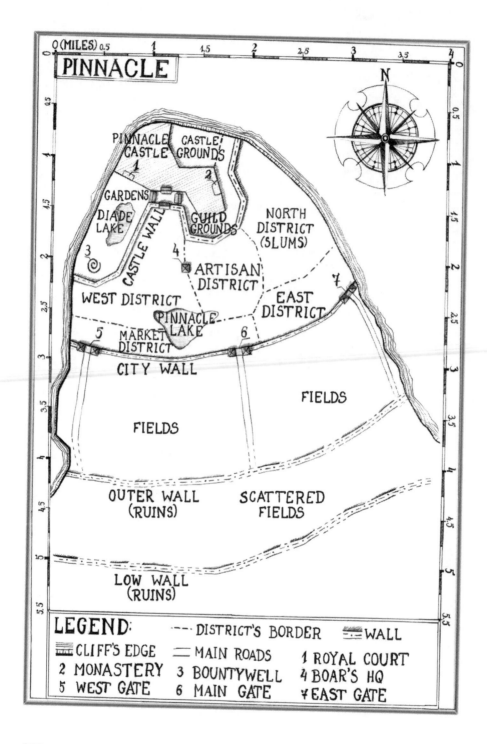

71: Wakening

— Day 154, the night before Phoebe left Haven for the city of Pinnacle

Rodrigo awoke in darkness, lying on cold, dry clay and hearing a throbbing ring in his ears. He rolled onto his back, grimacing at the soreness and ache from nearly every part of his body.

He remembered. He stilled himself and listened, trying not to think of his helpless plight in these vast, dark tunnels. Thoughts of his early days intruded forcefully on his mind—wandering the dark with the shadow of fear hovering about. But he took a breath, willed himself to calm, and closed his eyes, concentrating everything on his hearing. He rubbed his neck and the ringing in his ears faded slowly.

To his surprise, he heard voices, faint but clear. He opened his eyes, trying to get a bearing on the sound. At first he thought his vision might be trying to play tricks on him, for there seemed to be a measure of light—just the barest flicker. But the flicker stayed, and danced slightly in the manner of firelight, proving itself real.

Rodrigo worked at getting to his feet. Something sticky like blood clung to his clothes and they reeked of fish. Every muscle felt like it had been thrashed with a club. His ankle worked stiffly. He staggered forward, feeling for the wall, and he found it—rippled, smooth rock, as though a river had long ago passed through the tunnel.

This must be an offshoot from the pumice tunnel. How did I get here?

Memories of the battle came to him. He was in the act of thrusting his sword at the closest sliver when the nightmare creature struck hard from behind…

Of course! The slivers and the monster must be natural enemies and they clashed immediately after I fell, leaving me knocked aside and forgotten.

Staggering forward, he felt his muscles ease and loosen as he worked them. The firelight grew brighter and more direct. By the time he turned a last corner and caught sight of the torches, he felt almost human again.

But he had no idea where he was.

The light came from a host of torches in a small cavern crowded with dozens of people. One well-armored man stood on a ledge, his bald head throwing off a torchlit glow. He spoke to the crowd in a hushed, hurried tone, waving around a weapon as he talked—a long spike sticking sideways from a metal axe handle, like a one-handed pickaxe.

"We're late, so we need to move it. Keep your calm and listen carefully. We have only a few hours before the blackspawn get active. It's three miles to the fields and another two miles to the Pinnacle gates, so pace yourself, but move fast. Don't talk and don't make noise. If we do meet spawn, run, don't fight. You'll just attract more. Got it?"

Rodrigo glanced back at the dark tunnel behind him. He wondered whether these blackspawn were what he knew as slivers, and if any were close by.

"You said we'd be safely in Pinnacle long before the spawn woke up," said a visibly agitated, frightened young man near the front. "We aren't that late getting here. You lied to us!"

"Watch your mouth!" hissed the bald man. "You knew the risks. You don't like it, go right back down that tunnel."

Rodrigo wandered up to the back of the crowd. A sturdy woman with short, spiked hair gave him a glance, then a second. "Who're you, then?" she whispered.

"A straggler," said Rodrigo, giving her a reassuring smile. She scowled.

"You know very well that we can't go back down the way we came!" spat the frightened young man. "The spawn would have us long before we got back to Drift."

Drift. Rodrigo snapped alert, looking about at the crowd, hoping that no one turned around and recognized him.

"Then shut up and let's move," commanded Baldy. He didn't wait for a response but set off down the tunnel, followed by the crowd. Rodrigo took up station at the back of the line.

The tunnel twisted and turned, and grew narrower and shorter until Rodrigo hunched and finally crawled. The smoke of the torches burned his eyes, and his knees hurt from the loose, round gravel and stones layering the tunnel floor. But before long, Rodrigo received an unexpected shock.

The scowling woman in front of him took on a slight bluish glow as she crawled through a small entrance, and then she stood up. A fresh breeze passed through the tunnel when she moved out of it. Rodrigo followed her, stood up, and took in a startled breath.

Midnight blue tendrils drifted overhead in a starless sky and stretched out in every direction. No cliff interrupted the view. He stood at the top of the world. Scattered lines and bunches of glowmoss snaked across the broken plains, tracing hundreds of waterways. Far away—five miles at least, if Baldy was correct—the fires of a city glowed dimly.

Pinnacle.

He remembered when the end had come to him in the pumice tunnels, and the crushing weight of that nightmare creature. Those tunnels could not possibly have been anywhere near the surface of this grand mesa. He'd been miles away

314

from Drift, heading in the opposite direction. How could he possibly have gotten to the surface near Drift?

Considering the strange nature of the pumice tunnels and their odd light bursts, perhaps they'd transported him here, just before the creature had been able to bring him to the ground and dispatch him. He knew the erratic power of the great aircraft-swallowing hole below the lake. The pumice could have similar exotic effects. It may have saved his life, but it had thrown him far away from his friends. Yun, Scarlet, Rip, Hope, even Ed—he recalled their faces, and an uncomfortable loneliness sank in.

He had to find them again.

The group set out toward Pinnacle, each with a lantern in one hand and the unusual pickaxe weapon in the other.

They covered only half the distance when the hiss and bone-clatter of black-spawn sounded behind them.

72: Chase

Rodrigo ran. Despite a twinge of pain in his ankle, he soon outdistanced a half-dozen of the others in the fleeing group, his lean frame navigating the broken, rolling terrain better than the more heavily burdened others. The abundance of streams, the heavy growth of glowmoss, and the heave and roll of the land prevented clear sight, and so he heard more than saw the chaos around him.

Most of the others ran in silence, but some could be heard shouting in confusion—or crying, or screaming. The blackspawn hiss rose and fell, slowly becoming more distinct as they closed in from behind and to the left. The world narrowed to Rodrigo's sprinting feet and the few paces of ground in front of him as his mind fell into a tunnel vision of fear and terror. He felt as though he had never known anything but flight from these merciless blackspawn—mile upon mile, never stopping and never resting, death just a few paces behind him.

And yet a part of him began to focus, as though it were evaluating the rest of him. He noticed that, despite the dull pain in his ankle, it felt healed and gave him little actual trouble. Had more time passed than he believed—time enough to heal his wounds? It seemed like only hours ago since the final battle in the pumice tunnels, caught between monsters and monstrosity. He remembered charging the line of blackspawn, shouting and holding his sword high before the crushing end. But yet his sword was back in its scabbard. How had it returned there? If he had been mysteriously whisked away by the pumice tunnel lights, why would his sword be in its scabbard?

A true, agonizing scream erupted from somewhere behind him. The blackspawn had run down their first kill. The scream spurred Rodrigo on, faster, risking a painful fall should he stumble in his sprint. None of them would be able to keep this pace for long, certainly not for several miles.

His vision fell on something ahead—a pickaxe, perfectly outlined in a mounded patch of reddish glowmoss. Its owner must have tossed it away in the interest of faster flight. A sudden anger flared in Rodrigo, and his tunnel vision faded. He angled toward the pickaxe, scooped it up, and raced on.

To his left, a man began shouting for help, his voice increasingly terrified and panicky. Rodrigo caught a glimpse of him on the next rise, and, behind him, a flashing patch of blackness outlined in the scatter of glowmoss. Rodrigo angled to the left, sliding his sword back into its scabbard. He jumped a small stream, sprinted up a rise, and topped out just as the spawn passed. The monster loped forward, its concentration fully on the shouting man ahead of him, its grotesquely massive neck and jaws and powerful front shoulders all but dragging its small hind legs along.

At the last moment it seemed to sense Rodrigo and tried to spin to face him. Rodrigo brought the pickaxe in a sideways stroke, burying it just in front of the monster's hip. He thought momentarily about trying to wrench it free as he ran behind the creature, and he held on slightly too long. The grip of the weapon twisted Rodrigo backwards and he lost his footing, tumbling into a shallow stream. The creature flipped sideways, its rear flank a black fountain.

Rodrigo regained his footing quickly and sprang back onto the path of the shouting man, the fate of the spawn left to the darkness behind him. He could see the man ahead, stumbling in exhaustion. An exhilaration filled Rodrigo as the success of his surprise strike on the spawn set in. He had saved a life, at least for now.

"Slow down," said Rodrigo as he fell in step with the man. "You will be too tired to fight."

"You slow down," said the man, his face set in a pained grimace and his rounded cheeks slick with sweat. He tried to speed up, but lost his footing instead and pitched headlong into a scattering of rocks. He yelled in agony and clutched his ribs.

"Get up!" Rodrigo tried to lift the man. He could hear a hiss off to the right and saw the silhouettes of two men and a woman. They were no longer running. Pulling the hurt man to his feet, he slung one bloodied arm over his shoulder and began to make his way to the group. He managed only a dozen paces when he saw a pair of monsters close on the three.

He dropped the man, drew his sword, and sprinted toward the battle, pleased at the realization that he wasn't yet that winded. As he closed in, he splashed through a wide stream, alerting the two spawn to his presence.

One of the men appeared to be down but struggling to regain his feet. The woman swung wildly with her pickaxe at a low, scuttling spawn, while the other man retreated in the face of a big six-armed smasher the size of a draft horse. Rodrigo lunged toward the scuttler, hoping to catch it from behind, but to his dismay the monster had no real behind, built vaguely like a pair of scorpions stuck together end to end. One of its swinging arms caught Rodrigo in the leg and flipped him to the ground, but not before Rodrigo's bull sword had passed through the arm.

The scuttler hissed wildly and retreated, but the woman's pickaxe buried in an arm on the other side of the creature and it flailed in disintegration. Rodrigo regained his feet and looked for the basher.

The struggling man was on his feet again, but the other man lay prone under the basher as it pounded him savagely. Rodrigo closed in from the side, shouting to draw its attention. It turned to face him and lunged forward. Rodrigo backed away, aiming his sword for the flailing arms. He caught one and the sword bit home, but the force of the blow ripped the weapon out of Rodrigo's hand. Despite the leaking black wound, the monster pressed forward, throwing the blade away with a toss of its damaged arm. Rodrigo tried to keep a small spire of rock between them, but the spawn slid around it and aimed a series of swings that came within inches of taking Rodrigo's head off.

Rodrigo cast desperately about for a weapon. He could see the woman doing the same, and the surviving man staggered away, apparently interested only in flight to far-off Pinnacle.

The spawn lurched forward and gave a violent hiss. It spun about, a pickaxe buried in its ankle. Behind it, the round-cheeked man with the hurt ribs backed away, his face twisted with fright. "Nicely done!" cheered Rodrigo, and he tried but failed to catch ahold of the pickaxe as the monster's leg swung by.

Nursing two wounds, the monster did not press the attack, and when Rodrigo circled around to pick up his sword and join the woman and the grimacing man, the spawn had retreated.

Rodrigo glanced at the shattered body of the other man. "We had best be moving," he said to the two others. The woman found a pickaxe. The grimacing man held his side, but didn't seem to have much difficulty breathing or moving.

The three took off at a trot. Smasher did not follow, and Scuttler was nowhere in sight. For a couple hundred paces they heard little. The lights of Pinnacle seemed closer, almost possible. But then hissing broke out to their left, and they increased their speed to a dead-run.

Dozens of blackspawn loped and lumbered in from the side. Rodrigo struggled to decide whether to fight to the death with his two companions, or outdistance them and leave them to their fate. He sped up. It mattered little as the faster spawn could easily overtake him.

A pair of tall men appeared in front of him, each with a wide russet strip of cloth wrapped around one leg and another tied around their shoulder. They lifted their arms and threw. Javelins streaked past Rodrigo, and then the two joined him in flight.

More men appeared, throwing javelins and retreating until a line of russet-marked soldiers came into view, arrayed along a stream bank.

The oncoming line of blackspawn hit the human ranks of spearmen as Rodrigo reached the men, and the world twisted into a confused melee. He lost his sword again, recovered it, and took a painful blow to the chest, flattening him out among the glowmoss and rocks.

His head struck against a stone. The sky whirled drunkenly above as he fought disorientation and the clash and cries of battle surged around him. Then

318

the hiss of blackspawn and the sounds of battle quieted as the terrors broke and ran. A face hove into view, staring down on him with a widening, triumphant grin.

"Rodrigo! I am delight to find you."

It was the face of Boar.

73: Unpleasant Reunion

The soldiers herded the surviving immigrants of Drift together, stripped them of weapons, and set them moving. Boar himself took Rodrigo's sword and scabbard and tied the boy's hands with a short rope lashed to a pole. After collecting the wounded, the formation set off for Pinnacle. To Rodrigo's surprise, Boar led the column of soldiers.

Boar threw the pole over his shoulder and pulled Rodrigo along. The deadly killer was in high spirits.

"I have itch, right back here, behind ear, when something important to happen today," said Boar. "Today I itch bad. Because of you, I think?"

"Give me my sword back," said Rodrigo. "I'll scratch it for you."

"Ha-ha! You like sword. I keep it for you. Children should not have dangerous toys." Boar pulled the sword from its scabbard and inspected the blade. "How do you come all the way here from little nest at lake?"

"I walked."

"Dangerous walk. Where did you find way out?"

"Through a hole."

Boar shook his head. "I am friend, Rodrigo. Best friend. And Yun?"

"Safe."

"At lake?"

"Safe. How did you turn up here?"

"I walk too."

"Where did you find troops?"

"I win them," said Boar, flourishing arrogantly. "I have great personality."

"Why did you disarm the Drifters?"

"We go to Pinnacle. Only friends allowed in Pinnacle, and no one is friend until they prove themselves. Of course, you are good friend, and we will have good times together." Boar turned around to give Rodrigo another stare. "Just you and me. The last time we talk, we make promises, da?"

"Da," said Rodrigo. "Something about stabbing each other."

"Ah, yes. I was quite angry, but I do not hold grudge. Today, I promise you will not die. Soon."

Those last words ended in a tone not to Rodrigo's liking.

Boar swung to face his column and bellowed to a captain, who came running forward. The two conversed about patrols and spawn signs. Rodrigo noted the respect and obeisance given to Boar by the captain, and the natural way in which Boar dominated the soldier. It became clear how this Dustie could rise to command in such a short time.

Boar handed Rodrigo over to the captain. "I must speak to other captains. Take this one and make sure he has pleasant journey." He turned to the boy. "I was wrong, Rodrigo." His fist drove into Rodrigo's stomach, a short, clipped punch that slammed Rodrigo's wind from him.

Rodrigo dropped to his knees and Boar bent to him.

"I do hold grudge."

The captain jerked painfully on the pole, pulling Rodrigo back to his feet.

———

An hour passed. Rodrigo's wrists bled from the ropes and his stomach muscles knotted painfully. Each step blended into the next—a long agonizing blur of glowmoss, streams, and rocks.

They marched through the thoroughly wrecked ruins of a low fortified wall, broken, neglected, and abandoned. Beyond it began scattered fields of glowmoss, savaged by the scars of battle. Ranks of soldiers patrolled the fields, but Rodrigo could see no prepared breastworks or fortifications. He wanted to ask the captain about the lack of defenses, but thought better of it.

The lights of Pinnacle grew larger as they marched. They passed through a taller wall, also abandoned and in ruined state, beyond which the glowmoss fields began in earnest. In the distance rose the city wall proper, aged and worn but still sound and lit here and there with watchfires. The silhouetted spires and fortifications of an impressively tall, immensely wide castle thrust up into the midnight blue sky from beyond the wall.

Boar reclaimed Rodrigo from his captain as they approached the towering iron-banded gates of the city. The main gate stood closed, but a smaller door opened within the structure of the larger gate, and the procession entered Pinnacle.

They moved through wide streets, past elegant but aged and unkempt buildings. Scattered glowmoss grew along the multitudes of culverts, canals, and fountains, but the scarcity of lamps left much of the city in half-lit gloom.

The streets were busy with citizens and soldiers, but not crowded, as were the shops and pubs and markets lining the street—at least, those that looked inhabited. Every street they traveled had its share of dark, derelict sections, and some appeared all but deserted. It occurred to Rodrigo that Pinnacle was a city desperately in want of people.

A disturbance broke out in a market ahead. Rodrigo could see a squad of soldiers piling goods onto a cart. A man and several women tried to stop them. The man took a spear butt to the stomach and crumpled over, and the distressed women dragged him back into the maze of the market stalls. After a few coarse threats, the warriors resumed their looting.

"I see your soldiers are making friends," said Rodrigo.

"Not mine," said Boar. "Blueboys." He pointed to the dark blue half-capes worn by the looting soldiers, then pulled at the russet sash on his shoulder. "I command Hunters."

A young woman stepped close to Rodrigo, her eyes black pools of sorrow. "Andrea Tate," she said, clutching at Rodrigo's shirt. "Please tell her that her mother loves her. She's seven now. Andrea."

A soldier behind Rodrigo shoved the woman aside. Rodrigo turned and watched her repeat her words to several of the soldiers and Drifters, suffering rebuffs from the soldiers with each attempt. Boar swung Rodrigo back around with a pull of the rope.

"Has she lost her child?" asked Rodrigo.

"Not at all," said Boar, giving Rodrigo a sarcastic grin and nod, then pointing at the spires of the great castle. "Child is with Temma, Greatmother and Queen of Pinnacle."

"A queen over the city," said Rodrigo.

"And king, and king, and king," said Boar. "And someday you might even meet them. But today, you and I, we enjoy day together, da?"

They reached a long row of barracks and a blocky, fortress-like Hunter command quarters. Boar and the officers entered the fortress and, once inside, Boar unlocked a thick door. Beyond it, a flight of narrow granite stairs led down into an unlit gloom. Boar lit a lamp, untied Rodrigo, and motioned to the stairs.

Rodrigo gave Boar a sideways stare. "I am surprised that you untied me."

"I am surprised that you do not try to run," said Boar, fingering the hilt of his long, double-edged sword. The soldiers in the barracks drew closer.

Boar leaned in close to Rodrigo, the heavy smell of his sweat penetrating Rodrigo's senses. "These soldiers of mine, they get curious now, they make bet like soldiers do. They say, 'Will Rodrigo come back alive once he goes down there?' Those who say yes, they try for the long odds."

Rodrigo peered down into the darkness. "You control the payoff, Boar. What *are* my chances?"

"This is no longer your worry," said Boar. "Your future is mine to choose."

"Fair enough," said Rodrigo, and he descended into the chambers below. Boar followed, locking the door behind him.

When Phoebe reached the top and stepped out of the rail cage, blue-clad troops escorted her immediately to the city of Pinnacle, less than six miles away. The soldiers allowed her a day to settle in before fetching her hastily to the magnificent, shadowy bulk of Pinnacle Castle, through the thick keep walls, and along stately but sparsely decorated halls to the vaulted immensity of the royal court.

Seated by her escorts in the wait-wings to the left front of the four thrones, Phoebe settled in to watch the ceremony already in progress.

Temma, Queen of Pinnacle, spun slowly to allow the four boys holding the long train of her royal dress to keep it precisely draped behind her. Four girls arrayed in crisply pleated green skirts arranged the matching green drapes and pillows on her throne. She fussed at the arrangement, prodded the bundle of silver-blond hair atop her head, and scolded one of the girls before settling into her seat of power. To Phoebe, the queen seemed youthful in movement, but the lines in her sharp, aristocratic features hinted at the approaching onset of middle-aged maturity.

Three kings were already seated, awaiting the completion of the queen's ceremonial entrance. Like Temma, each wore not a crown but a plain circlet of very bright metal, like polished silver. King Awkley hunched on his blue-draped throne with simmering impatience, shaking his creased brown head and shifting his midnight eyes to and fro around the assembly. King Morten leaned sideways in his copper-draped throne, his head resting on one hand and his sharp-featured, pale face reposed in what could be mistaken for a drowsy apathy, his own coal-black eyes half-closed. Balding, mousey-faced King Scribbs jotted furiously in a thick journal, paying not the least bit of attention to the queen, one hand battling wisps of straying blond hair. But when the assembly master announced the presence of Shoca and Rafe, and the two titans entered, he did look up, his large hazel eyes giving him the appearance of being perpetually surprised.

Phoebe's mouth opened in awe and she breathed out a long "Ohh my."

Everything about the two titans radiated magnificence. Over twice the height of a man, their long strides brought them swiftly past the thrones, escorted by a dozen lean tantyrs. Although the steps of their bare feet sent slight vibrations through the stone floor, they moved with a surprising grace and silence. They wore only a gray robe draped over one shoulder, their pearly skinned bodies rippling with herculean strength. Neither had the least bit of hair on head or body, with brows layered instead with short bony growth.

They might have looked human but for the extended torso and the two pairs of arms that set the titans entirely apart from the tiny humans in the great hall.

"Greetings, Rafe," said Awkley, standing up on his throne seat and giving the first titan a sweep of invitation with his arm. "And greetings, Shoca."

The one named Rafe studied those he passed with large amber eyes, his delicate aquiline features flashing a pleasant cordiality. Two long, slightly curved blades rested in scabbards that crossed behind his shoulders. The other, Shoca, had a blockier shape and a squarer head. His darker but no less amber eyes narrowed regularly, as though he carefully appraised everything and everyone he met. Strapped to his back were a large mirror-polished shield and a heavy sword, among other smaller weapons.

The two titans took their places on marble ledges along the vaulted wall, behind the thrones of the humans. They remained silent.

King Awkley rose to speak, posing in such a ridiculous fashion, and adorned with such a pompous oversupply of royal attire that Phoebe fought to keep from giggling. "Now that we are properly gathered," he announced, flicking his eyes at Queen Temma, "we can *finally* commence with court."

It appeared to Phoebe that the gargantuan hall could hold as many as two thousand in the lower audience. A second level, and a third, opened upward, but both were lost in unlit gloom, except where water flowed through fountains and pools down to the lower levels and the ever-present glowmoss spread. The awesome splendor of the architecture kept Phoebe's mouth agape. It all appeared quite ancient, though still in good shape. She wondered if the entire castle had even been built for humans in the first place, considering the height of the ceilings in the corridors and the immensity of this chamber.

Half of the lower audience seating sat empty. Many of those present wore either blue-caped uniforms or copper sashes. Most of the others wore fine clothes.

For a time, court turned out to be just that—a chance for citizens to air their grievances and for the royals to pronounce judgment. The relationships among the four royals became immediately apparent to Phoebe. The loud, eccentric King Awkley argued at length with the scolding, prudish Queen Temma over the finer points, while King Morten seemed mostly content to let them battle, becoming interested only when the subject of punishments arose. King Scribbs paid little attention, scratching endlessly in his journal and voicing his opinion at odd times.

Now and then, one of the titans would offer up concise words of wisdom, their rich, bell-clear voices bringing even the royals to immediate silence.

Phoebe noted this show of respect toward the giant creatures and picked out other scraps of interest. A commander wearing the blue half-cape of the Blueboys sat next to Awkley, while a copper-sashed brute sat confidently next to King Morten—two kings, two armies. Queen Temma surrounded herself with her eight attendant children and one sour-faced matron. Scribbs sat alone.

"Enough!" shouted Temma. Over an hour must have passed since the queen had first taken her throne. "The complaints are endless, and I am sick beyond words of hearing them." When the herald tried to suggest a short break, she waved him off in irritation. "No more! Did the Phoebe girl arrive yet?"

Phoebe jumped.

She saw the herald pointing at her.

"Girl, come forward!" insisted the queen. "Let us have a look at you."

Phoebe rose and walked hesitantly to a spot in front of the queen. Her hands were gripped tightly together, and she forced her arms to her side. She remembered to curtsey, then stood quietly for far too long as the queen appraised her in front of all.

Queen Temma sighed and sat back. "You've an uncivilized, back-country look about you, girl, but a countryside beauty to match. You're a scrawny little thing, as well. But they say that you can shoot a bow better than any man?"

"A crossbow, ma'am," said Phoebe. "Haven favors the crossbow."

"As does Pinnacle," said the queen. "Then let us put you to the test. Awkley, Morten, get your best crossbowman up here."

"I'm afraid I left my cross-" started Phoebe, but a blue-clad soldier came forward and placed Lightning in her hands before she could finish.

The three squared off—Phoebe, a tall smirking Blueboy, and a decidedly handsome Hunter. Queen Temma ordered that three tightly stuffed targets, in the shape of dragonheads, be placed on the far wall. The evil-looking eyes were each painted with a 10 score, the toothy mouth given a 7, and the rest given a 5.

"Ladies first," spoke Blueboy, turning to Phoebe and bowing.

"Ladies last," commanded Queen Temma.

"Of course," nodded Blueboy. He took leftmost and first, while Phoebe walked to the rightmost.

Blueboy balanced his long, custom-designed crossbow at hip level, staring intently at the dragon. Then he brought the weapon crisply up to his shoulder, breathed out, and fired. His bolt sank into the dragon's mouth. A cheer erupted from King Awkley's blue-clad men.

The Hunter brought his smaller, lighter crossbow to his shoulder, aimed for a longer time than Blueboy, and fired. He too struck the dragon's mouth.

Morten and the other Hunters cheered loudly, trying to beat the former volume of the Blueboys.

Phoebe checked Lightning, glanced around at the crowd and the royals upon their throne, and aimed. Her finger came smoothly and slowly down on the trigger until the bolt loosed, striking the center of her own dragon's mouth. At first there came scattered clapping, then a swelling roar of approval from the soldiers of both kings.

Blueboy went for his second shot, heckled by a few Hunters and even his own Blueboys.

"Just a little girl, nothing to worry about, boyo!"

Blueboy struck the dragon mouth again and gave his hecklers a confident sneer and a few words back. The Blueboys erupted thunderously.

By the end of the third round, the crowd noise had become deafening. Chanting accompanied each shot, and the wild revelry after each loosed bolt shook the stone. But the cheers came less for Phoebe. Both Blueboy and Hunter had sunk three mouth shots in a row. Phoebe had missed her second and third shot by a fraction, gaining only five points each. The best she could hope for now were misses by the men and hits by her, resulting in a tie.

Queen Temma's mouth curled down, sourer and sourer.

An emotion rose up in Phoebe, almost causing her to cough. She could not stand the idea of losing—a vile, wretched thought that she revolted at. She closed her eyes, trying to drown the sound of the crowd, but to no avail. She opened her eyes, saw that it was her turn, and whispered to herself, "It's *my* noise."

She took aim, seeing her intended target steady down the length of the bolt. As she concentrated, the target seemed to become larger and larger, until it filled her whole vision. A last breath, and she fired.

The bolt embedded itself to the feathers in the left eye of the dragon. A judge leaned to the target, checked it, and cried, "Eye ring!"

At first the crowd quieted, then muttered appreciatively, then clapped. A fine, lucky shot to nearly even the score. Blueboy and Hunter both had four mouth hits for 28, with Phoebe trailing by only one at 27.

Blueboy took his last shot, fell errant into the 5 ring, and suffered the collective groans of his fellows. Hunter struck true, reaching 35 points and a perfect string to the mouth. The Hunters whooped in exaltation and cajoled their defeated rivals.

At the height of the jubilation, Phoebe brought Lightning up and fired. The bolt sank in, and her dragon lost its right eye.

Silence fell until the judge called the hit, and then the crowd erupted—especially the Blueboys, who brought the derision back double-fold on the Hunters. Phoebe had won, 37 to 35.

Phoebe curtsied, and then her mischievous side got the best of her and she did a little skip with her heels, smiling girlishly at the audience. Blueboy and Hunter alike erupted with applause and more than a few whistles.

Behind her, Queen Temma's demeanor brightened considerably. She motioned to her matron. "Fetch Phoebe's things and see to her accommodation in the Cherrywood Suite."

"Sandrova is housed in Cherrywood, m'lady," said the matron.

"Sandrova can find a chamber on the third floor," snapped the queen. "Do as I say."

The matron left as the furor over the contest began to die down. Queen Temma rose, put on a motherly smile, and motioned for Phoebe to approach. She glared at the crowd for silence, which she slowly received.

"Let it be known that a woman is the finest shot in Pinnacle!" she announced. There was little more than a scattering of applause, which appeared to make the queen irritated. Phoebe glanced about, embarrassed by the queen's heavy-handed statement.

Temma gestured to a cushion next to her throne. "Well done. Take your place here, for now."

Phoebe knelt, carefully arraying her dress. The queen turned back to the crowd to speak. She opened her mouth and had uttered her first syllable when the doors at the right of the chamber burst open and a squad of Blueboys entered.

They were not alone. Someone walked within their protective circle. Several pursuing Hunters tried to break through the circle and get at the person. The Hunters inside the chamber saw this and moved to help. Blueboys did the same.

"Stand down, Hunters!"

The words came with such volume and authority that Phoebe jumped, as did half the audience and King Scribbs. She turned and saw King Morten's powerfully built Hunter commander step forward and bellow the command again.

Blueboy and Hunter alike obeyed. The formerly surrounded squad moved forward despite Temma's repeated complaints about a lack of order. The squad parted, a man dressed in a bloodied linen shirt stepped forth, and Phoebe gasped.

Rodrigo!

———

He looked a mess—swollen and bloodied in the face from a recent beating. Crimson stained his shirt. But he didn't hesitate or stagger. He moved straight to the Hunter commander, and Phoebe had the closest seat in the chamber to witness their confrontation.

Rodrigo tossed a ring of keys at the Hunter commander's feet. "Thank you for your hospitality, Boar, but I will be seeking quarters elsewhere."

Boar! He must be the one that Yun told stories about...

Boar's eyes squinted and he ground his jaw. "How did you...? But it does not matter, nyet? I see you reclaimed your sword."

Rodrigo tapped the bull-inscribed sword at his hip. "It knows its owner." Rodrigo turned to the royalty, bowing crisply to each in turn. "My apologies, Your Highnesses, for my appearance. I have Boar to thank for it."

King Awkley rose. "Why is this—boy—interrupting our court?"

The Blueboy commander standing next to King Awkley stepped forward. "Captain Zales!" he shouted. "Why did you bring this man here?"

One of the squad of Blueboys who had escorted Rodrigo came to attention, his broad, ugly face and bald head reminding Phoebe of a shaved bulldog "Because the Brownies did not want us to, sir! He was running from Brownies near their stronghold, and he asked for an immediate audience. So we brought him in."

Some of the Hunters in the crowd muttered. Apparently they disliked being called Brownies.

The commander glanced at King Awkley, and the king waved a hand dismissively. "Sit down, Commander Sheare."

Phoebe saw a flash of anger in Commander Sheare's eyes as he slowly returned to his place.

Awkley studied Rodrigo a moment. "Boy, am I right in believing that you escaped the chambers of Commander Boar, and the Hunter stronghold?"

"Your Highness is correct."

King Awkley rose and paced around Rodrigo. "And why were you taken there in the first place?"

Rodrigo dabbed at his face with his cuff. "I was with a group of Drift immigrants caught by slivers—blackspawn, I should say. Commander Boar's troops came to our rescue. Boar and I know each other. As you can see, we are not the closest of friends."

Awkley kept his pacing, looking from Boar to Rodrigo and to the other royalty. Morten appeared amused, and Temma pursed her lips and mumbled in irritation at the distraction, but it was Scribbs who put down his journal and stood.

"Having this hall turned into an archery training ground for killers is hard enough to bear," said King Scribbs, his bloodless face tight with anger. "Suffering a violent feud between your uncouth bands of murderers is quite another. Is this what we have become?"

"Patience, Scribbles!" shouted Awkley. "We'll get to your tedious poets and bards soon enough."

Scribbs worked his mouth but apparently thought better of it. He sat down in a huff, picked up his journal, and scribbled furiously. Phoebe tried to imagine the words being scorched into the journal by the irate, silent king. She turned back to Rodrigo, wondering when—or if—he would notice her.

King Awkley stood in front of Rodrigo, eying him appraisingly. "Can you fight, boy?"

"Well enough," said Rodrigo.

"Have you fought blackspawn?"

"I have killed my share, My King."

Awkley stepped away, pacing again. "Well then, since Commander Boar cannot be trusted with you, I leave you in the hands of Commander Sheare. Welcome to the Blueboys."

The Blueboys applauded and came forward to escort him away, but Phoebe noticed that Rodrigo's attention remained on Awkley. The king's face appeared cordial enough, but Phoebe caught something unnerving in his eyes—a suspicion that he left unvoiced. Beyond him, Boar's hard, cold gray eyes shifted between the king and the boy.

Rodrigo's escorts spun him away and toward the doors. Phoebe watched Rodrigo pass by, wondering if he would notice her. But as he drew close, his eyes darted sideways to her and he shook his head ever so slightly before quickly returning his gaze forward.

75: CHILDREN OF PINNACLE

The next morning Phoebe found four girls—all dressed in the green of Queen Temma—attending to her room and her needs as she awoke. The room in which she slept was fit for royalty—ornate furniture of fine reddish wood, paintings, and other fine art layering the walls, and even a small pool in which to bathe, fed constantly by a spout in the shape of an egret.

Phoebe tried to strike up a conversation with the girls, but they appeared embarrassed and a little frightened by her questioning. The youngest, however, was less timid.

"My name's Kinna," said the girl to Phoebe's prompting. "I'm not supposed to talk to elders."

"Well I am delighted that you broke the rule," said Phoebe. "I'm going to guess that you are eight years old."

Kinna's eyes brightened. "I am!"

"Are you an orphan, Kinna, or do your parents live in the castle?"

"I used to have parents," said Kinna, "but now I have the Greatmother."

"I am sorry to hear that."

Kinna scratched her ear. "Sorry for what?"

"That you lost your parents."

"They aren't lost. They live in the city."

"But you said you used to have parents."

"They aren't my parents anymore, not since I turned six. Everybody knows that."

Phoebe didn't know what to say. So she bathed, dressed, and ate, all with the dutiful but subdued assistance of the girls. Phoebe disapproved of their slave-like devotion and would have preferred solitude, but she decided not to press matters further until she learned more. Much more.

She spent the morning exploring a small part of the immense castle. She found children everywhere—sitting quietly in classes, laboring in the kitchens, cleaning the extensive hallways, all dressed in the ever-present green. Wherever the children could be found, there also were matrons seeing to them, overseeing their studies and labor. She asked many about Petra, Ana, and Ardi, but received no positive answer.

As lunchtime drew near, Kinna and the girls met up with Phoebe and led her to the east side of the castle. Her mouth gaped as she passed through a tall archway and entered a vast dining area that extended onto the open grounds for many paces. Small boxy lanterns lit many rows of tables, but more than half were left dark and unused. Even so, the dining area that was lit could easily hold several thousand.

The entire castle must come here to eat, thought Phoebe.

Children began filtering in, led by their matrons, in orderly, quiet lines. Phoebe took up position at what appeared to be the main entrance, only to discover four other entrances spaced around the grounds. A matron came for Kinna and the girls.

"I am glad that we could serve you, mum." said Kinna gave a small curtsy, and fell in obediently behind the marching matron. Phoebe had no chance to thank her.

The entrances filled swiftly—line upon line of children guided by their caretakers. Phoebe heard the tread of many feet but little else as the children moved to their seats. Older teens came also, but clearly the matrons held less control over them. Groups of older girls and boys moved through the tables, surreptitiously bullying the younger children that happened upon their path.

Phoebe turned to take in the view of the large courtyard, but stopped abruptly.

An older boy stood close to her, staring at her, sliding one bony thumb through his oiled dark hair. His eyes—one nearly black and the other a cloudy gray—shone with such malevolence that Phoebe caught her breath.

"You're new," he said.

She tried to think of something—anything—to say to remove herself from his presence, but she managed only a nervous cough and a slight nod.

"You don't have a name? My name is Quait."

Then he stepped in close, his shoulder to hers. His long fingers reached up to touch her hair. "Do you see the matrons, how they don't look at me? They're afraid, as they should be. You'll learn to be afraid too. But you'll also learn to obey me."

He lifted a finger to his lips and gave her a crooked, knowing smile.

Phoebe turned away from the terrifying boy, sickened and frightened. She moved quickly through the crowd, but she could feel the gaze of those unbalanced eyes following her.

———

Close to two thousand children surrounded Phoebe in the dining hall, but based on what she overheard from the passing matrons, this was only the first of two groups. And when they all gathered, each in front of their stool, they paused.

Queen Temma appeared on a balcony overlooking the grounds. She stood at the low railing, cast her gaze right and left, then raised her many-jeweled hand. "To the bounty of Pinnacle!" she shouted.

"To the Greatmother!" chorused the many children, and they sat down to eat. A swell of voices rose from the crowd as the younger children gained permission to speak.

Phoebe's mind pieced it together then, though she could not believe the truth. Every child of Pinnacle above the age of six lived in the castle—taken from their parents and brought here, under the wing of the so-called Greatmother.

Phoebe raised a hand to her mouth and turned to view the thousands of children. She could think of nothing so heartbreaking as this—this mass kidnapping. She stopped a tear with her finger, blinked, and turned to find Temma's sour-faced head matron at her side.

"We have not properly met," said the matron, lacing her aged fingers in front of her. "I am Imirette, and I see that I have arrived just in time to save you misunderstanding."

"They are all here, aren't they?" said Phoebe. "All the children of Pinnacle."

Imirette turned and began walking slowly through the tables, placing a hand on each child as she passed. "Yes, and this is for the best."

"How can you possibly say that? How is the 'best' served by taking them away from their parents?"

"This is a world of Sleepers, my dear," said Imirette. "There is little loyalty here, little familiarity, little responsibility, and little love. Parents willingly give their children. It is a burden gladly escaped in an evil world."

"Such was not the case in Haven," challenged Phoebe.

"Haven!" sniffed Imirette. "You use that den of thieves and traitors as your counter point? Do you not search for three children who were given away by that very city? And for what? A small pile of the Queen's gracious bounty and a few livestock?"

Imirette's truth struck home to Phoebe, and yet it raised the girl's hopes. "Do you know where they are? Are they here?"

"Of course." Imirette turned and gestured with her hand.

Close by, Ana sipped at a drink and chatted happily with the more subdued girls next to her. Across from her, Petra smiled primly, a content, relieved smile playing across her face as she stared up at Phoebe.

Phoebe gasped with joy, but before she could move, Imirette grasped her arm. "Greet them, but do not show open affection. Not here."

Phoebe ignored her. She pulled herself from Imirette's grasp and rushed to the girls. Ana saw her, squealed with delight, and jumped the table. Phoebe and the two girls formed a tangle of tightly clasped arms, tears, and overwhelming joy. Phoebe began to ask where Ardi was when she felt the boy wrap himself around her hips.

Imirette's wrinkled hand gripped Phoebe's shoulder and forced her around. The matron signaled upward with her eyes. Phoebe's gaze followed that gesture.

In the balcony above, Queen Temma had come to her feet and stood near the rail's edge, staring down at the disruption. With one hand, she motioned discreetly to Imirette.

Matrons brought the three children back under control and Imirette pulled Phoebe close, whispering in her ear.

"I warned you."

———

Queen Temma did not immediately invite Phoebe to sit. She completed her meal first, glancing not once at Phoebe. Only after a slight motion from the queen's hand did Imirette signal for Phoebe to take a seat in front of the queen, toward the back of the balcony.

Temma motioned a hand toward the grounds below. "How many children would you guess are in the castle, Phoebe?"

"Several thousand, Your Highness."

"Three thousand five hundred and fifty-eight," corrected the queen. "How many did you greet with such passion?"

"Three."

"And how many did you ignore and treat with contempt?"

"Your Highness, I do not understand-"

"That is clear, you foolish girl!" snapped Temma. Her face flushed red and one hand trembled. "Were you raised selfish and cruel?" The queen cut off her next sentence, composed herself, and smiled coldly. "I can see that you will require proper training in civility and behavior. You do not wantonly show such passionate favoritism toward a selfish few in full view of the thousands that you ignore. And what should be obvious," she finished, stabbing the last remains of her food with each word, "is that such cruel and mean-spirited behavior is inappropriate at any time."

"I did nothing more than-"

"Enough! I can see you will not be quick to learn. You will not speak to those children again—at least until you have learned how to properly treat children."

Phoebe stood, clenching her fists at her side. "I have every intention of speaking with them again!"

Queen Temma regarded Phoebe silently, her pale green eyes narrowed and sly. "You were brought up from that Haven slum for one reason, which you demonstrated last night. I had hoped for more from you, but that is currently your one and only value here."

"And that is a value that you will never witness again unless I am reunited with those children," declared Phoebe, her anger and desperation over the children bolstering her courage just enough to allow her to meet the queen stare for stare.

The queen shook her head and smiled sadly, rising to her feet. "Perhaps it is better if I have you done away with. I can see you will be trouble."

"Imagine how the kings will gloat, knowing the queen's triumph of womankind ended so feebly and quickly," said Phoebe.

"The triumph has already been demonstrated."

Phoebe raised her eyebrows. "Can you hear the kings? That silly one—Awkley, isn't it? 'Just a dumb, lucky fluke,' he'll say. 'How embarrassing for desperate Queen Temma!'"

For a moment, Phoebe thought the queen would strike her. She decided to simply allow it, tensing for the pain and closing her eyes. But the blow never fell, and Temma eased off, erupting in a laugh.

"There is more to you after all! Not a complete waste. Very well, I will grant you two hours a week to meet with those children—in private."

"My aim is bound to suffer faced with only two hours. Ten hours will improve it considerably," said Phoebe.

"Six hours will do."

"Agreed, reluctantly."

"And," warned the queen, "you will mind your passions when you are around them. Never forget, those three children were bought with a price, and they are entirely mine. They must be brought up correctly. The future of Pinnacle depends on it."

Phoebe nodded silently.

Queen Temma turned back to the balcony. Imirette took Phoebe's arm, leading her away.

76: WALLS OF PINNACLE

— 14 days later

The ascending row of eleven clock fires burning high on the far central tower of Pinnacle Castle went dead, signaling midnight. Cold, damp air flowed sluggishly through the city, sprouting tendrils and pockets of mist. Despite the late hour, Rodrigo's day had just begun.

The boy leaned over the edge of the formidable city wall of Pinnacle, admiring its height. Beyond the wall, glowmoss grew like veins along the many wandering streams, turning into straight, orderly rows of fields off to the right. The shadowy bulk of the ruined and abandoned outer wall could be seen a mile farther out. The eerie blue of the sky tinted everything, and Rodrigo paused to watch the strange mist-shapes pass far overhead.

"Don't look at them. You'll draw down unwanted attention," said the person to his right.

Rodrigo turned to the speaker—King Awkley's head commander, Sheare. "What do you mean?"

Commander Sheare kept his head down but peered upward at the sky. "They watch us."

The odd, fearful look on Sheare's face set Rodrigo's nerves on edge. For some reason, the commander had chosen to immediately bring Rodrigo on as his aide, dismissing his former aide harshly and without cause. Over the past fifteen days, Rodrigo had ample opportunity to discover Sheare's erratic nature. In fact, while Rodrigo did not wish to describe the man's eccentric behavior as insanity, it became more difficult to avoid that conclusion.

"Are the mists alive?" asked Rodrigo, carefully avoiding any telltale disbelief in his voice.

"Check the lamps and mind your work," snapped Sheare, suddenly all business. "We're not here to chatter."

For the past hour, Rodrigo and the squad of six men under Captain Zales had worked a night patrol along the city's southern wall, checking the oil supply and condition of the war towers. The lean towers were topped with a lookout post and a large tank of oil reserves for the watchfires. Taking Sheare's command to heart, Rodrigo made his way along the wall to the skeletal steel struts of the next tower where Zales oversaw the inspection.

"Why do you check the oil supply when the watchfires are not even lit?" asked Rodrigo.

"Procedure," said Captain Zales, scratching his bald head with one meaty hand. "Meaningless tasks keep the fighting spirit at its peak."

Rodrigo smiled. Unlike Sheare, Captain Zales demonstrated both command ability and a sarcastic soldier's wit. Since rescuing Rodrigo from recapture by the Hunters, Zales had clearly taken a personal interest in the boy. He had lobbied strenuously with Sheare to have Rodrigo moved under his command. When that failed and Sheare had suddenly appointed the inexperienced boy as his personal aide, Zales had continued to lobby to train him. Sheare consented.

The Blueboy that had climbed the lantern tower called down the oil level. Full, as expected.

Rodrigo recorded this in the log and edged closer to Zales. Rodrigo had many questions, but he carefully paced them.

"One watchman every hundred paces seems rather ineffective."

"Watchwomen," corrected Zales. "The city watch are all Temma's Greencloaks. But the lack of watchwomen hardly matters. We cannot use this wall as a defense."

Rodrigo raised one eyebrow. "Why not, sir?"

"Procedure. It was decided years ago that neither of the city's outer walls would be rebuilt." Zales waved a hand toward the far-off ruins. "Without that, the fields could not be defended. So we fight the blackspawn on the open mesa."

The patrol continued, inspecting the wall, a few scattered siege machines, and the lantern towers. The lone Greencloaks that they passed ignored them. Rodrigo moved again over to Zales while they walked. "Why would the walls out there not be rebuilt?"

"Honor," answered Zales sourly, "imposed by the royals after the coming of the tantyrs and the titans. Part of the purging of our dishonor in the war against the cliff cities." He scratched his head and sighed. "I can appreciate merit in a bold stance, and I understand how a defensive mindset can lead to despair and self-defeat, but I hate losing men in unnecessary open battle against an enemy."

"The kings have never reconsidered?"

"On the contrary. Our forces have grown with increased levees from Haven and Drift, and the blackspawn attacks are not as strong as they once were. The kings are contemplating an offensive into the tunnels or down south at the Karrock ruins…"

Zales let his voice trail off, and he stopped, peering out over the network of streams below. Rodrigo stepped to the parapet, trying to see what had caught Zales's attention in the patchwork of glowmoss and darkness. The drifting strands of ground mist made it difficult to catch movement. He kept quiet. A minute passed, and the rest of the patrol continued to the lantern tower ahead, not yet noticing that their captain had paused.

"I saw movement," whispered Zales.

They were close to where the wall met the east cliff. Much of the terrain below consisted of broken heaves of rock constricting the streams to thin, fast flows, poor for glowmoss cultivation and therefore less illuminated. The low, muted sound of water taking its long fall over the cliff side made hearing difficult. Rodrigo had neither seen nor heard anything.

Zales straightened and sighed. He started to move forward again, then leapt back to the parapet, pointed down and cried, "There!"

Rodrigo looked. A dark, flowing shape darted to the base of the wall and began to climb at a shocking speed, straight up toward the lantern tower ahead.

An arrow of fear lanced into Rodrigo. He knew without doubt what came for them—the monstrosity that had struck him down in the tunnels.

His hand went to his sword, though he immediately recognized the futility of it.

Zales ran forward, yelling at his men. Rodrigo followed. They had made it less than halfway when the terror boiled over the lip of the wall and smashed into the tower.

Rodrigo heard screams, saw the lamps of the men ahead scatter. He raced forward, trying to catch the sprinting Zales. Then a ghost flew past them going the other way—the pale, bloodless face of Commander Sheare, his eyes rolling in terror and a continuous moan pouring from his strained lips as he rushed by in the opposite direction. His spear lay cast aside farther on, and Rodrigo picked it up.

There came the squeal of protesting metal and the lantern tower twisted sideways, toppling across the length of the wall to the parapet edge. A line of fire formed at the base of the wreckage, then erupted into a maelstrom of smoke and flame. Rodrigo caught sight of a massive shape beyond the fire, but the smoke quickly obscured it.

He closed on the tower, rushing past Zales, who was pulling a Blueboy to his feet and yelling at another, who staggered back away from the flames. His eyes caught movement—the silhouette of a man dangling from the wreckage, out over the wall's edge, and his mind focused there. His hand reached back to his satchel, pulling forth a small bundle of rope.

Jump there, there, and then there, said his mind. His feet leapt him up onto the parapet edge and he soared out onto the shattered roof of the fallen tower's oil basin. The torn section proved less than sturdy and threatened to topple him, but he gained his balance long enough to step onto a twisted steel girder and fall forward. The dangling Blueboy hung directly below him. He reached out from both sides of the small girder, flung a length of rope around the soldier's wrist, and tied it securely to the girder before grabbing for the soldier's other hand.

It was only after the Blueboy had a relatively secure position on the girder that Rodrigo remembered his dislike of heights.

"The trick with the rope—it's almost as if you practiced for that," said King Awkley from his throne.

"A good friend taught me the value of a little rope," said Rodrigo. "She saved a life in that same way."

The royal court had assembled in haste to discuss the monster, but no audience other than the royals' favorites were allowed. Phoebe sat beside the throne of Temma, Boar towered next to Morten, and Rodrigo, Captain Zales, and Commander Sheare stood in front of them all.

The private court had been in progress for over an hour, with Zales and Sheare giving their accounts of the incident. The testimony of Sheare deviated from reality at several key points, particularly regarding his headlong flight from the battle. During the conversation, King Scribbs mumbled something about "this new terror" and Awkley was certain he had said "newt horror," and before long the name simply stuck—Newt.

Awkley leaned back, glancing over at the other royalty. The titans sat passively behind them, silently observing. "Captain Zales, are you absolutely sure of the Newt's path?"

"Positive, my king," said Zales. "My men and I followed it north. It retreated quickly once the explosion seared it. I lost sight of it past the gate junction, but I could see down all of the connecting walls and streets. My guess is the sewers. The protective grate barring that section of the sewer river has long been broken. The tunnel is plenty big enough for the Newt to gain passage."

During the incident, Zales had engaged in a vengeful, foolhardy chase of the monster along the wall before it crawled over the side, down to the city proper, and into the swirling waters of the fast-flowing sewers. The Newt had apparently carried away one of Zales's men and a watchwoman along its path. Another of the Blueboys had fallen to his death, and one lay injured. The bitter anger at his loss was evident in Zales all morning.

"It's been hours," said Queen Temma. "My Greencloak should have been found by now."

"I'm sure the Newt is enjoying his hard-earned meal," said King Morten with a lazy smile. "And it appreciates a mix of tastes—one man, one woman."

The queen gave Morten a disgusted stare, and Zales clenched his jaw, red-faced but silent.

"And now the Newt is nestled under a giant pantry," said Awkley. "There are a hundred ways out of that sewer."

"The fire hurt it, and I am fairly sure I hit it with a spear throw," said Zales. "It's big and demon-fast, but I know my men can kill it."

"So ready to kill," mumbled Scribbs. "We know nothing about it. It might have even been benevolent, had you not attacked it-"

Zales again grew red-faced, but Awkley quickly broke in. "Oh shut up, Scribbles. I don't mind so much the fact that you're boring, but your stupidity is unforgiveable…"

"Shut up, yourself!" hissed Scribbs, who appeared ready to fling himself out of his throne onto Awkley.

"And you call yourself a scholar?" continued Awkley. "Have you found anything in your dazzling collection of books about the Newt? Of course not. Maybe you wrote something in your endless journals that might make sense of it."

"Enough!" shouted Queen Temma. "Not just the Blueboys, but your men as well, Morten, should be immediately engaged in finding and killing this invader. If that monster reaches any of my children…"

"Wouldn't miss it," said Morten. "Will make excellent sport."

"We are agreed then," said Queen Temma. "I suggest we retire and allow our commanders to devise a plan."

"One moment," said Awkley, who rubbed his hands and settled into his throne. "You may leave if you wish, but I have a puzzle to pick at, and you might find it interesting. I've called for Ancimoden."

———

None of the royalty left. The name of Ancimoden clearly struck their interest, and though they asked Awkley for the reason, he responded only with jokes and useless hints until the doors opened and a tall, green-clad tantyr glided in. It quietly took its place to one side, its handsome, exotic features relaxed and its amber eyes stoic.

"Step forward, Captain Zales," said Awkley.

Zales glanced nervously at Commander Sheare and stepped forward.

Awkley stared at him silently for a moment. "No, Zales, Ancimoden is not for you," he said finally, chuckling, his little joke on the captain completed. "You behaved admirably. I will remember."

"Thank you, my king." Zales stepped back, with a sigh, to the audience seating.

Rodrigo noted with interest that Commander Sheare's face clouded over, contemplating dark thoughts. Rodrigo had heard rumors that King Awkley changed commanders often, based on whatever fickle whim struck him, and

Sheare would be exposed if the truth of the incident came to light. Rodrigo wondered if Ancimoden—for whatever purpose he served—was here for the commander.

"Rodrigo, step up. Let's have a chat."

―――――

Rodrigo hesitated, not expecting to be called upon again. "Yes, my king," he said, taking his position in front of the thrones.

Awkley steepled his fingers and looked Rodrigo over, a smile playing across his face. He turned to Temma. "A handsome boy, wouldn't you say, my dear?"

"Yes," said Temma, smiling kindly. "And brave."

"From the queen's own mouth," said Awkley, raising his eyebrows in feigned admiration. "I wager that you did not know this, Rodrigo, but I have taken a distinct fascination with you, ever since you arrived. Do you know why?"

"I could not hazard a guess, my king."

Awkley smiled broadly and turned to King Scribbs. "He could not hazard a guess. Scribbs, did you hear that?"

Scribbs glanced sourly at Awkley, but he put his journal down and looked at Rodrigo.

Awkley settled deeper into his throne, making a show of getting comfortable. "You have a nice sword, boy. How did you come to own it?"

"Merely a providential discovery, my king. You could almost say that it found me."

"You found it in Drift?"

"Below Drift, my king-"

"Gads, boy, leave off the 'my king' bit. Just have a chat with your Uncle Awkley."

"Yes, my...yes," said Rodrigo.

"Below Drift? What do you mean?"

"I lived in tunnels below Drift, by a small lake. I was alone for some time, but eventually found and woke a few other Dusties—Sleepers as you know them. We worked our way out, to Haven and Drift."

"We'll come back to that, boy. For now, what do you think of King Morten?"

Rodrigo gave Morten a momentary appraisal and a nod. "From what I hear, he is a hawk among men. I would say that it would be far safer to serve under his banner than to face it in conflict."

Awkley produced a pleasantly surprised face. "Admirable words! What say you, Morten?"

"I will have it engraved on my sword," said Morten, smiling slyly but clearly struggling to dig through to Awkley's game.

"And how about lovely Queen Temma? What do you say of her?"

"She has my deepest regard," said Rodrigo. "She holds her own against three kings."

The queen nodded impassively, but all in the room clearly knew that the words had struck a responsive chord in her.

Awkley laughed. "And how would you rate our old scholar and prophet Scribbs here?"

Rodrigo bowed slightly to Scribbs. "He speaks little and therefore hears much. I greatly admire his desire to seek peace whenever possible, even though I do not entirely share his absolute commitment to non-violence."

"That is regrettable," said Scribbs, but his tone was softer than usual.

"Beautiful sentiments," said Awkley, working up a great mock sigh. "You can even make Scribbs's withered, dead old soul quiver a bit. But I saved the best for last, and that would be me." Awkley spread his hands wide and closed his eyes, awaiting Rodrigo's words.

Rodrigo did not respond immediately. Awkley opened one eye and cocked his head.

"You are a ferret," answered Rodrigo. "Playful, inquisitive, and very keen of mind. But behind the charm sits a mouth full of very sharp teeth."

The room remained silent for a moment. Awkley put his hands down, opened his other eye, and raised his brows, smiling.

King Morten began clapping. "Bravo! You have Awkley by the tail, boy. And now I think I understand Awkley's game."

Awkley looked surprised. "Do you? I hope so. It should be so very obvious." He rose and walked down toward Rodrigo, his face turning stern and commanding.

"Look at you! Can you even grow hair on your face?" said Awkley.

"A bit of stubble, given time-" started Rodrigo.

"A bit of stubble, given time," mocked Awkley in a mumbly voice. "Listen to you! Say something stupid and clumsy."

"I-"

"Say something sarcastic and obnoxious. Pretend I'm your drunk pappy who is spewing meaningless gibberish about your choice of trousers."

"I doubt that my father-"

"By the worthless gods, I rest my case! You can't do it! Boys *don't talk like you.* Everyone your age is foolish to the very hilt!" Awkley stepped around Rodrigo from a distance, as if he were a tailor appraising Rodrigo's clothes. "I noticed it right away, of course. How does a boy stand up to the formidable Commander Boar so confidently? And Commander Sheare has taken excellent notes on your unusual manner over these past weeks."

The king paused and paced the other direction. "So, what, exactly, are you, I wonder?"

Rodrigo drew in a breath and clenched his teeth. "Sir, I can remember nothing past a hundred seventy days ago. Your question is as important to me as it is to you." Rodrigo's voice rose slowly. "I simply wish a welcoming hearth and a quiet bed."

"Oh...touching," said Awkley, clicking his tongue. "A poor, weary soul. And such a handsome young lad. The perfect port to lure vessels of sympathy. Wouldn't you say, Temma?"

"Leave the poor thing alone," said Temma. "Really, Awkley, your paranoia can be insufferable at times."

"Ah, what she really means is that she would like to take you under her wing and console you." Awkley moved in on Rodrigo to stare at him squarely. "A greater danger to you than my playful bantering, I assure you, boy."

Awkley moved off again, heading to his throne. "You are a puzzle, Rodrigo. One I must solve." He took his seat and nodded to Ancimoden.

Four guards brought a chair forward, placed Rodrigo in it, and strapped his arms and legs into place. Rodrigo did not resist, but he fought a wave of panic when they brought a strap tightly across his chest and pinned his arms to his sides. His mind flashed back many days ago—squeezed into thin cracks while trying to find a way out of the cavern of the artesian geyser, fighting to keep his fear of tight places from overcoming him.

The green-clad tantyr moved forward to Rodrigo. "Have you faced scourging before?"

"You intend to take a whip to me?" said Rodrigo, his breathing labored.

"Not at all," said Ancimoden. "Relax yourself. This will not be difficult unless you resist."

"Could you undo this chest strap? I am having trouble breathing."

Ancimoden moved forward and undid the chest strap. Rodrigo sagged forward, breathing heavily.

Morten waved his hand and smirked. "This is a scourging, Ancimoden," he said smoothly. "There are expectations."

Ancimoden turned and regarded Morten for a moment, then nodded.

"In fact," said Morten, rising, "let's stand him up."

Temma clucked her tongue. "There's no sense in being cruel, Morten."

"Nothing cruel about it." Morten turned to look back at the two stoic titans. "Whether traitor or patriot, this young man must be tested. Wouldn't you agree, Rafe?"

The titan Rafe eyed Morten, then nodded. "The boy is indeed a puzzle, and may even be a threat, considering the looming possibility of the Final Assault. Hold nothing back in his scourging."

"If he is loyal to humanity, the scourging will serve to temper and strengthen him," added the titan Shoca.

Scribbs shook his head. "There is no possibility that a Sleeper can have anything to do with the Final Assault. That's foolish talk, Rafe."

Rafe bowed his head to Scribbs. "Of course you are right, Lord Scribbs. I did not mean that the boy was connected to the Assault. I simply meant that we must be watchful for hindrances or sympathies. This is a very dangerous time."

"Everyone is aware of that," snapped Scribbs. "One would wish our enemies saw the wisdom in living peacefully with us."

"At least let him sit on the floor," said Temma. "He might bloody his nose otherwise, or even crack his head."

"I want him standing," insisted Morten.

Awkley slapped his armrest. "Stop the yammering and let's get on with it! Stand him up and give him your fullest, Ancimoden."

The guards unstrapped Rodrigo and returned him to his feet, facing Ancimoden.

"Brace yourself," whispered Ancimoden.

The world slid closed, and another slid open.

———

Rodrigo rocked gently in a small boat, little more than a skiff. It floated down a slow stream bounded by pleasant woodlands. A warm, bright sunlight bathed everything, delighting the sun-starved Rodrigo.

An angel shared the boat with him, reclining in the bow and trailing one long hand in the clear water. Its amber eyes blinked serenely as it regarded Rodrigo.

"It is a beautiful day to be on the river," said the angel. "But a storm is close. I hope that we can avoid the storm."

"That would be good," said Rodrigo dreamily, feeling his muscles relax under the gentle warmth of the radiant sunshine.

"I am glad to be with you," said the angel. "But I do not know your name."

"I am Rodrigo."

The angel shook its head and laughed. "Forgive me, I misspoke. I meant your real name. The one you share only with those who journey closely with you, like myself."

"Oh, yes, I see. But that is also Rodrigo."

"Are you sure?" said the angel. "The river can sense these things. It would be dangerous for us if your words did not ring true."

"We are safe then."

The angel nodded silently, slowly. Rodrigo splashed his hands delightedly in the clear water.

In the royal court, Awkley and Morten laughed quietly as Rodrigo sat down on the floor, rocking slightly, with Ancimoden sitting next to him. "We are safe then," said the boy, and flopped his hands off to the side as though he were splashing them in water. Queen Temma smiled slightly in veiled amusement.

"Do you think this river flows past your home?" said the angel.

"Only if we go over a very tall waterfall," said Rodrigo.

"Why?"

"My home is deep down."

"By a lake?"

"Yes."

"Who else lives by the lake?"

"No one now. We all moved away."

The angel nodded and looked off into the woodlands. "How long ago did you move to the lake?"

"I was born near the lake, or above it, in a place called Drift," answered Rodrigo.

Around the boat, the water roiled and pushed them on faster. Clouds rolled in over the sun, and a chill seeped into the air.

"The river!" warned the angel. "Are you sure you were born in Drift?"

Rodrigo wrapped his arms around himself to ward off the chill and wished for the sun to return. "I was born there, or near there."

Rodrigo heard a dull rumble that grew louder and louder. The angel turned. "Look!" it cried.

Downstream, the river turned angry, boiling and crashing in white-crested rapids and descending with a thunderous roar into a misty valley.

The angel turned to look closely into Rodrigo's eyes. Misted water trickled down its lean face and over its cloak. "The river will kill us unless you tell it where you were born."

"But I have told it!" yelled Rodrigo over the roar. "Why is it not listening?"

With a sickening lurch the small boat canted sideways into the rapids, flung from one swell to another. Rodrigo lost his bearings and his body slammed back and forth as icy water cascaded over them.

With embarrassment and disgust, Phoebe watched the entertained faces of the royalty as Rodrigo thrashed wildly about the stone floor, with Ancimoden hunched, frozen, over him.

"It must be told or we will drown!" yelled the angel. "Tell it before it is too late! Where were you born?"

"Above the lake! It was above the lake!"

"Where were you before you were born above the lake?"

Rodrigo took his eyes off the terrifying rapids and the water filling the boat and peered at the angel. "Why are you asking that? How could I be anywhere before I was born?"

"The river knows better, Rodrigo! Of course you remember. What color was your home?"

"Color? I...I do not remember."

"But you remember your mother. You remember her name."

Rodrigo shook his head for a time. "No. I cannot remember!"

346

The boat lost its battle with the rapids and sank. The angel took hold of Rodrigo, but apparently it could not swim, and it dragged at him.

"We're drowning! Why did your father let you go to the lake?"

A surge of water entered Rodrigo's throat and he choked raggedly at it. "I cannot—I cannot remember!"

Rodrigo screamed out the last word as he sank below the raging whitewater.

He awoke lying in the mud on the riverbank, coughing water and shivering from the cold. The angel waded in the backwater, lifting and emptying the boat of water. "We must move on, Rodrigo."

Rodrigo worked himself to his feet, stumbled into the water, and collapsed into the boat. The angel joined him, and they again drifted off through sluggish waters.

"How old are you, Rodrigo?"

"I do not know."

"Are you seventeen or eighteen?"

"Eighteen, I should think."

"Humans live just down the river," said the angel. "Do you want to see the humans?"

"I do not understand."

"Are you afraid of humans?"

"Of course not. I am human."

The angel looked surprised. "You are? Are you sure? It is dangerous to be in this swamp if you are not human."

"Then I am in no danger-"

Something swift and sleek erupted from the water and struck at Rodrigo's hand. He cried out in pain and tried to pull his hand back, but the toothy mouth of some serpentine creature engulfed it. Its eyes glittered evilly at Rodrigo, and its teeth worked up a little farther on the boy's wrist.

"Quickly, Rodrigo, before it is too late. Why does this swamp serpent believe that you are not human? What are you?"

"I do not-" Rodrigo cried out in pain as the sharp teeth inside the monster's throat began grinding through his fingers. "It should not be attacking me!"

"I can heal your hand, Rodrigo," urged the angel, "but you must tell me what type of creature you are before I can remove the serpent."

"I told you! I told you!" screamed Rodrigo as the serpent swallowed his severed fingers and started up his arm.

"Ancimoden!" commanded Queen Temma, standing.

The angel rose over the serpent and smashed it back into the water. Then it placed a hand on Rodrigo's stump and it grew swiftly to wholeness. The pain eased and faded away, and Rodrigo fell back into the boat, exhausted and soon sleeping...

Queen Temma crossed to Rodrigo, lifting him and petting at his hair.

"It seems you have acquired for yourself nothing more than a very remarkable young man," she said to Awkley.

After removing the disoriented Rodrigo from the royal court, and after the other royals left the hall, Queen Temma turned to Phoebe. "Your duties here are not merely for entertainment, girl. You are a masterful shot, and you are a woman, and, therefore, I intend to place some trust in you as a bodyguard—on a trial basis, of course, to see if you are brave enough and obedient enough for the task."

"I am honored," said Phoebe. "I will do my best-"

"Do you have the stomach for killing?" asked Temma pointedly.

"I..."

Temma leaned back and sighed in disgust. "I'm beginning to doubt your value, girl. I will have you guard my head matron, Imirette...for now. At least you're pretty enough to maintain the standards of my entourage. But remember this—there are many pretty faces around this castle, and you can be replaced if no other value is found in you."

Phoebe nodded silently.

The queen stood. "Tomorrow morning you must be ready by the sixth hour. You will accompany me to Bountywell."

"What is Bountywell?" asked Phoebe.

Temma waved her hand with a flourish. "Bountywell is why I am queen."

———

Phoebe paused, staring down into the massive, fortified sinkhole that was the entrance to Bountywell. From the open-air windows of the royal court, Phoebe had often caught a view of the far-off pit—a great ring beyond the neglected maze of glowmoss gardens, a depression surrounded by lanterns and heaps of glowmoss, and guarded heavily by tantyr forces.

Queen Temma strode down the rocky spiral path with Phoebe and an entourage of a dozen children, several matrons, and twenty city laborers in tow. The well-worn path circled the inside of a large pit, just inside the western wall of the castle. At regular intervals, gates and fortifications guarded the path, manned by stoic tantyrs. It appeared to Phoebe that the fortifications were designed not to keep someone out of the pit, but to keep something in.

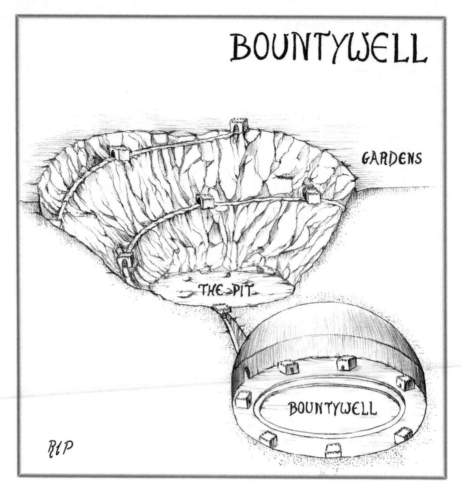

BOUNTYWELL

GARDENS

THE PIT

BOUNTYWELL

RIP

At the pit's bottom, tantyrs raised a battered portcullis, and the entourage descended a wide, smooth, steep tunnel that eventually opened out into a place that seemed eerily familiar to Phoebe—at least by description.

The immense size of the cave into which they entered disoriented Phoebe's mind and eyes. The ceiling above glowed with a thousand wandering white streaks, illuminating the entire extent of the perfectly circular cavern that stretched out for hundreds of yards. Terraces of glassy stone encircled the center, but unlike those described by Rodrigo around the Big Hole in their old home, the five or six terraces here descended shallowly, more like steps. The extensive center was not a pit, but a perfectly flat stone plain, two hundred yards wide. This vast flat was entirely empty of any object or marking.

Fortifications lined the terraces around the edges, manned by a hundred or more tantyrs. Phoebe could only guess at the dire nature of the threat that this cavern represented.

Far out on the ceiling, at the center of the cavern, Phoebe noticed one unusual feature—a dull, red circle of light, like a dying star.

Queen Temma glanced back at Phoebe. "Have Imirette explain," she stated, then moved swiftly down the terrace to the great flat expanse of stone. Imirette and Phoebe lagged behind at the edge of the plain.

Imirette managed a smile—the first that Phoebe could remember. "Our queen has many gifts. This is her greatest. It is here that she conjures forth the treasures of Bountywell."

Temma's entourage remained in a tight, orderly column behind her. The laborers maneuvered large, two-wheeled carts into position. Temma stretched out a hand, tilting her palm at different angles and slowly sweeping the arm right and left. Several minutes passed and nothing unusual happened.

Phoebe glanced at Imirette. "Patience," said Imirette.

More minutes passed. Phoebe sat down on the glassy stone of the terraces. Temma wandered from her initial location by some distance when she twisted both arms out in a strange, intricate pattern. A band of white light, at least twenty paces in length, erupted along the floor's surface and crawled rapidly across the stone.

In its wake, things materialized from thin air—buckets, piles of hay, saddles, a wildly alarmed cat, an anvil on a stand, numerous tools and tack. But most importantly, there appeared seven horses. The city laborers went to work, while the children gasped excitedly and gaped at the horses.

The horses scattered, and for the next twenty minutes there ensued a long, chaotic chase around the plain. To Phoebe, they brought forth a strange sensation, a sense of loss and nostalgia. As one white-rumped paint mare circled its way around close to Phoebe, she could no longer resist. She stepped out to meet it, clicking her tongue. The paint stopped, tossed its head, then walked quietly to Phoebe's outstretched hand.

"Well now," she whispered, touching the paint's speckled nose.

A shock of disorientation struck her mind. She could see a barn, small but well stocked, with strong morning light filtering in through the cracks and the slightly open door. She gasped and tried to look about the barn, but the vision flashed away and she steadied herself against the horse's shoulder.

It was a memory, she was sure of it—a place with proper day and night, and the comforts and smells of home. She found her heart racing wildly and she tried to catch a breath.

"I see you know horses...*ehm*...Phoebe, is there something wrong?" said the approaching Imirette.

Phoebe worked up a nonchalant smile. "No—quite all right. I do like horses."

A laborer came to walk the paint away, and Temma continued conjuring forth more treasure—sacks of grain, a neatly stacked pile of lumber, an entire bedroom of sturdy furniture, oddly fashioned clothing with strange devices made of a glossy material, a large wooden workbench with a scattering of tools, a tangle of wires and electric lights, and more. Hours passed, and the valuable treasures piled up.

Temma put her arm down and turned silently for the exit. As she passed, Phoebe saw the strained weariness in the queen's shoulders and face. There was apparently a price to be paid for this bounty.

80: MEETING OF MINDS

The next afternoon, after Phoebe had entertained the court with her ever-improving shooting skills, she happened to make eye contact with Rodrigo. Rodrigo had yet to acknowledge her. Frustrated with not knowing why, she held up seven fingers and then steepled her hands as if in prayer, hoping that Rodrigo would understand.

At the seventh hour, Phoebe took Ana, Ardi, and Petra to the great sanctuary down the long hall from the royal court. Although the tall chamber appeared designed as a place of prayer, its stylish stained-glass windows and the rich ornamentation made it an excellent location for a museum—in this case, a museum devoted to the current kings and queen. The children chatted quietly with her, but they clearly sensed her distraction. She did not tell them her real purpose here. If Rodrigo did appear, she would explain.

Would Rodrigo come? Phoebe looked up at the array of stained-glass windows lining the upper walls. The bluish cast of the midnight sky was not enough to illuminate them, so whatever scenes they conveyed remained a secret. *The bright sun on my face, even for just one minute*, wished Phoebe, remembering her vision of the barn.

She counted five others in the sanctuary—not unusual. The only ones allowed to wander the main level of the castle proper were the royalty and their trusted assistants, laborers, and guards. The many children kept to the levels above and on the extensive castle grounds, which acted almost as a city within the city. The castle grounds had its own wall, a guild commons with all of the smithies and shops necessary, and enough living space for at least ten thousand. Queen Temma put this space to use for children, and put the castle wall to use keeping the real mothers and fathers away from those children.

Ana scooted up next to Phoebe and whispered in her ear. "Who are we waiting for?"

Phoebe gave the girl a surprised look and a pat on the back. "Am I that obvious?"

"Ardi guessed," said Ana. Behind her, Ardi nodded.

"He's clever," whispered Phoebe. "We are waiting for someone."

"A boy?"

"Yes, a boy," said Phoebe.

"Is he handsome?"

"Very."

"Do you like him?"

"I didn't know him long. We spent our time arguing. But at least he's a familiar-"

Rodrigo stood in the high-arched open doorway, wearing the uniform of a Blueboy. He surveyed the room slowly, appreciatively, but his eyes flicked frequently to Phoebe.

"His name is Rodrigo," said Phoebe. "We must pretend not to know him, so don't look his way."

Phoebe walked the fingers of both hands quickly across her grey glowmoss dress, one following the other, keeping distance between the hands. She repeated it, not looking at Rodrigo. Then she stood, took Ardi and Petra by the hand, and walked out. "Follow," she breathed as she moved past Rodrigo.

Phoebe moved through the castle corridors, trying to appear unhurried. At one bend she glanced back and breathed a sigh of relief as she caught sight of Rodrigo. She continued up, past the more inhabited lower floors. The upper levels of the castle above Queen Temma's domain had few residents and many scattered rooms and towers, providing plentiful locations for privacy. Like much of Pinnacle, there remained evidence of past violence and destruction in these desolate upper regions. Phoebe lit her personal lamp and turned right, into an ill-treated corridor. She moved along through the scattering of rubble, waited at a side archway until she saw a lamp appear at the corridor behind her, and ascended a long stairwell.

They came out a trap door and up into a small watchtower with a roof but open walls. Close by to the south rose the tall clock tower and its ascent of fires designating the hour. The tall gas-lit flames—seven at this hour—lit the watchtower's interior brightly. A rocking chair and a small library of books rested to one side.

"My home away from home," said Phoebe.

"How did you find this place?" asked Ana as she went for the chair and Ardi went for the books.

"I tend to wander," said Phoebe, dousing her lamp.

Footsteps arose and a lean form appeared from the stairwell.

"It is good to see you well, Rodrigo," said Phoebe.

"And you, Phoebe." Rodrigo bowed slightly. "How are Scarlet and Trace?"

They quickly related to each other everything that had happened since they parted in the pumice tunnels.

Ana immediately took to the dark-haired older boy. "You're a gold soul, I can tell," she said to him, and led him to the chair, but he insisted that Phoebe take the seat while he paced around the watchtower, closing the trapdoor to the stairs so that he wouldn't accidentally fall through.

"Why did you avoid me?" asked Phoebe.

"I do apologize," said Rodrigo. "This is a treacherous, uncertain place, as you must have noticed by now. For some reason the rulers here are interested in who I am and what I know, and, as you saw, they are not gentle about asking."

"Have you recovered from the scourging? That was truly awful to watch."

Rodrigo nodded, his face turning grim. "Somehow Ancimoden reached into me, whether in spirit or mind. An effective way to carve out secrets. It was…unpleasant."

"And you believe I would be in the same danger? Is that why you didn't want me to talk to you?"

Rodrigo nodded emphatically. "They would have handed you over to Ancimoden. However, the danger may be past now. Ancimoden's work seems to have satisfied them. But, just in case, we need a way to tell them that I know you without stirring up their suspicions again."

"Easy enough," said Phoebe. "Tell them that we have not been on speaking terms."

Rodrigo smiled slightly and swallowed. "A bit severe, but that is an elegant solution."

Phoebe coughed and picked at a nail. "Rodrigo, I know you have a belief that we and our Dustie friends are somehow different, or meant to be together. But we are no longer at the lake, and I have only one concern now—to see to these three children. Do you understand?"

Rodrigo nodded slowly. "I have been expecting it, for all of us. The lake was not a true life. We have found cities now, and lives of our own."

Phoebe's brows furrowed for a moment. "You must have arrived in Pinnacle the same day as I, did you not?"

"Yes, that same evening."

"How did you know enough about this place to decide to keep our past relationship secret?"

"That is very perceptive," said Rodrigo, smiling diplomatically. "I cannot tell you how, not now."

Phoebe spread her hands in disappointment. "You seem to prefer being an enigma. But it was good to speak with you again, and hopefully we will remain friends."

Rodrigo bowed. "It is an honor to know you, Phoebe."

They shook hands and exchanged a few more pleasantries. Ana and Ardi held each other's hand while the scene played out, clearly dismayed at the formality of the conversation. Petra wandered about the watchtower, looking out through the battlements.

"Why do you suppose they built this tower?" said Petra.

"It is a watchtower," said Rodrigo absently.

"But it's too dark to see much, and the clock light is in your eyes," said Petra.

Rodrigo and Phoebe wandered over to the normally quiet young girl, who stood on her tiptoes to try to see down.

"This is a very old castle," said Phoebe. "Perhaps they built the tower before the clock was installed…" Her voice trailed off, and she remembered…

"Stained-glass windows!" she cried, a little too loudly, and put her hand to her mouth.

Rodrigo and the children turned to her, puzzled.

"If you are an artist in this place, why would you ever create stained-glass windows?" said Phoebe.

Rodrigo looked out over the battlement for a moment and he began nodding with increasing emphasis. "Or watchtowers at this distance! Gracia de Dios, there must have been a sun!"

"Rather, there must *be* a sun," said Phoebe. "There should have been no doubt—how can a world exist without a sun? But why can we not see it? Or are we simply dreaming?"

"It does no good to believe we are dreaming. We have no choice but to act as if it were real-" Rodrigo stopped suddenly and smiled. "Apologies, I went round and round the subject with Scarlet."

"Then these clouds—or whatever they are—must be blocking the sun completely," said Phoebe.

"Makes sense," said Rodrigo. "It is a bit lighter in that direction, in the east, though why it simply stays that way, I do not understand. Everyone I have met here talks like the sun does not exist at all. But if it has not been seen in lifetimes, then perhaps a missing sun would seem normal." He rubbed his chin. "I wish Yun were here. Are there libraries in Pinnacle?"

"In the castle, yes. Many books, from who knows where. Do you know about Bountywell?"

Rodrigo shook his head.

"There is a large cavern in a pit, off that way." Phoebe pointed. "I went there with Temma. It sounds very much like the Big Hole pit down in Lakeside, but this a large flat area. Queen Temma can conjure up things—ordinary things, buckets and horses and such. A long band of light runs across the floor and—*snap!*—things appear. And the things are related. Temma's first 'catch' was everything that you would find in a nice horse barn. It's as though she locates a place out there somewhere and transports everything in that area through Bountywell."

Rodrigo considered that. "That fits. This whole mesa—the Spire, they call it—must have a natural capacity to reach out and take hold of things. The people and the birds and planes, turned to stone. Random possessions scattered all through our old home. And remember the bits and pieces of rooms in the tunnels of the cringers?"

"Best if I could forget that place." Phoebe shuddered.

"I wonder if all the royals can work Bountywell," said Rodrigo.

Phoebe raised her brows in excitement. "I wonder if I could do it."

"I wonder if you could do it in reverse."

"You mean, send us home? I don't dare hope."

"We have a new common goal then," said Rodrigo.

"And without our usual bickering," said Phoebe.

"There's someone on the roof," said Ardi.

"What?"

Ardi pointed to the roof.

Everyone went still and silent. For some time they stayed that way. Only the light fire-hiss of the clock and the faint sounds of activity in the city intruded on the silence. Rodrigo moved to the battlement and leaned out, looking up, but the roof's overhang prevented any view up top.

"Are you certain, Ardi?" whispered Phoebe.

Ardi nodded, keeping his eyes on the roof. To Phoebe he looked concerned, but not frightened. Ana fidgeted and grinned, looking neither concerned nor frightened. Petra stood unmoving, her hands clasped and her face fearful but still set in her perpetual, melancholy repose. Phoebe found her hard to read.

They were all gathering around Rodrigo as he tried to find a way to look, when they heard the trapdoor rise. Rodrigo reacted instantly, leaping around and drawing his sword, knocking Petra sprawling in the process. They all gasped.

A shadow hung over the trapdoor, pulling it open, but it was not trying to come in, it was trying get out. They could not see it well except for its outline, as its skin appeared to be the deepest black. Two large golden, owl-like eyes reflected the light of the clock. It looked little taller than Rip, but a concealing cloak hid its outline.

While Rodrigo hesitated at the fallen Petra, the creature dropped its hold on the trapdoor and brought up, out of its short black cloak, a small crossbow of unusual design, leveling its aim at Rodrigo's midsection.

Rodrigo kept his sword tip pointed at the creature. The two stared at each other in silence, neither moving.

Rodrigo raised an eyebrow and shook his finger in the air. "Ahhh, you are Owleye—Boar's little demon friend, are you not?"

"I am de*mon* like you are de*mon*," spoke the creature in a high-pitched voice, its accent placing emphasis on unusual syllables.

"I'm no demon," said Rodrigo.

"We *hit* same tar*get*," said the creature.

Rodrigo glanced at Phoebe, confused. She shrugged slightly in response.

"There are children here," said Rodrigo. "I want no fighting. I will lower my sword." His sword point dropped slowly to the floor, but the crossbow remained on target.

The creature leaned down to the trapdoor, levered it up sufficiently to wedge through, and slipped away.

Rodrigo gathered up Petra, who hadn't moved after falling. "My deepest apologies, brave one," he said to her, seeing the scrape on her hand and kissing it. He looked into her frightened coal-black eyes and brushed back her equally dark hair. "You did very well tonight."

"How so?" said the girl, her eyes lowering. "Ana's the brave one, and Ardi's clever. He heard the thing on the roof."

"You asked the right questions—about the watchtower, I mean. Because of you, we discovered something important."

"About the sun?" said the girl.

"Yes," said Rodrigo.

Petra looked like she was about to cry, and she nestled into Rodrigo's arm.

Rodrigo held her gently and looked up at Phoebe. He gestured at the children.

"You have chosen a nobler goal than all the kings in all their campaigns. The Lord of All will bless you for it."

81 : Fair Warning

— 8 days later, the same evening that Hope fell into the gnarled hands of Scare-face and Mole down in Haven

Captain Zales sprinted through the vast, bright rows of glowmoss fields outside Pinnacle, found Rodrigo returning from a patrol inspection, and pulled the young man aside.

"We've got trouble," sputtered Zales, trying to catch his breath. "Awkley plans to promote you."

"To what?" said Rodrigo.

"Commander," said Zales.

Rodrigo started a cautious smile, awaiting the joke. "He already has a commander."

"He's had three commanders so far this year, and two dozen in the last five years. Awkley goes through commanders like I go through socks."

"That makes no sense. I am far too young. I am certainly not commander material, not yet."

"Neither were most of the past Blueboy commanders. Not meaning to insult you, but our good King Awkley cares little for actual expertise in his command choices. What he cares about is entertainment."

Rodrigo shook his head. "What do you mean?"

Zales's voice grew quieter but harsher. "Don't be fooled by King Awkley, Rodrigo. He is as bloodthirsty as King Morten, but he likes to hide it behind laws and rules. His new commanders must prove themselves worthy of the position by combat."

"Meaning?"

"Meaning you have to fight Commander Sheare."

"What type of fight?"

"The kind where someone dies."

"This is insane," said Rodrigo, shaking his head in disbelief. "Does Sheare keep his command if he wins?"

"He does."

Rodrigo rubbed at his chin. "Awkley expects me to be killed in the fight."

"That's my thought," said Zales. "Commander Sheare might be completely boggled, but he knows how to fight. Don't let his flight from the Newt throw you off; he's just as likely to go into a berserk rage."

Rodrigo paced, trying to make sense of events, and of the king, and of his situation. He had felt like a puppet on Awkley's string since he arrived in Pinnacle, and now it appeared the strings would be cut. He could not make sense of Awkley's high level of both interest and suspicion toward him—a boy, and a Dustie at that.

Rodrigo turned to the captain. "Why, Zales? I am nothing more than a boy. Why is Awkley in for me?"

Zales laughed his humorless laugh. "I was a Haven man, Rodrigo, awakened down in the tunnels. Came here to Pinnacle five years ago. They bought me with a little bag of coin and the empty promises of the kings. This city eats you from the soul out. You've been here long enough, don't you see it? Everyone's out to survive. You try to make something of yourself, or make things better, you are singled out and beaten down. The kings and queen want no competitors, and we, the soldiers, are right there helping them."

Zales stepped away a moment, then turned back to Rodrigo. "That's why I wanted to be a soldier. Not to defend Pinnacle, but so I could lord it over the unfortunate citizens and so avoid being an unfortunate myself. I'd like to think I've changed a little since then, but I honestly don't think by much.

"Then you come along, little more than a boy, but you don't act like it. You act honorably simply as a habit…*and* you escaped—somehow—from the lair of that sadistic pig, Commander Boar, and then made a fool of him in front of the royalty. Priceless! And you've been here only three weeks. You are *not* normal.

"So you've got Awkley's attention. And you've got our attention. You *must* win that duel, Rodrigo, because Pinnacle needs you. My men need you."

Rodrigo blinked and took in a breath, wrestling silently with his thoughts for a time.

He turned and gripped Zales's shoulder. "I'll need your help."

"You have it!" Zales's solid cheeks wrinkled up into a pugnacious grin.

"Tell me about Sheare," said Rodrigo.

Zales nodded and tapped at Rodrigo's scabbard. "As the challenged, you got the choice of spear or sword. Don't choose spear. Commander Sheare is superb with it. He's good with a sword, and he uses a parry dagger like you, but he overcommits. I've seen you in practice. You anticipate your opponent better than any I've seen. That's the advantage that gives you a fighting chance."

Rodrigo nodded and faced Pinnacle, wiping the sweat from his hands onto his hips. Atop the imposing bulk of Pinnacle Castle, the clock blazed ten.

A minute passed in silence. Zales watched as Rodrigo's brows slowly relaxed, and a small smile flickered on the boy's lips.

"You got a plan?"

"No, but I see an opportunity," answered Rodrigo.

Zales nodded. "Long as you get past the surviving first."

"Indeed," said Rodrigo quietly. "Well then, just enough time in the day left to settle the matter."

82: DUEL

In some more prosperous and enlightened distant past, the artisans who built Pinnacle Castle had lavished their finest work on the open parade ground atop the main keep. Despite the decay of age, the long years of neglect, and the fact that he could be dying in his own blood in a very few minutes, Rodrigo couldn't help but gaze in appreciation at the detailed stone-laid murals that covered nearly the entire surface of the grounds.

Rodrigo had barely entered the city when a castle page intercepted him and ushered him up to the grounds. Kings Awkley and Morten awaited him there, with the silent presence of the two imposing titans standing passively to one side. Commander Sheare brooded at Awkley's side, while Commander Boar leaned back smugly by King Morten, his pale eyes following Rodrigo's every movement as the young man stepped in front of Awkley and stood silently. Above them, the great gaslight clock tower brought a new jet of flame to life, signaling the eleventh hour.

"Ah, the main attraction," announced Awkley. He gestured toward a dark stain, spread over the stone tiles near Rodrigo's feet. "You missed the contest of innocence between two thieves."

Rodrigo noted other, older stains marring the murals nearby. He chose to remain silent.

Awkley rose, gesturing to Commander Sheare and then to Rodrigo. "You've been summoned here because I have questions about the leadership ability and fighting spirit of my current commander. I choose you, Rodrigo, to replace him. As a verification of my decision, you must face Commander Sheare in personal combat, until death settles the issue. Are you following what I am saying, and are you prepared?"

"What are the options?" said Rodrigo.

"Sword or spear, your choice."

"Begging the king's pardon," said Rodrigo, "but I meant, what are the options for a more peaceful resolution?"

"Peaceful?" Awkley adjusted the cuffs of his royal-blue shirt.

"Combat is not necessary," said Rodrigo. "I yield the field to Commander Sheare."

Awkley shook his head, visibly disgusted. "I do not remember explaining any such option to you. You seem to be having trouble understanding the way of Pinnacle, boy. My rule is absolute, and you live—or die—at my discretion. So it has always been, and so it will always be. Now, instead of complaining and hinting at cowardice, you would be wise to take this night as the high honor that it is. Despite your tender age, you are on the threshold of acquiring lordship over an army, with all of the benefits and privileges of rank. Really, your lack of gratefulness depresses me."

"This is indeed an honor," said Rodrigo, bowing slightly, "and I meant no insult. However, considering my youth, my lack of experience with the ways of Pinnacle, and my dislike for bloodshed—which might be mistaken for cowardice—I believe it is clear that I am not in any way qualified for the role of commander."

Awkley grimaced and turned to King Morten. "This is very difficult to deal with, Morten, really. What would you do?"

King Morten waved a hand in the general direction of Rodrigo but did not look at him. "I do enjoy listening to the boy; he has a way with words. And he does make a solid point about his lack of qualifications. But your selections for commander are always entertaining. I just hope that he provides a decent challenge for Sheare."

Awkley turned back to Rodrigo. "Sword or spear, boy."

Rodrigo pretended to consider and wandered over in the direction of the titans.

"Titans," he called up to them, "it is clear that this is little more than blood sport. How do you-"

Awkley burst from his throne, anger twisting his face. "Silence!" he shouted as King Morten rose with him. "You do not address the lords of the tantyrs! Know your place!"

Rodrigo turned back, giving one final glance at the silent titans. He approached Sheare. "I will not take a life at the whim of anyone, king or no," he said.

Commander Sheare lifted his head to stare into Rodrigo's eyes. "I will take your life, king or no," he half-whispered.

Rodrigo breathed a heavy sigh. "Sword," he declared.

He moved slowly back to the combat area in front of the two kings, drawing his bull sword and testing it. He settled a square-pronged parry dagger in his left hand. When he turned, he saw Commander Boar next to Sheare, whispering in his ear. Sheare nodded and Boar returned to Morten's side, smiling knowingly.

"What are the rules?" asked Rodrigo, bowing and presenting his sword to his slowly advancing opponent.

"First one to die loses," said Awkley. "I would think that is obvious."

Sheare moved in with a flurry of strikes high and lunges low, trying to trap Rodrigo's own sword with his forward-pronged parry dagger. Rodrigo retreated, keeping his weapon close and knocking aside thrusts only when they posed a clear danger. Sheare had a strength advantage over Rodrigo and knew it, and he clearly intended to disarm Rodrigo if possible. Sheare lunged high and Rodrigo riposted, sliding his weapon down for a strike at the commander's arm, but Sheare's prong caught his blade. Only by a quick retreat did Rodrigo hold on to his blade as the man tried to twist it from his grasp.

A feral grin appeared on Commander Sheare's face. Rodrigo could understand why. They both realized that the commander had a small but decisive superiority in skill.

Sheare stepped in with a wild, powerful side swing. Rodrigo caught it with his dagger and tried a swing of his own, but the force of the commander's blow knocked him off balance. Rodrigo felt a stab of pain in his forearm as Shear's dagger lanced in and slid out.

Rodrigo fell back, gripping his forearm and gritting his teeth against the pain. "Piece by piece, boy."

Sheare lunged in again, but twisted at the last second and landed a side-swing to Rodrigo's hip. Rodrigo felt the powerful shock of the blow but little pain. He stepped back, discovering that his scabbard had been cut deeply while only a light slash appeared on his flesh.

Sheare shook his head. "Lucky."

Rodrigo lunged, throwing several feints low before trying for a slash at Sheare's hand. His strike missed by a thread, and Sheare's counterattack knocked Rodrigo to the ground. The boy scrambled out of the way of Sheare's determined assault, surviving only when his flailing weapon caught Sheare in the knuckle. Sheare winced and recovered, but Rodrigo escaped to his feet.

Zales was right, thought Rodrigo. *He pays attention mainly to his own offense.*

Rodrigo shifted side to side and took in a nervous breath. Sheare grinned and moved in, readying another powerful side-swing. The swing came in waist high and Rodrigo dove, extending his sword in a stretched thrust before rolling to the side. He felt his sword bite deeply and saw Sheare's own sword point slam into the stone a few inches from his hip. Had he missed, Sheare would have had him.

But he hadn't missed. When he regained his feet, he saw Sheare clutching his calf above the Achilles tendon. Sheare attempted to take a step and grunted in pain and frustration, and his face reddened as a wild anger took hold of him. The commander screamed in rage as he tried a second step and fell to one side.

Rodrigo walked away.

Awkley rose, his expression difficult to read. "Finish him."

"Commander Sheare is down," said Rodrigo. "It is finished."

Awkley drew his jewel-encrusted blade. "Finish him or I will run you through."

As Awkley finished his sentence, the rush of fighting adrenaline in Rodrigo turned to anger. He dropped his sword and tore at the front of his shirt, baring his chest. "You are king. Do as you wish."

Awkley advanced on Rodrigo.

A long, lazy laugh sounded from King Morten. "I changed my mind, Awkley. This boy is positively delightful. I haven't been this entertained in decades."

Awkley looked from Morten to Rodrigo. At first his face showed dreadful seriousness, but slowly a perk of humor spread.

"He is an interesting case, isn't he?" said Awkley to Morten. "There's something that disturbs me about him, and yet it's exciting to see what he'll do next. And now, wonder of boy-wonders, he's my commander! I wasn't prepared for this."

"He bared his chest!" laughed Morten. "Temma will be incensed that she missed this. I suppose someone should dispatch Sheare."

"Ah yes." Awkley strode, sword in hand, to the downed commander, who continued to sputter in incoherent rage and pain. But he stopped short and turned. "I'm terribly rude, Morten, did you want the kill?" He gestured to the wounded man.

"Not at all," said Morten. "It's your duel."

In the eventful days since Rodrigo had first passed through the gates of Pinnacle, he had witnessed the many unusual and often unpleasant traits of the kings and queen. Despite this, the core of his nature stubbornly respected their royalty and right to rule. But this night, watching Awkley and Morten delight themselves so casually over a man's pain and death, his respect unraveled.

These two were nothing more than murderers in king's cloth, and Rodrigo resolved to stand against them.

Rodrigo followed Awkley to the downed commander. He began to speak, to confront this chatty monster at sword point if necessary, when the flow of events suddenly changed...

Sheare roared and leapt up on his knees with the ferocity of a wounded animal. His blade came up and out, and straight into the stomach of Awkley.

Awkley stared at the hilt of the sword as Sheare threw his weight into it and pushed it through the king.

But Awkley did not fall. Instead, he shoved Sheare sprawling with one hand. The king turned to his fellow.

"This hasn't happened to me in *at least* three years, Morten."

Morten shook his head slowly and clicked his tongue.

Wisps of yellowish smoke puffed from the front and back wounds surrounding the sword. Awkley's face reddened, and reddened further. Rodrigo backed up.

"This…this filth…put a hole—two holes—in my attire!" screamed Awkley.

"And he tried to assassinate you in the process," reminded Morten.

Bellowing in rage, Awkley pulled Sheare into the air with one hand and stormed toward the keep's edge, the sword still firmly impaling his stomach and the yellow smoke erupting in puffs from his body. Sheare roared as well, digging viciously at the king's face with his hands, releasing tiny drifts of the odd smoke with each gouge of Awkley's skin. The king reached the edge and launched Sheare violently into the darkness. He then wrenched the sword from his belly and flung it at the receding screams of the doomed commander.

Walking back from the edge, he breathed a calming breath and turned to Rodrigo, his body continuing to smoke lightly.

"Congratulations on your promotion, boy—eh, Commander. You will find your new braids of rank down on the street below."

83: Phoebe and Imirette

The next morning, Phoebe escorted Temma's head matron, Imirette, moving through the light crowd of market-goers on her way to the smithy. In the forty minutes spent walking through the streets, she felt herself fighting a cloud of depression.

Despite the desperation of the war with the blackspawn, the streets of Haven, her former city, had flowed with life—full of loud, cocky, but generally amiable, people. In her travel on the streets of Pinnacle today, she had not yet met eye contact with anyone. Men and women passed silently by, faces to the street. Only inside the archways of inns could normal conversation and a semblance of merriment be heard. Men, and a few women, in Hunter and Blueboy uniforms wandered by, apparently on city guard duty, though there seemed little to do among the subdued half-crowds.

Phoebe noted the large number of areas in the city that appeared deserted. Vandals had had their way, turning once stately old buildings into looted shells, their stone walls marred by graffiti chiseled into or whitewashed over them. One large message spanned an entire market front, reading:

BLACKSPAWN OR OLDEVIL,
MALFAER OR DEVOURER,
CHOOSE, FOUL GODS,
AND LET IT END

"What is this Oldevil?" asked Phoebe.

Imirette walked beside Phoebe. She had volunteered to escort the girl to the weaponsmith, and Phoebe was surprised by the bond that had somehow grown between the two. Imirette regularly expressed disapproval of Phoebe's actions, or dress, or mannerisms, or personal opinions, but her tone in doing so had become softer, more instructive, and interrupted with occasional compliments. Certainly Queen Temma had Imirette spy on Phoebe, and yet there seemed more interest on Imirette's part than simply that of a spy.

"I suppose you expect a history lesson," said Imirette.

"Yes, please," said Phoebe.

Imirette sighed, her creased face as disagreeable as ever. "Unfortunately the weaponsmith is inconveniently far still. Very well. The Spire holds a special place in the world, containing powerful magic to open portals to other lands, as you have seen. This city—the first city of the world—is many centuries old, ruled wisely by a line of kings and queens so old that it is lost in time. But from the dawn of the Spire, the chosen royal line has been bitterly opposed by many others. Foremost among these was a dark force that coveted the power of the Spire. It has had many names, but it is commonly known, now, as Oldevil."

"Frightening," quipped Phoebe. "I wonder if it originally meant 'Old Evil' or 'Ol' Devil.'"

"It is a terrifying power that seeks total domination," corrected Imirette sourly, "and no laughing matter."

Phoebe nodded, hiding a smile, knowing Imirette's narrow limits.

"Centuries ago," continued Imirette, "Oldevil won a victory and wrested control of the Spire, but only for a short time. Three great kings and an inspired queen confronted and defeated the monster, banishing it to another land. But before it was cast away, Oldevil buried its magic inside Bountywell, which has allowed it to temporarily open the portal at great cost. Do you remember the red glow, high above in Bountywell?"

Phoebe nodded.

"That is the eye of the magic. Oldevil has made the attempt eleven times over the last few centuries, each time pouring an army through Bountywell. But all have failed, and its buried magic is nearly broken. Only one more chance remains to it. We have now waited over a century since the last attempt. The length of time has certainly allowed Oldevil to build strength to its fullest. We know the attack is soon upon us, and the Seer-King Scribbs has prophesied its coming."

"Is that what he calls the Final Assault?"

"Yes."

"And the tantyrs are here to stop it?"

Imirette shook her head. "The tantyrs and the titans serve the royalty in restoring honor to the humans of the Spire. There was war between the cities, a decade before my own birth. The people did not listen to the kings and Queen Temma, revolting against their rule and committing shameful, traitorous acts, even allying with fiendish non-humans. The gods were infuriated, but in their mercy sent the tantyrs to instruct and restore the honor and loyalty of the people. Because the time of the Final Assault is so near, the tantyrs have agreed to stand in the breach against whatever comes forth from Oldevil."

"How long ago did you say that war between the cities occurred?"

"Over ninety years now."

"You are eighty, Imirette? You have aged well."

Imirette remained silent.

"Was the Queen Temma of that war the first Temma in her line?" said Phoebe.

Imirette actually smiled. "No. That is the Queen Temma of today."

Phoebe raised her lush brown brows and shook her head. "How is that possible?"

Imirette turned serious again. "You have not been told, I see. Did you know that I was a child under Temma's wing just as your three friends are today?"

Phoebe opened her mouth. "I—I don't understand."

"I was age six in the second year of Temma's inspired decision to become Greatmother. It is a matter of personal pride that I was one of the first."

"But—Temma, and the others, they look no more than forty, if that."

Imirette raised a finger. "You have not yet reached the obvious. Queen Temma, and the kings you know today, are the very same that defeated Oldevil centuries ago. My dear girl, they are immortal."

84: WHISPERS OF ROYALTY

— 3 days later

Queen Temma, Immortal Greatmother of Pinnacle, sat close to Awkley and Morten under a golden awning set up on the parade grounds atop the keep. She had spent the last ten minutes scolding the two for not inviting her to the duel between Commander Sheare and the young Rodrigo. Now, the three watched Rodrigo introduce himself to his Blueboy captains and troops—nineteen hundred men and women whose natural cynicism toward yet another commander was made doubly worse by Rodrigo's age.

"I am surprised to discover that this boy knew Phoebe," said Temma. "They both came from that same hole—that one with the lake."

"Oh?" said Morten. "There must be something in the water there. I saw Phoebe practice this morning. She has three crossbows now, all spread on the table. She's trying to pick up and shoot all three before the targets fall. Nearly did it."

"If her manners were only as polished as her archery skills," said Temma distastefully.

"If you tire of her, I would be happy to have her," said Morten with a predator's smile.

"Mind your own toys," scolded Temma.

"I wonder if the others are this unusual?" wondered Awkley out loud.

"What do you mean? What others?" said Temma.

"I've had Berylata's latest report," said Awkley. "The other people from that lake are all in Haven. I've asked her to keep watch on them. They sound interesting. Did you know one is an oriental beauty with a love for the archives?" Awkley smiled slyly.

The others looked at Awkley expectantly, waiting for him to complete his joke. Only a few weeks ago, Scribbs had descended into one of his prophetic trances, announcing that the Final Assault would not come until he had been wed. His utterances had described just such an oriental bride. But Scribbs had a spotty past with his prophetic talents, and none of them had treated this prophecy with any seriousness. Scribbs paid little attention to women, and no attention to social interaction, so the thought of him marrying was a matter of humor, not reality.

But now Awkley surprised them. His smile slowly vanished and he announced meaningfully, "I am deadly serious. Her name is Yun."

"That's odd," said Temma.

"Quite the joke to play on Scribbs if we brought her here," said Morten.

They fell into silence for a time, watching the boy commander make his first impression. He appeared to be holding his own so far.

"We must prevent her from coming here," said Temma.

The other two stared at her.

"You aren't serious," said Morten. "Scribbs's clumsy 'prophecies' are worthless rot. How many signs of the Assault have we heard? The haunting specter of the ray of twelve, thrice-forked lightning ascending to heaven, cattle and pigs rampaging, and—Awkley, what was the one about snakes?"

"Snakes? I thought it was wolves or weasels or whatnot," said Awkley. "How many thousands of prophetic guttertraps have we heard over the last century alone? They're so rarely meaningful."

"And sometimes they are," said Temma. "I don't like the feel of this one. Is she pretty?"

"Apparently she's an absolute heart-thief," said Awkley. "Odami's son is smitten with her, but she's torn between him and one of the Lakesider boys."

Temma shook her head. "We should get Berylata involved."

"I think you're overreacting just a bit." Awkley laughed.

"I'm not overreacting!" Temma ground her teeth before continuing. "The Final Assault, it's close and I feel it. If there's something, anything, to this prophecy of Scribbs's, I want us to act. If this girl marries Odami's son, she'll be out of reach. And that might delay the Assault."

"But why delay it?" said Morten. "Let's have Oldevil's last gasp while we have the power of the tantyrs at the ready. Then we can turn our whole attention toward eradicating the blackspawn. I say sit the girl in Scribbs's lap and be done with it."

"No!" insisted Temma. "In fact, I find it suspicious that this girl appears so conveniently close to the prophecy. How do we know she is not part of the Assault herself?"

Morten threw up his hands. "Ridiculous, Temma. Oldevil can only act through Bountywell. It is simply impossible. And even if Oldevil could, it would be throwing killers here, not bothering with little girls."

Temma shook her head. "I don't care. Bring Berylata into it."

Awkley snorted in exasperation. "You were the one who cut short Ancimoden's work on Rodrigo, Temma. Now you want to bring Berylata to bear on some ninety-pound bookworm?"

"Berylata does not need to scourge the girl," said Temma. "Just question her. Make her see the wisdom of marrying Odami's son."

Awkley waved a dismissive hand. "Fine, I'll not argue it anymore."

"Well, I will," said Morten. "I'm tired of waiting for the Assault. Oldevil is half-defeated anyway, at least as far as me and Awkley are concerned. I say we send the tantyrs to collect all of these Lakesiders and bring them up here. I'm intrigued, and I want to see if Scribbs even knows what to do with a girl."

Awkley held up a hand before the argument became heated. "Might I suggest that we have Berylata manage a gentle questioning of this Yun girl and then receive Berylata's report. We can keep tantyr scouts on watch and decide whether to snatch these Lakesiders out of Haven afterward."

The other two nodded sullenly in agreement.

85: WAR

—3 days later

Rodrigo gave his report to the royals at the court. The monster Newt had now been sighted twice and several more citizens were missing, along with a milk cow. But neither the Blueboy nor Hunter soldiers had found a trace of its lair.

Rodrigo had just begun to explain a new strategy for digging out the monster when the main doors burst open. All in the room turned at the intrusion.

A squadron of tantyrs entered through the open window arches, swiftly and in some disarray. It was clear from the abundant spatter of blood—a mix of purple tantyr and crimson human—that they had seen fierce battle. Everyone leapt to their feet.

The tantyr captain glided to Awkley and spoke quietly. Awkley fell back into his throne.

"Are they insane?" he muttered to the tantyr. "Three hours ago? Why didn't you report immediately?"

"What is it?" screeched Temma.

"The Havenites—they attacked the tantyrs sent to gather up the Lakesiders. They declared war on the tantyrs and Pinnacle," said Awkley.

"Are they insane?" cried a suddenly interested Scribbs.

"We covered that," said Morten. "This doesn't make much sense. Unless Haven has reunited with their old-time allies, they can't even reach us."

"But to attack the tantyrs," said Temma, shaking her head. "They set their faces against the gods themselves."

"We lost four tantyrs, and dozens more are wounded," said Awkley, "and Berylata is wounded, perhaps mortally. She is in the castle hospice."

"This is upsetting," said Morten. "We can't act against Haven with the Assault hanging over us, not to mention the blackspawn raids."

Other tantyrs arrived, carrying passengers.

When the tantyr set Yun gently down on the stone floor of the royal court, she staggered, found her balance, and stared around at the crowd of strangers. One stood crisply at the side of a throne, dressed in a blue military uniform with gold braids. He looked remarkably like a friend whom she had lost recently. And then the soldier grinned from ear to ear and raced toward her.

"Yun!" he yelled, and she knew the truth.

Rodrigo caught her up, clasping her tightly, remembering the smell of her hair and the lightness of her body. She managed to whisper his name, then she burst into tears. He held her until he felt more hands and arms around him, and he heard Rip's bell-crisp voice.

"Yeh Ballytoads! He's not nearly as dead as yeh promised!"

Rodrigo held Yun until she gained a measure of control. Then he whispered in her ear.

"Boar is here. Ignore him. Follow my lead."

She pulled back and looked into his eyes. He nodded confidently. She nodded back hesitantly.

Rip grabbed him then, and Rodrigo clapped his back, shouted in joy along with the small man, and then leaned in close. "There is danger here. Be small and unnoticed. I need eyes," he whispered.

Rip stepped back and laughed. "I hear yeh!" he said with a wink.

A hand grasped Rodrigo's shoulder, and Rodrigo found Scarlet at his side, his clothes and skin bedraggled and bloodied. They both shook their head in disbelief and clasped forearms.

"You look your usual," smirked Rodrigo at Scarlet's extensive wounds and bruises.

"Tradition," said Scarlet.

Rodrigo spoke quietly. "There is danger here. Say little. Follow my lead."

"Aye," said Scarlet, smiling grandly.

Rodrigo greeted Hope, Trace, and Ed in turn, warning each in whispers but enjoying the glowing moment of rediscovered friends.

―――

At their thrones, Kings Awkley and Morten and Queen Temma gathered together, watching the Lakesiders.

"My, they are a tightknit band, are they not?" said Awkley to the other two.

Temma gestured discreetly toward Yun. "Scribbs has already noticed the girl. I don't want-"

But Morten quickly stepped forward and announced himself.

"Welcome, Lakesiders. We have eagerly awaited your arrival. Commander Rodrigo, if you would introduce us."

Rodrigo announced the royals, then his friends. After he introduced Yun, Morten interrupted him.

"Ah, Yun, you are as beautiful as advertised. It comes as a welcome surprise among the typical slack-faced old scholars. I hear that you are quite the archivist."

Behind him, Temma flushed and clenched her fists. Scribbs leaned forward, his large eyes growing wider and wider.

Yun bowed and managed a smile, despite her tears. "It is my first love, my king." She held out Ravenhair in both hands. "As you can see, I have a book with me even when I am snatched out of the air."

"I caught her as she fell from the high tower of Odami," said the tantyr behind her.

"How so?" said Morten. "Were you pushed? Or were you attempting to flee from Odami's oafish son?"

"A bit of both, my king," said Yun.

"King Scribbs is a most dedicated scholar," continued Morten. "Yun, I suggest you take a place beside him."

Yun smiled politely and walked slowly to Scribbs's throne, sitting cross-legged on the floor. Scribbs stared awkwardly at her, as though he were seeing a ghost and an angel at the same time.

Morten turned and chuckled as he passed Temma.

86: REUNION

Yun's diary, Day 190

> You might say I went from frying pan to fire, but not so. King Scribbs almost worships me, quite literally, as though I were more than human. He is not handsome or ugly, but compared to that oaf Ikone, he is quite tolerable. He loves books, and his libraries are simply immense. I don't know where to start.
>
> Sometimes I miss our old home down in Lakeside, but I think I've found a new home here.

Many of the Lakesiders slept the entire next day away, the excitement of finding Rodrigo having been replaced quickly with the fatigue of their efforts in Haven and Old Haven. But two days later, the eight gathered in a dusty museum room off the castle's beaten path. They arrived an hour after midnight so that Yun could escape the infatuated but sleepy King Scribbs, and the conversation continued strong even after four flames lit the clock. Rodrigo considered this evening to be the greatest hours of his remembered life.

There were changes. Hope's eyes showed less self-assurance, and Rip seemed a bit more subdued and serious—or perhaps more maturity had settled in—while Scarlet had gained a measure of thoughtfulness. Both Yun and Ed displayed an unusual excess of cheer. Only the quiet, contentedly smiling Trace seemed to have avoided any significant change.

They each recounted their personal adventures. Scarlet told about the insane Rook Lord Grager, and repeated the memorized message several times before Rodrigo turned back to the subject of the Dalmar Wall. "Can you remember it?" he asked Scarlet.

"The whole thing was covered in some type of writing," said Scarlet. "I remember none of that. But the big symbols, I memorized those. There were sixteen spread out in a circle, and another big one in the center. Hmm—eh, Yun, I say, can Rip borrow your journal and charcoal?"

For the next twenty minutes, Scarlet, Rip, and Hope argued over the symbols as Rip made his sketch. Finally they all nodded or shrugged, and spun the journal around to Rodrigo and the others.

"The lever symbol in the Forge, and the lightning bolts from the firepoles," noted Ed.

"Exactly," said Scarlet. "For some reason we found five of these seventeen symbols on the things in our old home. Does anyone remember seeing any of these other symbols?"

They all shook their heads.

"And this Dalmar Wall is centuries old, correct?" said Rodrigo.

"So said the Uglies," remarked Scarlet.

"Then, other than us finding random artifacts devoted to this wall, it does not appear to mean anything," said Rodrigo.

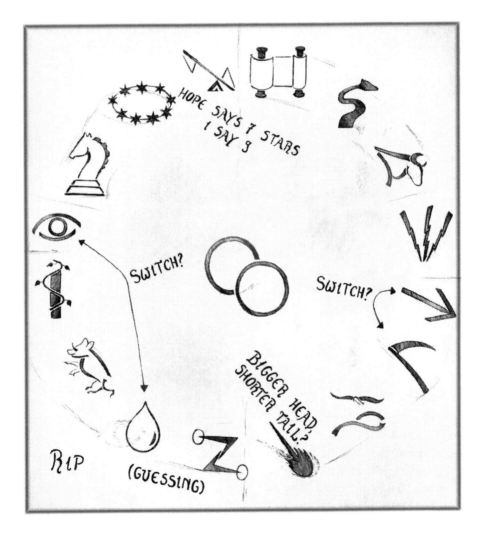

"The Uglies thought otherwise," said Scarlet. "They went to a great deal of trouble just to show us the Dalmar Wall."

"And eat us," added Hope.

Scarlet shrugged. "Perhaps. I'm unsure. It all ended abruptly."

A moment passed in silence.

"Well," said Hope, "from what you have said, Pinnacle is not a paradise. It appears to me that we all have little choice but to scratch out a living here. There is nowhere left to go, and little chance for improvement."

"It means we will likely go our separate ways," said Yun, "and this is as good a time as any to tell you. I am very happy to have escaped Odami's son Ikone. We have not been three days in Pinnacle, and I am already in the same situation with King Scribbs. But this time, I intend to pursue it and not try to flee it."

The others looked at each other. Scarlet nodded and stared at the floor. Rodrigo pulled Yun close and kissed the top of her head. "We understand," he said. "There is wisdom in doing so, and you will be safer."

"Wife to an immortal king," mused Rip. "Ahey, yeh'll be safe, for as long as yeh can keep his interest."

"I've thought about that," said Yun, "about when I am older. But that is a long way off yet." She turned to Scarlet, whose eyes remained fixed downward. "I am sorry, Scarlet."

"Think nothing of it," said Scarlet, who managed only a momentary glance up before returning to his study of the floor. The others fidgeted and exchanged looks.

"I might be able to shut down Bountywell," mused Ed. "Clip Oldevil at the shorts before he can even make his Final Assault."

"Oldevil..." said Hope. "The list of frightful forces threatening this world never ends, does it? At the risk of sounding defeatist-"

"No defeat," interrupted Rodrigo, startling them all at the seriousness and sternness in his tone. "The Spire is our home now, and together or separately, we have no choice but to make the best of it."

The others held silent for a moment, until Scarlet spoke. "Are you trying to propose something, Rodrigo?"

"Of course he's trying to propose something," said Ed. "He can't help himself."

"I know that," said Scarlet. "And before anything goes further, my vote is for together."

"We are already splitting up, Scarlet," said Hope. "Yun is merely the first, and Phoebe is under Temma's thumb, and you are a commander now, Rodrigo. You have duties."

"True," said Rodrigo. "But all of that might well aid us rather than hinder us. By extreme fortune, several of us are already highly placed. We have influence."

378

"Don't hold much to my influence," said Phoebe. "Queen Temma suffers my presence only because of my skills at the crossbow. She detests me otherwise."

Rodrigo turned to Yun.

"Yes?" said Yun in response to his stare.

"May I ask one favor?" said Rodrigo. "You have access to the wealth of Scribbs's archives. Are you willing to do a bit of research for me? About the Dalmar, for one, and this Daystar that the Uglies mentioned. Also, any history of the royals, and the blackspawn-"

"I understand," interrupted Yun, who smiled up at Rodrigo. "I'll snoop for you."

Rip whispered something to Trace, and they both suppressed a laugh. Rip looked at Rodrigo, and the command braids on his shoulders. "Yeh been dead for thirty-odd days, and we find yeh commander of an immortal king's army. I know not how yeh do it, Rodrigo, but yeh have the Hallow's gift of makin' things happen. And now I can see right into yeh, plain as rainwater. Yeh plan on doing something grand here in Pinnacle. All yeh have to do is fight off the blackspawn, survive some demon god's final attack, resolve a war with Haven, and overthrow four immortal rulers. Do yeh deny it?"

"I would not...well, if you put it that starkly..." stumbled Rodrigo.

"We get it right," said Trace, grinning like a child that had just won a prize at the fair.

"Ah-hey! Rodrigo, yeh haven't the faintest of prayers, but just tell us what yeh want..."

Rip's voice trailed off as his gaze drifted past Rodrigo.

One by one they turned and saw what had caught Rip's attention.

Commander Boar wandered through the exhibits and displays in the museum, his massive arms crossed and his pale killer's eyes taking in the artifacts of war and death appreciatively. Three well-armed Hunters and a tantyr held back near the doorway. Boar paid no apparent attention to the eight Dusties as he stopped within a few paces of them, grunting in approval at a giant brass-banded spear and shield in a large glass case. Then he turned slowly to them, smiling like a weasel in a mouse den.

"My family!" he said, opening his arms wide. "So many new faces, all happy together."

Trace moved forward, but Rodrigo stopped him, shaking his head.

"So Rodrigo make big plan, da? Wonder-boy make ambitions?"

"Speak your mind, Boar," said Rodrigo, "and then leave us be."

Boar nodded smugly. "I make plan too, Rodrigo. Plan to lure my enemy, catch him where he thinks he has me, but I have him instead. Deep plans, scary like Newt, all set and in place, nyet?"

"Nyet, Boar," said Rodrigo. "You do not frighten me, and I know you too well by now to be lured. So how do we put an end to this?"

"Hah!" grunted Boar. "Trust me, bad things happen, very bad for many here, I think. I do not hurt you, but your friends hurt first. Trust me, you watch them die, wish you could save them, but nyet, trust me. Then end come, and worst nightmare come, and you twist."

"Yeh need a dagger twisted in yer fat neck-" started Rip, but Rodrigo silenced him with a hand.

"This is between us, Boar, not these others. If you have nothing valuable to say, perhaps you should find another museum."

Boar looked back at his escort. "No problem. Always count on prying eyes and ears and minds, da? I see you again soon, Rodrigo."

He turned to leave, but swung around. "Girl Yun, and Hope, you *will* join me soon." He smiled his voracious smile, and walked away.

———

The Dusties looked nervously at each other.

"He's certainly as advertised," said Ed.

"We better off if he dead," said Trace.

Rodrigo shook his head emphatically. "No, Trace, absolutely not. He is commander of the Hunters and every bit as dangerous as he appears, trust me. You need to stay out of his path. We have a host of other dangers without tempting more."

Trace nodded sullenly.

"However," said Rodrigo, looking at Rip, "I would like to put our own prying eyes in place."

———

As the conversation continued, Scarlet noticed Hope withdrawing into puzzled thought, and he edged close to her.

"What are you thinking about?" he whispered.

"Oh, hello, Scarlet," muttered Hope. "Did you notice anything unusual in Boar's little speech?"

Scarlet let out a hushed gasp. "A speech…Aye, that's just it. It's like he rehearsed the words. Is that what you meant?"

Hope's nod of agreement turned slowly to a shake of concern. "He's up to something. But everyone is trustworthy here…right?"

Scarlet's eyes widened. "What are you saying?"

Hope pulled Scarlet farther back, away from the chatting group. "Boar is a killer, Scarlet. He clearly intends an end to Rodrigo. I am concerned that he may have help in doing so."

Scarlet began a laugh, but chopped it off. "Help? From one of us?"

Hope nodded slowly.

"Who?" asked Scarlet.

"Whoever he was trying to communicate with just now."

87: Watching the Garden

The next morning, Scarlet and Rodrigo took up position at a castle window overlooking the gardens. Queen Temma and her procession passed below them, on their way out to Bountywell.

"She does this every two days," said Rodrigo. "Conjures up treasures. Odd treasures. Real wood, spices, chickens and horses, furniture, weapons, on and on. Sound familiar?"

Scarlet nodded. "Like all the odd stuff scattered about in Lakeside, minus the animals."

"Precisely," said Rodrigo. "This treasure is how she buys soldiers from Haven."

"And orphans," said Scarlet. "I'll have to take a look around tomorrow and see where she squirrels up all this Bountywell bounty. Rip and I might see a need for some of it."

"Be careful."

"We will."

———

Hours passed. Rodrigo waved a hand out toward the garden, where Queen Temma's procession marched back toward the castle "This Bountywell is where the Final Assault is to take place, right? Why there?"

"From what I've gathered," said Scarlet, "Bountywell is Oldevil's power source. He can't 'clothe himself' in his power without coming though Bountywell. So he has no choice. No Bountywell, no power, no life."

"Ah," said Rodrigo, and he thought about that for a time as the two sat in silence. Finally he continued.

"And Rook Lord Grager mentioned the Final Assault?"

Scarlet sneered. "Yes, insane suicidal murdering kidnapper Lord Grager did mutter something incoherent about preparing for the Final Assault."

Rodrigo laughed. "You don't—didn't—like him much."

"You heard the murderer part?" snorted Scarlet. "And the abusing Phoebe part?"

Rodrigo pursed his lips. "Repeat Grager's message again."

"Again?" groaned Scarlet. "Fine. 'Time is short. Do not be distracted by the enemy on the far hill and fail to see the foe at your throat. Fear and chaos crouch in plain sight, readied to spring, their plans, laid long and patiently, come to fruition.'"

Rodrigo repeated it back to himself under his breath.

"You're taking it all too seriously," said Scarlet.

"Probably so," said Rodrigo. "I, for one, am not sure what it might mean. Has anyone else had a thought about it? Yun? Ed?"

Scarlet shook his head.

Rodrigo wagged a finger, his eyes darting about as they always did whenever his mind raced off on some thought. "What is your guess at Grager's words, 'If you fall, worlds fall'?"

Scarlet's head dropped. "Dash it, friend, you can't keep this up. You're grasping at a lunatic's tatters. And Phoebe wasn't exactly in a calm mind at the time. For all we know, Grager said, 'If you fall, we all...' and failed to complete the sentence before he did himself off over the cliff."

"I trust her to hear it right," said Rodrigo.

"Why? Because you actually think that you are responsible for worlds? We can barely keep our own skins alive."

Rodrigo stood up for a drink from his flask, slapping Scarlet on the shoulder. "Of course I agree. So the question is, what was Grager actually trying to tell us?"

"Lunatics tend to babble."

Rodrigo sat down in front of Scarlet, his eyes friendly but intense. "I have a theory. Would you-"

"I'd love to hear it," said Scarlet.

"What if Grager was not insane?"

Scarlet smiled like a man hearing a good limerick for the first time. "You're not serious."

"Quite serious," said Rodrigo. "Follow me. Let us say we are special in some way, and, for some reason, it is an important secret. Let us further say that Grager was a hidden ally of ours. You said that when he found you and Phoebe sneaking into his secret lair, into that tunnel with the suspended bridge, that he let you go."

Scarlet nodded. "Aye, that he did."

"That was kind of him," said Rodrigo. "Far too kind under normal circumstances. But if he was an ally, it would make sense. He couldn't tell you anything, and he wouldn't make it public, so he lets you go."

Scarlet's eyes narrowed, following Rodrigo's explanation.

Rodrigo raised and wagged a finger. "But, if he feels the need to be a *secret* ally, there must be enemies to keep the secret from. Say, perhaps, the former Rook Lord Ulth—the man that Grager killed.

"Now, let us follow that. Let us say Lord Ulth threatens the secret. Grager has no choice but to kill him. Not so much a murder as an act of war, and the golem Three did say there was a war going on. He did not say what kind of war, but secrets seem to be very important to it."

"This is becoming a very wild theory," said Scarlet. "How do you explain Grager's suicide?"

"Ah, that is the easiest part. We now know that secrets can literally be stripped from our minds, as Berylata and Ancimoden prove. What if the floating monster of shimmering darkness that attacked you and Phoebe at Desolation Point had the same ability? The way you described it, it sounded similar to Ancimoden's scourging of me—being drawn into a different reality. So, Grager senses the approach of the creature, cannot escape because of his stricken knee, and feels that there is only one course of action to keep his secrets safe. He jumps off the cliff."

Scarlet grinned. "That it?"

"For now." Rodrigo smiled. "You are thinking that I am merely weaving together events in a way that gives me more meaning than merely being a lost Dustie."

"Aye…just a tad."

Rodrigo laughed. "You could very well be right."

———

"Ah. Awkley is out and about for his little dalliance." Scarlet pointed down.

Rodrigo peered over the window edge. In the gardens below, King Awkley kissed the hand of a young woman and led her away, toward the lake at the garden's center.

"Did, eh…Hope share her little conspiracy with you?"

Rodrigo's brows furrowed. "Conspiracy?"

"Yes. She thinks Boar was trying to communicate secretively with one of us last night."

For a moment Rodrigo simply stared at Scarlet. Then, his mouth quirked up. "Why does she believe that?"

"His words came out rehearsed."

Rodrigo gave a single, emphatic nod. "Ah! I noticed that as well. But I took it simply as a planned and rehearsed confrontation by Commander Boar. All our friends are trustworthy."

Scarlet coughed. "Well, I talked that through in greater detail with Hope earlier this morning, and there is one possibility…"

Rodrigo's face turned to puzzlement. "What?"

"Yun." Scarlet's face stretched in apology.

Again Rodrigo stared at Scarlet, until he suddenly chuckled. "Yun? Are you serious?"

384

Scarlet held up his hands. "I'm just…listen, Hope says that an impressionable girl like Yun is easily dominated by someone like Boar, and he has tried to do just that from his very first days, right?"

"Tried and failed," said Rodrigo forcefully.

"Fine and fine," said Scarlet. "But Boar clearly intends you dead. I'm merely asking that you keep your eyes wandering and your ears twitching."

Rodrigo sighed. "I do not underestimate Boar's cleverness. If he is somehow working in league with one of us, I must rely on you to spot it and act accordingly. Agreed?"

"I'll keep watch," said Scarlet.

"I trust you will," said Rodrigo, staring at Scarlet with a slight smile.

Scarlet rose. "Look, sorry to leave, but there's something I need to do."

"What's that?

"I have someone waiting for me."

"Ah…Pretty?"

"Quite."

"Give her my regards," said Rodrigo, "whoever she is."

88: Bedside

— 2 days later

Yun's diary, Day 194

Scarlet and I have not talked—have not even seen each other—since that night in the museum. There is a barrier between us since my rejection of him in Haven, and it is probably for the best. Neither of us needs more pain. King Scribbs is claiming me. I will make the best of that.

Having not seen Scarlet for more than a day, Rodrigo asked palace guards, servants, and even tantyrs for Scarlet's whereabouts. When he finally received the answer from a tall female tantyr, he raised an eyebrow in surprise and found his way to the castle hospice.

Working his way through the rows of bedridden, ill children and the overseeing matrons and nurses, he reached a short hallway hung at the end with a thick drape.

He lifted the curtain slowly. Beyond it, Rodrigo found a small but elegantly furnished chamber containing four beds, a small waterfall, and a pool. One of the beds contained a female tantyr. Scarlet sat on the edge of that bed, his attention focused so tightly that he did not notice Rodrigo until his friend stood directly beside him.

"Hello, Scarlet."

"Eh—oh, hullo, Rodrigo."

No words followed. Rodrigo bent down to view the tantyr female's exquisite face more clearly, noting the fine white feathery hair of the frills to either side of her head and the golden tone of her skin.

"This is—Beratta, correct?"

"Berylata."

"Has she managed to awaken?"

Scarlet did not look up. "No. The healers don't know if she will."

Rodrigo straightened, cast an appraising glance toward Scarlet, and scratched his chin. He sighed, found a chair made of actual wood, slid it over next to the brooding young man, and sat down.

An awkward silence settled in.

Scarlet tried gamely to ignore Rodrigo's stare, but he finally turned and sighed. "You've come to talk, haven't you?"

"Only if an old friend wishes it."

Scarlet merely pursed his lips and cast his eyes back at Berylata.

"You and Yun were on the cold side toward each other," said Rodrigo.

Scarlet nodded.

"I know you once loved her."

"That's the essence of Yun, isn't it?" said Scarlet. "She falls in love with everyone and everyone falls in love with her."

Rodrigo nodded. "Very true. But I think she holds a special place in her heart for you."

"Possibly. But princes and kings seem intent on carving it out of her. She made her choice."

"She chose to protect you from their jealousy."

"I know. I've accepted that."

A silence passed as Rodrigo appeared to think through his next words.

"This is the tantyr that scourged Yun, is it not?"

"It is," said Scarlet.

"And scourged you, according to Hope."

Scarlet did not answer immediately. The subject had come. He should never have come to this bedside. But he simply could not stop himself.

Rodrigo continued. "I was scourged myself, by a tantyr named Ancimoden. Extremely unpleasant. And so I cannot fathom this. Here lies the creature that brought so much pain to Yun, and to yourself, and yet here you are, holding vigil over its bedside."

"*Her* bedside."

Rodrigo raised one eyebrow, a surprised little smirk crossing his face, as though he had opened an oyster and found a pearl.

The words were out—betraying words that Scarlet could not drag back. He had never made known what had passed between him and Berylata. He had intended never to let it be known. A part of him screamed to turn on Rodrigo, to tell him most emphatically to mind his own business and leave. He hated the threat to his secret. But when he turned and looked at Rodrigo's patient, expectant smile, his resolve failed.

"Dash it, you must promise not to-"

"I will tell no one," promised Rodrigo before Scarlet had finished. "You are my closest, most cherished friend, Scarlet. That is a sacred trust."

Scarlet nodded slowly. "Well, Berylata saw the seabird and vine symbols on the Dalmar Wall and went to scourge me, then and there. But the scourging didn't go...well, it didn't go as she intended. Or as I intended."

Rodrigo sat quietly, waiting for his friend to continue.

"Berylata came over me like a storm. I mean that quite literally. Did Ancimoden—?"

Rodrigo shook his head. "No, he used a less straightforward approach."

"Berylata was every bit the terror that Yun said. But when the storm struck me, I—well, I grew wings and flew."

Rodrigo raised an eyebrow.

"I flew, just like this gull, or hawk, or whatever bird it is," he said, pointing to his belt. "I flew right through her, and all around inside her. I know her now, intimately."

"What do you know about her?"

Scarlet shook his head. "No. I don't know anything *about* her. I know *her*. She is windswept skies full of purpose and pride in her skills and talents, while below lies a clammy, shifting fog of deception—not just deceiving others, but deceiving herself, trying to shut out some terrible pain. Below that is a hard, frozen surface of ice-cold determination and duty, but there were a few cracks, and in the cracks I saw the true depths—an entire sea of the most horrifying, final despair."

Rodrigo nodded, waiting for Scarlet to continue.

Scarlet's embarrassment escaped as a sheepish smile. "This is a bit embarrassing...eh, 'mushy,' you might say. Something girls titter about. Not for your comrades-in-arms, typically."

"I am no typical comrade. Please, go on."

Scarlet coughed. "Yes, well, I've thought it over for these past days, and it's something like this. A man takes a wife, and he believes he knows her well right from the start. But he discovers that he comes to know her day by day, layer by layer, until twenty years later the two feel like the same person. With Berylata, I went through those twenty years in ten minutes. Does that make sense?"

"Yes. You love her." said Rodrigo.

"No, I...I don't know what it is. I do know that I felt that sea of despair so deeply that I must find a way to help. And yet I can't, because I know that she might never, ever reveal the source of the despair."

"I understand. Perhaps we can discover the source together," said Rodrigo. "You did not plan for this to happen, and so it might be that the Lord of All did."

Despite Scarlet's deep regard for his friend, Rodrigo's immediate acceptance of Scarlet's secret burden took him aback. "Thanks, old boy. You have no idea what it means to find you among the living."

Rodrigo rose and clapped Scarlet on the back. "You are my brother, Scarlet. There should be no secrets between us. Stay here and do what your heart must. We can practice sword and spear another day."

As Scarlet stumbled through a goodbye, his friend walked away, back through the curtain.

———

Only once the curtain had fallen into place behind him did Rodrigo close his eyes and let out a troubled breath. He, Rodrigo, kept a greater secret than Scarlet's, and it shamed him that he had embarked on a path of daily deceit.

But he had no choice.

89: TIGHT PLACES

Yun's diary, Day 197

> I found Scribbs's writings, and I no longer doubt his immortality. In one vault there is a century's worth of journals, all in Scribbs's hand.

> Scribbs insists that I sleep in the room adjoining his master bedroom. My room is so large that when I cough, it echoes. Though he worships me, he has not treated me romantically. He seems nervous and distracted by something, and very tired.

> I thought I heard voices last night, but I think now that it's just that big room and the strange dreams that I've been having.

At first, the immortal kings and queen showed interest in the new Dusties, but this faded quickly. They had no use for Hope's healing, as they did not worry about death or sickness. Ed's engineering, while useful, did not evoke any fascinating conversation. Trace provided soldier material and nothing more.

Rip expected the same suspicion as he received in Haven, but the royals gave him surprisingly little inspection. "I am just a very short human," he decided to say, waiting for the disbelief. But the royals simply shrugged or nodded, and Scribbs raised a finger and said, "Ah, I've heard of your kind."

After this, Rip played hard at being dull-witted and silly, and the royals quickly gave up on him, turning their attention to the flamboyant Scarlet, who proceeded to make a small legend of himself in dazzling the crowd of young ladies of the castle with his dash and wit. A rumor circulated that Scarlet had fallen into a torrid love affair with a beautiful tantyr, but to this he would only say, "The angel who will carry away my heart will not have wings," and then he would tilt his brow and curl his lips just so, and the hearts of the young maidens in attendance would flutter about on their own wings.

It was masterful, and quite an act, for Rodrigo had put him up to it. And for that Rip was grateful.

With Scarlet diverting all of the attention away from Rip, Rip made himself uninteresting and receded into the crowd, keeping to himself during the day. He desperately missed his chapeau, and when the castle children teased him about his size and his ears, he gagged down his pride and told the clumsy ettin brats that he "just grew wrong."

Rip prowled. Hour after hour, passage by passage, he explored the extensive castle. He sketched his maps, compiled pages of notes, but even without them his mind took naturally to remembering every nook and cranny. It was as though he could "see" the whole castle, could spin it around and pull it apart in his mind then set the pieces all perfectly together again. The joy of it took hold of him, and he neglected both sleep and food—at least, until he knew where all of the kitchens and storerooms were, and then he helped himself.

On this night, Rodrigo had asked Rip to find a way to look in on Yun. But while most of the castle was unguarded, Rip knew that a tantyr held post at Scribbs's suite of rooms. Having no wish to tempt fate against such a fearsome creature, he considered alternate routes.

While giving thought to the problem in a nearby washroom, Rip happened upon his most valuable discovery.

Set high in the wall, water poured from a large oval pipe. Many rooms in this castle had flowing water—for washing, for pools, and for light from glowmoss. He recently found the source of this bountiful supply when he climbed a tower at the center of the castle complex and discovered an immense basin, boiling over with a river of water that fed a staggering array of pipes, and he wondered what engines below were driving such a powerful flow to such a great height.

Rip loved water, and fish, but he disliked getting wet when he wasn't intending to. He left the washroom and managed to reach ten paces before he set his fists on his hips, harrumphed, and turned around. Before he could change his mind again, he leapt up on the washbasin, jumped for a handhold on the pipe, and pulled himself in.

The pipe turned out to be wider than Rip had judged, though the low ceiling made him hunch down as he crawled along, thoroughly drenching himself. The water flowed slowly, seeping through a bed of mostly reddish glowmoss, lighting the tight surroundings in a deep crimson. He soon discovered that the pipe itself had a firm but slightly pliable feel—as though it were made of some tough form of glowmoss. A steady draft blew through the tunnel, rustling his mop of curled hair. Before long, the path branched, then branched again, until up ahead he could see a more open area where a small waterfall fell out of a pipe onto a shelf of hard, crusty moss. Two rats rose up on their haunches, uttered a few squeaks, and trotted off past the falls. He followed.

Spinning and aligning the castle map in his head, he chose a multitude of turns, zigzagging his way toward the chambers of King Scribbs. He met many more rats, as well as a few large hopping mice with big hind feet. They all looked fat and content as they nibbled along the edges of the abundant glowmoss. He was wondering why the tunnels weren't simply overflowing with the rodents, when he saw the eyes.

There were three pair, each set close together, and they approached down a side pipe. Rip moved forward to a concealing corner, readying his long knife in case the owners of the eyes proved to be unfriendly.

A snout appeared, and a long wedge-shaped head, and finally a lean body. It peered up at Rip, sniffing about uncertainly before leaping across the water and appraising Rip from the other side of the pipe.

Weasel, or ferret, or some such, thought Rip.

A second appeared, then a smaller third. The small one turned right into Rip, setting foot on his hand before jerking back in alarm. It cocked and shifted its head from side to side, trying to take measure of the obstacle, until it noticed that its parents had moved on and it quickly bounded away after them.

"Find dinner, mates," whispered Rip, and crawled the last remaining distance to Scribbs's room.

The king snored. Rip eased his head out of the pipe into Scribbs's room, seeing below him the extravagant series of pools gracing the king's chambers. Beyond the semicircle of pools, the outlandishly sized bedroom contained no light. As Rip pondered whether to risk checking the room for Yun or trying a nearby room first, he heard a voice from Scribbs's bed:

"The king sees, the king knows, the future is clear."

The voice lilted, as though it were being chanted, spoken so softly that even Rip's ears had to strain:

"Today I wed, and the day I wed will be the day that Bountywell rends
its last."

Rip dared not move for fear he would splash the water. Over the small noise of the water falling to the pools below, he could not tell whether the voice was Scribbs's. It continued, chanting the same words about the king and weddings, over and over again.

Then the voice ceased, and Rip picked up movement. A shadow flickered across the room and leapt to the pipe on the other side of the pools. Although the elaborate decoration of the room blocked much of his sight, he could tell that the intruder was small, dark, and cloaked, and it deftly pulled its way into the pipe.

Rip did not hesitate. He backed quickly to the first intersection in the pipe and turned right, driving himself on at a rapid, head-bumping clip—left, right, and another left—until he found disturbed glowmoss. He followed the trail of disturbance, holding his knife ahead of him, until he reached a small waterfall as before.

The disturbed glowmoss ended here, which meant that whatever he followed must be climbing up. Rip peered cautiously up into the pipe, noting that the water fell erratically. The intruder was there, tantalizingly close, but not visible in the cascading splash.

Rip knew that the pipe passed upward into the domain of Temma and the hosts of children. If this intruder reached the bedchambers of the children and found itself desperate as Rip chased it down...

"Catch yeh next time," muttered Rip, and he backed away.

90: The Insanity of Kings

Yun's diary, Day 198

It's the dead of night. I had a terrible dream. Something is very wrong.

Water trickled through cracks in the passageway's ancient ceiling at irregular intervals, leaving small clusters of glowmoss light that only served to accentuate the stretches of total darkness. The long-abandoned escape tunnel beneath Pinnacle Castle exited onto a growth-choked ledge outside, near a cattle pen. A farmer and two of his cows were missing, but a blood trail led down the dark, broken passage.

In the tunnel, two male figures with booted feet followed the trail of crimson—slim, dark-eyed King Morten and the imposing Commander Boar. Boar strode confidently, but not hastily, carrying a torch, carelessly treading on the smears of blood and the heaps of dead glowmoss torn away by something massive moving ahead of him. King Morten walked with much greater care, careful not to soil his boots more than necessary.

A third figure walked with them—Boar's small companion, dark and lean and cloaked, moving along slightly behind the men, its large golden eyes searching the darkness and its ears picking out faint sounds ahead.

On they walked, until a stench rose in the air, and they found the remains of the cattle. Low clicking rose from ahead, and the torch revealed movement. A massive shape spun around, tentacles and blades and razor claws coming to bear.

They had found Newt.

Commander Boar lifted his torch and grinned ferociously. "How is your hunger, my friend?" he said to the horror.

"As great as mine, I do hope," said King Morten, his eyes fixed on the terrifying creature with a mixture of awe and delight.

"Where is our Queen Temma?" Scribbs asked of Imirette.

"Detained with matters of the children," responded Imirette coldly.

"Ah…I thought she would be at Bountywell today."

"In the afternoon. What do you wish of her?"

"Oh, nothing at all." Scribbs smiled. "Nothing of importance."

Imirette turned away from the despised king, suspicious of his sudden willingness to speak to her. Her suspicion would have become true alarm had she turned back and seen the devilish stare lanced her way from Scribbs.

———

"I heard it a'least ten times," said Rip. "I could not help but remember it. Ready?"

Rodrigo and Trace, who were sparring with spears in the training hall when Rip found them, both nodded.

"The king sees, the king knows, the future is clear. Today I wed, and the day I wed will be the day that Bountywell rends its last."

"That is not much of a riddle," said Trace.

"Not at all," said Rodrigo. "And you say Boar's demon friend, Owleye-"

"I think it's a gablin, Boss, not a demon," said Rip.

"A gablin?" said Trace.

"Ahey. Sneaky little biters, and tough."

Rodrigo selected a longer spear, testing its balance. "You believe that it was Owleye who was whispering this to the king?"

"While he slept," said Rip. "Then it skittered off into the pipes and went pop-pop right up to Temma's level, it did. Those pipes will be a real boonie. Can't wait to explore more. There're rats and mousies and weasels all through them. I'd show yeh someday, but the pipes aren't fit for ettinkind."

"You think Final Assault today?" said Trace.

"Hardly," said Rodrigo. "They say Scribbs has botched the prophecy over a dozen times so far. It is a joke with the other royalty."

"Ahey, and this one isn't even a prophecy. Just a sleep-suggestion whispered by the local sneak," said Rip.

———

Yun kept to her promise of a breakfast with her friends, despite Scribbs's insistence that she remain close. Hope, Phoebe, Trace, Rodrigo, Scarlet, and the three children gathered in an ale hall near the royal kitchens. The children demanded a Ravenhair story from Yun, who gladly consented.

"Is it my turn to pick a number?" said Petra. Ana nodded and Ardi shrugged and Petra held a finger to her lip and thought until Ana gave her an impatient little shove. "Okayyyy!" pouted Petra, obviously nervous. "Seventy—ummm—seven."

Yun turned to the seventy-seventh story of Ravenhair and read while Phoebe and Trace prepared the morning meal of glowmoss with a small ration of eggs and ham. The story involved a particularly scary monster named Bhalereton, which delighted the children but seemed to discomfit Yun enough that Scarlet took over the reading of the story.

"Come into the light, Bhalereton and show me true!" cried Ravenhair. "You stalked the night and shadowed the day, and scared all of the Nymphs away!"

Then came a voice, most hideous and foul. "It is not my want to frighten the Nymphs, nor my desire to commit dark acts, for while my skin and flesh have been twisted, I tell you truth, Ravenhair, there's no twist of my soul."

"There are twists in your deeds, monster, both dark and terrible," called Ravenhair. "Deny it if you wish, but the Satyrs and Bulls come in vengeance to twist away your life!"

"Bhalereton you called me," cried the foul voice. "But don't you see? Untwist my name, Ravenhair, and free me."

Breakfast came to the table as Scarlet wrapped up the story. Ravenhair saved the day—and the monster's life—by untwisting the name Bhalereton to Nobleheart. Ana harrumphed and complained when it turned out there was no scary monster after all, to which Petra sniffed and said she thought it was a very beautiful story.

While the others ate and the children argued about the story, Rodrigo shifted over closer to Yun. "You look troubled," he whispered.

"Bad dreams," said Yun. "Reading too much. I have a puzzle."

"Oh?" said Rodrigo.

"I've read hundreds of books and journals by now. And do you know what I've never found? Something that I could *not* read."

"What do you mean?"

Yun parted her hair absently with her hands. "There are Dusties here from everywhere, every land and people, and books pulled from all over. But every one of them is in the same language—my language, I guess. Why are there no other languages? And have you talked to anyone who didn't understand you?"

Rodrigo's brows furrowed farther and farther as he pondered this in silence. "That is very strange."

"And yet lots of people say certain things—certain words—that I don't know, and they have different forms of speech. You say Gracia de Dios, for example."

"Grace of God, yes," said Rodrigo.

"Why?"

"I wish to honor my Lord."

"I mean, why do you say Gracia de Dios instead of Grace of God?"

"Ah, I see what you mean. I do not know."

Yun shrugged and stretched her arms. "I'm afraid I haven't found much else of obvious importance. I couldn't find anything about the Dalmar Wall or Old Haven. I learned some things from Scribbs's journals—like, that Awkley and Temma used to be in love, and that Morten and Awkley are 'safe' from Oldevil's assaults, and that it was the titan Rafe's idea for Temma to become the Great-mother, and that Scribbs is really, really mad at the other three. Oh, and sometimes it looks like Scribbs kind of loses it, and doesn't write coherently."

"Why are Awkley and Morten safe?" asked Scarlet from across the table.

"Scribbs wrote that Morten's tortures made them safe," said Yun, keeping her eyes away from Scarlet's own. "Just a mention. That's it."

Rodrigo glanced at Yun and Scarlet, his brows still furrowed. "You two are friends. Whatever else is lost, your friendship need never be, unless you throw it away yourselves."

Yun's eyes flicked up and met Scarlet's. "Sorry. Rodrigo is right."

Scarlet smiled slightly and nodded, and Yun turned to the children and involved herself in the argument over Bhalereton.

"Thanks, Grandfather," whispered Scarlet.

Rodrigo lifted his cup in mock salute.

After breakfast the Dusties broke up to pursue the day's activities. Hope decided to accompany Phoebe to an audience with Queen Temma, wishing to request approval for, and financial assistance with, a new hospice on the south side of the city.

Hope regretted that decision.

The queen scoffed at the idea, expecting Hope to instead become a matron in the castle. Hope responded with more sarcasm than was prudent. The words were barely out of her mouth when Temma flew into a senseless, fury-driven tirade, ordering the healer out of the castle immediately.

The queen then left for Bountywell, taking Phoebe with her and leaving Hope alone to pack.

———

Rodrigo met Hope at her door as she placed the last of her modest belongings into a cloth case. She flashed him a false smile and tried to hide the moisture in her eyes.

"Always knew my tongue would land me in trouble," she said, her eyes fixed down at the four cases on her bed—the sum of her possessions.

"Rip is waiting for us at the castle gate," said Rodrigo, lifting each case experimentally to find the two heaviest.

The walk to the gate progressed silently, both Hope and Rodrigo lost in their own thoughts. But upon exiting the gate, Rodrigo looked left, and a small quirk of a smile lifted his lips.

Rip sat atop a mule-pulled wagon, grinning.

Hope walked up to the wagon, full of suspicion. "Where did you get this?"

Rip tipped his sag-brimmed hat. "I purchased it fair with good money. Where d'yeh think?"

"And where did you get good money?" she said.

"The queenie is most generous." Rip grinned and hopped down with a small case. He opened it in front of her. Gold and silver coin reflected the bright light of the moss-pools.

Hope shook her head, but a smile came to her lips.

"Enough for a good building, and a hospice," said Rodrigo. His eyes flicked up over Hope's head and toward the castle gate. "But we are not about to let a beautiful young friend cart a chest of coin behind an expensive mule alone in this city…"

Trace lumbered up to them, newly dressed in a Blueboy uniform not quite large enough for him. "This pinches," he mumbled, pulling at the buttons that strained at his chest.

"Yeh look like a blueberry," suggested Rip.

"Yeah, I'm a Blueberry Boy." Trace tapped at the sewn insignia on his shoulder. "I am boss now, aren't I? People do as I say?"

"Just protect Hope," said Rodrigo. "If anyone tries to give you orders, tell them you're my aide and to talk to me."

Trace nodded and pulled his muscled bulk onto the wagon seat.

"Come see me," said Hope, her eyes moistening again.

Rodrigo surprised her then by taking her shoulders and kissing her lightly on the forehead. "I will always be close."

The mule started forward with Trace at the reins. Hope turned for a final wave and caught a troubled, almost haunted, look on the boy-commander's face. He brightened quickly and waved goodbye, but she knew that the cheerful smile that he gave her was nothing more than a mask. Something agonized him.

———

The third flame of the afternoon clock lit the sky. In the royal court, Scribbs and Yun quietly entered as Awkley discussed the campaign against the blackspawn with the titans, Rafe and Shoca. The other thrones sat empty, with Temma in Bountywell, and Morten having disappeared to his own concerns.

"My captains are convinced that the attacks have fallen off," said Rodrigo. "I have not been in the field enough yet to confirm that. There is one change, however. If I understand, in the early days, the blackspawn all awoke for only a short time in the day, and all at the same time. True?"

Shoca nodded, while Awkley chattered on about the issue. Rodrigo waited quietly for Awkley to taper off, but Scribbs did not. "I have had a vision," Scribbs announced, speaking too quietly to make much impact.

Awkley glanced back at Scribbs in annoyance, allowing Rodrigo to continue. The boy addressed Shoca directly this time. "Today there are blackspawn active every hour of the day."

Awkley began to scold Rodrigo for speaking directly to the titans, but Shoca answered directly to Rodrigo. "The world changes those who come. This would explain their altered habits and their gradual weakening."

"Hear me!" shouted Scribbs, standing up, the blood rising in his pale cheeks. "I will speak, and it will be now!"

Awkley threw up his hands. "Scribbles, you sniveling child, we are plotting the end of the blackspawn-"

"And I am prophesying the end of our greatest enemy, Oldevil!" cried Scribbs. "I see, I know, and the future is clear to me. Today I wed, and today will be the day that Bountywell rends its last!"

The poet-prophet-scribbling-king drew a long thick sash from his waistcoat pocket. He flourished it clumsily, holding it aloft and spinning to reveal the significance of the ornamented wedding sash to all in the chamber—Rodrigo, Awkley, the two titans, a few impassive tantyr guards, and Yun herself.

Scribbs turned to Yun, holding the sash above her head. "This sash represents your devotion to me, your reverence to me, and your duty to me. Do you accept?"

———

Despite the night of poetic whisperings that Rip had witnessed recently in Scribbs's chamber, neither Rodrigo nor Yun expected that this moment would come today. Scribbs had said nothing to Yun about marriage. Now, standing before the sallow-faced, half-crazed king, watching him make a mockery of a true wedding, Yun thought of running. She turned her eyes to Rodrigo. He stared at her, his eyes pained and helpless, and shook his head sadly, at a loss.

Together, at that moment, they shared the depth of despair that crushed the citizens of Pinnacle. Like everyone in the city, they were pawns and playthings for three men and one woman, whose bodies had gained immortality and superhuman power, but whose humanity had rotted away centuries ago.

Yun closed her eyes and thought of Rodrigo, and her mind tried to change reality, to see the polite, handsome young gentleman holding the sash before her, speaking words of true love and true matrimony, with friends surrounding her waiting for the moment in hushed expectation. But reality remained—the pale light of the chamber and the pale, immortal monarch standing before her with a sly smirk on his face, as though this whole event amounted to nothing more than a cruel joke. She knew that if she tried to run or if she rejected him, she and her friends would suffer unspeakable vengeance, for while Scribbs often spoke peace, she had watched him act with casual indifference and petty cruelty toward those who served him.

Her lie died. She had, in fact, landed in worse hands than Ikone's.

In her mind, Rodrigo smiled at her and kissed her lightly on her forehead. "I accept," she said.

Scribbs grinned triumphantly and looped the sash around Yun's neck. "You are bound to me then. Come, sit at the foot of my throne and witness the end of the world's greatest and oldest threat, Oldevil himself. And perhaps the end of others as well."

Yun followed Scribbs back to his seat of power. The king bounded up to his throne and sat back excitedly, like a child awaiting a puppet show. He fixed his gaze out the tall open windows that faced westward over the castle gardens and to the firelit pit of Bountywell beyond.

Awkley steepled his hands and shook his head. "That was the most painful two minutes of my considerable life. You have embarrassed yourself many times, Scribbs, but this might never be topped. Can we move on now?"

Scribbs scratched at his thin, straying hair and kept his attention out the great windows, at the ring of fire that burned around the pit of Bountywell. "It is a shame that you have protected yourself from Oldevil, Awkley. Poor Temma is not so lucky."

Awkley stared at Scribbs, then began a chuckle that rose to a full-throated laugh. "This is what our grand pacifist has become? Skulking about, thinking up ways to murder his fellows? Oh, this is rich! You put this poor girl through a mockery on the inane belief that you actually are a prophet, as if you could actually provoke Oldevil into his last gasp at the very moment that Temma is in Bountywell? You stupid, worthless fool! The girl is a beauty, Scribbles. I can think of a far better reason to marry her. Not that I would bother marrying her, mind you-"

From far off, a hollow, quavering wail penetrated Pinnacle Castle and crawled into the ears of those in the royal court. Scribbs jumped to his feet, a triumphant exhilaration building in his countenance. Awkley sputtered to a stop, appearing utterly confused and struck dumb with rising alarm.

There was no hesitancy in the titans, however. They rose instantly at the sound, barking orders to the tantyrs in the chamber.

"Third rotation to the pit, first rotation here!" commanded Rafe.

"Evacuate the soldiers from the city!" commanded Shoca.

The intensity of determination and concentration in the stone-like faces of the titans surprised Rodrigo. "Is this the Final Assault?"

"Yes," said Rafe. "You must evacuate."

"Why are you evacuating the soldiers?" said Rodrigo.

"They would only get in the way."

"I want Rodrigo here," said Awkley.

"You know the plan," said Shoca. "He must evacuate."

"I know that I wear the crown," said Awkley angrily. "And he stays."

"Very well," said Shoca. "You understand that if the Assault does make it this far, Rodrigo will likely be killed."

"Tragic," said Awkley, "but I insist."

"As you wish," said Shoca without any apparent hard feelings. "However, you and Scribbs must remain on your thrones and not move. They can sense you, so there is no value in running."

Awkley rolled his eyes. "Yes, yes, I have been through more of Oldevil's cursed Assaults than you, Shoca. And what do you expect to do yourself?"

"Stand in front of you," Shoca drew his sword and mirrored shield, "and hope that the tantyrs of Rotation Two can hold Bountywell."

The one hundred and eighty-six tantyrs that comprised Rotation Two dutifully manned their positions within Bountywell as Queen Temma completed her final "catch" of the day—a mountain of potatoes, freshly sacked. Laborers struggled to cart out the tremendous loot delivered up by the conjurations of the queen, and Phoebe wondered what it would be like to have such power along with immortality.

I would be different, thought Phoebe, but then her mind began to wonder whether she really would be, after five hundred years.

Phoebe positioned herself on the raised outer ring in the vast chamber. Imirette stood mutely beside her. The old matron seemed lost in her own thoughts, having spoken little in the walk to Bountywell.

Phoebe finally chose to break the silence. "The queen seems more and more ill-disposed toward me. Worse by the day. What is it about me that offends her so?"

Imirette sighed, as though she had been expecting the question. "She is not pleased that you dote on the three children. She also feels that you promote yourself too much. But there is something more. She says that you 'smell sour.' I did not pursue the topic."

"Hmph," snorted Phoebe. "Other than a bar of soap, I do not know how to cure that."

"I doubt that you can cure it," said Imirette with a strange finality in her voice.

Was that a warning? thought Phoebe. "Am I in danger?"

"An insect is always in danger of the tread of a man, or a queen."

Alarmed, Phoebe started to press Imirette for more, when she sensed a change in the great chamber—a steadily increasing reddish hue that bathed the walls and fortifications in crimson. Phoebe looked up. There, high up, where the small deep red circle of light had been, an angry red star grew slowly into intense brilliance.

Imirette gasped. A wail erupted from the stone plain, and Phoebe spun around.

The wail came from Temma herself. The queen abandoned her entourage of children and laborers, sprinting with her inhuman strength toward the entrance as though she were a practiced runner. "No! No! No!" she screamed as she flew past Phoebe and Imirette, her royal robe cast off, followed quickly by her emerald high-heeled slippers. A ghastly, clenching fear froze her face into a terror-mask and she ran as though Oldevil himself were behind her.

Imirette followed her queen, but old age prevented her from anything more than a fast walk. Phoebe remained at her side.

"Is this it, then? The Final Assault?" asked Phoebe.

"Stop asking fool questions—and stop following me! See to the queen!" said Imirette.

Phoebe nodded and ran after Temma, her long forest-green skirt whipping against her legs. Others converged on the queen as well, as many of the tantyrs abandoned their fortifications to form a protective ring around her. A horn filled the air with a long wail.

The world around Phoebe turned red. Scarlet bands of light flashed across the stone plain, and where they passed, a menagerie of monsters flared into existence. One red band swept directly beneath her feet, and she felt as though she were falling. Closing her eyes for a second, she bumped into something that had not been there one second ago.

She staggered back and looked up. A cat stood before her—not a cat, but an upright creature covered in a dense, short fur banded with shades of magenta. It swiveled around, flaring wide its wickedly long silver claws, and struck her. Phoebe felt the claws pierce her shoulder. It came so swiftly that it seemed as though she had only been shoved lightly, until she saw the blood.

She felt herself being picked up, lost her sense of direction, then realized she had been flung through the air. Her superb agility saved her as she twisted around, managing to land at an angle and roll before sliding along the polished smooth stone of the outer ring. She came to rest against the brick-laid wall of a fortified tower.

For a time she lay there on her side, stunned but feeling little pain, even from the shoulder. On the stone plain in front of her, monsters swept by in the direction of Temma and the exit—a scattering of the not-cats surrounded by a horde of short, toothy lizard creatures sprinting along on two rangy legs, their speed and movements so fast that they seemed to blur. At times a low, flat creature, like a scorpion with rhino hide, plodded by, as large as a plow horse but shorter than a man. Each had cases of javelins tied to their flat backs, and with their long, tentacled tails they grasped the weapons and flung them with whip-cracking force over their bodies.

The monsters trampled over scattered bodies, including the tangled, broken form of Imirette, thrown not far from where Phoebe herself lay. Phoebe looked away, struggling to come to grips with the violent death of a person who had conversed with her not seconds before.

A second flare of red rent the stone plain, and hundreds more of Oldevil's minions appeared, searching for enemies. Phoebe found her feet, leaning against the wall for support. Her heart threatened to pound from her chest as she realized that within seconds she would be torn to pieces. Spinning, she ran to the back of the tower and found a thin ladder leading up to the tower's battlement. She began climbing, becoming aware of pain growing in her shoulder.

Halfway up, a pair of the lizards appeared below, spotted her, and leapt. Phoebe let out a stifled scream as the two reptiles landed on the rungs directly below her and began climbing with quicksilver speed. Phoebe closed her eyes. Claws dug into and through her dress and she screamed fully, nearly losing her grip on the ladder. Pain seared her as she felt the skin tear on her legs and sides and arms. The horses flashed through her mind, and the barn, and the dream of her brother and sisters, and she tried to hold on to those thoughts rather than accept what was being done to her, rip by rip and tear by tear.

Sobbing and crying out, it occurred to her muted mind that the tearing had ceased. Slowly she raised her head and discovered that she was alone on the ladder. She looked up.

One of the lizards returned downward, falling past Phoebe with its head no longer attached. Above her, the whipping tail of the second monster lifted high and a tantyr appeared, bearing the lizard to the edge and flinging it outward. Then the tantyr stiffened, felt for the javelin that had pierced it through from side to side, and toppled over the battlement.

Phoebe climbed, her mind folding inward, her vision narrowing to the few rungs above. Her tattered willpower moved one hand and then the other, until at last she stood at the battlement. She staggered forward, nearly losing her balance before steadying herself on a swivel-mounted spear-thrower. Blood trickled lightly down her arm, but the scene below gripped her attention.

Near the entrance, a sea of combatants tore at each other. Ranks of tantyrs just outside the entrance pushed slowly forward, expertly slicing through the press of reptiles and not-cats but losing a few of their number with every step. Twenty paces separated them from an encircled island of tantyrs protecting the green-clad Queen Temma. Reptiles flung themselves upon the surrounded tantyrs, leaping into the host only to be cut down. Yet their suicidal charges distracted the tantyrs enough for their allies to find openings and make a killing thrust or cut. Phoebe could hear Queen Temma screaming out useless orders in the midst of the chaos.

Several tantyrs tried to fly in from the entrance to help the surrounded force, but two were pierced through with javelins from the scorpion-like beasts and fell helpless into the massed enemy. A few towers remained in action, firing their own deadly spears into the slow-moving scorpionids. Everywhere she looked, she witnessed merciless savagery as wounded were dragged into the ranks of enemies and slaughtered.

Red flashed again across the plain, filling with hundreds more enemies. Phoebe noticed that this time the horde contained few of the reptiles but many humans who rushed into the battle with a wide array of weapons and armor—bows, crossbows, swords, maces, and short spears. They fought expertly in close coordination with each other, unlike the disorganized but lightning assault of the reptiles. The tantyrs clearly outmatched their foes singly, but the much greater numbers of the enemy at first stopped then pushed back the relieving force of tantyrs. Temma's own surrounded force shrank steadily.

And then a fourth red burst surged across the plain. This force contained nothing but humans, including two warriors who stood out from the others. Crimson flashes snapped around them like tiny bolts of lightning. They dashed forward with an effortless grace of movement, flanked by dozens of protective troops bearing long thin swords in each hand.

Temma let out a piercing scream. The tantyrs that had surrounded her were utterly overcome, and the queen fought back alone, her inhuman strength scattering enemies about her. The press of invaders fell back, avoiding direct conflict with her. A not-cat called frantically to the newly entered humans, and one of the crimson warriors rushed forward.

Phoebe, her body bloodied and torn and her mind wracked with terrors, nevertheless focused on the singular event below. Queen Temma was in true danger, and the crimson warrior who advanced swiftly toward her represented that danger. Phoebe held no love for the queen, nor for any of the deranged royalty, but a resolve grew within her—she could not allow this savage horde a victory that could spell the death of every human in the city.

Something slid across Phoebe's mind—a strange, liquid-clear focus that flooded her pain away—and she acted. She checked the spear-thrower on which she leaned, found it cocked and loaded, and swung it around on target. Steadying the machine with one elbow and hip, she drew her aim through the double peep sight, pulled a last breath, and brought slow, steady force on the trigger. The spear-thrower swiveled by the barest fractions, following the target. And then the trigger reached its release point.

The spear flew outward and down. A sword-wielding bodyguard caught sight of the projectile and threw himself toward his crimson-charged master.

But the spear slid by, over his outstretched arms, and sank deeply into the red warrior, who pitched forward and fell against the stone, unmoving.

A hush fell over the humans. They turned to look at their fallen leader. And then, in a vengeful rush, they overcame Queen Temma and slashed her apart.

406

No flesh remained of the queen—only a fading cloud of wispy yellow smoke and a shimmering star of blue light as her circlet flashed out of existence.

The enemy force surged on toward the exit, but a few turned their attention to the tower from where the killing spear had come. Phoebe's eyes grew wide and she ducked below the battlement wall. Had they seen her? They would know the direction of the spear in any case.

The dizziness and the raw pain of her wounds took hold. Her arms and legs were cut but not flayed, but the tear in her side and the puncture wounds on her shoulder looked more serious. She fought back the panic and nausea, tearing pieces from her already shredded dress and wrapping them around her waist as well as she could.

The sounds of battle slowly muted—no less intense but shifting to the pit outside. Above that rumble, the tower ladder creaked. Phoebe's breath caught in her throat. She looked around for a weapon but her vision spun and she sank against the stone parapet. She pressed her hand against the wound at her side and choked back a cry of agony.

A furred hand gripped the ladder top and one of the not-cats vaulted itself up onto the battlement, crouching into fighting stance immediately. It saw the small, wounded human female and cast about for other enemies, but none were present. Slowly it turned its focus on Phoebe, its large violet eyes wide and fierce, and its lips folded back in a ferocious snarl. Phoebe lowered her head and closed her eyes. She felt the heat of the not-cat's breath on the top of her head, heard the spear-thrower swivel slightly, and then the creature let loose a powerful, guttural roar and slammed its claws violently through Phoebe's hair on either side of her head, nicking one side of her neck.

Phoebe cried out and opened her eyes, staring directly into the violet wells of rage in the creature's face, inches from her own.

Terror and pain overcame her, and she slid sideways, helpless. The creature gripped her head tightly with one hand and lifted his other high, claws outspread.

Behind him, a second not-cat appeared, barked harsh orders, and moved forward. The first reluctantly released its grip on Phoebe, snarled fiercely at the second, and retreated to the ladder.

For a moment, the second not-cat stared at the young woman, seeing the oozing flow of blood from her shoulder. A low growl issued from his taut, emotion-quivering lips. Glancing back toward the now empty ladder, he stepped to Phoebe, tore a long piece from her dress, bound the shoulder tightly, and loped back to the ladder, sliding lightly down.

When the wail of the Bountywell alarm lanced through the city, Hope was in the south markets, on the dimly lit second floor of a building available for rent. Beside her, the building's owner gave a yelp of shock, gasped out something about her uncle, and ran for the stairs without a word to Hope.

Hope descended the stairs and exited out onto the front landing. The wide street, so subdued a moment ago, had become panic personified.

Market-goers and sellers screamed, shouted, and ran into each other in their haste to get home, or out of the city, or into the cellars of their stores. Many Blueboys and Hunters, knowing their orders to leave the city at the sound of the alarm, and more than willing to comply, immediately looked to their own needs and began looting the market of useful supplies and transport.

Hope tried to catch sight of Trace, who had gone into the markets on the other side of the street to find a new belt. Not seeing him, she retrieved her package of newly purchased medicines from within the doorway and started making her way back to her wagon.

But the wagon had new occupants.

———

In the chaos, three Blueboy soldiers found a mule and the unattended wagon it pulled, and began filling it with the loot found nearby. Hope walked toward them hesitantly.

"Hey, lookit," said the first Blueboy, his squinted eyes roaming over Hope.

"She's got healer supplies in her hands, don't she?" said the second, trying to pull on a pair of newly acquired boots.

"Sure does," said Squinteye. "You thinking the same thing?"

Boots nodded. "Useful. Not bad looking either."

"You two crazy?" said the third Blueboy.

"Crazy?" said Squinteye. "By blazes, it's the end of the world! It's us that matters and nobody else."

"Besides," said Boots, his long face contorting into a lopsided leer, "we'd be saving her life getting her out of the city. And later, she can thank us proper."

The third Blueboy shook his head, but the other two acted. They slid from the wagon, smiled nicely to the confused healer as they approached, and threw a tarp over her head. The young woman cried out muffled shouts until Boots silenced her with a powerful backhand clout to her covered face. Squinteye held her limp form as Boots looped a cord around the tarp and trussed her tightly.

Throwing the stunned woman into the back of the wagon, they started to hop back on when they noticed a large Blueboy standing at the mule's head. He held the reins, having yanked them out of the third Blueboy's hands.

Squinteye and Boots immediately bailed back off the wagon and confronted the big man, having become used to bullying over the years. The size of this stranger gave them pause, but they brought their spears to the ready.

"Wagon's ours," said Squinteye. "Get your own."

"I like mule," said the large man, who pulled at the collar of his too-tight shirt. "I like wagon. I don't like you."

"Get lost or we'll pin ya," said Boots. He pushed his spear point forward until it pressed against the big man's chest.

Squinteye chuckled. Everyone around the market knew that the big oaf had made a serious mistake.

The big man's voice changed slightly, becoming smoother, quieter. He leaned into the spear point and tapped it, staring into the eyes of his would-be killer, Boots. "I thank you for the permission," he said.

Boots dropped his brows in confusion and contempt. "For what?"

"For this," whispered the giant. In a flash, his large hands snatched the spear from Boot's hands so forcefully that the rogue was momentarily lifted in the air. And then the spear passed through Boots's chest. Squinteye shouted in disbelief and backed up, not used to being opposed and generally relying on Boots when it came to violence.

The giant continued to stare at Boots until his struggling ceased. Then he lowered both spear and man to the ground and turned to Squinteye.

Squinteye fled.

The giant turned his gaze on the third Blueboy sitting on the buckboard.

The third nodded and tipped his ragged beret. "Old boy had it coming," he said. "Wagon is yours. There's a woman in the back. You should make sure she's okay. I would have taken care of her." He stepped off the buckboard and walked away.

Trace took the reins and drove the wagon out of the city.

Forty minutes after the wail of the Bountywell alarm, not a single tantyr of Rotation Two or Three remained alive within a javelin's throw of Bountywell or the pit leading into it. Despite the difficulty of overcoming the many fortifications, and having lost thousands at the hands of the four hundred tantyr defenders, the Assault horde now bore down on the long-neglected garden gate of the castle. Although the Oldevil attackers brought forward small but wickedly designed siege engines, they had no need, for the rotted old gate could not even be properly shut and barricaded.

The tantyrs of Rotation One and a few survivors of Rotation Three struck desperately at the now-diminished horde, exacting a brutal toll but losing their numbers by ones and twos. The attackers pushed past the castle courtyard, through the halls now choked with bodies and pooled with blood of several colors, and finally reached the threshold of the royal court itself.

A thin, final line of tantyrs held momentarily, wavered, and broke. The assault pushed through dozens of its own dead and expanded into the room, bearing down on King Awkley, who watched with hands in lap, and King Scribbs, whose white knuckles pressed at his throne's arms and whose fingernails bent against the stone with the pressure of his seizing fright.

Between them, Rafe, Shoca, and a line of thirty handpicked tantyrs waited.

The horde smashed into the final tantyr line, wounding several with ranged weapons before the court fell into a tightly pressed melee. Rodrigo stood beside Awkley, his heart racing at the fierceness of the fighting taking place only a few paces away. Conflict tore through him—an overriding drive to fight and defend the city, yet at the same time a darker desire to see an end to the royals, even at the city's peril.

Awkley watched him out of the corner of his eye.

As the battle closed tighter and tighter on the two titans, Rodrigo's eyes widened and his attention became consumed by a mixture of shock and amazement—for the titans entered into full battle.

Never had Rodrigo seen, or even considered, anything like what he saw. Rafe and Shoca struck back and forth across the battle line like lightning strokes, their four arms engaged in a blurred dance of bloodshed, the two coordinating their efforts with deadly efficiency. At times a blow or dart from their tiny foes landed, but these did nothing more than draw bloodless scratches against their tough hide. Bodies piled high along their line of attack, and as the tantyrs slowly fell, the two titans surged faster and more furiously.

Then Rodrigo realized that little more than the titans themselves remained against a force of no more than a dozen enemies wielding thin dual swords. The two forces smashed into each other in a last violent spasm of fury. And in that moment of whirling chaos, the last crimson-charged Assault captain appeared at the court threshold.

He sprinted across the body-strewn stone, vaulted a wounded tantyr that tried to slice him, bounded through the pile of dead, and leapt high, straight at the fear-struck Scribbs. His hand reached out, grasping at the silver circlet atop Scribbs's head.

But his fingers stopped less than an inch from the circlet as Rafe's top left hand gripped the captain's shoulder and neck. For a moment the captain was suspended in place, his fingers trying desperately for the circlet. And then Rafe lowered him and raised one sword.

"Don't kill him!" screamed Awkley. "Rafe, no!"

Rafe heard and stopped his blow within inches. He gripped the captain in two vise-like hands and turned back to the battle.

To Rodrigo's surprise, no enemies attempted to rescue their captain. The small remaining contingent of Assault forces had fallen away from the two titans and were roaming wildly among the bodies, slaughtering any wounded tantyrs that they could find. Shoca roared and raced through their final numbers, cutting down the remainder with breathtaking speed and efficiency. The few standing tantyrs gave equal quarter to the wounded enemy, dispatching them with vengeful violence. Rodrigo found himself nodding grimly. *No quarter given, no quarter taken.*

"Crump!" yelled a voice from the small servant's door to Rodrigo's left. Rodrigo jumped, realizing that he had been crouched tensely with hand on sword throughout the battle. He turned and saw King Morten hurrying in, sword in hand, followed by Commander Boar. Both looked upon the piles of dead with changing cycles of elation and pained disbelief. The grand, final battle for which King Morten had been waiting a century had come and gone in the space of an hour, and he had completely missed it.

"Morten, my friend, where in the blazes were you?" shouted Awkley, breaking from his own stunned condition. "I've never witnessed anything like it, not in five centuries! Our titans are absolutely unstoppable!"

Morten gripped his head and danced about in rage. "I was in my place of study...I cannot—ughhh!—how can..."

"Scribbs came this close, Morten." Awkley held up his hand and squeezed his finger and thumb together. "*This* close! And I mean that quite literally. Rafe caught the Oldevil cur in mid-leap. If I had been behind Scribbs, I could have but tapped his head forward a bit and the deed would have been done, the crown captured. I almost wish I had."

He gave Scribbs a cruel leer, which slowly transformed into confusion.

Scribbs sat on his throne, unmoving, his eyes cast upward and his mouth agape, as though he had been frozen in time at the moment of the enemy's leap.

"Scribbles!" shouted Awkley. "You can quit your fit of cowardice. The long game is finally played out, and we've won!"

Scribbs shivered, blinked his eyes, and muttered something under his breath, but he continued the mortally shocked look and the terrified skyward stare.

The two kings and their commanders moved in closer to the fear-stricken, catatonic king. Awkley waved a hand in front of Scribbs's face, then slapped him casually. Scribbs remained staring, and Rodrigo noticed that the king's hands shook in spasmodic waves.

Awkley grunted. "Looks like the little toad has gone useless," he said.

"Has been useless for a long, long time," muttered Morten.

"Well, if we're lucky, he'll stay this way," said Awkley. "His brand-new bride can drag him back to his chambers."

"No, leave him here," smiled Morten, "at least for now. It's amusing to see the pitiful coward transfixed like this. Payback for all those years of sniveling. And, that reminds me…where is our Oldevil assassin?—ah, Rafe, you've caught a bug."

Rafe held the struggling enemy captain in three hands and wielded one sword in the fourth as he moved through the piles of bodies, dispatching wounded enemies with deft, casual strokes. The fierce oriental face of the Oldevil captain bobbed upside down between two of the giant's fingers, blushing with effort, glowing red with the crackling glow of his Bountywell energy, and stained crimson with blood smeared across his bald head. He made no attempt to speak to Morten as the king moved close, but instead continued his hopeless struggle.

"Come, Rafe, bring our prize along. I have many months of labor ahead to mold him to my liking." Morten grinned nastily at the Oldevil captain. "My friend, you are about to embark on a long, unpleasant journey."

King Morten turned and led Rafe away into the corridors.

95: Celebration

— 3 days later

Yun's diary, Day 201

This world is a never-ending parade of cruel jokes. I am wed now to a lump of flesh. An immortal, quivering lump of flesh.

Days passed. Of Oldevil's hordes, no survivors could be found, expending themselves completely in their single-minded effort to reach Scribbs, their wounded having been dispatched by order of the kings. Blueboy and Hunter captains sought to regather the evacuated troops and quell the anger of the citizens who were targets of the widespread looting and brutality of the undisciplined soldiers. Those who complained too bitterly were forced to clear the battle of corpses and cleanse the castle of blood. Hundreds of tantyr dead burned on the pyres and the thousands of slaughtered enemy burned in the death-pits.

The royalty prepared a great festival.

Oldevil—greatest and most ancient of threats to the Spire—had been finally, totally, defeated. Of Oldevil's red star in Bountywell, no trace remained.

Queen Temma returned to life, elated and full of her own tales. Most of the children and servants that had attended her had died in the attack, but this did not appear to dampen her spirits.

Scarlet and Rip found Phoebe in the castle hospice. Hope arrived as well, insisting on seeing to Phoebe's wounds. So, despite having been thrown out of the castle by Temma, she walked past the castle guards and into the hospice aided by the presence of both Trace and Rodrigo.

At the tenth hour the festivities began with Awkley announcing to the host of select soldiers and citizens, "After centuries, victory has come!" The gathered citizens of Pinnacle responded with a ragged wave of cheers and shouts, and a clamor for a more abundant flow of the great store of spirits brought forth for the occasion.

Among the Dusties, little could be found to celebrate. Yun sat next to Scribbs's throne, her head down in numb embarrassment, unable to shut out the mocking comments spoken too loudly nearby. She and a few servants took care of the catatonic king, returning him to the throne at the insistence of Awkley and Morten.

Rodrigo, Trace, and Captain Zales kept in a tight knot near Awkley's throne, discussing the trials of the day in dealing with the ill behavior of a great number of Blueboys. Rodrigo had responded sternly to his rebellious soldiers, throwing many in prison, having others flogged, and even wounding one officer who refused orders and attempted to strike him. Word circulated that Rodrigo, like many other commanders before him, was already reaching the end of his service, to be cast aside by Awkley. The boy-commander now eyed Boar with some measure of envy as he drank and reveled with his devoted soldiers.

Rodrigo did not bring discipline against Trace, despite the killing of a fellow Blueboy. While many agreed with Trace's actions, others considered it nothing better than murder. Whispers of favoritism filtered through the ranks.

Scarlet and Rip stayed in the wings and shadows of the room, not wishing to bring themselves to the attention of the royals for fear that they would be dismissed like Hope.

Phoebe and Hope remained in the hospice. Phoebe's wounds were cleaned, sterilized, and stitched. Although she insisted that she would be fine, Hope commanded bed rest. Phoebe fell asleep soon after, far more exhausted than she would admit. Queen Temma made no mention of Phoebe's spectacular and royalty-saving shot with the spear-thrower. Phoebe wasn't certain that anyone had actually witnessed her killing act, and she had no desire to bring it up herself. In fact, a gnawing, terrible sense of guilt pulled her frame of mind downward. Despite the understanding that she had saved the queen, she had pierced the life of another human being, and that split-second decision now haunted her. Tears came to her eyes often, and she vowed never to take a life again, even if it meant losing her own.

Of Ed, there had been no trace for four days. None of the other Dusties concerned themselves with finding him, assuming that he had once again discovered something more interesting than human beings.

———

As the clock fires extinguished for midnight and the revelry turned drunken and clumsy, King Awkley returned to his throne, leaned back into the soft thickness of the draped fabric, and hugged himself, his face relaxing into a lazy smile.

His eyes closed momentarily, and he thought once again of Oldevil vanquished. This time he imagined the monster as a giant spider, its gnarled legs curled and its hideous, bloated body shriveling as its life and power drained away.

He drew in another satisfied breath and opened his eyes.

With Oldevil no longer a concern, he could turn his attention to other troubling matters.

414

His eyes once again found Rodrigo in the crowd.

———

Despite the abundance of heady drinks available at the festivities, the normally appreciative Scarlet and Rip did little more than sip at their short, fat cups. Captain Zales had downed rounds with his soldiers but left it at that, and the few glassfuls swallowed by Trace had small effect on the giant man.

Their thirst had all been cut short watching Rodrigo, who in the past hour had ceased his good-natured banter and had started staring into his cup, clearly caught up in wrestling over some thought.

"I think I'll check in on my men, sir," said Captain Zales, scanning over the sea of uniforms in the large hall. "Give them a few tall tales to keep their minds off brawling."

"Keep them by your side, Captain," said Rodrigo.

Zales paused. "Expecting trouble, sir?"

Rodrigo smiled. "Trouble in a mixed sea of high-spirited Blueboys and Hunters?"

Zales nodded slowly. "Aye, sir, that's always trouble." He gave Rodrigo an appraising stare, then strode away, all evidence of revelry having left his face.

Rip took a stand on a chair next to Rodrigo. He let go a laugh and raised his cup, but his voice came low and quiet, "The royals have been bugging their eyes at yeh all night. And whispering away."

Rodrigo displayed a grin. "Did you manage to catch any of their talk?"

"Neh. They clap up their lips quick if anyone gets close."

"Keep watching." Rodrigo nodded and turned to take another look over at Yun, who sat cross-legged at the foot of Scribbs's throne, as she had done all night.

———

King Morten leaned on the arm of Awkley's throne, his lips near to Awkley's ear but his eyes roving over the drunken press of humanity.

"Five centuries, Awkley. Is it just a dream?"

These same words had been spoken by Morten at least ten times that evening, and yet King Awkley never tired of hearing them. His smile grew into a gloating grin once again. "No dream, old friend. We outlasted the monster. The demon is no more."

———

Rodrigo stooped once again to Yun. "Are you certain you do not wish to join us?"

Yun lifted a hand to his knee and managed a weak smile that died quickly. "I can't, Rodrigo. My place is here now, when I am in the royal court."

Rodrigo bit at his lip. He wanted to yell at her, to explain to her—no, to demand that she see—the mockery that was her so-called wedding to Scribbs—this cruel, abusive monster that now sat helpless in his throne.

Rodrigo's hand touched at his sword hilt. One swipe of its sharp edge, and King Scribbs would be a satisfying cloud of yellow smoke...

His hand came up, and his finger swept the hair at Yun's ear. "Would you mind if we came and sat with you?"

She tried to smile, but her lip trembled and a tear welled up and fell from her delicate round cheek. "That would be...nice."

Rodrigo caught the attention of Trace, Rip, and Scarlet, and they gathered around her.

———

King Morten smiled again—a thin stretch of the lips that showed no teeth, but King Awkley could tell something gnawed at his friend's mind. "What could possibly be bothering you at a time like this?"

"You don't find it difficult believing our immortality is now forever?" said Morten. "That our enemies are no more?"

"Oh, Morten," groaned Awkley, rolling his eyes in a showy display of disgust. "You are ever the pessimist. Our enemies? Oldevil was our only true fear."

"And that Devourer Abberatas," corrected Morten.

"Abberatas?" Awkley laughed longer than necessary. "Abberatas was never more than a worry—and a worry trapped forever, thanks to me."

Morten nodded in agreement, but some unspoken thought clouded his eyes. "Still, it is hard to imagine, immortality forever and ever."

"Do you intend to continue your studies?" said Awkley.

King Morten cast a careful gaze back toward Queen Temma and King Scribbs, and his smile turned into a cruel grimace. "Oh, every intention, my friend. My studies are so very important. If I can find the key to our immortality, I can bring an end to those two, and we can both wear two crowns. Imagine our power then."

Morten's words subdued Awkley's cheer. "Really, Morten, I'm quite adequately powerful enough already. Your studies could easily be turned against us."

Morten gave no answer to that.

"But, no matter," sighed Awkley, glancing past Morten. "Temma is coming over here. Mind your words."

———

Scarlet finished an outrageous tale that successfully wrung a genuine smile out of Yun. She had kept her eyes on Rodrigo during the storytelling, and now she tapped his foot with her own.

"What's wrong, Rodrigo?" she asked.

Rip flipped a hand dismissively. "He'll not say, been clammy all-"

And then Rodrigo spoke, pointing a finger at Trace. "Why did they have the soldiers evacuate from the city during the Final Assault?"

"Rafe and Shoca ordered it, so us humans don't get hurt," rumbled Trace. "Battle too scary."

Rodrigo glanced at the two immense titans, who sat like marble statues at the back of the royal court. "I know that is what they told us, but what if there is another reason?"

Scarlet's lips curled in a smirk. "Seems straightforward to me. You have an odd theory, haven't you?"

"I do. What if the titans and kings feared that the soldiers would side with Oldevil? After all, humans fought for Oldevil as well."

Trace wrinkled his face in disgust. "Never heard any Blueboys want Oldevil."

"Nor I," said Rodrigo, "but the royals do not need any truth to fuel their suspicions."

"But they've treated their soldiers well in the past," said Yun.

"Except those they used for blood sport, like Awkley's commanders. Like me," said Rodrigo.

Yun leaned on Rodrigo's arm and clutched it.

He gave her a reassuring squeeze on her shoulder, regretting his sharp reply. "You are right, Yun. They have treated the soldiers with some regard. But that was before this week."

"Before the Final Assault?" said Scarlet. "How does that change things? With the tantyr forces all but destroyed, the royals need their soldiers more than ever."

At this, Rodrigo smiled. "Everyone agrees that Oldevil was the greatest fear. In fact, it sounds like Oldevil was the only threat to the immortality of the royals. But the Final Assault failed. The royals now fear nothing."

Agreement came with emphatic nods and grunts.

"So," said Rodrigo quietly, "what will our insane, bloodthirsty, immortal rulers do with soldiers—or Dusties—that they neither trust nor need for protection?"

96: TREASON

Queen Temma approached Awkley's throne. Kings Morten and Awkley greeted her warmly.

"Here's to forever!" said Awkley, raising his glass.

"Yes, and setting things right," said Temma sourly. "The safety of the children must take greater priority."

"Oh, agreed!" said Morten sarcastically.

Temma swept her eyes over the celebrating crowd. "I can no longer accept your soldier brutes in my castle. Only my Greencloaks are allowed here, starting tomorrow."

"Your Greencloaks!" laughed Awkley, sighting his cup at the revelers. "Your oh-so-proper Greencloaks are cavorting strenuously with my Blueboys as we speak. I reject your proposal. Morten?"

"Rejected," quipped Morten.

Before Temma could begin building a flying rage, Awkley pointed a finger at her. "But...you *will* like this."

Temma managed to calm herself.

Awkley waved them in closer. "Now, we agree that there's something not right about those Lakesiders. Not right at all. And their presence here might have poisoned the minds of others."

"Agreed," said Temma. Her eyes wandered to the small knot of whispering Lakesiders gathered around Yun. "And I don't trust your Blueboys after you stupidly put Rodrigo in charge."

"Ah!" gasped Awkley. "That's it exactly. I don't trust all my Blueboys either. I did try to kill Rodrigo, if you remember. Commander Sheare failed me quite badly. But now, I think Temma is wise. Let's do away with Rodrigo, and give my Blueboys the test. What do you say?"

Morten agreed with a smile of expectation.

Temma pursed her lips in silence for a moment, until she arched a finger at Awkley in the manner of a lady addressing her peasant. "Very well, but if there's bloodshed, it's on your hands."

"Oh, of course," grinned Awkley, washing his hands of imaginary blood as Temma retreated back to her throne.

———

Rip was the first to speak after Rodrigo's chilling statement. "What do we do then? I'll not curl up and wait for the axe on meh neck."

"We need to return to Lakeside, at least for now." Rodrigo's eyes wandered to the three whispering royals gathered around Awkley's throne, and for a second it seemed that Awkley met his gaze. He looked away quickly. "And I think it would be wise to hurry."

Scarlet flared his eyes. "We've been awake two hundred days and managed three separate death penalties in three different cities. Is it just me or does that sound above average?"

"Ettins!" spat Rip. "Your stinking cities can all go stick their heads in the drop-pot. To Lakeside, I agree."

"How do we possibly get back to Lakeside?" said Scarlet.

Rodrigo stroked his chin and shook his head, his eyes boring into the stone floor.

"I don't understand the titans," said Yun. "Surely Rafe and Shoca would help us. They're here to uphold honor."

Rip laughed sarcastically. "Those two lumps? They've lifted n'hardly a finger against the royals' wishes since we got here."

Scarlet raised his hand. "Let's get back to getting back to Lakeside. Seems important."

"Climb down to the tunnel entrance from above," said Rip.

"Easy, if there wasn't a mesa full of Pinnacle troops and nasty blackspawn in our way," said Scarlet. "And some of us can't climb."

"I fall off ropes," explained Trace.

The three escalated the discussion among themselves, leaving Rodrigo to his furious thoughts and Yun clutching his arm.

"Rafe and Shoca," she said to herself, and she managed a pleased smile.

"Hmm?" said Rodrigo absently.

She leaned up and whispered in his ear.

He turned to her slowly, his brows furrowing.

"Odd, isn't it?" she said.

What's odd?" said Scarlet.

"Oh that-"

Rodrigo's hands clamped tightly to Yun's mouth and the back of her head, silencing her. She strained her eyes sideways. Rodrigo held her tightly a moment, utter shock on his face.

The others froze.

Scarlet gave an uncertain smile. "What are you..."

Rodrigo's lips came to Yun's ear. "I did not mean to scare you. I will remove my hand now. Do not repeat what you said to anyone. Promise?"

She nodded slowly, and he removed his hands.

"Count to five, then get up. Walk through the kitchens and out to the hospital. Get Phoebe and Hope to the Watchtower hallway. Phoebe knows what that is."

Yun's breath came quickly. "We're in trouble, aren't we? Real trouble?"

He smiled warmly. "Start counting."

Rodrigo laughed, turning to the other three. "Count to twenty. Then get to the children's dorms and find Ana, Ardi, and Petra. Take them to the Watchtower hallway. The children know where that is. You should find Yun and the others there. Then get out of the castle, find an abandoned house, and stay hidden."

Yun stood, turned stiffly, and headed to the kitchens, her head down and her face hidden behind her bangs.

"What about you?" whispered Scarlet as he watched Yun pass, his lips in a cheerful grin but his eyes pleading for understanding.

Rodrigo smiled then—a genuine, grateful expression, and he took each of their hands, careful not to be seen doing so. "Take care of them for me."

"That's not an acceptable answer," warned Scarlet.

But Rodrigo had already stood and turned away from them.

———

Rodrigo strode toward the tables holding the wine barrels. He lowered his cup to a spigot, watching the last of the wine dribble into it. He felt as if he had a memory then, a comforting flash of home and family and old wine brought from the cellars for a joyous feast. Wherever that dream drifted, he wished then that he could reach out and draw himself far, far from here.

But he turned then, and his steps took him slowly, deliberately, toward Awkley and Morten.

———

"No one will lift a finger to help Rodrigo," said Morten with confidence.

"A wager then." Awkley raised a finger. "The boy has friends. I'll say at least twenty will foolishly stick their necks out for him."

Morten tapped the stone confidently. "A thousand coin on that. If there are only nineteen fools, I win."

Awkley steepled his hands pleasantly, as if in prayer. "Fair enough."

"And how will you accuse the boy?" said Morten.

"Oh..." said Awkley, rising and spreading his hands confidently. "That is so very easy."

Awkley turned, found Rodrigo close by off to his left, staring at him. Awkley paused, gave the young man a gentleman's nod, and then raised his hands to the sky.

"Hear me!"

———

Scarlet, Rip, and Trace were halfway to the court's east archway exit, pushing their way through revelers, when Awkley stepped away from the huddle of rulers and shouted, "Hear me!"

The crowd, despite its drunken state, quieted quickly. Scarlet turned and found an open spot to better see the king.

"It is with deep regret that I announce today that we have a traitor among us," continued Awkley.

Those who had not yet fully given their attention to the king lowered their cups and took note.

Awkley strode to the edge of the platform, leaning out and offering up a splendidly traumatized expression. "During the Final Assault, this traitor stood casually by as our loyal allies, the tantyrs, died fighting against Oldevil's savages. Despite being allowed a position of honor defending our dear fellow King Scribbs, this man did not lift a finger as Oldevil's demon minion stretched out his hand to rip the crown from our royal Scribbs. In fact, it seemed as though this man sympathized with Oldevil itself."

"Who?" said a voice from the crowd.

"What's this about?" came another.

Awkley brought up his hand, and his voice rose in intensity. "I regret to inform you that this foul traitor, this deceiver, is none other than my current commander, Rodrigo."

When Scarlet heard Awkley's outrageous lie and accusation, he acted instantly, understanding the mortal danger that suddenly confronted them. Awkley clearly intended a purge, and that would include all of Rodrigo's friends. Scarlet discreetly urged Rip and Trace along toward the exit, his head down, but he turned for a last glance at the platform. He spotted Rodrigo standing near Awkley, doing nothing more than sip at his wine cup.

And then Scarlet's eyes locked momentarily with Awkley. Awkley's outstretched finger, currently pointed at the accused Rodrigo, swiveled toward Scarlet.

"Stop them!" yelled the king. "Stop that giant and the midget and—and that weasely looking fellow!"

Soldiers followed where he pointed, spotted Trace's hulking figure, and closed in.

Ten paces separated the three from the archway. "Push it!" shouted Scarlet to Trace. Trace nodded and stormed forward, holding his spear sideways. A squad of still-confused Hunters scattered out of the way of the lumbering giant, but the Hunters behind them reacted with drawn weapons. Scarlet drew his own sword and rushed forward past Trace.

Scarlet's heart sank when he saw the elite Black Huntsman insignia on the eight Hunters at the archway. The three had little chance against Boar's best, especially with others closing in behind and to the side. Scarlet's mind made a snap decision, and he lowered his head in a full rush. Trace and Rip could get through if he could break the line.

His shoulder bumped into someone else. Startled, he found Captain Zales of the Blueboys running next to him. The captain's entire command of sixty soldiers were following, charging beside them toward the archway.

There was no time to think after that. Scarlet slammed into a Hunter, barely blocked a swipe to his head, stumbled headlong into the hall, and felt a piercing pain in his thigh. He looked down to see a spear point slide away from his leg, leaving a gash. The fallen Hunter next to him tried to reorient his spear, but Scarlet caught him in the head with his boot heel.

"Left-left-left!" yelled Scarlet as he scrambled back to his feet. "Leftward!" he heard Captain Zales repeat. The company of mutineers and the three Lakesiders sprinted down the hall and up the curving stairway toward the next level of the castle, leaving nine of their number dead or captured at the archway.

Rodrigo watched in apprehension as the chaotic, violent jumble at the archway quieted. The chase moved on, deeper into the castle. Black Huntsmen dragged dead, wounded, and captured from the hallway—all Blueboys of Zales's command, but no more than ten. It appeared possible that his friends had escaped, and with a last hopeful glance and a muttered prayer, Rodrigo turned to face the kings and queen.

Awkley took his eyes off the archway as well. Turning to Rodrigo, he folded his arms and gave a half-shake of his head, as if to say "I knew it."

"Clear the court!" shouted Temma.

The court emptied with surprising speed, the staggering drunks driven to lively action by a cadre of Temma's Greencloak guards not permitted to engage in the festivities, and therefore motivated to punish the revelers.

A squad of Black Huntsmen dragged their four unwounded Blueboy captives to the front of the court. Three tantyrs moved forward to surround Rodrigo. Awkley returned to his throne, leaning back and rocking his dangling legs like a small child on a porch swing. He looked satisfied, as though a stubborn itch had suddenly cleared up.

"And now, let's get to the bottom of things. What have you been plotting, traitor?" said Awkley.

Rodrigo bowed stiffly. "I am plotting merely to keep my friends safe, nothing more."

Awkley snorted. "Your greasy friends deserve no safety. Decent fellows don't bolt and run when they've been unmasked."

Rodrigo remained silent, but his mind prowled the twisted paths ahead of him.

Like a lamp to darkness, Yun's whispered words had revealed the truth to him. That, and the rant of an insane murderer, Lord Grager of Rook Clan.

The scattered pieces of the puzzle fell readily into place, and Rodrigo knew then why Pinnacle had fallen so swiftly into decline—and why every man, woman, and child living within the city could be dead in a matter of days.

He would need to act with extreme care, yet time was running out.

Rodrigo glanced over at Commander Boar, who stared back at him, his face clenched in an ominous grimace.

"Your Highness," said Rodrigo, "the only real enemy I have is Boar. You must believe me. Allow me the right of challenge by combat."

Boar burst to his feet, knocking aside his spear. "I am fully prepared for you, Rodrigo. Fully prepared!"

Rodrigo took a step toward Boar, his lips twisting in anger. "Even if Rafe and Shoca themselves stood between us, I would bring you to the ground, brute!"

"Even Rafe and Shoca?" Boar smiled in amusement. "Are you sure?"

"Without doubt," said Rodrigo. "Does that give you pause?"

Boar did pause, prowling in front of Morten. "Whatever secret power you wield, Rodrigo, even the power to do what you say, I can match it. I would come at you sudden, sideways. I would lure you. And when you think you know, you find out you don't, and I strike from above, da? Remember what I tell you before. Your threats, they change, but what I promise before is still true."

"Then are you a coward who will not face me?" said Rodrigo.

"You are arrogant child," said Boar, laughing. "You have no right of combat. You are prisoner—my prisoner."

"He won't be alive long enough to be your prisoner," said Awkley. "I've tip-toed sufficiently around this fellow—played the game, smelled him out. He reeks of trouble."

"You won't harm the boy yet, Awkley," said Temma testily. "Wait until Ancimoden returns."

Rodrigo's heart sank. Ancimoden! Why did that soul-ripping tantyr have to be one of the few survivors? If he got a chance to scourge Yun...

Above everything else, Rodrigo could not let that happen.

"Let me take care of the boy," said Morten. "I have just the place for it. Do you remember-"

"Yes, Ancimoden for all of them," said Awkley to Temma. "Tear every shred of truth out of Rodrigo and all his ghastly friends."

Temma snapped her fingers in enlightenment. "Ghastly, how true. I suspect they are scouts for one of our old enemies. That nasty little runt with the freakish ears is most certainly a Malfaer in disguise."

"Malfaer? A mist-lurker?" said Awkley. "I highly doubt that. Those sniveling cowards don't leave their mists."

"I'm telling you-" tried Morten again, leaning forward in frustration.

Temma continued on loudly, apparently unaware that Morten was even trying to speak. "Well, they can't be Devourer minions. Devourers have long since lost their power."

"Lost their power?" scoffed Awkley, twiddling his hands mockingly. "Just because they lost their armies does not at all mean they are without power."

"The Devourers were never a match for the Malfaer, and certainly not a match for us!" snapped Temma.

"The Malfaer are sniveling cowards hiding in their mists," said Awkley. "Not so the Devourers! It took everything I had to defeat them."

"Oh, not this story again!" groaned Temma. "You imprisoned one Devourer—one! Out of pure luck, I might add-"

"That's a lie! If I had not trapped Abberatas-"

"Well, I was going to tell you…" started Morten angrily.

Temma pulled at her hair. "Yes, Abberatas, Abberatas, Abberatas…I get sick of hearing you spout on about your one, lone, lucky victory!"

"…but now you two can just hang it!" ended Morten in a shout.

The three stopped, pouting like spoiled children at a birthday party gone wrong.

Rodrigo wondered how many had suffered and died under these four royals. Could they even remember what evil they had done over the centuries? Was there any curse worse than immortality? The body might live on, but the soul was not so hardy.

"We are vulnerable," said Temma.

"*We* are anything but vulnerable," said Awkley. "Our worries are permanently over."

"Yes, but the children are not safe. If the armies mutiny…"

"If the armies mutiny, Temma, we hand them over to Rafe and Shoca," said Morten. "Or my new friend," he added with a smile.

"Temma's right," said Awkley. "We have exactly nine tantyrs standing. It astounds me that over four hundred tantyrs could be killed or wounded in battle in less than an hour. Less than *one* hour! Astounding. The whole event is burned into my memory."

"Yes, shut up, I missed it," said Morten bitterly. "Shoca, you promised more tantyrs. When?"

"A new host will be called," said Shoca, his bell-clear voice commanding attention, "but months will pass. However, the tantyrs are not the concern. You are once again on the path to dishonor."

The royalty all turned to face the titan. "What do you mean?"

"The blackspawn are ripe for destruction," said Rafe, his lighter, more elegant voice turned harsh and commanding, "and yet you allow your forces to rot in the city. That rot has reached to rebellion, with enemies now in your very castle. The tantyrs sacrificed their lives in noble fashion to defend this realm against Oldevil, and here do the humans sit, cowering from a much weaker enemy. This is to your shame. Now is the time to push your strength advantage. Take the Pinnacleer army south and crush the remaining blackspawn. Shoca and I will lead you."

Awkley huffed and raised his arms, having no way to defend his honor. Morten muttered, "That's not entirely fair," and looked over to Temma, who stared back disapprovingly at the two men.

"Rafe is right," said Temma. "The titans and I have been insisting for months now about digging the blackspawn out of their holes, and the two of you have done absolutely nothing."

Awkley sputtered, shaking his head and bugging out his eyes. "You? You've done nothing but prattle on about "protecting the children" and "barbaric violence" with your tight little lips pursed up like a wet scab! Granted, you weren't half the annoyance that dear old Scribbles was...but at least he has the decency to keep his mouth shut at this moment."

"He's drooling at the moment, you fool," sneered Temma, glancing at the catatonic king.

Morten stood up and put his hands on his waist. "Right, this is exactly the course of action I have been advocating. The Hunters are ready for an immediate offensive, unlike the Bluegirls. Commander Boar, ready your men."

Boar stood and muttered something in Morten's ear, his lips curling into a cruel grin.

"Oh yes, this will be a banner day for my new friend," said Morten back to Boar in plain voice. "In fact, perhaps we could delay the march so that you can come watch?"

"What new friend?" said Awkley.

Morten grinned cruelly. "Oh, just you wait and see. You'll never believe it."

Boar took a step back and bowed lightly. "New friend will have no problem taking care of situation. But, I *must* ready army."

"Of course. A shame," said Morten.

Boar turned and strode out, a smug, arrogant grimace building on his face.

Awkley turned on Morten. "The Blue*boys* are in far better shape-"

"Really?" crowed Morten, pointing to Rodrigo. "You mean, other than this traitor that you put in as commander, and the equally traitorous captain Zales who is running around our castle threatening the children..."

"The children!" gasped Temma, leaping to her feet. "You worthless fools, stop standing here and *do* something-"

"...and the fact that half of your lowlife troops are good only for guard duty!" continued Morten.

Awkley waved Temma off, leaning toward Morten with his arms akimbo. "*I* have already prepared *my* troops for battle, Morten, and a new commander will be in place today. As for the rebels, they stupidly trapped themselves in the castle and will be hunted down within the hour."

"Do something!" screamed Temma, making fists.

"You do something!" shouted Morten. "Where are your useless Green-cloaks?"

Rodrigo shook his head at the ease with which they were manipulated. Why could there not be more time, and more options beyond the fragile, twisted way forward? So much hope rested on a plan with a thousand points of failure, with failure at any point ending in the death of his friends.

No, even success would likely mean the death of my friends.

And to make it worse, he was merely the puppet on the strings, the bait on the hook. He was left to play his part, and play it convincingly. But to do so, his secrets could never, not for a second, be betrayed.

And then Rodrigo saw green-cloaked, grim-faced Ancimoden and three of the other surviving tantyrs leading Yun, Hope, and the limping, pained Phoebe into the court. Yun had not reached them in time.

And she was now in the hands of Ancimoden, the tantyr with the power of soul-entry.

Rodrigo closed his eyes.

You dull-witted fool, could you not have seen the truth sooner?

And yet I am alive, so there remains hope, however desperate.

One choice remains. Can you do this? Not likely, Rodrigo, but you must. No—you have no choice. You must.

Awkley clapped. "Ancimoden, by the worthless gods, you found them!"

The tantyrs brought the three girls forward and placed them before the royalty, shoving them to their knees. Phoebe staggered, and Ancimoden caught her, laying her gently down on the stone floor. Then the tantyr leader stood and faced the royalty.

"Yun went to warn these two and the three were fleeing the hospice when we found them," he said.

"Excellent!" crowed Awkley. "We'll have all of the rabbits back in the hutch in no time. Rodrigo! I offer you a deal, man to mortal. Tell us who you really are and why you are here. If you do, the lives of these three precious, tender young things will be spared. If you do not, then Morten and I have a thousand amusing activities on hand, and you can watch as we perform all of them on your traitorous little maidens—day after day, month after month, until their strength and minds are ultimately spent."

Rodrigo met the gaze of each of the kings, then turned to Queen Temma. "Is this your desire as well?"

"It is not for me to interfere in this matter," said Queen Temma aloofly, closing her eyes and leaning back.

"In that case," said Rodrigo, stepping forth and drawing his sword, "it is my wish to spare innocents. The girls are merely pawns. I used them to gain entrance to Pinnacle and gain influence with you, and they performed admirably." Rodrigo gripped his sword by the blade and held the hilt high. The firelight and moss-glow glinted off the silver sign of the bull.

"I am The Bull of the Dalmar, and I know the secret to stripping immortality from all of you."

———

In reality, Rodrigo didn't know exactly what his bold lie would cause. He was essentially throwing a bomb at his feet and hoping for a beneficial explosion. But no matter what else happened, he needed one specific result...

The royals responded with silence. Morten returned to his throne, rubbing his hair, a truly puzzled look on his face. Awkley spun back and forth between Temma and Morten, searching for answers with his usual overly dramatic shrugs and eye rolls. Temma simply wagged her head back and forth, as if looking at

Rodrigo out of the corner of her eye would help matters. The tantyrs surrounding Rodrigo had readied their weapons when Rodrigo had drawn his sword, but apparently to defend themselves and not the immortal royalty.

As usual, Awkley found the need to speak first. "You're the bull of who?"

"The Dalmar," repeated Rodrigo, his hand tiring of holding up the sword.

Awkley went back to shrugging at his immortal companions. "Does anyone?—No?—I'm sorry, dear boy, I'm sure this is quite a pronouncement for you...but we're not clear on exactly what Dalmars and cows have to do with anything."

Rodrigo lowered the sword slowly, desperate options spinning through his head. "That is my *secret*."

Awkley threw up his hands. "All right, then, one step at a time. Give your pointy sword to the tantyrs or we'll have to order them to kill you."

Rodrigo handed the sword leisurely to the tantyr next to him, hilt-first. "If you kill me, then my *secret* is lost to you."

For the love of mercy, how many times do I have to say the word?

"Oh!" Morten pointed. "There's a bull scrawled on the hilt!"

Awkley slapped his hands to his forehead and pulled at his heaps of tufted hair. "By the worthless—are you *sleeping*? That's the whole point of him raising the sword like that! Temma, please tell me you saw the bull?"

"*I'm* not stupid," said Temma.

"Ah, wasn't there some group called Dalmars in Haven?" Morten's eyes squinted down in concentration.

"When?" said Temma.

"Oh, four or five centuries ago?" answered Morten.

"How do you remember anything that far back?" said Temma.

"Can we move on?" said Awkley, striding over to stand above Yun, Phoebe, and Hope. "Now, for which of these three fine maidens does your heart sing?"

"I care deeply for all of them, Awkley. Harm any of them, and my *secret* is lost to you," said Rodrigo.

"My, aren't you the playboy," said Awkley, shaking his finger. "Fine, random one then. This one—Phoebe, correct?—she looks a little worse for wear. Bring her here—oh, wait. Temma, do you mind?"

Temma scratched at her nose for a moment, looking down along it at the wounded girl. "Not at all," she said.

"But...but I saved your life!" protested Phoebe, struggling at the grip of the tantyr that held her. "I fired that spear!"

The royals paused. Temma continued to tap at her nose. "That was a fine shot, girl, really. No one else could have done it. I should have known it was you.

But that was days ago, and with Oldevil put to rest I truly doubt you could help me again. To be honest, I am quite glad to be rid of you."

Phoebe gasped and cried out as she struggled with the tantyr.

Awkley drew his sword. "Now then, I am tired of dealing with you, boy." He stepped down and gripped Phoebe's long brown locks, pulling her head back. "Enlighten us, or I slit this pretty girl's throat and you can watch."

The sword pressed up to Phoebe's skin, drawing a thin line of red. An agonized, choking cry came from her. Rodrigo's furiously flailing mind struck deadends in every direction.

"Awkley," said the titan Shoca, "killing any of the traitors might be unhelpful. They may know important information. Have you forgotten Ancimoden?"

Rodrigo's heart leapt with hope. *Gracia de Dios! Finally! Thank the Lord of All for one reasoning mind in the room!*

"Yes, exactly." Morten eyed Phoebe. "You're far too hasty, Awkley. We had plans for the girls, remember? Hardly any entertainment found in your rash bloodthirstiness."

Awkley rolled his eyes and dropped the sword point to the stone in exasperation. "Fine! Really, though, I am getting the itch to end this quickly. Ancimoden, do what you do. And don't bother being gentle. Strip their minds to rags."

Ancimoden moved toward the three women. Rodrigo stepped forward quickly and stood in his way, the tantyrs behind him jumping ahead and laying hold of him. Ancimoden placed his hands on his two elegant short swords and drew one out.

"You will need to be fresh to scourge me this time," said Rodrigo.

"As you wish," said Ancimoden.

"Do the little bride first—Yun, correct?" said Awkley.

"You'll need everything for me," insisted Rodrigo, challenging the tantyr to lock stares with him.

Ancimoden cocked his head slightly, his amber predator's eyes narrowed. "Rodrigo will be first," he announced, ignoring Awkley's protest. "Close your eyes. It will go better if you do."

Ancimoden positioned himself in front of Rodrigo, sheathing his sword. Rodrigo closed his eyes, hoping beyond hope that he had guessed correctly. The tantyr guards released their grip and moved back.

And the world faded, as though a heavy shade slid down a window. A new world appeared with such force and vividness that Rodrigo staggered and shielded his eyes.

430

99: ANCIMODEN

There was a sun, high in the sky, giving off a warmth that made Rodrigo lift his face in delight. The meadow of flowering lupine around him gave way to thick forest and a mirror-smooth lake that reflected the jagged, snow-lined peaks backing it. Rodrigo closed his eyes and breathed in deeply.

Someone stood beside him—a tall angel with strange amber eyes. "So beautiful," said the creature, looking out at the valley. "A precious jewel. And so long as it lasts, we are safe and content."

The angel took hold of Rodrigo by the shoulders and flew, lifting the boy slowly upward. Excitement rose in Rodrigo as he anticipated the vast panorama of beauty that would open before them.

But the beauty stopped. Beyond the meadow, the small forests, the lake and the mountains, black rock spread out in all directions, split with angry red fissures and geysers of lava. But for this tiny oasis, the world writhed in flames.

"This world senses the corruption in your soul, Rodrigo. You can save this last valley, but the corruption must end. No more deceit. No more lies."

Rodrigo nodded. The angel's wings slowed, and they drifted back into the lupine valley. A soft breeze caught the field. Rodrigo breathed deeply. The angel strode slowly around him.

"Do you know how to strip away immortality?" asked the angel.

"I do," lied Rodrigo, wandering lazily toward the lake.

"Does anyone else know?"

"Not yet."

"How do you strip away immortality?"

"I cannot tell you," said Rodrigo.

"Why?"

"Because if *they* found out how, *they* could prevent it, and then nothing could take away their immortality, ever."

"The world hates secrets, Rodrigo. Tell me how to strip away immortality."

"I do not think I should."

A reddish glow and a wash of heat struck Rodrigo from the right. Fire advanced through the forest, consuming it in a wind-whipped maelstrom. The flowers of the lupine wilted, and Rodrigo tried to cover his face from the waves of searing heat. He retreated toward the forest on the other side of the valley.

"See, Rodrigo! The world dies because of your selfishness. Tell me the secret, and the meadow will bloom once more."

Rodrigo turned in alarm and saw patches of fiery glow appear in the other side of the forest.

"Tell me before the last forest dies!"

"But…I should not," said Rodrigo weakly, fright twisting his eyes this way and that as the conflagration arose in the other forest. The heat seared his skin, causing him to groan and cry out. He turned and ran to the lake, sinking with relief into its cool depths.

When he broke the surface, the angel hovered before him. "It is a beautiful lake, Rodrigo, and your very last refuge. If you will not take the honorable path and speak the secret, then there will be a final death. Is that what you wish?"

Rodrigo did not answer. The angel cocked its head, puzzled.

"Even now the lake dies, Rodrigo. Tell me!"

Lava poured from fissures in the snowy mountain, throwing up great gouts of steam where snow met heat. The molten rock poured into the lake, and the temperature of the water rose.

"Rodrigo, you have no more time."

Rodrigo did not answer, standing stoically in the neck-deep water.

The angel's eyes narrowed. The temperature of the water reached the point of scalding, and the boy groaned in agony. Still he did not speak.

The world of flames began to fade, drawing them toward a softer, cooler place. But that new place shattered as though a brick hit a mirror, and the world of flames and scalding heat snapped back into focus.

The angel's amber eyes grew wide in alarm. The boy cried out in terrific agony, then his chestnut eyes opened and he stared at the angel, gritting his teeth as he choked out these words:

"You—you will not remove us from this, Ancimoden. I will not leave, and you cannot force me, can you? You burned the world—and I choose to die in it. Wait for me…"

The boy screamed once more in mortal agony, and sank below the boiling waters, his body writhing in scalding torture.

In the royal court, Rodrigo ceased his screaming and his eyes snapped open. He lay curled on the floor with Ancimoden leaning over him, frozen. In an instant Rodrigo leapt to his feet, pulled both of Ancimoden's short blades and drove them through the tantyr's ribs.

The tantyr guards, caught entirely by surprise, leapt forward.

"Stop!" yelled Awkley at the tantyrs. "Stop!" roared Rafe. The tantyr guards slitted their eyes in fury but retreated.

Exhausted and bathed in sweat, Rodrigo rested one hand on Ancimoden's shoulder. The tantyr slid to the floor and Rodrigo caught him, trying as well as he could to bring the large creature down to the floor gently. Purplish blood stained his hands and clothes.

It felt like murder. Despite the contest of wills and the clear intent of Ancimoden to cruelly torture Rodrigo for as long as it took to tear the truth out, this killing act stabbed Rodrigo's soul.

"I am deeply sorry," he whispered, his brows knitted and mouth set grimly.

Ancimoden's eyes turned his way. "Do not be. I…I embrace death. But I do wish to know…who *are* you?"

Rodrigo leaned down and whispered in the dying tantyr's ear. "The truth is this, Ancimoden. I am a man who does not wish his friends to die. Beyond that, there is nothing extraordinary about me."

Ancimoden's mouth opened and he chuckled, leaking a thin dribble of purple from the side of his mouth. "Yes there is," he choked out. He pulled Rodrigo closer, and the two spoke for a moment. Then Ancimoden slid down onto his back, his amber eyes open and unseeing.

Rodrigo stood and faced his enemies, his features set in both anguish and determination. His one critical act had been accomplished. Everyone in the room was now free of the threat of Ancimoden's prying mind. So long as Berylata remained in her death-sleep, they were all safe from discovery.

Unless, of course, true and ordinary torture proved to be more effective.

With Rip's excellent navigation, the fugitive band of Lakesiders and Blueboys managed to avoid capture, and found a long, partially burned corridor in the deep levels of the castle that served as an excellent choke point against their Black Huntsmen pursuers.

Unfortunately, their flight had led them far away from the place where they were to meet Yun and the girls.

"They're staying back," said a breathless scout to Captain Zales.

Trace and Scarlet crouched next to the captain, just within the chamber where the corridor ended. An exit behind them continued on into the castle's depths. The only two Blueboys armed with crossbows braced the archway beside them.

"How many out there?" asked Zales.

"Three, maybe four," said the scout. "Not many, but they're the original Blackies."

"Crossbowmen?" asked Zales.

"Only one. The Blackies were as ill prepared as we were, sir."

Captain Zales peered down the dark, rubble-strewn corridor from which they had come. The corridor ran straight ninety feet, with no rooms or exits. It made for an excellent choke point, but with the exception of a tiny patch of glowmoss near the far archway, it was dark.

"We need to set a lantern out there, about thirty feet," said Scarlet.

"None to spare," said Zales. "Can they flank us?"

"Yes, but I doubt they know how," said Scarlet. "Behind us is an old abandoned monastery on the east side of the castle. This is the only connection into the monastery except for a set of stairs lower down and a tiny hidden door out onto the guild grounds. Not likely that anyone knows about either."

Zales nodded. "Perfect. We'll collapse the corridor here. How did you know about the monastery?"

Scarlet checked the oil in his small personal lamp. "Rodrigo sent me and Rip out on exploration the second that we arrived in the castle. Thought it might be useful. I get the feeling he expected something like this."

"He's amazing," said Zales. "So far beyond his years."

Trace smiled. "That's why we call him Grandfather."

Scarlet chuckled and closed up his lamp. "Once Rip finishes giving your soldiers a guided tour of the monastery, we three have a little foray to make. Be sure your men explore and make maps; whoever built this place had fun with it. You can get lost easily."

Captain Zales nodded. "It's a standoff here, so you might as well go."

"Right. Good luck, Captain."

———

Trace and Scarlet sped down the opposite corridor and through several patches of rubbled ruins until they reached the entrance to the monastery. They wound their way through the dusty maze of the corridors until they reached the central worship hall.

A strong draft blew through the high-vaulted chamber, producing a chorus of moans and sighs among the shadowy remains and sculptures. *If there were ghosts in the castle, this would be their favorite haunt,* thought Scarlet.

"I wonder who they worshipped," he said.

"Oldevil, probly." Trace pointed to the abundance of flames and reddish suns worked into the mosaics and ornamentation of the monastery.

"Cheery thought," said Scarlet, trying hard not to think that he was back in Old Haven. He kept one wary eye on the abundant nooks and corners buried in shadow. "So much emptiness in this castle—in the city, for that matter. I wonder what it was like back when it was bustling. Their builders were masterful."

Footfalls approached as fire glow appeared in the far archway. Rip and a squad of Blueboys entered the hall, their voices echoing up into the darkness of the high vault. Scarlet wondered if the Newt could fit up there, in the gloom. He decided to wander over to the covering protection of a low archway.

"Hahlay, ettins!" called Rip, crossing over to them. "The soldier-boys are all snug like rabbits in a warren and ready to bolt if pressed. Time to snatch up the three kiddies."

Rip, Scarlet, and Trace hurried through the monastery to the steep, narrow stairs next to the wine cellar. The stairs wandered down into a maze of wet, aging tunnels and chambers. After nearly half an hour of twisting through the dank maze, and as Scarlet and Rip began arguing about who got them lost, they came upon a familiar, highly ornamented room containing a narrow spiral staircase set into the wall. It appeared to have been meant to be secret, but the panels that hid it had rotted away long ago.

"Mind yer step, cally-pads, this goes up and up," said Rip. "I'll go first. Don't want an ettin to squish on me."

The staircase was not built for comfort, with narrow steps so alarmingly steep that Trace held onto the steps above him with his hands. The big man barely fit in the tightly wound spiral, scraping his shoulders on the stone. The stale air made breathing difficult, and when they at last pushed open a bookshelf and scrambled out of the hole into a dusty study, Trace stayed on his knees for a moment and uttered some incoherent exclamation of gratefulness.

"And here we be," whispered Rip. "All we have to do now is walk a league's worth of halls past guards and mugly matrons to the children's nest. How do yeh plan that, Scarlet?"

Scarlet smiled and waved them on. "Time for a bath."

Many hallways beyond, Ana and Petra padded quickly down the corridor toward their dormitory, their slippers slapping against the smooth stone, their nightdresses billowing back and forth as they hurried along.

Ana knew that they faced trouble, no doubt about it. While they'd bathed, one of the other girls—a stupid toady who always tried to impress the pack of cruel older girls—had tossed their slippers and gowns onto a high ledge, and now they were many minutes late after recovering their clothes. The others would already be in their beds, and a furious matron awaited them.

"Why would she do such a thing?" said Petra, near tears.

Ana clicked her tongue, as much at Petra's delicate nature as at the answer to the question. The answer would be Safiria, a green-eyed, flame-haired older girl who'd feuded with Ana since their first day, and who certainly put that other girl up to it. Safiria ruled the dormitory, and Ana didn't like to be ruled.

"Just come on," she said. "And you let me talk to Matron Habald."

They hurried past the Lookout—a fissure in the wall where the children could see to the outside—and into the corridor that passed along a short section of abandoned, fire-damaged rooms.

As they passed one of the rooms, four figures jumped out from the doorway and pinned the girls to the ground. Ana found a hand around her mouth and bit it.

"Owww!" yelped the boy who held her.

"Shut up!" whispered another. "C'mon, move it!"

The attackers half-carried, half-dragged the girls into the doorway, through a ragged hole in a wall and into a long narrow room where a rivulet of water cascaded out through wide gashes in the outer wall. The midnight blue of the sky filtered into the room through the ragged gaps.

Rough hands threw Petra to the ground, and she landed hard on someone's leg. She looked over and saw Ardi lying next to her, his cheek swollen and his lip split and bleeding.

"Keil, go keep lookout," said one of the boys, his voice like the velvet of a tarantula's back.

"I did last time," said Keil.

"Do it," said the other, smoothing a thumb through his slightly disarrayed black hair. His misfit eyes glinted in the dim light of the glowmoss—one shadowy black and the other a pale gray.

Keil sulked off through the hole in the wall. "Fine," he said, "but someone else next time, okay, Quait?"

Quait didn't bother answering. "Let's wait for our other guests," he said, grinning evilly at Ana.

———

"Are yeh daft?" huffed Rip.

"All of the children should be in bed by now," said Scarlet.

"I can *hear* kiddies in there," said Rip.

"Most all," corrected Scarlet.

The three had squeezed into an alcove behind a statue of a winged angel. Their attempt at stealth lacked merit, considering that most of Trace stuck out beyond the angel.

"Look, this is ridiculous," said Scarlet. "I'll nick some clothes for you."

Scarlet peeked around to the girls' bathhouse. He sighed relief and raised a hand. "All clear, back soon," he whispered, and passed through the bathhouse archway.

Rip and Trace heard a muffled scream and edged out from behind the angel statue. Scarlet darted around the corner carrying a bundle of whites.

"Time to move on," he whispered as he scrambled past them.

Ten minutes later, after much coaxing and threats, Rip emerged from the dusty study wearing a girl's white nightdress.

"Sweet," said Trace, grinning.

"Shut yer yammer hole!" said Rip, pulling at a restricting fold in the nightdress. He had managed an admirable job with the towel on his head. Except for a few wisps of hair sticking out of his slippers, he looked every bit the bedtime lass.

"Walk!" he said, waving them on.

"Right. Sell arrogance, Trace," said Scarlet.

The three moved off at a rapid clip, the two men escorting the girl between them. When they turned a corner and saw a Greencloak guard, they moved past without so much as a glance, their faces hard set. The corridors and hallways passed by, and though one matron did finally challenge them, Trace gave her an angry stare and they passed on, hoping for the best. No pursuit came.

"I'll wager no one up here even knows about our mutiny," whispered Scarlet. Trace nodded.

Rip stiffened. He grabbed at Trace's leg and waved them to a dimly lit side hall. He raised his finger to his lips.

Voices could be heard, hushed but excited. Two older teen girls turned a corner, one stocky and dark haired, the other broad shouldered and tall with flame-red hair. They glanced around warily and passed on, murmuring to each other.

"Follow them," whispered Rip.

"Why?" said Scarlet.

"They mentioned Ana, and not in a nice way," said Rip.

———

Quait turned his mismatched eyes toward one of his boys—a bulky fellow that the others called Gurster. The pudgy brute grabbed Ana up off the floor by one arm. "What're you lookin' at, spitty?"

"Watch it," warned Quait.

"She's makin' faces at me," said Gurster, "like she can get away with it."

"Then teach her a lesson," said Quait. "Just don't mark her."

"Yeah," said Gurster, licking his lips. He grabbed Ana by both arms and pushed her backward against a ruined armoire. "You wanna make faces?"

"No, please don't hurt me," said Ana, squirming weakly. "I am so frightened."

"You don't know what frightened is yet, spitty. Wait till I suck your eyes out, heh?" Gurster licked his lips, flipping spittle on Ana's face.

Ana twisted a forearm to point at Gurster. "You keep doing that."

"What?" said Gurster.

"Your lips. You keep licking your lips."

"You makin' fun of me now?" Gurster reddened with anger. "You think I'm kidding?" He let go of her arms and grabbed her by the throat, flicking his tongue out at her eyes.

Ana bent her knees, braced against the ground, and rammed her palm up under Gurster's chin, sending his upper and lower teeth to meet halfway through his tongue. His hands went to his mouth and her knee went to his groin.

Gurster fell sideways, trying to scream.

"You little-" shouted Gurster's thug-mate Maabo, charging at her. Ana tried to dodge past him, but his fist caught the back of her head and she went sprawling.

Ana caught herself and spun around. Maabo blinked, clearly surprised to see a smile on her face.

"You should check your friend," she said. "He's choking."

Quait chuckled. "I like you. Ana, right?"

Ana's challenging eyes turned on him, her lips curled in a combative grin. "My name's Ah-na. And...ugh...you're a real baddie. I can see."

"Well, Ahh-na, it's a shame you're about to get messed up."

Two girls stepped through the hole in the wall. Safiria, her green eyes on fire, took in the situation, wincing in annoyance at the cries from Gurster. "Somebody shut him up!" she whispered harshly. "What happened?"

"She happened." Quait grinned wolfishly and pointed at the cornered Ana.

"Really," said Safiria. The two girls moved in on Ana.

Quait strode over to look down at Petra, who cried openly. She peered up at him and tried to crawl away.

He sneered at her. "Now where do you think you're going?"

———

Keil peeked out the archway. Sure enough, someone was coming—a girl dressed for bed, like the other two. When the girl came close, he couldn't help but step out and stand in her way.

"You shouldn't be here," he said, trying to grab her arm.

The girl's piston-like fist compressed Keil's midriff by six inches, forcing the air out of his lungs.

"Yeh don't say," said the girl—Rip—who pulled the towel off his head, dropped it on the back of the doubled-over bully, and passed through the archway.

When Rip popped through the hole in the wall, no one in the room noticed. He stepped up behind a boy that was bent over Petra, put his slipper on the thug's conveniently placed hindquarters, and shoved. The boy pitched over forwards.

"Hahlay!" shouted Rip. "Who wants a pounding?"

A girl and a boy turned on him. He could now see Ana in the corner, her face terribly battered, yet bearing a feral smile. A dark-haired girl knelt on the floor nearby, clutching her nose in pain, and a screaming boy writhed on the floor beside her.

"What's the pipsqueak doing here?" said Maabo.

Quait regained his feet, his miscast eyes burning at Rip. "Doesn't matter—this one dies," he said, moving in on Rip.

Scarlet bent through the hole in the wall, and the young thugs froze in place. When Trace squeezed through, they stepped back.

Scarlet moved forward and picked up Petra, who quieted her sobs.

"Are you all right?" he asked her.

"Y-yes," she stammered, trying to straighten her hair. "I'm okay."

Ardi appeared next to Scarlet. "Me too," he said quietly, his manner calm despite his kidnapping and the split in his lip.

440

Scarlet guided the two children back to Trace, then pushed through the thugs to Ana, who worked at tying her hair back and wiping the blood off her chin. He knelt and gently took her arm. "Ana, you okay?"

"Oh, yes." Ana looked around and cracked a bloody grin. "I think I could have won."

Scarlet's brows rose. He jacked a thumb toward the injured thugs. "You did this?"

Ana shrugged. "They started it."

He grinned in amazement. "You sure knocked down your share of baddies."

"I hate baddies," Ana walked through the thugs without looking at them. Scarlet followed her out. Trace kept his eyes on the thugs until everyone had passed safely out of the savaged room.

"They'll be brought back, you know," said Quait as Trace turned to leave. "And I'll have them again."

Trace turned back to face the boy. "You need friends who fight better," he said.

"I can find others to serve me," said Quait, his eyes glittering.

Trace, who had again turned to leave, spun back around and scooped Quait up by the neck. "Now, that is an odd thing for a mere boy to say," he said quietly, holding Quait up against the wall.

Their return to the monastery went swiftly and uneventfully, and they placed the three children in the care of Captain Zales. Scarlet shook his head as he watched Ana climb around the platforms and ledges of the worship hall.

"Take care of them," he said to Zales. "Ana, you stick around here, okay?"

"Sure," she called. "This place is great!"

"She's a handful, watch her," he said, and returned to Trace and Rip.

"We need to find out what happened to Yun and the girls, see if we can slide them out of harm's way as well," said Scarlet.

"Scampering up to the Watchtower hallway where we were supposed to meet them will be a nimbly trick," said Rip, and then he snapped his fingers. "Ah, but I can make a quick climb from the outside. I'll nip right back."

Rip left the monastery through the small door out to the Guild Grounds. An hour later, he returned. "No girls. Not a stitch nor sight."

Scarlet bit at his lip. "They might have been snapped up. If so, they are likely with Rodrigo."

"Where do yeh think they'll stuff Rodrigo?" said Rip.

Scarlet shook his head. "We'll have to duck as close as possible to the court and try to pick up a clue. I found it strange that the castle isn't swarming with pursuers. Zales says they've made no further attempts to get in here."

Rip picked at his towel-ruffled hair. "The closest we can get is to wend-away through the lower tunnels, pop up through our museum, and try to sneak a bob from there."

"Right," said Scarlet. "Zales's men will watch over the children."

"And Ana will watch over them," said Rip. "Never knew ettin lasses were so fiskety."

"She's definitely an exception," said Scarlet as they headed once again down the staircase and into the soggy maze.

———

So accustomed were they to the abandoned emptiness of the lower corridors that they started in shock upon hearing a splash ahead. They backed quickly into the half-shadows of a drier side tunnel and hid among the debris. Scarlet and Trace laid out flat to stay hidden while Rip peeked through the grating of an old sewer entry.

Scarlet heard the foot splashes of several people pass by and turn at the corner just beyond their hiding spot. One voice growled deep and sounded familiar. The other spoke in a strangely clipped higher pitch. Scarlet shrugged at Rip.

Rip snuck a look and his eyes grew large. Turning back to Scarlet, he grabbed his arm and flexed it with a grim, haughty look, then mouthed a name.

Boar. What in blazes is he doing down here?

The voices faded, and the three rose.

"Boar and that little black owl-eye thing I chased in Scribbs's room," said Rip.

"He might know where Rodrigo is," said Scarlet. "He might even have Rodrigo in some dungeon down here. We'll need to follow-"

"I will," interrupted Trace, and turned to leave.

"Hang on," said Scarlet. "Take Rip with you. He knows these tunnels. Good luck."

"We'll do more than follow him if we get the chance," growled Trace, and he turned and hurried after the Hunter commander.

Scarlet continued through to the flight of stairs that angled up close to the museum. He had just left the landing when a Hunter hurried by, his attention so focused that he failed to see Scarlet ducking away. The Hunter stopped at a room up ahead and two other Hunters came out to meet him.

"What'd they say?"

"Same thing. Get the whole command out on the fields for assembly, do it like snap or else."

"Yeah, but everyone? Who'll get the Bluegirl traitors?"

"'Leave them to the Greencloaks,' they said. Ain't that a laugh!"

"I just know the whole command is getting called up, guards and everyone."

"We finally going after the blackspawn nests, I hope?"

"Sounds like it. They plan on march-out in the morning, not that we'll be ready by then."

"Yeah, 'specially the Bluegirl screw-ups. Hope they don't have our flank."

"At least we get to put the final screws to the blackspawn..."

Scarlet ducked into the museum's small east archway as the conversation outside devolved into coarse boasting.

As he moved through the various displays, he came across broken glass and a ransacked display case containing a large round shield of banded brass. Empty supports showed that something else had lain in the case, but had been taken.

That's odd, he thought. *Who would smash up our museum?*

Something caught his eye in the ruined display—an object hanging out from behind the shield.

As he pulled it out, a peg holding the shield in place gave way and it rolled free, crashing through the remaining glass and slamming to the stone floor with a deafening bell-like clang.

Scarlet panicked, trying to find a place to hide. He slid under a table of piled crest banners just as the Hunters rushed in.

"Get the other door!" yelled one. Scarlet saw legs sprint past.

"No one out here," came the eventual reply.

"Right, just stay there in case they try to bolt."

The table gave Scarlet little cover. If one of the Hunters simply bent down and looked along the floor, they would see him. His hand reached up on the table and grabbed at the banners.

Another set of legs passed nearby and stopped at the case. Scarlet tried to bury his hand in the fabric.

"Shield rolled right out of this case! It's huge, look at this. That must have been it."

"Yeah, look around anyway."

Scarlet saw the knees of the guard start to bend and he quickly flipped a banner down so that it hung to the floor, closing off his vision.

The wandering Hunter continued a haphazard search while his two mates guarded the exits. Scarlet looked at the thing that he had pulled out of the display case.

An armband, elaborately engraved, with a rampant boar set with rubies as the centerpiece.

The boar looked familiar.

As Scarlet stared at the armband, his flexible mind spun memories, loosed in a cascade like an avalanche triggered by a snowball.

He remembered the Dalmar Wall and its chiseled circle of symbols, including a rampant boar exactly like that on the armband. And then later, when Boar threatened them in this very room, he stood admiringly at this very case just before he made his threats.

What was in this case? A sword—no, a spear. But the spear was giant.

So is Boar.

Boar had said, with his typical self-satisfied mug, "I make plan too, Rodrigo. Plan to lure my enemy…"

Odd. No one sets a trap and then starts giving their intended target hints about it. Granted, Boar is full of himself. And why 'my enemy?' He was threatening Rodrigo, the person standing right in front of him.

What else did he say? Remember his little rehearsed speech?

Boar's words came back to Scarlet. "Deep plans, scary like Newt, all set and in place, nyet?"

All set and in place. In the deep.

Boar had stood there, at the display case. Hunters and a tantyr had hovered behind him at the entrance, watching him. "Always count on prying eyes, and ears and minds, da?" said Boar.

Prying minds. Ancimoden…

Blazes and cauldrons, it was Rodrigo! Boar and Rodrigo have been communicating secretly. Coordinating secretly.

What had Rodrigo said only days ago as they watched the castle garden from the high window? "I do not underestimate Boar's cleverness. If he is somehow working in league with one of us, I must rely on you to spot it and act accordingly."

Oh, Rodrigo, you clever…you knew I would sniff it out.

Scarlet's mind returned to the museum, the night of their reunion gathering. Trace was angry after Boar left. "We better off if he dead." Rodrigo had then turned quickly on Trace, greatly concerned. "No, Trace, absolutely not…You need to stay out of his path."

Rodrigo was trying to keep trouble away from Boar. And Trace is stalking Boar right now, deep down underground. Deep down.

"I have deep plans, Rodrigo," Boar had said.

Whatever Boar planned with Rodrigo, he might very well be putting it into motion right now, deep down in the lower corridors.

And Trace is about to get in the way of Boar's plans…

I have to stop Trace!

In a sunless land, the world's background is shadow. So it was in the museum. Although the carefully placed fountains and gutters provided sufficient moss-glow to function in the room, it left many pools of shadow. Scarlet turned on his belly and scanned the room's floor. Watching the wandering Hunter's feet, he waited for them to turn, then crawled carefully toward a long, low table full of figurines, replicas, and journals, grateful for the scabbard on his back rather than at his waist.

Reaching the table, he popped his head up slightly, took inventory of the display's contents, shifted over and carefully hefted a pitted, rusting idol of a pregnant and busty goddess off the table.

Come along now, keep circling right, Hunter…

And the Hunter did, coming round the display, perusing the museum's contents before he leaned down and took a look underneath.

Scarlet rose behind him and brought the idol down on the small of his back—a strong, measured blow that sent the Hunter to his knees.

"Hullo!" called Scarlet to the other two. "I must depart, the queen awaits me in her private chamb—oh dash!"

Scarlet ducked as the Hunter at the main hall archway brought a crossbow to bear and fired. The bolt penetrated the nose of *Emperor Morten at Repose*, a colorful but uninspired painting. Scarlet jumped up and sprinted for the crossbowman, hoping that the other was not similarly armed. The Hunter began reloading his crossbow, but realized his mistake and pulled on his sword. Scarlet flung the idol at him, hitting him in the chest and knocking him down. He tried to rise but took a foot to his stomach as Scarlet vaulted him.

Scarlet heard the other Hunter race for the exit behind him. But he was too late. Scarlet had already sprinted around the hallway to the stairs and was taking the steps four at a time back down into the wet maze.

After the royalty recovered from their alarm and disbelief at the death of Ancimoden, Morten declared forcefully that it was his time to deal with the issue, and that he had a surprise for them all, deep down below. Awkley and Temma agreed that the issue must be handled quickly and effectively. Rafe and Shoca agreed that, for the murder of Ancimoden, the only honorable and just outcome was death in return—unless Rodrigo were to cooperate fully and willingly.

Rodrigo politely refused.

King Morten displayed his serpent's-smile. "Then, you are mine." And he had Rodrigo bound and led away to his domain in the lower regions of the castle.

———

For the three-hundredth minute, Rodrigo coaxed himself to remain calm. Eight straps held him fast to a hard wooden table, pinning his legs and arms down so tightly that he could barely wiggle his toes and fingers. The strap across his neck made breathing difficult. His fear of tight places leapt at his mind repeatedly, like a leopard uncaged and angry.

He couldn't lose control, couldn't scream. The women needed strength.

Phoebe, Hope, and Yun sat curled up in tiny, filthy metal cages at the other end of the low-ceilinged room, unable even to stretch out or lift their heads. Yun cried off and on, Hope muttered to herself, and Phoebe lay listlessly, clutching her bandages and staring vacantly. A sweating torturer busied himself nearby, scraping the rust from an ominously shaped contraption of metal. Morten had seen fit to decorate the room with sufficient artifacts of his cruelty, so Rodrigo kept his eyes safely on the ceiling.

A man's muted cry of agony drifted through the stone walls of Morten's dungeon retreat. His cries could be heard when Morten's torturers had strapped Rodrigo to the table, and had not let up since. The terrified, heart-rending screams of a woman started up soon after, but to Rodrigo's great relief faded to silence after an hour.

Only now, as a participant, could Rodrigo witness the full extent of Morten's sadistic depths, and the terror that it brought to the city on which he preyed.

"Rodrigo," called Hope. "Rodrigo?"

"Yes," he croaked, hoping his strangled voice could be heard.

"We must remove Phoebe from here. Her wounds will become infected, if they haven't already."

Rodrigo smiled in spite of his situation. He never could figure out Hope. So many contradictions in one soul—bossy and humorless one moment, sly and flirtatious the next; openly selfish until someone truly required help, then willing to pour heart and soul away on those in need; harshly suspicious of the men around her, yet intensely interested in how they ticked.

And now, she was concerned about Phoebe's comfort, as though they weren't all soon to die without hope of escape. Rodrigo could not bring himself to speak the truth. There was a possibility, however slight, of Rodrigo surviving. He could not say the same for the girls. He could only hope for a miracle.

Lord of All, bring them away to safety. Rescue them with Your angels—real angels.

There sounded a clang of metal, a grinding of gears, and a thick metal gate swung ponderously open to admit Morten and two thick-muscled torturers.

"Good news, Rodrigo! Your time of resting comfortably is at an end. A shame that we must rush this. I would have appreciated a relaxing pace to more properly entertain these dear, bored girls."

Rodrigo kept silent.

"Let me explain today's agenda," continued Morten. "As a murderer, your life is forfeit. But these girls have done nothing wrong. They will live if you talk. Simple. You can start now if you wish."

"Please don't hurt them," begged Rodrigo.

"Tell me the secret, and they won't be hurt."

"Please, don't."

Morten shook his head in disgust. "Weaklings beg, Rodrigo. I thought I would get better from you. On your feet, then."

The torturers unstrapped Rodrigo. They dragged out the girls, bound them and hooded them, and did the same to Rodrigo. Morten led them out of his private chamber of hell and along a twisting, downward route. Rodrigo tried to keep track of the turns and failed quickly.

The hoods were removed. Rodrigo stood in a tall corridor. Ahead of him, Morten greeted Temma, Awkley, and the two titans, Rafe and Shoca. Behind them were three tantyr guards, a half-dozen Hunters, and the four captured Blueboys of Captain Zales's command.

Morten welcomed them heartily, barely able to contain his passion for what was to come. "Let us discover old haunts, shall we, Awkley?"

They descended into the castle, lower and lower, following Morten.

"Have yeh thought some care into this, Tracie?" whispered Rip.

"No," rumbled Trace.

"Good then," sighed Rip. "Yeh can never be too under-prepared."

He stopped whispering. The other two up ahead had already heard them.

Boar and his small owl-eyed companion turned around. The little gablin-creature brought up a crossbow, while Boar dropped an immense brass-banded spear off his shoulder and placed it on the ground.

"Who is this?" said Boar. "Ah, the one who is too big and the one too small."

Rip chuckled. "Yeh do see the irony in that insult, don't yeh?"

Trace strode right up to Boar, within arm's length. Neither flinched. They simply looked each other over appraisingly. Rip did the same to Owleye, raising his hands disarmingly. The gablin stood almost exactly Rip's height. Its giant golden-yellow eyes stared out at him from its black cowl, the crossbow leveled at Rip's chin. Rip's immediate desire was to find cover, but a greater desire to show Trace his toughness had forced him to walk up to that crossbow.

"Where is Rodrigo?" asked Trace.

"I go see him right now," said Boar. "You are not invited. Your feet, they make, eh, slappy noises on stone."

"No, I go see him right now," said Trace. "Because I will drag you there by the hair if you do not tell me where he is."

Boar laughed and ran a hand through his short-cropped reddish bristle. "Hah! You have good grip, da, to get ahold of this?" He folded his impressive arms. "So, you want fight?"

"I want fight," said Trace.

"If I may," said Rip lifting an already raised hand higher. "I have a crossbow in meh face, and nothing but a nice knife that I like to keep clean. I rather not want fight, if it is to start with meh face getting shot through."

Neither Boar nor Trace took their eyes off of their opponent. "Impi, go sit down," said Boar. "Keep little Rippie company. This not take long."

"Not long at all," said Trace, waving Rip off.

"Excellent!" said Rip, presenting a hand toward a layered pile of paddle-like glowmoss. "Are yeh the wagering kind?"

"Water drips down," spoke Impi in a lilting voice, surprisingly refined. The creature settled in nearby, the crossbow resting on his lap.

"Ahey, water does that," mused Rip, confused.

The gablin rummaged in a satchel and brought out a handful of gems. He put a fat garnet down between him and Rip.

"Raiding the palace, I see," said Rip, but the gesture held obvious meaning. The gablin was, in fact, the wagering kind. Rip pulled out a pair of gloves and laid them next to the garnet. "The queen's own!" he crowed, and wiggled his stocky fingers. "She has thin little sticks for fingers, not like me. You?"

Impi plucked up the gloves and slid one onto his bony, rough left hand. He let go a toothy smile and held up his hand. "Fit like glove," he said.

"Heh, now that I understood," said Rip.

Boar stepped back and stretched his arms. "We fight like men, or like killer?"

Trace threw his spear aside. "No need for this to get nasty."

"Da, good!" said Boar. "We just break a few bones, no need for anything serious."

Trace's gaze became distracted. He pointed down. "This your spear?"

"Da, my beauty, had my eye on her for while now." Boar picked up the behemoth weapon and tossed it to Trace, who caught it with little effort.

Trace hefted and balanced it, grinning appreciatively. "Very nice! If you die, I take it," he said.

"Sure, no problem!" said Boar. "And if you die, it probably because I kill you with this spear. See the handle, it has my-"

And then Trace dropped the spear and punched Boar. Boar ducked just enough for the blow to land on his forehead, and he staggered back, shaking his head. Trace shook his knuckles.

"You fight dirty!" said Boar, grinning. And the two went at it.

Rip and Impi stopped their chatting, their eyes widened a little, and their jaws went slightly slack as they witnessed the fight. Every now and then one would exclaim. The two behemoths pounded against each other like sea and cliff, raining kicks and blows mercilessly and without pause, tossing each other like giant sacks of cement. Trace had eighty pounds and nearly a foot on Boar, but Boar held an edge in fighting skill.

"Glad I'm not a cally-pad," said Rip.

"Cally-pad?" said Impi.

"Big and clumsy, like them," explained Rip.

"Yesss, cally-pad," said Impi, taking a bite of some form of glowmoss-wrapped fish cake. Rip gave it a look, and Impi broke off a piece. Rip nibbled at it and his face turned sour, spitting out the raw fish. "I like meh fishies put over the fire, but thankee anyway."

Impi raised a finger and brought out another wrapping, handing it over. Rip took a bite of the superbly smoked fish and his eyebrows rose in delight. Boar landed heavily next to Rip and Rip guarded the fish.

"So, where's the best fishies?" asked Rip after Boar roared and stormed back to his feet.

"Big water," said Impi.

"The city lake?"

"No, big, big water," said Impi, finishing off his wrap.

Rip wondered where big, big water could be on the Spire. But he hadn't further time to think about it. Trace roared in pain on the ground, holding his thigh.

Boar stood nearby, breathing heavily and wiping blood off his face. "Good fight! You, Trace, tough, tough man. Your thigh, good in three weeks, no problem! But Impi and I go now." He pointed at Rip. "You stay, take care of friend. You follow, Impi shoots you in face."

"I'm following…whether Impi tries to shoot me or not," said a voice. Scarlet approached, breathing as if he had been in a long sprint.

"Do not interfere," said Boar, his face growing deadly serious.

"I know you and Rodrigo have been secretly coordinating something," said Scarlet. "I'm going with you. I'm doing what you tell me, when you tell me, but I *am* going."

"What I tell you, when I tell you. You are light on feet, sneaky like weasel, da?"

"Not happy with the weasel bit, but aye," said Scarlet.

"Then we go, no time," said Boar, picking up his spear and striding quickly down the corridor. Impi snatched up his garnet and new gloves and scampered after.

"Take care of Trace," said Scarlet to Rip. "If things go badly, take care of the children."

"Do yeh expect bad things?" said Rip, his brows wrinkling in concern.

"Not a bit," said Scarlet, "but I'm irrationally optimistic."

Unlike the darkness of the abandoned, desolate upper regions of the castle, the lower depths were well lit by rampant growths of glowmoss that choked the passageways. Water flowed and pooled everywhere, and all three royals complained bitterly of the danger to their majestic clothing. "If this is a joke by Morten, I will surely test his immortality," grumbled Awkley, who grunted in anger each time he looked at his muck-caked boots.

"I assure you this is worth the toil," said Morten. "I wish Boar could be with us. He has been such an inspiration. A guide, even. But the destruction of the blackspawn is at hand and the army needs its commander."

Rodrigo felt a gnawing sense of alarm. Boar was missing. Had he already marched south to fight spawn?

They soon reached a wide corridor and a wider set of shallow steps up that led into an immense, high-vaulted chamber. Small rivulets of water flowed down the walls in a few places, pooled together and ran through the archway that they had entered, providing just enough glow-light to dimly make out the structure of the room.

The chamber reminded Rodrigo of an oval stadium. Terraces of stone seating curved high up around the walls on one end, with a wide ledge of stone running overhead like a horseshoe, containing the rotted remains of lavish wooden box seating.

A flat expanse occupied the other half of the chamber, scattered with wreckage and heavy metal cages, and divided from the seating area by a fence of woven metal three times the height of a man. Three wide tunnels exited this half, descending gradually into gloom. Rodrigo shook his head slightly and leaned toward Yun. "An arena," he whispered. "A gladiatorial arena."

As they approached the arena floor, Morten smiled broadly and held his arms up high and wide. "Do you remember? Remarkable! I haven't been here in— why, it must be at least a century."

"Your arena!" congratulated Awkley.

"Built with my own hands," said Morten, breathing in appreciatively. "And the hands of quite a few slaves. Those were the days of glory, my friend."

"If I recall, first they built it, and then they played in it," said Awkley, looking impishly at Temma.

The queen rewarded him with a shake of her head. "Do you two never tire of your bloody vices?"

"Bravo! The queen remembers those days," added Awkley.

"I remember a terrible waste of humanity," said Temma. "A shameful waste."

"Says the queen who spent many a night right up there." Awkley pointed to the decayed box seats high above.

"Shut up," snapped the queen. "Did you call us here for a reason, Morten, or did you simply want us to relive your past follies?"

"Someday I must find a way to end your life, Temma," said Morten, smiling lazily. "Which, if we are fortunate, could be today. But until then, let us share in a new adventure! I give you…" Morten flourished a hand toward the large center exit of the arena.

"The Newt."

Within the darkness of the dry exit, Rodrigo imagined another, greater darkness. And then he heard the low, staccato clicking. Visions of the nightmare creature that had poured over him in the pumice tunnels washed through his memory, and he unconsciously took a step back.

"This is insanity," he said to himself.

"Yes," mused Morten, turning to look at Rodrigo with an appraising eye. He stepped close to the boy and whispered, "Tell me your secret, and I will see to it that you all live like royalty in Pinnacle. You might even be able to take Scribbs's place, if you can touch his circlet without your life being snuffed away. And perhaps Temma's place, for one of your dear girls."

Rodrigo turned to the king's ear. "And your place, as well," he whispered.

Morten shook his head in exasperation. "You have much to learn about the realities of life, you stubborn young fool. Unfortunately, unless you can find some measure of flexibility very soon, the only lesson coming to you is the finality of death."

"Do your worst," said Rodrigo. *Where is Boar?*

Morten straightened and stepped back, giving Rodrigo a resigned nod and a wave of his long-fingered hand. "As you wish," he said. "This is all upon your head. I wonder how that god you cry out to feels about your selfish willingness to see others die to keep your violent secret."

"I imagine that He is becoming angrier with you by the minute," said Rodrigo.

Morten shook his head, raised his hands, and clapped them together. "Time for a demonstration! Please, everyone, make yourselves comfortable near the fence. Hunters, bring the Blueboys."

"This fence will not keep the Newt in," said Rodrigo.

"It does not need to," said Morten. "The Newt is no animal." Morten tapped the side of his head. "It is smart, clever—a creature born to serve a powerful master. Since its awakening here it has searched for a suitable master to serve. It found me."

Morten gripped the fence and shook it. "No, my dear boy, this is to keep the *prey* in."

The Hunters dragged the four Blueboys to the front. Morten levered open a small gate in the barrier, through which the Blueboys were tossed. Rodrigo recognized one of their faces.

"Toronado, who is with you?" called Rodrigo.

The Blueboy named Toronado turned to Rodrigo, holding a wounded forearm. "Graves, Adanpuri, and Belosh, sir." The three others nodded and saluted.

"You will not salute!" yelled Awkley. "He is not your commander and you are no longer Blueboys. Traitors!"

"Shove a crooked stick in it," growled Adanpuri. "Remember us, Commander," he said to Rodrigo.

"Avenge us," added Belosh.

Rodrigo nodded, but he had no way at hand to avenge them. Only Boar could have, and he was gone. Was he, in the end, a clever liar as well?

"Gentlemen," said Morten, "you are warriors. There are weapons all around you. Defend yourselves. If you are victorious, you have my word that you will be freed."

There were weapons—old rusty relics scattered across the arena, left to rot for hundreds of years. The four began casting about for ways to defend themselves, muttering at the callous irony of Morten's words. They separated, scavenging through the debris.

In the gloom, the staccato clicking drifted from one of the side tunnels.

"Brace yourselves, everyone," announced Morten, his eyes wide with excitement and anticipation.

Rodrigo heard Adanpuri call out for the others to regroup around him. The Blueboy had gained a height advantage by climbing onto an old platform atop a large cage, his silhouette showing that he had found a spear as a weapon. Graves ran past, close by the fence, holding two blades, heading toward Adanpuri.

The clicking continued, lightly, indistinctly. A small stone fell and clattered among the debris.

"Above!" shouted Rodrigo. Awkley bludgeoned him in the stomach.

Adanpuri's silhouette spun about, and then another silhouette snapped down upon him, smashing the man prone—a long, ropy curling thing that lifted Adanpuri from the platform and into the darkness of the ceiling. His shouts turned to screams and abruptly chopped to silence.

Awkley clapped, as if applauding an opera. "Magnificent, Morten! I am almost afraid, quite seriously!"

Rodrigo noticed that fear touching everyone. Temma stepped away and leaned backward with a look of wavering shock and amazement. The Hunters huddled, weapons at the ready. Of the girls, only Hope watched. There seemed no expression on her face at all, simply a clinical detachment in her hazel eyes.

A minute passed. The clicking rose and fell, barely audible and difficult to pinpoint. The three remaining Blueboys assembled with their backs to the bars of the cage where Adanpuri had been snatched away.

And then it came, making no pretense of stealth, a black mountain flowing across the floor, twice the height of the men and five times the length, a curling mass of tentacles and scythe-like mandibles tapering off into a lean body and a thin, whip-like tail. Rodrigo realized that he had become rooted and frozen with a numbing fear, despite his experiences with the nightmare creature before. The poor lighting only enhanced the effect, so that the monster could be seen just enough to allow the terrified imagination to fill in the unearthly details.

Morten must be bursting with pride.

The three men fought, but it made little difference. Their cries and screams rose and fell, and their three silhouettes rose simultaneously in the air, entangled and helpless, as though the monster wished to show off its trophies. And then the three disappeared, engulfed in the black mass. For a moment it ceased its movements, as if relaxing. Then it flowed away into the gloom.

Silence fell on the arena.

"Bravo," whispered Awkley. "That is easily the most frightening thing I have ever witnessed. Pure killing essence!"

Temma looked as though she wanted to run. "Are you certain that it is safe? I mean…"

"Quite safe," beamed Morten. "When Boar first introduced me to it, it tried to kill me. No end of weapons inside that mass, I assure you. It smoked me in seconds. Took me two days to resurrect. After I came back, it worshiped me. Never has it had an immortal master."

"But, how did…" said Temma hesitantly.

"My dear Morten," interrupted Awkley, "you really must re-open this arena. Don't change a thing! The lighting, the gloomy atmosphere—perfect! Of course, you'll need to figure out how to challenge this monster. I doubt even twenty well-armed men could properly test it in battle. Even Rafe and Shoca would have their hands full, no doubt."

"No doubt!" said Morten. "Now that would be a battle to witness." His voice trailed away and he peered through the gloom of the arena. "I hope my Newt didn't wander off. There's more to the feast today…unless, Rodrigo, you see reason now? There's no need for this to go further. You could even become commander again. Right, Awkley?"

"Most assuredly," said Awkley cheerfully. "Everything forgiven and forgotten. Just tell us your secret, and where your friends might be hiding."

Rodrigo wanted to answer, to crow about their failure to find Scarlet and scream at their poisonous souls, but he dared not. His rage threatened to snap free, to throw him into an incoherent, murderous fury that would serve only to fulfill and delight these hideous monsters and to shatter the already fragile mindsets of the girls.

Morten pressed close to Rodrigo's face. "Take a minute to think, Rodrigo. It's an important minute, because this is it. No more threats. In one minute, one of your friends goes in the cage and I will make sure you watch."

Rodrigo read the cold man's eyes and sober expression, and knew that he meant it. *Think, Rodrigo! There must be a way!*

He tried to think, to pull a life-saving strategy together. He remembered his past words to the others, his hopes for somehow restoring Pinnacle, and he almost laughed with the raw futility of it.

Stop pitying yourself and think!

He found himself spinning slowly, looking from face to face—Temma's intensity, Awkley's boyish excitement to witness more killing, Hope looking at him placidly, while Yun hid under her bangs, and Phoebe clutched her bandages and shivered, the two titans standing back, deep in whispered conversation.

And then something crept slowly into his mind. Awkley and Morten were exactly right—the Newt could be a danger to the titans. Were the titans discussing that very possibility right now? He doubted that even the monster could be a serious threat to the titans, but if he could find a way to engage them...

"I wonder if there are more of these creatures," said Rodrigo, loud enough to interrupt the titans. "Even Rafe and Shoca would have to watch their backs, and check every shadow. Morten might find he likes Newts as lapdogs better than the meddling titans as busybody overseers."

"What are you—?" said Morten, puzzled. Then his eyes widened. "Ahh, I say, masterful! Try to pit the big boys against the Newt. Won't work, of course. Rafe and Shoca are far smarter and wiser than you. Have you made up your mind?"

Rodrigo looked at the titans. They had stopped talking and were watching him impassively. Morten was right. What words could he speak?

"I cannot-" he began.

"Right!" said Morten, the veins on his forehead bulging with his rising anger. He pointed at Phoebe. "Throw the hurt one in." He levered open the door with a grinding, rusty clang.

The Hunters rushed back to their positions to comply, but Hope stepped forward. "Not her. It's my turn."

"Oh, such a noble one. Showing off for your love?" said Morten.

"You talk too much," said Hope. "I've realized that there's nothing to you. You're a spiteful little appetite in fancy clothes. I can understand your cruelty, to strike back at all of the people who compare favorably to you."

"Typical of a woman," snorted Morten. "Can't even die quietly."

Hope's mouth stretched in a sneer. "It must frustrate you to be immortal, to know that you can't ever end who you are. How many times have you tried to kill yourself, Morten? Is that why you want Rodrigo's secret?"

Morten gritted his teeth, stepped forward, and swung a vicious backhand. But, to his surprise, Hope deftly ducked it, and he stumbled over himself. When he turned around, she had stepped through the gate.

Temma laughed. "The healer read your soul, Fancy Clothes."

"Shut up!" shouted Morten, flecks of spittle spilling from his lip. He slammed the gate shut. "I'll enjoy this!"

"Of course you will," said Hope calmly. "It's the only purpose that you have left." She walked toward Rodrigo and placed her hands on the fence. He moved to the fence as well.

"You were everything that I knew did not exist in men," she said. "And you're only a boy."

"Time has passed," he said. "Am I really still the boy?"

Hope shook her head. "You're right. You've grown up, grown more than all of us. Shouldered more than all of us."

From somewhere in the arena, the clicking sounds drifted in the dank, still air.

"I am sorry, truly sorry. I failed you," he said, taking her fingers in his through the wire.

"You're a great man," she said, and her mouth quirked. "But sometimes you overestimate yourself."

A roiling black mass arose quietly behind Hope. Rodrigo's eyes were pulled to the nightmare that took shape in front of him. Seeing this, Hope closed her own eyes, knowing what came behind her.

Rodrigo could not move, mesmerized. The mass of tentacles loomed over him now. At face level, two glinting eyes studied him like pools that sank to the underworld. The razor-lined mouth split sideways, braced by a long pair of sword-like mandibles and a smaller pair of scythes. Short feeder tentacles and spikes writhed in anticipation around the quivering mouth.

Rodrigo forced himself to look at Hope. "May the Lord of All enfold you, Hope."

She opened her eyes. "He had better do it soon."

The tentacles closed around her, slowly, almost hesitantly. They pulled her back, tore her hands away from the fence. She let out one subdued groan, and was engulfed by the black mass.

Rodrigo watched in numb shock as the Newt retreated slowly and silently back into the darkness. He turned to Morten, his eyes burning but his chin steady. "You are a damned soul in a living hell, Morten. I pity you."

"I didn't think it would change your mind," said Morten, trying to return to his sophisticated facade. "And it does not matter. No one wants you alive anymore, Rodrigo. You aren't worth the trouble. Let all your secrets and all your friends die with you."

The door clanged open. The Hunters threw Phoebe and Yun through, and Morten grabbed Rodrigo by the throat and tossed him in.

Rodrigo stumbled to his feet and spun, waiting, however futilely, to defend himself. But the Newt had retreated back into the shadows.

The end had come, and there was no Boar. Rodrigo had made himself bait for Boar's hidden plans, and he now found himself on the hook with no one holding the pole.

Boar had betrayed him.

––––––

On the day that Boar had taken the captive Rodrigo down into his personal dungeon at the Hunter stronghold, he did not torture the boy as his captains had assumed. Instead, he explained the nature of Pinnacle—the twisted insanity of the royalty, the decay of the city and its soldiers, and the hopelessness of the people. His surprising passion for making things right in Pinnacle struck a natural chord in Rodrigo, and the two agreed to at least delay their feud for another day.

To make this odd relationship function, Rodrigo chose to overlook Boar's definition of "right." The warlord had clearly desired to rule the city, and his strong, charismatic, brutal talents had quickly brought him to leadership and to the attention of the sadistic Morten.

By coordinating with Boar, Rodrigo believed that swift change could be effected. But there were dangers, of which Ancimoden ranked foremost. It would be critical to keep the secret from all their friends, in case they revealed the plans under Ancimoden's scourging. This meant that they must keep up the ruse of being mortal enemies, and, because both were regularly watched and spied upon, they could only communicate by hints and code words during their verbal clashes.

Boar then proceeded to punish Rodrigo's face, leaving him realistically bruised and bleeding for their first dramatic confrontation in front of the royalty. Boar led Rodrigo out of his dungeon by a secret tunnel and left the boy to find his own way to the castle without being recaptured.

Despite the discovery of the royalty's immortality, it became increasingly clear that the royals had vacated much of their responsibilities, living more and more isolated from the city. And in those gaps of responsibility, Rodrigo and Boar—the crusader and the warlord—hoped to build a new power to confront and circumvent the royalty.

All wasted dreams.

Rodrigo remembered the smug, cold Commander Boar standing with arms folded, giving the signal that his plans were set in motion.

I make plan too, Rodrigo. Deep plans, scary like Newt, all set and in place, nyet? I am fully prepared for you, Rodrigo. Fully prepared!

Whatever those plans were, they disappeared with Boar. Perhaps he had misread the man. Perhaps this was Boar's way of removing Rodrigo and exacting his revenge.

And yet, something nagged at him. Something about Boar's threats...

In the tunnel behind Rodrigo, the clicking echoed. It sounded strange, hollow. His fear began to rise, but he struck it down harshly and went to pick Yun up off the ground.

To his surprise, she smiled and hugged him. "We had a good journey, my brother," she said. "Would you hold me—until it comes, I mean. I don't want to look."

He stroked her raven hair and kissed the top of her head. "Of course," he said. He glanced down at Phoebe, wishing to help her too. She looked ill and shaken, but she began staggering to her feet against the bars of a cage. It mattered little now. A minute, perhaps less…

"You were brilliant, you know," he said to Yun. "Rafe and Shoca, Fear and Chaos." He remembered the late Lord Grager's words, the ones he commanded Scarlet to memorize above all else:

> *Time is short. Do not be distracted by the enemy on the far hill and fail to*
> *see the foe at your throat. Fear and chaos crouch in plain sight, readied to*
> *spring, their plans, laid long and patiently, come to fruition.*

And Yun's swift mind had caught it, had unscrambled the names, and it was those unscrambled names that Yun had whispered in Rodrigo's ear during the celebration. Rodrigo had known then who the real enemies were—the titans, the enemies hiding in plain sight.

"How did you think to unscramble their names?" he asked Yun.

"It just came to me," said Yun. "I am good with words, you know. And this language, it has unusual…*magic* to it. I wonder if the two titans even know their names do that. But Loa smiled on us, because we just happened to read the story of Bhalereton and how his name unscrambled to 'Nobleheart.' After that, I started trying to unscramble everyone's name, just for fun. I couldn't make anything from your name, by the way, except Drogori. Doesn't mean anything, just sounds neat."

Rodrigo's mind wandered back to the museum. Boar's threats—the filler talk between their clues—ironically turned out to be truer than the clues themselves.

> *Trust me, bad things happen, very bad for many here. Trust me, you watch*
> *them die…trust me. Then end come, and your worst nightmare come, and*
> *you twist.*

Rafe and Shoca. Fear and Chaos. Bhalereton and Nobleheart.

The great, unanswered question came to his mind. *Why am I not a corpse in the pumice tunnel, crushed between blackspawn and Newt?*

And then the answer came, suddenly, obviously.

Gloria ardiente de los ángeles en el cielo! You stupid, dull-witted cousin of a mule and an ass!

"Yun!" he whispered in her ear. "Get down and make yourself invisible. Take Phoebe into the debris. Get in a cage if you can. Do not ask questions, just do it!"

Increíble! I've been led by the nose to water, and I refused to drink! What am I to do now?

I'm the bait.

Just wiggle on the hook for as long as you can.

"Before I die," he called out, stepping up onto a block of stone, "I am willing to give up a secret. Would you like to hear it?"

The clicking from the tunnel grew slightly louder, more insistent.

Awkley raised his hands. "By all means, boy. I wouldn't suggest you take too much time, however."

"Thank you, my dear Awkley," said Rodrigo, as if they shared a close friendship. "If you will answer a quick question, then...What was Pinnacle like a hundred years ago?"

Awkley and Temma looked at each other. "You are about to be eaten," reminded Awkley. "How does the answer help your predicament?"

"Consider it a last request," said Rodrigo, his eyes glancing secretively about the chamber. "How was it different?"

"We were at war with the other cities," said Temma. "Not the best of times."

"And yet the city was active and noisy and teeming with people, wasn't it?" said Rodrigo.

Awkley shrugged and looked to Temma. Temma nodded. "I think, yes," said Awkley. "Temma has a better memory than me. Is this meaningful?"

"And what of your armies?" said Rodrigo.

"Stronger, to be sure," said Temma. "That was before the blackspawn."

"True," said Rodrigo. "But it was also before the titans."

"Get to your point, boy," said Morten.

Rodrigo's turned serious. "The titans and their tantyr allies have been patiently destroying you, bit by bit. It was they who persuaded Temma to become the Greatmother."

"Which ushered in the golden age of Pinnacle," cried Temma.

"Which threw you into decline," said Rodrigo. "What mother wishes to see her children stolen away?"

461

Temma sputtered in anger.

"And who persuaded you to fight in the open against the blackspawn rather than repair and man your defenses? How much have you bled needlessly?"

"That was for the best," said Morten, "to keep us bold and aggressive."

"And your armies are now bold, aggressive, and a ghost of what they were. The city guards openly loot and pillage, and the city falls deeper into ruin every year. You are afraid to let Haven and Drift see your decline. You share some of the blame, but the titans expertly manipulated you into oblivion."

Silence, but for the clicking.

Then Awkley chuckled. "A last, desperate ploy, Rodrigo. Very entertaining." He turned to the titans. "Surely you two haven't been misbehaving?"

Rafe and Shoca did not immediately respond, standing passively like two imposing marble statues. And yet their faces changed subtly, slowly, until Rodrigo could not help but shudder at the cold malevolence of their stares.

The Hunters edged away from the giants and the tantyrs moved to guard their titan masters.

Shoca slid his long sword from the scabbard at his back and tested its edge. "Decade laid upon decade, and today, at last, comes the end of the human blight of Pinnacle. The other cities will soon follow you into extinction. We are the new heirs."

"By the worthless gods!" Awkley gaped, then pointed a long finger at the other two royals. "If you will recall, I was against allowing these giant rabblecaps into the city in the first place."

"That was a century ago," said Temma. "You do hold score, don't you?"

"It matters not a bit. These two fools seem to forget our immortality," said Morten.

Rafe drew his two swords, spinning them expertly so that the points tapped lightly together as they met on the apex of the swing. "You may be immortal, but you can be 'smoked.' I relish the thought of doing so each day. You will be a never-ending source of entertainment."

"You would not dare touch me!" cried Temma.

Rafe's intense stare turned on the queen. "So long as you bring what we demand through Bountywell, you will be spared. We may even spare some of the little ones to comfort you."

"Don't you dare touch the children!" Temma screamed. "Awkley, Morten, stop them!"

"You've seen them fight," said Awkley. "I might last a moment, but they would smoke Morten on the first pass."

462

"I've bested you repeatedly!" cried Morten indignantly. "And personally I would find the castle quite the more pleasant without those annoying brats squirming about like maggots."

"You disgusting...*You* are the maggot!" yelled Temma.

"I haven't lost a single duel to you in a month," said Awkley to Morten. "Really, you have selective memory."

"*Be silent!*" boomed Shoca, growling in exasperation. "A century of you! I have been in the tortures of Gundre for ninety-one years listening to you four. I can wait no longer!"

Shoca took a step forward, but Rafe held out two of his four arms to stop him. "One moment, I have several curiosities. Rodrigo!"

"Yes?" called the boy.

Rafe paced around Shoca, casually maneuvering his swords together in a delicate dance. "It is strange to me that on the very eve of our victory, you happen to unmask us."

"Yes," said Rodrigo, "that should concern you."

Rafe laughed, his musical voice clashing with his cruel expression. "I did not say that it concerned me. Do you truly consider yourself the Bull of the Dalmar?"

"Quite so," said Rodrigo.

"But of course you are not," said Rafe. "The Dalmar are long past, having faced the same extinction that you do now. Their great hoax could succeed only once. However, if you are willing to tell us who you truly are, you and your friends will be spared."

"Ah, that is your plight," said Rodrigo. "You are playing king of the hill against—what?—a dozen?—a hundred?—other factions, fighting for control of this Spire. Who am I, you wonder? Do I represent a threat on the order of Oldevil, which you successfully defeated? Congratulations on your victory, by the way."

"I thank you." Rafe bowed. "Oldevil was the greatest threat to us—to all of us. Now, *our* time is at hand. We have built up our forces for long years. There are no other powers that can compare to us or our masters. And, while these kings are immortal, they suffer the ravages of being so. They are lazy and stupid and self-obsessed."

"I had noticed," said Rodrigo.

"So easy to manipulate that it became tedious," said Rafe.

"I believe you," said Rodrigo.

"Can you imagine the pain of sitting idly behind these four as they chatter on and on about everything and nothing for hours every day, year after year, for a century!"

"It is a wonder that you maintained your insanity," said Rodrigo.

Rafe stopped his pacing and cocked his head at Rodrigo. "You are a bold one. Do you even know who we are, I wonder?"

"Not the slightest idea," said Rodrigo, "other than this—a man that I choose to trust once told me to stop you. And so I shall."

"You are about to be eaten," said Rafe. "I believe you will have difficulty stopping us."

"I agree," said Rodrigo, his eyes scanning the chamber. "So, if you would be so good as to impale yourselves, I would be forever in your debt."

And as he finished his sentence, he caught a glimpse of movement, barely noticeable, high above. And yet the hollow, echoing clicks continued from the tunnel behind him.

"I offer this one chance, Rodrigo," said Rafe. "You and your friends can live in luxury and comfort under our rule, or you can be consumed by the monster—final choice. Choose quickly, before you are torn apart."

Rodrigo allowed the tiniest quirk of a smile.

"I choose the monster."

From the box seat ledge high above, a long, thin shape appeared—a mammoth brass-banded spear arcing outward and downward, thrown by an unseen hand. At the same time, an immense black shape dropped from the dark reaches of the ceiling above Rafe.

The Newt had found larger prey.

The spear struck half a second before the Newt, piercing Shoca's shoulder near the neck. Despite the massive size of the spear and the gathering power of its flight downward, it was not able to penetrate completely through to Shoca's barrel chest. The titan did not cry out. Instead, his head arched back, and a wavering hiss erupted from his widened mouth.

Rafe, his blades already drawn, reacted like a lightning stroke. He somehow sensed the fall of the monster toward him and launched himself sideways. The Newt brushed past, landing on the stone, its tentacles flailing for a grasp upon Rafe. Rafe's blades whirled back and forth, and three dismembered tentacles writhed furiously until their remaining lifeblood drained from them. Dark blood gouted from the Newt's severed stumps.

But other tentacles found a firm hold. The Newt drew itself to Rafe and embraced the titan. Rafe hissed fiercely and struck deeply into Newt's body with his blades. The embrace held for several seconds, and then the Newt staggered back, limping and heeling sideways.

Rafe's hiss contorted into an eerie screech, like boulders sliding across steel. His body convulsed, pierced deeply in a dozen places by the savage weaponry of the Newt. But he did not bleed. Instead, the wounds bulged and twisted, spreading and growing, bubbling out like a mud pot. Rafe opened his mouth wider and wider, his screech stuttering to a stop.

And then his head fell from his shoulders. It bounced off the quivering mass of his body and dropped to the stone, flattening as though it were made of warm butter.

Behind it, the headless body boiled and shuddered. From out of his flesh, arms twisted into shape, and legs, and stingers. A trio of spiny insect-like heads thrust themselves from a thigh, and a bloated human-like head arose from the opposite shoulder. With the heads came shoulders, and torsos, and soon what had been Rafe was now two monsters joined like Siamese twins, each ferociously working to free itself from the other. The two battled against each other violently before they broke free, showering pale gray globs onto the stone. The globs formed themselves into ghastly creatures and scuttled away.

Where the titan had stood, there now crouched two bone-pale monsters—one lean and wickedly spiked, its long, stingered tail whipping about its three razor-frilled insect heads, the other a mocking half-replica of a human, one half bulky and fat, the other lean and wiry.

Shoca reached back and tore the spear from his body. The wound gushed pale monsters and gray spawn essence. Shoca tilted forward awkwardly as if hunchbacked, and the wound slowly closed over.

In shock, Rodrigo understood. The titans were spawn.

The chamber devolved into chaos. The three tantyrs hounded the Newt, slicing and hacking at the monster. A tentacle found the leg of one, pulling it close enough for the wickedly fast strike of a long claw to tear away the tantyr's life. Shoca roared a command and pointed at Rodrigo. The two tantyrs broke off and climbed away on their light-wings, turning for the boy.

Rodrigo looked about desperately for a weapon, but could see nothing handy except a rock and a few old boards. "Gracia de Dios, no!" he shouted to himself, realizing that he had run out of chances. He turned to sprint to the nearest cage, knowing that he would never make it.

The two tantyrs angled in to intercept. They came within ten paces, when Rodrigo heard a thrumming noise behind him. One of the tantyrs clutched at a bolt in her side and peeled away. Rodrigo felt someone slam against him and turned to defend himself. Strong hands gripped him and steadied him.

"Now there, Commander, not as dead as you might think," said the Blueboy Adanpuri, alive and well and sporting a long spear. The other three Blueboys drew next to Rodrigo and presented a wall of spear points to the onrushing tantyr. The creature veered high, barely dodged a second crossbow bolt, and sped back toward Shoca.

Rodrigo turned to find the crossbowman. Atop the rock on which Rodrigo had made his earlier speech, he saw Boar's small friend, Owleye, its black cloak waving about as it deftly worked another bolt into its weapon. It brought the weapon up, gave a slight nod to Rodrigo, and aimed for a shot at the stinger-tailed spawn.

Stingertail tore wildly at the two kings and a single Huntsman. Two other Huntsmen lay dead at its feet. Awkley slammed his long blade into the monster's thigh. Morten aimed for the darting tail and missed, but one spiked claw of the monster caught the king and held him long enough for the tail to pierce him through and lift him. The monster's claws tore at the king until Morten became nothing but a cloud of yellowish smoke and a tatter of clothes. A flare of bluish light erupted as his silver circlet disappeared in a small implosion.

"Gods, Morten! Embarrassing!" yelled Awkley, ramming his sword through the nightmare's foot. The creature caught a crossbow bolt in one neck, staggered on its pierced leg and crashed sideways, its wounds twisting and spewing smaller spawn.

Beyond, the half-bulky spawn chased two Huntsmen and the screaming Temma as they fled out of the entrance.

Rodrigo saw a rope fall from the ledge above. A figure leaned off the ledge and began a swift descent on the dangling rope. *Scarlet?* A second figure followed. *Boar!*

Shoca circled the Newt, his mirrored shield raised and his sword arm cocked. The Newt tried one advance and lost another tentacle in the attempt. It retreated and circled as well.

Rodrigo and the four Blueboys raced to the gate, but it was closed.

Awkley turned to look at Rodrigo, his arm absently stabbing his lean blade through the rat's mouth of a collie-sized monster. He strode over, picked up Morten's sword, and yanked the gate lever over. "Welcome to the free-for-all, boy! The fun's on this side of the fence tonight." The king who had tried to murder Rodrigo and his friends only minutes ago beamed excitedly at the boy and threw him Morten's weapon. "Oh, it's your Blueboy friends. The Newt wasn't dining on you after all. Sneaky. Plenty of mayhem to go around, boys—wade in!"

Stingertail had splintered into half a dozen horrors that immediately beset Awkley and the Blueboys. Rodrigo stabbed at one and ducked to the side, trying to see Scarlet, but Shoca and the Newt blocked his vision.

The Newt and the titan continued to circle each other. Newt bled freely from a half-dozen wounds and lost limbs, while Shoca hunched forward on his bent back. Neither could easily advance without opening themselves up to a deadly strike. The unwounded tantyr hovered nearby, uncertain what to do.

"Fly at him! Strike!" growled the titan to the tantyr. Without hesitation, the tantyr flew into the maw of the Newt, her swords flashing. The Newt swept the tantyr down and ripped the life from her, but Shoca charged, driving his sword deep into the tentacled monster.

The Newt writhed violently, caught one of the titan's legs, and savaged it. Shoca stabbed again and again, and the Newt shuddered and lost its grip.

Shoca readied a fourth blow but suddenly arched back, hissing and squealing. Beside him, Boar roared, his neck bulging with veins as he rammed the giant brass-banded spear deeper into the titan's side.

Shoca swiped with his shield, smashing Boar in the shoulder and head and sending him sprawling twenty feet. Behind Shoca, the Newt rose up and plunged its razor-sharp mandibles into the titan's back. Newt and titan fell sideways, and as Shoca shuddered and deformed, the Newt slashed at the resulting monstrosities, and they tore at it.

Scarlet pulled the shaken Boar to his feet. "Well done, big man!" he shouted.

Boar staggered and shook his head, grabbing Scarlet by the shoulders and leaning heavily on him. "Rawf!" he growled loudly, letting out a heaving breath. And then Boar's eyes rolled up into his head and he pitched forward unconscious, falling over on Scarlet and pinning the boy to the ground. By the time Scarlet worked his way out from under the unconscious warrior, the Half-Bulk spawn had rumbled back into the room, having lost interest in the fleeing queen.

The monster went straight for Awkley, flailing its large arm like a sledgehammer. Awkley dodged, but the monster took a long step and swept its arm sideways at the Blueboys in a surprisingly deft move. Their spears pierced the arm, but not before it crashed against Belosh and crushed him against the fence. Scarlet drove in and stabbed the thinner leg, barely avoiding being stepped on. Awkley stood at the other leg, piercing it repeatedly until it kicked back and sent him flying. Stung by Scarlet's blade, it turned, but found Rodrigo directly under it and aimed a blow at the young man.

Rodrigo retreated, collided with Adanpuri, and spun through the gate of the arena fence. He looked up and his heart skewed in sickening circles.

Hope—alive and well—stood at a cage nearby, next to Yun and Phoebe. None of them were looking at Rodrigo. Instead, they stared at the tantyr female in front of them, who earlier had been pierced by a bolt from Owleye. Owleye lay at the tantyr's feet, unmoving.

"No!" yelled Rodrigo and rushed at the tantyr.

The tantyr raised a sword to strike Hope, but the healer fell back and away, and the tantyr did not have enough time to correct her stab before Rodrigo was on her.

The tantyr's second blade parried Rodrigo's outthrust sword point and sliced him across the forearm, but Rodrigo slammed into the protruding shaft of the crossbow embedded in her side. She grunted and fell sideways. Rodrigo stabbed at her, but the tantyr dodged the blade and swiftly regained her feet, less one sword. She clutched at her bleeding side.

"It is finished!" shouted Rodrigo, pointing with his sword to the fighting beyond the cage. "Lay down your weapon."

Her face fell into bleak finality. "Only death can finish it," she said, and lifted her sword high, rushing at Rodrigo. Rodrigo nicked her leg and rolled sideways, hoping to escape her revenging cut, but her weapon slashed across his shoulder.

468

Stunned from the pain, he rolled over and saw the tantyr standing over him, weapon ready.

And then a crossbow bolt erupted from the side of her neck, her weapon slipped from her grasp and she pitched forward, her breathing ragged and rasping. She tried to reach for her sword but Rodrigo kicked it away.

Scarlet stood at the gate, lowering a lean crossbow. Rodrigo rose and nodded to this friend. No words were necessary between them, and Scarlet returned to the slaughter of the Titanspawn.

"Hope, you are needed!" Rodrigo called, keeping his eye on the tantyr.

Hope came up behind Rodrigo to look at his shoulder.

"I'm fine," he said. "See to him."

She bent to examine the tantyr, but Rodrigo stopped her again.

"Not her," said Rodrigo. "Him." He pointed at Owleye.

The tantyr twisted face up, her side and neck leaving a pool of purplish blood on the stone. Her eyes turned to meet Rodrigo's, and they stared at each other until her chest stopped falling and her eyes lost focus.

The surviving lone Huntsman and the three remaining Blueboys rushed about the great chamber, eradicating the last of the small remaining monsters. Everywhere, the tiny crab-like spawn essence flowed like gray sand dunes, seeking hiding places in the debris and darkness, scuttling away from the patches of glowmoss. Rodrigo and Scarlet met near the gate, keeping an eye on any of the scuttling monsters that might threaten the girls. Scarlet brought great relief to Phoebe when he shouted to her that Ana, Ardi, and Petra were safely out of the queen's clutches and hidden away.

Awkley walked up to the two young men, still beaming excitedly, his royal clothing ragged and tiny wisps of yellow smoke drifting from his numerous cuts.

"How do you do it, Rodrigo? Always alive at the end of a tight spot."

"Many of those spots brought about by you," said Rodrigo.

"Too true!" laughed Awkley. "I'm actually quite glad to see that I haven't succeeded at doing away with you yet."

Awkley stepped up on a stone platform, took in a deep breath, and swept his arms in a circle. "Ahh, glory! This day put Morten's old arena games to shame, I can tell you that. Sad that he ended up being smoked. Now I have to wait until he springs back to life to gloat. But then, if he hadn't been smoked, I wouldn't have as much to gloat about, would I?"

He laughed and took another deep breath. "I have been waiting and planning for this day for a very long time. Oldevil finished. The titans and tantyrs erased. It's all working out quite splendidly."

"I did not know that you were working from a plan," said Rodrigo.

"Of course!" said Awkley, gazing out on his field of victory. "Everything turned out as I had foreseen. I knew that the titans were no good, but I could not convince the others. So I patiently put up with them, all the while convincing them into being the force to stop Oldevil. I even seeded in their minds a mistrust toward the human troops, so that I could evacuate my Blueboys out of harm's way when the assault came. In the end, Oldevil and the titans canceled each other out quite nicely, as I knew they would."

"Congratulations, you are a wonder," said Scarlet sarcastically, glancing sideways to Rodrigo.

Rodrigo shrugged and gave his friend an uncertain look. Of all the royalty, there was something dangerously clever about Awkley that put Rodrigo on his guard. So, while the king's boasts were likely lies, Rodrigo could not be certain.

"Well," said Awkley, turning and slapping at the dust and debris on his clothes, "a change of attire is called for. I couldn't help but notice Commander

Boar is here, which I find very odd." He glanced suspiciously at Rodrigo and stepped down from the platform, heading toward the entrance. But after a few steps he called over his shoulder, "I think Morten would approve if I left Boar in charge here. Please be so good as to tell your sworn enemy that he has command over the field of battle."

Rodrigo's newly awakened sworn enemy approached the three women. Hope and Yun glanced at each other in alarm. Boar stopped in front of them, his face grim. He pointed to the small, still form of his servant, Owleye. "Is he alive?"

Hope nodded. "He's gravely wounded. He is alive for now. I do not know."

"His name is Impi," said Boar. "He will live. You will whisper this in his ear every hour, da?"

Hope nodded.

"And you slap him in face, each time? Soft, like this." Boar slammed his face with one meaty palm, launching droplets of sweat. "You do that because I tell you, da?"

"I'll keep that in mind," said Hope.

Boar turned to go but saw Phoebe standing nearby, leaning against the cage bars. "Ah, this is Phoebe, nyet? You shoot like man." He inspected her wounds and her frame rather indelicately, and she shooed away his hand. "You live, I think. Grow up, have many babies that shoot like you."

"I have three children," said Phoebe.

Boar scratched his chin and looked her over questioningly. "Three? And who is father? Rodrigo? Scarlet? Both?"

"Your timing is in question," she said, cocking her head, her teal eyes challenging him.

"Timing? Da! Of course, not many days, no time enough." Boar flexed one impressive arm, clenched its bloody fist, and then tapped her forehead. "No matter. You strong in head, I know, strong like man."

"If I am to birth babies, sir, I will need to be strong like woman," said Phoebe.

"Da!" laughed Boar. He stepped back and looked away, his eyes lost in thought. "I go now. Must say goodbye to friend."

Phoebe tisked and folded her arms, wincing at the pain in her side. "Why do they always tease me about babies?"

Behind her, Hope gave Phoebe a sly, disbelieving look. "If you think about it long enough, I'm sure it will come to you."

———

A "Hahlay!" rang over the field of victory and Rip slid down Scarlet's rope. Above, Trace limped to the edge and waved happily, but made no attempt at the rope.

Rodrigo and Scarlet greeted their small friend, who swung around in a circle and gasped at the many remains of the titanic battle.

"M'thinks I'm glad to have missed this," said Rip.

"I am most glad to have survived it," said Rodrigo.

Rodrigo ordered the surviving Blueboys to bring oil for burning the spawn, then stepped through the spreading pool of Titanspawn essence that marked the point of death for Shoca. Centered in Shoca's remains spread a darker stain surrounding the limp bulk of the Newt. The three friends stepped hesitantly around to the monster's tentacled front, shocked by the severity of the creature's wounds. All but a few of the great ropy tentacles were now nothing more than stumps. Ragged wounds opened to raw flesh everywhere, and the buried head had fared even worse, with one side of the vertical mouth torn free and the double set of mandibles sagging and twisting brokenly.

But there remained a glitter in the two unharmed eyes, and they seemed to shift as Rodrigo stepped close. Rodrigo heard steps from behind, and Boar strode up next to him.

Boar placed a hand on the feeder tendrils next to the mouth. They shifted slightly, slowly, enfolding his hand.

"No one could have done what you have done, friend," said Boar. "I am proud to have stood by you in battle. You die atop your crushed enemies. I will do the same one day."

Boar stood there for some time, his face hard set, the tendrils wrapped around his hand. *Is he crying?* thought Rodrigo. Rodrigo found it difficult to fight back the rim of moisture in his own eyes. Without this terrifying, lonely beast, the lives of everyone on the Spire would have been lost.

"He looked the evil monster, and so we treated him as such," said Rodrigo. "Just like Bhalereton—Nobleheart—in the story."

"Newt is smart," said Boar. "He knew heart of Morten, knew his ferocious look and ferocious acts would impress king. Knew that he could lure in the titans through Morten."

Rodrigo placed his hand next to Boar's. "Well done, Nobleheart," he said.

Moments later, the flicker died in the black eyes, and the tendrils went slack. Death came to Nobleheart.

"How did this happen, Boar?" said Rodrigo. "How did you befriend him?"

"It is strange that you ask," said Boar. "I know his father."

"There is more than one?" said Rodrigo. "Ah, the clicking! I heard it in the tunnel behind me just before Nobleheart sprang on Rafe.

Boar shook his head. "No, boy. *You* are his father. *You* woke him."

"What?" said Rodrigo, blinking.

"In tunnels near Drift, my friend Newt appeared as stone like us. People there, they get very frightened, think demons come to get them. Not smart in head, people in Drift, scared of everything. But Newt stay stone, so they start getting used to him there. And then, you come and wake him up with touch and big burst of BOOM!"

"Gracia de Dios!" said Rodrigo. "I do not remember!"

"You get knocked down, bad knock on head. And my friend Newt not quite right in head then either, just wake up, hurt some Drifters, kill some Drifters." Boar shrugged. "Did not mean to, but they blame you. Over the falls you go."

Rodrigo swallowed, trying to determine how Newt fit into any of his assumptions. "How did you find this out?"

Boar smiled. "When I was in Drift, of course. You are boogeyman in that city."

Rodrigo thought back to the battle in the pumice tunnels. "Ah! Newt was trying to help. That explains why I am alive after I was trapped between Newt and the blackspawn. He was not attacking me; he was protecting me. And Newt must have been trying to reach us down in the tunnel under the gargoyle, and caused Raeder to fall. We never imagined that something so terrifying would be an ally."

"Da, he always try to capture first," said Boar. "That way, plenty time to explain while he has your attention. Otherwise, nothing but running and screaming and no listening."

Rodrigo shook his head. "I told Scarlet that only one could see this through. I meant you, Boar. I did not know that it would be Newt."

"*And* my spear, *and* these ultimate weapons," said Boar, slapping his arms. "You do not forget. It go badly for you."

"And our feud?" Rodrigo straightened the tattered edges of his shirt.

"No problem, unless you make me angry again."

A man approached Newt—a short, stocky, dark-skinned fellow with placid eyes and a welcoming set to his face. Boar's eyes lit up. "Ah, here is other Newt! Rodrigo, this is Conee, mason of Pinnacle. He is second person that my friend 'eat' in city."

Conee nodded, his face turning downcast as he moved up to touch Nobleheart.

"Most people not really like kidnap by monster," said Boar. "Conee, he okay with that. Show Rodrigo your stones trick."

474

Conee turned and nodded. "How do, Rodrigo," he said, pumping Rodrigo's hand. "I've a knack for stone, sir." He put two large flat stones in his hand and struck them together rapidly in a rocking stroke, producing the hollow Newt-clicking that Rodrigo heard earlier.

Rodrigo smiled. "Masterful, Conee! I was hearing you in the tunnel behind me. I thought the Newt was still there."

"Rafe and Shoca think same," said Boar, grimacing smugly. "I told you I set trap, no one get out. You remember that."

"And I survive traps," said Rodrigo. "You remember that."

"So the Newt was capturing people, not eating them?" said Scarlet.

"Da!" said Boar. "He eat glowmoss like everyone else. And some cows and things, but people he only capture to make name for himself as terrible servant of evil. It catches Morten's attention, nyet?"

"Clever animal," said Scarlet.

"Not animal," said Boar. "Maybe smarter than you."

"Your spear," said Rodrigo, seeing it half-buried under Newt's bulk. He tried to pull the giant weapon out from under the body, grunting with exertion. "This weighs like an anchor," he said.

"Spear not for you," said Boar, stepping over and dragging out the weapon. He hefted it with one hand, as though he were readying to throw it. "This spear for man, for one man—Boar."

He rotated the spear until the two boys could see a brass ornament near the spearhead—a stylized wild boar, rampant, in exactly the same form as that on the Dalmar Wall.

Scarlet started to speak, but Rodrigo elbowed him. Conee stood nearby. Rodrigo turned to him. "Conee, as a mason, do you think that you could build a monument, right here—a mausoleum dedicated to Newt, the Nobleheart, the savior of the Spire?"

Conee smiled and nodded. "That would be an honor," he said, his eyes appraising the stone floor and the nearby structures.

"We will leave you to it then," said Rodrigo, and nudged the others through the gate and back toward the girls. Rodrigo had Boar show the spear's ornamentation to the women.

"Apologies, Scarlet," said Rodrigo, "but we need to be careful in discussing things like the Dalmar Wall around others."

Scarlet nodded and pulled something from his belt case—the arm band with the wild boar set in gems. He handed it to Boar, who whistled appreciatively and tried it on. It settled in perfectly.

"Not to be spooky-sounding, Rodrigo, and I know what you said before in the museum, but I doubt that's coincidental," said Scarlet.

"I certainly agree now, but not because of some prophecy," said Rodrigo. "These are pieces fitting into place, and someone is placing those pieces in front of us."

"What do you mean?" said Hope. "Who?"

Rodrigo's lips curled into a hunter's smile. "Whoever gave those carefully crafted words of warning to Rook Lord Grager. Whoever wrote an entire instruction book, apparently just for us—Ravenhair."

Yun's eyes brightened. "I knew there was more. It's just...special."

"Where is the book now?"

"In Scribbs's chambers, under my bed," said Yun.

"We have to protect that book at all costs," said Rodrigo.

"Yes, but, why so sneaky and secret?" said Rip. "Why have Lord Grager give us a riddle? Why not the whole tale, bright and fine?"

Rodrigo shook his head. "I'm not entirely certain, but I do know secrets are hard to keep here, with soul-rippers like Berylata and Ancimoden around. So, my guess is that whoever is pulling at our strings plays a dangerous game of dropping hints and hoping we figure it out in time. I wonder whether that is why secrets are buried so deep in the Ravenhair book."

Scarlet tapped at his gull-emblazoned belt buckle. "But how could this— whoever—know we would even find the book? And besides making me look fantastic, what good is this belt, or these other Dalmar things?"

"Speak for self," said Boar, hefting his spear.

"Clearly our mysterious friend—or friends—wish to remain hidden, for whatever reason," said Rodrigo. He turned to Yun. "Remember when we found the Ravenhair book? What were the chances of you not seeing and taking Ravenhair in that library?"

"None!" said Yun. "It's perfect!"

"Exactly," said Rodrigo. "You love books, you love fairytales, and that bright blue cover among all of those boring dusty brown tomes in that library. You— and you alone—would never have let that pass. And your belt, Scarlet, and my sword, and Hope's healing kit—all things that would catch our hearts."

Rodrigo leaned in closer. "Which means that whoever this person is, he knows us very, very well."

"Yes," said Phoebe, "but *how* could he know us that well? We were nothing more than statues until just recent—oh, sakes! He knew us before we woke!"

Rodrigo nodded meaningfully.

"We are not Dusties. We were planted here."

476

111 : PROMISE

Yun's diary, Day 205

> We are all together, all alive, hidden away in a large monastery. I've
> gotten lost in the maze of corridors twice already. Hope is busy caring
> for the wounded—Rodrigo's shoulder and Trace's hip and Phoebe's cuts
> and a knot on Boar's head the size of my fist. One of the Blueboys,
> Belosh, died last night. Hope didn't give him much of a chance anyway.
>
> Impi, the little black-skinned creature that follows Boar, is not yet
> awake. Hope is surprised he is alive.
>
> No, I realized we are not all here. No one has seen Ed.
>
> I have to find a way to see Scribbs. Everyone says that we aren't
> married, and that the ceremony did not count. I don't know if that is true
> or not.

Rodrigo stood in front of the royal court, as he had on so many other occasions over the past month. Two days had passed since the battle against the titans, and while all of the other Lakesiders had joined the children and Zales in the monastery for safety, he and Boar walked brazenly into the court, welcomed with open arms by Awkley, with faint praise by the newly resurrected Morten, and with screaming fury by Temma.

"They *stole away* my children!" she howled, "and cruelly tortured and wounded other children in doing so! You cannot allow them to live, much less remain as your commanders. Are you *insane?*"

"Why," shrugged Awkley, "I feel saner than I have in a century, thanks in part to these two rapscallions. You, Morten?"

"I have no intention of giving up the toughest commander in living history," said Morten, bowing slightly to the smug Boar. "Besides, we have an offensive against the blackspawn to conduct, and bygones must be bygones."

"I will have my children back or I will execute Rodrigo until he gives them up!" screamed the queen.

Morten looked at Awkley and smiled, his emotional frump fading. "You're not making much sense, Temma. Perhaps you should go lie down."

Temma leapt to her feet. "I will not stand to be part of this any longer. It is clear that my Greencloaks must be strengthened, and I intend to do that *right*

477

now!" Without another word, she stormed out of the court, her entourage of children and her new head matron following her nervously.

"A shame that she will miss saying goodbye to our useful, traitorous tantyr friends," said Awkley as the vibration of wings rose from outside. A pair of tantyrs floated down onto the ledge of the great open windows, their green and amber eyes gleaming in the bright light of the court. Rodrigo shook his head slightly. *Such incredible beauty, and graceful skill—and implacable enemies.*

"We have given our wounded the final honor," said the lead tantyr. "They have fulfilled themselves, unlike we who survive. However, we could not find Berylata. You must return her."

The two kings glanced at each other, confused. They looked at Boar, who shrugged his folded arms.

Scarlet, what have you done? Rodrigo stepped forward.

"Berylata is the remaining leader of those who betrayed this world," said Rodrigo. "She must answer for your treachery."

"You intend to kill her?" said the tantyr.

"Berylata will be no more," said Rodrigo.

"Then we will depart for now," said the tantyr. "A new host will return to destroy you, though I doubt it will be necessary."

"Do not return," said Rodrigo, "or your fate will be sealed."

"Our fate was sealed long ago," said the tantyr. The two rose and willed their light-wings to life, and the surviving tantyr retreated from the Spire.

All but one.

"Why does Rodrigo always end up taking over the conversation?" said Awkley.

"Could you have said it better?" said Morten

"Of course not! It's why I love the boy!" crowed Awkley, rising to his feet. "And now, we have an army to lead. Commanders, be at the gate by the eighth hour, and be prepared to ride."

Rodrigo nodded. *Time enough to do what needs to be done.*

———

"Where is she, Scarlet?" said Rodrigo.

In the dim light of the monastery hall Rodrigo could see Scarlet's face at first try to brighten for a cheery and naive smile, but then sink to resignation. "You made a promise to help her," he said.

"Take me to her."

For a moment, Scarlet hardened, but then he sighed and looked around. Certain that no one else was nearby, he swept his hand toward a side hall. "Follow me."

Scarlet brought Rodrigo through twists and turns to a small, dark monastery cell, one of many along this particular block of corridor. The cell contained a living space with a tarp-covered archway at the back. He motioned for Rodrigo to enter, moved to the tarp, and lifted it, revealing a sleeping area. On the ground, upon old blankets and rugs, lay Berylata.

Rodrigo went to draw his sword. Seeing this, Scarlet tried to land a punch, but Rodrigo had expected Scarlet's reaction and ducked, flipping his friend over his back.

Rodrigo knelt on Scarlet's chest, his sword point at his friend's neck.

"Choose, Scarlet," he said. "Berylata, a traitor to this world, or everyone else here. Choose!"

Scarlet said nothing for a time, nor did he struggle. Suddenly his eyes filled with tears. "You promised to help her," he said.

"Choose. Her, or everyone else," repeated Rodrigo.

Scarlet struggled within himself, his tears draining to the floor. "At least let me leave," he managed finally through sobs.

Rodrigo shook his head. "No, Scarlet, stay," he said, "but do not interfere."

Rodrigo turned and knelt by Berylata. "Can you hear me?"

"I am awake," said Berylata, lifting one weak hand, her eyes slitting as they looked upon the boy. "I have heard. I am prepared."

"No, you are not," said Rodrigo. "You do not escape so easily, Berylata of the tantyrs, whose name means Betrayal. You are the last of your kind here, for now, and it will be you who repays this world for all of the pain that you have caused."

Rodrigo raised his sword above the tantyr. "I will have a promise from you, or I will take your life. And if your life ends, then Scarlet, who loves you, will live on in a waking hell. I have, myself, made a promise to Scarlet to find a way to help you, and I made that same promise to Ancimoden as he lay mortally stricken. I keep my promises, Berylata. Whatever terrible hold has been placed on you and your people, I will break it. And now, swear by Scarlet that you will serve me in the purpose of my promise, no matter how little you believe in that promise now. If not, you will die, and this hope for you and your people, however slim, slips away. As does Scarlet."

Is it true? wondered Rodrigo. *Is my guess correct? What a terrible, slim razor on which I stand, and which readies to cut Scarlet to the heart if I am wrong.*

Berylata closed her eyes for a time, and Rodrigo thought that she may have fallen back into unconsciousness. But then her eyes slitted open and she began to laugh, a musical, terrible, heart-wrenching laugh. Rodrigo's face fell and his heart knotted.

"You foolish boy. You have no idea of what you speak. You know nothing, and yet you make bold promises. And here I lay, ready to die, to fulfill the terrible duty placed on my people, so that my kit and clan will not suffer the Hanging. I need only say, 'No promise!' and all will be as it should be."

She quieted and closed her eyes again, and Rodrigo gripped his sword tighter, ready for the downward thrust.

When the green slits opened again, tears flowed from them. "And yet the titans are dead. How is that possible?"

Her hand reached up, found his shirt collar, and gripped it tight. "You *swear* to me that you will never cease to find a way. You *swear* it!"

"I do not swear it," said Rodrigo. "My answer is simply yes. Until death takes me, I will not tire or cease."

"Then I promise by Scarlet, whom I love as a brother of the womb, that I will serve you."

Rodrigo clenched his jaw and brought his sword down. The blade sliced through the bedding, nicking her shoulder. "Then Berylata is slain! I give you a new name—Promise. This will remind you of your oath to me, and through me to Scarlet, for the remainder of your life."

The newly sworn Promise pulled in a heaving breath and her eyes grew wide and anguished. "I have condemned my own kit and clan to oblivion!" she cried. Her voice choked off then, and she sobbed—a terrible, very human sob that cut Rodrigo's heart like a knife. He fell back, away from her, shocked and pained. Scarlet's hand dropped to his shoulder, and he moved past Rodrigo to comfort her.

There remained nothing left to say. Rodrigo found a deserted storehouse, fell back against the wall, and cried for the pain that he had witnessed in Promise, and for all of the pain and terror and sorrow that he had shouldered upon his back for two hundred days.

112: THE VICTORIOUS RIDE

The army, assembled upon the field of Pinnacle, swung in column and marched toward the far side of the Spire, where the blackspawn, now leaderless, had so long felt safe in their holes. Ahead of the vanguard swept patrols, and ahead of the patrols rode a tiny contingent of scouts mounted upon precious horses. Forefront among these were four riding together—the two kings and their two commanders.

"If I am smoked, you must promise to stop your slaughter until I return," shouted Awkley, riding his horse with a fair amount of skill, propped forward and straight, with a grand, delighted grin on his face.

"We'll not stop for a minute," said Morten. "You'll simply have to guard your life like all the ordinary mortals."

"Says you!" laughed Awkley.

"This army needs focus," said Boar. "When battle is over, no more Blueboy and Hunter. One army, one resolve, one fist."

"With you as commander of all," said Rodrigo.

"Dah," said Boar.

"It's a new age," said Awkley. "I can feel the change in the wind. A new golden era for Pinnacle. We have been asleep on our thrones too long, Morten!"

Morten did not respond. He peered forward, trying to focus.

Rodrigo followed his gaze. Nothing but darkness and moss-glow registered for a moment. Then his eyes picked out movement and a dull glow—a deep violet stain among the riot of moss-glow colors.

Awkley stood up in his saddle and raised a long glass to his eyes. "By the worthless-" he gasped. The glass threatened to slip from his grasp, but Rodrigo rescued it. The young man brought the spyglass to his own eye.

Across the horizon, line upon line of blackspawn advanced, many thousands strong, some glowing a brilliant, powerful purple. Packs of dark, swift scouts spread forward from the main lines. The overwhelming army advanced straight toward them.

"Morten, we are undone!"

Morten grabbed the spyglass, followed by Boar. Before Boar could lower it, the kings spun and fled for their immortal lives, cursing to the dark skies.

Rodrigo and Boar looked at each other.

"Rafe and Shoca," muttered Rodrigo.

"This is why they wanted my army to march south," growled Boar. "To be annihilate once and for all."

"What now?" said Rodrigo.

"I will die on mountain of enemy dead, like warrior, like man," announced the warlord, stretching in his saddle. "But you are child. It is good for you to run."

"Third choice," said Rodrigo. "Return to army, get it to safety, then make mountains of enemy dead without dying on top."

Boar's eyes searched over the distant mass of oncoming spawn. "We are leagues from city, boy. We don't make city in time."

"Perhaps if we run like royal cowards?" said Rodrigo.

Boar ground his teeth. "No good, but—da."

They shook their heads in disgust, set their heels to their mounts, and followed the course of their panicked masters.

Scarlet's diary, Day 208

> We had a good run. Nothing to be ashamed of. But the enemy is truly at the gates now—the host of spawn that Rafe and Shoca boasted about, though we did not understand.
>
> The titans must have been laughing even while their lives fell away.

EPILOGUE

It was a dark, dry place beneath the city of Pinnacle, but Ed found enough food in the old, cracked tunnels nearby on which to live comfortably. He wasn't sure how long he had been down here, under the city, but his mind dwelt on other things.

He didn't have much oil left—perhaps enough for several more days. But having to leave this discovery for something as mundane as lamp oil offended him, and so he pressed on.

For the past nine hours he had struggled with a large metal object—a piece of machinery like a curved pipe but dotted with knobs and vents—trying to wrestle it into correct position, but having been in its current position for a very long time, it refused to budge.

There, in a corner down at the end of a shattered hallway, he discovered a long bar of metal—a bracing, broken away from the wrecked wall. He dragged it step by step, grunting with each strenuous pull, until the end of the bar lay under the great pipe. Finding a stone of reasonable shape, he pushed it near the pipe, lifted the bar over the stone and upward with a desperate surge of strength, and then pulled down. The bar caught on the pipe, braced atop the stone, and Ed hung from his makeshift lever, yanking at it.

The pipe shifted slightly. Ed laughed and yanked harder until it swiveled into position. "I can move the world!" he crowed to himself.

Sounds grew around him. He shouldered aside the bar and searched among the other machinery. Yes, this needs pushing, and that needs pulling, and a tap over here.

A glow arose, washing his face in a yellow-green bath of light, followed by bluish flickers. "Aha! Yes!" he shouted. "You are one big, ugly, Hephaestian beauty!"

More sounds. There arose a heavy grinding of rock and metal, a long, low rumble, and the ground shook.

"Off! Down! Sit!" he shouted, and he ran for his life.

37239516R00273

Made in the USA
San Bernardino, CA
13 August 2016